PRAISE FOR O LI
BETHLEHEM

"Elizabeth Boyle has always had a rare gift for giving us people to care about, but she's put her whole heart into this beautiful, magical story that caught my heart completely in its spell. Absolutely enchanting!"
~ SUSANNA KEARSLEY
Author of *The King's Messenger* and *The Vanished Days*

"Every so often, a book arrives just when you need it. *O Little Town of Bethlehem* by Elizabeth Boyle is perfect for those yearning for a tale of friendship and a sense of hope, set in a quirky small town held together with a bit of magic and a lot of love."
~KATE MACINTOSH
Author of *The Champagne Letters*

"Boyle's story of placemaking and letting go of the past is sure to enchant readers."
~ *Kirkus* Reviews

"The magic of Bethlehem is impossible to resist. This captivating tale pulls you right into the feisty heart of the town alongside Madeline, and you never want to leave."
~CJ HUNT
Author of the *Rivers End* romance series

ALSO BY ELIZABETH BOYLE

The Rhymes with Love series

Along Came a Duke

And the Miss Ran Away with the Rake

If Wishes Were Earls

The Viscount Who Lived Down the Lane

The Knave of Hearts

Six Impossible Things

Have You Any Rogues?

The Bachelor Chronicles series

Something About Emmaline

This Rake of Mine

Love Letters from a Duke

Confessions of a Little Black Gown

Memoirs of a Scandalous Red Dress

How I Met My Countess

Mad About the Duke

Lord Langley is Back in Town

Mad About the Major

The Marlowe Series

His Mistress by Morning

Tempted by the Night

Best wishes,

O LITTLE TOWN OF BETHLEHEM

ELIZABETH BOYLE

Elizabeth Boyle

O Little Town of Bethlehem. Copyright © 2024 by Elizabeth Boyle.

Cover design by 100Covers.com

First edition 2024

Publisher's Cataloging-in-Publication
(Provided by Cassidy Cataloguing Services, Inc.).

Names: Boyle, Elizabeth, author.

Title: O little town of Bethlehem / Elizabeth Boyle.

Description: First edition. | [Seattle, Washington] : [Elizabeth Boyle], [2024]

Identifiers: ISBN: 978-1-7336765-9-5 (hardback) | 978-1-7336765-4-0 (paperback) | 978-1-7336765-8-8 (ebook) | LCCN: 2024910029

Subjects: LCSH: Women--Wyoming--History--20th century--Fiction. | Wyoming--History--20th century--Fiction. | Strangers--Wyoming--History--20th century--Fiction. | Friendship--Fiction. | Female friendship--Fiction. | Christmas stories. | LCGFT: Historical fiction. | Christmas fiction. | BISAC: FICTION / Women. | FICTION / Historical / 20th Century / General. | FICTION / Holidays.

Classification: LCC: PS3552.0923 L58 2024 | DDC: 813/.6--dc23

To Terry
For everything. Always.

CHAPTER 1

Thanksgiving eve,
Present day

It was supposed to be a night filled with magic.

"When will I learn?" Madeline Drake muttered as she stood at the end of the driveway in near-blinding snow. Stomping her feet and shivering, she tried to get some feeling back in her toes. She'd stood here for nearly thirty minutes, her luggage looking like the parts of a toppled snowman.

She dug out her cell phone. Again. The service was spotty at best, but the last text she'd gotten from her assistant, Mindy, said she'd managed to get her a ride to the airport and a plane to pick her up.

Behind her, the twinkling lights of Emerson's "mountain modern" monstrosity, his Jackson Hole retreat where he liked to "rough it," sparked with warmth, but she stubbornly held her ground. She wasn't going back inside.

Dumped. Out. Humiliated.

The news banners that had scrolled onto her screen earlier this morning and sent her hightailing it to Jackson to confront Emerson offered a hint of what awaited her back in LA. At least this time the disaster hadn't been her fault.

Not that anyone would listen.

Then again, if her ride didn't show up quickly, she'd most likely freeze to death right here in this snowbank. If there was any comfort in that scenario, it was that she wouldn't have to face the landslide of mortifying opinions that were already being bandied about by pundits and social media trolls.

One would think that, after all these years in the spotlight, Madeline would be used to weathering the comments and slurs and ugly suppositions that came with the very public dissection of every aspect of her life.

But this time it weighed too much, and she felt herself slumping toward the ground until she heard her grandmother Gigi's sharp tones. *Straighten up. You're a Drake, for Christ's sake.* Gigi had hammered that canon into her. Thus reminded, she sucked in a deep breath and dashed her nearly frozen fingers at the tears threatening to fall.

"I'm Madeline Drake," she reminded herself.

Whatever that meant.

As if in answer to her prayer, she heard a heavy wheeze. Out of the swirl of flakes and bitter wind, a pair of headlights bounced up the lonely road.

An old pickup truck, all patched and rusted, pulled up the drive, until the headlights left her all but blinded. They flipped off even as the truck grated and ground to a shuddering stop. The driver, a mere silhouette inside, leaned over and shoved open the passenger door. "I'm guessing you're her."

This was her car service? Mindy had never let her down before, but this must be what she had meant by "it's the best I can do."

The wind blew the door shut, the *clank* snapping her back to attention. Even if there had been a way to call for someone else, it was freezing cold and snowing hard, so she went to open the door—but it stuck.

The irony did not escape her.

"Got to jiggle it a bit and then give it a good tug," the voice inside encouraged.

After a few attempts, the door finally opened. No, this certainly wasn't her usual ride.

"You Maddie?" A small, thin man bundled up in an old sheepherder's jacket sat hunched behind the steering wheel, looking her up and down with no small measure of skepticism. As if there were half a dozen other people clamoring for a ride.

"Yes, I'm Madeline Drake," she corrected. She glanced down at her phone. *His name is Shandy.* "You are . . . ?"

"Shandy," he confirmed, grinning at her. "Get in. I'm freezing to death." He was already shifting the groaning engine back into gear.

"My bags," she said with a nod toward the lumps in the snow.

"Best get them in the back," he told her, jerking his thumb toward the rear of the truck. "I left bingo at the VFW for this."

He left bingo . . . Madeline bit back a sharp retort only because she wasn't convinced he wouldn't drive off without her.

She hefted in one bag then the other, carefully setting them well away from the empty beer bottles, a sandbag, an old cooler, and the rusty shovel decorating the truck bed. The only things missing were duct tape, rope, and a tarp to make this the perfect opening to an episode of *Forensic Files*.

When she opened the door this time, she realized her seat was otherwise occupied.

Rather a metaphor for the day, since she'd arrived in Jackson to find Emerson occupied with someone else.

The interloper this time was a large dog, of sorts, as scruffy as the driver and sporting the same mismatched patches of color as the truck. The mutt had the nerve to stretch out a paw, if only to take up more space.

"Um—" she began, not sure how to proceed.

"Don't mind him. Picked him up on the way out here. Poor fella. Abandoned on Thanksgiving." He paused and tugged an old-fashioned pocket watch from his coat. "Yep, after midnight, so it's Thanksgiving. Can you imagine being that mean?"

She could. Still, she hardly wanted to start a club. "Is he safe?"

"The better question is, does he have fleas?" the man chuckled, wrapping his hand around the dog's middle and pulling it over to make some room. "I'm pretty sure he does, but I can hardly put him in the back, now, can I? He's near-frozen as it is."

A gust of wind blew through her thin coat, leaving Madeline scurrying toward the meager warmth of the cab. "Does he have tags or a collar?" she asked, casting a suspicious glance at her seatmates. Both of them.

"Nope."

The heater blew warm then cold in errant gusts as the driver shifted into gear and the truck groaned and heaved into motion.

"Best hang on," he advised.

She scrambled to find a seat belt, a handhold, anything. He gunned the engine and the truck shot forward, the rear end fishtailing on the snowy road. She had no choice but to take a breath and shove her fingers into the grimy depths of the seat in search of a seat belt. She freed a buckle from its hiding spot as they blew through a stop sign and went roaring down the road.

Finding the rest of her seatbelt took on new urgency. Madeline reached over her shoulder and, after a couple of pulls, released the strap so she could click it into place. To her relief, it seemed to hold.

Clearly, it was the only thing about this truck that actually worked.

He turned again, this time onto the road that led to the highway, and Madeline tried to settle in, but her thoughts returned to the hours before.

You can't cut me. Not now. Not for her.

Babe, you gotta understand, it's all business. . .

She shivered.

"Should have waited in the house," the driver pointed out. "'Specially in that getup."

"I'm not used to winter. I'm from LA." She glanced out the window and tried to see anything in the darkness and snow.

"LA." He snorted. "You one of those fancy-pants actors who comes here and drives up all the prices? Builds them big houses"—he jerked a nod back toward Emerson's place—"then leaves them empty most of the year?"

"That house belongs to my—" She nearly said *boyfriend.* "Former business partner."

"What sort of business?"

Madeline drew a deep breath. "Movie," she replied. "We were supposed to be making a movie."

"So fancy-pants actors," he repeated, as if he'd won the argument.

"I was going to co-produce and star in it," she corrected. A quake rattled inside her. *Star in it.* A light flickered out on all the possibilities that this film might have opened.

"Was?"

"Yes. He's decided to go in a different direction," she said, thinking of when she'd arrived and found him and Gemma in a definitely different direction.

"That why you're in such an all-fire hurry to leave, on Thanksgiving and all? Want to get back to your glamorous life?"

Great. She'd gotten the nosiest driver in all of Wyoming. "I don't have a lot to be thankful for tonight." She wanted to tell him that this glamorous life of hers was a giant, lonely lie. A façade of smiles and spotlights. "And I don't know about the glamorous part," she told him. "You aren't catching me on my best day."

He coughed out a bit of a laugh. "I rarely catch people on their best day."

Meanwhile, the dog had inched closer, settling his head on her lap. She wasn't too sure what to do, so she patted it awkwardly, her fingers brushing over his ears. The dog sighed and laid his head in her hand, trusting that she wouldn't abandon him. Something inside her thawed just enough to let all those roiling emotions spill out.

"Have you ever wanted something so badly that you'd do anything to get it? A chance to do something beyond anything you've ever been offered?" She took a breath. "To be someone?"

There it was. The admission that had clawed its way forward. She wouldn't be in Emerson's biopic of Amelia Earhart, the sort of movie the Academy loved. Months of reading, flying lessons, watching old newsreels, doing everything and anything to slide into the elusive flyer's character and finally charm all the naysayers, all the critics. "I've lost everything today. I don't even know who I am."

"Have you tried being yourself?"

"That's rather hard when you're an actor."

"How's that?"

"When you slip into a role, one you play for a long time, that character becomes a part of you. The longer you play it, the more they seem to take over your life."

Even now, one of the lines she'd recited earlier that day haunted her.

Time is a river. A river with currents that run so fast they will sweep you away, drown you.

If only it would. Just sweep her away.

"You say 'slip.' I say it sounds like you use them roles to escape."

Right now she wanted to escape this ride. Escape tomorrow and the day after that. Everything was in the toilet. She'd even argued with Nate when she'd left the *Star Bright* set earlier, her hair on fire and more than ready to murder Emerson given the news that he'd cut her out of *Earhart*.

This time, maybe Nate would make good on his threat to fire her. Tears welled in her eyes as she thought of him—her best friend. He'd written the starring role in his series just for her, given her a chance when no one would hire her. And how had she repaid him?

"Actor, huh? Done anything good?" Her driver glanced at her, but his expression showed no sign of recognition.

After a day of insults, this was the final straw. "I'm on a series," she supplied, dashing away the tears still threatening to spill over. "A show, *The Star Bright*. I play the saloon owner, Calliope Corfield. Before that I played Casey Jones in a detective show for kids . . ."

This earned her a noncommittal shrug.

"You haven't heard of *The Star Bright*?" It was actually rare when someone hadn't. It streamed all over the world. And *Casey Jones, Girl Detective*? She doubted the reruns would ever end—as her mother, Dahlia, gleefully reminded her twice a year when the residuals were tallied up and she got her stage mother's share.

"Nope, can't say that I have. Then again, never had a TV."

Of course not. He barely had a truck. She'd be surprised if they made it to the airport.

Speaking of the airport, Madeline tried to figure out where they were. Except for the tunnels of shifting, flickering light from the headlights, darkness surrounded them.

"What's yer show about?"

His question dragged her out of her reverie. "My what?"

"This show yer in. What's it about?"

"A small town. Here in Wyoming, as a matter of fact."

"Which one?"

A flicker of a smile warmed her as she thought of the set. "Bethlehem. Though it's not real."

He chuckled. "You sure?"

"Yeah, I'm sure. My friend Nate writes and produces the show— so he makes it all up." Nate's beautiful lines had given her a leg up, but when she'd tried to branch out between seasons, she'd found herself boxed in once more. First Casey, now Calliope.

"Huh. So who are you?"

She took a deep breath. "I told you. I'm Madeline Drake."

He nodded. "But *who* is *that*?"

Good God, she was in no mood for a philosophical dissection by a bingo-loving rideshare driver.

She reached for some other subject, for anything else to talk about, but as she looked out the windshield, the snow nearly blinded her as it tumbled this way and that, making it impossible to see anything other than a kaleidoscope of flakes.

How could he even see the road? Especially at this speed.

She curled her hand into the seat, unable to pull her gaze away from the road—given what little she could see of it, the snow whirling in the headlights, endlessly twisting and falling.

A river with currents that run so fast they will sweep you away . . .

The lines swirled back up inside her like an eerie premonition. "Do you have to go this fast?"

"Fast, you say?" Shandy chuckled. "Hardly fast enough. Not if you want to make it in time. Like I said, I left bingo for—"

Out of nowhere, something flew in front of them.

She cried out even as she saw it. An owl. A huge white owl, its great snowy head turning slowly toward them, its serene flight hardly ruffled by the rattling, rumbling old pickup barreling toward it.

Shandy said something, a prayer of sorts, and swerved.

Then the truck turned upside down, and Madeline reached for the shore as everything was swept away in the raging river of time.

CHAPTER 2

Bethlehem, Wyoming
Thanksgiving, 1907

*S*omething always changed this time of year, Savannah
Clarke mused as she paused outside her house. It wasn't that
the cottonwood and aspens all stood bare, the grasses brown and
withered, or the way that the draughts nipped around the door frame.

All around her, the physical world had fallen asleep, while the
mortal one awakened. People opened their eyes, blinking in wonder
and joy at this brief pause between the hurried labors of harvest and
the beckoning of spring plowing.

For what lay before them was the happy prospect of holidays.
Thanksgiving. Christmas. New Year's.

But to Savannah, this change was like that unexpected, fragile
moment before one drifts off to sleep. An inescapable trap wherein
one is powerless to stop the transition from the commonplace and
everyday into the darkness and the unknown.

Savannah tightened the black shawl around her shoulders and

hurried up the steps, the leaden clouds behind her moving silently over the mountains.

They promised snow.

She pursed her lips as she came inside. The warmth was a welcome relief. A better relief would be a few feet of snow to cancel all the celebrations planned for later.

Yet not even that would stop the people of Bethlehem from gathering. She stowed her hat on the hall tree and hung up her coat. St. Michael's had been cold but the Thanksgiving Mass thankfully short. Father O'Brien, like everyone else, was looking forward to the festivities tonight.

Thanksgiving. She'd argue this day was no holiday, but rather a harbinger.

A bowl clattered in the back of the house, and she followed the echoing refrain to the kitchen.

"Looks like it's going to snow," she remarked, knowing full well her dour prediction would elicit an emphatic response.

Inola looked up from the pie crust she was mixing. "It wouldn't dare."

"You haven't even looked. Why, the sky is—" Savannah crossed the kitchen to the windows running across the back wall.

Inola ignored her and returned to her mixing. "I don't have to look." She pinched and pressed the lard and butter into the flour. Her dark hands moved with a sure, fluid motion, so hypnotic it was hard not to watch. Then she stopped and smiled because she knew Savannah was watching. "How was Mass?"

"Cold." Savannah glanced down and realized she'd forgotten to take off her gloves. Tugging them off, they revealed her own pale fingers, compliments of their Irish father. The world that saw them as so opposite, despite the parentage they shared. "Father O'Brien asked after you."

"He did?" Inola went back to her mixing.

"I told him you were too busy making pies to attend Mass."

"What did he say?"

"Something about 'thank the Lord.'" Savannah looked at the chaos of the kitchen—bowls, spoons, open tins of flour and sugar and spices, and sighed. She itched to roll up her sleeves and reach for her apron, if only to bring a bit of order to what was usually her domain.

"I told you my pies would absolve me."

Rather than examine the turmoil around her—and within her—Savannah looked toward the copse that ran on either side of the stream behind their house. Bare white trunks stood in quiet solidarity, rooted in place, ready for winter.

Soon snow would cover everything. Conceal so much.

"It isn't going to snow," Inola repeated, as if she could hear Savannah's dour thoughts. "My bones tell me so."

"You might want to listen to your nose. That pie smells like it's about to burn."

"Tarnation." She glanced at the small clock on the shelf and tapped the face. "Does this thing ever work?" She hurried to the oven. "You could help," Inola scolded over her shoulder as she pulled the pie from the oven.

"I could." But she wouldn't, even with all the work that clearly needed to be done—like packing the dishes, silverware, and tablecloths that were haphazardly gathered on the dining room table beside a row of baskets. Not to mention the pies, all of which would need to be carried over to the Opera House.

In the heat of summer, in the dead of winter, they worked side by side. But as Thanksgiving came closer, they drew apart.

Their annual estrangement, as Savannah had taken to thinking of it.

Then again, if she'd dared offer to help, Inola would most likely call in the doctor.

Inola finished her examination of the hot pie, nodded, and, having made her decision, returned it to the oven. "Just a bit longer," she said, more for her own benefit, before turning back to Savannah. "After all this time, why do you insist on being so . . . so . . ."

Inola, most likely, had compiled an entire encyclopedia of things to say and kept it at the ready, starting with *obstinate*.

To her credit, she didn't finish that sentence. Instead she opened the lid to check the firebox then, satisfied, closed it with a *clank*, though her silence rang louder. Not that anything she could say would change Savannah's mind.

Then again . . . Inola, bless her heart, was just as obstinate.

"It's Thanksgiving, Vanna." Cajoling, cozy words.

"I'm well aware of that." Savannah glanced around the ransacked kitchen. "You've all but emptied the larder to prove the point."

Unrepentant, Inola turned the pie crust she'd been mixing onto the floured workbench. "How can you be so hardheaded?" Apparently, even her legendary patience had run thin.

"Thanksgiving!" Savannah's nose pinched at the very mention of it. "I do not celebrate Yankee holidays."

Inola snorted. "Listen to you. There haven't been Yankees for a long time."

"Not to me." Savannah surveyed the kitchen. The open tins of spices filled the close quarters with a thick air of memories.

Holidays past. Holidays lost.

It nearly drove Savannah out of the kitchen, out of the house. For that sweet bite of cinnamon, that tang of fresh-scraped nutmeg, was too haunting. Despite her annual resolution to ignore the festivities, the scents of the season filled her.

What was it about this time of year, that a hint of ginger could carry her back across the years? It didn't happen in April. Nor in July. But now, on the very edge of winter, it was as if that spiced thread tugged at her memories with the fortitude of an iron chain.

Savannah shook her head slightly. "How can you forget what they stole from us?"

Inola stilled. "How can you forget what they gave me?"

"You were already free." This subject always curled like a knot inside her.

"Was I?"

At least Inola hadn't added the other part. *Were you?*

This being an old argument, Inola changed course. "You could come along just for the turkey dinner." If that wasn't enough, she added, "Mr. Badger was by this morning with more firewood and said the turkeys are extra fat this year." Her sure hands moved quickly, efficiently as they brought the shaggy dough together and then flattened it out into an even disc.

"No. Thank. You."

Inola reached for her rolling pin. "Mrs. Viola Kinney Livingston always says, 'The holidays are meant to be spent with cherished ones and family.'"

Savannah was unmoved by the famous columnist's advice. "I always thought that was a rather back-handed bit of counsel. Is the family cherished or not?" She smiled back. "Besides, doesn't she also say, 'Never press an invitation on a reluctant guest?'"

"'An invitation is an honor that a lady gives due diligence,'" Inola quoted in response. "And Mrs. George L. avers that Mrs. Livingston's advice is as close to gospel as one can find these days."

"She is a bothersome know-it-all," Savannah replied.

"Which one?" Inola did like to be exact.

"Both."

Inola's nose tipped up. "I take that personally."

Savannah slanted a glance at her. "You should."

Whatever Inola muttered as she went back to rolling out the dough in even sweeping movements, Savannah didn't hear, lost as she was in watching Inola's hypnotic motions. One. Two. Three. A little adjustment and then, like some rare bit of alchemy, the crust appeared, even and round.

An almost magical transformation of flour, salt, water, and lard. Simple ingredients into something perfect. Inola made it look so easy. Her skill reminiscent of the sleight of hand practiced by the street entertainers on the busy corners near their childhood home in New Orleans.

"I don't know why you go to all that fuss and bother," Savannah said.

"It's no fuss or bother," Inola told her. More like prodded her. *If you were just willing to try, Vanna* . . . "Folks like my pies. And I like these folks." She paused for a moment and then gently laid the crust into yet another pie tin.

"That pie," Savannah said, nodding toward the oven, "is going to burn."

Inola sniffed, brow crinkling. "I've never burned a pie. Not once. 'Sides, what does it matter to you? You won't be there to eat it." Still she moved quickly to open the stove and peer inside. A slight smile tugged at her mouth.

Potholders in hand, Inola pulled out the tin, tipping it slightly so Savannah could see the perfectly browned edges, the sweet-potato filling just set.

No doubt it would be the first pie tin on the dessert table to be emptied.

"I might remind you that Mrs. George L. only asks you to bake those pies so she doesn't have to."

"Who'd want to eat something that old hen baked?" Inola set the hot pie on the rack and returned to the empty crust. "Everyone knows I make the best sweet potato pie in all of Wyoming."

Savannah smiled despite herself. "West of the Mississippi," she corrected.

"West of the Mississippi," Inola agreed.

"Still, why do all this work for that woman? It isn't as if she'd invite you inside her house."

Inola trimmed the edges and began to flute the crust. A pinch and turn. Pinch and turn. No one else crimped an edge like Inola, leaving no doubt as to exactly which pies were hers.

"Why would I want to go in her house?" Inola asked, huffing just a bit. "Probably no different than this one." Wiping her hands on her apron, she paused. "You'd probably get invited out more as well if you'd be a bit more civil."

That sent a bristle up Savannah's spine. "When have I not been civil?"

Inola's deep brown eyes sparkled. "Should I start at the beginning, or will just this week do?"

Retreating from what was sure to be a rout, Savannah ignored her by gathering up the dirty dishes and settling them into the wash pan. This might qualify as helping, but she decided to leave such hairsplitting to lawyers and other pettifogs. The way she saw it, dirty dishes were just an ongoing obligation. "I declare, Inola, I don't know where you get these notions of yours. I am always civil."

"You might try asking Mrs. Bergstrom for her thoughts on that subject." Inola studied the crust and gave the pie tin another turn. "What was it you said to her last week as we were leaving the mercantile?"

"I didn't say anything to her." It was a poor defense. Her words had been meant for Inola's ears, though they hadn't been all that cautiously spoken. "That woman is expecting her fourth child—"

"Fifth," Inola corrected.

"Exactly. Whyever is she continuing to add to that unruly horde when they can barely feed the ones they have? Bah! And I thought the Irish were irresponsible."

Inola shook her head. "We're Irish."

"Only half."

"Which half is that?"

Savannah went back to the subject at hand. "As I said, having more children than one can feed is irresponsible."

"So you said, and rather loudly."

Savannah tucked her nose in the air. "It isn't like Mrs. Bergstrom speaks a word of English. She had no idea what I was saying." Taking up the kettle, she brought it over to the deep tin sink and began to pump the water.

"You certain about that?" Inola looked up.

"Well, she does have too many children," Savannah muttered as she returned the heavy kettle to the stove and set it to heat.

This left her with nothing more to do but stand and watch. And wait. Even the clock seemed to wait.

Savannah took another look around at the cluttered mess. "How many pies have you made this week?"

"Never you mind," Inola scolded. "Most likely not enough."

"You know very well we can't afford to feed the entire town," Savannah remarked, one eye still on the kettle. "Bad enough you sneak meals to every vagrant and woebegone beggar who comes along."

Inola didn't look up. "I hardly ever—"

"You sneak meals to that boy."

"Dobbs," Inola said firmly. "His name is Dobbs."

"Yes. Dobbs. You feed him." Savannah would have stopped there but remembered someone else to add to her list. "And that awful man." She didn't need to use his name.

"Mr. Badger?" Inola shook her head as if she'd never heard such nonsense. "He's not awful. He's right kind and smart. If you ever got down from your high horse and said more than two words to him, you'd know he talks like an educated man."

Savannah's lips pursed together. *Badger.* What sort of name was that? And talk to him? Heavens, no! "That man is a fright to behold. I've never seen a more ragged coat. More patch than whole cloth. And that great mess of a beard and shaggy hair." She shuddered. "I tell you, Inola, there is something wrong about his eyes."

Bright blue and piercing. As if they could cut through the very darkness, all the way into one's soul.

Inola blew out a breath. "He's been right kind to us."

"He'd be a might kinder to the entire town if he merely bathed a bit more often."

"True enough, but there's always extra when he brings our firewood. And he fixed the screen door last summer without me even asking. He's a good man."

The argument slipping from her grasp, Savannah returned to the real bane of her ire. "You've emptied the cupboards when we haven't even enough to—" She bit her bottom lip to stop the flow of words.

"Don't bother saying it. I can hear what you're thinking. 'Inola, that is good money out for cream and lard and butter and sugar, all of which we can ill afford.'"

Well, there it was. They couldn't afford any of this.

"You know we need to be careful. Mr. King has been gracious about our account so far, but even his generosity is going to run out. We need to economize."

"As if I don't know that." Inola huffed. "Yet if we are quibbling here, which I don't want to do, I would point out I paid for all this with my money."

Her money.

That stung. Because it was always Inola's money that kept the roof over their head. Food on the table. Their account at Mr. King's nearly always paid in full.

Until lately.

Inola continued on with her usual confidence. "We won't starve, Vanna. We never have. We never will. Not as long as we stick together." She carefully filled the crust with her secret mixture of finely mashed sweet potatoes, eggs, butter, sugar, and cream. Then she picked up the grater and ran a nutmeg against it so a fine dusting of spice rained down atop the pie.

Despite her best intentions, Savannah inhaled again. Deeply.

Heavens, it did smell good.

Inola noticed. "Come for the supper." She paused before adding those two magic words. "Roast turkey."

Savannah held her ground, despite the fact she truly loved a well-roasted turkey. And, drat it all, Inola knew that. Nor was she done.

"Cornbread stuffing. That fancy orange relish Mrs. George L. has sent up from Denver. Miss Minch is most likely bringing biscuits. At least she better be. And I heard tell that Mr. King is having oysters expressed in. Oysters, Vanna."

Her conviction wavered, for she did love oysters. That is, until she remembered what this day was. Thanksgiving.

The very day they'd found themselves here.

So no, not even for oysters. There'd be too many people. The clamorous symphony of children running about. Well wishes and laughter. She shook her head and looked toward the mountains again.

How those high hills pulled at her. Beckoned her with a dark enticement, as if they knew what she'd done in the world beyond. One day, when she was ready to climb their steep slopes, they would welcome her and allow her the grace of slipping into the barren darkness they promised.

"Aren't you tired of living all stuck and angry?" Inola's quiet question nudged her to come back. Then she stepped closer and unhitched Savannah's hands from the edge of the counter. Savannah hadn't even realized she'd latched onto it, if only to anchor herself to the here and now.

Inola knew her too well, covering her hands in a warm grasp to ease her out of that cold place. "We're safe here. You're safe here."

The kettle began to rumble, and Savannah pulled her hands free and fled to the other side of their small kitchen, catching up the hissing kettle and pouring the hot water into the dish pan, letting the steam rise around her.

Not that it hid anything. Not from Inola.

"You might even make a wish."

A wish? Savannah shivered at the very thought. Another foolish town tradition. Writing down wishes for Christmas and tucking them in a mason jar.

She picked up the washrag and began scrubbing.

Inola wasn't about to give up. "You could put your name in for the Christmas tree drawing."

"Oh, not that," she said, shaking her head. "This town takes choosing their Christmas tree far too seriously."

"They do, don't they?" Inola agreed, but she sounded rather pleased with the notion. "I suspect you'd pick a right pretty one." She slid the fresh pie inside the oven and closed the door carefully. "Then, come Christmas Eve, I wouldn't have to listen to you complain that the tree isn't right."

"I don't complain—" she began, until Inola's brow lofted at that all-too-familiar angle that said *don't even bother*.

But Savannah did. Especially on this subject. "Not even you can say that the tree Mrs. Baumgarten chose last year was anything but a horror. All crooked, and not enough branches. 'Esoteric and artistic,' my corset."

Inola shook her head and pressed her lips together, doing her best not to laugh.

"And what about that monstrosity Mr. Cochrane chose two years ago?" Savannah shuddered. "I don't know what was worse, the size of that tree or the fact that the foolish man chopped the top off to make it fit into the Opera House." Now it was her turn to arch a brow. "He chopped off the top of the Christmas tree. Why, any fool knows you chop from the bottom."

Inola's eyes sparked at the memory, and her lips twitched. Then both of them began to laugh.

Oh, that poor tree, and how people had gaped as they'd come into the hall that night.

They continued to giggle, a thread of companionship trying desperately to knit them back into a whole cloth. Yet a single thread was hardly up to the task, especially on this day, of all days.

With the last of her pies now in the oven, Inola gathered up the little tins of spices and put them away in the cupboard. "Come along with me tonight, put your name in, show 'em all how it's done."

Savannah planted her feet. "As tempting as that might be, I will not."

Her hard words shooed away any lingering echoes of humor.

"It is a turkey dinner in the company of our neighbors. Whatever are you afraid of?"

"I am not—"

"You are. Afraid. Down to your soles." Inola rose to her full height. "Everyone else in that room arrived as we did, more or less. Coming with their secrets and failures and sins. But they find a new path, a new life."

"I'm not afraid of anything," Savannah declared.

"Mark my words, Vanna. One day you're gonna wake up and find you've missed everything. Everything that matters." She wiped her hands on her apron and then straightened it with a swoop of her steady hands.

Then she glanced at the clock and tapped the face once again. When it sat silent and obstinate, she checked the watch pinned to her shirt, then hurried along into the dining room, saying over her shoulder, "I give up. I'm in no mood to keep pushing your wheelbarrow of regrets up that lonely mountainside. If you are determined to spend your days mourning a life long lost—a life, I might add, that wasn't all that praiseworthy to begin with—there isn't anything more I can say that hasn't already been said." With that, she began packing up the baskets. Silver clattered. Dishes rattled. "I'm taking the extra china and our best blue tablecloth."

Words meant to challenge Savannah to say something. Anything.

She nearly did open her mouth—but if she did, then she'd have to *do* something.

So she went back to washing up what was in the sink and ignored that she was doing that much.

There was another huff from Inola, then the swish of her skirts as she swept through the kitchen. "I'll be back before those pies are done."

Savannah didn't look up until she heard the back door close with a decided thud. As it did, something yanked at the knot inside her. Inola's boot heels, hard and determined, punctuated everything that had been left unsaid as she went down the steps.

By the time she finally found the right words, Inola was already picking her way through the copse of aspen.

So once again, as Savannah did every year, she reminded herself why she didn't want to go.

She had nothing to wish for. Nothing to be thankful for.

Inola had the wrong of it, she would tell her. She woke up every morning knowing that she'd lost everything. A life, a place, that could never be found again.

Nothing would ever ease the emptiness that filled her each winter and left her as bare as the pale, flickering aspen branches wavering in the dreary gray light, awaiting their blessed covering of snow.

CHAPTER 3

*M*iss Parathinia Minch carefully picked her way across the icy street and sighed. It had snowed during the afternoon, but only enough to ensure that the entire population of Bethlehem would be giddy with holiday cheer.

Except her.

As the town's postmistress, she preferred the orderly rules that guided her small realm. Postage rates, prompt deliveries, regular hours. Even the rush of Christmas, with its messy and at times overwhelming piles of parcels and postcards and letters, was never truly bothersome.

Parathinia prided herself on handling it all with steady perseverance.

Until this morning. This particular Thursday. This Thanksgiving.

Something was different today. She decided to blame it on Mrs. Mercer's book, which had arrived yesterday.

An Improved and Forthright Life for the Modern Woman.

She'd stayed up far too late reading, and despite all of Mrs. Mercer's exhortations of *Exorior!*, Parathinia had awakened to a singular question. Rise forth to what?

She hardly knew, so she continued toward the Opera House, basket in hand, every step dogged by the irrational sense that something monumental was about to change—and that no amount of rules and regulations would be able to rein it in.

Perhaps she should have stayed home, warm and solitary in her beloved kitchen, rereading her favorite Austen novel.

But you promised to bring biscuits for the supper, she reminded herself. Scolded, really.

That, and there was that *other* matter. Parathinia nearly turned and fled, but since it was Bethlehem, she'd already crossed town and found herself standing in front of the Opera House. Inside, the lights twinkled and the buzz of conversation hummed through the walls.

There would be supper and toasts and well wishes, and then . . . she'd be called up to the stage to draw the name for the Christmas tree.

She quaked. This "honor" had been bestowed upon her after the scandalous year Miss Dorothy Braken had deliberately drawn her sister's name two years in a row—the final straw after years of accusations of cheating and favoritism and outright bribery. Instead of bringing the town together, the Christmas tradition was dividing them.

So when Shandy had declared her the most honest woman in town, and no one could argue the matter, Miss Minch had been appointed to pull the name from the jar, and had been so tasked for more years than she cared to count.

She took another breath. It wasn't the drawing so much as the standing up in front of the entire town. She much preferred standing behind her post office counter.

Or was she just hiding behind it? Oh, heavens, the realization rather startled her. Mrs. Mercer would have definite opinions on *that* subject.

Not ones, Parathinia was certain she was ready to hear.

Bracing herself, she made her quiet entrance into the Opera House. She'd always thought it quite an ironic name, since she doubted anyone in Bethlehem had ever heard opera, though Mrs. George L. Lovell claimed to have heard it sung in Denver.

Nor was this squat hall at the end of Main Street—the hallowed gathering place for the citizens of Bethlehem—as glamorous as its name implied. It was—if she was feeling charitable—a serviceable hall that sufficed for community dances and bazaars and town meetings and suppers.

Like this one.

Which, judging from the clamor within, sounded as if everyone had already gathered. A room full of people that she knew. Intimately. Their favorite newspapers and magazines. Their unanswered letters. Debts in need of payment. Sins unforgiven.

Claiming the last empty hook in the foyer for her coat and hat, she steeled herself for the main room, basket in hand.

Almost immediately, Dobbs appeared at her side. "Miss Minch, let me take that."

She wasn't fooled—though, to his credit, the boy was always willing to help—but today his eagerness had more to do with the contents of her basket.

If she wasn't mistaken, he'd grown a bit of late, so he was most likely hungry.

He took the handle and grinned as he inhaled. "Biscuits." The word came out in a reverent rush. That alone should have been a point of pride for her, but it had stopped being so years ago. Now it was just another unchanging expectation.

Miss Parathinia Minch. Postmistress. Spinster. Biscuit maker. Most honest woman in town.

Dobbs carried off the basket as if it were gold, leaving her alone to take a measure of the busy scene before her.

The Presbyterian Ladies Benevolent League was in charge this year, and Mrs. George L.'s hand was evident at every turn. She stopped at nothing to ensure they outdid Mrs. Neville Norwood and the Catholic Women's Auxiliary, who managed the decorating in even-numbered years.

Under Mrs. George L.'s fastidious and exacting specifications—and her all-consuming rivalry with her nemesis, Mrs. Norwood—the hall stood gloriously festooned with bright garlands of fall leaves and russet ribbons, while smaller arrangements of wheat and corn decorated the tables.

Mrs. George L. would not be outdone.

Of course, at the end of the supper table sat the mason jars. One blue and one green. Slips of paper lay around them, scattered like little piles of autumn leaves alongside the bare stubs of pencils. And a line of people waited to fill out their names for the Christmas tree drawing and add their annual wishes to the blue jar.

Parathinia made her way to the other end, where Inola was already unpacking the biscuits. It struck her for the first time that Inola lived a rather solitary life, the only other people of color around being Dobbs and Elias Turner at the hotel.

Was she lonely? Parathinia wondered. It wasn't like she was included in the various clubs or organizations, though no one objected to her help when there was a large project at hand. Nor did she socialize all that much, outside of her life with Mrs. Clarke.

Yet she never lacked a smile or a kind word. Inola, Parathinia suspected, would understand far better than she did what Mrs. Mercer meant when she urged her readers to fill their hearts with the spirit of *Exorior!*

Having set the last biscuit on a large platter, Inola smiled warmly at Parathinia. "There now, the table is complete. No one wanted to start filling their plates until your biscuits were here." She tipped her head toward the queue forming at the other end, where the high school boys jostled each other for position, while their mothers scolded them out of the way of their elders.

"Now I feel quite bad for being late."

"Never mind that, honey. It's good for them." Inola laughed. "Still, you do have a way with biscuits. Are you certain you aren't Southern?'

Parathinia shook her head. "No, I was born in Wisconsin."

"You sure do cook like a Southerner."

"My mother's recipe," Parathinia said as she glanced down the table, overflowing from one end to the other with viands. Another table sat adorned with a selection of pies and cakes. "One of these days, you'll teach me how you make your pie crust so perfect."

"Making pie crust isn't taught, Miss Minch. You either know how or you don't."

"Every man in this town is thankful that you do, Miss Inola," Mr. Archimedes Thayer remarked, leaning over Parathinia to reach for a biscuit. "Miss Minch, you have once again taken the humble biscuit and raised it to new heights."

Parathinia grappled for the right words but found herself quite flustered. Mr. Thayer always left her stumbling over her own tongue. Perhaps it was his patrician Bostonian manners, or his handsome features, the kind not usually seen in these parts—dark eyes with a wry light, and well-trimmed black hair that in the last few years had begun to show a bit of distinguished gray around the temples. And now here he was, smiling at her.

Unwittingly, her gaze fell on the blue jar at the end of the table, and suddenly Parathinia knew exactly what she would wish.

I want someone to call me Ninny again.

Like when she was a girl. When life had lain before her wide and open, like the plains beyond the high mountains, an expanse of wavering green grasses and wildflowers dancing in the breeze, beckoning her to romp and tumble within their tall, undulating embrace while, just ahead, Papa drove the wagon, the horses plodding along.

She'd been Ninny then. Before Shandy had guided them here. She was still Ninny in her heart, but when the world looked at her, they saw only Miss Minch. And she was Parathinia only to a mere handful.

When she glanced up, she found Inola and Mr. Thayer looking expectantly at her, awaiting an answer to a question she hadn't heard. *Oh dear.*

What had been said?

Why, even Inola looked at bit undone, smiling and glancing away. No wonder Mr. Thayer was such a good lawyer—he could sway anyone's heart with his effusive words and kindly looks.

"Yes, well, I suppose I should hurry along before the pies are gone." The man bowed his head slightly to the both of them, murmuring a polite, "Ladies," before continuing down the table.

"Oh, that man is a devil," Inola remarked, fanning herself. "He always leaves me feeling like my petticoat is knotted up."

Parathinia wanted to ask what had been said but couldn't find the nerve, so she just nodded in agreement. She stole another glance at the man, strong-jawed, so very tall and dashing . . . and yet she often wondered how a Harvard-educated man had ended up here, at the very end of the road in Wyoming.

That question could be asked of just about anyone in Bethlehem. Whatever did you do to end up here? What forgiveness did you seek to find this place?

But asking such a thing was never done.

The line continued to move, and Miss Minch found herself being edged aside as Mr. King came forward, plate in hand, his daughters trailing after him. The youngest, Francine, reached around and took two biscuits.

"Is Mrs. Clarke here yet?" Mr. King asked Inola, glancing around the room.

Inola's jaw set for a moment. "I'm sorry, Mr. King, she isn't coming tonight."

"No?" The man glanced toward the door in vain while his oldest two nudged each other knowingly.

"She's feeling a mite poorly today." The words came out with a wry note.

Miss Minch wished she could be so lucky.

"Tell her I hope she's feeling better soon," Mr. King offered.

Inola huffed a breath. "Oh, I imagine she'll be quite improved by tomorrow." She paused for a moment and then looked over the girls. "Why, Miss Myrtle, you've gotten taller this winter. I say, you and Miss Minch are just the same height, and both so willowy. I am envious."

At this, Mr. King turned slightly, his eyes widening as he realized that Parathinia was right there, for he clearly hadn't seen her.

"Oh my! Miss Minch! Do join us," he offered hastily, remembering his manners.

"Yes, Miss Minch, please do," his middle daughter, Myrtle, added as she came around him to get a biscuit. "We have room at our table."

Parathinia smiled slightly and turned back to Inola. "Do you need any help?" It wasn't a question as much as a plea.

"Oh, no, Miss Minch, you go on and have your supper," Inola told her. "Mrs. Higgins is going to come spell me in a little bit so I can go eat with Mr. Turner."

Well, at least someone got to do things how they wanted, Parathinia mused as an empty plate was pressed into her hands and the chatter of the King girls surrounded her. As much as she longed to make her own excuses and go home, she spied Mrs. George L. rising from her chair at the table up front, an empty spot reserved beside her.

Oh, heavens, no. She'd have to spend the evening complimenting every detail of the decorations—and comparing them favorably against those Mrs. Norwood had chosen the previous year—if only to remain in Mrs. George L.'s good graces for next twelve months.

Honestly, the rivalry between the two women was exhausting.

"I would love to join you," she told the Kings, quickly filling her plate and ducking behind Mr. King so Mrs. George L. couldn't find her. Well, not easily.

Safely ensconced at their table, with Goldie on one side and Francine on the other while Mr. King and Myrtle sat across from them, their party soon increased as the Hoback family joined them.

Quickly the conversations took familiar roads. Speculation on the weather. The price of butter. Mrs. Hoback fussing over "you poor motherless girls," a designation that had Francine pulling faces whenever the woman wasn't looking.

Halfway through dinner, Mrs. Bergstrom went into labor, but it was such a common occurrence that it was barely noted. Grace Wilkie, the town's midwife, hurried forward to walk the woman home and tend to things while Mr. Bergstrom and the rest of the Bergstrom children stayed put, happily enjoying their Thanksgiving feast.

As the lines for seconds and thirds ebbed and flowed, others milled around the jars at the end of the table.

Francine reached around Parathinia and poked her sister. "You owe me a penny."

"How is that, Frankie?" Goldie was, like her name implied, shiny and bright with golden hair and a regal bearing.

Francine nodded toward the front door. "Look who's here. Told ya Badger was coming."

They all looked up, and there was the very familiar figure of the town recluse, Badger. The man paused hesitantly at the doorway, as if he expected to be sent packing, but after a brief lull in conversation, he ambled toward the supper table. Inola stepped up immediately to offer him a plate, the pair chatting amiably as he filled it.

They were two rafts adrift in a sea of judgment.

"Told you he'd be here," Francine continued to crow. Having caught the attention of the much younger Hoback children, she leaned forward. "I heard tell he killed a man in Laramie."

"It was not Laramie, but Texas." Goldie glanced over at him. "I do hope he's bathed. The last time he came into the store, I nearly fainted."

"I don't think Mr. Wu has that much hot water in his entire laundry," Frankie added.

"Enough of your gossip, girls. Badger always pays his account in full." Mr. King's sharp words brought the pair of them upright, and the sisters nodded in concession.

Apparently this was the highest praise their mercantile father could heap upon his fellow man.

"Look there, Miss Minch," Goldie said, tipping her head slightly. "Mr. Thayer is smiling at you."

Parathinia swore the sharp-eyed girl never missed a thing. "Oh, hardly." But, unable to help herself, she looked anyway, and indeed there was Mr. Thayer, seated at his vaulted spot at the Lovells' table, smiling in her direction. Not so much with good humor but rather with a droll tip of the lips that might be taken to mean "help."

She wasn't the only one to notice.

"He took two helpings of your biscuits," Goldie added.

"So did Frankie," Myrtle remarked, though no one paid her much heed.

"Look, he's getting up." Goldie turned toward Miss Minch, her face alight with excitement. "Do you think he's coming over here?"

Parathinia tried to say something, but her tongue seemed glued to the roof of her mouth.

Not that the King sisters seemed to notice.

"Maybe he'll ask you to dance," Goldie speculated, her eyes getting that dreamy sort of look that came with being just twenty.

The girl's delighted hope sent a bolt of panic through Parathinia. "I certainly hope not."

That got everyone's attention. After all, Mr. Thayer was the town's most prominent lawyer. Granted, there were only two lawyers in Bethlehem, so it wasn't much of a contest, but still . . .

As it turned out, Mr. Thayer was seeking something else— seconds from the supper table.

The girls all let out a sigh, but none more so than Mrs. Hoback, who had other opinions.

"No wonder," she remarked. "Poor man never gets a home-cooked meal. I was just saying to Mrs. Jonas the other day that I thought Mr. Thayer appears quite worn of late." She shot Miss Minch a pointed glance, as if this were her problem to solve, and then turned back to threatening her youngest to finish his green beans or "there would be none of Inola's fine pie for him."

The King sisters—at least Goldie and Myrtle—frowned with disappointment at the man. Parathinia, for her part, was nothing but relieved. At one time such a moment would have been everything to her. But she'd learned in the last twenty-some years not to let her heart get distracted with such vainglorious folly.

Still, she stole another glance at Mr. Thayer and had to agree with Mrs. Hoback. He did look a bit thin.

"I wonder if Mr. Thayer ever killed anyone." Francine took another bite of pie and considered the idea.

"Don't be ridiculous," Goldie told her. "He's a gentleman. If he'd killed someone, Miss Minch would know."

They all turned toward her.

"Me? How would I know such a thing?"

"Because you're the postmistress. You know all the town's secrets," Francine said matter-of-factly.

Now all eyes at the table turned toward her.

"Is it true, Miss Minch," Goldie asked, leaning closer, "you see all the love letters?"

Francine rushed to add, "And who has a wife tucked away in a sanitarium?" The girl read far too many penny dreadfuls.

"Or who has outstanding debts?" Myrtle said with a practical air.

"Listen to you all." Parathinia managed a nervous laugh. "This is hardly Cheyenne with such goings-on."

"But you see all the mail," Goldie pointed out.

The love letters. The debts. The secrets. Yes, she did. All of them passed through her hands. Quietly. Silently. Never remarked upon. Secrets were her stock, but never her trade.

"Indeed, I do," she told them. "But I only see what is on the outside," she reminded them firmly. "Not the inside. What I do see on an envelope is of no mind to me. Just that it gets where it's intended."

"But aren't you ever curious?" Francine persisted.

She shuddered and shook and her head. "Oh, heavens, no." Secrets came with a price, one she was of no mind to pay ever again. But she added, with all the authority granted to her by the United States Postal Service, "I would remind each of you that regulations are very clear on the matter."

Goldie opened her mouth to continue, but her father cut her off.

"Girls!" Mr. King spoke sharply. "Leave poor Miss Minch alone. She is our postmistress because she is the epitome of honesty and, more importantly, discretion. You would do well to follow her example."

"Yes, father," came a trio of echoes.

After a few moments of silence, Goldie ventured back to their earlier subject. "Promise, Miss Minch, you'll stay for the dancing." She smiled toward Mr. Thayer, unwilling to give up all hope just yet.

"I'm not much for dancing," Parathinia demurred, picking up her fork and making a great show of eating the piece of pie in front of her. As good as it was—and yes, it was *that* good—she had a hard time enjoying the sweet slice of heaven, what with the clock ticking away.

All too soon it would be time for—

"Miss Minch," Francine began, "do you put your name in the Christmas tree drawing?"

She shook her head. "That would hardly be fair."

"Why not?" Francine's fork sat poised over a slice of pie. "Everyone can enter, and it seems to me—"

"Frankie, it wouldn't be fair if she were to enter," Mr. King pointed out. "Remember why she does this! Miss Minch selflessly gives up her chance in order to keep the drawing fair and honest. We owe her a debt."

They all looked down at their plates, thus chastened. But not for long.

"At least you can make a Christmas wish," Francine persisted. The girl was, if anything, fearless. "You make a wish, don't you?"

Parathinia shook her head. "I gave up Christmas wishes a long time ago."

Goldie shot her little sister a glance that spoke volumes. *Do be quiet.*

Of course, Francine ignored her. "Oh, golly, Miss Minch. There's no reason not to. Everyone does. You gotta have something you would wish for, don't ya?"

I want someone to call me Ninny.

But she could hardly say such a thing. Not out loud. Why, they'd think her nothing more than a foolish spinster.

If they didn't already. And yet, here it was, this notion to be Ninny again. Oh, what was it with this day? She was starting to think she shouldn't have gotten out of bed.

Having found no sport in Miss Minch's silence, Francine turned back to her sister. "Why don't you tell us what you wished for, Goldie? Or should I guess *who* you asked for?"

"Whom she wished for," Myrtle corrected, pushing her spectacles back up her nose.

"Stop that right now, both of you." Goldie set down her fork, glaring at her sisters, a telltale blush rising on her cheeks. "Shandy isn't likely to bring you that motoring car you want, Frankie—not when you persist on wearing dungarees everywhere."

"He's not going to get Peter Bergstrom to kiss you either," her little sister shot back, her face smug with victory.

Goldie's face flamed. "Francine King! Wishes are private!"

An unrepentant Francine smirked. "Then don't write so big."

"Girls! Please!" Mr. King shook his head and turned back to his discussion with Mr. Hoback as to the fluctuating prices of heating oil.

All three bowed their heads and continued to eat, slanting glances at each other that promised more was to be said later on all accounts.

After a modest interval, Myrtle ventured forth. "Do you think, Miss Minch, it is proper to wish for someone to kiss you?"

Instead of erupting into a cacophony of questions and taunts, the three sisters turned in unison to Parathinia. Apparently, there were no boundaries with sisters, and for this moment, they were holding her to the same tenet.

Gracious heavens! They actually expected her to answer? "I-I-I, that is, I've—"

Thankfully, Mrs. Lovell and the Christmas tree committee chose that moment to rise from their places and make their way to the podium. That was enough to still the roomful of conversations.

"Zooks!" Francine whispered. "It's time."

Time.

Forget being Ninny again. If Parathinia were to make a wish, she'd divine a sick headache like Mrs. Clarke. Or even Mrs. Bergstrom's excuse. But there was no saving her now from the most humiliating five minutes of the entire year.

"You are so lucky, Miss Minch." Francine grinned. "You get to know who the winner is before everyone else."

Parathinia wished with all her heart she could just hand the task over to someone else, then be like snow in the spring, melting and disappearing into the depths of the earth.

As she rose, Francine tugged at her sleeve and whispered, "When you pick, look out for one with bent corners. I saw Josephine Lovell deliberately bending down the corners on hers."

Before Parathinia could respond, Miss Elda Barrett, the town's schoolteacher, raised her baton in front of her gathered students, and the school band began a deafening refrain of squeaks and squawks in a poor attempt at a Sousa march. Parathinia had no choice but to make the long, humiliating procession to the stage.

Worse, there was an enthusiastic round of applause, so if anyone hadn't been looking at her before, they were now. What if she tripped? That terrifying thought was added to the laundry list of her greatest fears.

One foot after another, Parathinia made her way to the front—all in one piece—and was quickly flanked by the Christmas tree committee, Mrs. George L. Lovell, Miss Cora Stafford of the *Bethlehem Observer,* and Mr. Bohlen, the mayor. His wife, Mrs. Bohlen, stood off to the side. She wasn't part of the committee, but she never missed an opportunity to remind everyone she was the mayor's wife.

That, and she was wearing a new hat.

Mr. Bohlen smiled at Miss Minch and looked ready to speak, but Mrs. George L., unwilling to relinquish the spotlight, stepped in front of him, filling the space behind the podium, waving her hands for everyone to settle down.

"My dear citizens of Bethlehem, I do hope with all my heart you found your Thanksgiving meal satisfactory." She made her greeting with a modest, demure air, as if she'd cooked the supper herself. Not that anyone was fooled, but they supplied her with a roar of loud applause as well as a few whoops from the miners in the back.

"Now for the moment we've all been waiting for," she continued, thrusting out the green mason jar stuffed with names. "Miss Minch, will you do the honors?"

As if Parathinia had a choice.

Her hand wavered over the jar. Plunge it in and pick. It was so simple. Yet she couldn't. Instead, she looked up and let her gaze sweep over the assembled crowd, the sea of familiar faces, the happy families gathered together.

She scrupulously avoided such intimate moments only because they reminded her of how alone she truly was—a postmistress who daily watched the world slide through her fingers yet had no real place in it.

Shaking off that thought, she slid her hand into the jar, into the mishmash of paper. Exactly as Francine had said, here was a piece with bent corners. She shook her head slightly and pushed her hand in deeper.

Honesty and discretion. Everyone here trusted her to do the right thing.

"Parathinia," Mrs. George L. hissed under her breath, "draw a name."

That nudge pushed her to hastily catch hold of the first slip she could wrangle and draw it out. The entire room quieted as she opened it.

Then, much to her horror, another slip fell from the first, fluttering to the floor of the stage, an errant butterfly out of season.

"Parathinia, what have you done?" the chairwoman hissed, even as Parathinia scooped them up.

Indeed, what had she done? She'd drawn two names.

She took a furtive glance at the slips in her hand, and the two names came into clear focus. Oh, if only she'd tripped on the way up and knocked herself senseless, for the shock of what stared up at her left her flabbergasted. What were the odds?

She straightened and looked out at the expectant crowd, now a bit restless as whispers of her mistake spread quickly.

"Two. She's drawn two slips."

"Well, who are they?" someone shouted from the back.

Who? Hastily she crumpled the slips in her hand and frantically tried to form the names caught in her throat.

"A name, Parathinia. Choose a name," Mrs. George L. whispered in a demand both sharp and disapproving..

Pick? She couldn't. She wouldn't.

Her indecision was suddenly met by something far more powerful than even Mrs. George L.

Exorior!

Good heavens, this was not a time for Mrs. Mercer's goading, and yet it was like a memory from the past, a happy whisper from the girl who danced in the wildflowers. The sense that everything was about to change if only . . .

"Archimedes Thayer," she declared. Immediately people began to politely clap. Yet that wasn't right. So she spoke up again, this time with a burst of something she couldn't explain.

Rise forth. And she did, in a moment of unparalleled defiance.

"Sterling McCandish Densmore."

All around the room, the citizens exchanged bewildered glances.

Now, everyone knew Archie Thayer. But Sterling McCandish Densmore? People mouthed out the name as if saying it would jog their memory.

"Who's that?" one of the miners in the back shouted.

All eyes looked once again to Parathinia, for if there was anyone who knew everyone, it was their postmistress.

"There is no such person," Mrs. George L. announced, clearly uneasy with the misdirection of the proceedings, especially on her watch. "Mr. Densmore, indeed." Then she went to snatch the slips of paper from Parathinia's hand if only to put these proceedings to rights.

But before she could, there was a shuffle at one of the back tables, and a chair scraped loudly against the wooden floor. "Oh, aye, that's me," Badger announced in a deep Scottish burr, lumbering to his feet and glaring at one and all, daring anyone to contradict him.

Of course, Mrs. George L. rather insisted on doing just that. "This cannot be," she whispered to the committee, her tone askance at having the town derelict anointed with such a high honor. She reeled around so her back was to the room, and she faced Parathinia, who had slid the pieces of paper into her pocket. "There's no mistake about it. You picked Mr. Thayer first."

"But did she?" Cora Stafford tipped her head and gave it a slight shake. "I'm not so certain."

"Well, I'm always certain," Mrs. George L. shot back.

"Indeed, she pulled out two names," Mrs. Bohlen chimed in, clearly without thinking and always too eager help.

At least by Mrs. George L.'s estimation. "Obviously," the woman said, in a voice low and withering enough to send Mrs. Bohlen shrinking back and wishing her new hat wasn't quite so prominent.

Not to be outdone by his wife, Mr. Bohlen stepped forward and spoke in a stage whisper. "It looks like we have a competition, now, doesn't it?" He rubbed his hands together and winked at the crowd.

"Absolutely not!" Mrs. George L. declared, but her words were drowned out by a new round of cheering. She whirled back to Parathinia. "Just say which name you chose first."

"I don't know," she answered in all honesty.

"Do you want to be the reason Christmas is ruined?" Mrs. George L.'s brows arched to punctuate what she was really saying.

Choose Mr. Thayer and remedy this disaster.

"Yes, I have to agree. In fact, it appears the majority of the committee is in agreement," Cora Stafford said, her eyes sparking a bit. "You'll just have to choose, Miss Minch. Will it be Mr. Thayer or Mr. . . ." She dug out her ever-present notepad and a stub of a pencil.

At the very sight of them, Mrs. George L. groaned.

Not that Cora cared. Like a fisherman dangling a baited hook over a plump trout, she smiled kindly at Parathinia. "What did you say Badger's real name is?"

Parathinia took a step back. Knowing Cora, she'd probably already drafted her headline for next Thursday's edition of the *Observer*, something along the lines of "CALAMITY AT CHRISTMAS."

And in a typeface large enough to take up the entire top half of the newspaper.

Oh, whatever had she done? "Well, I think . . . That is, I think I should . . ." Parathinia gazed out over the sea of expectant faces, but all she saw clearly were two.

Mr. Thayer, calm and smiling as if awaiting his expected anointing, and Badger, arms crossed over his chest and a merry twinkle in his eyes.

Daring her. He was daring her to defy them all. As if he'd heard that odd whisper as well.

Exorior!

Then the Opera House door swung open with a bang and a swirl of wind and snow. With it came Dobbs, skidding to a stop, breathless, snow crowning his dark, closely shorn head.

"Shandy's back! He's here." The boy drew a deep shuddering breath, wildly glancing around the room before he continued. "Doc, you got to come. There's trouble."

That brought everyone to their feet.

Old Doc Groves pushed his way forward. "Outta my way, you fools," he complained. "Where is he, Dobbs?"

"In the Star Bright."

That gave half the room pause. The female half. They reared back nearly in unison.

Even the doctor stopped. "What? The saloon?"

"Yes, sir. The sheriff is with him."

"Well, fetch him round to my office, boys," the doctor ordered a couple of the larger youths.

But Dobbs wasn't done. "That won't do. He ain't alone. Shandy's brought someone new with him."

CHAPTER 4

*A*s Madeline came to, hushed conversations ebbed and flowed around her. And when she finally willed her eyes open, the voices stilled, and she found a dozen or so faces staring down at her.

"Doc, she's waking up," someone said.

Crap.

Sadly, this wasn't the first time she'd come to with a crowd around her.

Madeline tried to turn, but a sharp pain rifled through her head, and she scrunched her eyes shut against flickers of memories that made no sense. An owl. Swirling, blinding snow. Metal scraping and grinding.

Darkness. Stillness. Something, someone, reaching out for her.

She yanked her eyes open.

The crowd around her parted slightly and an elderly man, with a neatly trimmed white beard and a deeply lined brow, came forward and knelt beside her. "There, there. Easy now. How are you feeling, miss?"

Before she could push out an answer, someone else spoke for her.

"Well, hell, Doc. Pretty bad, I reckon. Look at that goose egg she's sportin'."

Doc shook his head ever so slightly, but it was the younger man at his side who spoke first, and with some authority. "Be quiet, Denny. Let the doc do his job."

She managed to keep her eyes open this time, even as she raised her hand and found the painful spot. She winced. Yep, a goose egg of a bump.

The doctor took her hand, checking her pulse and prattling on with long-practiced ease. "Careful there. Looks like you took quite a blow. Do you remember what happened?"

She tried to gather the tumbling pieces together—glass breaking, being tossed like a pair of tennis shoes in a dryer, the grinding of metal.

Holy shit, the truck. The snow. The icy road.

She'd been in an accident. A bad one.

The air seemed to leave the room. *Don't panic. You're still alive.*

Yet something wasn't right. Here she was, surrounded by total strangers, so why wasn't anyone shouting at her? There wasn't a single cell phone out. Or the usual chatter that rolled over her like errant waves of disgrace.

She's drunk again.

Who'd she punch this time?

Think I can get a selfie before she comes to?

Madeline struggled to sit up, and the crowd reeled back as if she were a jack-in-the-box suddenly sprung from captivity. She blinked, even though it hurt to do so, straining to fix her gaze on her surroundings. Antlers on the wall, lights flickering near the bar, stained glass twinkling in the cabinets, extras in turn-of-the-century costumes.

She breathed a sigh of relief. She was on the *Star Bright* set . . . and yet . . . she'd left the studio, hadn't she? Despite her muddled senses, she had a very clear memory of Nate's glower as she abruptly abandoned the final hour of shooting to catch a last-minute chartered flight Mindy had booked so she could go confront Emerson.

And while everything here seemed so familiar, it wasn't. Yes, the extras were all here, but the cameras and crew were missing. And there were four walls, not just three.

And the air . . . She sniffed. Old cigars. Spilled beer. Dust. Someone who really, really needed a shower. Perhaps more than one person.

Somewhere she heard a door creak open, and the wind rushed in, nipping everything in its path with a chill that wasn't manufactured.

The set was always hot, but here, the cold seemed capable of seeping into one's bones.

"Good heavens! Let me through." The words held a haughty air of irritation and expectation. "This is a terrible place to bring a new minister."

The crowd parted in due haste, all except the young man by the doctor's side. He alone stood his ground.

This latest arrival came into view, his round, florid face scrunched into a moue of dismay as he pointed a short, thick finger at her. "That is not a minister."

"You added that up right quick for a banker, Mr. Lovell," someone said with a laugh.

The man ignored the heckling. "Sheriff Fischer, I'll have an explanation of this!" he said to the young man at the doctor's side.

Madeline turned toward him as well. *Sheriff Fischer*. The name suited him somehow. As if he'd been perfectly cast. Why, he looked like a young John Wayne, all scrubbed and brushed.

And she'd know—she'd watched *Stagecoach* more times than she could count with Gigi.

"You're complaining to the wrong man, Mr. Lovell." Why, he even spoke like a young John Wayne: carefully, slowly, all steady authority.

But his matter-of-fact answer found no favor with the older man, whose jaw worked back and forth. "Mrs. Lovell will not be pleased. Not in the least."

"When is she ever?" someone in the back muttered.

"Forget about his wife," another added. "Who is going to tell Poppy?"

Mr. Lovell's bushy brows furrowed like fat exclamation points as he issued another edict. "I will have an accounting of this from Shandy."

Inadvertently, he opened a floodgate of memories.

Emerson's betrayal. Her life upside down. That horrible pickup.

Madeline found herself swept again into a vast darkness of currents and torrents, and the only thing she could latch onto was that one name.

Shandy.

THE HOUR HAD GROWN LATE. At least Savannah assumed so as she knitted away with a fierce consternation. The clock on the parlor mantel had stopped working not long after Inola left. Fool thing was never reliable.

Click. Click. Click. There was none of the usual calm that surrounded her as the stitches moved from one needle to another. That, and the parlor was chilly. She should have settled into the kitchen where it was warm, but tonight the stiff furniture and orderly room suited her mood.

Thanksgiving, indeed. Whatever did anyone in this town have to be thankful for?

Her pace continued unabated, even when the back door opened and brought with it a gust of November wind that reached deep into the house for every bit of warmth it could snatch.

Click. Click. Click.

Finally a pair of voices managed to prod her out of her solitary tower. Words full of warmth and good cheer, belying the falling thermometer.

Inola's laughter came first. "Just bring in that basket and leave it on the dining room table, Mr. Turner. I'll put it all away in the morning. Lordy, I'm worn out."

Savannah glanced up. So Inola wasn't alone. At least she'd had the sense to ask for help. Hadn't Savannah told her she was doing too much? Not that Inola ever listened.

"And that last piece of pie . . . ?" Mr. Turner's drawn-out question carried with it all the warm, drawling notes of home.

Home.

That familiar cadence, a reminder of the vast distance between then and now, stretched so thin that she feared if she dropped even one stitch, all her precious memories would unravel and be lost forever. Yet she couldn't help but reach for the echoes of his words, so very intimate, a flickering light drawing her closer to something she couldn't quite reach.

Inola's footsteps, as familiar as her own, echoed in the kitchen. "Don't you serve pie at that hotel of yours?"

"Not like yours." Mr. Turner had arrived in Bethlehem not long after they had, and had set to work opening and running a hotel by the railway station. "If you ever want to come cook for my guests . . ."

How long ago had that been? Savannah shook her head. Time here in Bethlehem was as odd and patchy as a tinker's wares. She tried to count the years, but they blurred together.

An inelegant snort was the reply. "Oh, yes, it always starts with a bit of cooking. And then what will you be wanting, Mr. Turner?"

"Now, Miss Inola, don't you think, after all this time, you could call me by my given name?" he cajoled, his voice full of charm. Not surprising. He'd been a porter on the railway before . . . before
. . .

Savannah tugged at the ball of yarn, winding the strand through her fingers as she sought to find her way again. *Before.*

Oh, how that one word marked the lives of the citizens of Bethlehem. A dividing line between the lives they'd had and the ones they'd been given when Shandy brought them here.

For Savannah, that wavering "before" was like the flickering images from Mrs. George L.'s fancy stereoscope, the one she kept prominently displayed in her parlor.

Click. A house in New Orleans.

Click. Papa's estate far up the river, with its wide lawn that ran endlessly up to the grand columned house.

Click. A child laughing as he tumbled along after her, gamboling like a puppy around her wide hooped skirts.

Click. War and darkness. Everything light and good obliterated into one endless horizon of hardship and calamity.

In the kitchen, Inola's laughter hauled her back into the light, tethered her from falling. "Elias Turner, you keep your hands off that pie. I saved that piece for Mrs. Clarke."

"So you keep saying." There was yet another shuffle of boots and then the rattle of dishes as the basket settled on the table. "Seems to me if Miz Clarke can't be bothered to come to Thanksgiving—"

"Now you just shush right there. She's got her reasons. Not good ones, mind you, but she's got her reasons."

"Still, how's she to know you saved that one for her?" His words were persistent. Teasing.

Then again, it was one of Inola's pies. Savannah wasn't so proud not to admit that she'd wheedled once or twice for an extra slice.

"Oh, go on with you. Get out. I'm not going to listen to such talk," Inola was saying. "'Sides, I know how many pieces of pie you ate tonight."

Yet there was no retreat toward the back door, for clearly the lure of that last piece of pie—or was it something else?—had Mr. Turner staying put.

Savannah's knitting stilled. What was this?

"Why stay here, Inola?" Words spoken from the heart. "I don't understand why you won't get married. Have your own house, have a—"

"A what? A family?" Inola finished, with the sort of scoffing note that should have put an end to this all-too-personal inquiry. "I'm too old for such a thing."

Not that Mr. Turner was listening. Then again, he *was* a man. "Hardly," he continued in earnest.

"I don't expect you to understand," Inola told him. "No one does. As for Mrs. Clarke, well, she's all the family I got. The only bit of home I care about."

Savannah's fingers faltered, the yarn falling away. She shivered and began winding the yarn back onto the ball with tight, sure circles so it didn't come loose again, holding at bay her regrets and twinges of responsibility.

They were here because of her.

"What do you need, Inola?" Mr. Turner's question came out not with the coaxing air of a man after the last piece of pie, but with an intimate whisper of understanding, words strung together like a line of those new-fangled Christmas lights Mr. King had hung in the window of his mercantile, twinkling bits of hope and promise.

"Go on with you, Elias Turner," Inola told him with a laugh. "The only thing I need is sleep. And when I say sleep, I mean just that, *sleep*."

The man chuckled, and his boots shuffled across the floor. Savannah looked up at the parlor door, the one that cut her off from the scene playing out down the hall.

Inola's boots clicked against the floorboards. "I'm too tired for your foolishness. I've been on my feet since before sunrise."

"You don't fool me, Inola Charles. You would have danced all night if they hadn't called it off."

"Might have. Say, why don't you go see what all that fuss is about?"

He laughed again. "I just might. And if I have a mind, I'll be back." The back door creaked open.

"I'm sure you will be, Mr. Turner. You're as certain as death and taxes."

"Far more pleasurable, I assure you."

"Don't you have a hotel to see to?"

Another chuckle echoed in the kitchen, and the trod of boots was followed by a firm thud of the back door closing.

Jolted out of her eavesdropping, Savannah rather clumsily poked at the next stitch in her knitting.

"Just sitting there being stubborn, I see," Inola remarked from the doorway. "You didn't eat anything, did you?"

"I wasn't hungry."

Inola sniffed at this. "Don't know why I even bother." She turned and then paused. "I saved you a piece of pie. Best come and eat it, or I'll give it to one of those vagrants I'm so fond of feeding."

"Like Mr. Turner." The words came out sharper than Savannah intended, and immediately she regretted them, but before she could say anything resembling an apology, Inola stalked back to the kitchen in high dudgeon.

Savannah's shoulders sagged. When would she learn to govern

her tongue? She stowed her knitting in her workbasket and made her way to the kitchen. "I'm sorry."

"For what?" Inola asked. "For not coming with me tonight? For sniping at me over a leftover piece of pie? Clearly I should have let Mr. Turner have it." She wiped her hands on her apron. "Don't even pretend like you weren't listening."

Savannah had the good sense not to. Their house wasn't that big.

Inola huffed and began to unpack one of the baskets on the worktable. "Better still, I've got half a mind to give that piece to Badger's old dog."

"You wouldn't dare." But she knew Inola would if she set her mind to it, so Savannah quickly picked up the plate and a fork before settling down at the small table in the corner.

Inola grinned at her. "Thought that would get you out of your sulks."

"I am not sulking," she replied between bites. Nutmeg, buttery crust, and sweet potatoes all collided together. It was pure heaven. She might have groaned a little.

Not maybe, for here was Inola chuckling as she laid out the silver on the dining room table so it could be sorted and put away in the morning.

Savannah finished eating quickly, guilt prodding her to do more than sulk, and once she'd settled her plate and fork into the sink, she turned to the last basket that needed unpacking. Yet when she pulled the cloth free and looked inside, she jumped back, pointing at the basket with a shaky finger. "What is *that*?"

"What is what?" Inola came over to take a look, and did the same double take. "Well, I'll be." Unlike Savannah, she reached inside. "You mean this?"

Savannah backed up as if Inola held a snake.

"Not surprised you don't know what this is," Inola said, setting the blue mason jar down on the table. "That there is a bona fide jar of wishes."

The word came out before Savannah could stop it. "*Wishes?*"

Inola blew out a breath. "Yes. You remember those?"

"I know what wishes are," Savannah shot back, frozen in place as she eyed the jar. Shandy's jar. She retreated behind her armor of reserve and disdain. "What a foolish waste of time and paper. Why, that old jar probably held sour pickles last week." She sniffed again. "Whatever will the people of this town come up with next?"

"Only time will tell," Inola replied.

"That still doesn't answer as to what *that* is doing *here*."

Inola shrugged and went to unpack the rest of the basket. "I don't rightly know. There was one hullabaloo after another tonight."

"Really?" *In Bethlehem?* Giving the jar a wide berth, Savannah picked up the stack of dessert plates and put them away in the china hutch in the dining room. Her gaze slid toward the window. Beyond the copse, the lights from town sparkled. "What was this hullabaloo about?"

"What do you care?" Inola replied as she stacked dinner plates.

"I care," Savannah insisted as she gathered them up, curiosity being an odd sort of hunger.

"Since you asked . . ." Inola said, letting her words hang there.

"I did," Savannah replied, carrying the stack of plates into the dining room.

"Mrs. Bergstrom went into labor."

That hardly warranted a stir. "When isn't she having baby?"

Inola's gaze rolled upward and she made a sort of *tsk-tsk*, continuing her work in that stony silence she favored when she disapproved of something.

Savannah pursed her lips, for she couldn't stand Inola's silence or her censure. "How was she faring?" she finally asked, doing her best to sound contrite.

"I don't know, but Grace is with her."

Savannah nodded, and drew a deep breath that settled heavily in her chest. Childbirth. There was no easy way about the business of a pushing a new life into the world, but if it was any solace, Mrs. Bergstrom had done this before, and Grace Wilkie was a good midwife.

Still, that was no guarantee.

Every woman who'd ever walked that lonely, painful road knew the very real fear that arrived hand in hand with the pangs of labor.

There was nothing to be done 'cept get on with it and pray, as Inola's mother used to say.

"Babies come all the time." Savannah glanced again out the window before adding, "Especially in that house. Hardly seems like much to get in a foment over."

As it was, Inola had more than one card up her sleeve. "Oh, the stir had nothing to do with Mrs. Bergstrom. The real scandal was Miss Minch."

Savannah straightened. "Oh, now you are teasing. You expect me to believe Miss Minch caused a scandal? Really, Inola."

"Oh, it's possible." She began sorting through the empty pie tins. "I don't know the particulars 'cause I was in the kitchen finishing up the dishes. Afore I could find out anything, word came about Shandy. Well, nearly everyone got up to go see him, and Miss Minch was quite forgotten."

Savannah settled the pie tins on the shelf. Bother Inola, she was deliberately leaving out the good bits, and worse, she was going to make Savannah beg for them. So she feigned indifference. "I don't see why Shandy's arrival would cause any sort of stir. He arrives most years. Right around supper time."

"Suppose so."

Finally Savannah could stand it no more. "So are you going to leave me in suspense all night—"

"Gonna have to," Inola told her, wiping her hands on her apron and surveying her work. "'Cause I didn't see who he brought."

Savannah stilled. "You didn't think to tell me that first?"

"Nope."

"Why not?" If there was one thing she could count on from Inola, it was the gathering of information. She loved the town's prattle as much as anyone.

"Well, I've never set foot in that place, and I don't plan on doing so any time soon—not even to satisfy your curiosity. Or mine." There was a note of indignation to Inola's words.

"Good heavens, whatever are you going on about? There isn't a square inch of this town that you wouldn't set foot in . . . . 'cept . . . ."

Except one.

The surprise must have shown on Savannah's face. "You don't mean—"

Both women glanced out the back window, past the huddle of aspens and cottonwood toward the main street of town, where a confluence of lights twinkled where there shouldn't be any at all.

"Oh my," Savannah finally managed, her world shifting beneath her feet.

Out of the corner of her eye, she swore that horrible mason jar winked in the lamplight. She shook her head and turned to Inola. "But you sent Mr. Turner to—"

"So you were listening."

"You weren't particularly quiet, and it's a small house."

Inola's lips twitched, but she didn't say another word. At least not on that subject. As she turned from the window, she spoke softly and quietly. "What do you think it means?"

Savannah slanted a glance at her. Inola looked fair worn out. She'd done all that work without any help.

That in itself plucked at her. *You should have helped.*

And what had Inola told Mr. Turner so adamantly? *She's all the family I got.*

That went both ways.

Another look at Inola's tired features and Savannah reached over and took the last stack of dishes from her. "You've done too much today. The whole week, I imagine. Go get some rest. I'll sort this all out."

"So now you notice?"

"I always notice."

"Well, then." Inola untied her apron and hung it on a hook. She had to be tired if she was giving up without even a scrap of an argument. "If you don't mind—"

"No, I don't. Suppose it is the least I can do." After all, there was no use arguing over today when it was nearly over.

Inola took one last glance out the window and shook her head in a sort of resignation that came from a lifetime of facing the silent, unrevealing dawn. "Good night, Vanna."

"Good night, Nola." Savannah watched her leave even as she

considered what needed to be done and where to start. But even as she reached for the first stack of pie pans, her gaze strayed toward the window and that odd bit of light that shouldn't be there.

That building had stood in the middle of town for years, without a proprietor, without a purpose, and now . . . Well, it was like looking up and finding some long-forgotten star suddenly sparkling overhead, like Mr. Halley's comet come early.

Not that any of it was her concern. She swept her hands over her skirt, turned, and did the last thing she'd ever want to do—she bumped into the corner of the table and sent a jar flying.

That jar.

The one she wanted nothing to do with. Yet here it was tumbling over, and her scrambling and flailing to catch it before it hit the floor. Time slowed as the jar spun in the air. Her hands dipped and dove, until she'd nearly consigned herself to the inevitable shatter of glass.

But catch it she did, a hair's breadth from the floor.

Still, the incident hadn't been without casualties.

The strips of paper inside had found freedom, falling like bits of New Year's Eve confetti all around her feet.

Savannah froze, the blue jar safe in her hands, her feet glued to the floor for fear of trampling someone else's heart's desire. After a few fluttering heartbeats, and assured that Shandy's jar was whole and safe, she gave a sweeping glance at the drifting slips of paper.

Scraps, really. Hardly as terrifying as the pounding of her heart would lead her to believe.

They were, after all, only words on paper.

Nor were they her wishes.

Not that anyone had listened to hers that long-ago night. *I will have no part of this place, sir. Better you leave me to die.*

Bother Shandy and his interfering ways. Savannah almost felt sorry for this new lost soul. Almost. Because no one came here without some sort of grievous sin on their shoulders. Something to atone for.

She knelt down, her black wool skirt pooling in a stormy cloud around her. She did her best to ignore the frayed hem that seemed more evident against the bleached wood of the floor. The skirt needed to be made over. Yet again.

Stuffing the first handful of wishes back in the jar went easily enough, but when she reached for another, a child's scrawling handwriting caught her eye.

Please bring candy for Christmas.

Oh, she couldn't help herself. Savannah smiled. How could she not? Some things never changed. Children always wanted candy for Christmas.

Hadn't she? Christmas had always brought the sweet scent of rich, buttery pecans toasting in a skillet. Fluffy white piles of divinity stacked on the counter, just out of the reach of small hands.

Auntie Vanna, will there be pralines?

Whatever do we need pralines for, sugarplum, when you are the sweetest thing ever?

Savanna closed her eyes, pressed her lips together, and shuttered her lashes tight, as if that might blot out the pain, the sudden rush of hot tears. Such a simple wish that had been so impossible. There hadn't been any sugar then.

And she wouldn't make a promise that she couldn't keep.

Then came the year when there was no one to ask her for pralines.

Yet that very same wish now hung in the air like the sharp scent of sugar as it begins to caramelize—not quite burnt, but coming close.

Swiping away a sudden welling of tears, she caught up another handful of wishes and crammed the slips into the jar, this time careful not to look too closely.

Wishes, indeed. Foolishness, really.

And, just like that, they were all back in Shandy's jar where they belonged.

Suddenly she felt as tired as Inola had looked, as if all those years, all those lost Christmases—and, yes, even Thanksgivings—had exacted their toll.

Looking around, she shook her head and decided it might be better to finish this once the bright light of day had chased away the shadows of memories.

But as she gathered up the lamp, something caught her eye.

Two more slips of paper, just near the stove leg.

When she went to pick them up, a worrisome weight settled on her shoulders, leaving her oddly transfixed.

These aren't wishes for candy, a wry, old voice warned.

"They are naught but paper," she reminded herself firmly, feeling foolish that she even needed to be told as much.

She whisked them up, yet as her fingers curled around the torn slips, it was as if she'd freed some wily bit of magic into her tidy, ordered life. And that whisper of warm Christmas wonder beguiled her into forgettting one very important thing.

Don't look.

She took a glance at the first wish, and regrets filled her nearly as fast as the words rushed up to meet her. A child's wish for candy was such an ephemeral desire, but the one staring up at her held a lure capable of finding a home inside her abandoned heart.

It was a wish she'd made so many years ago, one that had utterly changed her life. Now someone else had been reckless enough to dare such a yearning. To take such a chance.

"No," she whispered back, and, without thinking, shoved the slips of paper not into the jar but into the pocket of her skirt. Then she hurried upstairs, those words, that wish, chasing her the entire way.

A wish that had found purchase so deep inside her, she wondered how she'd ever root it out.

A new dress for the Christmas ball.

CHAPTER 5

*M*adeline woke again to stillness, the buzzing chatter thankfully gone. She thought she was all alone, yet as she struggled to push aside the cobwebs in her head, a quiet conversation from somewhere across the room cut through the shadows.

"Where did you pull her from, Shandy?" That voice, she recognized it. Solid and steady. The younger man with the stern expression.

"Jackson Hole." This voice she knew instantly. The odd driver who'd picked her up.

So he'd survived as well. Good. She had a few choice words for him.

"You know exactly what I mean. What year?"

What year? What the hell did that mean? Madeline tried to stir, but it was like pulling herself from a deep dream, thick and heavy layers holding her in place.

"Oh, sometime after you. Thereabouts."

"And you brought her here?"

"She needed a place. Granted, it was a risk, but she has some experience."

"Experience?" Disbelief filled the younger man's question. "I'm afraid to ask."

Madeline lay still and listened. Whatever did he have to be annoyed about? At least he knew where he was.

"Ah, Wick, when will you learn not to judge a bird by its feathers?" Shandy replied. A chair scraped, and boots scuffed against the floor. "Well, looky here. She's come around again. Welcome back, Maddie."

This time she managed to push herself up, and as she did, something slid from her shoulders. A heavy sweater of sorts.

The sheriff stood a few feet away. Wick, Shandy had called him.

He nodded to the sweater. "Had Dobbs get that for you from my place. Thought you might be cold." He glanced down at his feet, then slowly looked back up. "You can hang onto it. You'll need it."

He certainly didn't, Madeline thought, what with his heavy sheepherder's jacket and jeans.

"Thank you," she managed, shrugging her way into it, finding the wool soft and warm. At her feet, she felt, rather than heard, something move. *Thump. Thump. Thump.*

She edged back, and peered cautiously toward the far end of the old-fashioned sofa.

The lost dog. From the truck. His honey-gold tail fluttered tentatively.

"Hey, there, fella," she said softly. "You made it as well."

The dog blinked sleepily at her, then gave a contented sigh and leaned happily against her.

"What's his name?"

Madeline looked up, having forgotten the sheriff for a moment. "I have no idea. He said—" she began, then she nodded toward Shandy. "It's a stray."

"Looks like he's yours now," Wick said, his expression softening for a moment. Though it probably had more to do with the dog than her.

She shook her head. "No. That would be a mistake. I'm not one for dogs."

Wick chuckled. "He doesn't think so."

Canine opinions aside, she reached for the poor mutt, her hand moving from the dog's head to his back. She wasn't so much petting as searching. Miraculously, everything seemed to be in its place. How had this dog survived such a horrific crash unscathed?

For that matter, how had she? And where was she?

The large room around her sat cast in shadows, except for a circle of light from a kerosene lamp on the bar. From what she could see, this place was a close replica of the *Star Bright* set.

Except this felt so very real. Solid, even.

Like the way the dog's stiff fur ruffled as she ran her fingers through it, or how, when she stopped, he ducked his wet nose under her elbow. *More, please.*

"Looks like you've both made it all in one piece," Shandy said, coming to stand beside Wick.

She pointed a shaky finger at him. "You! You brought me here."

"Lucky for you," the sheriff replied.

Lucky? She did her best to remain calm. "Where am I?"

"Wyoming, miss," Wick told her. "Bethlehem, Wyoming."

Madeline tamped down a growing sense of panic. Bethlehem wasn't real. "This whole thing—the bar, the extras from before, the historical attention to detail—is amazing. I'm flattered, really," she rambled, her fears clawing at her need to stay calm. But it was no use. The walls closed in around her, panic pushing her to her feet. She swayed as she straightened but stubbornly held her ground.

The pair gaped at her.

"I appreciate your help, but I need my things. I need to get going." She paused for a moment, half expecting them to try and stop her, but neither man moved.

Until she wavered again, her head protesting.

Wick took a step toward her, but Shandy caught him by the arm and gave a slight shake of his head. *Leave her be.*

If that was the case . . . Madeline took one tentative step, then another. Neither man moved. Her four-legged friend, however, stayed right at her heels. Tugging the sweater tighter around her shoulders, she was struck by the scents enveloping her. Strong soap. Woodsmoke.

So real. So very, very real.

She continued toward the door, glancing behind her every few steps to see if they were going to stop her.

They hadn't moved.

Whatever doubts she had about this place, she knew one thing: this was no Burbank back lot. Definitely not the manufactured conjurings of a set designer. Because you could dress up a set to look like anything, but you couldn't make it smell like this.

Like old cigars. Like spilled beer and flatulent men. Like winter. Yes, it smelled like winter here. That couldn't be faked.

Madeline made it to the door and caught hold of the knob, half clinging to it as she twisted it open. The door came swinging toward her, caught in a gust of wind that nearly knocked her off her unsteady feet. Whatever bit of warmth she'd gained, the wind ripped it away, along with the cobwebs clouding her faculties.

The dog shivered from its nose to its tail. Then he looked up at her as if to say, *You've got to be kidding me.*

Undaunted, she stepped outside, blinded at first. She blinked frantically to find a point of reference, a route of escape, but with the snow dancing drunkenly on the intemperate wind, she couldn't make out anything solid. There were no streetlights casting a warm circle of safety. No headlights.

There was nothing but darkness.

Her chest clenched. Even surrounded by the wind, she couldn't seem to breathe.

No, she definitely wasn't on a set.

Backing inside, she closed the door. Her heart skidded again, ramming against her chest as she clung to the doorknob.

"Where am I?" she whispered to herself.

Then her gaze strayed to an old-fashioned beer advertisement on the wall beside her. A cheerful Gibson girl held up a large mug in greeting, smiling winsomely at her audience above a calendar.

Greetings 1907, it announced in a great swirling script.

1907? Oh, she'd hit her head harder than she'd imagined. No, it was impossible. This was all a hoax. An elaborate, well-planned one.

Slowly, she turned around. "Where exactly am I?"

"As I said before, miss. Bethlehem, Wyoming." Wick went over to the bar and held out a mug for her. "You look like you could use something."

She came closer, drawn by the heavenly scent of coffee—now that was definitely real. But instead of reaching toward it, she sidled past him, making her way to the refuge of the sofa. She wasn't about to take anything from these two. Not until she had some answers. Nor was she about to admit that her venture had left her exhausted and shaky—like she'd just crossed a dozen time zones.

The cheery girl on the poster smiled at her from across the room. A hundred or so years' worth of time.

No. No. And *NO.*

"I'm Madeline Drake, but I assume you already know that," she said, watching the sheriff closely.

"Why would I—" He looked over at Shandy, who merely shrugged.

"Sure, we'll go with that." Madeline sat on the edge of the sofa, straight and tall, trying to appear in control. "How far are we from Jackson?"

Both men exchanged a glance.

"You didn't tell her?" Wick groaned. He caught up one of the chairs, dragged it over to the sofa, and sat down, setting the mug of coffee on a small table nearby.

As enticing as it smelled, Madeline ignored it.

"Didn't have time." Shandy scratched at his craggy chin as he got his own chair. "'Sides, I didn't think she was ready."

"Who is?" Wick huffed a sigh. "I sure wasn't."

"Ready for what?" She took another breath, even as the room tilted a bit beneath her. "And how am I not in a hospital? How is this dog here without the least sign that he's been in a wreck?" Then she got to the heart of it, the question that rose up from her gut. "How am I alive?"

Shandy, it turned out, was well practiced in evasion. "The better question, Maddie, might be, why am I alive?"

"Stop calling me that," she snapped, ignoring the rest of his words. "I don't even know you." The only person who called her 'Maddie' was Nate.

He hardly blinked. "That lump is bad. We met in the truck, don't you remember?"

"I remember. You kidnapped me." She turned to Wick. "If you're really who you say you are, Wyatt Earp, do something. That man kidnapped me."

Wick drew a deep breath and crossed his arms over his chest, apparently used to the vagaries of kidnapped women. "Well, miss, in a manner of speaking, he saved you."

"Saved me? What does that even mean?" She looked from one to the other.

"It means I can't arrest him."

She'd heard enough male bullshit—especially in the last twenty-four hours—not to be stonewalled easily. "Can't—or won't?"

"Both, I'm afraid." He nudged the coffee mug closer to her. "What do you remember?"

She'd humor him for now. "I was in Jackson Hole. I needed a ride to the airport. My phone wasn't working." She stopped right there and looked around, her hands automatically searching her pockets. "My phone . . ."

Shandy shrugged. "Everything got left in the truck. Well, what's left of it. Not that it would work here anyway."

"How convenient," she shot back. "No service, I assume."

Wick's brow furrowed, more in puzzlement than anything else. "Only because they haven't strung the lines this far yet."

Lines? That dizzy feeling swirled around her again, and she avoided looking at that smiling girl on the wall and all her 1907 nonsense. "I want to be taken back to the airport. Now."

"Airport?" Wick said the word slowly, as if surprised by the sound of it. "Don't you mean an airfield?" Yet before she could correct him, the sheriff swung around. "Shandy, when did you bring her from?"

"Why do you keep saying 'when'?"

"Because you keep saying 'airport' and something about leaving your phone in the truck." Wick paced a bit, hands shoved into his pockets. "What does that even mean?" This he directed at Shandy.

"Like I said, she needed a place, and she's got some experience with all this." As Shandy waved his hand around the room, the lamp burned a little brighter, chasing away the shadows, the illumination following his direction like a conductor.

For the first time, the rest of the room came into clear view. Tables, chairs, a piano against the far wall. A billiard table, those big front doors, and that calendar.

Greetings 1907.

Then the backbar lit up with an uncanny magic. It was a gloriously carved and elegant piece of cherry wood, sporting a grand figurehead of a winged siren with bared breasts and flowing hair. Tall cabinets on either side of the large mirror beneath this temptress sported stained-glass panes—shooting stars glowing in their prison of lead.

She shook her head. The Star Bright.

The *real* Star Bright.

Her gaze flew back to Shandy, but whatever magic he'd managed was gone, and he'd shriveled back into that sort of scruffy extra casting usually found in some dreary dive in the old part of Vegas.

Madeline drew another breath, deep and slow to calm her pounding heart. This wasn't the Star Bright. Just a very good reproduction.

And this pair, and the others? She eyed them both. They displayed all the earmarks of fanatical fans. Every show had them—though most didn't resort to kidnapping.

Until now. She shivered.

This Wick, whoever he was, noticed, and to his credit he got up and added more wood to the stove like it was the most natural thing to do. Brushing off his hands, he asked nonchalantly, "Miss Drake, what do you remember about getting here?"

Was he was actually trying to get to the bottom of this? Because something told her he was as unnerved as she was.

"Do you remember anything useful?" he prompted.

Madeline closed her eyes. "It was snowing. Hard. I couldn't see anything." Her lashes fluttered open, and she cast an accusing gaze toward Shandy. "You were driving too fast."

The man shrugged, completely unconcerned about his complicity in all this.

"I told him to be careful, but he ignored me."

"Yeah, he's good at that," Wick agreed.

The rest of it came back to her in a flash: the way the truck shuddered and fishtailed across the narrow road, the sound of metal crashing, glass shattering, and the abrupt, hard impact.

Yet where there should have been pain, she recalled only a sense of plunging, like when you start to fall asleep. One moment you're drifting, and then abruptly there's nothing beneath you and you plummet into an abyss.

But the bottom . . . the landing . . .

Again, her breath caught in her throat. They should all be dead.

Shandy's question twisted inside her like the crunch of metal. *Why am I alive?*

As if in answer, a faint image fluttered through her. "There was an owl."

Methodical and slow, the creature had flown in front of them as if caught outside the world barreling toward it.

"An owl?" Wick asked.

"No, let me finish." She closed her eyes, trying to grasp hold of the rippling threads. "The truck skidded off the road. We rolled. The next thing I remember, I woke up here, surrounded by a bunch of judgmental . . ."

Wick snorted, smiling for the first time. "Now look who's being judgmental."

Madeline's temper flared, but before it could burst to life, Shandy stepped between them. "You were lost, and I found you."

"Lost? The only thing lost is my career if I don't get back to LA as soon as possible."

Wick's brow puzzled. "Career?" His disbelief rankled her.

"Yes. Career. I'm Madeline Drake."

He blinked, yet there wasn't even a hint of recognition. He truly had no idea who she was. Didn't anyone in Wyoming watch television?

Meanwhile, he'd turned to Shandy. "Was I like this?"

Shandy chuckled. "A fair bit."

The sheriff ran a hand through his hair. "I don't recall."

"Well, you did spend the better part of a year . . ." Shandy tipped his head toward the bar.

Madeline waved her hands at the pair. "Hello? This is my crime scene. Reminisce on your own time."

"Hardly a crime," Wick told her. "You see, this place is sort of a miracle."

"A waystation of sorts for lost souls," Shandy added.

Miracles? Lost souls? Madeline stopped listening. It was all nonsense.

Next they'd be telling her George Bailey and Uncle Billy lived next door and she was about to have a wonderful life.

Madeline laughed. Rather hysterically. The horrible sound crashed out of her. Because she didn't believe a word of it. "I should be dead. We should all be dead." She took a moment and then looked at Wick. "Well, not you. You weren't there."

Shandy leaned forward, hands resting on his narrow knees. "Believe what you will, Maddie, but this is your second chance."

"To do what?"

Shandy smiled. "What you were meant to do. Live."

Live? She barked a laugh. "I think I've managed that. Ask my mother. Or my lawyer. Or every troll on the internet."

Shandy chuckled a little. "You don't have to worry about them anymore. There is no internet here."

"Right. Because this is 1907." She wagged her chin toward the calendar.

Wick's gaze narrowed as he turned around from the bar where he'd gathered up his hat. "What year should it be?"

Madeline shook her head. This was getting ridiculous. Like when a dream careens off into weirdness. "I'm in a coma, aren't I?" Not that she expected either of them to pipe up. *Why, yes, Miss Drake, how wise of you to discern this. We'll get you back to your regular life immediately following this necessary medical intervention.*

"And you two," she continued, until the dog nudged her. "Well, you *three* are some sort of guardian angels, I suppose."

Wick reeled back a little. "I assure you, I am no angel. But like the doc said earlier, that's quite a bump you got. You need some rest, Miss Drake. Things will seem clearer in the morning. Always do." He shot another pointed glance at Shandy then stalked out the front door.

"Well, I suppose I scared him off," she told Shandy.

"Might not want to do that. He got that sweater for you, seeing as you aren't really dressed for the occasion. That, and he fetched you supper." Shandy tipped his head toward the bar, where a plate sat covered by large white napkin.

Having lost all sense of time, she couldn't even remember the last time she'd eaten. But just the sight of the plate had her stomach growling to life.

She got up and crossed to the bar, gingerly lifting the napkin.

There waiting for her was a generous meal. Turkey slices. Mashed potatoes. Gravy. Green beans. A large spoonful of cranberry sauce. Off to one side, on a smaller plate, sat a hefty slice of sweet potato pie —she knew it was sweet potato because it was what Nate always made.

Nate. Madeline closed her eyes and winced. Why hadn't she listened to him and stayed in LA? Right now they'd be sitting on his couch, laughing over every bit of gossip they'd heard at his infamous Thanksgiving dinner.

"I'm so sorry," she whispered, hoping that somehow he'd understand why she'd missed his annual celebration. That he'd forgive her for arguing with him. For leaving him worried sick. Because he would be, and she hated the thought of him not knowing what had happened.

Shandy ambled over to the bar and gathered up his hat. "Go ahead. You'd best eat something. The turkey is good. But if I were you, I'd start with the pie." He smiled. "Inola made it, and you've got the last piece in town. Or so Wick said." He smiled, that odd twinkle back in his eyes. Then he turned to leave.

"Where are you going? You can't abandon me here," she said, following him.

"I'll be back," Shandy assured her. "But for now, you need to eat and get some rest." He paused at the door. "Your room is upstairs."

Madeline took a step back, for even as he said the words, images flitted through her.

A brass bed. A crazy quilt. A wide dresser topped by a large round mirror. A stovepipe running up through the middle of the room. The roof sloping down. A pair of narrow windows tucked into the eaves.

The memories were so real it was as if she'd lived in that room all her life. But how could that be? The show had never shown Calliope's room. It was a running joke.

"Where's your room, dahlin'?"

"Upstairs."

"Care to show me which one?"

"If I can find the time." Then she'd smile coyly over her shoulder at her latest love interest.

But Calliope's room and what was up that staircase, well, Nate had chosen not to show it, leaving her character's private life a mystery.

Yet Madeline saw the room with a rush of clarity. The bits of silk and velvet in the quilt, a hint of violets in the air, the click of the door as it closed.

She shook her head and focused on Shandy, standing there hat in hand, his head tipped ever so slightly as if he knew what she was trying to puzzle out.

"Don't fret," he told her as he began to open the door.

Fret? That barely framed the panic running through her. "You can't leave me here. *Alone.*"

"You aren't." Shandy glanced down at her side. "You got him."

"That is not my dog."

"Let's see." Shandy whistled and patted his leg. "Come here, boy."

The dog stayed at her side, tail thumping against her.

Shandy chuckled. "Not that I blame him. It's awful cold out. Good night, Maddie." Then he opened the door and slipped into the darkness.

Oh, hell no. She grabbed up the lamp, chasing after him.

Out the door. Into the night.

Yet in that swirl of snow, there was no one there. No Shandy. No fresh set of footprints.

She held up the lamp, trying to cast some light out into the dark street. When that failed, she hurried down the steps until she was utterly surrounded by the whirling flakes. The dog had followed her, but he had other intentions, doing his business and then ambling back inside.

"Shandy! Where are you? Come back here right now!" Madeline puffed a few breaths, but the darkness closed in right up to the edge of the lamplight. Beyond that illuminated circle, the world plunged into nothing.

From the porch, the dog whined, and a renewed creep of panic brought her back to her senses.

She scurried back into the spare warmth of the saloon, then threw the bolt that locked the door. Settling the lamp on the end of the bar, Madeline steadied herself against the solid wood, even as the smell of turkey and gravy rose up to welcome her senses. Then the sweet hint of pie. Her stomach rumbled.

Beside her, the dog's expressive brown eyes said quite clearly, *If you aren't going to eat that . . .*

Poor bedraggled thing. She picked up a piece of turkey and carefully offered it to the shaggy beast, who gulped it down.

"That good, huh?" Madeline picked up the fork, took a bite, and sighed. Even cold, this was just as good as one those fancy organic birds Nate got every year.

"More?" she asked him as she portioned out the turkey slices between them. When that was gone, she eyed her choices and bypassed the potatoes, heading straight for the pie—just as Shandy had advised.

Nor had he been wrong. Cinnamon and nutmeg warmed her tastebuds even as the crisp layers of crust melted in her mouth. She stood in front of the bar, fork in hand, marveling at how anything could taste this good.

Reasoning that pie, even imaginary pie, was probably not good for dogs, Madeline climbed onto the barstool and began eating in earnest.

She tucked into the cranberry sauce and green beans then found, wrapped in another napkin, a biscuit like nothing she'd ever eaten. When she was done with that, she put the plate down on the ground and let the dog finish off the mashed potatoes and gravy, neither of which had ever been her favorites. The dog was more than happy to help out, wolfing down the leftovers.

As he licked at the now-empty plate, cleaning it thoroughly, she remembered what Shandy had said.

You'll find everything right where you left it.

Madeline glanced up at the tin tiles covering the ceiling, and an oddly familiar laundry line of images fluttered through her thoughts again.

A brass bed. A crazy quilt. A jar full of buttons.

"There's only one way to find out," she told the dog. Gathering up the lamp, she rounded the far end of the bar. Just behind the cabinets, tucked in where no one would see it, a staircase ran up to the next floor.

What if she went up there and it was just as she'd envisioned? She glanced over her shoulder. She could stay down here on the sofa by the stove. Where. It. Was. Safe.

Then again, when did she ever do what was safe and sound?

In the end, as Nate liked to say, curiosity always leads the way. Besides, the dog held no qualms and trotted up the stairs.

Steadying herself with the handrail, she climbed one steep step. Then another. The dog sat at the top, patiently watching her slow progress.

"Tomorrow I'll wake up in some hospital and this nightmare will be over," she told herself, doing her best to sound confident. Yet already that ever-present dread curled around her heart. For when she woke up, there would be a throng of paparazzi outside, shoving and pushing to be the first with a picture of her latest disaster.

"Then again, 1907 has its appeal," she confessed to the mutt. For if this was the Star Bright, she'd escaped to a place well away from the never-ending cycle of mean-spirited posts on social media and celebrity headlines.

Are They a Couple?

Dating!

In Love?

Mad Madeline Engaged?!

Secretly Married?

Dumped!

Off the Rails Again.

She paused near the top of the staircase, clinging to the railing. She was tired of life. Tired of headlines. Tired of broken promises. Filled with a torpor that dragged at her soul and spirit.

Rounding the corner, she found herself staring down a long, dark corridor. She raised the lantern higher.

The dog sat waiting at the end, in front of a door that stood cracked open. Her four-footed friend nudged his way through and disappeared into the darkness. Madeline followed, her steps slowing, because a large part of her didn't want to open that door. Didn't want to see what was beyond.

Don't just stand there, Gigi would have railed. *You're a Drake.*

She pushed open the door, its rusty hinges groaning as if it had been years since they'd moved. Then she raised the lamp to illuminate the shadows of a forgotten life.

CHAPTER 6

Friday, November 29

A *new dress for the Christmas ball.*
The words snapped Savannah awake early the next morning and sent her catapulting out of bed.

That is, until the nip of November shot chilblains through her bare feet and sent her scurrying back under the quilts.

A new dress for the Christmas ball.

The refrain taunted her, like the unwanted remnants of a bad dream.

"Go away," she muttered, pulling the covers higher.

A new dress . . .

Good heavens, it was as if that wretched thing were hounding her from right there in the room.

And then she remembered it was just that—right here in the room with her.

From beneath the covers, she peeked out at the hook on the wall, where her skirt hung harboring an unwanted fugitive.

"Not for long," she muttered, throwing back the covers. Gritting her teeth against the bite of the cold floorboards on her bare toes— gracious heavens, how was it that she always managed to kick off her bed socks during the night?—she hurried over to her skirt and dug her hand into one pocket and then the other. But she stilled when she brought out not one wish but two.

She'd all but forgotten that second slip of paper. After the first, she'd panicked and . . . well, never looked.

Her gaze dropped to the fist that concealed the hidden desire of that second wish.

Nipping back a waxing curiosity, she reminded herself that one wish was bad enough.

Only a simpleton would open Pandora's box twice.

There was no course but the most expedient one. Put these wishes back in that old mason jar and then see that all the mischief contained therein was returned to Shandy.

Immediately.

Satisfied with her plan, she hurriedly got dressed.

A new dress . . .

Ridiculous. What was she even considering? She didn't even know who had made the wish. Though one thing was certain: a wish so filled with yearning could only come from the younger set.

Why, more than a dozen young ladies in Bethlehem could have written those foolish words. Nor was it like Savannah could invite them all over for tea, hold up the paper, and ask who'd authored such folly.

She had a word or two to spare when it came to stitching one's heart's desire into the threads of a new gown.

A new dress . . .

"I will not," she said aloud, as if that ended the matter.

She went downstairs, but to her consternation there was Inola, turning the crank on the coffee grinder and filling the air with the smell of freshly ground beans.

"You will not what?" she asked.

"Nothing," Savannah said, moving around her and making a

beeline for the basket atop the table. "I didn't think you'd be up so early."

"I've been up early every day for a week, so I guess I just got used to it." Inola eyed the grounds and then turned the crank a few more times. No one was more particular about her morning coffee than Inola.

Savannah surreptitiously slid her hand into her pocket and curled her fingers around the slips of paper, feeling like some sort of thief.

Goodness' sake, she was returning the errant bits, not stealing them. All she had to do was . . .

She glanced inside the basket, yet, to her horror, it was empty.

No jar. Nothing. Not even a stray spoon.

She looked around the kitchen and found no sign of that wretched blue jar—how could this be? It couldn't just hie off on its own. And she couldn't ask Inola without it turning into a long discussion on a subject she had no desire to mire herself in.

Wishes. Dreams. Living.

So she casually glanced around the kitchen, while a growing, gnawing panic roiled inside her.

The jar was gone.

Savannah clenched her teeth. *Shandy*. This had all the earmarks of his meddling. Well, she'd have none of it.

"What's the matter?" Inola asked, pausing over the coffee pot, a measure of freshly ground beans at the ready. "You look like you've lost something."

"Hardly," she said, her gaze straying to the stove and the door to the firebox.

WEAK WINTER LIGHT stole through the lace curtains as Madeline woke the next morning. She'd practically fallen into the bed, exhausted by the time she'd gotten upstairs, and now here it was morning.

How could that be? She'd slept the entire night through. The *entire* night. She never did that. Even more amazing? She felt rested.

Her head ached a bit, but the swelling on the lump seemed to have gone down. Some.

She pushed herself up, and almost immediately there was a *thump, thump, thump* from the other side of the bed.

Rolling over, she found herself nose to nose with the dog. "You're still here, huh?"

The reply was a staccato of happiness as the dog's tail beat furiously against the bed.

"Yeah, I've got the same question," she told him. "Where are we?"

Now that she was awake, the room turned out to be just as she'd imagined it, right down to the wide dresser with a round mirror against one wall. A small writing desk sat tucked in one corner, a highboy dresser near the door. Hooks on the walls held a selection of clothes.

As if she'd walked into someone else's life.

Absentmindedly, she reached out and scratched the dog's ears. "I think our first order of business is to get home." Before her disappearance became more of a scandal. A broken relationship, being recast—those her publicist could explain.

Disappearing into time? Not so much.

But given that was the least likely scenario, perhaps her first step ought to be to contact Nate—then apologize profusely and beg for his help.

She glanced over at her new partner in crime. "I'll find you a good home. I promise."

The dog's adoring gaze suggested he'd already decided the matter.

As she slid out of the cast-iron bed, her feet hit a thick carpet. It wasn't fancy or elegant, rather worn at the corners with loose threads popping up like crabgrass, but the deep nap greeted her toes with the familiarity of an old friend.

Ignoring the sensation, Madeline made her way slowly around the bed, her fingers tracing over the crazy quilt, a collage of knots and lines and flowers embroidered into a prism of silks and velvets.

The fabrics should have looked aged, worn with time. Yet the colors were too bright and shiny to be more than a century old. They looked almost new. As if it were . . .

Greetings 1907.

Madeline took a deep breath. Someone had gone to great lengths and expense to make this look real. Or perhaps—in the words of the childhood drama tutor her mother had hired when she'd been turned down for the lead in a potentially lucrative series—she'd finally "surrendered her entire being to the role."

"So, Calliope, this is what your room looks like," she whispered to the character she'd embodied for the last four years.

She drew a deep breath and came to a sudden realization: this was no coma, for she needed to use the bathroom. *Across the hall*, came a whisper of memory. Her bare feet danced over the cold floorboards as she opened the door and found an old-fashioned but fully equipped bathroom across the narrow hall. Rather than dwell on the weirdness of her entire situation, she made use of the facilities.

At least she hadn't conjured an outhouse.

When she returned, the dog greeted her with another round of tail wagging and those big brown eyes.

"I suppose you need to go too," she replied as looked around for her clothes.

She was wearing her T-shirt and underwear, but her jeans were gone, as were her boots—her brand-new boots straight from the runway. "Someone is going to pay for those," she advised the dog, even as her gaze strayed to the clothing hanging on the hooks by the door. Crossing the room, she sorted through the selection: two plain white cotton shirtwaists and a striped one, a gray wool skirt as well as a black one, and a white linen apron.

Well, since it was too cold to wander about in next to nothing, she took down one of the white shirtwaists, turning it this way and that. There was nothing modern about it—sporting all the old-fashioned details, from the pearl buttons to the delicate hand stitching around the collar.

Then she tried it on, only to find it fit. As if Lily, the *Star Bright* costume designer, had sewn it herself. Madeline held out her arms and marveled at the way the cuffs stopped right at her wrists.

Of course they did.

Reaching for the gray wool skirt hanging beside it, she found it had no zipper, only hooks and buttons for fastenings. She held her breath as she stepped into it. The hem fell exactly to the floor.

Ignoring a ripple of premonition, she went over to the dresser. Atop it sat the usual set dressings—a brush and comb, a few pots, but also an old canning jar full of buttons and coins. For a moment, she wondered at the colorful collection, some with threads still attached.

Something to explore another time, she told herself as she shivered again. Rummaging through the top drawer, she found a pair of thick, warm stockings and tugged them on—then remembered she'd need garters to hold them up. Hunting around in the drawer, she found those as well and added them to her costume.

Shaking out her skirt, she glanced up at her reflection in the round mirror over the dresser. The lump at her temple was very much evident, as was a growing bruise that ran down to her cheek.

Lovely. Perhaps there was a way to hide some of the damage.

She'd never had much of a talent for doing her own hair, but still, having had it done professionally nearly every day since she was eleven, she'd learned a thing or two. Within a few minutes—and using the hair roll she found in the drawer—she had managed a serviceable Gibson that dipped down with a delicate swoop.

Not quite as good as the one her friend in the beer ad sported, but good enough. Better yet, it hid the lump at her hairline. The bruising was entirely another matter. Her fingers traced over the greens and purples already blooming there.

Her face would be a mess for a while. *Great.*

Eyeing a pair of half boots tucked up against the wall, she caught them up and gingerly put her foot into the first one only to find it was exactly her size. Winding the laces around the hooks, she ignored the rather alarming realization that these weren't someone else's shoes. The sole curved to her foot.

Everything you need . . .

Another ridiculous tremor of panic rippled through her—*oh, shit, this is real*—so she pulled on the other shoe and laced it up, willing herself to ignore the perfect fit. Getting to her feet, she took one last look around.

Ah, the only thing she was missing: the sheriff's sweater.

Hers now. She tugged it on and snuggled into the thick gray wool. As cozy as a blanket. Wick Fischer might be part of this odd dream, but one didn't turn down a well-knit sweater on a snowy, bitter day.

That very thought stilled in Madeline's gut. Born and raised in southern California, what the hell did she know of snowy winter days? She looked up and stared into the round mirror. The old-fashioned glass shimmered in the weak light, making her image sharpen and ripple, as if she and Calliope were being stitched together in this strange nightmare.

"Don't get used to it," she informed the shifting reflection. "I'm going home."

Hurrying downstairs, the dog trotting along at her side, she discovered she wasn't alone.

"How did you get in?" she asked as she came to a stop behind the bar. For here was Shandy, seated in what she couldn't help but think of as his spot. On the bar between them sat a basket, and from the smell, she suspected bacon lurked somewhere inside.

Her stomach growled. *Bacon.* Bribery at its most elemental. She glanced up at Shandy. "I locked that door last night."

"But not the one in the back," he told her, with a jerk of his head toward the other side of the saloon.

"Good to know. Still, now that you're here, you can take me home."

The old codger heaved a sigh. "This is never going to work if you don't try a little harder, Maddie. If you prove me wrong—and none of this works—Mindy will be the devil to—" He stopped and snapped his mouth shut.

Madeline's hard stance fell apart. "Mindy? As in Mindy McClean?" She rounded the bar and stood in front of Shandy, leaving him no escape, no way to just vanish into thin air. "Are you telling me my assistant had a hand in all this?"

Over by the stove, the dog lay down and tucked his nose under his paw.

Shandy's jaw worked back and forth as he slid a hand through his thinning hair. "Now, you shouldn't blame her. I chose you. Well, I didn't exactly choose you. And Mindy, well, she's more of a . . ." He scratched at his chin. "An intermediary."

"You're telling me my personal assistant is an accessory to kidnapping?"

"She's really more my assistant than yours." He rushed to add, "So whatever you are plotting, I would prefer you didn't. Good assistants are hard to find."

Oh, the irony.

"Rather than quibble over the details," he continued, "how about some breakfast?" He reached for the napkin.

She pushed the basket out of his reach. "I'm not quibbling. Take me home."

There was another long sigh. "You are home, Maddie. You've been given the refuge you were looking for."

Despite Wick's warm sweater—or perhaps because of it—she shivered. The words she'd delivered on set earlier in the week echoed with eerie clarity.

. . . and sometimes the river of time stands still, so sweet and poignant, you hope the current never catches up with you . . .

"How can I be here, let alone belong here?" She chucked her chin toward the front door. "If that calendar is right, I won't be born for nearly ninety years."

He tucked a napkin under his chin. "Time isn't a line that only runs forward, rather, time is—"

Before she could stop herself, Nate's words came bubbling up out of her, caught on their own current. "Time is a river."

The old man brightened. "Exactly. There you go. Mindy said you were going to be a stubborn handful, and here you've gotten to the very essence of all this."

"I didn't come up with that nonsense," she shot back. "Nate did. They're his words."

"Yeah, I know. Where do you think he learned 'em?"

"From you?" Now it was Madeline's turn to guffaw, but something about the clarity in Shandy's eyes, the set of his jaw, told her he was telling the truth. She blinked, and suddenly he wasn't some grizzled old drunk spouting mad conspiracy theories at the TV over the bar. He seemed both illuminated, and grounded in something much higher.

An inescapable river.

Her question came out slowly. "How do you know Nate?"

"He's a good fella. Right smart."

"True enough," she agreed cautiously. He'd been her champion since the first day they'd met on the set of *Casey Jones*. Always bailing her out of trouble.

"He's probably worried sick. You need to let me call him," she said, trying a new route. "I promised him I would be back in time for Thanksgiving. Now you've forced me to break that promise. Stranded me here where I don't belong."

"Where you don't belong?" He chuckled and nodded at the wide cherry-wood space between them. "Then what are you doing?"

Madeline paused and looked down. Without realizing it, she'd cleaned the entire bar top. It was one of those things she did automatically during her scenes to make the shot look more natural. She wiped the bar. Cleaned the beer pints. Said her lines.

She didn't know when or where she'd picked up the cloth, but she dropped it. "Nothing. I'm doing nothing."

Outside, the jangle of bells pulled her attention toward the windows. Madeline watched as a man drove by in a large horse-drawn sled laden with logs, like something out of an old Currier & Ives Christmas print.

Shandy forgotten, Madeline walked toward the door, her gaze fixed on the scene outside. A sense of urgency pushed her to hurry, and she fumbled to unbolt the door. Then she dashed down the steps. "Please stop! Help me."

The large man, hunched in a thick coat with a knit cap pulled low over his ears, pulled at the reins. Slowly the plodding horses came to a halt. He looked over his shoulder, and his eyes widened before his gaze wandered over Madeline's shoulder toward the saloon.

"Oh, aye. Good day to you, Shandy." He spoke with a thick Scandinavian accent.

"How's Mrs. Bergstrom this morning?" Shandy asked.

"Well enough. We've a new boy. Though he's small." He shook his head and glanced away.

"He'll grow with time, Mr. Bergstrom, you'll see," Shandy offered.

While Madeline's attention had been busy taking in the world that had been hidden in shadows last night, her breath now huffed out in a great cloud. If this was a hoax, someone had spent a lot of time and money to make it appear real. There were power lines strung between the collection of brick and wood low-slung buildings, while on the poles sat large glass insulators.

There wasn't a single car in sight. The only conveyance was this man and his sled-load of logs.

"Can I borrow your phone?" she asked as she approached him.

He looked from her to Shandy and then back at her. "Miss?"

"Your phone. Can I borrow it?"

He shook his head. "A telephone? Oh, no. The lines, they haven't been strung."

"No, your cell phone."

"My what?" The man pulled back, looking up and over her shoulder. "Shandy?" It was more a plea than a question.

"She took a bit of a bump on the way here." Shandy tapped his skull to emphasize the problem.

"Sorry to hear that, miss," Mr. Bergstrom said, before shaking the reins and saying to the horses, "Walk on." Which they did, the sled lurching forward.

Madeline took two steps to follow. "But, but—"

"You might want to come back inside," Shandy advised.

With no one else in sight, no one else stirring, no hint of modern life, Madeline had no choice but to follow.

When she closed the door, she leaned against it. "You're telling me I'm in Wyoming, and it's 1907, and all this is real?"

"Yep." He settled down onto a barstool.

"That isn't possible."

"There is far more possible than most people are willing to believe."

She paused for a moment, but then shook her head. "Well, right now I don't believe. The only thing I want is to wake the hell up and go home."

"Why?"

"Isn't obvious? I can't just disappear. I have work and a career. A life." She paused for a moment. "Do they have cappuccinos here?"

"No, can't say that I've ever had one—not here."

"Well, that is a deal-breaker." That, and a myriad of other things, like the lack of central heating and a good sports bra. "I don't belong here, whatever 'here' is."

"Bethlehem," he corrected. "This is Bethlehem, Wyoming."

"This can't be real. It's a dream." She leaned into the bar—the solid wood hardly helping her convictions. "It's a parade of a TV show inside my head. Like my shrink used to say when I was a kid, 'an illusion colliding with my sustained reality.'"

His brow furrowed. "What does that even mean?"

Madeline's jaw worked back and forth. "How was I supposed to know? I was seven at the time."

"Sounds rather foolish to me," he said.

"Says the man trying to convince me this is 1907."

"Well, if this is all a dream, just wake up," he dared.

Wake up. Could it be that easy? Like when you realize you are drowning in a nightmare and wrench yourself awake? But, try as she might, Madeline couldn't reach the surface. "How?"

"It's *your* dream." He climbed off the barstool and straightened slowly.

"*You* brought me here."

"Me?" He shook his head and smiled. "You give me too much credit. I'm just the help. The driver, in this case."

"Well, you're a terrible driver," she shot back. "You missed the airport by more than a hundred years. Nor are you going to like the one-star review I leave."

He heaved a sigh and bundled deeper into his rough coat. "In the meantime, until you 'wake up,' I've got other things to see to. Your arrival is causing a proper stir." He chuckled and started for the door.

"Oh, no, you don't." Madeline hurried after him. "If you're going, you're taking me with you."

She stood there, firmly planted to the solid floor beneath her feet, trying with all her might to find some force within her to make this all go away.

Into this steely silence came a quiet, reedy voice. "Shandy?"

Madeline turned around even as Shandy's hard expression softened and widened in greeting.

"Dobbs! I was wondering where you'd taken yourself off to. Good morning, lad." Shandy let go of the doorknob and ambled over to a small, slight figure who'd arrived through the back door.

The one she needed to remember to lock.

Madeline couldn't make out the kid's features because atop his head sat a round, flat-brimmed cowboy hat that had seen better days. The boy held a large stack of wood in his arms.

"I brought more firewood, like you asked," the boy said, with a shy sort of shrug. Shandy gave the kid's hat a friendly tousle and then began unloading the offering into a wooden box beside the stove.

"Well done, Dobbs," Shandy said.

As for the kid, he slanted a glance at Madeline, his dark brown eyes large with curiosity, but only for a moment, for right then Shandy opened the stove and began adding wood to the coals inside. As the heat welled outward, the kid turned greedily toward the fire.

It was then she noticed his thin coat and ratty mittens—hardly much against the snow and wind outside.

"Why don't you warm up a bit?" she suggested, nodding at the stove, a strange curiosity pulling her toward this newcomer, prodding her to take a closer look.

He hesitated, but only for a moment, before he stripped off his mittens and held out his thin brown hands, skin tight against the bones.

Too thin. The words hit her, and she took another, longer look at this latest arrival.

There was something so familiar about him. As if she knew him. Those big brown eyes—tentative, wide, curious. That shy smile. He was at that wobbly point in childhood where his wrists outstripped his jacket and he was on the verge of shooting up, filling out.

Learning that the world wasn't always so shiny and bright. Not that it appeared it ever had been for him.

The stove door shut with a loud clank.

"He brought you firewood, Maddie." Shandy prompted.

"Oh, yes, thank you . . ." Madeline leaned down to get a better look under that impossibly big hat.

"I usually get a jitney for delivering wood," he told her.

This took her aback, and she glanced at Shandy. "A what?"

"A nickel," Shandy supplied as he dug into his pocket, pulling out a coin and tossing it to him. The kid caught it like a pro.

"This here is Dobbs," Shandy supplied as he made his way back to his spot, nodding at the boy to take the seat next to him.

But the boy's attention had shifted elsewhere. "Is that your dog?" A smile rose all the way to his eyes.

The dog's tail thumped happily, and then the pair of them looked to her for confirmation.

"No, I'm afraid not."

Indeed, his face fell a bit. The tail thumping stopped.

"Never you mind what Miss Drake says, Dobbs. That there dog thinks differently."

Suddenly something occurred to her. Shandy could spin all the tales he wanted about it being 1907, but this kid . . .

"Hey, Dobbs. What's your favorite video game?" She folded her arms over her chest and smirked at Shandy. She had him now.

But instead of the anticipated blanch of panic or concern, Shandy just shook his head.

"My wha-a-a-t?" Dobbs asked, looking from her to Shandy.

"Video game," she repeated. "What's your favorite? I'm still trying to master Fortnite."

He bit his lip and peered up at her. "Is it like checkers?"

"Checkers? No, it's a video game." She glanced at Shandy, and he was still shaking his head. "I thought you were leaving."

"Not now. I want to see how this works out for you." He settled back onto his barstool.

She tried again. "Checkers, huh? Is it hard to learn?"

Immediately his eyes brightened. "It ain't that hard at all."

"Like Batman hard or Superman hard?"

"Huh?" Dobbs reeled back and eyed her with an air of suspicion.

Over by the bar, Shandy huffed. "Really?" Then he laughed a little. "Hungry, Dobbs?" Shandy pulled the napkin off the basket and nodded again toward one of the stools, which the boy happily climbed up on.

"Yes, sir." Dobbs wiggled in his seat, a grin rising immediately.

"Good. It appears Mrs. Pingree gave me a couple of extra biscuits this morning. I told her you were helping me." Shandy divvied up the plates, one for each of them. The old codger had planned this from the start.

Of course he had.

From inside the basket came a plate stacked with biscuits, then a small pot with a large pat of pale butter. A pile of bacon strips came next, all browned and crispy.

Over by the stove, the dog rustled to life, nose in the air. He ambled over and sat down beside her, his tail sweeping the floor.

Madeline looked over at Dobbs. "What are you waiting for? Go on."

The boy didn't need any more invitation than that. "Thank you, ma'am." He quickly loaded up his plate, even as he was filling his mouth.

Madeline took a biscuit and a piece of bacon, splitting them and handing the dog half of each. He took it in one gulp—much like Dobbs, who seemed to be inhaling his breakfast.

So the comic book reference hadn't worked. Nor the video game. She'd have to try a Star Wars quote at her first opportunity.

Shandy ate slowly, with a deliberate pleasure. "I do like Mrs. Pingree's biscuits."

"They aren't as good as Miss Minch's," Dobbs pointed out.

"No, they aren't," Shandy agreed, "but they come a pretty close second in my mind." He reached inside the basket and brought out a large mason jar of peaches. "I told her you might be here, Dobbs, so she sent these along. She says you like them."

The boy nodded, and watched happily as Shandy opened the jar and spooned out a couple of halves. They lasted about as long as the bacon had, though in fairness, he'd shared his last piece with the dog, grinning a bit when the mooching hound caught it in midair.

"Hey, Dobbs," Madeline began, choosing a new tack, "How old does your mom say you have to be before you can have a phone?"

"My mom?" Any delight on his face crumbled away. "I don't have a mom."

"Maddie," Shandy warned.

She ignored him, ignored the haunted look on the kid's face. "Your dad?"

Dobbs shook his head and looked away.

"Stop pestering the kid," he told her. Then he turned, a gentle smile on his face. "Dobbs, why don't you take that dog out back and let him see to his needs?"

His forehead furrowed. "His what?"

"His needs," Shandy repeated, lowering his voice. "He's been inside all night."

"Oh." Dobbs slid off the barstool and walked toward the back of the saloon. "Come on, fella," he said, patting his leg.

The dog sat in place, turning his head to look up at Madeline.

She took a deep breath. Both child and dog were waiting for her blessing, as it were. "Go on."

The dog went slowly after the boy, glancing back every few steps as if to check and make sure she hadn't changed her mind.

Meanwhile, Shandy had packed up the now-empty dishes into the basket. "That wasn't very well done, Maddie. Then again, Mindy warned me you don't know when to stop." He moved toward the door with the same direct haste Dobbs had shown the bacon. "That kid has no parents. So don't do that again."

"What are you talking about? Of course he has parents—"

"No. No one. They were lost."

Her temper got the better of her. "I thought that was your job. Lost souls and all. Weren't you supposed to save them? Or did you screw that up as well?"

He reeled back at her sharp words like they had punched him in the gut. "I tried," he ground out. "But by the time I got there, they were gone."

There was something about the finality of that word—*gone*—like the *whoosh* of air rushing out of a blown tire.

Her voice dropped to a whisper. "Gone, as in . . ."

A short sharp nod then a single word. "Yes."

Madeline backed up a step as an ache, an unfamiliar need to help nudged at her. None of this is true, she reminded herself, going back on the defensive. And not because she didn't know when to stop. But because she needed the truth. And she wasn't one to offer assistance. Not when she was already in over her head.

Still, she couldn't help asking, "Who takes care of him?"

"He does. For the most part."

She took hold of the bar. "How can that be? He's what, eight? Maybe nine. This is all insane."

"Yet it happens. You know that."

Which she did. Nate had been on his own. In and out of foster care. On the streets. Until he'd gotten lucky and landed with the right family.

"Why hasn't anyone taken him in?" She chucked her chin at the window. "What about all those people last night?"

"There aren't that many folks around here who look like him, if you get my meaning."

"Of course I get your meaning, but he's just a kid."

He took another long, patient breath. "Haven't you been paying attention? This is Wyoming in 1907, Madeline. It matters. You, of all people, know that."

Racism in all its ugly forms had been a recurring storyline on the show. Nate had never shied away from examining the worst of it. Segregation. Lynchings. If this was real . . . then . . .

Shandy nodded, as if leading her to finish that thought.

Someone needed to look after him. She shook her head. "Listen, I don't know the first thing about—"

Before she could say anything more, the back door opened with a bang. The dog came bounding in from the back room, and Dobbs followed, hot on his heels. Both of them wore looks of pure joy on their faces.

Shandy tipped his hat to the boy. "You'll help Miss Drake now, won't you, Dobbs? She's going to get this here saloon up and running again."

"Yes, sir." Dobbs looked around the room, eyes bright and grinning from ear to ear as if he'd been dropped into the middle of Disneyland.

Madeline's attention swiveled. *"Run this place?"* She shook her head. "Now hold on—"

Shandy grinned. "None of your naysaying. Dobbs believes, don't ya?"

"Sure do," the boy said, nodding emphatically.

Shandy rapped the bar with a knuckle. "I always say, follow the child. After all, 'tis the season of miracles and children, isn't it?"

Then he was out the door, and the sharp cold breeze whistled around her.

"Oh, hell. Not again." She rushed after him—and smacked right into a wall of a chest.

"So you're still here," Wick Fischer remarked, the words like a sigh of regret.

Her hands splayed out across this very masculine wall as she steadied herself.

Real. Definitely real.

CHAPTER 7

"*Y*oo-hoo! Oh, yoo-hoo! Miss Minch!"

Parathinia wished she had the nerve to hasten her pace and pretend she hadn't heard Mrs. Jonas, but from the huffing and puffing growing louder behind her, the intrepid gossip was determined to bend her ear. Short of stature and quite stout, it was always amazing just how fast Drucilla Jonas could move when there was gossip to be had.

The lady rumbled to a halt, wheezing a bit and trying to both catch her breath and get a reckoning. "Goodness, gracious heavens! It must be something important indeed to draw you from the post office at this time of day, Miss Minch."

"I merely overlooked a parcel for Mr. King," Parathinia admitted. If she'd had her way, she'd have stayed safely ensconced behind the counter, but an undelivered package was the worst sort of sin in her estimation—well, nearly the worst.

"How fortuitous! I was on my way to the mercantile as well. Shall we?" Mrs. Jonas smiled and continued on, leaving Parathinia with no choice but to keep in step with her.

As she did, she found Mrs. Jonas squinting as she tried to read the shipping address on the package Parathinia was carrying.

She turned the package so the label rested against her coat and out of sight.

After a sniff of dismay, Mrs. Jonas began anew. "Well! Overlooking packages. That is hardly like you, Miss Minch. Of course, you know that I, of all people, would never condemn you for such a lapse in duty. After all, it has been *quite* the morning. Has it not?" She peered up eagerly from beneath the brim of her wide, feathered hat, ready for whatever tidbits or rumors might fall her way.

"Yes, it seems everyone has been out and about today," Parathinia replied, hoping such a mundane response was enough to dent the woman's appetite. "I have high hopes of spotting Dobbs. I need some kindling. You haven't seen him, have you?"

"Dobbs?" She shook her head. "Best to check with Mr. King."

Parathinia nodded in agreement as she fixed her gaze on the mercantile, which had never seemed so far away.

Mrs. Jonas blithely continued. "Perhaps this package disaster will give you the perfect excuse to post your choice about the Christmas tree drawing."

It isn't a disaster, Parathinia wanted to protest and feared if she didn't, by the time they got to the mercantile, Mrs. Jonas would have this wayward parcel underscored as a plague of biblical proportions.

"After all, you were most cruelly interrupted last night. Your moment to shine, snatched from you. I hold the deepest sympathies— as I have told one and all. Especially what with all the pains you'd taken to draw two such names."

"Mrs. Jonas! I would never—" Parathinia sputtered.

"No, no, of course not!" Mrs. Jonas agreed with a sly smile. "As I told both Mrs. Pingree *and* Mrs. Bohlen, 'Parathinia Minch is the epitome of honesty. How could anyone think her capable of such a machination?'"

Machination? Parathinia rushed to set the record straight. "Mrs. Jonas, it was nothing more than an accident."

Mrs. Jonas's gloved hand fluttered dismissively. "And certainly everyone who knows you understands. You are the last woman in this town anyone would accuse of trying to curry a man's favor. Besides, as I told Beryl Smith, the likelihood of drawing Mr. Thayer's name right along with Badger's . . . Well, the odds are uncountable." Mrs. Jonas drew a breath. "Though between you and I, I feel it an obligation to warn you that Mrs. Norwood will make the most of this failure. She'll have Mrs. George L. at her wit's end that such a catastrophe occurred on *her* watch. Poor, dear Columbia! I haven't dared visit her to see how she is bearing up in the face of this tragedy."

Parathinia tried a direct approach. "It is hardly a tragedy, Mrs. Jonas. Merely a mishap."

Mrs. Jonas's mouth pursed. "Merely a mishap? Miss Minch, how can you say such a thing?" She ruffled from head to toe. "Why, with the Christmas tree drawing in a shambles, the dance was canceled—"

That wasn't exactly the way Parathinia recalled the previous evening's events, but there wasn't an opportunity to correct the woman, for here she was going on at length.

"—the poor broken-hearted young people. They'd so counted on the dancing. My darling Pinky"—referring to her daughter—"cried herself to sleep last night, jangling my every last nerve. I can't even imagine the state Mrs. George L. is in. Until you make a choice, why, the entire town will be embroiled in seething conflict. Sides will be drawn."

Parathinia's head began to swim. However did this woman spin such grand webs with merely a breath? "I don't think—"

"Yes, yes, of course," she tut-tutted, patting Miss Minch on the arm. "Why, it is almost as bad as . . ." she slowed and then came to a stop.

They were, Parathinia realized, in front of the saloon. But only for a moment. "As upstanding members of the Bethlehem Temperance Union, we must vehemently oppose this treacherous turn of events." Mrs. Jonas shook her skirts and marched onward, leaving Parathinia to hurry after her.

She nodded in agreement more by rote, but still stole a glance over her shoulder at the twinkle of light inside the saloon, a defiant refulgence where there had been darkness for too long.

A newcomer. The notion sent a shiver through her.

"Disgraceful!" Mrs. Jonas complained. "What was Shandy

thinking, bringing such a creature here?" She shook her head. "I can confide in you, Miss Minch, because you are the font of discretion, that Mr. Jonas went over to the saloon last night."

Parathinia turned to her.

"Yes, I can see the shock on your face."

It was hardly shock. Parathinia would have been shocked if the man hadn't gone. He'd probably been the first one through the saloon door, and most definitely at his wife's behest.

Mrs. Jonas patted the brim of her hat. "I was in a state of utter despair over the implications of his presence, yet I have been assured that even Mr. Lovell attended. Worse, Mr. Jonas arrived home bereft of information. Bereft, Miss Minch! Imagine my disappointment." She drew another breath. "He learned only that the newcomer is a young woman, and that she was wearing a man's undershirt and dungarees. *Dungarees!*" This was followed with a decided *tsk-tsk*.

They had come—finally—to the distinctive building at the corner of First and Main. The tall false front declared in large, ornate dark green letters that they had arrived at King's Mercantile. Mr. King always made the most of his corner location, using the broad windows for artful displays of merchandise that the city's occupants and visitors could not live without.

And at Christmastime?

"My word!" was all Mrs. Jonas could say.

Parathinia had to agree.

One of those fancy new strings of lights hung overhead, while below them on threads swayed fanciful lace snowflakes. Stacks of colorfully wrapped packages sat in the windows, fenced in by a paper chain of green trees that ran through the display like a forest. Sitting atop the various packages were all the things that made perfect Christmas gifts: brushes, picture frames, ribbons, notebooks, pens. Or so Parathinia was told.

It had been a long time since she'd received a Christmas gift. Most years she did her best to ignore all the pretty packages, but something about this year had her looking over the possibilities with a sliver of envy.

"Goldie King has outdone herself this year," Mrs. Jonas noted with a nod of approval. Though her demeanor changed as they came up the walkway and found Wellington, Badger's infamous dog, sitting beside a stack of pine wreaths.

Infamous because the thing was larger than a small horse. Some sort of Scottish dog, Parathinia had heard. The beast barely took note of either of them, his soulful eyes fixed on the door.

Which meant only one thing: Badger was inside.

"Well, if this isn't an unfortunate turn of events, I don't know what is," Mrs. Jonas said, shaking her head. "Not to worry, Miss Minch. I will not allow that man to bully you into making an ill-advised choice—"

"I don't think—"

Mrs. Jonas leaned closer. "I hear tell he robbed banks with a most cutthroat band of thieves before coming here. Why the sheriff hasn't arrested him is beyond me." She huffed and seemed to gird herself as they went up the steps. "Best lock your doors in the meantime, Miss Minch."

Whatever did Mrs. Jonas think Badger was going to do? Suddenly go on a rampage? In between the odd jobs he did around town, Christmas was probably his busiest season, making wreaths and garlands and delivering trees.

As they got to the door, the heady scent of pine and fir surrounded them.

Even Mrs. Jonas approved. "Well, if there is one grace, the man does have a way with a fine wreath," she noted. "Do remind me to buy one before we leave. They sell so quickly." She reached for the door, then turned once more to Parathinia. "I would not be your friend if I didn't warn you . . . Mr. Jonas is convinced there will be fisticuffs before this is all over." Her brow furrowed as if it were an already scheduled event. "You know Mr. Thayer doesn't like to lose . . . Then there's the dreadful reputation of his opponent." She nodded once to indicate she was passing on this responsibility and was well glad to be rid of it.

Fisticuffs? Oh, no, that would never do. Parathinia bundled the package tight against her chest and hurried past Wellington.

Whatever had she gotten herself into? Then again, this was

Drucilla Jonas, a woman who could make a mountain out of porch sweepings.

There was no need to panic.

At least she hoped as much.

The bell over the door jangled with a holiday cheer matched only by the expectant air inside. The store was packed with customers.

"Miss Minch," Mr. King called out in greeting from behind the cash register. "What brings you here this time of day?"

"It seems you did get a package after all," she told him, handing over her bundle. "My apologies. I don't know how I missed it, but I hope you can forgive me."

"How can I not when you are ever the reliable steward of our community?" he told her, accepting the package and then passing it to Goldie. "You wouldn't happen to have anything else to deliver, would you?" He slanted a wink at their audience.

Oh, dear heavens, they expected her to make her announcement right this very moment, with Badger standing there near the stove, his hands held out to the warmth, apparently not giving a care. If that wasn't bad enough, Mr. Thayer leaned against the counter with his usual sardonic grace.

"Yes, I do, Mr. King," she said, taking a gulping breath. The entire room seemed to lean closer. She scrambled to come up with something, and finally a truthful answer tumbled forth. "If you see Dobbs, will you ask him to stop by? I'm nearly out of kindling." She bobbed her head and fled, a rather poor example of Mrs. Mercer's *Exorior*.

Then again, perhaps Mrs. Mercer had never done what Parathinia had: stood up on a holiday stage before her neighbors and friends and told a bare-faced lie.

SAVANNAH DREW a deep breath as she paused in front of King's Mercantile. She never liked going in the place. Especially when it was crowded.

As it was today.

Half the town appeared to be inside—but what had she expected? It was the day after Thanksgiving, and now everyone would be mad for Christmas.

Christmas. There was no avoiding it now.

A moment of guilt tugged at her. Yes, she'd tossed those Christmas wishes into the stove with a cavalier disregard for another person's hopes and dreams. No, it wasn't the best solution to the problem, but better than the nagging reminder that there were still wishes to be had in the world.

The door jangled open, and down the steps came Miss Minch, who barely spared her a glance as she flitted past like a lost sparrow.

Savannah looked over her shoulder and wished she could take flight as well, flutter back to the quiet solitude of her home. And yet, would she find refuge there now? Not when, deep in the stove, the ashes of those wishes stirred together.

A new dress for the Christmas ball.

Oh, for goodness' sake. She turned on one heel only to find herself face to face with the Winsley sisters.

"Mrs. Clarke!" they said in unison, immediately flanking her.

"How lovely to see you," Miss Theodosia said.

"Yes, lovely," Miss Odella echoed.

"Was that Miss Minch we just missed?" asked Miss Theodosia, glancing after the postmistress.

Before Savannah could answer, Miss Odella replied, "But of course it was, sister. Who else has that dull brown hat?"

Theodosia clucked. "How inconvenient. I had hopes of discovering how things fared last night, since we left early."

The sisters were of an indeterminate age—like so many of Bethlehem's residents, having been deposited here some time past, courtesy of Shandy.

Despite their years here, their pale blue eyes retained a bright spark, and the sisters shared a youthful outlook that defied the hints of gray in their hair. Curious and academic, they dressed like a pair of schoolmarms— with the exception of Odella's singular love of grand plumed hats, which she wore even when they went on their scientific rambles.

"We missed you last night, Mrs. Clarke," Theodosia informed her, wrapping her hand under Savannah's elbow and effortlessly guiding her up the steps of the mercantile.

"Yes, indeed." Odella closed the trap and caught hold of her on the other side. "We were quite distressed when Inola said you wouldn't be attending."

"A sick headache, wasn't it?" Theodosia prompted.

At this Odella shook her head. "Sister, perhaps it was something else. Another sort of ailment." She looked away, for fear they might have trampled into some intimate female affliction that was entirely unmentionable.

Theodosia examined Savannah carefully, blinking behind her spectacles. "You seem quite revived today, Mrs. Clarke, if you don't mind me saying."

"Still, you look cold," Odella said, from beneath the wide brim of today's spectacular hat. "Doesn't she look cold, sister?"

Theodosia, the younger by a mere a ten months—Savannah's stepmother would have declared them Irish twins, and not in a kindly way—nodded emphatically in agreement. "Inside is the only place for you, Mrs. Clarke. One mustn't risk chilblains."

Odella opened the door, and the bell overhead rang cheerfully as they entered the egalitarian world of a small-town mercantile.

At the back of the store, a gaggle of men stood around the stove, gossiping like old hens, while a varied collection of matrons wove their way through the long center aisle, chattering amiably with all they passed.

"A newcomer . . ."

"Shandy couldn't have . . ."

"Whatever was that man thinking?'

"Who would wish for a . . ."

The Winsley sisters eagerly followed the flow of conversation, towing an unwilling Savannah along with them.

"What is this?" Theodosia Winsley asked the first lady they came to. "A newcomer?"

The lady tipped her head. "Indeed! Shandy brought someone new last night, and—" The poor woman had no chance to continue, for already Theodosia and Odella were off and running with the slimmest of threads.

"Someone new?" Odella repeated.

"Oh, I do hope it is a minister," Theodosia declared.

"A proper one," Odella noted.

"Sister!" Theodosia admonished.

But Odella remained firmly unrepentant. "Well, it isn't that Reverend Belding isn't a *proper* man of the cloth, but he is getting on in years."

There was more than one nod of agreement from the assembled company.

"And," Odella continued, realizing she had an audience, "wouldn't it be stirring to have someone young and full of vigor, who could light the fire of redemption under the sinners of this town?" She looked around the room, but to her obvious dismay couldn't find anyone upon whom to pin her gaze.

"Tut-tut," Theodosia corrected. "Mother always said a lady mustn't judge."

"True," Odella agreed. "Nor did she ever shirk her duty. If Shandy has done us the kindness of bringing a new minister, a pound social is in order."

Theodosia shook her head. "We can hardly proceed without consulting Mrs. George L. She will have opinions on the subject."

"Oh, she will," one of the old men near the stove muttered, leaving more than a few of the old codgers chuckling behind their beards.

Savannah's ears pricked. Whatever was this about?

"But in the meantime," Theodosia announced, straightening slightly and ignoring the rabble, "we will need to consider what we can spare."

"We cannot be miserly, sister."

"No, indeed not. Our obligations are clear. It just needs to be decided whether flour or sugar should be offered."

"Sugar is quite dear right now," Odella pointed out. "But if he is a *good* Presbyterian—"

"Then sugar would be quite in order," her sister agreed.

"Yes, exactly." She tipped up on her toes and looked over toward the cash register where Mr. King stood. "Sir, I believe we will want to add a pound of sugar to our usual order. For the new minister."

With the sisters entirely diverted, Savannah made her escape, only to turn around and find someone else in her way.

"Ma'am," Mr. Thayer said, nodding politely as he edged his way around her to address the Winsley sisters.

"Miss Odella, Miss Theodosia," the lawyer began, tipping his hat to the sisters. "Before you make any hasty purchases, I think you should know that there is some doubt that the newcomer is a good Presbyterian."

Odella blinked. "Not?"

The lawyer shook his head. "No."

"Oh, how can this be?" Theodosia looked around the room as if searching for the answer. "Mrs. George L. will never approve. Dear heavens, what if he is a Baptist?"

Miss Odella wavered.

"But a minister, nonetheless?" Theodosia persisted. "Certainly a Methodist might do in these trying times."

There was another round of chuckles from the men by the stove, and Savannah grew impatient with the lot of them.

"It isn't a man," Mr. Thayer told them, folding his hands behind his back and rocking on his boot heels. It was a stance, Savannah imagined, he used in the courtroom.

At this, Odella frowned. "If it isn't a man—"

"Then we haven't a new minister at all," Theodosia finished. She heaved a sigh and looked around. "Oh, dear, this will be a crushing blow to Mrs. George L."

"Yes, indeed," Odella agreed quickly.

Savannah hardly heard them. She was still fixed on Mr. Thayer's disclosure. *It isn't a man.* Her gaze went unwittingly across the street to where the old saloon sat, its windows all dull with grime.

If not a man, then the question became, what sort of woman . . .

"If we haven't gained a new minister, then I fear a pound social is quite out of the question," Theodosia noted.

Odella sighed. "At least not a 'pound' social."

Theodosia took her sister's arm. "We haven't had a good pound social in an age, and it is such a lovely way to get to know one's new neighbors."

"It is indeed," Odella agreed.

"Perhaps . . ." Theodosia began.

Odella brightened a bit, tipping her hat back so she could see her sister clearly. "Yes?"

"What if we were to consult with Mrs. George L. as to whether or not an exception can be made?"

Odella tapped her lips. "Oh, do we dare?"

Theodosia shrugged. "I don't see how we could do otherwise."

"No, indeed." Odella looked around as if she'd quite forgotten they were standing in the middle of the mercantile. "Think of it. A new lady in town."

Mr. Thayer began to cough, that is until Mr. King prodded him in the ribs, confirming the worst of Savannah's fears.

Their new citizen wasn't a lady. Not in the way the Winsleys thought. Of course, the male half of Bethlehem was enjoying this fine joke at the sisters' expense.

Theodosia, though, took no notice of the snickering, for she was far too enraptured with her visions of a kindred spirit. "I can see her now. A modern young lady."

"In a manner of speaking, Miss Theodosia, you are quite right," Mr. King told her, looking as if he too was enjoying this far more than he ought.

"University educated, I imagine," Odella prophesied. "Do you think she might be persuaded to read our paper before we send it to Dr. Judson? If only to give us her honest appraisal of our findings?"

Theodosia nodded vehemently. "Indeed! Oh, consider, sister, how her learned viewpoint might give our theories the right polish."

They both looked over at Savannah. They had hinted at this often. That perhaps Mrs. Viola Kinney Livingston might review their papers.

Savannah did what she always did when someone intimated as to her connection to the infamous authoress—she ignored them, this time by taking an intense interest in a rack of thread.

"We must speak to Mrs. George L. immediately," Theodosia declared. She glanced at the pocket watch pinned to her coat and frowned. "Goodness, this cannot be correct." She tapped the glass, looked up at the clock that sat behind the counter, and then reset her watch, her brow crinkled as she wound the hands to the correct time. When she finished, she turned and ran right into Savannah. "Oh, Mrs. Clarke, there you are! I fear we cannot stay—"

"No, we cannot," Odella added for emphasis. "Mrs. George L. will want to be apprised of the situation without delay."

Theodosia paused at the doorway and turned to the counter. "An extra pound of sugar, if you will, Mr. King. We'll return after we've spoken to Mrs. George L."

They left in a whirl, and for a moment, the entire store seemed to take a collective breath and let it out. Then the pressing matters of lists and shopping took hold once again, the chatter beginning anew.

Savannah reached into her pocket for her list and, when she unfolded it, found two crumpled slips of paper within.

The wishes.

No. She gaped. *However had they . . . ?* Oh, she knew exactly how. Shandy! That devil of a man. Her fingers curled shut around them. Tight. And her lips closed into a hard line.

"Mrs. Clarke?" Myrtle step forward. "What can I help you find?"

A new dress for Christmas.

For a moment, she feared she'd said those words aloud, but apparently not, for here came Myrtle's sister, Francine, echoing the Winsley sisters. "Mrs. Clarke, you were missed last night," she began, sidestepping Myrtle's sharp elbow. "You didn't get your Christmas wish in—"

Wish.

Savannah straightened. Turning toward the impertinent girl, if one could call her that, for here she was, in the middle of the day, wearing the most horrible pair of dungarees and a flannel shirt that looked like it should be on the back of a tie hack. "I have no need for wishes."

Undaunted, Francine replied with a firm certitude and an air of youthful challenge, "Everyone has a Christmas wish."

"I do not," she replied in a tone sharp enough for Myrtle King to step in front of her younger sister, order book in hand, and ask, "Mrs. Clarke, how can I help you today?" Then with hardly a hesitation, her glance slid toward her sister. "Frankie, have you unpacked the boxes that came in this morning like Father asked?"

Francine sniffed, muttered something both her sister and Savannah chose to ignore, then slunk off. Myrtle shook her head slightly—a disapproving tremble that suggested she had no idea what could be done with such a child. Then, in the blink of an eye, she was back to business, a sensible trait that had always impressed Savannah. "I'm so sorry, Mrs. Clarke. How can I help you today?"

Savannah went to retrieve her list, but her hand stilled for fear of unleashing the other trouble stirring in her pocket. Instead, she chose to recite it, not that it was a labor, for they ordered the same things every Friday.

Heavens, Myrtle probably could retrieve their meager groceries by rote.

Then, to her horror, a whisper of something curled around her, an impulse—a wish, if you like—and she spoke without thinking, the words in no way her own. "I would like to look at some silk. A good length. For a dress."

Savannah snapped her mouth shut. Whatever had she just said?

Meanwhile, Myrtle's speedy pencil stilled, and she glanced up from her order book as if she too wondered where such a notion had come from. "I'm afraid we don't have any black silk at the moment. Is there anything else?" Again the pause, her pencil ready.

"It doesn't have to be black," Savannah hurried on, the words tumbling from her like the rush of water sliding through her fingers. "That is, I don't think . . . and actually . . . well, black wouldn't do at all."

Myrtle nodded as if she understood exactly. Which was good, because Savannah certainly didn't. "Oh, I see. For Inola, then. For Christmas?" Before Savannah could utter a reply, Myrtle turned and efficiently wove her way through the press of customers to take her place behind the dry goods counter.

Savannah shunted aside her muddled thoughts and followed quickly, determined to put an end to this folly.

Myrtle leaned over. "Did you hear? Mrs. Bergstrom had her baby. A little boy." She pushed her spectacles back up on her nose.

"A happy day for the Bergstroms," Savannah said mechanically. Another mouth they could ill-afford to feed was more like it.

Then she noticed that Myrtle hardly looked buoyant over the news. "Actually, Mrs. Wilkie says he's very small. Not apt to live."

Not apt to live. A pang of guilt wormed through Savannah. "And Mrs. Bergstrom?" she asked, regretting her intemperate words from the other day and her errant thoughts moments ago.

"As well as can be. Or so said Mrs. Wilkie. She was heading home as we were opening up this morning." Remembering herself, Myrtle got back to business. "So a new dress . . . I have just the length you might like." She wrestled the tall roll of fabric out of the barrel and laid it on the table. Unrolling it slowly, the chartreuse silk undulated as it went, like the first blush of spring shifting in the breeze.

But in her very Myrtle way of doing things, she set down her notebook and pencil and straightened the length, letting the fabric shimmer in the light. It might appear she was merely being neat and tidy, but she was her father's daughter, and she knew how to show a piece of merchandise. Every pull on the fabric only emphasized its eye-catching spark amidst the more reserved hues of the everyday wool and checked muslin they primarily stocked.

But to Savannah, the green hue sparked only that old memory of the dress she'd worn at the last ball at Larkhall. The one she'd chosen so carefully in hopes of catching Lucius's eye. The only dress she'd kept all these years.

As a warning and a reminder of the dangers of errant wishes.

"No, no," she murmured. "That won't do at all. It would be all wrong for—"

That was the problem. She didn't know who this dress was for. Or, for that matter, what she was doing—looking at silks she could ill afford. One glance at the hem of her own skirt announced the state of their finances.

"You might be right. I'm afraid it is rather dear, though I do love this color," Myrtle said. She leaned in again. "I'd sell it to you, but Father says—" The girl stopped, nipping at her lower lip.

Savannah knew exactly what Mr. King might have said . . .

A kindly version of *you're overextended.*

"I suppose I'll have to think upon it," Savannah told her, stepping back from the counter as the mortification of their situation drained through her, right down to the patched heels of her wool stockings.

"Yes, ma'am. That might be best," Myrtle offered as she rolled up the length.

Yet when Savannah looked up, she found herself face to face with Shandy. Where had he come from? More to the point, how was it he always turned up where he was least wanted?

Which was anywhere in her vicinity.

"Mrs. Clarke," he said, tipping his battered old hat. "Done with your shopping so soon?" He glanced at her clenched hand and then at the roll of fabric. "Have you found what you were looking for?"

A new dress for the Christmas ball.

Ignoring the shiver running down her spine, she pushed her shopping list back into the recesses of her handbag and leaned in close, lowering her voice. "I want nothing to do with you and your parlor tricks."

Shandy had the audacity to wink, a trickster's twinkle in his usually rheumy eyes. "I'll have you know, Mrs. Clarke, that I am never invited into the parlor."

Whatever had she expected? She sent a curt nod to Myrtle. "I'm so sorry to have wasted your time, my dear. Will you have our regular order sent over?" Then she spared a glance at Shandy. "Good day." With that, she hurried out of the store.

After a moment, Myrtle shrugged. "How odd."

"Not really," Shandy told her. "But promising."

CHAPTER 8

Savannah got no further than the bottom of the steps where she found herself mired in the inescapable quicksand that was Bethlehem's own grand matron.

"Mrs. Clarke, we missed you last night," Mrs. George L. Lovell said, or rather announced. She never really said anything, or conversed for that matter.

She announced.

"I was having one of my headaches," Savannah replied automatically, pulling at her mittens and looking for an escape route. "Speaking of missed, the Winsley sisters . . . They had a matter of some import to discuss—"

"I doubt it," the woman said. "Actually, it was you I had hoped to see."

"Me?"

"I was thinking of you as I was reading my new issue of the *Woman's Home Companion.* I was so struck by Mrs. Livingston's column—you've read it, of course." She smiled in confidence. "You must know how much I take her excellent advice to heart."

Blast the woman and her attempts to ingratiate herself. Savannah did her best to smile.

"And while I know you prefer to dole out advice in a more public forum, do you mind if I offer you a modicum of counsel?"

As if Savannah had a choice. She inclined her head slightly.

"If only you would avail yourself of Dr. Timonius Stevens's powders as I've advised you on so many occasions. They are the perfect restorative." She took a breath before proceeding almost modestly—if that word could be used in connection with the woman. "I only share this with you because I believe most emphatically that we ladies of quality must look after each other, mustn't we?" She raised her brows.

Savannah unwittingly reached up to straighten her hat.

"How thoughtful you are," she managed to bite out. "I shall endeavor to look into them." She went to move to the right, but the matron was one step ahead of her, again blocking her path.

"Mr. Hoback carries them." Mrs. George L. tipped her head in the direction of the druggist. "I would go with you, but as you might have heard, we have a new resident." This was punctuated with a distinct sniff of disapproval.

Savannah's ire got the better of her. "Yes, indeed," she said, smiling widely. "Myrtle was just telling me that Mrs. Bergstrom had her baby last night. A boy."

Mrs. George L. fluttered her hand in dismissal. "Babies arrive all the time in that household. Five children in seven years. Not that they last, poor things. No, I'm speaking of the other delivery."

Hearing a whiff of her own words gave Savannah pause—even, daresay, a moment of shame. Had she sounded that ugly when she'd uttered them? No, certainly not.

But a frisson of truth found a foothold. Well, perhaps a little.

"Am I to understand correctly," Mrs. George L. began, "that this person Shandy has foisted upon us is not a minister?"

Savannah smiled, rather too pleased to be able to say, "It seems you've been informed correctly."

The lady's lips thinned. "I hardly see how difficult it can be to find a good minister for our flock—not that I suppose such matters are *your* concern."

Savannah being Catholic, after all.

Ignoring the woman's religious barbs was always the best choice. There were not so many women in Bethlehem that they could fully divide their ranks along sacred leanings—not that Mrs. George L. wasn't above the occasional rosary joke or complaint that "if only we had a good minister, Mrs. Norwood wouldn't always look so satisfied on Sundays."

"I fear I did not express my opinions clearly to Shandy," Mrs. George L. was saying, as if such an event were even possible. "However, I will have a full accounting as to how this grievous mistake happened."

Savannah almost felt sorry for Shandy and his meddling ways. Almost.

Then again, it might teach him a lesson if he ended up in Mrs. George L.'s proverbial sights. Savannah happily nodded at the door behind her. "You are in luck, Mrs. Lovell. Shandy is inside. You'll be able to lodge your complaints with him directly."

Mrs. Lovell's nose once again tucked up in the air. "I never complain. It is unbecoming of a lady."

"How true that is," Savannah agreed, tipping her head politely and trying yet again to make her escape.

"Will we see you Tuesday at the Ladies Aid meeting, Mrs. Clarke?" Again, it wasn't really a question. "We will be gathering names for the booth assignments for the bazaar. Every pair of capable hands will be needed to make this year a success." She shook her head, the feathers in her hat trembling. "'Many hands make light work,' as Mrs. Livingston oft reminds us."

The Ladies Aid Society. Savannah wanted to groan. "I have so many obligations at the moment—"

But her words were cut off as a bareheaded young woman Savannah did not recognize pushed past Mrs. George L., earning herself a hard glare of indignation from the matron.

"Excuse me," she murmured as she went.

For a second, Savannah locked eyes with this newcomer, and she was struck by the young woman's frank expression—angry, determined, fiery, like she could stop a train with just a glance.

It was an odd thing to see yourself reflected in another after so many years. See the trouble headed in her direction.

And Mrs. George L. was the very definition of trouble.

Savannah had no idea why, but she made a slight shake of her head, warning this stranger not to tangle with Mrs. George L. And the girl continued on without another word.

"Well, I never," Mrs. George L. sputtered, all glowering indignation. For a moment her dark stare followed the young woman into King's. "Did I just mistake the matter? Was that shameless creature parading about with no hat? No gloves?"

And wearing a man's sweater, Savannah would have added.

Not that Mrs. George L. missed such a detail. "Whatever is the matter with young ladies these days that they feel the need to parade about in men's clothing?" Her brows furrowed into battle trenches. There was another grand shake of lace and feathers as the matron shed the unwelcome interruption and returned to the matter at hand.

She never liked to leave anything unfinished.

"Dr. Timonius Stevens, Mrs. Clarke," she admonished, gathering together the remnants of her parting sally. "He has captured the elixirs of ancient Egypt and distilled them into a cure for all the modern ailments. I trust you will heed my advice."

"How can I not?" Savannah replied.

Then, as luck would have it, the sheriff came hurrying past, and Mrs. George L. was off.

"Mr. Fischer, a word with you!"

"Excuse me," Madeline murmured as she hurried past a pair of women at the foot of the steps. She would have stopped to ask them for help, but they were deep in discussion, and the one with the big feathered hat didn't appear to be the helping sort, if her scowl was anything to go by.

Certainly not when Madeline's apology was followed by an indignant, "Well, I never!"

She considered telling the old gal, "Same here," but the other woman with her, the one all in black, looked at her as if she'd seen a ghost and shook her head slightly. A warning. In no mood to tangle with anyone who couldn't get her home, Madeline turned toward the crowd inside the store, which was, according to the golden script painted on the glass,

King's Mercantile
B. T. King, Prop.

If this B. T. King couldn't help her, certainly someone among the press of people within would be willing to break her out of this crazy cult.

Sparing a glance at the stack of wreaths outside—nice touch, she thought—she opened the door to the scents of spices and soap and people.

A lot of people—every single one of them looking as if they'd shown up for a *Star Bright* fan con.

Immediately, every conversation stopped. Every jaw dropped.

Great. A room full of starstruck fans. This could be helpful or a disaster.

Madeline held her head high. If they wanted Calliope Corfield, she'd give them Calliope at her most regal. "Does anyone have a phone I might use? I seem to be stranded."

No one moved.

Then out from behind the counter came a tall, middle-aged man wearing a kindly expression and a large white apron. A touch of gray marked his temples, and the corners of his eyes crinkled as he came closer.

"Mr. King, I presume?"

"Indeed," the man replied. "How can I help you, Miss—"

"Miss Drake," she supplied. "I hate to inconvenience you, Mr. King, but might I use your phone?" As Gigi always said, polite and to the point gets the business done.

Mr. King's easy veneer shifted, and, ever so slowly, he took a gander over his shoulder. Madeline followed his gaze to the back of the store, where a few men stood huddled together, warming themselves by the stove.

One in particular. *Shandy*.

Madeline buried her consternation. "Mr. King? A telephone?" she prompted, drawing his attention away from Shandy and working her smile until it glowed.

The store owner shook his head and got the same confused, apologetic look they all wore. "I'm sorry, ma'am. We don't have one yet. The lines—"

"Yes, yes, the lines haven't been strung. So I've heard." She smiled again and took a deep breath. Someone here had to be willing to help her, if only to gain their fifteen minutes of fame. "A cell phone, perhaps? There must be a tower nearby."

Their gaping faces showed nothing but stupefied confusion. As if they truly hadn't any idea what she was talking about.

Then her gaze lit on a little girl standing in the shadow of her mother's skirt. Madeline leaned down toward her. "Who's your favorite pony? Rainbow Dash or Pinkie Pie?"

The little girl's eyes widened as she shook her head.

Undeterred, Madeline turned to a sturdy little guy a head taller, whom she presumed was the girl's brother. It might not have worked on Dobbs, but this kid would only be an extra. "What game do you play on your mom's phone?"

Again, all she got was a look that screamed *what is she talking about?*

These kids didn't know. Either they were the best little actors in the business, or . . .

Real. This is all real.

Madeline wavered a little and did her best to ignore a wary sense that she'd been dropped off in more than just the wrong place.

The wrong time.

For his part, Mr. King blinked, then took off his old-fashioned glasses and wiped at the lenses with a white handkerchief, clearly taking his time to compose a response. "Miss Drake, as I said, the lines haven't been strung. Not yet. Why, we can't even agree on where to put the exchange." He followed this with a companionable chuckle.

Though no one else laughed.

Nor was Madeline in the mood for a chummy moment. Turning from the store owner, she faced the collection of customers. "I need a ride to the nearest town. One with a telephone or cell service."

She got back crickets. As in nothing. Just blank stares. Oh, for God's sake, didn't any of them want a bit of viral fame for returning her to civilization?

"A ride?" she pressed. "Please? Anyone?"

"Well, miss," one of the men offered, "it's snowed fairly deep if you haven't noticed."

There were nods all around, as if that finished the matter.

Madeline forced a smile back on her face. "Surely someone has four-wheel drive or an ATV to get out of here."

She might as well have been speaking Klingon.

Looking back at the kids, she made one more desperate attempt to get them to crack. "Honey, where did your mother park her car?"

The little girl swallowed. "We walked."

"Leave her be," her mother said, pulling both her children behind her before she turned to Shandy. "Shame on you, sir." Then she hurried for the door, where she was nearly run over by not one, but two new arrivals.

Of course, the sheriff had followed her from the saloon, after she'd given him a few choice words about his unwillingness to help her get home.

But the woman behind him, the grand one from outside, wasn't just any customer, Madeline quickly realized. For here was Mr. King hurrying forward, everyone else forgotten. "Mrs. Lovell, how may I—"

"None of your charms today, Benjamin King," the woman barked as she barreled in, gloved hand waving him away. She paused as she came alongside Madeline, her gaze sweeping in a quick yet thorough head-to-toe inspection. At its conclusion, she sniffed and continued on, the crowd parting for her.

"Shandy, a word with you," Mrs. Lovell said as she continued unimpeded toward the stove.

If Madeline wasn't mistaken, Shandy cringed.

Good. She suspected he was about to get filleted and roasted. Now that was nearly worth the price of admission.

"Mrs. Lovell," Shandy said, tipping his hat as he looked toward the door.

"I requested a minister be brought. A minister, sir." She paused, and when Shandy didn't reply—not that she seemed to expect one—she continued with hardly a breath. "A Presbyterian one, if you recall—"

"I do," he managed to get in. "But as I told you—"

"None of your prevarications or shenanigans, sir. You have failed this community. Worse, you've brought into our innocent midst a . . ." She paused there, nose pinched, lips curled, as if the word on her tongue might just be too distasteful to utter.

But Madeline was soon to learn that the indomitable Mrs. Lovell was willing to muster all sorts of words in defense of her notions of dignity and order.

"A trollop," the woman declared, to the collected gasps of the other women in the room. Their gazes swiveled toward Madeline and now shared Mrs. Lovell's scorn.

"Whoa, lady," Madeline said. "Standing right here."

"Now, Mrs. Lovell." Wick held up both hands. "Miss Drake."

Mrs. Lovell ignored them both, her ire solidly fixed on Shandy. "This is malfeasance, sir. You were told to bring a—"

"I was told?" Shandy straightened. "Contrary to your assumptions, Mrs. Lovell, you don't make these decisions."

Mrs. Lovell's jaw flapped.

Madeline used the lull to add her own two cents. "I'm more than happy to leave, lady."

Mrs. Lovell turned back to Shandy. "You heard her. She wants nothing to do with us, and the feeling is more than mutual. Take her back to where she came from."

Shandy's lips arched slightly, into something of a sly smile. "You know the rules, Mrs. Lovell, as well as anyone."

"There are rules? Nobody told me about any rules," Madeline complained, though no one seemed to be listening to her.

"Thanksgiving to Christmas," Shandy supplied. "And, Mrs. Lovell, don't even try. She stays." He ambled toward the door—making good his escape while everyone stood there, speechless.

"Christmas?" The word came out of Madeline in a gust as cold as anything outside. Why, that was weeks away. He couldn't hold her here until Christmas. She caught him by the sleeve and spun him around. "I'm not staying here until Christmas."

"Those are the rules, Maddie."

"To hell with your rules, and to hell with all of you," she shot back before she turned and marched out.

They all gaped after her, and then, one by one, they all looked toward Shandy.

Mrs. Lovell wasted no time catching up with Shandy and wagging her finger at him. "Christmas, indeed. She will ruin us all before then, you troublesome fool."

Shandy grinned. "Even you, Columbia?"

CHAPTER 9

Sunday, December 1
The first Sunday of Advent

Parathinia got up Sunday morning and glanced out the frosty window. Freshly fallen snow blanketed everything she could see. The world felt new and clean and ready for winter.

It was exactly the sort of day to get one's life in order.

Which was exactly what she'd do this morning after church. She'd straighten out this mess she'd gotten herself in. Why, she'd never told a lie in her life until last Thursday.

Most likely, she'd have to tell another one to get herself out of this muddle, but then this entire sorry business could be forgotten and settled without fisticuffs.

Coming downstairs with an eye toward a bit of tea and toast, she found the kitchen stove out. Not even an ember from the previous night.No wonder the house held an extra chill this morning.

Ninny pursed her lips. So it was going to be *that* sort of morning. And Dobbs hadn't been by, so she'd have to chop some kindling.

Oh, why hadn't she done this yesterday?

Because she'd been hiding. That was why.

Sighing again, she donned her father's old coat and went to step outside, only to come to a fumbling halt.

"Well, my word," she said as she caught hold of the door jamb. There at her feet sat a large bundle of kindling, perfectly cut and neatly tied with a heavy jute cord. Dry twigs, bits of old branches, a nice mix of pine cut to fit inside a firebox. All just perfect to get a quick blaze going.

This wasn't Dobb's handiwork. Dear boy that he was, he just tumbled the kindling into the box on the back porch and knocked for his payment.

Ninny looked around, but saw no one, not even footsteps.

Whoever had left it had done so before the snow had begun to fall.

As she looked again at this most welcome surprise, she spied something tied to the top—a few twigs of holly wound with a bit of red ribbon. How lovely and thoughtful. So very much like a Christmas gift.

Ninny paused. A gift? But whatever for?

She looked down at the pretty bit of holly, and a feeling of wonder whispered inside her. Her fingers grazed over the ribbon as she tried to recall the last time someone had given her something special enough for such a pretty bit of trimming.

But who . . .

Then she remembered what Drucilla Jonas had said. *You are the last woman in this town anyone would accuse of trying to curry a man's favor.*

"My heavens!" It was the only explanation, given that she hadn't received a Christmas present since Papa had died.

Then she remembered. She'd asked Mr. King to send Dobbs around, and both Badger and Mr. Thayer had been in the store at the time.

This was no gift. Why, it was nothing short of bribery. Gathering up the bundle, she fled into the house, closing the door quickly behind her. Good heavens, what if someone had seen it?

She shivered and glanced over at her cold stove. Bribery it might be, but she wasn't so foolish as to look a gift horse in the mouth. In two shakes, she'd assembled a pile of kindling in the stove and was touching a match to the dry twigs. As a bright flame rose up, the crackle of pitch sparking to life, and the heat reached out to envelope her, an odd warmth blossomed inside her, bringing a glow to her cheeks.

As if awakened by this quietly offered and most thoughtful gift.

Bribery, she reminded herself. And it needed to end this very day.

"HEY, WAKE UP."

The sharp command, followed by a good shake, dragged Madeline out of a deep fog.

She batted aimlessly at the offender and tried to roll away, but whoever it was kept insisting, shaking her until she thought her teeth would rattle loose.

"Where's Dobbs?" The question tolled like a bell.

She opened one eye and looked up to find Wick Fischer towering over her. Another quick glance revealed the rest. She'd passed out on the sofa by the stove.

She'd spent two days trying to find a way out of this place, and yet the weather and the entire town conspired against her. She'd knocked on nearly every door, asking for assistance—but all she got was a hurried slam in her face or a lecture about her questionable morality.

Clearly, even without modern technology, news traveled fast.

Yet it was the tiny glimpses into these homes and businesses that had left her with a growing conviction.

This was all real.

The night before, she'd taken to ransacking the saloon for any proof of the twenty-first century.

Her search had turned up a different proof: a case of rum. Not her usual poison, but when in Bethlehem . . .

"Are you even alive?"

She groaned as she rolled over and tried to get her feet to the floor, but she ended up kicking an empty bottle and sending it rattling across the uneven boards.

"Dobbs?" he prodded. "You seen him?"

Madeline winced. "No. Not since last night."

"I imagine not."

She straightened, doing her best to feign indifference as to how hungover she must appear. Hell, she wasn't even sure she was hungover yet. It had been a long night of pacing the floor, drinking, and trying to figure a way out of all this madness.

As her blurry gaze focused, she found the sheriff all spiffed up and polished, his hair brushed back, wearing a dark coat instead of his usual heavy jacket. She slanted another glance and realized he was also wearing a tie.

"You've cleaned up. Going to a funeral?" She swayed as she struggled to her feet.

"On my way to Mass." He turned his attention toward the stove and added a few pieces of wood to it. "I see you've been putting your time to good use."

Before she could shake her head, Dobbs—as if on cue—came racing in from the back. Like the sheriff, he'd cleaned up as well. He'd scrubbed his face and wore a neatly mended pair of pants and a somewhat clean shirt. The jacket, like everything else he wore, was too small for him. "I got breakfast—"

"There you are," Wick said. "Good lad. Now we won't be late."

Dobbs glanced from him to Madeline. His eyes widened as he took in her bedraggled emergence back to life. "Do I have to go, Sheriff? I think I might be needed here." He cast a longing glance at the bundle he'd deposited on the bar.

From the smell of it, fresh bread. Normally that would have had her looking for a knife and one of those little pots of butter, but not this morning. She closed her eyes and tried to ignore the way her stomach twisted uneasily.

"You want some before you go?" she offered, hoping he'd eat it all.

Dobbs slanted a quick glance at the sheriff's stern expression and reluctantly shook his head.

"You look very handsome this morning," she added, hoping that might improve the dour mood in the room. Her own attitude notwithstanding.

"Maybe I should stay here with Miss Drake," Dobbs said in an aside to Wick, before he lowered his voice further. "She doesn't look so good."

Madeline thought to argue the point but caught a glance of herself in the bar mirror. From the bruise on her face to her hair sticking out in every direction, she looked like she'd just rolled out of a gutter.

Nor was her sorry state winning any points with the sheriff. Wick ruffled Dobbs' hair. "Nice try."

"It's not like I understand most of what's said," the boy complained.

"That's because it's in Latin."

"Latin?" Madeline stopped tucking the evidence of her solo pity-party beneath the bar. "Why is the Mass in Latin?"

Wick's brows furrowed. "What else would it be in?"

Madeline opened her mouth to argue. But if it was 1907, then Vatican II was about sixty some years away. She shifted the subject. "I didn't know you were Catholic, Dobbs."

The kid shrugged. "Don't rightly know what I am, but the sheriff says I gotta go to church every Sunday, so I go."

"So *you're* Catholic," she said to Wick, who was still frowning at the empty bottles. She added "altar boy" to his list of Dudley Do-Right traits.

"He's Irish Catholic," Dobbs corrected. "What are you?"

"As it happens to be, Catholic," she told him, taking up a rag and wiping at the bar top. Out of the corner of her eye, she could see Wick's brow arch. "When she was alive, my Gigi used to take me to Mass with her—just like Mr. Fischer takes you. She rather insisted I go."

Dobbs tipped his head. "What's a Gigi?"

Madeline laughed. "It's what I called my grandmother. She didn't like anyone knowing she was old enough to have grandchildren."

Having considered this, Dobbs pressed on. "You can still go. Even without your Gigi."

She slanted a glance at Dobbs, his face scrubbed and expectant. "I don't have time to get cleaned up, kid."

He looked her up and down, measuring what would need to be done. "I suppose not."

She laughed a little, not sure whether to be insulted or relieved.

"Come on, you charmer," Wick told him, pushing back from the bar and nodding toward the door. "Time to get going. Father O'Brien doesn't like latecomers."

The boy grumbled but, to his credit, led the way out the door.

The opening brought with it a rush of cold air, an emptiness that filled the saloon whenever she was alone. And this morning, she didn't want to be alone.

"Mr. Fischer, I've been meaning to thank you for the meals," she rushed to say, following in his tracks toward the door.

"Oh, now, I didn't do—"

If Madeline didn't know better, she'd say the man was blushing.

"Dobbs told me."

His mouth set even harder, and he glanced out the door toward the kid waiting in the street below.

Now she'd done it. Gotten the kid in trouble. "He has a good heart," she insisted. "He deserves better."

"He does."

"If you help me leave, I'll take him with me and see that he gets a good home. I don't belong here, and clearly he doesn't either."

"You're right about the first part. You don't belong. Hell, I've got half a dozen complaints on my desk attesting to that fact."

Given the number of slammed doors she'd met over the past two days, she was surprised it wasn't more. "If they want me gone, why won't they help me?"

He sort of smiled, a wry tip to his mouth. "Because you've got to help yourself, Miss Drake. That's how it works around here."

"What works? I don't get any of this. It's all batshit crazy."

He glanced again at the empty bottle. "Yeah, well you won't get any argument from me on that." He put on his hat as he went out the door. "I will leave you with this bit of advice *my* grandmother gave *me*: while a river might choose its course, it always ends in the same destination. Your choice each day is to find your path, your course, or to spend your precious life paddling against the currents. Either way, you'll eventually end up in the same place."

She was too hungover for either a philosophy or geography lesson, yet a question begged its way forth. "What choice did you make today, Mr. Fischer?"

He stopped at the top of the steps, still and tense. "The same one I make every day, Miss Drake."

"What is that?"

"Stop fighting the current. I suggest you do the same."

"WHY, MRS. CLARKE, THERE YOU ARE," Mrs. George L. called out, waggling her fingers before she tucked them back into the large fur muff she carried. She hurried through the press of parishioners coming out of Mass. "Oh, how fortunate this is."

Savannah tacked a smile on her face even as she knew fortune had nothing to do with this encounter.

"Lord have mercy," Inola muttered under her breath.

Here was the one place in Bethlehem—the front steps of St. Michael's Catholic Church—that Savannah would have wagered her soul she was safe from Mrs. George L.'s meddling. But already the matron's sharp gaze was halfway through her usual assessing sweep, and Savannah braced herself for another pointed remark about her diminished appearance. But for once, Mrs. George L. nodded slightly in approval. "I see you took my advice, Mrs. Clarke, and consulted with Mr. Hoback. Why, you look quite restored this morning, I must say."

Savannah did her best not to look at Inola, though she could all but hear the question forming on her lips. *Advice? What advice?*

"I'll say it again. Dr. Timonius Stevens is a miracle worker," Mrs. George L. enthused. "Your frail constitution aside, I must ask something. A matter of some delicacy." She glanced over at Inola with a purse of her lips and an arch of her brow.

As if Inola didn't know when she wasn't wanted. But she did like to press the issue, and stood beside Savannah as unmoving as the mountains around them.

As much as Savannah enjoyed the pair's occasional game of wills, it wouldn't do to rile Mrs. George L., no matter how much they disliked the woman. "Is something amiss in the Athenian Society?" she asked, sounding entirely innocent, but knowing such a hint would prod Inola along.

After all, it was Inola who had badgered Savannah to accept the offer of membership in Bethlehem's most exclusive ladies club.

I will not spend my afternoons with those ridiculous women, she'd protested.

But think of the books, Vanna. We'll have our pick of books.

Since Bethlehem hadn't a library, the Athenian Society offered the only access to a variety of reading material.

"I daresay I must be getting home," Inola said to no one in particular. "Mrs. Lovell." She inclined her head and left, casting one long backward glance full of questions.

With Inola's departure, Mrs. George L. was once again summer sunshine and radiant smiles, taking Savannah by the arm and leading her away from the curious glances of the milling crowd. "Dear Mrs. Clarke, you wouldn't believe the week I am having."

The woman launched into a confessional of problems—the poor state of the various Ladies Aid committees, the rumors of the saloon being reopened, something about Mrs. Bergstrom's new baby, how Mr. King just couldn't seem to stock a decent selection of postcards for Christmas . . .

Savannah knew this was all a prelude to what would be some trifling, nagging request—make that demand—for her time. One she had every intention of demurring. Just as she was trying to do with those wretchedly stubborn wishes.

She'd let them flutter into the wind on her way home from the mercantile on Friday only to find them tucked in her skirt pocket Saturday morning. A second trip into the flames hadn't worked any better than the first, for they'd managed to find their way into the sugar bowl.

So this morning, she'd tucked them into the collection basket. Let a higher power manage them. But much like Mrs. George L., Savannah suspected they wouldn't take no for an answer.

Meanwhile, Mrs. George nattered on, while Savannah nodded when necessary and murmured the appropriate responses at the correct intervals.

Dear heavens, Mrs. Lovell.

How inconvenient, Mrs. Lovell.

I couldn't agree more, Mrs. Lovell.

None of which she meant, but it was enough to satisfy the woman, who really wasn't listening to anything other than her own voice.

Instead, Savannah kept glancing in the direction of the young girls, gathered in knots just beyond the steps of the church. The young people in town held none of their elders' preconceived notions of dividing lines. Released from their respective houses of faith, they had threaded together according to their own pecking order.

On one side stood a few of the more prominent young ladies: the Garland sisters, the Bohlen girls, Edith Higgins, and, at the center of it all, Miss Josephine Lovell, with the ever-present Pinky Jonas at her side. Josephine held a lovely fox fur muff, while Pinky appeared to be showing off new gloves.

Oh, they might have appeared to be a discussing fashions, but like a line of sparrows on an electric wire, they each took turns warily glancing over at the boys gathered near the church lawn, roughhousing as much as their mothers would cotton on a Sunday.

Some things never changed. Girls and boys, a gulf between them, and none quite sure how to cross the gaping divide.

They'd learn. Savannah knew that. They'd finally summon up some bit of courage to begin to cross that expanse.

And, speaking of divisions, across the brown lawn stood Myrtle King and her circle of friends.

Here were the real sparrows, clustered apart, feathers more worn and less showy than their well-plumed counterparts. Dark Eton jackets and sensible skirts left them all but invisible, especially when compared to the other young ladies.

But not immune.

For here was Myrtle turning from her conversation with Addie

Sullivan and stealing a glance toward the boys, a look of longing flitting ever so briefly across her face—but oh, that spark. That bright, brief flicker was enough to nearly stop Savannah's breath, for it said one thing.

Him.

Savannah tried following that glance, but to which of the boys it was aimed she had no idea. The entire lot of them was pushing and showing off in a writhing knot of masculine bravado.

Travis and Walker Stafford were trying to catch each other in some sort of wrestling hold that had their Aunt Cora chiding them not to "break anything again." All the while, the illustrious Junior Lovell—much like his sister Josephine—held his own court in the thick of it, calling out warnings to Walker and encouraging Sam Bohlen and Peter Bergstrom in their friendly shoving match.

Then the Lovell heir shouted something about a football game, and it was enough to lure the rest of the boys close.

"Mrs. Clarke? Are you listening?" Mrs. George L.'s insistent voice pierced Savannah's surveillance.

She turned to the matron, who was looking at her with nothing less than an expectation of immediate agreement.

"Yes, yes, of course," Savannah replied without thinking. After all, it was the only reflexive response she hadn't used yet.

"Excellent. I knew you would rise to the occasion. As Mrs. Livingston always says, 'Find a woman of integrity and talent and your labors are eased tenfold.'" Then she smiled in that ingratiating way of hers, as if they shared a most secret, special bond.

"It is most opportune," the woman continued, "that it is your turn."

"My turn?" Savannah managed, scrambling to put all the pieces together.

"Why, yes. When I realized the task fell to you, my confidence was restored. After all, I read Mrs. Livingston's October column. Twice."

Savannah rather wished she had as well.

Mrs. George L. paused, tipping her head and studying Savannah.

"Are you certain a basket of this order won't be too taxing on your circumstances?"

"A basket?" she managed, ignoring the false concern about her current financial situation.

Savannah would have to pick at that burr another day, for right now she was trying to sort together all the tumbling bits from the woman's earlier prattle.

Shoddy Christmas cards . . . Merely a trifling case of the sniffles . . . Yet another baby . . . A tendency to melancholy . . .

Baby. A basket. Savannah looked up, and the shock of it must have shown. She'd just agreed to provide the baby basket for Mrs. Bergstrom's newest arrival.

"Yes, yes, I know," Mrs. George L. was saying with a weary flutter of her hand, entirely missing Savannah's dismay. "I declare Mrs. Bergstrom has single-handedly run through every charitable nerve in my body! Five births in seven years."

"Four. I do recall one of those births was twins," Savannah offered mildly, struggling to think of how she and Inola would manage such a thing. It wasn't just the basket, but all the things that went inside it. Not to mention the meals.

Now tasked, she and Inola would need to see to it that the younger children were fed and that supper was on the table until Mrs. Bergstrom could manage it again all on her own.

"Well, luckily this time it's merely a single boy. A small one, Grace says. Probably won't last to the new year. Poor wee thing, but we must do our Christian duty, Mrs. Clarke, especially since Mrs. Bergstrom can become a bit, shall we say, susceptible to the doldrums. And it is, after all, *your turn.*"

Poor wee thing . . . won't last . . . your turn . . . The words tolled inside her, and an old panic, one she'd held at bay all these years, began to rattle ominously.

Poor wee thing . . . won't last . . . all your fault . . .

Bethlehem's major-domo continued on, blithely ignoring that her orders might cause even a moment of consternation. "I shall ask around and see that whatever can be spared is brought to the Ladies Aid Society meeting on Tuesday." She patted Savannah's arm. "That ought to save you from bearing the entire burden." She blinked and looked over Savannah's shoulder. "Ah, there is Miss Minch. On to my next bit of business."

Before she tottered off, she lofted one last bit of advice. Or was it an admonition? It was always hard to tell the difference with Mrs. George L.

"We are all tasked with what we can manage, Mrs. Clarke."

Savannah suspected this was yet another quote from Mrs. Viola Kinney Livingston. When she got home, she had a word or two of her own for that illustrious authoress.

WITH EVERYONE in town having gone to their respective houses of worship, a solemn silence descended upon the street. Madeline felt it right down her toes.

Stop fighting the current.

"This isn't real," Madeline muttered under her breath as she paced in front of the large windows. "This isn't real."

Somewhere in the distance, a train whistle blew a lonely note that pulled at her with its haunting wail.

"I just need to wake up," she repeated, hoping that might be enough to stir herself to consciousness. "Just wake up." She closed her eyes and waited.

After a few moments, she opened her eyes to find she was staring out at the same cold, empty street. It had started to snow again, the tiny bits swirling and dancing down from above, cold and indifferent to where they fell.

Cold.

That was it. Madeline shivered as a sort of delirium unfurled inside her. There was no way she could freeze to death if she was dreaming. Besides, soon everyone would return from church, and this rollercoaster would begin its slow climb back up the rails.

It was time to get off this ride.

Maybe she was still drunk. Or she had, as the tabloids had long suspected, finally gone mad. Pot-valiant, as Gigi liked to say. But one way or another, she was getting out of this nightmare.

Wake up.

She pulled off Wick's sweater and let it fall to the floor with the same insouciance as a flake of snow. Instantly the chill of the room rushed in, eager to replace the warmth that had cradled her.

Then she unlaced her boots and kicked them into the growing pile. As she passed the bar, she picked up the last bottle with anything left. Taking a swig, she carried her confidence with her.

The dog trotted to her side. Even as her hand closed around the doorknob, the brown, grizzled mutt nudged her with his wet nose.

"In this together, are we?"

The dog sighed, as if resigned to her folly.

So Madeline opened the door. Cold, bitter, and raw, the wind slapped her in the face. Yes, this was exactly what she needed. "Let's go home."

CHAPTER 10

When Parathinia finally exited the church—having studiously avoided everyone else by offering to stack the hymnals—she found her path outside waylaid by her waiting neighbors and fellow citizens.

"Miss Minch, a good day to you."

"Miss Minch, have you done something different with your hair?"

She hadn't, but her hand still went to the mousy strands if only to check they hadn't gone awry.

All this attention left her rather unsettled.

Made more so when Mrs. George L. announced, "Miss Minch, might I have a word with you?" Then, in her indomitable fashion, the matron elbowed her way to the forefront. "If I have a particularly large and most generous Christmas package *for my sister in Denver*"—she emphasized this latter part so everyone might be reminded of her esteemed family—"would I be better served mailing it this week or next? For I am most partial that it arrives in a timely fashion. As one knows, such a decision is of the utmost importance."

Parathinia paused, seeing the various ladies tip their heads in her direction as they tried desperately (albeit discreetly) to follow the conversation from a modest distance, all watching and listening like buzzards.

"It is always good to mail early during the holidays," she provided, more from rote postal training than a sense of self-preservation.

For she knew only too well that this scene wasn't about the package for Mrs. George L.'s sister in Denver, which she—having taken in said package annually for the past two decades—would hardly describe as large. Nor had she ever had any suspicions of the contents being generous.

"Then I suppose it might even be a good idea to make such a decision *today*," Mrs. George L. said to her audience, though her arched brows were aimed at Parathinia. "It is never good to delay the inevitable, am I right?"

Heads all around nodded emphatically.

Then, none other than Mr. Thayer came by, doffing his hat. "Miss Minch, how rosy and bright you look this cold morning. The sight of you has quite warmed my heart." That oft-mentioned twinkle in his glance was hers and hers alone, and it left her rather blinded.

Then he bowed to the other ladies and continued on his way.

Parathinia just stood there, staring after him. Bright. Warm. *The kindling.* Hadn't he said as much, without saying it at all? Why, it must have been him.

But she had to be certain.

Ignoring a stammering Mrs. George L., she hurried after him.

The circle of ladies fluttered then followed like a swarm of bees, humming and circling as if they weren't sure where to go, lured only by the prospect of *gossipus neverendus.*

"Mr. Thayer," Parathinia called after him. "A moment."

The man stilled and turned as if he had been expecting just this. "Yes, Miss Minch?"

"That is to say—" she began, but that was the problem. She didn't know what to say. What did one say to a man who quite took her breath away?

Choose him, she could almost hear the ladies behind her urging. *What are you waiting for?*

Yet as she looked into Mr. Thayer's beaming gaze, the same vainglorious spark behind her first deception lent her another wicked notion.

Once you choose, this will be all over.

Which was exactly what she wanted, she reminded herself, glancing over her shoulder at the sea of expectant faces.

A sharp bark from near the front door of the church stopped her meandering thoughts, followed as it by that deep, familiar voice.

"Come along, Wellington." Badger, bundled in his great fleece-lined coat, a battered hat pulled low over his ears, continued strapping on his skis.

As busy as he was, Parathinia wasn't fooled. This man—this loner, this outcast—was waiting to hear her pronouncement along with everyone else.

Taking a deep breath, she began, "Mr. Thayer, I would like to thank you for the bundling of kindling you left me."

Mr. Thayer's handsome and carefully set features faltered. "Kindling?" His brow furrowed, and he glanced around as if his witness had just confessed to some as-yet-unnamed crime.

This gave the waiting bees their first taste of honey.

"Kindling?"

"Left a bundle?"

"Did you hear that?"

Parathinia took another breath. "Yes, the bundle of kindling. It was ever so kind, but quite unnecessary."

Mr. Thayer looked up at the waiting crowd, then stepped closer and spoke quietly. "But Miss Minch, I didn't leave you anything."

Parathinia's cheeks flamed. He hadn't?

Over by the stairs, Badger made a rather loud, inelegant snort, then tramped his skis against the snowy ground. The glance he threw her way suggested he'd thought better of her.

"Oh, no!" she whispered as Badger turned his back to the entire lot of them and begin to ski away. She'd been so certain a few moments ago. The holly . . . the ribbon.

"Seems I'm not the only one who seeks to gain your favor, Miss

Minch," Mr. Thayer remarked as he edged closer. "Though I certainly wish I'd thought of it first. Obviously, I am going to have to rise to the occasion if I am to gain your consideration."

Oh, this was going from bad to worse. Parathinia scrambled to correct him. "Oh, no, I wouldn't presume . . . Actually, I fear this is all a bit of a misunderstanding—"

"No, no, say no more," he told her. "The holidays aren't the holidays if they aren't fraught with a trial or two. Besides, I do enjoy a good challenge."

Before Parathinia could find the right response, Dobbs came bursting through the tangle of spectators. "Sheriff! Sheriff! You gotta come quick."

Mr. Fischer waded forward. "Ho, there, Dobbs. Where's the fire?" he asked as he caught the boy by the shoulder.

"There's no fire. It's *her*, sir."

"Her?" the sheriff asked.

Dobbs tipped his head. "You know, *her*. Miss Drake. I went straight back to the Star Bright and found her . . . outside. She won't come in."

The sheriff tipped his head. "What do you mean?"

"She's outside freezing and won't come in," the boy supplied. "She's shivering something fierce and talking crazy."

Outside. Freezing. Parathinia looked down the street but didn't see what everyone else saw, didn't hear the words in the same way.

Please, Machias. . . Let me in . . . I'll freeze out here . . . Absently, Parathinia began to shiver.

"How long has she been outside?" This came from Cora Stafford. A story was a story, even if it was being witnessed by most everyone in town.

Dobbs, unwittingly, wrote the first few lines for her. "I don't know," he told her. "She already looks a lot like Old Billy Johnson did after he died last winter, 'cept with less clothes on. At least that's what Mr. Brassard said to Mr. Hubert."

At this, a collective gasp arose. The sheriff's face darkened like storm clouds. "And no one has done anything?"

The boy shook his head. "No. They're just standing around gaping. Mr. Daggett says she's sure as shooting gone mad."

"Well, shit," the sheriff muttered under his breath.

Parathinia flinched, but she couldn't blame the man. Truly, what was wrong with people when they wouldn't offer some help to a newcomer?

Even if she was a fancy woman living in the saloon.

As the press of people hurried along, Parathinia stood rooted in place, voices from the past begging insidiously in her ear.

Please, Papa, let her come inside.

She's made her choice, daughter.

Machias . . . please.

Someone ought to help the poor woman. Something ought to have been done days ago.

Parathinia Minch turned from all the hullabaloo and hurried toward the post office, each step filling her with a fiery indignation. This, she assumed, was what Mrs. Mercer meant when she exhorted her readers to heed that clarion call of *Exorior!*

She certainly heard it now. And on a Sunday, no less.

INOLA GLANCED up from her desk as Savannah came in the back door. "You gonna tell me?"

"Tell you what?" She tugged off her mittens and let the warmth of the room surround her cold fingers.

"Tell me what that dreadful woman wanted. What did she mean about you going to see Mr. Hoback?"

Savannah had finished unbuttoning her coat and paused for a moment to see if that was the last of it.

It wasn't.

"You sick?"

"No." Then she tried changing the subject. "I thought you weren't going to work on Sundays. Mrs. Livingston would hardly approve."

Inola frowned, clearly caught off guard at having the tables turned. "Even Mrs. Livingston has to pay her bills."

"So you *are* working." Savannah shrugged off her coat and hung it on the hook by the door.

"Well, yes, I suppose I am."

"Then I'll start dinner." Savannah continued into the kitchen to finish warming up by the stove. Of course, Inola got up and followed. She was buzzing with questions now that Mrs. George L. had gone and kicked a hornet's nest, as it were.

"Well?" she prompted.

Savannah looked over her shoulder. "It is our turn to provide a baby basket for Mrs. Bergstrom."

"I suspected we were getting close again."

"Past due, apparently." She pulled her hands back from the stove and went over to the sink to fill the kettle. She'd gotten rid of those wretched wishes only to be saddled with an even more troubling obligation. Standing in front of the sink, she stared out at the copse of bare white aspens behind the house. "I don't see how we'll manage."

"We always do."

Savannah didn't turn around. "It's not just the basket—it's the meals as well. And—"

And Mrs. George L.'s cavalier assessment. *A wee thing. Might not last to the new year.*

She closed her eyes, tremors rising inside her, tears stinging with insistence, her hands clinging to the unmoving cast iron of the sink.

Might not last . . .

When she thought she couldn't stand it any longer, there was Inola's warm hand closing over hers.

"I know, Vanna. I heard," she soothed. "Poor thing."

"I just can't. Not if the baby's not likely to live. Not again."

Inola nodded. "Then be there for poor Mrs. Bergstrom as only you can."

"You weren't there. You don't know what it's like." Savannah began to shake, her arms crossing her chest to stop herself from rattling to pieces.

"I'd know if you would tell me," Inola said.

Savannah shook her head, unwilling to let that nightmare gain any purchase. "I can't do this."

"Course you can. 'Sides, that was all a long time ago." Inola took a long breath and sighed. "You spend too much time in the past, Vanna. There's nothing there."

"Not to me," she whispered to the solemn row of bare aspens, lined up like the bars of a cell.

"WAKE UP. WAKE UP," Madeline mumbled to herself, even as she shivered violently, her teeth rattling. "Wake up." She'd been so certain this was all a nightmare, the sort where you realize the zombies chasing you aren't real and all you have to do is jolt yourself awake to escape them.

She'd gone outside, past the snow piled up on either side of the street, and stopped right there in the middle, letting the wind cut through her, letting the weather do what she couldn't seem to manage herself.

How long she'd been standing outside drinking, she didn't know. Long enough to attract an audience—though a silent one, all bundled up in their long coats and woolen hats and gloves, gaping at her.

She blinked as she tried to make out their faces, their expressions, but they stood like a fence around her, faceless and unspeaking, while she . . . well, she shivered and concentrated on keeping upright.

"Wake up," she mumbled again, the bottle slipping from her fingers, landing with a plop in the piling snow.

The only consolation in the staring crowd was that none of them had phones. Not yet. Not for another ninety years. That alone made her laugh, but it came out all garbled.

"Wake up," she told herself, trying to concentrate on the mechanics, but nothing seemed to be working. Her hands moved clumsily, and her legs wavered beneath her. Who knew that cold could seep right into your chest, into your brain, until it too started to thicken and freeze like a tray of half-done ice cubes.

Madeline blinked and tried to focus on the horrified faces surrounding her.

"I know what you all are thinking," she told them. She tried to wag her finger, but instead her hand just flopped about. "But you aren't real. So take your disapproval and dismay and curiosity and shove it—" The rest of her planned, expletive-laden speech stopped when she eyed a woman in a plain blue tam, strands of red hair poking out from beneath it. Standing just to one side of her fellow citizens, she steadily jotted in a notepad even as she kept one eye on the scene before her.

The 1907 equivalent of a livestream.

She wanted to laugh again at the absurdity of it, but all her body offered was a rattling shiver, as if her bones wanted to free themselves and find warmth on their own terms. She looked around and tried to remember why it was so cold . . . so very cold.

Tipping her head back, the snow came twirling toward her, a dizzy, silent chorus of restless flakes tumbling headlong toward the ground, where they'd become just snow.

That was what she wanted. To be just snow. Not the flake. Not the one that stood out, but the one hidden in plain sight.

She yawned and swiped at her mouth, realizing that was the problem. She wasn't asleep. How could she wake up if she wasn't even asleep? A gasp rose from the crowd as she fell more than knelt into the street. Somewhere off to her right, a dog began to bark.

Dog? She turned toward the noise, and then she heard it.

"What the . . . ?"

Madeline knew that voice. Please, not now. Not when she was so close to waking up. He'd ruin everything. She curled up tighter, trying to hide.

"What the hell are you doing?" he persisted.

She opened one eye and saw only the dark gray of his pants, the polished leather of his Sunday boots. As her gaze rose higher, a wavering vision came into focus.

"Mr. Fischer." Though it came out more like "Midder Fissure" because her tongue refused to work. "Go 'way. I'm dead."

"Not yet, Miss Drake." He knelt behind her. "Time to get up." The stubborn man hoisted her up, her stocking-clad feet pedaling in the air.

"Noooo," she managed, shaking her head, trying to be decisive. In charge. But her muscles abandoned her when she tried to stand, and the ground welcomed her anew.

To her chagrin, those solid hands were once again under her arms, and this time they left nothing to chance, catching her beneath her legs and sweeping her off her feet, cradling her against his chest.

"There you go," he said, and not the least bit nicely. More like he'd picked up a stray dog inclined to bite.

As he pushed his way through the crowd, the faces stared back at her, a blurry collage of shock and wariness.

"A word, Sheriff—" the woman with the pencil asked.

"Not now, Cora."

"Just a few lines."

The sheriff came to a quick halt. His speech wasn't just for the reporter, but for all the curious. "Nice way to welcome a newcomer. You should all be ashamed." With that, he stomped his way toward the saloon.

Each step jolted her, all of her—her arms, her legs, her hands—and the painful shock brought her back to the one place she didn't want to be. Here.

"Leave me alone," she said, making a futile attempt at escape as he juggled her up the steps. "Just let me die."

"Not your time," he told her.

"How do you know?"

"Because you are here instead."

"I don't want any of this."

"Listen to me," he told her, rattling her good as he shifted her weight. "You're alive. Be thankful for that." He hardly sounded happy.

Ahead of them, Dobbs was already opening the door.

Once inside, a calm silence blanketed her, as if the saloon itself sighed at her return. Dog headed quite happily to his spot by the stove.

As they passed the bar, the backbar mirror reflected a spectacle she'd seen too many times. Disheveled, wrecked, drunk . . . lost.

So nothing had changed. No matter the century.

"What the devil were you thinking?" Wick scolded as he

deposited her on the sofa—more gently, she realized, than he had when he'd gathered her up.

"Will you stop yelling?" she told him, rubbing at her ears.

"You haven't heard me yell," Wick told her. "Yet."

"Then yell. Wake me up from this coma."

Dobbs had gathered up the various articles of clothing she'd dropped like breadcrumbs, until they were piled up in his narrow arms. Wick picked his sweater off the top and settled it over her.

Immediately, it enclosed her in warmth, the kind that began to chase away the bitter cold.

"No." She shrugged it off. "I want to wake up." She struggled to get up, but the moment her feet touched the floor, a thousand pins and needles stabbed her. "Ow! Oh, ow!" She fell back on the couch.

"Hurts? Well, that's a good sign." Wick caught up her feet and put them back on the sofa.

"If I could just wake up—" Yet she hadn't the power to get up. Her limbs were dull, and where they weren't, they burned with a reckoning.

"Wake up? How about not dying? At least not on my watch." He shoved the sofa—with her on it—closer to the stove and its cozy welcome. He turned to Dobbs, his tone softening. "Hey, chap, go upstairs and find a couple of blankets, would you?"

The boy scrambled away, clearly happier with something to do.

"Maybe I am already," she muttered, more for herself.

"Already what?" Wick asked as he poked a few more pieces of wood into the stove.

"Dead. Is that why I can't leave, because I'm really dead?"

"You aren't dead," he told her.

"How do you know?"

"I don't usually find the dead so stubborn." He filled a tin cup with hot water from the kettle, wrapped it in a rag, and handed it to her. "Sip that."

She shook her head. Stubbornly.

"I assure you, Miss Drake, for whatever reason, you are alive, and whether you like it or not, it's 1907."

"Oh, heavens, she is in a bad way." The speaker caught them both unaware, having arrived via the back entrance. "Imagine not even knowing what year it is."

"I've got to remember to lock that door," Madeline muttered. This latest interloper was a woman of an indeterminate age, bundled up in an unremarkable dark coat with a plain, utilitarian hat plopped atop her head.

"Miss Minch! This a surprise," the sheriff was saying.

"To you and me both." The woman surveyed the room like a wary robin—all dips and bobs, turning her head this way and that, until her gaze lit on Madeline. Her eyes widened, and then, as if catching herself staring, she looked away.

As if the sight of her was just too much. Something so private it shouldn't be witnessed.

"I just thought . . . Well, I don't want to interfere with your duties." She held out a plate covered with a napkin and a small tin pail. "But I thought these might help Miss . . . Miss . . ."

"Drake," Wick supplied.

"Miss Drake, then." She glanced over and offered a timorous smile.

It was on the tip of Madeline's tongue to make some sharp observation, some wry comment about this woman's ulterior motives. She couldn't count the number of times photographers had posed as gardeners or delivery people to get past the high walls surrounding her house.

But the woman's kindly nut-brown eyes shone with a different light. She hadn't come to gape and witness Madeline's unraveling. She come to offer some help. A bit of kindness.

Gratitude sent an unfamiliar flicker of warmth through her, and Madeline struggled to sit up a bit. "Please, call me Madeline."

Miss Minch made quick shake of her head. "Oh, dear, that would hardly be proper." Instead, she offered the plate again. "I made these earlier for my . . . oh, never mind that. I thought they may be of more help here."

Dobbs came down the back stairs just then, arms full with the quilt from her bed, his nostrils flaring as he breathed deep. "Are those biscuits, Miss Minch?"

The woman nodded. "Perhaps our new . . . well, guest . . . might be hungry after . . . well, after what she's been through this morning. There's also soup. It will help warm up those chills after such an adventure." She surrendered her offerings to the sheriff and took another fleeting glance at Madeline.

"Miss Minch, this is most kind of you. So thoughtful," he said with no small measure of surprise and wonder, as if she too had strayed from her usual path.

At this, the lady demurred, looking down at her boots, yet her cheeks glowed with a pale flush. "Oh, it's hardly anything. But I should be going. I have Sunday hours to see to." She took a step back.

"I suppose I can't talk you into using the front door so you won't have to wade through the snow out back." Wick nodded toward the wide double doors.

"The front?" Her eyes widened. "Oh, no. I think not. I—I just couldn't." She took another tentative glance at Madeline. "My dear girl, do try to eat something. The world always looks better once one is properly fortified. Or at least so Mrs. Mercer always says." A trembling smile rose on her lips, and then she turned and darted away as quickly as she'd arrived.

Dobbs leaned toward the plate and sniffed. "Biscuits."

"Miss Drake first," the sheriff reminded him.

Slowly, she reached for one, her fingers finally working again, thanks to the cup she'd been cradling. She inhaled first, letting her nose fill with the scent of butter and baked goodness, just like the one from Thanksgiving night. And here she thought she'd imagined that.

Then she bit into it.

"Oh, my." These were real. *Very real.* She looked up at Wick, only to find that he was watching her. "This is all true, isn't it?"

"Yes."

"This is 1907?"

"What year should it be?" Dobbs asked, looking over at the plate.

"Indeed," Wick agreed, holding out the biscuits for him.

Like a magpie, the boy quickly pocketed two of them while somehow tucking a third one into his mouth.

She reached for another one as well. "I'm not going to stop trying to get home." It was a reminder more for herself than him. "I can't wait for Christmas. I have to get back or I'll lose everything."

Wick smiled, as if he expected nothing less from her. "Though I gather not before you finish that plate of biscuits."

"No one is that foolish," Dobbs remarked, reaching for another one.

CHAPTER 11

Monday, December 2

*M*adeline had stayed up most of the night considering what to do next.

Find her own course or paddle against the current.

She wasn't too sure which she was doing right now, blowing on her hands to warm them and feigning indifference to the crunch of boots up the steps to the train platform.

Him.

She'd spent the last hour here at the train station, ticket in hand, and had expected him much sooner. Still, here he was, even as the conductor began to call for the passengers with a booming "All aboard."

"Mr. Fischer, if you think you can talk me out of—" She turned around and came to a complete halt.

For there stood Shandy.

"Thought you'd left town," she said by way of greeting.

"I never really leave."

"Because you can't?" There was a sniping peck to her words, but the only hint that Shandy had heard or cared was the slight tip of his head as he looked out from under the brim of his battered hat.

"I can go. So can you, if you have a mind to, come Christmas Eve." He settled down on the bench and reached down to scratch the dog's head. "But not that way," he added with a nod toward the train.

"Oh, yes I can. I have a ticket," she told him, holding it up.

"So you found the gold?"

"Gold?" she scoffed. "I emptied the button jar on the dresser and used every last coin in it."

"Resourceful."

She'd thought as much as she'd sorted the oddly familiar bits and bobs in the jar. "Christmas Eve doesn't work for me. There's too much at stake." She took a step toward the train, half expecting him to stop her. "I'm going now."

"So you said." He stuck his legs out in front of him, his boots as beat up as his hat. "But the real question is, go where?"

"Laramie, as it happens to be. Both of us," she told him, nodding to Dog, who sat beside her. He'd followed her willingly enough to the station, though he now eyed the train sitting atop those long, unbending tracks with the same skepticism as Shandy.

"Do you even know what's out there?" he asked.

A thread of doubt wiggled inside her, asking to be pulled so the question could unfurl inside her. Expertly, she ignored it. "A way home."

"What about the people here?"

Madeline couldn't help but look back toward town for some sign of Dobbs. She'd explained her plans to him last night, thinking he'd be delighted with the prospect of leaving, of finding a good home.

Instead, he'd become quiet, asking only one question. "What if I don't wanna?"

Now she saw that his reluctance had been a different sort of refusal. For when she'd gotten up this morning, he was gone. She'd looked for him for as long as she dared, and when she couldn't find him, she'd penned a note for him and for the sheriff. She'd find a way to help him once she got back home. At the very least, Nate would know what to do. He'd come out of the foster system and found his way.

"You know very well I don't belong here," she said.

Shandy finally spoke. "You belong here, Maddie. More than you realize. Like it or not, you're a part of this town now."

"Hardly. They don't like me."

"None of them?" Shandy asked, before he leaned closer. "They might not realize it yet, but they need you."

And you need them. The sentiment whispered at her stubborn determination to go home.

"I'm not good with people." Or with agents. Or producers. Directors. The strangers on the streets Nate helped without a second thought.

"Not yet," Shandy added as if he'd heard her list.

"I don't have the time to wait for that miracle," she told him. "My career will be in the toilet if I don't get Emerson to change his mind."

"There is nothing there for you. You need to try harder to find your place *here*. Not by drinking or complaining or parading about in your—" The words stopped, and his jaw worked back and forth.

Madeline watched the old coot blush. "Go ahead," she dared him, chucking up her chin. "Say it."

"I'd rather not." He rose slowly in that stiff way that showed his age, whatever that might be. "You've got talents, Maddie. Planted long ago. All they need is for you to give them time and space."

"I'm not much of a gardener."

"Ever planted a seed?"

"No." She shook her head. "Wait. I did grow a plant from an avocado pit once."

He nodded. "Did you expect it to blossom overnight?"

"Of course not."

The man smiled. "Exactly. You gave it time. You let the roots find their way. Eventually it bloomed."

"Are you saying I'm going to bloom like an avocado?"

"You only need to give yourself some time," he advised.

Time.

He acted like it was an endless well. She supposed it was, but not for her.

"Why don't you just tell me what I need to do here so I can get home that much quicker?"

Shandy shook his head. "I keep trying to tell you. There is no quick path in life."

"All aboard!" the conductor called again. The last handful of passengers climbed on.

"Come along," she told the scruffy mutt as she walked toward the train, but the dog refused to budge. "I'll leave without you."

Dog looked as if he wanted to share with her a bit of sage advice. Something pithy and to the point. Like *warm stove*.

"You can't stop me," she repeated, not sure if it was for Shandy's benefit or Dog's.

"Not my job." Shandy ambled toward the end of the platform.

"What exactly is your job?" she called after him. "Besides kidnapping and time travel?"

"I think you know exactly what my job is, even if you are danged determined to make a mess of things."

She took another glance down the tracks, suddenly ill at ease as an all-too-familiar coil of foreboding tightened inside her gut.

The platform was nearly empty. The other passengers had climbed aboard without any hesitation.

Still, she couldn't help but take another glance at the singular line of tracks that led down the valley until they met the edges of the mountains on either side, the swirling snow swallowing the rails in a dark shadow.

Suddenly she had to know. She turned to Shandy, now poised by the steps. "What is down there? That is the way to Laramie, isn't it?"

He tipped his head and looked as well. "Don't rightly know."

She crossed her arms over her chest and waited.

He shrugged. "That's the truth. I don't go where I'm not wanted."

"I don't belong here. None of this is right." Notably, she didn't say *real*. "They slammed their doors in my face and then stood in a circle as I nearly . . . very nearly . . ."

"All of them?" His quiet question prodded her.

Fine. She'd had some help. The sheriff. Dobbs. That rather odd Miss Minch.

Madeline's heart squeezed a bit. Would she have done the same for a complete stranger? How often had she admonished Nate for wasting his money on some homeless wreck outside a coffee shop, always stopping to buy them a sandwich and something warm to drink. Taking the time to find out their name and if there was a way he could help.

The shame that washed over her held the same bitterness as the wind. Yes, perhaps she'd been wrong about that.

Still, it was time to go home. It had to be. It was the only path she knew.

"Come on," she said to the dog.

The animal, who had been her shadow for days, refused to follow, lying down and whining, his expressive eyes morose with worry.

Oh, for the love of Pete, she wasn't going to be blackmailed into giving up her future by a pair of sad brown eyes. "Suit yourself," she told the mutt. And then to Shandy, "He's yours now."

Before she could be beset by any other objection, she hurried aboard the train without another glance back. Settling into a seat, she wiggled deep into the cushion, trying to ignore the strange panic filling her.

I'm going to Laramie. I'm getting out of here.

Laying her cheek against the chill of the window, she looked ahead, toward the shadows misting around the end of the valley, beckoning like a dark doorway. The snow fluttered in the wind and curled into the train's smoke, a whirligig of swirling eddies.

Nate's lines whispered in her ear like a warning . . . *an unending circle from which you cannot escape.*

"Last call," the conductor shouted, then began to make his way on board, even as the train whistle blew a sharp, haunting note like the one she'd heard Sunday. Just before . . .

She shivered and looked back at the platform. To her surprise—or maybe not—Shandy was gone. But Dog remained, looking up at her with those trusting eyes.

This is not your river. Not your course.

This time when the whistle blasted, it shot through her, propelling her out of her seat. The next thing she knew she was bolting from the train. Just as she hopped off, the train jerked and pulled from the station. Caught up in the stirring of wheels and iron and the intemperate wind, the whistle wailed one last time, cajoling her to follow.

Madeline closed her eyes and planted her feet until the last notes faded into nothing. When she finally opened her eyes, the tracks stood empty, and a strangling silence surrounded her.

What have I done?

But as she began to breathe again, this odd place in which she'd found herself stirred anew, its ordinary noises wrapping around her. The *clip-clop* of horses pulling sleighs and wagons. The bustle of people. A door closing somewhere.

Madeline shivered—not from the cold, but from something else. A tiny, rare sense of accomplishment.

She turned from the tracks, faced this new horizon, then looked down at the ever-present shadow at her side.

"Come on, fella," she said. "Apparently there's more than one way home."

CHAPTER 12

Tuesday, December 3

*P*arathinia stood in the doorway of Mrs. George L.'s parlor and searched for an open seat. It was hardly surprising to find the large room filled to capacity given that this was the last meeting before the Christmas bazaar on Saturday.

But she'd had a long line at the post office, so she'd arrived late.

It wasn't just the added parcels and postcards and letters of the season. This year, every customer insisted on adding to their transaction a mailbag's worth of speculation about Shandy's latest arrival.

Not that any of their gossip fit the poor young woman Parathinia had met.

Yet, to her shame, she hadn't corrected anyone.

Setting the record straight would have required admitting that she'd met this infamous newcomer and, further, gone into the saloon. Not that Parathinia regretted taking her dinner over to Miss Drake, the poor dear with her bruised face and tattered spirits.

No, not at all.

But she had to question what had come over her of late. First the tree drawing, and now Miss Drake. Not to mention that she'd thanked the wrong man for a gift of kindling.

Ninny sighed and laid the blame exactly where it belonged: on Mrs. Mercer's book and her exhortations of *Exorior!*

So far, that singular notion seemed capable of unraveling her carefully structured life, leaving her exactly as she was now, lolling about in the doorway of Mrs. George L.'s parlor like some uninvited guest—a status sorely noted by her hostess and the Ladies Aid chairwoman.

"Miss Minch, if you will, please be seated." Mrs. George L. gave an imperious flutter of her hand as she rose to her feet, a sign that the lady was in one of her moods. Her expression nearly matched the mounted elk heads placed on opposite sides of the room. The pair had been shot, as the story went, by Mr. and Mrs. George L. on their honeymoon.

Parathinia had always rather pitied the poor creatures stuck on the walls of this house, trapped in an eternity of glaring at each other.

Rather like the Lovells.

Edging into the only empty spot, the one beside Odella Winsley— no surprise there—she leaned over to ask the sisters, "Whatever is wrong?" For despite her hurried entrance, she hadn't failed to notice that there wasn't a single lady with her work out. With the impending bazaar, why wasn't every pair of hands busily finishing items for the booths?

"According to Mrs. George L.," Odella whispered back, "there seems to be a dreadful emergency that requires our utmost attention."

As Odella drew a breath, Theodosia hurried to add, "A scourge is upon us, Miss Minch. A dreadful one."

Before either sister could finish, Mrs. George L. Lovell called the meeting to order with a solemn announcement. "Ladies, dear friends, I fear the most grievous misfortune has befallen our fair town." She paused to survey her audience, but also to give everyone a good look at her brand-new day dress.

"I have convened this meeting not as a Ladies Aid Society

gathering, but rather as an emergency meeting of the Temperance Union," Mrs. Lovell announced. She drew a shaky breath before continuing. "We face a terrible state of affairs that cannot wait until Thursday." There was another grand pause. "I have every suspicion that the Star Bright will be reopened by this dreadful creature of Shandy's."

Mrs. George L. knew her audience and waited for a long moment before slowly settling into her grand chair, solemnized by the morose elk overhead.

The reaction, as she'd anticipated, was immediate.

"No!"

"What is he thinking?"

"Can it be our place to question Shandy—"

To Parathinia's horror, all the ladies turned toward her. Dear heavens, had those fateful words truly come out of her mouth?

"I mean to say . . ." She looked around for someone, anyone who appeared to be sympathetic to her sentiment.

Bad enough that the elk's gaze seemed to fix upon her, but here also was Mrs. George L.'s beady stare.

"Perhaps it is merely an error," she managed to cobble together.

"There is no error!" Mrs. Jonas said with a finality that quieted the room. "Just yesterday afternoon, that shameful creature was in the mercantile buying a broom and a jug of vinegar." Recognizing her moment in the sun, the lady preened and sat up. "She even told Mr. King, and I quote, 'After I get things cleaned up, I shall be back for supplies.'" Mrs. Jonas nodded for emphasis. "Supplies, ladies! There is no doubt what she meant."

A general murmur of agreement and discussion ensued.

Then Miss Theodosia cleared her throat and spoke up. "Might I propose a pound social as an opportunity to explain our concerns?"

Mrs. George L. waved her hands back and forth in a hurried effort to restore order. "Ladies! It is imperative that each of us who are full-fledged members of the Temperance Union"—her gaze flickered over the few ladies who were not—"sees that this affront never happens."

"However do we do that?" Parathinia clamped her lips together.

Tight. Whatever was wrong with her that she kept speaking out of turn?

Mrs. George L. straightened. "We must confront this deranged Jezebel and demand she leave town."

That silenced every tongue in the room. Not once had anyone whom Shandy had delivered to their doorstep been driven out. And there had been some very questionable arrivals over the years.

"Has anyone addressed these concerns to Miss Drake?" Parathinia looked up to find every pair of eyes fixed on her.

A solitary brow arched as Mrs. George L. spoke. "Miss Drake? You've met her?"

Parathinia suddenly knew exactly how the elk had felt just before that fatal shot rang out.

"I, that is, she introduced herself to me. On Sunday." Parathinia glanced around again. "After that unfortunate incident. I took over some soup— Well, I took it to the sheriff, and he . . ."

She should have stopped before she began. There was no reason to load Mrs. George L.'s hunting rifle for her.

"Unfortunate incident, indeed." Mrs. George L. Lovell sniffed. "Yet . . ." Hand pressed to her ample bosom, she shared the sad truth. "Ladies, I cannot, as the president of the Bethlehem Temperance Union, set foot in such a place. Why, it would be unseemly. Rather, we must nominate a committee to address our concerns." She smiled slightly. "I put forth the name of Miss Parathinia Minch to be the chairwoman."

For a moment, Parathinia sat speechless. A committee? A committee of her own? Then she realized just what was being asked. For her to organize a mob to run a young woman out of town.

Not just any woman, but Miss Drake.

Madeline. Please call me Madeline. As if they were dear friends. An urgent tremor ran through her.

"But I—" Parathinia began to protest, yet here was Mrs. George L., already tapping her fan against the arm of her monstrous chair.

"If, as you say, Miss Minch, you have already been introduced to this person, you are the perfect choice to lead the committee." She paused only for a breath. "All in favor of Miss Parathinia Minch heading the Star Bright committee, please raise your hand."

A show of hands went up with all the haste of a crowd scampering out of a burning building.

No one wanted to be anywhere near this mare's nest. Save one foolhardy soul.

"Madame Chairwoman," Odella interjected, "I would be remiss if I didn't point out that Miss Minch has a far more pressing matter to attend to at this time."

"Another matter?" Mrs. George L. asked. "I can't think of one."

"The Christmas tree," Theodosia hastened to add, glancing around as if she were surprised that anyone could have forgotten such an important issue.

"Excellent point, Miss Odella, Miss Theodosia," Mrs. George L. conceded. "But that matter can be concluded with just a word from Miss Minch." She turned her full, unwanted attention back to Parathinia. "Miss Minch, have you made your choice?"

Once when she was a child, when she was Ninny, she'd stood on the train tracks and watched the express come toward her. Closer and closer it had roared, the engineer blowing his whistle, her father shouting at her as he ran down the hill.

But still she'd stood there, held her ground, lost in the thrill, in the inherent danger. Those brief moments had been lived.

Lived in incautious arrogance, if she was being honest.

Rather like the singular bit of defiance that now prodded her to say, "No, I have not."

At the very least, she needed to thank Badger for the kindling and apologize. Then . . .

"So." Mrs. George L. surveyed the room again. "We have a motion on the floor. Do I hear a second?"

It was quickly seconded and then voted upon, hands shooting in the air along with a chorus of ayes. Mrs. George L. made a nominal show of counting the votes as if she had to be certain.

Parathinia, for her part, abstained from voting. Not that there was any doubt the count would be anything other than a landslide.

Miss Theodosia, never one to leave well enough alone, spoke up.

"Miss Minch can hardly do this on her own, Madame Chairwoman. It would be improper to send her into such a den of iniquity alone."

Mrs. George L. turned from instructing Beryl Smith, the Temperance Union secretary, how she wanted the vote noted in the union records. "Indeed, Miss Theodosia, an excellent point. I therefore further nominate you and your sister to assist Miss Minch with her efforts. All in favor."

The vote carried again along the same lines, though this time with three abstentions, including a thunderous Odella, who glared at her sister for landing them in such wretched straits.

Savannah and Inola had spent most of Sunday afternoon cutting old sheets and towels for nappies, and that evening, Inola had taken over a large pot of soup to help the family through. If anything, this basket business, as Savannah had taken to calling it, helped keep her mind off the other pressing problem in her life.

That bothersome wish.

A dress for the Christmas Ball.

She'd thought she'd washed her hands of the matter when she'd tucked the wishes in the collection basket Sunday, but they had since appeared three more times—all when she'd least expected them—the final time this morning when she'd opened the tea tin.

She'd tucked them once again in her pocket and was of half a mind to tuck them beneath the cushions of Mrs. George L.'s settee, however, pressed in as she was between two other matrons, she barely had room to breathe.

That, and the elk on the far wall, with its uncanny gaze, left her a bit unnerved.

Not only was there the usual clutch of matrons and mothers about the room, but for some reason it seemed every young lady in Bethlehem was also in attendance. The girls sat in knotted clusters in all four corners, or beside their mothers, most with their hands folded demurely in their laps, striving to appear the epitome of grace and manners.

Clearly, she hadn't been to a Ladies Aid meeting in some time.

For her part, Savannah had only come to the meeting to see if Mrs. George L. had made good on her promise to put the word out that a baby basket was in need.

She hadn't expected much—after all, Mrs. Bergstrom was a rather frequent subject of baby basket aid—but to her surprise, the Ladies Aid Society of Bethlehem lived up to its name. There was already one basket filled when Savannah arrived, and by the time Miss Minch hurried in, Savannah had at her feet a full selection of jams, baked goods, two jars of Mrs. Daggett's bone broth—"most restorative," she'd assured Savannah—nappies, hand-me-downs, and a beautiful new hood and wrap from the young Mrs. Nash.

The former schoolteacher had lost her first baby the previous summer, and had silently added a lovingly knit baby gown to the pile, her fingers making one last, fond trace over the stitches before she moved on to take her place beside one of her neighbors.

Savannah found herself transfixed by the lacy pattern and the tiny pearl buttons, most likely clipped from a special dress.

It was too much to give. Especially when this baby, this new arrival, probably wouldn't . . .

"Mrs. Nash, you ought not—" she began, reaching for it, but Mrs. Baumgarten, who sat beside her, stayed her hand.

"Let it be, Mrs. Clarke. It's her way of letting go."

Savannah wanted to tell her that letting go wasn't so simple. Clearly Mrs. Baumgarten had never lost a child.

"Ladies, dear friends, I fear the most grievous misfortune is upon us," Mrs. George L. began, calling on those members who also belonged to the Temperance Union to heed her on a matter *most urgent*, while the younger set shifted with impatience, catching Savannah's attention.

"I wish she would just let us sign up for the booths so we could leave," one of the girls whispered.

"I need to practice my piano lesson," another complained. "I'm supposed to have it done before Papa comes home."

"I'll write your name down," her friend offered under her breath.

Write your name down.

As much as she considered eavesdropping its own sort of wickedness, those words prodded Savannah.

"And let you sign me up for kitchen sundries, Hazel Smith? I don't think so."

A tiny chorus of giggles erupted, as if this was the most dire fate they could imagine.

An older girl leaned in. "You don't get to sign up for the booth you want, you ninnies. You only sign up to help. Then stuffy old Mrs. Pelham assigns you to a booth."

"And then only after Josephine Lovell is assigned the best spot," Goldie King pointed out. "She always gets first pick."

"And a new dress."

Sighs of envy encircled the tight knot of girls. *A new dress.*

Savannah tipped her head slightly so she could look at them— Hazel Smith, the Daggett sisters, the middle Hoback girl, and one of the Sullivans. They all wore their best day dresses, but the hems showed wear, and a few revealed signs that the seams had been let out.

Hand-me-downs. Something Savannah knew more about than she cared to admit, looking at her own worn hem. Most of the girls in Bethlehem wore hand-me-down dresses from their older sisters and cousins, or even remade frocks from their mother's saved dresses.

But a new dress? Oh, that was an occasion of note.

So who had taken the time to put those words to paper?

She glanced again. It could be any of them.

"Now that this distasteful business is concluded," Mrs. George L. was saying, "and all the committee chairs reported in as they arrived, I do believe everything is in order for our annual Christmas bazaar and supper dance. So shall I ring for refreshments?" She reached for the bell sitting on the table beside her.

Savannah could feel as much as hear the dismay running through the girls as they looked to each other in a bit of a panic. Yet not one of them had the nerve to stand up and make a protest.

Every single one had come with the intention of signing up for the booths at the Christmas bazaar. Write down their names and . . .

Write down their names.

She glanced once again around the room. There was no way to tell which one of them wrote that wish by looking from one youthful face to the next.

But their handwriting. She thought of the almost familiar copperplate hand on that slip of paper. Well, one of them might provide a clue . . .

Prodded to her feet by forces she didn't understand, Savannah spoke up. "Madame Chairwoman, the booth assignments?"

Mrs. George L. blinked. "Well, my heavens, Mrs. Clarke, you are a godsend. In all this indelicate business, I forgot." She glanced around the room. "As it is, Mrs. Pelham is currently indisposed with some trifling ailment and won't be able to fulfill her duties this year."

Nearly every woman in the room looked away, at her gloves, anywhere but at Mrs. Lovell's searching gaze. They all knew what was coming.

But oh, curiosity was a dangerous thing.

"So I will have need of a volunteer to—"

"I'll do it," Savannah offered.

Mrs. George L. peered over the top of her spectacles. "You, Mrs. Clarke?"

The rest of the room stilled.

Savannah did her best to look utterly unruffled in the face of their collective disbelief. They needn't look at her like she'd suggested a round of sherry. "Why, of course. I don't mind. Not in the least. As you reminded me the other day, many hands lighten the work." She tried to make it sound as if she stepped in all the time.

"Well, then," Mrs. George L. said, "our junior members should see Mrs. Clarke if they would like to help with a booth." With that, the membership was adjourned to the dining room where refreshments had been set out.

Sometime later, Mrs. George L. made her way over to Savannah, who now had a full list of willing participants.

"You needn't go to too much bother," Mrs. George L. began, pressing a paper into Savannah's hands. Then she lowered her voice, quite confidentially. "While it is nice to make a public show of being egalitarian, you can simply use the assignments from last year."

"Thank you, Mrs. Lovell," Savannah said, recalling what one of the girls had said earlier. Clearly the preferential assignments weren't as much of a secret as Mrs. George L. thought.

"As for Mrs. Bergstrom," the woman continued, "you should call on her with some alacrity. It is all well and good to send over Inola with a pot of soup, but that poor woman has had . . . difficulties, shall we say, in the past. She will need your singular attentions." She sighed, as if lifting the weight of the world from her shoulders. "I must insist you call on her personally, Mrs. Clarke. Tomorrow at the latest."

❄

MADELINE STEPPED BACK to admire the gleaming mahogany bar, the swept floor, and the sparkle of the stained-glass cabinets. It was a good start.

If only she could figure out how to get the ornate clock over the backbar working. She'd have to ask Wick who might be able to fix it.

As it was, she'd come back from the train station on Monday and taken a closer look around. If she must remain in Bethlehem, at least for the time being, perhaps she should do as Shandy said, and cause a proper stir.

If there was one thing Madeline Drake excelled at, it was making herself most unwelcome.

Not that going home didn't pose a whole other set of problems. How would she ever explain her disappearance?

Knowing her mother, Dahlia had immediately circulated some self-serving press release stating that her "poor, troubled Madeline" had finally sought treatment, then ended it with a plea for "prayers and privacy" during this difficult time. Then she'd hire a new pool boy.

But it was Nate who had her in a real turmoil. He was probably frantically looking for her this very moment.

She wished she could just text him and tell him she was fine. Glancing around the bar, she suspected he'd be jealous, for here she was in a living, breathing example of turn-of-the-century Wyoming.

The Star Bright Saloon. All hers. Or so Shandy had said.

And while Madeline might excel at making messes, she also hated living in one, so she'd started cleaning. When Dobbs showed up, she'd bribed him into service—that is, after he'd volunteered to get them both dinner from Mrs. Pingree's.

Now, a day later, Madeline had to admit she liked the transformation. Yet she was missing one essential thing.

"Booze," she said aloud.

"What?" Dobbs asked as he came in the door, dragging a chair with him, having finished cleaning the grime from the outside of the front windows.

"I'm going to need to stock the bar. Beer, rum, whiskey, vermouth —" She silently ticked off the bottles she recalled from the set, as well as her own research into vintage cocktail recipes.

"Oh, I can get all that for you," Dobbs offered. He positioned his chair in front of one of the windows and surveyed the task ahead.

Madeline laughed. "You can't go buy liquor."

His brows furrowed as he looked over his shoulder at her. "Why not?"

"You're a kid."

The boy's puzzled expression never changed. "Never stopped me before."

She realized he wasn't joking. "Before?"

"I buy bottles for Mr. Thayer all the time." Dobbs crossed his arms over his skinny chest. "When he's fixing on some important matter, he sends me over to Mr. Hoback's for a bottle. Of course, I get a jitney for the errand."

A jitney? Oh, right. A nickel. She'd circle back to that one while making a note to talk to this Mr. Thayer. Some moral example he was. "And Mr. Hoback is . . ."

"The druggist. He has the shop down at the end of the next block." Dobbs nodded. "Says I'm his best customer. Gives me a cut as well."

"Really?" She had to admire Dobbs' entrepreneurial talents. That, and he was single-handedly keeping her fed and warm—with baskets of food (conveniently with enough to share) and a full wood box every day. Not to mention, his cheery, chatty company. She loved listening to his stories about the town and the people passing by. The kid truly had no filters, and gave his unvarnished opinions in a matter-of-fact delivery.

He'd quickly become the brightest, most welcome part of her day. Madeline owed him a real debt, for she'd never have managed any of this without him.

Dobbs happily chattered on as he began wiping the inside windows. "I buy bottles for most of the men in town. So their wives don't find out." He paused. "Well, not in the case of Mr. Thayer, on account of him not having a wife."

Oh, good heavens. Madeline looked up from her list. "Dobbs, what *don't* you do around here?"

"I don't know," he said with a shrug, getting back to his cleaning. "I just do whatever needs to be done. Run errands, chop kindling for folks, like Miss Minch."

"Miss Minch? She runs the post office, doesn't she?" Madeline had her on her list as well. She needed to return the woman's soup pail and thank her for her kindness.

Dobbs scrubbed at a particularly grimy spot. "Yeah, she runs the post office, even though she's not supposed to."

"Not supposed to? How's that?"

He stopped wiping, staring at her as if the answer was obvious. "Because she's a lady. Ladies shouldn't run post offices. Or so Mr. Hoback says."

"Are ladies allowed to run saloons?"

The lines on his brow ran deeper as he considered it. "I s'pose not."

"So you don't want to work here?"

"Oh, I want to work," he told her, getting back to his scrubbing.

Madeline grinned. She liked this kid. He'd taken Shandy's request to help her out to heart and had become her lifeline. But what was his life here? Then something occurred to her. "Helping me won't interfere with school, will it?"

"School?" He shook his head. "I don't go to school." He went back to cleaning the window, now with a bit more intensity.

Up until she'd asked the question, she hadn't really thought of it. She'd taken the kid's presence for granted. A bolt of shame shot through her.

"Don't go? Why not?" She was certain she'd seen a school the other day.

"'Cause." This was followed by another of those shrugs, like the answer was obvious.

Not to her. She crossed the room and took the rag from him. "'Cause why?"

He opened his mouth to say something, but words stuttered to a halt. "'Cause. I'm . . ."

"You're what?"

"Colored."

Madeline paused. "What has that got to do with going to school?"

"There are no colored schools here." He chucked his chin up a notch. "That's why I'm saving my money. To go to the colored school in Cheyenne."

The light suddenly dawned on her. 1907. Segregation. Aw, shit. But if she remembered correctly . . . "We're in Wyoming, aren't we?"

"Yeah."

"How many kids of color are here?"

"Just me, I suppose," he shrugged.

"So you can go," she told him. Nate had always insisted on historical accuracy in his scripts. "Wyoming law states that you can go to school." They'd done an episode on that very point.

"But Mr. Hoback says I can't go. He's on the school board and all."

So misogyny wasn't the man's only sin.

"You don't need to go to Cheyenne. You just need a lawyer."

Her tone had Dobbs climbing down from the chair. "Oh, no. You can't. Mr. Hoback won't like that. He'll lower my cut."

"Never you mind about Mr. Hoback. From now on, I'll be purchasing the liquor. You work for me. No more buying bottles for others. If they want a drink, they can come here."

That brought a shake of his head, as if he'd never heard anything so foolish. Then he cocked his head. "What's my salary?"

"Name your price," Madeline offered.

Dodd's eyes narrowed, and she could see him calculating what he thought he could get. Then he named his price. When she nodded in agreement, he asked, "Have you got that much?"

That rather stopped her. She hadn't even gotten around to the issue of money yet. Mr. King had, albeit reluctantly, given her credit after she'd lied and assured him that Shandy had promised to cover all her expenses.

But opening this place would take more than a bit of sleight of hand at the mercantile, that is until something else occurred to her. It might be that Shandy had unwittingly given her the key the other day.

So you found the gold?

"Shall we see?" Madeline went around to the back of the bar, her gaze sweeping over the elaborate woodwork of fancy cabinets until she saw what was she was looking for—a solitary shooting star carved into a thin panel.

She traced her finger over the little bit of ornamentation. *No. It couldn't be.*

Taking a deep breath, she pushed the panel. It clicked and then sprang open.

Dobbs had come around the bar, and he gaped at the opening. "How did you know it would do that?"

She shrugged, and reached inside to pull out a small, sturdy strongbox. "Our secret, eh, kid?"

He nodded solemnly.

She reached under the other counter and—yes, of course—found the key hanging on a nail. Opening the box, they both looked inside. All the gold she'd need.

Dobbs whistled in appreciation. "That's enough for all the liquor in Mr. Hoback's back room."

"I don't think we need that much."

He grinned nonetheless. "Are you really going to open up this place?"

"I mean to split this entire town wide open."

He let out a long breath, but conspiratorial twinkle lit his dark eyes. "Folks are going to be fiercely unhappy with you."

"Dobbs, I've spent most of my life with people being fiercely unhappy with me."

"Really?"

She nodded again.

"That doesn't seem fair."

She realized he was speaking from experience. "Neither does not letting you go to school." She wiped her hands and took off her apron. "Shandy brought me here for a reason, and I say we owe it to him to stir things up a bit."

CHAPTER 13

Wednesday, December 4

*P*arathinia Minch had always longed to be named the head of a committee, but certainly not one the good ladies of Bethlehem had quietly dubbed the "Get Rid of That Harlot" committee. Yet here she was, on the front porch of the Star Bright Saloon, about to execute its directive.

"Do you think, Miss Minch, that the front door is a proper entrance for us?" Miss Odella Winsley peered out from beneath her grandest hat, seasonally re-trimmed in red ribbons and sprigs of holly.

Parathinia suspected that none of this was proper. But there it was.

On her other side, Miss Theodosia shifted the large basket she'd insisted on bringing.

When the woman caught Parathina looking at it, she sighed. "Please don't say anything to Mrs. George L. I doubt she would approve. But it hardly seems right to visit a new neighbor without offering them a basket. Especially when one must ask them to . . ."

Vamoose? Scram? Pack up and leave? Parathinia hardly knew.

"Indeed," Odella agreed. "Not at all neighborly."

They had paused here, in front of the double doors, but not one of them possessed the wherewithal to step forward and open one of them, or knock, or whatever it was a lady did to enter a saloon.

"You've done this before," Theodosia reminded Parathinia, nodding toward the door. "Gone inside." Odella, too, looked at her expectantly.

"I suppose I have, but I must admit I came in from the back," she explained. She'd also been filled with an unusual abundance of *Exorior!* that currently eluded her.

"Well, it is reassuring that you survived your brush with this den of iniquity," Odella said matter-of-factly.

"I fear it isn't quite as wicked inside as one might suspect," Parathinia replied.

"Oh," Theodosia murmured, sounding more disappointed than relieved.

Just then the door swung open and, to their shock and amazement, the sheriff stuck his head out. "Ladies, it's too cold to be standing out in the wind. Come in and get warm."

Theodosia brightened immediately. "Well, if the sheriff is here, that lends a measure of respectability to all this, don't you think, sister?"

"Indeed," Odella said, brushing past Parathinia to make her way inside. Theodosia needed no further prompting and followed close on her sister's heels.

"Miss Minch?" the sheriff prompted, still holding the door open.

"Yes, I suppose," she said, gathering her shawl tighter around her shoulders, annoyed with herself that she was the last one in.

As the committee chairwoman, she should have been first. This was her duty, like it or not, so she hurried inside and came to a stop beside the Winsley sisters, who stood stock still as they took in this foreign shore.

For her part, Parathinia realized that when she had been here on Sunday, she hadn't looked around all that much, for certainly she would have remembered the beautiful stained glass—a tumbling array of shooting stars—in the cabinets overhead. Why, they were as beautiful as the windows in the Catholic church.

Odella's gaze seemed fixed on the carved figurehead that was the centerpiece of the elaborate bar, a bare-breasted woman whose smile could only be described as beguiling.

"Heavens!" she whispered, before lowering her shocked countenance and turning to Miss Drake, who stood beneath the figurehead with an equally beguiling smile on her face. It was marred, though, by those terrible bruises.

"Oh, my," Theodosia gasped, her free hand going to her own cheek.

"Sister!" Odella whispered under her breath, and Theodosia's hand dropped.

Despite the bruises' new hues of yellow and green, Parathinia found Miss Drake looking quite recovered, hardly the same dismal creature the sheriff had plucked out of the snow. She stood behind the bar fresh-faced and lively. Very much so. A restless energy surrounded her as she finished wiping the top of the bar and came around to greet them.

"Miss Minch!" she exclaimed. "How nice to see you again. I've been meaning to come over to the post office and return your tin. I'm certain I have your kindness and soup to credit for my full recovery. It's around here somewhere . . ." She went back around the bar and began to rummage beneath it, even as Parathinia felt more than saw the Winsley sisters swivel toward her.

"So it *is* true," Odella whispered to her sister.

Parathinia tamped a moment of indignation. Did everyone think she'd made up her earlier visit? Yet now was not the time to fret over such skepticism, for here came Miss Drake, wiping her hands on a clean rag and giving her apron a tug into place. "I'm so sorry. I can't find your tin right now. But when I do, I'll—"

"You don't need to—" Parathinia began.

"Oh, it's no problem. I just want to be neighborly," she said, casting a glance at the sheriff. "And you've brought friends. Wonderful!" She stuck out her hand to Odella. "I'm Madeline Drake. A pleasure to meet you."

Odella glanced at the proffered hand and then gingerly put out her own. "I'm Miss Odella Winsley. It is nice to meet you, Miss Drake."

"No, no, please call me Madeline." She gave Odella's hand an enthusiastic wag. "When you say Miss Drake, it makes me sound like my mother."

Odella's brows rose as she began to work out the particulars of this introduction. If her mother was a "miss," then that meant . . . Hastily, she turned and passed the problem along. "Miss Drake, might I introduce my sister, Miss Theodosia Winsley."

"Theodosia. And Odella. What lovely names," she said, smiling at the pair.

"Oh, my." Theodosia actually dimpled into a blush. "Our mother thought much the same, while our father argued that more utilitarian monikers would be—"

Odella nudged her, a reminder that this wasn't a social call, so Theodosia's explanation halted into a rather awkward silence, leaving all five of them shuffling a bit.

The sheriff, arms folded over his chest, leaned forward, peering around them. "Is that a welcome basket I see, Miss Theodosia?"

Theodosia looked down at her hands, blinking as if surprised to find it still there. Then, with a stiff arm, she stuck the basket out in offering. "Well, it isn't a proper basket. Certainly not to the order of generosity that sister and I are known for, and while I had such high hopes of a . . . that is . . . usually a pound social would be in order, but Mrs. George L., that is Mrs. George L. Lovell . . . I don't suppose you've met Mrs. George L., have you, Miss Drake?"

"Large, overbearing woman with a disagreeable personality?"

While good manners—and a well-honed sense of self-preservation—demanded the three of them deny this appraisal of their Temperance Union president, they all found themselves nodding in agreement.

"Then, yes, I have," Miss Drake said, with an impish grin.

Theodosia, a veritable high tide of help, hurried to flood the void before another troublesome silence invaded the room. "Yes. Well, this basket hardly makes up for a pound social. I hope you will believe it is well meant."

After a nod from the sheriff, Miss Drake set down her cleaning rag and came forward to take the offered basket. "Thank you very much." She glanced again at the sheriff as if looking for direction.

Parathinia had to wonder where Miss Drake had come from, for she acted as if she'd never been offered a basket before, even one as poorly presented as Theodosia's.

Then it became apparent she never had, for she abandoned it on one of the tables and continued on as if nothing of note had happened. "Since I don't know how long I'll be here, I've been cleaning. At least I've made a dent in things," she told them with a sigh, waving her hand at the mismatched chairs, the collection of glasses and bottles on the bar, and the bare windows. "Anyway, cleaning and sorting seems a much better use of my time than day drinking and taking long walks in the snow. Eh, Wick?"

The sheriff just shook his head, his eyes rolling upward.

Day drinking? Parathinia had to imagine it was some sort of modern slang, for the Winsley sisters appeared just as befuddled.

For her part, Miss Drake laughed, but she was the only one. And when she realized it, she smiled a little brighter and turned a questioning glance at Sheriff Fischer, as if she was as unsure as her visitors.

Theodosia, of course, recovered first. Which was hardly a blessing. "Mrs. Drake—"

The young woman shook her head. "It isn't Mrs. It never has been."

Odella peered out from beneath the brim of her hat, ribbons all aquiver. "Never?"

"Oh, no," Miss Drake said, picking up a rag and wiping at the table around the basket. "I've been engaged twice. . . No. Three times, if you count that weekend in Las Vegas. Though I try not to, if you know what I mean." Miss Drake leaned closer, confidentially. "He was awful in bed."

Engaged thrice? In bed? Parathinia was quite certain not even Mrs. Mercer would approve of such a problematic state of affairs. At least she didn't think so. She still had three chapters left to read.

Shaking off her errant thoughts, she struggled to get to the point of their business. But before she could, the situation veered downhill quickly.

"Yes, well, where are my manners?" Miss Drake had returned to the bar and was now sorting through the madcap jumble of bottles atop it. "You ladies are in luck. Just earlier I found an unopened bottle of applejack that is begging to be sampled."

She set the brown bottle on the bar. *Plunk.* Then *plink, plink, plink,* she added three glasses beside the two already there. All lined up like passengers waiting for a train.

A runaway one.

"Oh, we couldn't." Parathinia tried desperately to find the brakes on all this, to no avail.

"It is no trouble. The least I can to," Miss Drake told them. "I was just telling the sheriff I make a mean Applejack Sour, and now I can prove it."

"Are you suggesting a cocktail?" Theodosia whispered in a desperate little squeak.

"I'm not suggesting," she told them as she brought out a seltzer bottle and a sugar bowl. She went over to the ice box. "I'm insisting."

Odella turned. "Miss Minch. Do something!"

The offer of a libation at—what?—ten in the morning *was* rather alarming . . .

"Is there something else you wanted to say, ladies?" Sheriff Fischer asked, his lips quirking.

Why, the wretched man was enjoying all this. He knew exactly why they were here. Of course he did. The entire town did.

With the singular exception of the woman now fixing cocktails for a Temperance Union committee.

Parathinia huffed a sigh, drew herself up, and directed her words toward Miss Drake, ignoring the sheriff and his smirks. "Miss Drake, if you would . . . That is . . . We are here to . . ."

Meanwhile, at the bar, Miss Drake had finished shaking this unholy potion of hers. "I know what you are going to say," she began as she poured the amber liquid through a strainer into each of the glasses.

"You do?" Theodosia sighed. "Oh, that is such a relief, isn't it, Miss Minch?"

"I'm not so sure," she told Theodosia as she surveyed the glasses in front of them.

Miss Drake eyed her concoctions and then, seemingly satisfied with her work, smiled at her guests. "This time of year, one usually puts a little grated nutmeg on top of an Applejack Sour—just to be festive—but I don't have any." She pursed her lips. "I'll have to add that to my shopping list." She pushed the glasses forward. "On the house, as they say."

Odella stepped forward, not knowing what else to do, until Theodosia caught hold of her sleeve and gave it a tug, her eyes alight with panic.

"I came to suggest, that is, *we* came to ask . . ." Parathinia found that words failed her, for here was Miss Drake, smiling at them, looking so proud of the pretty cocktails she'd managed to put together on such short notice.

Even without the missing nutmeg, Parathinia had to admit they did look very festive.

The sheriff finally waded in. "Miss Theodosia, do I smell your famous ginger cookies?" He wagged his chin toward the basket. "I think they will add to this party, don't you?"

"Well, it would hardly be proper—or neighborly," Theodosia sputtered, slanting a wary glance at Miss Drake, "to come to ask such a . . . thing, and not—"

"Bring cookies?" he finished.

The words just rushed out of her. "I am so glad you understand, Sheriff Fischer."

"I wish I did," Miss Drake said plainly.

Here was the opening Parathinia had been waiting for. "Miss Drake, we are here on behalf of the Temperance Union—"

The younger woman's brow furrowed, and then it was as if a light flickered on inside her. "Oh, now I understand. The cookies are to sweeten the bargain."

Parathinia let out a breath. Perhaps her committee wasn't going to be a complete failure after all. "So you do understand?"

Miss Drake nodded. "Of course. But if you needed a donation, all you had to do was ask."

"A-a-a-a—" It was as far as Parathinia got.

"Or a place to meet?" Miss Drake continued. "Once I get the back room cleaned up a bit, I thought it might be fun to hold a dance there. We did that on a few episodes of the show. But it would also work as a meeting space, that is if your group needs a place."

"Meet here?" Odella choked out, her pale blue eyes wide with alarm. "The Temperance Union?"

Miss Drake glanced around and came to a different conclusion. "Yes, I suppose it doesn't seem like much now. But again, once I get it cleaned up, it will be perfect for the ladies' side." She paused and looked over at them. "That is what it's called, isn't it?"

The ladies' side? Parathinia blinked. Had Miss Drake just suggested that ladies might come to a saloon?

Apparently she had, for here she was, opening the door to the large room in the rear for them to inspect. "Would this be enough space for your group to meet?"

"Oh, my," Theodosia managed, sadly never lacking in words no matter the situation, "I fear we could never . . . I mean to say, how could we go back to Mrs. George L. and suggest—"

Odella shuddered from head to toe. "Why, it would be impossible."

Parathinia knew exactly what specter had prompted such paroxysms of horror.

The three of them standing up at tomorrow's meeting, reading the following report:

After Miss Drake offered us libations, she kindly suggested the use of her back room for our future meetings . . ."

Miss Drake shrugged. "Perhaps we can just start with a donation."

"Yes," the wretched man replied mischievously. "Five dollars ought to do it."

"Five dollars?" squeaked Odella and Theodosia in unison. It was an outrageous sum.

The young woman brightened. "That I can do," she told them. She walked over to the cash register, and, after she poked at the buttons and turned the crank until the bell rang, the drawer popped open.

As she came back, money in hand, it struck Parathinia that Miss Drake walked with purpose. Her stride came with confidence.

Miss Madeline Drake—like Mrs. Mercer—would never let a committee under her leadership go awry. "I hope this helps whatever it is your organization does." She handed the coin over to Parathinia.

"The Temperance Union," Odella supplied, leaning over to inspect the offering.

Parathinia looked down at the gold half eagle as well. Not knowing what else to do, she resorted to habit and good manners. "Thank you, Miss Drake." And she dropped it into her purse.

"My pleasure, Miss Minch. Whatever I can do to help." Then Miss Drake smiled in a bright, welcoming flash, the sort that warmed even the coldest of days.

Now how could Parathinia tell this kind young woman she wasn't wanted?

She just couldn't. So she thanked her again, nudged the Winsley sisters out of their stupor, and led her committee, as any good chairwoman might, out the front door.

"Is that truly a five-dollar piece?" Theodosia asked once they found themselves well away.

Parathinia dug into her purse and held it up for them both to see.

"I declare," Odella said with a bit of a whistle.

"Indeed," Theodosia agreed.

Parathinia tucked her unwanted donation out of sight and began a hurried retreat.

"Whatever are you to do with it, Miss Minch?" Odella asked as she caught up.

"Do with it?" Parathinia asked.

"Yes," Theodosia said. "However will you explain where five dollars for the fund came from?"

"I suppose," she began, "I could slip it into the Ladies Aid collection, perhaps when no one is looking."

"Would you dare?" Odella asked, looking at her askance—but with a bit of admiration.

Did she have a choice?

Theodosia shook her head, unconvinced. "What if Miss Drake says something to Mrs. George L. in the meantime?"

Parathinia waved off such a suggestion. "I doubt they will cross paths."

Odella nodded in agreement, yet had to add, "At least one can hope."

Theodosia was quiet for a moment as they continued down the street. "Those were bruises on her face, were they not? She would have such a pretty countenance, if not for those terrible . . ."

Odella blew out a puff of breath. "Sister! One doesn't speak of such things."

"Yes, but however did they . . ." Theodosia went no further in her supposition.

Parathinia shivered. *Come to be?* There were two ways. An accident or a man's fist. But in polite society, it was always the former that was offered as the respectable truth.

Sadly, even the Winsley sisters understood the distinction.

"Whatever are we to report, Miss Minch?" Odella asked. "Especially after Miss Drake was so affable."

"Well, she never said she was opening the saloon," Theodosia pointed out. "Not precisely."

Parathinia glanced back at the Star Bright. No, she hadn't.

Odella nodded. "She was just cleaning. And providing a space for meetings."

"A pound social would have made this difficult business so much more agreeable," Theodosia mused to no one in particular.

"THAT WAS ODD," Madeline remarked, head cocked slightly as she watched the door close. The morning was turning into a regular circus. First Wick drops by to check on her, then Miss Minch and her friends arrive. "Really odd."

The sheriff burst out laughing. "You have no idea."

Yet from the way the man was laughing, Madeline realized there was more to the ladies dropping by than a casual visit from the local Welcome Wagon. "What's so funny?"

"I just can't believe I was lucky enough to witness that," he managed between guffaws.

There was a word she never thought she'd use. *Guffaw*. But it fit. The man was laughing so hard he was wiping tears.

Madeline crossed her arms over her chest. "Witness what, exactly?"

"You and a committee from the Temperance Union. Oh, poor Miss Minch."

"Poor Miss Minch? I gave her five dollars. They brought me a basket. What am I missing?" Then Madeline thought about it. "Wait just a minute." The odd pieces clinked together like ice cubes falling into an empty glass. "Temperance as in prohibition—as in no alcohol? Did they come to shut me down?"

He nodded. "Yes. Best of all, you offered them a drink." He tipped his head at the line of cocktails on the bar and shook with another fit of laughter.

But Madeline's brow worried into a hard line. "I'll be damned. Here I rather liked Miss Minch." She glanced at the door again.

"Don't blame her. Most likely Mrs. George L. bullied her into it." He began rummaging in the basket.

So her plan *was* stirring things up. "What's inside that?"

"I'm hoping a plate of Miss Theodosia's ginger cookies." He dug deeper into the basket. "What I would give to be a fly on the wall at their meeting tomorrow. I should warn you, you've kicked a hornet's nest."

"I have a talent for that," she murmured. This unexpected development should have buoyed her spirits, but still, Miss Minch?

Not that he was listening, for he'd plucked his prize out and taken a bite. After a few contented chews, he popped the rest of the cookie into his mouth. His face glazed over a bit.

"Why are you here?" she asked as she reached over and took one of the cookies. As she bit into it, she was lost in pure sugar bliss.

"You've been too quiet the last few days."

"As I told my new friends," she said, reaching in and taking another cookie, "I'm giving this place a thorough cleaning. Top to bottom." She took a bite.

"Then what? Clearly the Temperance Union thinks you're about to open up." He picked up one of the cocktails, sniffed it, and then put it back down.

"They wouldn't be wrong."

He stilled. "What?"

"You heard me. I'm opening this place."

"You can't be serious."

"I'm dead serious. If those Carrie Nation fanatics think they can stop me, they're wrong. And you—stop stealing my cookies."

"There is one thing you and the Temperance Union don't seem to realize: you can't open without a license." He took another cookie. "Consider this your first fine for selling alcohol without one." He tipped it at her before devouring it.

Now it was Madeline's turn to laugh. "I didn't sell anything. Those drinks were on the house."

After a moment, they both laughed, and while they did, she slid the plate out of his reach since she doubted Miss Theodosia would be returning any time soon. At least not with cookies. "So where do I get this license?"

He winked at her. "As it turns out, from the sheriff."

"LORD ALMIGHTY! WHATEVER IS THIS MESS?" Inola swept into the room, bringing with her a righteous breeze.

"Oh, no!" Savannah exclaimed as she threw herself over the slips of paper in front of her before they scattered like leaves.

"What are you doing?" Inola gaped at her.

Savannah carefully stacked the slips back into a semblance of order. "Booth assignments."

"Booth what?"

"Booth assignments," Savannah repeated. "For the Ladies Aid bazaar."

Much to her chagrin, the sign-up sheet hadn't given her what she wanted—a match to the handwriting on the wish.

"Why do *you* have the booth assignments?" Inola's foot tapped against the floorboards.

Savannah reasoned the best course of action was the truth. Well, as close to the truth as she could manage. "Mrs. Pelham was sick, so I volunteered."

Inola's mouth opened and then shut. She paused to take a steadying breath before she asked, simply and slowly as if she hadn't heard correctly, "You? Volunteered?"

"Yes. But only to organize the booth assignments." Savannah tried her best to appear nonchalant, as if her taking on such a task was the normal course of business.

Inola pulled out a chair and sat down. "I'm not even going to ask."

"Truly?"

Inola shook her head. "Of course I am." She leaned forward. "Are you dying?"

This was rather the last question she'd expected. "Dying?"

"Well, something's got your skirts in a knot. Been that way for nearly a week now, and the only thing I can think is that you're dying." She folded her hands in front of her, mouth set in a determined line, and waited for the news.

Of all the ridiculous nonsense. "No. I'm not dying." Savannah straightened and began to sort the names anew, mulling each one as she went. *Pinky Jonas, no. Clemie Bohlen, no. Rosemary Tuttle, no. Miss Elda Barrett . . .*

Savannah paused as she looked again at the schoolteacher's name. Elda hadn't been there to sign up. Rather, her sister Libby had done the deed. How had she forgotten that? She looked at the slip again.

"Then why are you doing all this?"

Inola's sharp question startled Savannah. "I told you. Mrs. Pelham is doing poorly—"

She faltered to a halt as Inola's brows arched. Oh, she knew *that* look.

The one that said, *I don't believe a word of what you're saying, Savannah Adeline*.

Deliberately she picked up a slip of paper and put it atop a booth.

"Are you sure you aren't sick?" Inola pressed, reaching over and laying her hand over Savannah's.

"No. I am not sick." She pulled her hand free and started over once again. *Rosemary Tuttle. No.*

Inola barked a laugh and nodded at the chart. "You certain? 'Cause you just put that poor little mouse, Rosemary Tuttle, in the same booth as that awful Lovell gel. She'll get eaten alive. Along with all the candy." She came around the table to examine the big piece of used brown wrapping paper from King's, on which Savannah had drawn a diagram with the name of each booth: candy, raffle, aprons, lace, household goods, kitchen sundries, toys, dolls, mittens, and finally, baked goods.

As Inola's gaze narrowed with concentration, Savannah took another look at what she'd just done. Botheration. Inola was right. That would hardly do. "Dear me," she muttered under her breath as she swept the two slips back into the pile. What had seemed a relatively easy task was turning into an unyielding tangle.

"Dear me, indeed," Inola said, reaching over and retrieving both slips of paper. "You should put Josephine Lovell in charge of mittens. Serve that overly proud gel some good."

"Mittens!" Savannah shook her head. "Mrs. George L. would never stand for it. She'll want her darling daughter somewhere popular." Josephine went back down on a candy square.

Inola caught it up and put it back. "Mittens."

Savannah fetched it back and held on to it. "I know perfectly well what I'm doing."

There was that look again. "When was the last time you even went to the Ladies Aid bazaar?"

"I hardly see how that matters," Savannah told her.

"Then what are they serving for supper?"

"Pardon?" Savannah did her best to pretend like she hadn't heard, when in truth, she hadn't the least idea what was being served at the supper.

"What are they serving?" Inola repeated.

Savannah's lips pursed together. "Turkey."

"No," Inola told her as she returned to sorting the slips. Nor did she supply the answer.

After a few moments of silence, Savannah tried again. "Ham. That's it. It's a ham supper."

Inola blew out a breath. "While I don't like to say I told you so—"

"You live to say that."

"I do." Inola grinned. "But to prove my point that you don't know a thing, I will tell you this: Josephine Lovell likes to set herself up at the candy table and spend all her time flirting with the boys. When what she's supposed to be doing is selling that candy. Let her flutter her lashes over mittens." Inola picked up the girl's name and set it on *Mittens*.

Savannah shook her head. "Her mother won't like it."

"If you are going to cozen me with this nonsense about wanting to 'help out'"—Inola began plucking up the various slips, ignoring any protest—"I'm certain you can find some tall tale for that dreadful woman." She clucked her tongue and shook her head. "Lawd sakes, Vanna, you can't put Hazel Smith and Alice Bohlen together. They don't like each other." With a quick sort, she placed Hazel Smith next to *Toys*. "That will do the trick nicely."

Inola was right, of course. Savannah glanced over the stacks of names and the chart before her. She had no idea what she was doing.

"Who would you punish with *Aprons*?"

Inola's brows crinkled as she looked over the sheet of paper. "Pinky Jonas."

"Why is that?" Savannah asked as she put the girl's name down on the square.

Inola laughed. "That girl can't cook a lick. Neither can her mother. I do like the irony of it."

Savannah grinned back. "Well, there is some humor in that." She looked over the rest of it. "What sort of candy are they selling?"

Inola must have known what that admission cost her and answered matter-of-factly. "The usual, I imagine. Caramels. Fudge. Those mints Mrs. Pelham makes."

Savannah shuddered. Those mints were enough to turn one off candy until the end of their days. They were better off melted and used to fill the chinks in siding. "Divinity would be better," she replied. "Or pecan turtles. That would make things interesting." And edible.

"We could get out the kettle tonight," Inola suggested, "'cept we'd need sugar."

Savannah shook her head. "We can't afford extra sugar or the pecans. Mr. King is being generous about our account as it is, and now that we also have to see to the Bergstroms . . ."

A long silence spread between them.

"We've made do before," Inola said quietly, firmly. More slips of paper crossed the space between them.

"Yes, we have," Susannah agreed. But the years ahead would prove difficult if something didn't change. The gold and jewelry she'd brought with them from Mississippi was nearly all gone.

When she looked up, she found Inola smiling. "You could use less sugar in the cake you're baking for Josephine. That ought to let us make some divinity."

"That would be hardly fair to the poor boy who bids on her cake. He should get something sweet out of the bargain."

Inola laughed. "It certainly won't be Josephine's company."

Savannah nodded in agreement there. She had known far too many Josephines in her time.

"There you are," Inola said with a nod as she put down the last name. "All on your own." Her smile teased as much as her words.

"I concede I couldn't have done it without you."

"Nothing to concede. We both know that."

Savannah laughed and began transcribing the assignments to a plain sheet of paper.

With this completed, she was free to wash her hands of this entire wish nonsense, since she'd hadn't the least notion of how to find whoever made that wish.

But apparently the wishes were not done with her yet.

"Looks like you might have missed one. There's another slip down here," Inola said, bending over to retrieve a piece of paper from under the table. She glanced at it and then shook her head. "No, my mistake. Only the receipt from last week's groceries." She set it on the table. "Still, I can't get over this—you volunteering to help, and during the holidays no less. It's like a wish come true."

Wish.

That single word pulled her gaze toward the receipt, which was written in the same clean, clear lettering that had become the bane of her existence. No wonder the handwriting on that wish had seemed so tauntingly familiar.

She didn't see the list of groceries. *Sugar. Flour. Coffee . . .*

Savannah saw something else written there. *A new dress for the Christmas ball.*

Her mouth moved with a name that wouldn't come forth, as if her tongue knew that once she uttered it, this stubborn, impossible wish would need to come true.

Myrtle King.

CHAPTER 14

Though Madeline was hardly happy with Wick for outright refusing her a liquor license, she gave him a chance to redeem himself by showing her where she could get her laundry done. Sure, he was a judgmental, opinionated male, but much could be forgiven if one didn't have to wash out their underwear in the sink yet again.

"You have to agree that I was perfectly nice to those ladies, despite the reason for their visit," she said to Wick as they walked along the boardwalk.

"And if you'd known the real reason for their visit?"

Madeline didn't have an answer for that. When word got out that she intended to open the saloon, the Bethlehem Temperance Union would return. And not merely the kindly trio who had visited today.

Well, at least she'd be prepared.

They'd walked all the way to the edge of town, where the river ran alongside a row of shanties and rough houses. Wick pointed out the mill and the copper smelter in the distance.

"The smelter is why we have electricity," he explained.

Finally they arrived at a two-story ramshackle building with a large, crooked sign that read *Good uck Laundry*, the *L* in *Luck* having faded away.

Off to one side, a wobbly-looking staircase led to the second story, and yet another fading sign pointed the way up to the offices of *The Hon. Erasmus P. Quinby, Attorney-at-Law*.

A questionable laundry and suspect legal offices. Oh, this was reassuring. When she got home, she would never take her washing machine for granted ever again. Or her espresso machine . . . or her microwave . . .

She hurried inside after Wick, who at least had offered to carry her bundle. The moment she stepped through the doorway, she was hit with a blast of hot, moist air and the sharp scent of strong soap. A narrow counter sat between them and a blue curtain that concealed the workings in the back.

Both sides of the front room were lined with shelves stacked with brown paper packages—all tied in twine and each with a different tag. So apparently the laundry had customers.

Or it was the only one around.

"Sheriff," said a thin Asian man as he came out from the steamy environs beyond. Of middling years and wearing a white shirt with the sleeves rolled up, he tipped his head to Wick but barely spared her a glance. "Your laundry is not done. Come back tomorrow."

"Not here about my laundry, Mr. Wu. I've brought you a new customer."

Mr. Wu's sharp gaze narrowed in Madeline's direction for only an instant and then returned to Wick.

"Which I would receive with gratitude," Mr. Wu began, "under normal circumstances, but I have heard from others that *she* is not a proper citizen." He looked her up and down, his gaze finally coming to a stop at the bright yellow bruises on the side of her face. "I have standards."

Her hand went to her face unconsciously. *This is not my fault*, she wanted to tell one and all. *I was in an accident.*

But it was the later implication—*I have standards*—that sent a familiar surge through her.

"Not a proper—" Madeline began, until Wick put up his hand to stop her. Normally she wouldn't have let anyone run interference for her, but she decided to let the sheriff have the first stab at this, since she'd completely screwed up with the Temperance Union.

And stab he did. He leaned on the counter and looked the man right in the eyes. "Respectable establishment? You run a gambling den most nights back there."

"Sheriff—" Mr. Wu began to protest, holding up his hands and shaking his head.

Wick wasn't done. "The only reason I don't run you in is because you and Quinby would cook up some legal filibuster to wrangle you out of the multitude of charges I could file."

Mr. Wu nodded. "Mr. Quinby is a very smart man."

"He's a lawyer." Wick's reply could never be mistaken for a compliment.

The two of them stared at each other over this detente, until Mr. Wu straightened. "No laundry. Bad for business."

"Listen, she's just gotten off to a rough start. I'll speak to her character."

"No." He turned and parted the curtain that led to the back of the laundry, offering a glance of the room beyond. Laundry hung on multiple lines that crisscrossed the ceiling, but something else caught her eye.

Madeline spoke up quickly. "I'll pay in gold." To further her point, she laid down the money. The solid clink of the coins stilled Wu.

He turned around, his mouth open, as was Wick's.

Because she'd said the words in Cantonese.

She crossed her arms and stared the laundryman down. "I'm not crazy. I might not be as respectable as most, but I will pay up front. In gold."

Wick leaned over and murmured, "You speak Chinese?"

"Cantonese," she corrected. Switching back to it, she asked, "Do we have a deal?"

The curtain slipped from his hand and he returned to the counter. "How did you learn to speak Cantonese? You a missionary?" He looked her up and down.

Madeline barked a laugh. "No. Far from it."

"What's so funny?" the sheriff asked.

"He thinks I might be a missionary."

Now it was Wick's turn to laugh. "Definitely not."

"That's what I told him." Madeline pushed the money closer to the other edge of the counter. "Do we have a deal?"

Still, Mr. Wu shook his head. "No laundry. You're bad for business."

"Perhaps," Madeline agreed, again in Cantonese. "But were you welcome when you arrived? Are you now?"

The man's lips puckered, and he blew out a breath that spoke more than words.

Mr. Wu obviously had friends and allies. Wick, apparently. This Erasmus Quinby. All she needed was a way to include herself in that list.

"Who makes up your fourth?" She nodded toward the crack in the draperies.

"My what?"

"Your fourth for mahjong." Because that is what she'd spotted behind the curtain: a table set up with tiles. "Mr. Fischer told me you have two workers, plus you, which makes only three. So who is your fourth?"

"No fourth. We wait—"

"Wait no longer," she told him. "As it happens, I play." She paused for a moment and let that news settle in. "Though I warn you, I never lose."

"What are you saying?" the sheriff asked, clearly uncomfortable at being left out of the fast-paced back and forth.

She held up a hand as he had done earlier, her gaze never leaving Mr. Wu's. "Negotiating." Then, switching back to Cantonese, she sweetened the deal. "I win, you do my laundry."

The gold coin caught his eye. "When you lose?"

"You keep the money, and I take my laundry elsewhere."

"There is no elsewhere," he told her.

She shrugged slightly. "Then you keep your respectable reputation and my money."

❄

WHILE INOLA HAD SEEN to the Bergstroms over the past two days, Savannah could no longer avoid the obligation. Inola had settled an empty basket on the dining room table and pinned her with a no-nonsense glance. "I've got my own work to do."

Then she walked away.

Not even an anguished "Inola, please" had moved her to change her course.

There was nothing else for Savannah to do but gather up what she suspected they most needed and set out through the snow toward the small house near the river.

The Bergstroms lived in an old tie shack made up of thick logs and a sturdy roof. As the family had expanded, so had the house, until the original structure resembled an oyster covered in barnacles.

Yet, the closer she got to the house, the more Mrs. George L.'s words hung over her head, slowing her steps.

A wee thing. Probably won't last to the new year.

Savannah shuddered inwardly and was of half a mind to turn and make a hasty retreat when the door to the house opened.

"Mrs. Clarke?"

It was the oldest Bergstrom daughter. Oh, heavens, what was her name? Inola would know.

"I, um," she looked over her shoulder, still of a mind to flee, but when she turned back toward the door, fully intending to hand over her offering and take flight, another of the Bergstrom children poked her head around her sister's skirt.

"Where's Inola?" the child asked—no, demanded.

Savannah took a step back. "She was, that is, I—"

"Did you bring cookies?" the imp pressed. "Livia, tell her Inola promised."

Savannah looked up. *Livia.* That was her name.

"Berta! Don't be rude," A blush rose to Livia's pale cheeks.

But little Berta turned out to be a cheeky little monkey, ducking a cuff from her older sister and wheeling outside quickly, catching Savannah by her free hand and towing her inside, even as Livia took the basket from her and set it on the table beside a few sprigs of fir and pine and a snippet of ribbon.

Livia picked them up and set them in the windowsill. "I'm trying to make it feel a little more like Christmas . . . for the little ones."

Savannah glanced down at the hand holding hers. The small delicate fingers were as soft as old flannel. So trusting, so warm.

It should have filled her heart with that very same warmth, but she was suddenly chilled to the bone and pulled her fingers free.

To her horror, another child appeared, casting up a shy glance then making a beeline for the basket. Clearly she knew, far better than Savannah did, how this was done.

"Get Mrs. Clarke's coat, Margit," Livia instructed this new arrival, who was a mirror image of Berta.

Savannah shook her head and clung to her coat.

Not that the eldest Bergstrom noticed. "I am so glad to see you, Mrs. Clarke. I have a test to take this morning at school, and Pelle and Papa are at the mill, leaving me at my wit's end. Miss Barrett is an old trout over these sort of things."

"Pelle?" she asked.

"My brother, Peter," she explained. "As it is he went with Papa to work and I must go to school. And I can't leave . . ." She glanced over her shoulder at her sisters.

Was the girl actually asking her to stay? Here? With the children?

In this unholy state of a house? Dishes were piled in the sink and drainboard. The floor needed sweeping. A pair of ragged dolls littered the rug, while, beside the rocking chair, a sewing basket sat flung open.

Yet, unlike the discordant house, the basket was a shrine of organization. Tightly wound cards of thread and lace and ribbon sat side by side. Spools were lined up like soldiers awaiting orders. Needles and pins were tucked in a neat circle atop the pincushion. Scissors sat waiting in a leather case. Before Savannah could admire it further, a third child, a little girl, with the same round face and big blue eyes as her sisters, nudged her way to the forefront and climbed up on a chair to get a better look at what her sister was unpacking.

"Clara, don't crowd," Berta scolded. Once she'd finished glaring at the little interloper, she turned her attention back to the basket. "Livia, is there jam?"

Her sister nodded, even as she brought out the loaf Savannah had baked yesterday.

"Bread," Margit announced, while somehow inhaling happily at the same time.

The canning jars came next. "Mrs. Daggett's broth." Grimaces followed this announcement.

Livia dug in again and produced a small jar. "Jam," she told the trio. They seemed to hold a collective breath as the jar was turned and held up to the light, much like gold at the assay office.

"Miss Minch," Livia assured them. Happy sighs all around. Clearly Miss Minch's jam held a place of honor in their household as it was set next to the bread and well away from the bone broth.

"The children aren't all that difficult," Livia continued as the bread was cut and buttered and shared around with dizzying efficiency. With the three settled on the bench, they chewed happily on their meager feast. "Please. I'll be back as quickly as I can."

Savannah was about to relent, for the girl looked near tears, when a frail whimper rose from the corner near the fireplace. The cry rose to a weak wail, and not one of them moved, all their expectations resting on her.

Even without the midwife's assessment that the baby was not likely to survive, Savannah would have made the same judgment by listening to that thin cry.

A sad, tired little song that held no hope. She knew it only too well.

Something rustled behind her, and Savannah turned to find Livia slipping on her coat. "Your mother?"

Just the very mention of the woman had all three of them looking at the floor.

"She's sleeping," Livia said, the words coming out as if oft repeated and well worn. Her gaze slid toward the closed door on the opposite side of the room. A whole other sort of anguish resided in her blue eyes, as if she knew the truth of the matter and did her best to shield the others.

"Perhaps you could wake her?" Savannah looked toward that closed door as well.

"She won't come out," Berta said with finality, and then went back to eating her bread.

It was on Savannah's tongue to argue the matter. Of course their mother would come out. That sound, that note of anguish coming from the cradle, was for its mother and its mother alone.

Yet the door remained closed, not even a hint of movement behind it.

Oh, dear heavens. This was what Mrs. George L. had meant when she'd said something about a "tendency to melancholy."

Not likely to live. Had she meant the child or . . . ?

Drawing a breath through her nose, her teeth tightly set, Savannah crossed the room, determined to do the right thing. Until she got to the cradle and looked down.

Wee was not the word she'd use. The baby was scrawny, his scrunched face blotched red as he cried out.

Pick him up. Change him. Wrap him tight and hold him. Hold him until . . .

No . . . Savannah reeled back a step. Then another.

The crying started to weaken, having run its course. Or perhaps the poor thing had run through its strength.

It wasn't that she didn't know what needed to be done, and for the tiniest moment her heart trembled, came alive with a primal need to gather this child in her arms and will it to live.

But she also knew, only too well, how that investment of love and hope would end.

"Your father," she pleaded, just as she had to Inola earlier.

"He's working," Livia reminded her. But the hope in her eyes faded, as if could see that dark, empty shelf in Savannah's heart.

"It's just that—" Savannah began, glancing wildly around her. *No. Not this.* "I'm sorry," she offered as she fled out the door, the echo of the baby's weak cries chasing her all the way home.

❄

NIGHT HAD FALLEN, and Madeline grew restless in the quiet of the saloon. Dobbs was off helping someone named Elias, and that left only her and Dog.

Dog, while sympathetic, was no conversationalist. And without the option of binging the latest British mystery series or indulging in a restorative bout of online shopping, her gaze fell on the tin pail she'd set out earlier.

Miss Minch. As uncomfortable as it was to go apologize to the woman—that was decidedly not one of her talents—she did owe her that much. Probably more.

Tightening Wick's sweater around her shoulders and catching up the pail and the handle of the lamp, she strode out the door, Dog on her heels. At first she thought of taking him back inside, but when she looked around at the dark, empty street, she realized having the big lug beside her might not be a bad idea.

The post office, if she remembered correctly, was down toward the train station and then up the small hill. She hurried along the main street, glancing at the bits of light from the rooms above the various buildings.

As she approached the train station, where the buildings thinned out and the street widened, a bear of a man come lumbering out of the dark, his booted feet hitting the snow with purpose. He carried a pair of skis slung over his shoulder and a single thick pole in one hand.

Dog hardly seemed alarmed, which kept Madeline from turning tail and running for the saloon. Instead, she raised the lamp like a shield to get a better look. Almost immediately, she thought of the grandfather in that old Shirley Temple movie Gigi had loved so dearly. Which one was it? Oh, yes, *Heidi*. Because along with the great beard and huge coat, he had a gruff and wounded air about him.

As they drew closer, he shot a wary glance at her, as if she were the more frightening of the two of them.

Badger. The name came whispering along. She'd seen him a time or two around town.

"Excuse me, is that the post office?" She pointed at the building up the street.

"It is," he replied, coming abreast of her and continuing past, barely breaking his stride.

"Where Miss Minch lives?"

The heavy tromp of boots stopped. "Yes." One word, grudgingly offered. Yet she'd heard the burr beneath it, old and patrician. He dropped his skis to the ground and began to strap them on.

It was impossible to know what he looked like beneath the thick coat and the equally woolly beard. "What are you doing?"

"What does it look like?" he said. "I'm leaving."

"You can do that?"

He glanced up at her, once again wary. "Yes." He straightened, tested his skis again, and pushed off.

He could leave? He knew the way out of here? She raced after him, slipping and sliding on the hard-packed snow. "Hey! Please stop! Aw, come on—"

He paused, but he didn't turn around.

She faltered a few feet away from him. "What's out there? What's beyond?"

"Nothing." And then he let the void swallow him up as he glided into the night.

Madeline stood there in the silence and waited. He was there, and then he was gone. How was it that someone would willingly let that unnerving darkness envelop them?

She raised the lantern again, but this time, it seemed the circle of light had grown smaller, trembling at the edges. She could leave, just step into the night and go. It was a dizzying notion, an almost sensual pull, like the call of the train whistle.

Her boot edged forward, and she was about to give in to this strange tug into the oblivion beyond, but behind her, Dog began to growl. Then bark in earnest.

She blinked and looked up the hill, where a faint light twinkled from the back of the post office. That bit of warmth caught hold of her, nudged her to remember her errand.

So she turned and continued on, but every few steps, she found herself glancing back, still wondering what she'd find there in the empty darkness.

❄

It is the honest opinion of this committee . . . Parathinia shook her head at the blank sheet of paper before her.

Every time she tried to compose her report, she got no further than those few words. Whatever was she to say? The unvarnished truth?

Then again, perhaps Theodosia was on to something. Miss Drake hadn't said she was opening the saloon. Not precisely.

Ninny's gaze strayed to her knitting sitting atop Mrs. Mercer's book. Either would be preferable, though she suspected not even the esteemed Mrs. Mercer had faced such a problem.

She took a deep breath and tried to find the right words. *It is the sincere opinion of this committee* . . . Yes, that might do.

But, before Parathinia could pick up her pen, a knock at the door brought her head up with a jerk. At first she thought she'd imagined it, but there it was again. *Rap. Rap. Rap.*

She rose and stepped out of the comforting circle of light from the lamp. She had electricity, but it wasn't the same as the warmth of the old lamp. But now that she'd gone and gotten up, stepped out of that yellow halo, a chill assailed her. Whatever was she supposed to do?

No one ever called on her. Certainly not at this hour.

"Miss Minch?" A voice rang out from the back porch. "Are you home?"

Parathinia reached out and caught hold of the back of her chair. *Miss Drake? Here?* She couldn't help but glance around, as if someone might be watching from the wings. But of course she was alone. She was always alone.

"Miss Minch, are you okay?" The concern knit at Parathinia's heart like a row of purl stitches, all bumps and at odds.

If only she didn't have that other voice in her ear. It was as if Mrs. George L. were standing at her shoulder, admonishing her for even considering opening the door.

Parathinia Minch, turn this woman away. Immediately.

The words unspooled a memory of a long-ago night as snowy and deep as this one.

A cold shadowy kitchen. A single lamp burning low on the table. That furious spate of knocking at the door.

Please, Machias, let me in. I'm so very sorry.

Her father, his back ramrod straight, picking up the lamp and turning away from the door. He nodded at Parathinia, who sat on the stairs, clutching the railing to stop her slight frame from shaking.

Back to bed, child. She's humiliated us for the last time.

Parathinia straightened, her knuckles white as she clenched the back of her chair, shocked how this icy memory sparked a hot rebellion inside her. She hurried to the door, where even now she could hear the retreat of boots down the steps.

Catching up the lamp, she flipped the lock and flung open the door. "Miss Drake, please don't go."

The younger woman was already down the path. She turned around, her shoulders and dark hair dusted in snow, a leggy dog standing not far from her side. "Oh, you are home. I'm so sorry to disturb you. I just wanted to return your soup tin." She nodded toward the corner of the porch, where the tin now sat.

"Thank you. That's most kind of you," Parathinia replied as she gathered it up, not sure what to do in the raw silence that followed. Did Miss Drake know why she and the Winsley sisters had intruded upon her earlier?

"Miss Minch, I fear I owe you an—"

So she did know. "You needn't, Miss Drake. I'm the one who—"

The younger woman stepped closer, and then, as if remembering herself, she stopped in an awkward way that clashed with her bright confidence from earlier in the day. "Please, call me Madeline."

Certainly Parathinia couldn't—no, shouldn't—think of her as anything but Miss Drake. Not after such a short and tenuous acquaintance. Not after what she'd done. Or rather tried to do.

"Please forgive me for not opening my door sooner." Parathinia took another short breath of the biting cold. "You see, I don't get much company."

"The fault is all mine," Miss Drake rushed to tell her. "Usually I would have texted, or whatever it is you all do, but I haven't the least idea how these things are done here." She looked up, pleading her case with a wide-open gaze full of a rare sort of honesty. "I keep stepping in it, don't I?"

She bit her lip, then rubbed her hands together, and it was then Parathinia noticed the girl hadn't any mittens on. Bare hands. Bare head. Just the sheriff's sweater tossed around her shoulders, as if she'd left in a hurry, and now stood here shivering with the hem of her skirt caked in snow.

The bruises on her face.

The very sight of them flickered inside her, lighting memories she tried her best to keep extinguished. *Please, Machias. It is so very cold out here* . . .

That spark found the tinder it needed.

"You haven't stepped in anything," Parathinia assured her. "Please, come inside and get warm. You'll freeze out there like that. I'll make us a pot of tea."

"If it isn't any bother," Miss Drake replied. After a moment, she stepped gingerly in her previous tracks toward the steps, her mangy dog at her heels.

"None at all."

She stopped at the door and looked over at the animal. "I hate to leave him out here."

Parathinia nodded at the sorry-looking beast. "Do come in." She held the door open and the lamp high to light the way. "Both of you."

She set her lamp on the table and then turned it up a bit, if only to banish the remaining shadows. On the table, the blank sheet of paper stared back at her like an unspoken accusation.

Meanwhile, Miss Drake stamped the snow from her boots and shook out her hem, leaving the edging of snow outside. Finally, she came in, not stopping until she was in the middle of the kitchen, looking more than a little adrift. And shivering.

No wonder, Parathinia mused, *without a hat or mittens*. Why, one would think she'd never been out in winter before.

"Where are you from, Miss Drake?"

"California."

That explained much.

"You need a proper coat." Parathinia told her. "People will talk if you continue to wander about in the sheriff's sweater."

"I learned a long time ago that people will always talk. But no need to put the hook in the water, as my publicist likes to say."

"Certainly you didn't come all this way without one?"

Miss Drake shrugged, rubbing her hands over her arms. "I seem to have lost mine in the accident."

"Well, a proper coat is in order," Parathinia repeated. And mittens and a warm shawl. "Go stand by the stove, and then we'll have some tea." She shooed the girl toward it until Miss Drake was huddled in front, holding out her hands and letting the warmth fill her limbs.

The dog, it seemed, had better sense, having laid down in front of it with a contented sigh.

Satisfied that Miss Drake wasn't going to expire right in the middle of her kitchen, Parathinia emptied and refilled the kettle in the sink. Tea was not tea if it wasn't made with fresh, cold water. At least her mother had always said so.

When she'd been with them. Again Parathinia drew a steadying breath.

"May I help?" her guest asked.

"No, you just get yourself warm." Parathinia's thoughts ran in all directions. Tea. A coat. Mittens. Her mother asking for help. Forgiveness. She shook her head slightly at the tumble of wayward memories.

"The cold just gets into everything, doesn't it?" Miss Drake remarked as she gazed around the room, taking in every square inch of the kitchen.

Parathinia stopped what she was doing and looked around as well. Perhaps Miss Drake thought it quite a poor room. Or perhaps she felt slighted at being invited into the kitchen like some sort of poor tramp with his bindle slung over his shoulder.

But it was none of that. Once again, this odd young woman surprised her.

"What a lovely, charming place you have," she enthused. "How warm and homey. Thank you so much for inviting me in."

The younger woman's sincere words pushed aside any

remaining threads of reticence, because, after all, Parathinia loved her kitchen. It was her most favorite place in the entire world. "Thank you."

"I was going stir-crazy over at the saloon. It's just so dark and quiet and . . ."

Parathinia knew only too well what she'd been about to say. *Lonely.*

"Then I realized I never gave you back your tin, nor did I thank you for your kindness the other day. So I . . ."

"Came to call," Parathinia provided. She set the kettle on the stove. "Just stay there and get warm. I'll be right back." She paused for a moment, for truly, whatever was she thinking? If anyone found out.

Make that *when Mrs. George L.* found out.

Stop being so foolish, she chided herself as she hurried upstairs. *Where is your Christian charity?*

Unlike the kitchen, her small bedroom was neither cozy nor welcoming. The harsh single light overhead revealed her narrow bed against the wall, the tallboy on the opposite side, and a straight-backed chair near the window. All of it plain and neat as a pin.

The only thing out of place was the large orange tabby asleep at the foot of the bed. He opened one eye.

"There you are, Mr. Bingley. I wondered where you'd gotten yourself off to," she said as she knelt in front of the dresser, opening the bottom drawer. "You'd best stay up here. I don't think you'd like our company."

Quickly sifting through the drawer, she found two pairs of mittens, both old but still in good repair. She reached for the gray ones, but the red ones beckoned. She held them for a second, for it had been a long time since she'd taken them out. The wool was still soft, and the stitches were tiny and well-wrought. Quickly, she put the red pair back and retrieved the gray ones.

She turned to the small closet built into the corner and retrieved a coat hanging in the far back. She'd ordered it from a catalogue the year before, in a whimsical hope that having a new coat might make her feel . . . well, fashionable and young again. But when it had arrived, all she'd felt was ridiculous, and she'd tucked it in the back of the closet.

She took it out and shook it a bit. Yes, this would do. There was also the fact that no one in Bethlehem had ever seen her in it, so there wouldn't be any recriminations pointed in her direction.

Not exactly the brave defiance of an independent woman, as Mrs. Mercer liked to espouse, but then again, Mrs. Mercer hadn't Mrs. George L. as a neighbor.

In the meantime, Miss Drake had moved to the table. "*An Improved and Forthright Life for the Modern Woman*," she read, glancing up at Parathinia.

Ninny nearly dropped her bundle. Oh, of all the things . . .

"I like these sort of books," Madeline said, turning it over in her hand. "Is it any good?"

"Yes, well—" she began and then stopped, for she truly didn't know what to say. She was more flabbergasted by the notion that they had anything in common than she was at being discovered reading such a controversial text.

Yet here was Mrs. Mercer, bridging the gap.

Parathinia set the coat on the back of the chair next to Miss Drake and placed the mittens on the table. "These might keep you from freezing."

"Oh, what beautiful work!" Miss Drake exclaimed. "Did you knit these?"

"Well, yes—"

"I thought as much. I was looking at your project." She nodded at the knitting on the table. "I hope you don't mind, but your stitches are so even I just had to peek. I can never get mine that perfect."

"Oh, it is hardly anything," Ninny told her, trying not to blush. "You can take that as well," she said, nodding toward the navy coat and changing the subject.

Miss Drake drew back. "Oh, no, I couldn't take your coat. Why, that looks brand new."

Parathinia was already shaking her head. "I insist."

The kettle began to rumble a very welcome interruption. She measured loose tea from the canister into a pot, then filled it with boiling water. She carefully carried the pot to the table and settled a tea cozy over so it wouldn't cool while it steeped.

When she turned, Miss Drake was wearing the coat and mittens, a smile brightening her face. "How do I look?"

"Like a modern young lady," Ninny told her. Exactly how she'd hoped to look.

"Are you certain?" Miss Drake asked.

"Decidedly so," she told her as she put together a tea tray while Miss Drake set the coat and mittens aside and began once again thumbing through the pages of Mrs. Mercer's book.

"This is a hoot," she remarked. "A whole chapter on making a good first impression. I could have used that advice on Sunday before I . . ."

Parathinia glanced away. Oh, heavens, had she truly just brought *that* up? How could she not know that discussing such a personal subject was hardly done?

No matter that everyone in town was discussing it.

Miss Drake shrugged. "Perhaps I should get a copy so I don't make so many mistakes." She grinned and continued running her finger slowly down the table of contents.

Parathinia shook her head. If anything, Mrs. Viola Kinney Livingston's stodgy columns on decorum might be a better choice. "I don't know if that would be such a good idea."

Miss Drake looked up, her wide brown eyes full of questions. "Why not?"

Now Parathinia was backed into a corner. "Some people feel that Mrs. Mercer's ideas are a little *too* modern." She paused. "Quite a few people, in fact."

"Like that Mrs. Lovell?" Miss Drake made a sort of snort and shook her head.

"Yes, exactly like Mrs. George L.," Parathinia rushed to confirm —or rather, warn. Which, all things considered, was rather the same thing.

Miss Drake closed the book and settled it back on the table. "Why is she called that?"

"Called what?" Parathinia asked absently as she searched through the cupboard for her sugar pot and a tin of milk.

"Mrs. George L. I'm pretty certain her name isn't George, and why the need for the 'L'? It takes forever to say and seems rather pretentious."

Parathinia blinked and looked over her shoulder. "But that's her name."

"George?"

"No, of course not. Her given name is Columbia."

"That seems more fitting," Miss Drake straightened. "Columbia!" She announced with a flourish of her hand and no small intonation of drama.

Parathinia stopped what she was doing. "Oh, my! You could be an actress." Then she realized what she'd said. "I don't mean to—"

Miss Drake grinned. "Actually, I am one."

"One what?"

"An actress."

Parathinia looked at her again. "You are?"

"I was before I came here."

Parathinia had thought actresses must be glamorous creatures, like the Gibson girls in the magazines or that lovely Lily Elsie in London. But Miss Drake wasn't what Parathinia would call beautiful. She was striking, in an odd way, but not one of the beauties.

"What sort of things did you do?" Parathinia asked, the tea tray quite forgotten.

"I was in a . . ." She paused for a moment. "A dramatic show."

Parathinia sighed. "How exciting." Remembering the tea, she collected a pair of cups and saucers from the cupboard. "Did you know we have an opera house?" She hurried to correct herself. "There's never actually been an opera here, and it is really not much more than a hall with a stage, but we do have an Opera Society. They put on quite a gala just before Christmas." She glanced again at Miss Drake and thought it a shame that she hadn't been cast in the part given to Mrs. Vaughn. "Oh, if Mrs. George L. only knew we have a real actress amongst us."

"Would that improve her opinion of me?"

Parathinia thought about it. She could well imagine how such a tidbit would be received, say at the temperance meeting tomorrow.

While Miss Drake and I were having tea last night, she mentioned the most interesting thing about being an actress . . .

"Probably not," she said quite honestly. With the tea tray assembled, she carried it over to the table and found Miss Drake smiling yet again, but that bright light stood tarnished by the ugly bruises on the side of her face.

Miss Drake must have seen her staring, for her hand went to the side of her face.

"Do they hurt?" Parathinia asked without thinking. Immediately she wished her words back, yet it appeared Miss Drake hadn't minded her intrusion.

"No. Well, only when I roll over on them at night." She sighed. "I just wish they didn't look so awful."

Parathinia nodded. "Not awful, just unfortunate." She set the tray down on the table beside the blank piece of paper and her pencil. "They'll fade soon enough."

"Am I keeping you from something?" Miss Drake's gaze had followed Parathinia's toward the paper and pencil.

Parathinia shook her head. "No, not at all."

Miss Drake brightened. "Then let's get back to Mrs. George L. She pretty much runs this place, doesn't she?"

"In a manner of speaking, yes."

"Why is that?"

Parathinia paused, thinking of all the reasons she could offer, but in the end she went with the most obvious. "She's married to George L. Lovell. He owns the bank, so—"

"I get it. Gigi always said, 'Follow the money.'" After a few moments, there came the next question. "But why the 'L' part?"

"To distinguish him from his father, of course, and Columbia from the first Mrs. Lovell."

"No, kidding. There's another Mrs. Lovell?" Miss Drake shuddered.

"Yes. Her mother-in-law. Mrs. George J. Lovell." She reached for the biscuit tin on the counter, filled with the shortbread she'd baked for the Temperance meeting tomorrow. Mrs. George L. always set a brimming table. Her small addition would hardly be missed. So she piled up the pieces on a small plate and returned to table. Settling in, she plucked off the tea cozy, checked the tea, and, satisfied it was ready, poured it through the strainer into the cups.

Miss Drake added a dash of milk but otherwise seemed happy just to cradle the cup in her hands. "I also came over for another reason," she confessed, looking down at the swirl of milk in her cup. "I need to apologize." Then she looked up, indecision in her eyes.

And here Parathinia had thought her the most modern, forthright woman she'd ever met—momentary madness notwithstanding.

"Whatever for?" she asked, her gaze straying again toward the blank sheet of paper. She wasn't the only one who needed to ask for forgiveness. For right now she felt like the worst sort of Judas.

It is the opinion of this committee . . .

"I would never have offered you and your friends a drink this morning if I'd known that you were . . . Well, *why* you dropped by." She groaned a little and shook her head. "The sheriff had a good laugh over all of it, especially the donation part."

Parathinia's chest tightened like a row of stitches being tugged out of place.

"I thought I should tell you that had I known, I wouldn't have done that. I mean, it is your right to have your opinions on the subject—"

"Miss Drake, before you go on, you should know—"

"—and it isn't really necessary to get too worked up about the saloon, since Shandy says I can go home at Christmas."

Hope blossomed inside Ninny. "So you aren't opening it."

"Oh, I'm opening it. I intend to kick up the biggest fuss Shandy's ever seen so I can get an express ticket home."

Home.

"You don't want to stay?" Parathinia blurted out the words. She'd lived here most of her life and had never held a single desire to leave. Why should she, when the world came to her? Letters and packages bearing stamps and marks from Denver and Chicago and New York, even London—and a town in Sweden she couldn't pronounce but had often wondered about.

Miss Drake seemed not to heed her far-flung woolgathering. "No!" she replied emphatically. "My life is, well, far from here. I mean, don't get me wrong, it's a mess right now, but that's exactly why I can't wait. I must get home as quickly as I can."

"I suppose you miss your family," Parathinia offered.

"Dahlia? Hardly."

"Who is Dahlia?"

"My mother. I wouldn't wish her on anyone."

Parathinia decided the better part of valor was to shift the subject. "You must have someone special waiting for you?"

Miss Drake replied quickly. "Not at all."

Her words were so full of vehemence and hot anger they took Parathinia aback. "I'm so sorry. I didn't mean to pry."

Miss Drake carefully set her teacup on the saucer. "Actually," she began, her tone dropping, "until a few days ago, I did have someone. But he . . . well, we ended things. He ended things." Miss Drake's looked away, nibbling at her bottom lip.

Ended. Parathinia knew that disgrace only too well. Another piece, another connection, clicked together.

"I'm so sorry, Miss Drake." Those were the words she'd wished someone had said to her all those years ago. She pushed the shortbread plate across the table and nodded for her to take a piece.

"I do wish you'd call me Madeline. And don't be sorry. That asshole would have ruined everything eventually. Or so I keep telling myself."

Parathinia's mouth fell open. *Ass—*

Not that Miss Drake noticed, for she was intent on finishing her confessional lament. "I should have known better. I think I'm the third or fourth one he's led on in the last few years."

Parathinia slid the plate of cookies closer. "Truly? You knew?"

Madeline happily took another piece. "Sadly, I have a way of picking them. But it always ends up the same: me finding them in bed with some no-talent skank, and then I'm the one on every screen and browser." She paused. "Actually, I should be thanking Gemma

Lawson. Now she's stuck with him. And the joke's on her. He's so lousy in bed."

"In bed?" Parathinia gasped. She had heard things were a bit different in California, but she certainly didn't realize *how* different. Half of what the woman had said made no sense, but the latter part? She reached for a piece of shortbread and stuffed it in her mouth to stopper any more errant questions.

Then again, perhaps Miss Drake hadn't meant it as it sounded.

"Yeah," Madeline said, picking up her tea and cradling it in her hands. "Charming, great-looking, and then just awful at finding— Well, you know what I mean."

"I assure you I don't," Parathinia said, reaching for another piece of shortbread, her gaze straying to Mrs. Mercer's book. One of the lady's favorite tenets echoed in her thoughts.

A forthright life means speaking up.

Parathinia drew a deep breath. "If a man is a skunk, and this one certainly sounds like one, well, a lady must keep him at arm's length. Or so says Mrs. Mercer." She pushed the book across the table. "On second thought, you might like to read this."

Instead of being insulted, Miss Drake—no, Madeline—smiled in that friendly way of hers as she gathered up the book. "Thank you, Miss Minch."

Something warmed inside her. And it wasn't the stove or the tea that brought this glow. It was something that had been missing from her life for years.

"Ninny, my dear. My friends call me Ninny." Actually, no one did. At least no one had in a very long time.

But in this cozy circle of light, in her kitchen, she'd found that long-lost spirit once again.

CHAPTER 15

Thursday, December 5

"It is the sincere opinion of this committee that the aforementioned establishment is not in any danger of being reopened. The individual in question has expressed a desire to leave our fair town at her earliest opportunity, and no further deliberation on this sordid subject is necessary." Ninny drew a deep breath as she finished reading, then folded the blank page and held it tight. She'd done it. Gotten through the entire thing without so much as a tremble.

Looking up, she kept a measured expression on her face.

Unfortunately, the same could not be said for the rest of her committee.

Theodosia and Odella exchanged hasty glances, wide-eyed enough to catch Mrs. George L.'s sharp attention. After a moment's hesitation, Theodosia quickly folded the paper in her hand and tucked it into her purse.

Hiding the evidence, as it were.

"Miss Winsley, Miss Theodosia, is this correct? You appear to be at odds with your chairwoman."

Ninny had never been under any delusions as to why Odella and Theodosia had been assigned to this committee. The sisters were guaranteed to provide a full and unvarnished accounting to Mrs. George L. They wouldn't be able to help themselves.

So she rushed to speak first. "Madame President, I hardly see—"

"Miss Minch, I'm simply asking your committee to confirm your report."

A murmured ripple unwound around the room. After all, a confirmation was a highly unusual request.

But Ninny knew exactly what was wrong. She'd succeeded when Mrs. George L. had sent her to fail.

That, and the new issue of the *Bethlehem Observer* lay on the parlor table, bearing not one but three sensational headlines. *The Christmas Tree Debacle*—which Ninny supposed was better than "calamity" or "disaster" or "ruin," or a thousand other words Cora could have used. But good heavens, Ninny wished the newswoman had stopped there instead of continuing with the harrowing statements of *Christmas Canceled?* and *Newcomer Reveals More Than Glad Tidings*.

If Ninny hadn't felt like the elk on the wall before, there was no denying she was in Mrs. George L.'s sights now.

It would be her head on the wall next week, and she'd spend an eternity opposite the visage of Cora Stafford, murdered for her yellow journalism.

But right now, Ninny's real problem was keeping alive the illusion that their commission had been successfully completed.

"Miss Winsley? Miss Theodosia?" Mrs. George L. craned her neck to look around Ninny. "Is your chairwoman's report accurate? Have you signed it?"

Ninny had no choice but to let the Winsley sisters respond, and hope with all her heart they could refrain from digging a deeper hole.

For here was Theodosia looking all too ready to man the shovel, add a correction, or worse tell the *entire* story, but Odella placed a hand atop her sister's sleeve and answered first. "A signature? There was hardly time. Why, we just called upon Miss Drake yesterday, Madame President."

Mrs. George L. waved an imperial hand. "Of course. Yes, I suppose we must be satisfied it isn't as bad as was assumed." She pursed her lips, clearly vexed that her next words weren't a cry for the gathering of pitchforks and torches. Now that was a headline Mrs. George L. would have liked to see on the front page of the *Observer*.

The matron tipped her head and pinned her razor-edged gaze on the sisters as if deciding which one would most easily crack. "But the content of Miss Minch's report, Miss Theodosia, can you verify. . ." She paused and glanced around the room to ensure she had everyone's attention. " . . . its accuracy?"

The entire room stilled. This was unheard of. Oh, certainly Mrs. Bohlen was known to embellish her reports with grand expressions, but this?

"I do believe—" Theodosia began, glancing toward her sister.

"That is, it is our opinion—" Odella continued.

"Both our opinions—" Theodosia added, underlining her sister's words.

Odella frowned, for now it was up to her. After a long pause, she nodded. "Yes, it is accurate."

Ninny let out a slow breath. She hadn't realized she was even holding it. There. The entire matter was done.

But, lo, she'd underestimated Theodosia and her inability to let something remain unfinished. "If I could add," she began. "I would like to say that I found Miss Drake quite amiable. She even offered us a—" Her words came to a blinding halt as she realized what had nearly tumbled from her lips.

She even offered us a libation.

"A . . . ?" Mrs. George L. asked, her nose twitching like a terrier having caught a whiff of a rat.

"A thank-you for being kind enough to call," Ninny said, as coolly as possible. "It seems no one has yet to offer her any sort of kindness." She gave a firm, withering glance around the room, much like Mrs. George L. might, though she hardly had the same effect.

Most of the woman gaped at her as if she'd lost her mind for suggesting such a thing.

And since kindness and Mrs. George L. had never been properly introduced, the woman could only blink at this statement.

For certainly it wasn't—it couldn't be—a criticism of her.

"Yes, no one," Ninny repeated, feeling an odd bit of euphoria. It was the same dangerous tremor born out of the shaky notions that had prodded her along on Sunday, after that terrible blunder with the kindling. That had urged her to buy that coat, and to order Mrs. Mercer's scandalous book.

Pile enough kindling together, and eventually a spark will find it.

"Well, yes, but then again, no." Theodosia returned to the facts without thinking about the implications.

Ninny's breath froze. Oh, for heaven's sake, couldn't the woman just leave well enough alone for once?

"Sister is correct," Odella observed with the same blind faith in the truth. "Sheriff Fischer was there. Gave our entire business a rather official air—he being such a nice, respectable young man. It turns out he has been extending Miss Drake a helping hand."

This image lent itself more than a few sideways glances from the married women. A nice, respectable young man alone in a saloon with a woman of questionable origins?

With nothing being said, Theodosia did her best to fill in the void. "Of course, I do believe the basket helped."

Having accepted her defeat, Mrs. George L. had returned to her seat, but those innocent words—*the basket helped*—yanked her up once again into her domineering posture, like a tent pole hammered back into place.

"A what?" She slowly turned around.

"A basket," Theodosia repeated. She blinked and glanced around the room, taking in the expressions of avid curiosity and outward horror. "A welcome basket, though not as well represented as it might have been. It was all hastily done, and—"

"You took a welcome basket to a har—" There wasn't a woman in the room who didn't know exactly how Mrs. George L. had intended to finish that sentence.

Harlot.

Mrs. George L. swayed slightly, clearly at a loss for words. Mrs. Jonas rose immediately, scurrying over to support her dearest friend in this trial, but Mrs. George L. waved her aside and held her position. She took a deep breath through her nose and then slowly, ever so slowly, she began, "Whatever made you think . . ." But she couldn't go on. Couldn't fathom that this revolt of sorts was happening.

In her parlor, no less. And she swayed in this new wind.

She looked down, clearly searching for a way to grasp hold of the situation, put it to rights, but unfortunately—at least in Ninny's mind —so was Odella Winsley.

Odella, never one to be out of words, puffed up and said, "My sister thought a basket might help smooth the way. It clearly helped."

Then the Winsley well of good intentions ran over, with Theodosia bubbling forth, "Still, I'm of the opinion that a pound social would have been much more congenial, don't you agree?"

That was when Mrs. George L. toppled over in a dead faint.

CHAPTER 16

Friday, December 6

*D*uring a lull at the post office, Ninny saw an opportunity to go to the mercantile, and yet she hesitated, especially after the previous day's debacle at the Temperance meeting.

She'd hardly want to run into Mrs. George L. today. The woman's memory was notoriously long and unforgiving.

Still, there was no hope for it. If she was going to make biscuits, she needed baking powder. She'd promised a plate of them to Dobbs if he helped her later.

Hanging the "be right back" sign in the window, she hurried down the steps, pausing only a moment on the bottom one, which wobbled beneath her foot.

Yet another thing that needed to be fixed.

She sighed and plowed ahead, cataloguing how she'd gotten into this mess to begin with.

Whatever had possessed her to offer up that outrageous fiction yesterday?

She paused. How could she have done otherwise?

Madeline Drake hadn't done anything wrong. She'd been brought to Bethlehem against her will, and all she wanted to do was go home.

In the meantime . . . well, Ninny suspected she'd found something she hadn't had in a long time.

A friend.

It's wasn't until Miss Drake had settled into her kitchen and offered her trust and confidence that Ninny realized how much she'd missed having one. Over two pots of tea, Ninny had poured her heart out while Madeline had listened.

Actually listened to what she was saying.

So if she'd told a falsehood to help Madeline, then so be it.

Come Christmas Day, or more likely beforehand, Madeline would return to her home in faraway California, and Ninny would go back to her solitary life, while the women of the Bethlehem Temperance Union would continue to harangue about the evils of alcohol even as their husbands bought bottles of rye at the back door of Mr. Hoback's drugstore.

She nodded to Mrs. Samuel Cochrane, who had her two younger children in tow, yet the lady barely acknowledged her, especially after one of the little ones looked up at Ninny and, upon recognizing her, began to cry.

Ninny ground her teeth. She had a word or two for Cora Stafford. *Christmas Canceled*, indeed!

She'd made Ninny a pariah to every child in town, and probably a good part of the customers she spied filling King's Mercantile.

Worse, there was Wellington on the front step, which meant Badger was inside. At least she could make her apology to him regarding the kindling mix-up.

Exorior! she reminded herself, but that bolstering note fled as the bell jangled overhead, announcing her arrival.

A stillness greeted her, one that held an electric sort of buzz, like one of those new-fangled toasters Mr. King had in the window.

"Miss Minch," Mr. Thayer said, politely dipping his hat. He moved aside for her, and Ninny found herself immediately at the front of the counter without having to wait.

"Closed early, Miss Minch?" asked Mr. King, pulling her attention back to the business at hand. He smiled as he wiped his hands on his apron.

"No, Mr. King." She shook her head. "It was slow, so I thought I'd dash over and get some baking powder." She leaned closer. "I used all mine up for Thanksgiving."

"Of course you did," he said, turning and reaching for a can. "A fine use of baking powder it was—your biscuits make Thanksgiving special. You prefer the Rumford, don't you?"

"Yes. Thank you for remembering." She smiled and wished he would hurry along, for all ears seemed turned in her direction.

"Would you care for a ham, Miss Minch?" Goldie King asked. "We are taking orders for some lovely ones, and I know how much you like it." Her brow lofted, and her gaze flitted across the room to Mr. Thayer, who lounged near the stove where Badger was warming his hands.

The girl wasn't suggesting that one of them should buy her . . . Of all the cheek!

"No, thank you. Just the baking powder," Ninny said firmly.

"What are you making, Miss Minch?" Josephine Lovell moved out of the crowd like a sleek cat, and sliding in tandem came Pinky Jonas, just as done up in a smart new coat and a fashionable hat—both of them youthful mirrors of their mothers. Head tipped, Josephine studied the can on the counter. "Perhaps something for the cake dance tomorrow—what with your new admirer."

Pinky snickered and looked around for others who shared her amusement, that is until someone else by the door caught her attention.

Ninny glanced that way and found, of all people, Madeline Drake. When she'd come in, Ninny didn't know, but from the set of her mouth, Madeline had heard enough and looked ready to rise up in her new friend's defense.

Oh, that would only make things worse.

Ninny turned in a panic, only to find Badger watching her. His stern face was a mask, as it usually was, but his eyes held a defiance that whispered one word.

Courage.

Then that mercurial emotion swelled inside her, like he'd passed it along over a telegraph line with the firm and decided *clack* of fast-moving keys.

"I hadn't thought about it, Miss Lovell," she told the smartly dressed girl. "But now that you mention it, I still have my mother's recipe for a coconut cake. I haven't made it in years, but I might just have to give it a try."

She snapped her mouth shut, for there was no hope of reeling in those fateful words. Whether they were born of courage or too much time in the company of the Winsley sisters, she wasn't sure.

"You, Miss Minch? A cake?" Josephine sputtered, glancing around the room to make sure everyone was listening to her. "But the cake dance isn't for—"

Oh, the girl didn't have to say it when most likely everyone in the room was thinking the same thing: *old spinsters.*

"Why, of all the impertinent things to come out of your mouth, Josephine Lovell," said Myrtle King, her hands fisted on her hips.

"Golly, Josephine," Francine piped up, having joined her sisters behind the counter. "Who's baking your cake this year? Everyone in town knows you can barely boil water. Is it Annie, or have you gone and paid Inola to do it for you again?"

"Girls," Mr. King reprimanded lightly.

"Yes, Father," they murmured, but they hardly looked cowed as they smirked at their adversaries—a promise that this slight would not be forgotten.

Still, Josephine saw it as her opportunity to hazard a haughty, "My cakes are entirely my own creation." Which was an outright lie, but she tipped up her nose up in an uncanny imitation of her mother, as if that made it the truth. "This year, Myrtle King, do everyone a favor and remember it is a *cake* dance, not a *pancake* feed."

As Pinky tittered again, Myrtle blushed furiously, for indeed her cake the previous year had been a sunken disaster.

But it had been *her* disaster, and before the King sisters could fire back a trio of tart sallies—ignoring their father's warning—the bell jangled anew.

"There you are, darling," Mrs. George L. said as she stepped into the store. "I fear my conversation with Miss Stafford took longer than I thought it might. That dreadful scribbler hasn't the least notion of public decency. Mark my words, when the Eastern papers pick up her columns of lies, our humble town will be the laughingstock of the civilized world." She huffed and came sailing down the main aisle like a battleship, parting the crowd without a thought of . . . well, decency.

"Cancel Christmas, indeed!" Mrs. George L. tugged at her gloves. "Then again," she continued, "none of this misfortune would be happening if it wasn't for this unseemly bid for attention by a—" Her sweeping gaze landed on Ninny, and she faltered for just a moment until she regained her head of steam. She stalked forward, her finger wagging. "Miss Minch! There you are. I called at the post office and was shocked to find it closed. Perfectly shocked! In the middle of the day, no less. The situation is intolerable. It is bad enough there is no proper ladies' entrance, but that broken, rundown step is a public hazard. Why, I nearly broke my neck trying to enter the premises."

Someone in the back of the store muttered something about that being a public improvement, which garnered a few guffaws from the usual huddle near the stove.

Ninny ignored them and straightened. "I was just finishing here. If you care to—" she waved her hand toward the door.

"I do not! I shall not risk my neck again," Mrs. George L. replied. She turned to her daughter. "Josephine, are you and Pinky finished? I must see to the state of things at the Opera House. By now Mrs. Clarke will have the booth assignments posted, and there will be a myriad of other important details demanding my immediate attention."

"Yes, Mother," her daughter said, slanting one last triumphant glance at Myrtle.

As the pair swept from the store, Josephine turned and smiled sweetly at Ninny. "I look forward to seeing this coconut cake, Miss Minch. But it will be ever so sad if no one bids on it. Though I daresay you'll be in good company. Won't she, Myrtle?"

There was a parting titter from Pinky as she scurried after Josephine, the pair merging into Mrs. George L.'s wake.

The entire store let out a collective breath as the bell over the door jangled.

"Floozies," Francine King muttered.

"Frankie," her father warned. The girl looked ready to say more but nodded and stalked back to the storeroom. He managed a weak smile.

"You just ignore that lot, Miss Minch. If you do decide to bake a cake, I suspect it will be the belle of the auction." The consummate salesman, Mr. King took a package of coconut down from the shelf and set it beside the baking powder before adding a package of icing sugar. "Will you need some eggs as well? Mrs. Poole's hens can't seem to stop laying this winter, and Billy just brought in a basket."

Goldie was already counting them out. In a daze, Ninny couldn't find the words to protest these additions. Quickly, she counted out her coins and paid for her purchases, tucking the eggs in her coat pockets since she hadn't brought her basket.

As she hurried out the door, she shook with panic. Whatever had come over her to announce that she was going to bake a cake? For a cake dance of all things.

And in front of half of Bethlehem.

Ninny stopped in the middle of the street and blew out a breath. And yet . . .

A coconut cake. Just like her mother used to make. All white and fluffy and sweet. "Surely someone would bid on it."

"Of course they would," came an equally defiant reply.

Ninny whirled around. Good heavens, had she said that out loud? Apparently so, for here was Miss Drake—Madeline—looking as fierce and outraged as a Valkyrie.

She gave Ninny a long look. "That woman is a horrible old bit—"

"Oh, no! Don't say such a thing. It isn't proper," Ninny told her. Scolded, really. She towed Madeline by the elbow and beat a hasty retreat toward the post office. "Best to stay clear of Mrs. George L. and not make her more of an enemy than need be."

"If you say so," Madeline said, sounding disappointed.

Surely, there must be some sort of balance, Ninny reasoned. Somewhere between asserting oneself and not standing in front of a loaded cannon.

"Ninny?"

"Yes?" She blinked and glanced over at her.

"What exactly is a cake dance?"

WITH THE BOOTH assignments in hand, Savannah hurried toward the Opera House. Across the way, she spied Miss Minch leading that new woman away from the mercantile, their heads bent together in some hurried conversation.

She blinked and wondered if she was seeing things. Miss Minch?

She should be scandalized, and yet, as she watched the pair for a moment, a frisson of something moved inside her. Like she'd missed an opportunity.

Well, she had other things to worry about, and even as she turned up the street, someone fell in step beside her.

Myrtle King, with a pile of packages in her arms. Of course.

The girl paused as well, her gaze following the direction of Savannah's dismay.

"Poor Miss Minch," Myrtle began. "I fear Josephine gave her a devil of a time." Then came a big *sniff*.

Savannah took a closer look. Heavens, Myrtle looked like she was on her way to a funeral—her nose all red, her eyes all puffy, like she'd been crying.

In fact, she *was* crying.

She tried to stop herself, but the question tumbled out. "Myrtle, is something wrong?"

"Wrong?" Myrtle shifted the packages in her arms and glanced away as great round tears continued to well up in her eyes. "No. Well. It's just that—"

Savannah stopped. "What is it?"

"My cake—" Then the words tumbled out, carrying with them

every last bit of dignity she possessed. "I cannot bake, and now everything is ruined."

"Oh my," Savannah managed, looking around for someone more qualified to take over.

Inola would know what to do.

With no other choice, Savannah improvised, plucking out her handkerchief and handing it over. "It didn't turn out as you'd hoped?"

This brought out a wail of confession. "Not at all." *Sniff.* "And then Josephine Lovell was in the store." *Sniff. Sniff.* "She just had to bring up last year." *Sniff. Sniff.*

This was followed by a garbled explanation, punctuated by hiccups and sobs. Something about a pancake feed. And ending up an old spinster.

While most of it made no sense, Savannah got the general gist of the girl's lament.

"I tried last night and followed the directions in the magazine ever so faithfully, and still it came out flat." She hiccupped and tried to catch her breath. "I'll just have to sit out the dance. Again." *Sniff. Sniff.* "Not that anyone would have bought it. Not after . . ."

"Don't even think about it," Savannah told her, patting her arm and leading her along. "Those cakes in the magazines are all wrong. Haven't you your mother's old recipes? Or your grandmother's?"

Myrtle blinked and then looked away again. "Mother's things were all lost."

Honestly, she'd never given much thought to a Mrs. King, but certainly there must have been one once.

"Well, that is a terrible shame," she told her, meaning every word. After all, she'd left Mississippi in a indecent hurry, so she knew a thing or two about lost things. Taking a deep breath, she pushed aside that dark, awful night and continued on. "What sort of cake did you bake?"

Or rather tried to . . .

"It was supposed to be a Queen's Cake."

Savannah shook her head. A Queen's Cake? That wasn't a recipe for someone with limited skills in the kitchen. Though that was a discussion for another time. So instead, she said, "My dear, that isn't a cake for a man."

"It isn't?" Myrtle blinked from behind her foggy spectacles. "Oh, but it sounded so heavenly."

"Perhaps for the Ladies Aid meeting, but not to serve to a man," Savannah told her firmly. "Why, Inola and I had just this discussion" —make that argument—"this very morning while I, well, she, was baking a cake—"

"For Josephine Lovell," Myrtle muttered, more to herself.

Savannah waved her speculation aside. Josephine Lovell paid well to have that cake done. But the girl was a terrible pill. "I am not at liberty to say," she told Myrtle, "but a lemon chiffon was requested and provided. At the time, I expressed my opinion that a good solid apple cake would be much more to a man's liking." Savannah paused for a moment. A rebellious notion began to rise inside her before she could stop it. "Myrtle, I would love to prove Inola—and others— wrong, wouldn't you?"

The girl's brows knit together over her spectacles, and then she brightened. "I suppose—"

"I have the perfect recipe to do it. For an apple cake."

"An apple cake?" Myrtle pursed her mouth, clearly skeptical of such a homespun offering.

"Indeed, an apple cake." Savannah took another breath, a plan forming in her mind. For it was Friday. Which meant choir practice was this evening, so Inola would be out.

She couldn't hide the fact that she'd baked a cake—for, the moment Inola walked through the door, the house would reveal Savannah's clandestine baking in a warm, homey perfume of apples and spice—yet it was a small price to pay when she knew what Myrtle truly desired.

A new dress for the Christmas ball.

A wish Savannah couldn't afford to indulge. Rather a cake was a small price to pay when anything else was nigh on impossible. "Myrtle, our running into each other is serendipity," Savannah told her.

"Seren-what?" Myrtle blinked again.

"Serendipity," Savannah told her firmly. "I can help you bake a cake, and you can help me prove all the naysayers wrong. What do you say?"

"You and me?" A dubious note clouded Myrtle's question. As if the notion of baking a cake was suspect in and of itself.

"Yes." Savannah warmed to the notion that this simple act was the answer to all her problems. "Can you come by after seven?" Inola left for practice at ten before the hour.

Myrtle nodded, swiping at her nose and readjusting her packages.

She'd help Myrtle with the cake, and then this dress nonsense would be unnecessary. Or so she told herself as they came to a stop in front of the Opera House.

"Are you posting the booth assignments?" Myrtle asked, shuffling her feet and trying her best to nonchalantly change the subject.

"I am." Savannah held up the folded paper in her hand. She was rather proud of the *coup d'état* she'd managed with the assignments, albeit with Inola's intervention and insights.

Myrtle hardly looked excited. "I suppose Goldie and I are selling aprons again."

With Mrs. George L. nowhere in sight, Savannah smiled. "Take a look." She held out the paper and exchanged it for Myrtle's packages. "Be quick," she added, taking a furtive look around.

Myrtle's finger ran down the list, skimming over Lace, Bookmarks, Aprons, until . . .

"Candy?" Her gaze flew up, seeking confirmation.

"Yes, you and your sister."

Then Myrtle did something so surprising Savannah couldn't have anticipated it in a hundred years.

The girl gave her a fierce hug. "Oh, Mrs. Clarke!" In that brief bit of contact, something happened. Like when one is mending a sock and finally catches the loose threads from fraying further.

"There now, there now," Savannah told the girl, taking a step back before those delicate threads had a chance to knit together and completely patch the hole. "We can't have anyone thinking I'm playing favorites. Booth assignments are to be done with the utmost integrity. At least that is what Mrs. George L. told me." Then she winked.

When Myrtle looked ready to hug her one more time, she sidestepped the girl and added quickly, "Your thanks should rightly go to Inola. She thought you and your sister would be the most capable of seeing the candy sold properly."

Myrtle took one more look at the list in her hand, as if she couldn't quite believe her good fortune, but this time her finger stilled over a different entry.

"You put Josephine at Mittens?" Myrtle shook her head. "Mrs. George L. is going to insist Josephine be front and center, just like she always is." The smile that had brightened her features fell, and she exchanged the list for her packages with an air of resignation.

Savannah straightened. "You leave Mrs. George L. to me."

CHAPTER 17

*I*nside the Opera House, Savannah's valor wavered as Mrs. George L. ran her finger down the list just as Myrtle had done earlier. From across the room, the girl—who had scampered off to deliver her packages and then returned with the speed of a telegraph line—kept stealing glances at the pair of them, her face far from hopeful.

Addie Sullivan joined her, and the pair of them had their heads together. From their tight expressions, they didn't think their champion had a chance of lasting a single round.

"My dear Mrs. Clarke," Mrs. George L. said, adjusting the spectacles sitting pinched on her nose. "This will not do." Her finger stabbed at the list exactly where Myrtle's had stopped. "You've mistakenly put Josephine in a booth that is utterly unfitting for her station, her qualifications." Her head shook slightly. "You have Miss Barrett at the raffle. The raffle, Mrs. Clarke. The committee has high hopes of raising significant funds from that, and Miss Barrett is . . ."

"Perfectly qualified," Savannah told the chairwoman, and she raised her hand to stave off any protests. "My dear lady, I would never put your lovely Josephine at a raffle booth. Why, it would be unseemly!"

"Unseemly?" the woman stammered, her lashes beating behind her spectacles like moths at a lamp. "I'll have you know—"

Before she could gather a head of steam, Savannah forged ahead, drawing her aside. "Think of it, Mrs. Lovell. Your young, innocent daughter standing before a *bed quilt*, taking money from men. I can't imagine anything more . . . Well, I hate to use the word, but there is no other one to offer." She leaned in and lowered her voice. "I fear it would be suggestive."

This time, when Mrs. Lovell's lips flapped open, nothing but air escaped.

Oh, it was all ridiculous nonsense, but even the . . . well, suggestion had the woman's gaze flicking across the room to where the red-and-white quilt hung.

Savannah sighed, shaking her head. "It never occurred to me to put a respectable girl like Josephine—who clearly reflects your example of refinement and quality—in such a position. Miss Barrett, dear creature that she is, has a few more years on her shoulders and is such a plain girl. We can both agree she is unlikely to spark that wickedness that so often lurks in the hearts of men." Savannah nodded sagely. "As my dear mother—raised, as you might recall, in the elevated circles of New Orleans's most privileged citizenry—was wont to say, a lady should always strive to show a gentleman her finer traits."

"But mittens, Mrs. Clarke?" Mrs. George L. shook her head. "I think I see what you're saying, but if you might . . ." She let her words trail off, because she could hardly admit that she didn't understand genteel manners, considering she held herself as the very epitome of Bethlehem society.

Savannah took her by the elbow, leading her over to the booth that had been set up earlier.

"Her hands, Mrs. Lovell." Savannah picked up a mitten and held out her bare hand, turning it this way and that. "If Josephine is selling mittens, she can model her perfectly lovely hands, and there will be nothing in such an action that will inspire anything but an ardent admiration for her modesty." She smiled as if it was all so obvious— to women of good breeding, that is. "We *ladies*," she continued, with just the right air of distinction, "must always hold ourselves to higher, subtler standards than those ascribed to by persons of more common sensibilities."

Common. That word was enough to furrow the lady's brow. For if she were to argue the fact now, she just might look, well, common.

"Oh, I don't disagree with you, Mrs. Clarke, though . . ." Mrs. Lovell paused and leaned closer. "Well, let me be frank. Josephine has a new dress to wear, and she had hoped to sell candy—"

Savannah wrinkled her nose. "Candy? With a new dress? Heaven forbid. I don't need to point out that she'd have to wear an apron, which would hardly show that new dress to its advantage." With that, she dismissed the argument. "Besides, I never even considered her for *that* booth. It would be ever so mercantile for someone of Josephine's refinement."

Mrs. George L. straightened. "Mrs. Clarke, you have surprised me with your attention to detail. It does seem a risk, but . . ."

Savannah paused and looked at the lady as if she hadn't a clue why her plan wasn't the soundest and most moral route available.

Since arguing the decision would only lower her daughter from that lofty pedestal of privilege she claimed as her sole domain, there was nothing Mrs. George L. could do but post the assignments on the board near the kitchen.

Savannah folded her arms over her chest, brimming with victory, and when the others rushed over to see what spots they had been granted, she turned slightly and winked at Myrtle.

SAVANNAH HAD BEEN like a cat in a room full of rockers ever since she'd gotten home from the Opera House. Whatever had she agreed to?

But then Myrtle arrived at Savannah's back door promptly at seven, looking as if she were facing her own firing squad. Oh, weren't they a pair!

Myrtle set down the basket she'd brought with a heavy thud.

"Papa said I should bring along more than just myself. So I brought what I thought we might need."

Out of the basket came flour, sugar, a dozen eggs, a large pat of butter, a can of baking powder, a pound of pecans, and a collection of spice jars, along with a few apples.

Savannah gaped at the bounty now covering her table. "Why, Myrtle, I don't think your father meant for you to bring the entire store."

The girl blinked and then smiled a bit sheepishly. "You did say an apple spice cake, didn't you?" She quickly took an inventory. "Did I forget something?"

"Hardly, child," Savannah laughed.

"Is Inola going to help?" Myrtle asked, peering past the kitchen door and into the further reaches of the house.

Ah. So the girl didn't believe she could deliver on her promise. Whose fault was that? "Inola is at choir practice," Savannah told her.

The girl wrung her hands together. "I thought—"

"I can bake a cake without Inola, don't you worry." Savannah went to the cabinet and got out the mixing bowl.

Myrtle nodded. "I've always wanted to learn to bake a cake. You know, a proper one. Like the other girls bring. Not a flat one. But they have—"

They have mothers to help them. With cakes. And dresses.

Savannah ignored the way an entire army of loose threads began unwinding inside her, curling toward each other, all humming the same refrain, *this poor girl*. She snipped at them, hemming them back, even as she said, "We have no use for flat cakes in this house. So I promise you will leave here tonight with a cake that will be the envy of every girl at that dance."

"Oh, I know you'll try, but I really can't cook, Mrs. Clarke." Myrtle's words, so full of defeat, tugged anew. "I nearly burned down the store last winter trying to make a simple sponge. Goldie said I'll do the same here."

"You can stop that right now," Savannah instructed, taking firm command of the situation—despite a flicker of panic over the thought of her beloved house going up in flames. "Don't give your sister another thought." She certainly wasn't going to—though she made a note to keep the girl away from the open stove box. "Get your apron on, and let's get started. We have a lot to do."

So they began, and immediately Savannah realized she had her work cut out for her. For though Myrtle could tally a column of figures on an order slip in the blink of an eye, she couldn't measure, sift, cream, or stir to save her life.

So Savannah started with the basics, and then, after a few failed attempts at sifting, she took a step back to the bottom rung of basics.

She lost all sense of time until Inola came through the back door.

"What is this?" she asked.

A mess is what it was. Flour coated the floor, and the counters were littered with half-used ingredients and dirty dishes.

"Mrs. Clarke is helping me with my cake," Myrtle supplied, looking far prouder than her achievements warranted.

Inola lofted a brow at Savannah, who did her patent best to ignore it. "She is?" Even as she hung up her coat and took off her hat, Inola took in the state of the kitchen and grinned. "Did any of the flour make it in the bowl?"

Myrtle blushed. "Sifting is not as easy as it might appear. I fear I was a bit too enthusiastic. Those are Mrs. Clarke's words, not mine."

"That I don't doubt," Inola chuckled.

"Stop teasing, Inola," Savannah scolded. "Myrtle is our guest." She glanced at the clock on the shelf. "You're home early."

"No, that clock's just stuck again," Inola replied, going over to the shelf and giving it a tap. "What are we about to do here?" She paused at Myrtle's shoulder and looked down at the bowl.

"Creaming," Myrtle told her, that single word sounding like a surrender. "I'm a complete failure at this." Her lower lip wobbled a bit, and there was a sheen to her eyes.

"Nonsense," Savannah told her, trying to buoy her back up. "Just keep trying." She nodded at the bowl, and Myrtle dutifully stabbed at the contents with the wooden spoon.

"How are the lessons coming along?" Inola asked, doing her best to smile as she watched the girl's murderous efforts.

Savannah reached over and gently guided Myrtle's hand until she got the hang of pressing the butter against the bowl. "As I recall, when I taught you to cook, you weren't any better."

Myrtle's hand stilled. "You taught Inola?" Then, remembering herself, she went back to work.

"She did." Inola came over and looked into the bowl. "She's a far sight better at it than I am."

"But I thought—" Myrtle stammered. "That is . . . you both being from the South and all, that Inola was—"

"Ours was a house of a different sort," Savannah advised her. "I learned to cook at an early age."

Inola's eyes widened. *More different than anyone need know.* Then easily she changed the subject. "How is that creaming going?"

Myrtle looked down at the bowl and burst into tears. "All the girls love the cake dance, but for me, every year is a disaster. Goldie doesn't care, but she doesn't need a pretty cake to . . ." *Catch a man's eye.*

Inola leaned over Myrtle's shoulder. "Let's see what we got here. You see creaming is like a courtship. The butter and the sugar don't know each other yet, so it's up to you to push them with that spoon and then gently bring them together. Here, let me show you." Taking the wooden spoon, Inola demonstrated how to press the butter against the bowl, bringing the sugar with it. After a few strokes, she handed it back to Myrtle, watching and guiding the girl until she got the hang of it.

Savannah stood back, mesmerized by Inola's gentle words and lesson. She'd been trying to explain it for the past thirty minutes, and Inola had accomplished victory in two swipes of the spoon and just the right words. But she'd always had a way with words and people— something Savannah envied.

As the two disparate parts came together, Myrtle's brown eyes brightened. "How old were you when you learned to bake a cake, Mrs. Clarke?"

"I started helping in the kitchen when I was about five or six." The answer came out before she could stop it. Memories of that New Orleans kitchen, hot and always busy. But, oh, such a joyous place.

"So young?" Myrtle asked.

Savannah laughed a little. "When did you start helping in your father's store?"

The girl nodded in concession.

"My mémé didn't think I was going to turn out very pretty," Savannah told her matter-of-factly. "She said I should learn to cook so I had something in my favor." Especially given the rest of the girls in the house, including her mother and Inola's, were the reigning beauties of New Orleans's brothels.

"Mémé?" Myrtle asked.

"Grandmother, honey," Inola told her. "It's French." After a quick glance between them, Inola once again redirected the conversation. She'd wandered over to the table where Myrtle had deposited her bounty. "Where did all these eggs come from?"

Myrtle grinned. "Mrs. Poole sent them down from her ranch. It seems her hens have forgotten it's winter."

"Lucky Mrs. Poole," Inola muttered. "What, with all those eggs, you should have made a chiffon cake."

"Not for a cake dance," Savannah told her with conviction. "A cake dance is for making something a man will appreciate. Something he will bid for."

Inola huffed. "Then you should have made a chocolate cake." It was, after all, her favorite.

"Oh, chocolate," Myrtle intoned with a note of reverence.

"There will be half a dozen chocolate cakes at that dance tomorrow night," Savannah told her. "We are baking the sort of cake that will make a man sit up and take notice."

"Lemon chiffon always wins," Inola asserted, crossing her arms over her chest.

Savannah crossed her arms as well. "An apple is about to dethrone you."

Myrtle slanted a quizzical glance at the pair. "If you don't mind me saying, you two sound like me and my sisters." The girl was closer to the truth than she knew.

"You'd know," Inola offered. "You've got quite a pair of them."

"Tell me about it." Myrtle huffed, then cracked an egg into a dish and leaned closer to inspect for stray bits of shell.

"We sound like sisters," Savannah explained, "because we've been together all our lives."

"Really?" Myrtle shuddered. "I hope I don't have to spend the rest of my life with Frankie or Goldie."

Savannah reached over to stop her before she dumped the entire bowl of flour into the butter, sugar, and eggs. She nodded toward the cup of sour milk. "Only a third at a time," she reminded her. "Then part of the flour."

Myrtle nodded and slowly began to mix. A bit of the sour milk. Then part of the sifted flour and spices.

"There. That's how you do it." Savannah beamed at her. "Not too much more. The secret is to bring it together but not to beat it to death." After another quick glance at the bowl, she nodded toward the cake tins. "I think we're ready."

Myrtle looked down at the bowl. "Perhaps a bit more mixing?" She reached for the spoon.

"No," Savannah told her. "Mix it just until it comes together. No more."

Myrtle glanced at Inola. Clearly, she still didn't trust that Savannah knew what she was doing.

"Exactly," Inola agreed.

With a few careful words, Savannah guided Myrtle as she spooned the batter into the tins. Then she held her breath as the girl set them in the oven and carefully closed the door.

The house, thankfully, was still standing.

"Now what?" Myrtle asked.

"We wait," Inola told her.

"We clean up," Savannah corrected.

"I prefer washing to cooking," Myrtle said. "I can always be assured of getting a pot clean. But a cake baked . . ." She trailed off as her gaze drifted nervously toward the oven.

"You never mind that oven," Savannah told her. "Your apple cake will do what it is supposed to do." She filled a dishpan with hot water from the reservoir and set it in the sink, even as Inola collected all the dishes. They'd worked side by side in this kitchen for so many years that they did these chores by rote, while Myrtle flitted between them, her gaze always coming back to rest on the oven door.

Inola caught the girl's attention with a wide smile. "Myrtle, who do you want to bid on that fine cake?"

Myrtle's eyes widened. "Oh, I don't dare say. It would be bad luck."

Savannah crossed her arms over her chest. "Indeed, Inola."

Though now that the question was out, Savannah slanted a glance at Myrtle. Moments before, she'd been just a girl with her heart set on a cake and a dress.

Now . . . Savannah's insides quaked. She was the last person on earth anyone should ask about what happened after the cake and the dress.

Meanwhile, Inola had nudged Myrtle over toward the drainboard, and the two of them began drying the dishes.

Inola paused. "Now take a deep sniff and tell me what you smell."

Myrtle did as she was bid and a smile rose on her lips. "Apples?"

"Cake, child. I smell cake. And it smells ever so good." Inola glanced over at Savannah. "For an apple cake."

CHAPTER 18

Saturday, December 7

After Ninny had explained the archaic rules of a cake dance to Madeline and declared no intention of going, she found herself the very next morning stepping back to admire her handiwork as four perfect layers of cake cooled on the baking racks.

They were ever so lovely, and she couldn't help but grin with foolish pride.

Her mother's sponge cake. All they needed was frosting and a thick covering of coconut.

And then what? Carry it over to the cake dance and spend the evening in breathless anticipation?

Ninny shook her head. "Oh, what has come over you?" she muttered, looking at the cake with new eyes and a familiar perspective.

This might be the perfect cake, but she could hardly take it to the dance. Not unless she wanted to suffer everyone snickering behind her back—or, worse, to her face, as that wretched Josephine Lovell had done.

Hadn't she had enough humiliation for one week?

She glanced at the clock and realized she needed to get the post office open. Why, she hadn't even swept the steps. As she hurried to the front, catching up the broom as she went, a loud *whack* gave her a start. Then another. *Whack!*

Hurrying forward, she pulled the bolt aside and threw open the door, broom at the ready.

"Ho, there, Miss Minch!"

Ninny gaped, the broom slipping from her fingers and landing with its own whack on the porch.

At the bottom of the steps stood Mr. Thayer, hammer in hand. Instead of his usual suit of clothes, he wore a plain pair of wool pants and a heavy coat. An old cap sat at a jaunty angle on his head.

"Mr. Thayer." She gathered up her broom, clutching it close.

"I hope you don't mind," he began, "but when Mrs. George L. mentioned this step yesterday, I realized I've been shirking my civic duty by allowing it to continue to be a 'public hazard.'" His eyes twinkled a bit as he grinned at her.

Irish eyes, her father had called them. All blue and bright. Full of promises that wouldn't be kept.

"I'll have this fixed in no time," he was saying, pulling the old board free.

"Oh, but you needn't—" she began, glancing up and down the street to see if anyone was paying heed to the post office.

Not that there was the slightest chance such an act would go unnoticed in Bethlehem.

Mr. Thayer waved a hand at her and continued to work. "If Badger—that sly dog—can bring you kindling, then I suppose fixing this step rather evens the score."

"I assure you there is no score to be kept—"

"Oh, there is, Miss Minch. There is."

Having freed one of the boards, Mr. Thayer measured a new one. "Don't worry—I actually know what I'm doing. My grandfather was a carpenter. As a child, I spent my summers learning his trade on Nantucket Island—though my father had other plans for me."

"As parents do," she murmured.

Then Mr. Thayer's expression changed. Having taken a deep inhalation, his eyes closed to half-mast, an almost hypnotic smile rising on his lips. "Miss Minch, what is that heavenly air?"

She glanced back into the house. "I was, well, I was baking . . ."

"The cake you mentioned yesterday. Coconut, right?"

She managed a nod, a bit taken aback by the sheer delight on his face.

He sighed. "I'll be the first to bid on it tonight."

"Bid on it?" She shook her head. "Oh, it isn't for the—"

Mr. Thayer rose up. "But you must!" Despite the fact that she was shaking her head—now in earnest—he continued his argument. "Miss Minch, that smells like heaven on earth. If you don't bring that cake to the dance tonight, it will be a crime. A crime, I say. I shall report you to the sheriff for baking temptation and then withholding it from public consumption."

Ninny's cheeks grew hot, but it wasn't his cheeky words that drew the deep blush to her face. It was that he was actually serious.

"If my unerring civic duty hadn't brought me to your doorstep this morning, that heavenly odor would have done the trick in a trice." He took another deep inhalation. "You'll bankrupt me tonight, Miss Minch. So just in case I am outbid, promise me you'll save me a dance. A waltz, if you will—I'm not one for those newfangled steps. Just a plain old waltz." Before she could answer, he winked and then went back to work, whistling some jaunty tune as he measured the board for a second time. After he marked it, he nodded toward the broom in her hand. "Just leave that out and I'll finish sweeping up the other steps for you when I'm done." He tipped his cap. "Until tonight."

She backed into the post office, his cheery words chasing her. *Until tonight?*

Now what had she done?

※

IT WAS a question Ninny asked herself repeatedly during the course of the day.

Once the news of Mr. Thayer fixing her front step had spread, a good portion of the curious had suddenly discovered a need for stamps, bringing them in a steady stream to her counter. The unforeseen consequence was that they all got a whiff of the cake that was sitting in her kitchen, awaiting its robes of coconut and icing.

Are you bringing a cake, Miss Minch?

Do you think Mr. Thayer will bid on it?

Well, aren't you a dark horse, Parathinia Minch! I'm starting to think I made a mistake all those years ago.

That last impertinent remark had been from Mr. George L. Lovell himself, who'd come, most likely at the insistence of his wife, to survey the situation.

She remembered what Madeline had said yesterday, after Ninny had declared she had no intention of going.

Wouldn't it be worse if you didn't show up?

This was what she got for listening to the likes of Mrs. Mercer and Madeline Drake.

Especially now, as she cleared plates, surrounded by most of the town. It seemed even people who'd had no intention of coming to the fundraiser had shown up.

The bazaar booths had been cleared away and replaced with the supper tables, and it felt as if the entire town was now eating their fill of chicken pie while casting speculative glances toward the table of cakes proudly displayed on the stage. Hers sat in the back row, tucked to one side and overshadowed by Josephine's towering lemon chiffon beauty.

"Miss Minch, I hear one of them cakes is yours."

She flinched. "Yes, it is, Mr. Jonas."

"Well, indeed," Mrs. Jonas said with a sniff. "I always been of the opinion a cake dance is for, shall we say, more eligible ladies."

"Strike while the iron is hot, Miss Minch," Mr. Jonas urged her.

"Mr. Jonas!" Mrs. Jonas puckered and frowned. "Don't be vulgar."

At least he hadn't asked about the post office step.

Ninny gathered the plates and hurried toward the kitchen as the night's musical entertainment—old Gabe Lundy and his banjo, Mrs. Douglas on the piano, and Ira Wade with his violin—began a lively series of notes to announce Mrs. George L.'s stately arrival on the stage.

"Ladies and gentlemen," she began, and her words were met with a great cheer. She waved at them, fingers waggling with her usual feint of modesty.

Ninny took another glance at the cake-laden stage and panicked. Heart pounding, she fled toward the kitchen.

Inola met her at the door. "Let me take those, honey." She whipped the dirty dishes out of Ninny's grasp. "Don't you dare let that woman chase you away. You go back out and hold your head high. I've seen that cake of yours, and it is the finest one up there. Now, if you wouldn't mind . . ." She tipped her head toward the table in the back.

Ninny looked as well. Of course. Badger's table.

"None of the girls will do it 'cause those miners can be a rough lot, but I don't think they will give you any trouble," Inola continued. "Not with Badger sitting there."

"I can't— Why, it would look—"

"Like you're doing your job?" Inola reminded her. "Do you want me to send that pretty Bergstrom girl over there? Then one of those miners will get friendly, and her daddy won't take kindly to it."

"Well, when you put it that way," Ninny said, steeling herself as she made her way toward the back of the room.

"Now we have a lovely lemon chiffon creation baked by my own darling daughter, Miss Josephine Lovell."

As Josephine rose, there was a round of enthusiastic applause, for she was a very pretty girl despite her unfortunate mother. That, and most everyone assumed the cake had been baked by Inola, so it was guaranteed to be good.

Worse—and, much to Ninny's horror—the tie hacks and miners, most likely fortified by smuggled spirits, all rose to their feet and clapped and whistled, which drew every eye to the back of the room . . . right at the moment she arrived to clear their plates.

There was a bit of an awkward pause, but Mrs. George L. recovered quickly, holding the plate high for one and all to see and diverting the room with a call for an opening bid. "Who likes lemon chiffon?"

There was a roar from the crowd and the bidding began. After a moment, Badger tipped his head toward her. "Rumor has it you baked one of them cakes."

She nodded.

"Is it any good?"

Any good? Why, she'd have him know . . . Then she spotted the merry quirk to his lips.

"It's tolerable," she told him smartly. She imagined Miss Drake would be proud of her.

He snorted. "If it's anything like your biscuits, it will be worth every penny."

Ninny gathered up the plates and made her way to the kitchen in a bit of a daze. He wasn't going to bid, was he?

First Mr. Thayer, and now Badger.

Mark my words, fisticuffs before this is over.

Oh, heavens. What if, for once, Mrs. Jonas had the right of it?

SAVANNAH HAD SPENT the better part of the evening watching Myrtle King, especially when she'd arrived in a deep mustard dress that made her look positively jaundiced.

A hand-me-down from her older sister, Savannah assumed, given that the hue would be perfect with Goldie's blonde hair and ivory skin tones.

But not on Myrtle.

Heavens, the girl needed a proper dress, a problem all the more ironic when her father sold the very fabric necessary to see her in a flattering color.

More than once, Savannah had told herself this wasn't her problem, and she'd all but convinced herself as much—until the cake auction.

Not long after Josephine Lovell's cake—the one everyone thought Inola had baked—had gone for the princely sum of two and a half dollars, Mrs. George L. deliberately selected Myrtle's cake from the array of offerings.

"We have here an apple cake from Miss Myrtle King," she announced. She held it out, as if she were afraid it would fall like last year's offering. "Do I have an opening bid?"

To Savannah's horror, no one raised their hand. Not a single soul.

She looked to Inola, who stood at the kitchen door. *This is horrible.*

Isn't it?

"Anyone?" Mrs. Lovell asked, one might say gleefully . . . if one were being spiteful. Or honest.

Mr. King glanced around and looked ready to raise his hand, but Goldie stopped him with a disapproving shake of her head.

Worse than having no one bid? Having your father make up for the humiliating silence filling the room.

Myrtle, poor girl, was once again red-faced and looked ready to burst into tears.

Savannah looked around the room for someone to help until she realized the solution was right in front of her. The perfect young man.

Peter Bergstrom. Tall and handsome. He'd been outbid for Josephine's cake, which had the girl throwing spite-filled glances in his direction, as if she'd expected better of him.

Well, perhaps he could be someone else's hero.

She leaned over to the woman beside her and whispered, loud enough for the adjacent table to hear, "What a shame. Inola spent the better part of last night baking that cake with dear Myrtle. I thought they should have done a chiffon, but you know how men like a good, filling apple cake."

Peter's head swiveled toward the stage, where Mrs. Lovell held Myrtle's cake as if she had a rat by the tail. Then he glanced back in Savannah's direction. His gaze narrowed, glinting with one question. *Really?*

Savannah nodded at him. *Oh, yes, you heard me.*

Peter's hand shot up. "Fifty cents."

A moment of silence followed, then a chuckle from his friends rose around the room.

"Pan-cake," one of them reminded him, nudging another boy.

Across the room, Myrtle sat open-mouthed. As did her sisters, and nearly every other young lady in the room.

Peter's arm nudged higher. "Fifty cents."

There was another moment of silence as every boy in the room considered what was happening.

If Peter Bergstrom was bidding on Myrtle King's pan-cake, there must be something going on.

So they all wanted in.

"Sixty cents," Walker Stafford called out, his hand digging into his trouser pockets as he pulled out all his change and began counting coins to see how high he could go.

The rest of the boys scrambled to do the same.

"Sixty-three cents," Robbie Cochrane called out.

There was a hoot of good-natured laughter, and the bidding was off, leaving Robbie and his sixty-three cents in the dust as Walker called out, "Six bits."

Peter set his jaw and dug deeper into his pocket. "A dollar."

"A dollar and a half," Junior Lovell called out, much to everyone's surprise and his mother's great horror.

Peter's jaw worked, for he probably hadn't had the dollar to begin with, and now here was Junior wading in as he always did, with his father's money, claiming a prize without so much as breaking a sweat. Peter looked around at his friends. "How much you got? That cake is big enough for all of us."

The boys rallied around, emptying their pockets while Peter quickly counted. Even Walker came over and added his quarters to the pile.

"Another bid?" Mrs. George L. asked, clearly aghast at the idea of her son buying Myrtle's cake.

"Just a moment, ma'am," Peter told her as he tallied the pennies and nickels piled up in front of him. He named his price. With no one else bidding, he won the day, leading to a rousing cheer from his compatriots.

Savannah let out the breath she didn't realize she'd been holding and tried her best not to beam with pride. No use calling any more attention to the situation than necessary, so she moved on to gather more plates. But she slowed as a conversation between a pair of misses caught her ear.

"You'd think she'd look happier."

Both girls looked over at Myrtle with no small amount of envy.

"I'd be in heaven."

"I'd be in heaven if I had Josephine's new dress."

The gossipy conversation turned to the inevitable tide of fashions, leaving Myrtle's good fortune forgotten.

Savannah glanced back at Myrtle, who did indeed look utterly miserable with Peter Bergstrom on one side and Walker Stafford on the other, along with several others who were happily devouring the apple cake while the rest of the girls looked on wistfully.

Savannah straightened. Whatever was wrong? The girl should have been basking in the limelight. Hefting her stack of plates, she hurried across the room, if only to see what Inola made of all this.

But even as she came to the kitchen, someone stepped in front of her.

"Mrs. Clarke."

"Mr. King," she acknowledged, sidestepping him and carrying the plates into the kitchen.

To her shock, he followed her.

"Mrs. Clarke, if you have a moment," he persisted.

The kitchen, which had been a-clatter with the washing of plates and cheerful banter, paused as every pair of ears in the room turned toward this male intrusion.

The owner of the mercantile was clearly out of his depth, for he'd stepped into the swift currents of female territory. That he'd willingly waded in over his head said everything.

And drat it if Inola didn't come hurrying up and take the armload of plates from her, smiling at Mr. King and nudging Savannah closer.

"Yes, Mr. King?" Savannah asked, wiping her hands on her apron and ignoring all the curious glances.

Mr. King leaned in and dropped his voice. "Thank you for what you did for Myrtle."

"Oh, I didn't do anything. It was all—"

"I think you did quite a bit," he said quickly, glancing over her shoulder at all the help, who were agog at this unlikely tableau.

"Truly, she only needed a little help," Savannah assured him.

"Mrs. Clarke, I am very familiar with my daughter's cooking. There was more than a little help offered."

"Sir, you should give her more credit. She knows what to do, but only needs a bit of . . ." She paused, looking over his shoulder toward where Myrtle sat. In that moment, the perfect word came to her. "Encouragement."

"Which we all do from time to time, don't you find?" He smiled— he truly smiled—and Savannah sensed an odd undercurrent moving beneath her.

He wasn't suggesting . . . *Oh, good heavens.*

She took a steadying breath. "I daresay Myrtle brought over too much sugar and far more eggs than were needed. I'll return the rest of it on Monday when—"

"Don't you dare," Mr. King told her. "Consider it my gift for helping Myrtle. You've done my dear girl a kindness I shall not forget." He reached out and took her hand, giving it a squeeze and letting go of it as quickly as he'd taken it. "If you can't use it, then perhaps offer it to the Bergstroms."

Then he turned and left, leaving behind a roomful of gaping women, with Savannah teetering in the middle, her fingers curling together as if catching hold of something she'd thought was long lost. Forgotten.

"These dishes aren't gonna wash themselves," Inola announced in a voice that carried to every corner of the spellbound kitchen.

NINNY HAD DONE her best over the last thirty-five minutes to ignore the entire proceedings, but she'd been unable to stop counting down the cakes.

Josephine's. Myrtle's. Miss Barrett's. On and on, until there was only one left.

A ripple of anticipation ran through the room, for there wasn't a soul who didn't know who'd baked it. Mrs. George L. drew herself up to her full height, a commanding figure in most cases, but even more so tonight as she marched across the stage to take up this final offering.

"One entry left," Mrs. George L. commented, the note of disapproval clear to all. She sighed, as if this was just another inconvenience she had to contend with, and picked it up.

What happened next would be dissected in Bethlehem circles for years to come.

Those of a kinder bent were wont to say it wasn't the dear lady's fault—that her heel caught and it was all just an unfortunate accident.

Others—mostly those seated up close with a clear view of the proceedings—avowed that she'd done the horrible deed on purpose.

For as Mrs. George L. turned, cake in hand, the plate tipped, she stumbled slightly, and Ninny's glorious coconut cake toppled over and landed with a splat on the stage.

A collective gasp followed, then an aching hush that reached out and stole Ninny's wisp of a dream, now as ruined as her perfect cake.

But that mute shock didn't last long.

A heavy chair scraped in the back of the room, and a voice rose clear and strong. "Eight dollars."

No one moved, for most were certain that they hadn't heard Badger correctly.

"Sir, the cake is ruined," Mrs. George L. advised him.

"Not to me." Badger strode to the front of the stage. "I said eight dollars."

Then Mr. Thayer rose to his feet. "Nine."

AFTER A LONG EVENING playing mahjong and a bit of poker with Mr. Wu and his cohorts, Madeline wandered through the dark, empty streets of Bethlehem, Dog trotting along at her heels, until she came to a stop in front of the Star Bright. Further up the street, the tangy notes of a fiddle echoed. She had no idea what the song was, but her feet moved, and she began to slide along, singing at the top of her lungs, "Had me a boy, turned him into a man—"

Out of nowhere, a figure came striding out from the dark. "What the . . . ?"

"Shandy, you prevaricating bastard. I've been looking for you. Want to dance?"

His expression hardened as he spied the bottle in her hand. "Don't tell me you're drunk again."

"I'm not drunk," she said, trying to match his serious tone. "I'm shitfaced." She laughed loud and hard.

"Oh, good heavens," he muttered as she danced her lopsided way in a circle around him. "Why, Madeline? Why do you insist on drinking yourself into the gutter like this?" He shoved his hands in his pockets. "You'll stay stuck forever if you can't learn from your mistakes."

Mistakes. That word pushed past her whiskey-fueled fog. "Is that why everyone else is here? They've made mistakes?"

He nodded. "A good portion of them."

"Can they leave?"

His jaw worked back and forth.

She knew what that meant. *No.*

"Maddie, like you, everyone else is here because they got stuck— some for very good reasons, others for just being stubborn fools, some through no fault of their own. Sometimes they get unstuck, start moving again. They stay and grow, or they leave to go back and try again."

"Even the kids?" she asked, thinking of the ones she'd seen at the store.

"Nah." He smiled slightly. "Hardly fair to hold them to the sins of their fathers . . . or mothers. With a few exceptions, most can come and go. But even children can get trapped."

"In an eddy," she added.

He nodded. "Leave it all behind, Maddie. Leave it all behind you. That's how time works."

In time. Out of time. Those notions swirled in the muddy mire of her whiskey-soaked brain and found no mooring. She'd have to make sense of it all tomorrow.

If there was sense to be made of any of this.

But one thing stood out. She waved the bottle at the Opera House. "No one wants me here."

"It is any wonder when you persist in causing nothing but trouble?"

Now here was a familiar word. She grinned. "Trouble. Did you know that's literally my middle name?"

"Unfortunately, yes." He glanced back at the street, once again preoccupied.

"Shandy, relax. I've got new, dear friends at the Good Luck Laundry. Well, I had new friends." She shook her head. "It's an ironic name for a laundry, Good Luck, since Mr. Wu's luck at mahjong is not all that good." She leaned closer. "I cleaned him out. His wife is going to be furious with him." She laughed and staggered away.

After issuing a loud groan, Shandy paused. "Wait just a minute. Wu has a wife?" He shook his head. "Never mind that. What were you doing there?"

"I told you. Playing mahjong. Haven't played since Gigi died," she said, suddenly melancholy with memories of her grandmother's Sunday afternoon circle of friends, the tiles sliding across the table along with a steady stream of vicious, backstabbing Hollywood gossip. "I miss my Gigi."

Shandy swung back toward the laundry as if he expected to see something catastrophic. "Mr. Wu wasn't drinking, was he?"

She held up her bottle and eyed it. Since there was only about a swallow left, she promptly drank it. "Not anymore. I seem to have run out. By the way, that man cannot hold his whiskey."

He took a step back from her. "I am getting too old for this," he muttered as he caught her by the arm and steered her up the steps.

At the top, Madeline paused, for off in the distance, it wasn't the fiddle she heard but a train whistle. A long, lonely note that pulled at her. "Do you hear that?"

"The fiddle?" Shandy asked as he jiggled the door to get it open. "Ira's in rare form tonight."

"No, not that. The train whistle. I hear it at the oddest times."

He stilled and turned slowly toward her. "You hear that?"

"Yeah. I should just get up the nerve and take that train. Leave all this."

"Don't you ever learn?" He pushed open the door. "Stay here. Promise me—"

"Yes, yes," she said, her hand fluttering in dismissal. "I promise."

"Good. Go sleep this off."

"But I'm in the mood to dance," she told him, taking a tentative whirl around the chairs. "That's where everyone is, right? At that dance?" She paused for a moment. "I still don't get how you dance with cakes."

"You don't," he told her. "Now stay put while I go check on Mr. Wu." He hurried out the door.

Madeline glanced around the cold, dark room and sighed. This was why she'd gone out earlier. The quiet, added to her certainty that she wasn't wanted at the dance, had sent her scurrying to the laundry.

Because when she was all alone, the chorus in her head was the stuff of madness.

No one wanted her. Especially not here.

And back home? She was replaceable. Always.

It was a chilling fact her mother and agent had hammered into her throughout her years on *Casey Jones*, a sentiment doubly underscored by Emerson's recent recasting—personal and professional.

Off in the distance, a different sort of note pulled her out of her reverie and brought with it Shandy's words.

Leave it all behind.

She tipped her head and listened again to the keening notes of a fiddle. How was she supposed to learn from her mistakes if she didn't face them?

She went to the bar and retrieved another bottle. After all, Gigi always said it was bad manners to show up empty-handed.

Out in the alley, the cold, bitter air swirled around her, whispering words she couldn't quite discern. So she looked up at the bower of stars dancing overhead, offering a myriad of wishes.

"Just one dance," she whispered up to the distant, sparkling lights.

CHAPTER 19

"*I*'m so sorry, Mr. Thayer," Ninny exclaimed, after she'd trod on his foot yet again. "It's just been a long time since I've danced."

"Then I am the one who should be apologizing," Mr. Thayer told her as they whirled across the floor.

"How is that?" Ninny asked, doing her best to concentrate on where her feet needed to go. It was so awfully hard with everyone watching.

He tipped his head closer to her. "For not asking you long before this."

Ninny had no idea how to respond. After a spate of furious bidding, Mr. Thayer had won with the outrageous sum of twelve dollars and fifty cents, at which point every bit of satisfaction had drained from Mrs. George L.'s smug expression.

Nor had the woman's mood improved when, in a moment of gallantry, Mr. Thayer had taken his fork, gathered up a bite from the top of the wrecked cake, and declared it "the finest ever offered." He enjoined others to give it a try, causing a veritable stampede to the stage, all while Mrs. George L.'s murderous gaze remained fixed on Ninny.

This is all your fault, Parathinia Minch.

Worse, here was Mr. Thayer, who'd been unwittingly dragged into all this, and what had it gained him? One bite of a smashed cake and this terrible dance.

For the outrageous sum of twelve and a half dollars! Goodness, how could such a sum be afforded? Or repaid?

They turned, but her feet didn't follow, and she stepped on him again. For his part, Mr. Thayer smiled and winked at her, whirling her about the dance floor as if he were squiring a queen.

None of this would stop until she declared the winner of the Christmas tree drawing, and she needed to do that immediately. At the end of this dance, she'd make her announcement.

Yes, that was the best course, especially with Cora Stafford there watching their every turn about the dance floor. From her keen expression, she was most likely composing her front page, center column for the next issue of the *Bethlehem Observer.*

The Ladies Aid bazaar and cake dance benefit succeeded beyond their gentle expectations this year with the addition of a cake from Miss Parathinia Minch, a concoction of coconut and perfection, which drew the highest bid in the history of the benefit, the handsome sum of twelve dollars and fifty cents, courtesy of Mr. Archimedes A. Thayer, Esq., after a furious spate of bidding against his Christmas tree competitor, Mr. Sterling McCandish Densmore.

What will these two do next?

So lost was she in her own fanciful journalism, Ninny hardly noticed that the music had ended and Mr. Thayer was escorting her to his table. That is, until a large figure loomed in front of her.

"Miss Minch, may I have this next dance?" Badger asked, holding out his hand.

Ninny didn't know what startled her more—that someone else had asked her, or that it was Badger. Why, she didn't even know that he could dance. But here he was, brushed up as much as she'd ever seen, his beard not quite as wild and his hair combed back. He was still Badger, in his patched coat and trousers, and she could hear a few snickers behind her.

She could hardly say "no." She owed him the same courtesy, and the same apologies for dragging him and Mr. Thayer into her mire.

But before she could set this all to rights, Mr. Thayer answered for her in a low, firm voice. "I don't think so, my good man. If you'd wanted the honor of the lady's company, then you should have bid more." He took her hand and made a show of placing it on his sleeve. He was about to turn when Badger clapped his large hand atop the man's shoulder and held him fast.

"I don't recall asking you, Thayer. I was speaking to Miss Minch." He paused, cleared his throat a bit, and fixed his steady, dark gaze on her. "Miss Minch, will you do me the honor of a dance?"

Having read all of Miss Austen's novels more times than she could count, she didn't think Mr. Darcy or Captain Wentworth could have sounded any more forceful, and her heart hammered oddly.

Mr. Thayer glanced down at the hand on his shoulder and shrugged it off. "Perhaps you aren't familiar with the rules of a cake dance," he said, "but here in Wyoming, if a man wins the bid for a lady's cake, that gives him the honor of her company for the evening, if it so pleases the lady."

"Is that so?" Badger said, edging between her and the attorney so that he was nose to nose with the other man.

"It is," Thayer told him, straightening to his full height and widening his stance.

"Well, actually just for the cake and the first dance, if we are being particular," Ninny offered, hoping to quell the rising tension between the two.

Neither of them was listening, but then again no one was, for the entire room had gone still as the two contenders squared off.

"Thayer, I say the lady has a right to dance with whomever she wants," Badger told him.

"You're wasting your time," the attorney told him. "The lady is taken."

Badger leaned closer. "You can't dance if you're out cold."

"I don't think you'd dare—"

Why is it men don't have the sense to just stop? Ninny wondered, even as they both began swinging. Wellington appeared from the shadows and began barking furiously.

The sheriff pulled her out of the fray just as Badger came crashing down where she'd been standing.

He swiped his nose, grunted something, and got to his feet, barely pausing as he rushed like an angry bull, sending he and Thayer flying in the other direction in a hail of angry words and fists.

"Ho, there," the sheriff shouted, wading in and catching first Thayer by the coat and then Badger by the arm. He ducked to avoid being punched then, quick as lightning, caught the pair by their collars and yanked them together so their heads hit with a mighty crack.

Ninny thought it might be over, but it turned out neither was ready to concede.

"You son of a bitch," Thayer said, wiping again at his bloody nose.

"Really?" Badger growled. "I'll show you, you no-good—"

"No you won't," the sheriff barked, stepping between the two. Mr. Fischer was usually such a congenial man, but that mask had slipped away, replaced by a hard, unrelenting set of his jaw. "You're both going to jail."

"On what grounds?" Thayer bristled, yanking his jacket into place and swiping back his hair, once again the no-nonsense lawyer.

"Disturbing the peace, to begin with," the sheriff told him. "Property damage, and finally for being a right awful pair of jackasses."

"If you think—" Mr. Thayer began.

The sheriff moved in close. "Try me, Archie," he said, "and I'll hold the pair of you until the circuit judge arrives in January."

"Me?" Badger shook at the sheriff's grasp. "I'm not at fault here. He started—"

"That cell will be awful cold come January," the sheriff warned. "So let's go. I promised Miss Barrett the next two-step, and I mean to keep my word."

Mr. Thayer took a deep breath and then looked over at Ninny. "My apologies, Miss Minch."

"Ma'am," Badger said, tipping his head, before the sheriff marched them both out to a chorus of ribald comments from the miners and tie hacks.

Hastily, the musicians struck up another waltz, and it didn't take long for the couples to find their way back to the dance floor.

Meanwhile, Ninny remained rooted in place, trying to get her bearings. All around her, knots of ladies whispered amongst themselves, in between shooting censorious glances at her, as if she, Parathinia Minch, had done it all on purpose.

"She brought that cake to spite Mrs. George L."

"Set Mr. Thayer and Badger to bidding against each other."

"I declare, she turned our cake dance into a boxing match. I never."

The only one not glaring at her was Cora Stafford, who was grinning from ear to ear and furiously scribbling into her notepad, if only to make certain next Thursday's edition wasn't missing a single detail.

THE MUSIC LED Madeline into the crowded hall, where the good citizens of Bethlehem were too caught up watching the couples dance or conversing with their neighbors to take any notice of her.

She took a swig from the bottle of whiskey, the hot raw liquid running down her throat. She closed her eyes as her stomach quaked at the fire burning all the way down.

Yet when she opened her eyes, a flicker of light caught her uncertain gaze.

Strung up overhead, antique Christmas lights—at least antique to her—glittered with the same captivating incandescence as the stars outside, just out of reach and twinkling, fairy-like, over the dancers. The hall might not be anything fancy, but those lights lent a spark that drew her toward something unnamed.

Just out of reach but, oh, so possible.

From the haunting notes of the fiddle to the click of the dancers' heels as the couples turned and swayed, Madeline found herself pulled deeper into the community hall.

There was a magic all its own to this night, and it twined its spell around everyone.

Even her.

On the stage, a red-faced fiddle player stood beside a pale man with a banjo while a tall, wispy woman with a puff of gray hair at the back of her neck plunked at the keys of a battered piano. They played a sad song, at least it felt that way, and yet the music had people smiling and dancing.

Like cogs, the dancers turned and then, *click*, turned and slipped together, each one essential to the other.

Pieces of a grander order. All belonging. All in place.

How could they move together so easily? How did they dance so effortlessly without any mistakes?

Suddenly Madeline wanted . . . No, she *longed* to be part of this pendulum swinging in time, without faltering, without hesitating. Because she'd never belonged anywhere.

Always the star, cold and alone and far out of reach.

But tonight . . . a different light beckoned.

Right there she stopped herself. She was drunker than she'd thought. She wasn't meant to be here. She wasn't part of this.

She was about to reverse course when her ears pricked at a conversation between two older ladies behind her.

"Just as I predicted, Parathinia Minch made quite the goose of herself tonight," the first one was saying with a dismissive shake of her head.

"Yes, but who would have imagined men brawling over her?" said the one with the blue dress, adding a censorious wag.

"Well, I never! I don't know who looked more ridiculous—Miss Minch, or those two fools bidding over her cake."

Ninny had baked a cake? She'd told Madeline quite firmly the day before that under no circumstances would she do so. What had changed her mind?

A quiver of guilt, or perhaps responsibility, or maybe a good share of both, ran through her. She'd urged the kindly woman to bake a cake and make good on her vow.

Wouldn't it be worse if you didn't show up?

Apparently staying home might have been the better part of valor.

One of the women clucked her tongue. "Why Mrs. George L. hasn't taken the matter in hand, I don't understand."

"At least one man in this town has his senses back in order," noted the blue-gowned biddy, tipping her head toward the dance floor.

Madeline looked as well, only to find Wick and a young lady in his arms swirling past.

"The sheriff couldn't do better for himself than Miss Barrett. Mark my words, there will be wedding bells before spring, and we'll be looking for a new schoolteacher."

"Yet again."

Madeline's ears perked up. The sheriff? Had a girlfriend? She tried to find him, but he'd been swallowed up in the tide of dancers. However, she didn't miss the next comment, given that it was slung at her.

"He can't do better. Miss Barrett is a decent woman." With a sniff and huff, the pair moved off.

Madeline ignored them, still fixed on that one bit of information. Wick had a girlfriend.

Not that she cared, but he hadn't mentioned as much. Nor had Dobbs, who was a regular font of all things Bethlehem.

The dancers came around again, and Madeline remained rooted in place, unable to move as the sheriff swept past her.

Wick. Dancing and smiling and laughing. The aforementioned Miss Barrett, gazing at him with starry eyes.

The whole scene turned like the old flickering silent movies her grandfather had starred in, one fixed image after another.

Wick grinning. Tipping his head down to hear whatever Miss Barrett was saying. His hand resting protectively on the small of her back.

And with just a few notes, they were swept away again.

Something inside Madeline ached. This night was like every other night of her life, one frame in a long reel of flickering memories in which she reigned only for a momentary pause. Never long enough to latch hold and become part of the greater wheel.

The warmth of the room closed in around her, and the whiskey roiled inside her. Everything in her line of sight seemed to confirm how much she didn't belong here.

Straightening, she remembered what she'd told Ninny.

Wouldn't it be worse if you didn't show up?

Well, here she was. She'd come for one dance, and she was going to have it. Even if it meant she had to dance alone.

She moved to the edge of the dance floor and closed her eyes, beginning to sway in time to the music. As it filled her ears, carrying her far from her current predicament, she began to gyrate, move in time. Her time.

Yet just as her hips found the right roll, the music abruptly ended, and she opened her eyes.

To find she was the only one on the dance floor. She shimmied again, just to make a point.

"Stop that! Cease this very moment!" came a strident protest. "I'll not have another shameless display tonight. I will not!" The imposing lady herself, Mrs. George L., loomed before her. "Leave. Immediately." She pointed toward the door.

Madeline, having encountered more than her fair share of grand dames in her life, starting with Gigi and her brassy cadre of former starlets, wasn't easily cowed. "I want to dance."

"Oh, no you won't," Mrs. George L. told her. "No one else is going to ruin the remainder of our respectable gathering. It is bad enough you are determined to wreak havoc upon our beloved town, but now we all know you'll lower it to intolerable depths—" The woman wrinkled her nose. "Good heavens, you smell like a ripe still."

Madeline looked around to make sure she had the attention of one and all. "Speaking of wreaking havoc, I am opening up the Star Bright Saloon, and everyone in this town will be welcome." She turned to leave, but remembered one more thing. "And by the way, Mrs. High-and-Mighty Temperance Union, how do *you* know what a still smells like? Do you have some personal experience with one you'd care to share with your fine neighbors?"

Mrs. George L.'s mouth flapped open but nothing came out.

"Just as I thought," Madeline said, and she would have said more, but here was Wick striding across the empty dance floor. He certainly looked ready to say something. Probably a lot of somethings, by the set of his jaw.

Yet the fireworks his arrival promised were interrupted by actual rockets outside. The first shrieking streak and explosion stilled the room. One and all turned toward the row of windows, where outside, a telltale flash of light, and another *rat-a-tat-tat* and *bang* announced the next round of entertainment.

The sharp arch of Mrs. George L.'s brows indicated that this latest shindig was as unplanned and unwelcome as Madeline's arrival.

Outside, there was another volley of *bangs* and *cracks* that sent the cake dance crowd hurrying toward the door. Madeline got swept up in the rush and soon found herself outside. Dobbs twisted past her and came to a stop by Wick.

"It's Mr. Wu," Dobbs told him. "He's gone and gotten himself drunk. Shandy sent me to find you."

"Drunk?" Wick shook his head. "No. You must have it wrong."

Oh, no, he's right, Madeline stopped herself from saying, tucking her bottle behind her skirt.

"Good and drunk," Dobbs confirmed, as if that held some special significance. "He's got a crate of fireworks. Them big ones you told him he couldn't have anymore. Well, he's got 'em out in the street, and he's fixin' to shoot 'em off. All of 'em."

Then, like that, the entire sky lit up in a shower of sparks and lights.

Madeline had one of those moments, the sort her publicist liked to call an "oh, shit" reckoning.

Unfortunately, Wick also knew that turn of phrase.

"Ah, shit. He's going to burn down the entire town." Having completely forgotten the theatrics inside, he was now in Sheriff Fischer mode. "Who would be so stupid to give Mr. Wu a bottle?" he asked as his gaze swept the street for the guilty party. "Because when I find them, they're going to jail."

For some reason, all eyes fell on her. The newcomer. Because clearly they all knew better. Madeline straightened and tried to appear quite innocent of wrongdoing. And she might have succeeded if only she could stand straight and not waver so.

Really, someone needed to explain *all* the rules to her.

Then, somewhere off in the distance, the bright light and crackle of flames began to rise. The men began to move, running and calling to each other. "Fire!"

"Oh, shit," she muttered.

"YOU WERE WORRIED the cake dance was going to be dull," Inola remarked, as they walked down the street, having finished up the dishes after everyone left in such a hurry.

"Mrs. George L. quite outdid herself, don't you think?" Savannah said the words with a straight face, but it wasn't long before they were both laughing.

"And a fight over Miss Minch of all people. Well, I never," Inola said, shaking her head. "Whatever has taken hold of the people in this town?"

"Not what, who," Savannah said. "Why just the other day, I saw Miss Minch fraternizing with Shandy's newcomer. Now look at her! That creature has turned the town upside down since she arrived."

But Inola surprised her. "I rather like the look of her. And the changes."

Savannah stopped. "If she can corrupt Miss Minch, none of us are safe. She's trouble, that's what she is."

"Well, newcomers have a way of shifting things," Inola said. "It'd be rather dull if things just stayed the same." She slanted a glance at Savannah.

There it was again, that perceptive, searching glance, and Savannah shifted from one foot to another before marching forward. "I had no problems with the ways things were."

"If that were true," Inola told her, grinning, "you would never have given that boy a nudge so that he'd bid on Myrtle's cake."

"Inola! Where do you get such notions? I did no such thing."

"You did, and I saw you do it."

"Oh, for heaven's sake, Inola," Savannah protested. "I merely mentioned to the lady next to me that it was a shame such a fine cake was going to waste—"

Inola's brow cocked.

Savannah started walking again. "And I might have mentioned your name."

At this, Inola groaned.

Savannah stopped again. "What? It would have been a terrible shame to see a perfectly good cake go to waste."

"You are going to have every single one of those girls at our back door for the next dance, trying to finagle me into making their cake." Inola cleared her throat. "Miss Inola, I want a cake just like Myrtle's, if you could."

Savannah laughed, looked around, and then lowered her voice. "Since I am the one who bakes those cakes, and given Myrtle's success, I suggest we up our price."

Instead of laughing, Inola straightened. "I saw what you did. What you've been doing."

For a moment she wondered if Inola knew the truth and had discovered what she'd been really hiding. Willing to brazen it out, she tucked her nose in the air. "What is that?"

Before Inola could offer up some Mrs. Livingstonesque observation, somewhere down the road a thin wailing cry cut through the night. It wasn't anything that they should be hearing. Not outside, not on such a cold night as this.

They hurried down the road toward the river.

"Oh, dear heavens," Inola whispered, her words coming out in puffs of steam, her gaze fixed on the low-slung house, where a lone figure stood in the stark shaft of light spilling from the open door.

Mrs. Bergstrom.

The scene was made all the worse by the realization that Mrs. Bergstrom wasn't wearing a coat, or even a shawl. Just her nightdress, and the baby in her arms wrapped only in a thin blanket. She hardly seemed to notice its cries as she stood there in the snow, swaying back and forth, humming an unfamiliar tune while she shivered violently.

"Honey, what are you doing out here?" Inola asked gently as she approached. "That child would be much happier inside. So would you." She shot a sharp glance at Savannah. *Do something.*

Yet Savannah was too shocked to move.

Inola took the baby from its mother and hurried inside, leaving Savannah behind with a woman who didn't even seem to notice that she wasn't holding her baby any longer, her eyes unseeing as she swayed.

She'd never really met Mrs. Bergstrom, other than in passing. She wasn't too sure she even understood English.

Savannah looked back down the street toward the Opera House, hoping someone else was coming along, someone who would know what to do.

Like Mr. Bergstrom. Or even one of the older children. Yet now that the fire in Mrs. Wallace's shed had been put out, and the dancing had resumed, the festivities would continue for some time.

Inola reappeared in the doorway. "Vanna, what are you waiting for? Get her inside before she freezes to death."

She nodded. "Come along. Your baby is inside."

For a second her words brought Mrs. Bergstrom's eyes into focus, and the look she gave Savannah held only pain.

Then she said something in her own language, words Savannah didn't need anyone to translate for her.

Leave me be.

They were the very same words she'd begged of Inola that long-ago Thanksgiving eve. *Leave me be. Let me die.*

Ignoring the woman's plea, much as Inola and Shandy had ignored hers back then, Savannah gently took Mrs. Bergstrom by the arm, and when she drew her close, she realized how young the poor soul really was—still in her mid-thirties at the most. Why, she must have had her oldest when she was still a teenager herself. "Come along, my dear, it's too cold out here. You wouldn't want the children to see you like this."

Even though she imagined they had.

Mrs. Bergstrom walked woodenly into the house, where Inola hadn't wasted a moment. The wee mite was now bundled in an extra blanket and held close, and Inola handed a hasty cup of weak tea to Savannah. "Get her settled."

Savannah nodded and guided the woman into the bedroom. It felt wrong being in this intimate place, one that should be filled with warmth and love but right now held only a deathly chill and shadows encroaching from all four corners. It wasn't hard to wonder what had driven the woman outside to stand under the indifferent stars.

Savannah shuddered.

"Come along, a bit of tea and a warm bed will help." It was a lie, but she tried to make her words sound comforting.

Mrs. Bergstrom muttered something, but Savannah had no idea what she was saying. So she tucked her into bed as if she were a child. Then she took up the cup of tea and pressed it into her icy hands. "Drink a little bit. Try to find some warmth."

Whether it was the warmth of the cup or Savannah's tones, she seemed to come to, blinking and looking around, almost startled at the sight of a stranger in her bedroom.

Inola arrived with a hot-water bottle in one hand and the baby curled in the crook of her other arm. She handed the jug to Savannah, who quickly tucked the large ceramic jar beneath the covers near Mrs. Bergstrom's feet. "Poor child."

"Which one?" Savannah drew back from the bed.

"Both, I imagine," Inola said, practical to a fault. She fussed with the blanket around the baby. "This child needs to eat, or he won't live."

Savannah hadn't the heart to look at him. She didn't want to see that he hadn't improved since the other day. But one thing was for certain. "She needs to eat something as well. She's thin as a rail."

And as likely to die as that poor mite.

Savannah turned wildly toward the door. It was all too much.

Inola noticed. "Why don't you fix her something to eat? I'll see if she can nurse." In other words, *don't even think about leaving me with all this*.

Savannah caught her breath and nodded, relieved to get out, even if it was just to the kitchen. Building up the fire in the stove, she found a single slice of bread and set to work toasting it. There was only a bit of butter in the larder—all the food from the other day was already gone. A look through the nearly bare cupboards uncovered a tin of pears.

They were probably being saved for Christmas or some other celebration, but living was cause enough, Savannah reasoned as she opened the can and dished out the fruit, cutting the halves into small bites. She found a large plate and used it like a tray, carrying the small meal to the bedroom. As she passed the window, she broke a small bit of pine off the greenery Livia had put up the other day and added it to the plate.

Inola glanced down at the bit of frippery and cocked a brow at her.

"Thought perhaps a bit of Christmas would remind the woman that life was meant to be lived. Births celebrated. That the darkness could always be banished with a bit of light."

"You thought that?" Inola snorted.

"I read it in a magazine column."

As it was, Inola had worked something of a miracle herself. She'd gotten the baby and mother together, the little fellow latched onto his mother's breast, with Mrs. Bergstrom holding him. Her gaze might still be fixed on that faraway place only she could see, but at least they would both be fed.

Savannah set the tray down on the nightstand. "How could they have left her alone?"

Inola shook her head, her mouth pursed.

Soft noises gurgled from the baby as he sucked. So he was managing to get something.

They shared a glance. It was a wee bit of light in all this darkness.

"Do you want me to go get him?" Savannah said quietly.

"That's not likely to help." For Inola knew exactly what Savannah intended—to give that big Swede a tongue-lashing. Starting with the state of his household.

"Let them have their time," Inola said, pulling a chair up beside the bed. "You go along home. Get some rest. I'll wait with her until they get back."

"That might be hours. Morning, even." Dances often went until dawn, when it was light enough to drive a team and wagon home safely.

Inola's gaze had never left the baby. "I don't mind."

Savannah nodded. "I saw some oats in the cupboard the other day. I'll put them on so she and the children have something in the morning. I just wish there were some raisins in the house."

Inola shook her head. "Putting raisins in the porridge isn't going to fix what's wrong here."

CHAPTER 20

Sunday, December 8
The second Sunday of Advent

From some faraway place, Madeline heard the saloon door open. Then she felt it.

A cold, icy spike of wind stealing inside. In fact, it was blowing.

"Dobbs! Come on. Close the door, will ya?" She stirred, rolled over, and looked out from beneath the blanket she'd dragged over her sorry carcass after she'd stumbled home.

"Dobbs!" she complained again, as the raw breeze kept coming. She scrubbed her face with a fist and opened one eye.

Wick leaned against the bar, staring at her. Clearly, he'd left the front door open on purpose.

No, make that, wide open.

Madeline sat up slowly, her head pounding from the previous night's escapades.

He set his hat on the bar and looked about to say something, so she cut him off before he got going. "Don't lecture me. Just close the door, please." Preferably with him on the other side.

"You're lucky you didn't spend the night in jail."

"Jail? What for?"

"Public intoxication. Lewd behavior. Oh, and getting Mr. Wu drunk—those fireworks burned down Mrs. Wallace's shed. Someone is going to have to pay for that."

Madeline cringed. She usually turned these sorts of crises over to her publicist or lawyer. Or both, depending on the scope. "There's gold in the till. Help yourself," she told him. "Then please close the door." She waved her hand toward the opening, one that felt like an expressway directly from the North Pole.

He puffed out a breath and grinned. "Trust me, this place could use a good airing."

"Then close it on your way out," she suggested, rolling over and pulling the blanket back over her head.

"Crawling under that blanket isn't going to change anything," he told her. "Nor will it fix your mistakes."

Mistakes . . . Hadn't Shandy been nattering on about mistakes last night?

I brought you here so you could step out of time . . .

Madeline pulled the blanket up higher just to annoy him, but that didn't stop a deluge of memories from assailing her foggy thoughts.

People dancing. Laughter. A sense of longing for place and community.

"Why can't you just leave me alone?" With her mistakes. They were old and dear friends.

"If leaving you alone means letting you drink yourself into a bigger mess, then no."

"That's my business, not yours."

"It becomes my business when you put the entire town in jeopardy. Including this saloon."

She opened an eye and looked around, for it felt as if the very walls quaked at the suggestion. If she wanted a sense of place, then somehow this spot, this building, had claimed her.

Wick's gaze bore into her. "Do you think you're the only one of

Shandy's lost souls to rail and drink and moan about their situation? A situation, I would point out, of their own making? Everyone pays their dues eventually."

Madeline blinked. He'd unwittingly echoed Gigi's last words to her as she lay in that awful hospital bed, wracked with cancer.

One day, Maddie, there will be an accounting for the way you leave wreckage in your wake. Drakes always pay their debts. Eventually.

It turned out Wick had the same sort of philosophy. "Probably the very reason Shandy brought you here. Always throwing caution to the wind, I'd guess. Doing the same stupid things time and time again. Tell me if I'm wrong."

He wasn't. The same things. Over and over. Taking the wrong roles. Hooking up with the wrong men. Refusing to listen to the people who actually gave a shit about her.

Like Nate. Like Gigi.

She'd never listened. She'd given up trying to be like those dancers moving to the music with the precision of a clock ticking.

Because, as she would point out to Wick and everyone else, the music always stops. Everything does. Except time.

Time.

In the silence of the room, there was a click and then a tock, and then she heard the unmistakable sounds of the clock on the backbar grinding to life, measuring the unseen movement of that solitary word. *Time.*

Madeline sat up. *Tick. Tick. Tick.* She stood as the stubborn hands began to move. All that was missing was the lines from the last scene Nate had written just for her—or for Calliope, rather. They'd shot it just before she'd bolted to Wyoming.

"What is time? I'll tell you what it is, Sheriff." She didn't miss a trick as she picked up a bottle and poured a shot for the cowboy on her left. *"Time is a river. A river with currents that run so fast they will sweep you away, drown you."*

"You can always change course. Stop it. Dam it up," he argued.

"You can stop a river?" She shook her head. *"The river will*

always find its way back to its true heading. There is no stopping it. It always wins. Except . . ."

He leaned across the bar. "Except when, Miss Calliope?"

"Sometimes there are eddies, where the river moves one way. And that eddy? Oh, she's a dangerous and deceptive mistress, curling up and stopping the clock, pulling you from your given course, trapping you in an unending circle from which you can't escape. She'll tie you up in a place so sweet and poignant you hope the current never catches up with you. And it won't, until you find the determination to change your course." She paused and corked the bottle. "That's what you have to watch out for in life, Sheriff. The eddies."

The same mistakes over and over. The realization slammed into her.

"I'm trapped in an eddy," she said aloud, hugging the blanket to her chest. "This place, this time, it's an eddy." She'd nearly realized it before, but now it made sense, as much as anything here could.

He nodded toward the empty bottle on the bar. "If that eddy is made up of whiskey, then I suppose so."

She ignored him, putting this realization together with Shandy's lecture. In time. Out of time. Eddies. This all was some sort of eddy in time. It was the only explanation, crazy as that was.

Meanwhile, Wick, despite his claim of not wanting to lecture, was doing just that.

". . . drinking away your problems and taking no responsibility for your actions? Sure, you're doing a damn fine job of that. Let me lend you a little bit of experience. I wasted a fair amount of time feeling sorry for myself when I got here. And I wanted to be here."

That brought her head up.

"Don't be so surprised. I was in a far worse way than you are."

Madeline blew out a breath, about to make some flippant, scoffing remark, when once again she heard that lonely train whistle, far in the distance. A note so sharp, so piercing, carrying with it a finality that threatened to consume her.

She stumbled back and then looked up to find him settling his hat back on his head, the echoes of another time having retreated.

What the hell had she just heard? Was that Wick's eddy? Time at its end?

"Always so sure, aren't you, Miss Drake?" He pushed off the bar and crossed his arms. "If you ever bothered to open your eyes and look beyond yourself, you might find an entire world filled with people whose problems outweigh yours." He looked about to give her a list, but he didn't need to. Their names echoed in his rebuke.

Dobbs. Miss Minch. Me.

Him?

Madeline sputtered, trying to compose a crisp denial, but Wick's attention had already shifted to a point over her shoulder.

A stricken Dobbs stood in the doorway, looking as if he wished himself well away from this sharp-edged conversation and all the icy tension that came with it. Madeline's heart clenched at the sight of him.

"There you are, kid." Wick shifted his tone so it rang with a friendly toll, and his smile warmed the space between them. "Was wondering where you were. We'd best get going. You know how much Father O'Brien frowns upon stragglers."

About as much as the sheriff did, Madeline suspected.

"I'm ready, sir," the boy replied, hurrying past without really looking at her. He plunked a small tin pail on the bar. "Got you something for when you get hungry."

Wick was already out the door, but Dobbs paused when he got there and finally looked back at her. "You gonna be all right?"

Madeline nodded. "I really don't have a choice, do I?"

He shook his head slightly as if the answer was obvious. "You always have a choice."

NINNY SAT in her usual pew at church, wishing she'd never gotten out of bed. If the sideways glances and pursed lips of the Ladies Aid members weren't bad enough, the elbow jabbing by their husbands as they recounted the previous night's spectacle with their neighbors had her slinking down in her seat.

She fixed her gaze on the altar and did her best to ignore the congregation. But that only meant that her mind remained stubbornly fixed on her most pressing, nagging problem.

She needed to confess the truth. But then it would look like she'd staged the entire thing only to . . .

As if on cue, Mr. Thayer strode down the aisle and took his seat, with nary a hair out of place and wearing his Sunday best. He hardly looked the worse for wear after a night in jail. If it hadn't been for the fact that one eye was swollen shut and ringed in bright red and purple, he would have looked as if he were about to argue a case in front of the state court in Cheyenne.

A few minutes later, in came Badger. She didn't dare turn around and look, but she had no doubt who had arrived given the rush of whispers and head turning and the very distinct click of Wellington's nails against the wood plank flooring. Besides, no one else brought a dog to church.

Ninny, for once, gave all her attention to Reverend Belding's meandering sermon on "The Long Wait of Advent." Which was ironic considering how long his sermons could be, and even longer when he lost his place. (Rather than chance leaving anything out, he usually just started over from the beginning much to the chagrin of his flock.)

So she settled in. With any luck, his sermon would ramble on past Christmas and she would be set free from her obligation.

That is until Mr. Belding kindly extolled his community of believers with one question.

"What are you doing while you wait for the light that will illuminate your soul?" He paused and then asked it again. "What are you doing?"

It was as if he'd said the words for her and her alone. Ninny's eyes opened wide—for it didn't seem like anyone else had noticed or heard his question.

What are you doing?

Wallowing in indecision, if she was honest.

She should just pick and be done with it. She knew most of the town wanted her to choose Mr. Thayer.

Yet the idea of doing what was expected churned uncomfortably inside her. Something needed to change. Now. This Christmas. This season.

What are you doing?

Just then, Mrs. Belding's arthritic fingers found the piano keys for the last hymn, miraculously hitting most of the right notes, and everyone rose and began to sing "Come, Thou All Mighty King."

Then one voice rose above all the others, a deep rich baritone steadying the notes from Mrs. Belding's haphazard playing.

Even Mr. Belding paused and looked up.

Badger. Singing the solemn hymn with a voice that filled the church. Throughout the pews, people turned to each other.

"Heavens to Betsy, did you know?"

"No! Did you?"

With shrugs and shaking heads and open mouths, they listened as if the heavens had dropped an angelic chorus into their spare church. A voice rich and deep, rising up from this scruffy bear of a man.

After nearly half a verse, Mr. Belding remembered himself and solemnly processed down the aisle, all while Badger's song rose up to the rafters, his singing lending the familiar words new meaning.

He gave them light.

That realization, that note, settled in Ninny's chest, even as Mrs. Belding struck the last chord.

The reverend's wife glanced up, her rheumy eyes blinking behind her spectacles, and beamed, for here was the entire room, holding on to that last note as if it were grace itself. Deaf as she was, she hadn't heard a wisp of Badger's singing, so she breathed a happy sigh that for once her indifferent audience had paid attention.

Likewise, Ninny shook herself out of her astonishment and quickly gathered her things, especially since Mr. Thayer was coming toward her. Their eyes met, and the man's face brightened.

"Miss Minch! A word if you would."

Light was a funny thing. For it not only opened the way, but it could spark things long in disuse.

"I would not," she told him with as much tart as she could muster. Then she slipped into the line of people filing out and stalked toward the door.

Behind her, she could hear him as he pressed through the knots of people. "Excuse me, Mrs. Jonas . . . Pardon me, Miss Winsley . . . If you don't mind, Mrs. Lovell."

Apparently the ladies of Bethlehem were not making it easy for him.

Heartened, Ninny got to the door and down the front steps, where she found Badger, with Wellington at his side, waiting for her.

"Miss Minch—"

How had she never noticed the timbre of his voice before?

Perhaps she had . . .

She shook away that errant thought and straightened. "Mr. Densmore." She nodded and went to continue on.

After all, she needed to get the post office open. Sunday hours, especially during the holidays, were extraordinarily busy.

But before she could take a step, here was Mr. Thayer already at her side. The lawyer glared at Badger.

"Densmore."

"Thayer."

Ninny shook her head. She hadn't time for their foolishness. She had a post office to open. A new path to discover.

"Miss Minch," Mr. Thayer said as he rushed alongside her, his hat in his hand. "I wanted to take this moment to proffer a sincere—"

Ninny paused, as did Badger, who made a small snort. He stopped when she slanted a sharp glance at him.

"As would I," he rushed to tell her now that he had her attention.

"Then get on with it," Thayer shot back, edging closer to Ninny.

Badger shook his head. "No, no, you first, Thayer. I believe you have more to account for."

"Me?" His incredulous utterance was followed by a glance at the knot of people around them. "I don't recall that I had anything—"

Badger blew out a breath. "I must have knocked you down harder than I thought if you can't recall what you did."

Thayer's features flushed, but he recovered quickly. "So you admit that you hit me?"

"It wasn't all that difficult, what with you just standing there, blathering on. But I suppose that is what they teach at that supposed school you went to—"

"Sir, I went to Harvard—"

"So you say," Badger shot back, crossing his arms over his chest.

Mr. Thayer bristled. "I will not be insulted in this manner."

"I think you already have been," Badger pointed out, winking at his audience.

Thayer's nostrils flared, but then he seemed to remember himself. "My only intention here is to apologize to Miss Minch."

"Then do so," Badger suggested, "and then I can get on with walking her home."

Ninny's mouth fell open. She wasn't the only one gaping, for Mrs. Jonas goggled like a whitefish.

"Perhaps you should first inquire if the lady wants your company —which I doubt," Mr. Thayer told him, edging in front of Ninny and giving Badger a shove.

So much for cooler heads.

Badger drew up to his full height, like a grizzly awakened before spring. "You need to apologize."

"I would if you would get out of my way," Thayer told him.

"Keep talking, Thayer, and you'll have both eyes swollen shut."

"Not this time," Thayer told him, and then he swung.

Ninny got yarded out of the way by none other than Mrs. George L. The furious matron spun on her husband. "Mr. Lovell, *do something!*"

Mr. Lovell eyed the brewing squall and, having gauged the opponents, took a step back. "I don't think this is going to last long, Columbia."

His wife puffed out a breath, looking now for the real object of her ire. "Wherever is Parathinia Minch?"

Odella Winsley pointed down the road. "She left."

"Indeed," Theodosia added, adjusting her spectacles.

Sure enough, the lady in question was striding down the road toward the post office at a pace that was sure and steady.

Across the street, the Catholic church was letting out, and the curious papists mulled about to get a better look at the commotion, since Badger and Mr. Thayer were still scuffling and hurling insults.

Well, something had to be done.

Mrs. George L. strode between the two, caught them both by the collars, and, just like the sheriff had, knocked their heads together. "Enough of this! I won't have such a display in front of the Catholics."

THE CATHOLIC PARISHIONERS LEFT ST. Michael's only to find a ruckus taking place amongst the milling Presbyterians across the street—which was all well and good in Savannah's opinion, for it gave her the perfect opportunity to slip home without —

"Yoo-hoo! Mrs. Clarke!"

Savannah cringed.

"Oh, what a happy coincidence. Someone to walk home with," Mrs. George L. declared, as she wound her hand around Savannah's elbow and then tucked her fingers into her thick fur muff, effectively locking Savannah in step with her. But the lady faltered a moment, looking around. "Where is Inola? I hope nothing is amiss."

"Asleep," Savannah told her. "And Mr. Lovell?"

"He had some unfinished matters to take care of," Mrs. George L. said, making a point not to look back.

Savannah glanced over at the lingering mob. "Trouble?"

Mrs. George L.'s nose wrinkled. "Men and their follies." After another glance in that direction, she tacked back to her original query. "Is Inola sick?"

As much as she didn't owe the woman any explanation, for Inola's sake, Savannah rushed to her defense. "No. It's just that she sat up last night with Mrs. Bergstrom while the family was enjoying the dance."

"She did? Am I to assume there was a problem?" One could always count on Mrs. George L. to tug at any loose thread.

Nor was there any point in trying to weave it back in. She'd unravel the truth eventually. "Yes."

"I can see that my faith was not misplaced, especially given what transpired last night. Your help—and Inola's," she added grudgingly, "was nothing short of a miracle."

"More happenstance than miracle, I imagine." Savannah had been awake most of the night with the image of Mrs. Bergstrom standing in the snow, babe in her arms, and that expression—or lack of expression—on her face.

Pale, cold, lost.

"And more Inola's doing," she added, though Mrs. George L. wasn't listening. They had come to the middle of town, and across the way, the wide front door of the saloon opened and Shandy's creature, came out, broom in hand, with that straggly dog at her heels. She glanced in their direction and then began sweeping the snow off the steps, paying them no more heed.

Not that the same could be said on their part. "Truly, she isn't going to . . . ?" Savannah began.

"Unfortunately yes." Mrs. George L.'s withering statement was followed by a loud sniff. "It seems Miss Minch's committee report to the Temperance Union was in error." She ruffled and drew herself up as they hurried past. "Something will need to be done. Posthaste."

Savannah didn't ask if she meant the newcomer or Miss Minch.

Still, Savannah couldn't resist taking another look back at Bethlehem's newest addition. Like that morning in front of the store, their gazes met. Defiance and determination glared back at her. How was it that Miss Minch—of all people—had fallen into such company? Under such an influence?

Why, the postmistress was going to find herself ruined.

"Back to the matters at hand," Mrs. George L. announced, letting go of Savannah's arm to wave all else aside. "I fear you might be stretching yourself too thin. Of course I welcomed your offer to help with the bazaar, but this apparent interest in Myrtle King will not serve."

Savannah's head swiveled before she could stop herself.

"Certainly it isn't my place to say," the woman continued, "but don't you think such a charity is beyond your resources?" She let that cold sentiment settle over Savannah's shoulders before she made her most stunning foray. "That is unless—and of course I don't mean to pry—you and Mr. King have developed—"

Savannah gasped. "Mr. King?" She shook her head. "You cannot be serious."

Instead of showing any signs of contrition, the woman pursed her lips and looked horribly disappointed. "Still, Myrtle King? I'm not sure what can be gained by placing your attentions there. She is who she is."

She is who she is? Savannah worked to find the words to respond, but Mrs. George continued on, certain her sentiment was hardly worth batting an eye over. "As it is, the Bergstroms are quite a handful, and then there is tomorrow."

"Tomorrow?" she replied before she could stop herself. But even as she uttered the question, the answer came to her. "The Athenian Society!"

Mrs. George L., already a few steps ahead of her, paused and turned around. "I am looking forward to an elegant afternoon."

They'd come to the path where Savannah turned toward her house while Mrs. George L. would need to continue up the hill.

"Until tomorrow, Mrs. Clarke," the matron said. "And don't forget what Mrs. Livingston says: 'Goodness out, goodness returned.'"

"Yes, goodness," Savannah muttered, pasting a tight smile on her face as she marched up the path through the cottonwoods.

It was their turn to host the Athenian Society. How had she forgotten?

As she went to open the door, she realized someone had hung a pretty pine wreath there. She hadn't noticed it this morning when she'd left—her thoughts had been too haunted with the events of the previous night.

"Why didn't you remind me?" Savannah asked as she came in the back door. It opened into the stillroom that served as their sewing room, with just enough space for Inola's desk in the corner. There she was, in her wrapper, a cup of coffee before her. It might be Sunday, and she might have been up all night, but Inola worked every day to keep them from starving.

Nor did she look up from her pages. "I assume you mean the Athenian Society. Why would I? I'm not a member."

Savannah's gaze rolled upward. "You might not be a member in name, but you still gain the benefits of membership. I only belong so—"

Inola set down her pen and finally looked up. "Yes, I know why you belong. You remind me every month."

"Then you might have reminded me that we are hosting tomorrow."

"*We* are not hosting. *You* are." Inola picked up her pen and continued to scratch at the page.

Savannah glanced away. "I don't make the rules, Inola."

She sighed, and her shoulders sagged from their taut lines. "I know."

But there was an implication there. *You could change them. You could speak up.*

Savannah knew she'd been invited to join only because Mrs. George L. was under the erroneous impression that she, Savannah, wrote the wildly popular Mrs. Viola Kinney Livingston magazine columns and essays, thus bringing a "literary air" to their humble club.

Literary air. Savannah would have snorted if that didn't go against every ladylike grain in her body.

Yet she hadn't gone to any lengths to disabuse the woman of that notion.

No matter how much she loathed the meetings. A bunch of feather-headed women who got together on the pretense of culture and literature, spent ten minutes discussing their haughty notions of fiction, and then whiled away the next hour and forty-five minutes gossiping, eating, and drinking tea. Books, newspapers, and magazines exchanged hands, and then they all traipsed home feeling quite civilized.

Yet it was that exchange of well-thumbed books and new magazines that made the Athenian Society one of the most coveted memberships in Bethlehem.

One could join only by invitation and only when a new member was needed—with the membership capped at twelve ladies. While the outward justification for this limited number was so that each lady would have the duty of hostessing only once a year, Savannah suspected it afforded them an excuse to keep others out.

"Those less refined," as Mrs. George L. was wont to say.

So, twelve times a year, on the second Monday of every month, Savannah endured their onerous company for Inola's sake.

For the books and magazines they could ill afford. The ones Inola devoured voraciously.

Savannah took a deep breath and then stripped off her gloves and unpinned her hat. She looked up to find Inola watching her.

"This time make sure to get *The Return of Sherlock Holmes*."

"Didn't I get that last time?" she asked as she hung up her coat.

"No, you got *The Memoirs of Sherlock Holmes*."

"There's a difference?" Savannah teased as she added her hat to the rack.

Inola opened her mouth and then closed it, shaking her head.

Savannah remembered something else. "When did we get a wreath?"

"Mr. Badger brought it by late yesterday afternoon." Challenge tinged her words. Oh, there would be no stopping Inola once the Thanksgiving leftovers were finished. Soon there would be holly on the sideboard, and then the crèche would find its way to the mantel.

"Inola!" Savannah shot back. "We can't afford that."

"We can. Don't you remember when he needed his socks darned last spring?"

"How can I forget? It took a week to air out the house."

"It did," Inola agreed. "But it was a small price to pay for such a fine wreath, don't you think?"

Savannah twinged. After all, it was Inola's wreath. Still . . . "You wouldn't mind if—"

"You put it on the front door?" Inola laughed. "Here I told Mr. Badger you'd wait until tomorrow to ask."

"It is very lovely."

"I told him you'd say that as well, so he said he'd bring one by for you."

"If . . . ?"

"If you do some mending on a coat of his."

Savannah sighed and then nodded. So much of their existence came down to this sort of bartering. She took a step toward the kitchen. "Whatever are we going to serve?"

Inola got up and followed her. "Why not bake an apple cake? I hear your grandmother's recipe is quite popular."

Savannah swiveled toward her. "Oh you!"

In moments, they were both laughing.

"Truth is, if it hadn't been for Myrtle, we'd be in a bad way," Inola admitted. "We have enough sugar and eggs left over to make a lovely sponge."

Savannah grinned. "I was thinking the very same thing." Besides, she loved a good sponge cake—with a nice filling of raspberry jam.

Inola nodded. "Helping that girl was the best thing you could have done, Vanna. I don't know why you did it, but you should keep on with it. Though next time you might suggest a chocolate cake."

"Nola!"

She grinned back, a twinkle in her eyes. "Remember what Mrs. Livingston always says."

Savannah sighed. "Goodness out, goodness returned."

IN THE RUSH of getting everything ready for the Athenian Society, Savannah had no time to consider the tangle that was Myrtle's Christmas wish. Yet that very question returned to bedevil her as she finished up the dishes, but before she could do much more than curse her own circumstances there was a knock at the back door.

"You expecting anyone?" Savannah asked Inola as she hurriedly dried her hands.

Inola shrugged. "Mr. Badger, perhaps?"

"This late?" Savannah wasn't convinced.

"Won't know until one of us answers the door." Inola nodded toward the oven. "You see to those cookies. I'll get the door."

Savannah caught up the potholders and pulled the tray from the oven, smiling at the perfectly golden edges and the scent of cinnamon and sugar rising up. Just in time.

Meanwhile, Inola had opened the back door.

"Hi, Miss Inola," came a cheery voice from the back porch. "My ma sent me over."

Savannah turned to find Billy Poole in the doorway, holding a large pile of books. The youngest of the four Poole children, he was taking after his brothers and sisters more and more—long-limbed and upright. Someone had once joked that the family name was spelled wrong. It should rightly be P-o-l-e.

"That's quite a load you've got there, Billy," said Savannah, smiling. "Why don't you put those on the table?"

"Thank you, Miz Clarke." He set the books down but his gaze remained fixed on the tray resting on the rack. "Those smell real good."

"Now don't they?" Inola agreed, ruffling his cap. "You've arrived just in time to try one and see if Mrs. Clarke got the recipe right." She grinned over the boy's head as his eyes widened with alarm.

"Inola is a terrible tease," Savannah reassured him. "Nonetheless, you tell me if these are any good."

Billy didn't need any urging. He stripped off his mittens. "Mmm. Good," he managed through a mouthful of cookie.

The pure joy in his eyes rather warmed her heart.

Goodness out, goodness returned.

"Now what is all this?" Savannah asked Billy, blinking away the sudden flicker in her chest.

"It's for the Athens ladies," he explained once he'd gulped down his prize.

"The Athenian Society," Savannah corrected.

He nodded. "Yeh, that. Ma has to go out to the ranch at first light and wanted to make sure all the books and such were here. She saw your light was still on and sent me over." He tipped his head toward the door. "I got the rest of 'em on my sled outside." He went back out and brought in another full armload, and then a box of magazines.

Vesta Poole, as the society's librarian, managed the club's subscriptions and book orders.

"That was very thoughtful of your mother," Savannah told him, knowing full well Vesta's thoughtfulness sprang from a very real fear of running afoul of Mrs. George L. if the meeting convened and the new magazines she liked weren't ready and waiting for her.

"I hope nothing is amiss at the ranch," Savannah said, trying her best to be polite even as she wanted to hurry the boy along. Inola looked ready to burst—she never had an entire night to go through the society's collection.

"Something about the cows," Billy said, his attention still fixed on the cooling rack of cookies. Savannah reached for another one and then, after a moment, took two, handing them to the boy and nudging him toward the door.

"Thank you, Mrs. Clarke."

"Mind the steps, Billy," she told him. "I wouldn't want to add to your mother's problems."

"Hms, thannm yomm," he replied, mouth once again filled with cookies.

After she closed the door behind him, she found Inola gaping at her. "You're feeling rather generous tonight."

"Did you see him? He looks thin as a rail." Savannah huffed a sigh. "I don't think Vesta feeds him enough."

"If you say so," Inola commented, already head down in the first box and pulling out one novel after another.

It was only once a year that Inola got a look at the society's entire collection—when they hosted the December meeting.

Even then, she had to appear as if she were merely neatly arranging the choices, for some of the members would protest vehemently if they knew that she was actually picking out what she wanted to read over the next year.

Oh, the war between the North and South might have ended some time ago, but it still raged on in so many other terrible ways.

And would for some time, Savannah suspected—ignorance and hatred being, as it were, in a never-ending supply.

Yet, what could she do? Rise up?

Someone ought to.

Oh, yes, that would be beneficial. The last time she'd protested, she'd nearly died, and Inola along with her.

So while Savannah turned her cheek at the slights and comments, the sly remarks, the outright slurs, she had to wonder: when would it ever end?

"Here it is," Inola said, in a voice filled with wonder.

Savannah looked up to find her grinning, prize in hand. "*The Return of Sherlock Holmes*," she read aloud. "I suppose you'll be solving crimes for the rest of the night."

"Someone ought to be," Inola said, her apron coming off before she hung it in a dash on the hook by the cellar door. She'd already opened to the first page and begun reading as she made her way upstairs.

Someone ought to be.

Savannah shook her head and smiled as she carried a stack of books and a handful of magazines out to the parlor table.

But Fate had her own way of doing things, and one of the magazines slipped free, the pages fluttering this way and that, until it landed, wide open, on the floor.

She found herself staring down at a full-page illustration of the perfect dress for a young lady—or at the very least, the perfect dress for Myrtle.

No fancy laces, no ruffled trim, just a lovely chartreuse silk dress with neat pleats and a smooth line.

At least so the smiling girl in the illustration—a thoroughly modern creature, what with her Gibson do and her stylish hat standing before a sleek motoring car. There was something so confident, so utterly capable about the young lady on the page, as if she possessed the keys to this fast-changing world.

It wasn't Myrtle's dreams she saw staring up at her, but her own. Had she been that young once, so full of life, looking forward to the challenges ahead with nothing but confidence? Full of dreams and wishes?

She shook her head. Look at what her girlish yearnings had lent her—a life of sorrow and pain and guilt. A shadow life without color.

A life of waiting.

Savannah took a step back. Waiting for what?

Absently, she set down her armload, her gaze fixed on the windblown, winsome beauty staring up from beside a shiny motoring car. Who would have ever dreamt of such a monstrosity? Yet someone had latched onto that idea, that wish, and made it come true.

Now one could just speed forward—anywhere. They were no longer stuck in one place.

And while Mrs. George L. and others might think of Myrtle as stuck, Savannah realized that the capable young woman, who efficiently tallied all the orders in her father's store in her head, didn't deserve to be hemmed in. Yes, she held dreams close to her heart—for a new dress and, most likely, someone special—but there was no reason she shouldn't be allowed to speed forward in some dizzy fashion.

Why should Myrtle spend her life waiting?

Having discarded the other books and magazines, Savannah scooped up the magazine—the November issue of the *Delineator*—and sat down at the table and did something she hadn't done in quite some time.

She looked at the world beyond her own prison of lost dreams and wishes.

CHAPTER 21

Monday, December 9

Savannah had read the copy of the *Delineator* from cover to cover, as well as the latest issues of *Harper's Bazaar* and *Modern Priscilla*. It seemed she and Inola weren't the only ones who needed advice on economies, like reworking old gowns, and new forms of employment. Now there were typists and clerks and something called a "hello girl."

For the first time in, well, forever, she went to bed with a wish in her heart.

That she could make a new dress for Myrtle.

She even whispered a little prayer for Mrs. Bergstrom, but that seemed an almost impossible hope.

Yet she'd awakened to the cold reality that she could hardly conjure a gown from thin air. If anything underscored the perilous state of their finances, it was when she opened the tea tin, an hour before the Athenian Society meeting was due to begin, only to find it empty.

She looked in the canister again. They had no tea. At least none that hadn't already seen the inside of the teapot. Twice. Oh, of all the dreadful embarrassments. This would never do.

There was nothing to be done but make a hurried trip to the mercantile and hope for Mr. King's continued largesse.

She thought nothing of it until she opened the door, and all the conversations, all the attention turned toward her. After a long, pregnant pause, heads turned toward Mr. King and then back toward her.

She straightened and marched forward.

"Mrs. Clarke!" Mr. King enthused from behind the counter. His greeting broke the spell, and the conversations began anew. "Isn't this a pleasant surprise. Twice in as many weeks. To what do we owe the pleasure of your company this morning?" He pushed aside the collection of bundles and boxes in front of him.

"I need some tea," she told him, not daring to look around.

"Ah, the Athenian Society. You're hosting this afternoon, aren't you?" He made his way back around the counter and got out a large tin of tea from one of the lower shelves. He held it for a moment, as if hesitating, and then looked her directly in the eye. "Mrs. Clarke, I hate to say this, but . . ." He leaned closer. "It is getting close to the end of the year, and I've carried your account for far longer than I would anyone else's."

So much for his gratitude. What would she do if she had to entertain without tea?

Straightening up and picking at her gloves, she said, "I've been assured that there is payment on the way, sir." At least she hoped there was. She met his serious gaze and managed a tight smile. "I do promise to see our accounts paid in full before Christmas."

"I trust you will." Then he nodded and turned. "Myrtle, will you please help Mrs. Clarke with some tea?"

Of course. Savannah clamped her lips together to keep from cursing the Fates, and worse, here was Myrtle, clad in a plain brown skirt, white shirtwaist, and a brown apron, her hair primly pulled back. The girl, bobbing and weaving her way through the crowded store, couldn't look more like a bespeckled wren if she tried.

For a moment, Savannah saw her as she might be, in the perfect silk dress like the one in the magazine.

Then she reminded herself why she couldn't continue this farcical dream. She hadn't the money for the thread she'd need. Or the buttons. Or even a bit of lace.

Not to mention Myrtle's measurements.

After all, she was here to get tea she could ill afford—tea that hadn't been reused.

Reused. Like . . .

Like an old dress being remade.

A flitting memory of the pretty gown in the *Delineator* swept past her, however Savannah didn't have time to chase that bit of fancy, for the bell over the door jangled anew, and Myrtle came to an abrupt halt halfway down the aisle, her eyes widening and a quick rosy blush blooming on her cheeks.

Savannah turned to see what had stopped the girl's usually hurried tracks—only to find Junior Lovell striding in as if he owned the ground he walked upon.

Him.

Hadn't Junior had been one of the most avid bidders for Myrtle's cake? No wonder Mrs. George L. had made those disdainful remarks.

She is who she is.

Well, Savannah could agree with the woman on one thing: Junior Lovell was all wrong for Myrtle. The girl shouldn't pin her hopes on such an arrogant lout. For a second, Savannah was glad she couldn't help her.

"Mr. Lovell!" Pinky Jonas made a sudden appearance from a back aisle, her dark hair perfectly piled atop her head like one of the pretty models in *Modern Priscilla*, her coat nipped in at the waist, and a bright ribbon winding around the hem of her skirt, as beguiling as the girl beneath. "What are you doing out today?" She wound her way past Myrtle with a forward manner that suggested she was the only one in the store worth perusing.

Savannah did her best not to notice, but inside she was seventeen again, full of those fluttering longings as she stood at the top of the stairs while her stepsister, Sybilla, hurried past to greet their newly arrived visitor.

Lucius Maddox. Why, aren't you the most handsome fellow in three counties . . .

Savannah had spent the next three months watching in anguish while Sybilla flirted, danced, and then married Lucius, only to send him off to war. Sybilla cried prettily for all to see, while Savannah was forced to stand silently and endure the spectacle. *Her* Lucius.

Savannah straightened and gave her head a slight shake. Had he ever been hers?

He certainly hadn't been hers the night he'd come home from the war. Bitter. Defeated. His wife and child dead. He'd come to her room that night, bent on vengeance and . . .

Pinky's nasal tones snapped Savannah's attention back to the matters at hand.

"Are you and Jacob going up to the mine this morning?" Pinky curled her arm around Junior's and pulled him toward the stove, completely ignoring the young man who followed in Junior's wake. "Why, you might freeze to death," she said, following up with a *tsk-tsk* that was both censorious and inviting.

Junior pried himself free and handed over a list to Mr. King. "Mr. Norwood asked for this to be sent up today while it's not snowing." The merchant glanced over it, nodding as he went. "I'll see what we have, Junior. Why don't you and Mr. Kearns go warm yourself up over by the stove? Goldie, see about getting these boys some coffee."

"Yes, Papa," she said, smirking as she crossed paths with Myrtle and leaning in close to whisper something that had her sister blushing again.

Then it happened. Savannah's carefully stacked defenses toppled with one word.

As Goldie passed the counter, she asked, "Hey, Jacob. Two lumps of sugar, right?"

"Three," Myrtle whispered under her breath, half a second before Jacob said the very same thing.

Savannah looked from Myrtle to Jacob and back to Myrtle again.

The girl wouldn't have known that unless . . . unless her heart was set on Jacob Kearns.

A young man with studious features and a quiet determination so very similar to Myrtle's own restrained pride. If Savannah recalled correctly, he'd been outbid very early Saturday night but had added his coins to Peter's bid.

Oh, Inola was right. She should pay more attention to these matters.

With his spectacles fogged up in the warm air, and his heavy coat —covered with a crust of snow—creating puddles wherever he stepped, Jacob murmured his apologies and took a direct route toward the stove, hurrying right past Myrtle.

Without a word.

The girl let out the breath she'd been holding, and with a slight shift in her posture, gathered herself together and got back to the matters at hand. Notebook flipped open, pencil in hand, she returned to her usual unflappable efficiency. "Do you need anything other than the tea, Mrs. Clarke?"

"I need some good silk sewing thread," Savannah said, without even thinking.

After another moment, the rest of her wits came roiling forward. *What are you saying?* After all, however can one make a dress without fabric? Or measurements, for that matter?

Even as Myrtle opened the thread drawer, her gaze still tracked in the direction of the Kearns boy, dragging Savannah's attentions down that path as well.

"Something for a dress," she remarked absently. The boy was a decent-looking lad. None of Junior's bluster and bravado.

"Did you have a color in mind?" Myrtle had turned her attention back to the variety of spools the store carried, a veritable rainbow to brighten the dead of winter.

"Yes," Savannah repeated before she could stop herself. "Something pretty."

Myrtle smiled, then sorted through and finally selected a spool. "Like this?"

"Oh my." Savannah wanted to groan. A shade of green she knew so well.

Myrtle held on to it, turning it this way and that. "I love this color. Chartreuse, isn't it? Don't you think it would make a pretty—" She stopped as Goldie passed by, mugs of coffee in hand, toward the stove where the boys were warming their hands. A bit of longing flitted across her expression but she quickly recovered, as efficient a shopkeeper as her father. "Will this do, Mrs. Clarke?"

"I fear it would," Savannah admitted, leaning closer, until she glanced up and saw Mr. King watching the pair of them. Tallying one more debt. One she couldn't pay. "But I mustn't. Just the tea."

So there it was. She handed the spool back to Myrtle even as Shandy ambled in. Of course. The infuriating man had a way of showing up every time she found herself at these crossroads.

Well, she just wasn't going to be part of his Christmas shenanigans.

Mr. King, meanwhile, went over and greeted the town enigma enthusiastically. "What have you been up to this fine morning, Shandy?"

"Getting a bath at Mr. Wu's and a shave at Silvio's." He rubbed his chin. "I feel like a new man." His bright gaze lit on Savannah.

She ignored him as best she could.

"Wu's, you say?" Mr. King leaned over the counter. "Frankie, have you taken the laundry over to Mr. Wu?"

Francine King's expression curled up much like Savannah's mood. "No. I was going to help Mr. Grierson down at the smelter. The turbine is having—"

Her father was already shaking his head. "How many times I have told you? That is no place for a girl. Now take the laundry over to Mr. Wu so he will have it done before Thursday. And then come right back."

Francine looked ready to protest, but she was cut off as the door jangled anew. Mr. King was off toward his next customer, full of his usual effusive greetings.

"Don't forget my dress," Myrtle said over her shoulder to her sister. "The one I wore Saturday night."

Francine waved a hand and hurried toward the back.

Savannah stilled. Myrtle's dress.

She made the mistake of letting her gaze wander over toward Shandy and the wretched man had the nerve to wink at her.

No. This is all impossible, Savannah wanted to tell him in no uncertain terms. Whatever was she supposed to do? Waylay Francine in the alleyway to measure the dress? Or, worse, break into Mr. Wu's?

Of all the ridiculous notions. She glanced back at the spool of thread Myrtle was even now dropping into the drawer, in a shade of green she knew all too well.

Miss Savannah, don't you look as pretty as an April day.

Why, thank you, Mr. Maddox.

I was wondering if you were free for this dance?

As it happens, Mr. Maddox, I am.

He'd held out his hand and smiled, all charming and a bit wicked. *Then may I have the privilege of your company?*

I would be ever so delighted.

"Are you waiting for something else, Mrs. Clarke?"

Savannah blinked and found Shandy standing at her elbow, his gaze flitting between Myrtle behind the counter and Jacob cradling a cup of coffee by the stove. She stiffened.

"No, I have everything I need," she said as she turned toward the door.

"Or you will soon enough," Shandy said after her.

Are you waiting for something else?

Oh, bother Shandy and his implications, Savannah fumed, as she marched toward home. Never mind Myrtle's dress was on its way to Mr. Wu's laundry. It might as well be on its way to the moon—right next to the money they needed to pay their account at King's.

Her toe hit a lump of ice, and she stumbled. All around her the world was locked in winter, and she couldn't help but wish for the verdant kiss of spring—and right away she blamed that spool of thread for putting such a whimsical notion in her head. As she righted herself, however, she remembered how Myrtle's usually penny-plain expression transformed when she'd watched that Kearns boy. Anguish and desire. And her, trapped in her sister's hand-me-downs and a tide of doubts.

Hand-me-downs. Made-over silks.

Savannah stumbled again, this time over her own shock. Why hadn't she thought of it before? The green silk gown in her trunk! It would be perfect.

But there was the issue of Myrtle's measurements . . . That, and Mr. King's obvious dismay over adding even the cost of a penny spool of the thread to her account.

She huffed and looked up to get her bearings. She'd managed to miss the cutoff through the cottonwoods and ended up down toward the river . . . and in front of the Bergstrom house. She paused for a moment, lips pursed, as its small, sullen windows looked reproachfully back at her, reminding her of her other, more pressing obligation.

Savannah heaved a sigh. This obligation couldn't be repaired with a pretty spool of thread or a well-placed ribbon around a frayed hem. But as she waffled between guilt and indecision, her quandary was decided for her.

The door flung open and Mr. Bergstrom, as lofty and blonde-headed as a snow-capped mountain, stooped to come out and then rolled down the newly shoveled path. "Mrs. Clarke! Here you are. Like a miracle."

The next thing she knew, she was being hustled up the walkway and into the house, protesting the entire way. "Mr. Bergstrom, no, I cannot . . . I'm in a hurry . . . I've got—"

Obligations, she'd been about to say, but that was before she found herself face to face with a trio of obligations on the narrow bed in the corner, watching the proceedings with wide eyes and a hungry, resigned look.

A whimper from the cradle near the stove added to that number.

There was no sign of Mrs. Bergstrom, just that closed door. Savannah's teeth gritted together. Whatever was to be done?

But if the door seemed a permanent fixture, here was Mr. Bergstrom, shrugging on his coat even as he spoke in a hurried rush of broken sentences. Something about a problem at the mill, and Livia having a test at school, and she'd be back in no time.

"But Mr. Bergstrom," she protested, even as the dratted man flew out the door and it closed with a thud behind him. "Oh, my land! Men!" She glanced over at the children and around the room. Dishes sat stacked up in the deep sink. There were empty plates on the table, also in need of washing. Not to mention a trio of skeptical children.

"Where is Livia?" the little impertinent one asked, her round blue eyes threatening tears as she climbed down and toddled over to Savannah, boldly leaving her twin and younger sister to fend for themselves.

"School, your father said." Savannah took another glance around the disheveled house. "But I need to go home. I need to . . ." Her gaze landed on the closed door to the bedroom. She'd all but forgotten the children's names, that is until she got a bit of assistance.

"I'm Berta," the little girl told her. "That"—she pointed at her twin—"is Margit. We look alike, but she doesn't say much."

"I suspect you say enough for all three of you," Savannah told her. Astute little monkey, this one.

The girl grinned as if she'd just been bestowed the finest of compliments. "And the baby is Clara. Well, she's not the baby anymore," she added, with a glance at the cradle and the interloper it held. But Berta, pragmatic to the core, moved quickly to a subject nearer and dearer to her heart. "Did you bring cookies?"

Savannah shook her head, thinking of the plate of ginger snaps on the drainboard, waiting for the Athenian Society.

Oh, heavens! The Athenian Society! She glanced over at the cuckoo clock on the mantel. Yes, there was still time.

"I will bring some by later," she promised, replacing the apron hanging near the door with her coat, her need for order racing to the forefront. She marched over to the wood box, muttering, "There had better be . . ." And, thankfully, she found it full.

"Thank heavens for small favors," she told her towheaded

shadows. "First things first," she told Berta. "We are going to get you all cleaned up. Then we'll make the bed and do the dishes." Savannah went over to glance in the cradle, and Berta leaned over as well, her nose pinched.

"Nappy first," she directed, with all the sage wisdom of one pointing out a task that was not in their realm.

CHAPTER 22

*J*uggling a selection of her purchases and two wreaths—the rest having been promised to be delivered—Madeline found the uneven snow wasn't as much fun to navigate on the way back from King's mercantile as it had been on the way there.

"It would be helpful if you could carry something," she muttered at Dog as he ambled beside her. He wagged his tail and continued to lead the way.

She paused for a moment to rejigger her load when an older man, wearing a bowler hat and a wide, affable smile, approached her. He seemed well dressed—until he got close enough for Madeline to see the fraying on his coat.

Dog glanced over his shoulder at this latest arrival but gave him scant regard, clearly viewing him as no threat.

Madeline decided to trust the mutt.

"Do I have the privilege of addressing Miss Drake?" An Irish lilt touched his words. Without waiting for a reply, he tipped his hat and took the wreaths into his capable grasp.

She liked him immediately, for no other reason than he seemed a bit of a rascal.

"I don't know how much of a privilege it is," she replied, "but, yes, I'm Madeline Drake." She juggled the basket and wished he'd taken that instead. "You are . . . ?"

"Erasmus P. Quinby, attorney-at-law. At your service, madam." He bowed slightly and then fished out a business card that was well printed but worn around the edges, rather like the man himself. Dobbs had mentioned him once or twice, and always with a bit of awe.

"You have the offices above Mr. Wu's laundry," she said, reminding herself of the shabby sign and wobbly stairs.

He nodded. "I do. Don't mind the extra heat in the winter, but the summers can get a bit stifling."

"I'd imagine so," she agreed.

He fell in step with her. "Miss Drake, if it isn't an imposition, allow me to be quite frank."

"I would suppose nothing less of a purveyor of the law."

"Ah, you are a connoisseur of my trade."

"I've had the need from time to time." She shifted the basket, and the distinct clink of bottles sent his eyebrows arching upward.

"Given the makeup of that bundle"—he glanced at the basket— "might I assume the rumors are true that you plan to reopen the Star Bright Saloon?"

"They are." No need to pretend otherwise.

"So you'll be serving alcohol?"

Madeline gave the man a sideways glance. He wasn't part of the Temperance Union, was he? Then she remembered what Dobbs had said—that he frequently purchased bottles for Mr. Quinby, so that rather eliminated such a possibility.

"I simply beg a favor of you," Mr. Quinby continued. "Please, no more intoxicants for my good friend and tenant, Mr. Wu."

She flinched. "Don't worry, the sheriff has given me much the same warning."

"Oh, this is not a warning, just a favor being begged," Mr. Quinby said, striding over the ruts in the snow and going up the stairs of the Star Bright with the vigor of a man half his age. "As you might have witnessed on Saturday night—"

"I didn't know."

"No, that display wasn't your fault, nor do I blame you. Wu has a way of finding newcomers."

"I had no idea—"

"That he cannot hold his liquor?"

She shrugged.

"Precisely," Mr. Quinby said.

They'd gotten to the door, and Quinby, without missing a beat, hung one wreath on a nail on one side of the doors and placed the other on a matching hanger on the other side.

Now here was someone who knew this town. This saloon. Intimately. Much like Dobbs.

Satisfied with the placement, he reached over and opened the door, holding it for her. "Wu has an unfortunate lack of control when it comes to rum."

"And whiskey," she muttered under her breath as she closed the door.

"Pardon?"

"Nothing," she told him, making a beeline for the bar and hefting the basket up on top. The jars inside rattled anew.

His sharp gaze narrowed. "Mr. King or Mr. Hoback?"

"Excuse me?"

"Who sold you the liquor?"

"Mr. King."

Quinby shook his head. "Hoback will give you a better deal." He looked around. "Does my heart good to see this place reopened. This town hasn't been the same since it closed, and that was . . ." He scratched his chin and then shook his head as he settled onto one of the stools. "Well, I can't recall how long, but I'm dearly parched from waiting. Tell me, can you make a decent Manhattan?"

So he was going to test her. She turned to the backbar and took down a cocktail glass along with a tall bar glass. Chipping ice from the block in the box, she added the bits to both, then set aside the cocktail glass before quickly gathering the rest of her ingredients. When she got to the vermouth, she asked, "Dry or sweet?"

"You're the one who knows what she's doing."

She eyed him, and then made her decision. Dry. Measuring and pouring and finally stirring, she dumped the ice out of the now-chilled cocktail glass and strained her concoction into it. Pushing the finished drink across the bar with one finger, she nodded at him to give it a try.

He took a wary glance at the front door, then reached for the glass and brought it up for a tentative sniff. Apparently satisfied, he took a slow drink. His eyes widened, then he tipped the glass and finished it off. Every drop. After a short wheeze, he grinned. "You do have some experience in this line of work."

That surprised pronouncement made her grin. "Some." She'd prepared for the role of Calliope by working with one of LA's best bartenders, and over the years she'd become the darling of charity events, making drinks and posing for pictures.

He set down his glass. "Can you cook? You'll need some food. Nothing fancy, just something to bring the boys in for lunch or an early supper."

She hadn't even thought of that. Certainly no one wanted to eat her cooking. "Know anyone?"

He scratched his chin. "Well, the best cook in town is, bar none, Miss Inola. You'd have a stampede coming through those doors if you convinced her to cook for you." He leaned closer and lowered his voice. "She and Mrs. Clarke could use the extra money—not that you heard as much from me—though I highly doubt Mrs. Clarke will cozen to such an idea."

"Wouldn't that be up to Miss Inola?"

He laughed again. "You aren't from around here, are you?"

She shook her head.

He pushed the empty glass back across the bar and nodded for another. As she mixed, he got down to business. "Miss Drake, I would be derelict in my duties as your advisor and legal intercessor if I didn't warn you that you are going to kick a hornet's nest if you reopen this fine establishment."

Madeline grinned and began chipping more ice. "I've weathered my fair share of trouble."

"Really?" He shook his head. "I doubt you've dealt with the likes of Mrs. George L. Lovell. Columbia can be a veritable . . . ." He caught himself, as if suddenly remembering his audience.

She paused, spoon in hand. "Troll?" Having stirred the liquors together, she strained them into the cocktail glass and slid it back across the bar.

"Troll? I rather like that, though I do believe the *au courant* turn of phrase is busybody." Before he reached for the glass, he took another glance at the window, where the street beyond sat empty, before taking another long, appreciative sip. "I really shouldn't be imbibing so early in the day. Besides, if the sheriff were to see you serving—"

"—without a license. Yes, I know." She laughed a bit, until she saw Mr. Quinby's brow arch again.

So he was serious.

Quinby pushed back a little. "You mean to tell me you haven't a license?"

She shook her head and then realized he was both asking a question and giving her free advice. She quickly put the bottles under the bar.

He nodded and then tossed back the rest of the evidence. "I have no doubt Mrs. George L. and the Temperance Union will rather insist that the sheriff throw you in jail."

As if Wick needed another excuse. "Then I'd best get my license."

"Yes, but I will point out that you are currently not in the sheriff's good graces, or so say the prattling tongues of this fine hamlet."

"A temporary problem, I assure you. Leave the sheriff to me." Madeline wished she felt as confident as she sounded.

He pushed back from the bar and smiled. "Well, then, I see that my help isn't necessary." He grinned at her, gathered up his hat, and began to leave.

"Mr. Quinby?"

He glanced over his shoulder. "Yes, Miss Drake?"

"There might be another matter I need assistance with. A far more controversial one."

"More contentious than a single young woman of questionable origins running a saloon?"

She grinned. "Yes."

Erasmus Quinby tipped his head, studied her for another long moment, then settled himself again atop the stool. This time his expression took on a serious pall. "Just how controversial?"

So she told him.

❋

SAVANNAH HAD JUST GIVEN the bread dough a final knead when the door to the Bergstrom's cabin opened.

Livia hurried in and stumbled to a halt, open-mouthed at the sight that greeted her.

Everything had been picked up, cleaned, and swept. Dishes were stacked in the open shelves, and the table was tidy and ready for the next meal. There was a moment of stunned silence before the little Bergstroms clamored up, each offering their bit of news.

"Livia! Livia! Come look." Berta caught her hand and towed her to the middle of the room. "I had a bath."

"Me too," Margit added, in an uncharacteristic burst of speech.

"Oh, my," Livia breathed out, even as she gathered her youngest sister in her arms and settled her on her hip. "Mrs. Clarke! Did you do all this?"

Savannah brushed at the flour dusting her apron. She was tempted to similarly brush off the girl's shock and doubt with a tart reply, but what she'd assumed was disbelief turned out to be gratitude, evidenced by the sheen of tears in Livia's eyes.

Gracious heavens, she didn't know which way to look. So she got directly to the business at hand.

"I've mixed some bread, and it should be ready to bake in an hour." Savannah glanced around, taking a quick inventory. "I fed the children and, as you heard, gave them a bit of tidying as well."

Livia grinned at her little sisters, the twins preening especially at her attention.

Savannah continued, "I gave the baby some tinned milk—it was all I could find. And I tried . . ." She glanced at the bedroom door. *I tried with your mother.*

"Yes, well, Papa says patience is needed until she's recovered—" The ache in her words left the rest unsaid. *If she ever does.*

"I fear I must be going," Savannah hurried to say. "I've quite lost track of time, and the Athenian Society begins at promptly two o'clock."

"But Mrs. Clarke, it's half past two."

"Half past?" Savannah's gaze flew up to the clock, which read twenty to the hour—as it had the last time she'd looked. "That cannot be."

Livia's brow knit together. "That's odd. The clock usually keeps perfect time."

"Oh, no. Oh, no." Savannah tugged off the borrowed apron and hurried to the door, catching up her coat and hat.

"Cookies?" Clara reminded her as she straightened her hat.

"When I return," she told her, her words coming out a bit tart.

Too tart, apparently, for those blue eyes looking up at her filled quickly.

Oh, not another torrent of tears. Dear heavens! This family.

"I promise," she said as softly as she could manage, even as she had visions of Mrs. George L. storming about her parlor, calling for her head on a platter. Still, with the threat of tears before her, she leaned over and gave the child a kiss atop her downy head. "I promise, dear one. I will."

This time she would.

She hurried up the road, and as much as she wanted to sneak in the back door, she wasn't about to come stealing into her own house as if she'd done something wrong.

Still, she braced herself as she opened the front door, only to be greeted by loud whoops of laughter.

She didn't think she'd ever heard such merriment from the members of the Athenian Society. Ever.

"No! Such a simple problem—"

"'Cept if you are poor Mrs. T." More laughter followed.

"But certainly that letter isn't real?"

Letter? Savannah took another step inside, her hat still on her head.

"Mrs. Clarke! You must forgive us, we started without you." Mrs. Bohlen was the nominal chairwoman of the club, though everyone knew who was truly in charge—the lady seated in the best chair in the middle of the room.

Mrs. George L. Lovell. But even then, Savannah had to do a double take. The usually overbearing matron looked positively jolly. If she didn't know better, she'd think that Inola had been doling out her grandmother's holiday punch, wherein the celebratory part and main ingredient was elderberry wine.

But that wasn't even the most shocking sight. For here was Inola, seated to the right of Mrs. George L.

Inola. Seated with the Athenian Society.

Good heavens, just how long had she been at the Bergstrom's?

"Mrs. Clarke, why there you are. We were about to send out reinforcements," Mrs. George L. teased—yes, actually teased—for here she was winking at her audience.

The rest of the ladies lapsed into more whoops.

Savannah caught hold of the door jamb. "It appears I've missed quite a bit. My sincere apologies, but after I picked up the tea—"

"Tea?" one of the ladies said, giggling slightly. "I must say I much prefer this punch Inola was able to mix in a jiffy."

Oh, she hadn't . . .

"Divinely refreshing," Mrs. Jonas added, smiling sincerely.

Apparently she had.

Savannah looked over at the nearly empty bowl and then back at Inola, who just shrugged a "what did you expect me to do?"

She wrenched her gaze back to the collection of ladies and smiled weakly, hoping Inola hadn't used the entire bottle. For she suspected she'd need a very tall glass later. "As I was saying, I was waylaid by Mr. Bergstrom and—"

Mrs. George L. waved her hand, dismissing any further words. "Inola thought as much. She explained your deep and abiding concern for the situation—and how it has taken up so much of your time."

"Did she now." Her gaze took anchorage on Inola, who sat primly amongst the club members, hands folded in her lap, and a smile twitching on her lips as if she'd never had such a grand time.

"Indeed," Mrs. George L. replied. "That was when dear, dear Inola thought of the most wonderful way we could assist you."

"Assist me?" she managed, absently reaching up for her hat and unpinning it. "I haven't the least . . ."

Then she noticed what was off about the room, aside from the gaiety and good spirits, and Inola settled in amongst them like a graceful swan.

Not one of them held a book. Or a magazine.

Every lady had a collection of letters clutched in her hand or in her lap.

Savannah's mouth fell open and her gaze flew to Inola. Letters addressed to Mrs. Livingston.

Inola hadn't. She couldn't have!

Mrs. George L. tut-tutted at her shock. "Mrs. Clarke, you mustn't blame Inola. We quite winkled it out of her. Many of us have known for some time."

"Known?" she whispered, still fixated on the letters in their hands.

"That you are Mrs. Livingston, of course," Mrs. Jonas blurted out, earning a glare from Mrs. George L., who had planned on making the announcement.

"Mrs. Livingston?" Savannah managed, looking over at Inola.

"I didn't think you'd mind," Inola demurred.

Mrs. George L. nodded toward Inola, as if they were the best of friends and co-conspirators. "Inola thought we might be able to lend a hand with some of your more difficult letters."

"It's been our honor," Mrs. Bohlen confided.

"Exactly so," Mrs. Jonas agreed.

They all looked up at her expectantly, as if every one of them was awaiting her blessing.

"Oh, my gracious stars," she managed as she sank into the only empty chair.

Inola grinned to one and all. "I told you she'd be ever so gratified."

THE POST OFFICE door flew open, and the bell overhead jangled sharply, as a flurry of skirts and feathers bustled inside, bringing with it the sharp bite of December.

"Miss Minch! Miss Minch! We just realized the date."

Ninny wanted to cringe. Not the Winsley sisters, not now, and worse, in more than their usual panic.

She shot a warning glance over at Madeline, who had arrived a few moments before and looked ready to explode with some news.

Odella all but shouldered Madeline out of the way, laying down a flowery penny postcard that seemed out of place given the piles of snow outside. "We were cataloguing last summer's discoveries when Theodosia wrote down the date. The date, Miss Minch! I was ever so certain she was wrong—"

"Which I was not," Theodosia added with a sniff.

"No, you were not," Odella agreed and then turned back to Ninny. "You cannot imagine our horror."

Ninny could.

"We feared we were too late," Theodosia added, placing her postcard on the counter while Odella fished around in her purse for the necessary change.

Ninny had heard this question more times today than she could count. "No, not at all," she assured them. "Mr. Lovell has yet to pass this way, so your cards will arrive when he goes home for supper."

The ladies sighed in unison.

"Too late for what?" Madeline asked, arms crossed over her chest.

Odella glanced at her and then leaned across the counter and lowered her voice. "I fear she still might feel snubbed by its late arrival. It should have been mailed no later than Friday last." She glanced at her sister as her teeth worried at her lower lip.

Ninny exchanged the pennies for stamps and then smiled at the pair, hoping to soothe their feathers. "Not at all. You know I must be discreet, but let me say that yours will not be the only deliveries for Mrs. Lovell today."

Madeline leaned between the two sisters and looked at the postcard. "Many Happy Returns of the Day," she read. "How lovely. Is today Mrs. Lovell's birthday?"

"Of course not." Odella blinked in surprise, as if such thing should be common knowledge.

"Perhaps I should send her a card as well," Madeline teased.

Odella reached out and patted Madeline's arm, pressing her lips into a benevolent smile. "My dear, I don't think that would be advisable." After a moment, she returned to the business at hand. "The invitations haven't gone out, have they?" she whispered to Ninny.

"You know I cannot divulge such private post office business."

"No, no, of course not," Odella replied. Then she added, "I only ask because, as you know, one needs *time* for these occasions."

"To get things in order," Theodosia hastened to say.

"Invitations to what?" Madeline asked.

The sisters scowled, clearly wishing the town's latest arrival well away from *their private conversation*. But Madeline hadn't the least idea she was being snubbed.

If she had the sense of it, it didn't appear to matter. She stood transfixed, watching as Ninny added the postmark over the stamp carefully so the ink didn't smear, and then waved them in the air to dry before placing both greetings into the already crowded slot allotted for the Lovells' mail.

This wasn't the first time she'd had the sense that Madeline was watching ordinary events around her as if she had never seen such.

"This is the week that Mrs. George L.'s birthday party invitations go out," Ninny explained. "Wednesday, if Mrs. George L. remains true to form."

Of course, she would.

The Winsley sisters shuddered in unison. "One can always hope that this year . . ." They shared a glance as if neither knew what to say.

"You'll be invited?" Madeline prompted.

Theodosia spoke—as she nearly always did—without thinking. "Oh, heavens no. Quite the opposite." Her hand went to her mouth, but the cat was out of the bag.

Of course, Madeline had to ask. "What is so wrong with Mrs. Lovell's birthday party?"

"Mrs. George L.," Ninny corrected, more out of habit.

"Mrs. George L. Lovell's birthday party, then," Madeline amended. "How can it be so dreadful? Other than for the obvious reasons . . ."

"Oh, my dear, it is ever so much a trial," Odella supplied.

"Least of all what it does to one's nerves," Theodosia added, with a woeful shake of her head.

Madeline's brow furrowed. "But I thought everyone spent most of their time trying to curry her favor."

Ninny pressed her lips together. How Madeline just said things, out loud. She struggled to explain. At least before the Winsley sisters did. "That much is true, but her birthday party is an entirely different matter."

"How so?" Madeline continued.

Unfortunately, Odella was more than happy to expound, clearly forgetting that she was talking to Miss Drake. "It is the mark of social distinction to be invited, but . . ." She glanced away.

"But?" Madeline prompted.

Theodosia carried on. "It is always fraught with disaster."

"Fraught?" Madeline laughed. "That sounds fun."

The Winsley sisters shook their heads. "Oh, you wouldn't dare say such a thing if you had ever been invited."

Having warmed to the subject, Theodosia couldn't help but confide, "Every year there is some terrible disaster."

"Every year?" Madeline asked, looking toward Ninny for confirmation.

Which she provided. "Without fail."

"Such as?"

Of course, Madeline would want to know, and leave it to Odella to have an example at the ready. "Oh, heavens. There was the year when the oysters were not as fresh as they ought to be."

At this Ninny nodded and cringed. She remembered that year well.

"Oysters?" Madeline was asking.

"Mrs. George L. spares no expense for her birthday luncheon," Odella explained. "There are never fewer than seven courses."

Madeline took a step back. "That seems rather pretentious."

None of them argued.

"And there was the year Mr. Lovell's dog got into the cake before it could be served." Theodosia sighed. "Six layers of sponge and a nice buttercream filling."

Madeline nodded in agreement. "Now that is a disaster."

Theodosia brightened. "So you do understand."

"Bad oysters and a purloined cake. I mean, what else could go wrong?"

Ninny paused, opened her mouth, and then closed it again, while Odella and Theodosia grimaced.

"What?!" Madeline exclaimed. "Oh, come on! You can't just make faces like someone died and then not say anything." There was a hurried shift of glances, and Madeline's jaw dropped. "You aren't saying—"

"Old Mrs. Mott." Ninny closed her eyes and said a hasty prayer. As did the Winsley sisters.

"You mean to say she died?" Madeline whispered. "At the party?"

"Yes!" Theodosia supplied.

"How?"

"No one precisely knows." Ninny's brow furrowed. "She just nodded off during the speeches, and no one thought anything of it. She was known for closing her eyes as she composed her thoughts."

Madeline drew back. "Hold on. There are speeches?"

"Oh, yes. There is the toast, and then others are . . ." Odella paused as she searched for the right word.

"Compelled," Theodosia muttered.

"Encouraged, sister," Odella corrected. "Yes, encouraged to get up and give their personal salutations. It is all rather . . ." She searched again.

"Superfluous?" Madeline offered.

"Taxing," Theodosia provided, using the benefit of experience, though she garnered a reproving nudge from her sister. But that didn't stop her from adding, "Somewhere in the middle of all that adulation, Mrs. Mott expired. There she was, smiling and, for all we knew, dozing quite contentedly. But when we got up to go into the parlor for the recital—"

"There's a recital?" Madeline appeared to be keeping score.

"Of course," Theodosia replied. "What else would follow speeches?" She blinked and continued, "Once it became apparent that she wouldn't be joining us for the recital, Miss Lovell burst into tears. Poor thing, she'd been practicing her piano piece for weeks."

"A pity," Madeline offered.

Theodosia shook her head. "Oh, no, she played. Her mother insisted. It was rather uncomfortable, but it did pass the time until Dr. Groves could be fetched."

Madeline began to shudder with what looked to be the most morbid fit of laughter.

"You don't understand." Ninny's words were filled with rebuke, for she wasn't going to laugh. At least not in front of Odella and Theodosia.

"I might point out that last year Mrs. Brisbin went into—" Odella continued rather eagerly, until she got to the part where she had to explain. "Well, I do so hate to be indelicate—"

"I have no problems with indelicate," Madeline assured them. "Mrs. Brisbin didn't expire as well, did she?"

Which gave Theodosia her opening. "Poor Bessie was with child, and in the middle of her toast, she . . . Well, her—" Whether her courage faltered or she ran out of air, she resorted to a quick pantomime, fluttering her hands in a wide circle in front of her skirt and making a big grimace.

"You mean her water broke?" Madeline asked.

Odella nodded. "Right as she began her toast."

This time, Madeline laughed. Thoroughly. "That must have added to the festivities."

"You have no idea." Ninny shuddered at the memory. "She ought not to have come, but Mrs. George L. had asked her personally to give the toast."

Theodosia always hated to be left out, so she added, "I suspect nerves added to her distress."

Madeline bit her lips together, but, unable to stop herself, she laughed again, then Ninny did as well. Odella and Theodosia looked at each other as if they had no idea what could be so amusing.

"One shouldn't laugh at the misfortunes of others," Ninny advised —mostly herself.

"Poor Mrs. Brisbin," Madeline said, managing to get through it with only a small giggle.

"It wasn't so awful for Mrs. Brisbin—she was delighted," Odella pointed out. "After four girls, she had a beautiful baby boy." Then came the sad shake of the head. "But for Mrs. George L., it was all so vexing."

Theodosia supplied the rest. "She had to have her carpet replaced."

With that, Ninny and Madeline started laughing again.

Once they'd composed themselves, Madeline had to ask. "What was Mrs. Brisbin doing there so close to her due date?"

"How could she refuse?"

Madeline's brows quirked and she spoke very slowly. "By saying no?"

Odella sucked in a deep breath. "Miss Drake, one does not say no to Mrs. George L."

"Whyever not?" It was a question that had been asked around Bethlehem for some time, and yet the answer was obvious. At least to Ninny and the Winsley sisters.

"My dear, eleven invitations are sent out. Eleven only," Theodosia informed her. "It is a rare and distinct honor to be included."

"Only eleven?" Madeline asked. "I have a friend back home who throws a birthday party every year, and some years, there are so many people you can barely get in the front door."

"Mrs. George L. would consider that crass," Theodosia advised.

"The real reason," Odella rushed to advise, "is more practical. Her dining room table seats only twelve comfortably."

"There are no added tables or side tables for Mrs. George L.," Theodosia added. "She does not like to crowd her dining room and considers such practices uncivilized."

Or she just likes to keep the number limited to make the invitations that much more coveted, Ninny thought but didn't add.

"With Mrs. Jonas all but assured her spot every year at Mrs. George L.'s right hand, and Mrs. George J. at the other end of the table, that leaves only nine open chairs," Odella explained.

"The nine," Theodosia breathed, almost like a prayer.

"Sounds like a combination of Russian roulette and musical chairs," Madeline said. Before Ninny could ask what she meant, the young woman continued. "How is it I haven't met Mrs. George J.?"

"Not met her?" Theodosia's brows drew together. "That is rather surprising, considering Mrs. George J. is the—"

"Sister!" Odella hissed.

Ninny thought a good kick would have been a better admonishment. There was one rule that every lady in Bethlehem understood: you didn't bring up the subject of Mrs. George L.'s mother-in-law unless you absolutely had to.

Now the cat was out of the bag.

"Is this Mrs. George J. anything like her daughter-in-law?" Madeline asked.

"Oh, heavens, not in the least," Odella advised.

"I have heard that on occasion she likes to play poker," Theodosia offered.

"Sister!" Odella exclaimed. "Remember yourself. One could end up like Mrs. Garland."

"Let me guess: she was electrocuted," Madeline posed. "No, she forgot her speech."

"Oh, far worse," Theodosia explained. "Mrs. Garland bears the unhappy burden of being stricken from the guest list. Forever."

"To her great shame," Odella explained, "her husband recklessly proclaimed at a Masonic meeting that he'd voted for Theodore Roosevelt over Alton B. Parker. As one would expect, once Mrs. George L. heard that . . ."

All three women paused as if remembering a fallen comrade.

Mrs. Garland, for one. And Mr. Parker, if one dared.

CHAPTER 23

*a*n odd pounding at the post office door stopped Ninny halfway down the hall. She looked back at the clock and assured herself that she was justified in saying, "Closed for the day."

Another spate of pounding replied. Certainly whoever was on the other side of the door was determined.

It wasn't quite knocking, she thought, but more like hammering. "Oh, for the love of Pete," she muttered as she went to the door and yanked it open.

Badger stopped halfway down the front steps, wet and bedraggled. It had started to snow again, and the flakes were falling all over Wellington, who waited patiently at the bottom.

"Miss Minch, I thought you were closed for the day," he said, shuffling a bit. "Didn't want to intrude, but merely leave an apology."

She stood her ground. As much as she wanted to send him packing—postage due, mind you—she had to admit the man sounded sincere. Besides, she'd hardly be charitable if she sent him away without giving him a chance to say his piece.

She nodded for him to continue.

"Well, like I said," he began, stumbling a bit over the words, "I'm sorry."

Well, she hadn't expected poetry. At the very least, Wellington looked sufficiently contrite, looking up at her with those large brown doggy eyes.

Then Badger nodded to the side of the doorway. "I thought some Christmas cheer was needed." She looked over, and there hung on a new nail was the most beautiful wreath she'd ever seen. Truly it had had been put together with great care—cuttings of pine, fir, and spruce all blended together so their varied greenery created a feast for the eyes. Sprigs of holly stood out, the berries dancing like bright red stars amongst the deep green boughs.

"Good heavens," she managed. Perhaps fancy words weren't particularly necessary for an apology. Then she opened the door wide and stepped back. "Might as well come in and get warm."

What are you doing? Reverend Belding had extolled on Sunday.

Indeed, what *was* she doing? She glanced out at the empty street and felt a moment of relief that there was no one about.

Badger shuffled his boots a bit. "No, miss, I'm a muddy mess. I couldn't."

"I know how to sweep," she told him, tipping her head again. "I won't have it said I sent you off to freeze to death."

He tipped his head in appreciation and came inside, ducking as he went.

Ninny forced a smile to her lips and was about to shut the door when she looked down at his dog. "You as well. What are you waiting for?" Wellington didn't need any further urging. He was hot on Badger's heels and all but sighed when the door closed behind him.

"I was just about to put on a pot of tea," she remarked. "Why don't you come back and dry out a bit before you head home."

She didn't even know where his home was. Though she knew he had a solitary cabin up in the hills. Was it snug? Clean? Did he get lonely like . . . like . . .

She did.

She hurried toward the kitchen, sidestepping the accumulated Christmas shipments that lined the hallway.

"That's a lot of packages," Badger noted as he wove his way through the collection.

"That's only the beginning."

He glanced back and made a low whistle. "All of them for Christmas?"

She nodded. She'd learned over the years not to think of the gifts and surprises they held, the joy they promised. Yet it was nigh on impossible now, what with Badger eyeing them with open-mouthed wonder.

When she got to the kitchen, she hardly knew what to do. Certainly, it wasn't the first time he'd been in her kitchen. Over the years, Badger had done odd jobs for her. Brought her firewood, fixed the parlor door that stuck from time to time.

But this felt different.

"I've always liked this room." His quietly spoken confession rather soothed her ruffled sensibilities.

Ninny smiled and then remembered herself. "Thank you," she managed as she went to the sink to fill the kettle.

Badger stripped off his mittens and warmed his hands, his eyes half closed, while Wellington got as close to the stove as he dared before he settled down.

"Move over, you great ponderous beast," he told the dog.

But the animal gave him scant regard. The same couldn't be said of the feline occupant of the room.

Bingley sat up from his cushion and hissed.

"Really, Mr. Bingley," Ninny scolded. "We have company."

Wellington hardly glanced up. After all, he had the best spot in the room, at least by his canine estimation.

Bingley made an affronted circle on his cushion and then settled back into a loaf so he could keep an eye on this unwelcome arrival.

Ninny looked up at Badger to find his lips twitching, which only served to prod her own laughter, along with his.

"It seems they've found a way to get past their differences," he remarked.

Ignoring the implication, she finished filling the kettle. "Why don't you hang your mittens there on the pegs? They'll dry quicker."

"Thank you."

She nodded and set the kettle on the stove, sidestepping Wellington.

Without thinking, she lifted the lid of the pot on the back and gave the stew a stir. The smell of venison and onions and tomatoes filled the small kitchen.

Both man and dog closed their eyes and inhaled, though Wellington was not above turning his gaze expectantly to Ninny.

"I suppose it wouldn't do to send the pair of you away cold on the inside. You can apologize while you eat."

"I thought I already did," he said with a wry note.

"You want to eat?" Ninny had no idea where that waspish statement came from, but it elicited a snort from her guest.

"Then I suppose I'll come up with something more," he agreed.

Ninny nodded and gave her stew another stir, yet Badger remained at her side, peering into the pot.

"Whatever is that?"

"Spanish stew," she told him. "I found the recipe in this." She tipped the book so he could see the front.

"*The Methodist Ladies Companion Cookbook,*" he read.

"It has quite a number of perfectly good recipes—for Methodists, that is."

He chuckled. "Miss Minch, I didn't take you for a snob."

"I'm not, but Mrs. Jonas was raised a Methodist—not that she'll admit it now—and she cannot cook a lick, despite all her claims of her mother's prize-winning recipes."

"So you've condemned the entire faith because of Mrs. Jonas?"

"Have you met Mrs. Jonas?"

"There is that," he agreed. Nodding toward the pot, he asked, "What is in this Methodist stew?"

"Spanish stew," she corrected, and then flipped the book back open. "Oh, the usual that goes in a stew. Tomatoes and onions, but then you add cloves, sage, a bit of orange peel, and a large, finely chopped chili pepper." She peered down into it and smiled. "All that needs to be done is thicken it a bit and make some biscuits."

When she turned, she found the man had already decamped to the sink, sleeves rolled up, and was taking up the cake of soap.

"Let me wash up and I'll finish up the stew," he said. "I wouldn't want anything to hold up an offer of biscuits."

She laughed. "You?"

"I cook," he said, straightening a bit. "You can't eat beans from a can three times a day, so I've learned a thing or two." He glanced around. "If you can be so kind as to share your supper with the likes of me, the least I can do is help. Now, where do you keep the flour?"

As much as she wanted to shoo him out of her kitchen, she couldn't. Because those words—*the likes of me*—spoken so bluntly, left her at odds.

Whatever did that mean? Oh, she'd heard the rumors about Badger over the years. All of them. He'd murdered a man. He'd escaped a madhouse. He'd ridden with an outlaw gang.

But she knew he wasn't any of those things. Well, perhaps he had ridden with an outlaw gang once, but he was hardly that man now.

"The flour?" he asked, innocently enough.

She looked up and nodded at the canisters near the sink. "The tall one."

Certainly he had connections in London. Once a year he got a letter from a lawyer—rather a solicitor—with an address in Lincoln's Inn, but she hadn't the least idea of the contents of those letters.

She did know he never posted a reply. At least not from her post office.

As for Badger, he'd mixed a respectable-looking slurry of flour and cold water and was slowly adding it to stew.

But he was watching her.

"What?" she asked.

"Aren't you going to make the biscuits?"

"Oh, yes!" she exclaimed. "I fear you caught me woolgathering."

"About?"

"Postal matters." She turned to get her favorite mixing bowl from the shelf. So unused to having someone else in her kitchen, suddenly the room felt as close as a broom closet. She glanced over at Badger again, but all she saw was something else. "Those mittens of yours are more hole than mitt."

"I can cook, but I'm not much for darning."

"So I see." Having measured out the flour and the salt, she began cutting in the lard.

"I don't see anything fancy about the way you make your biscuits."

"They're just biscuits."

"The whole town knows that isn't true. Not when you make them."

"Well, now you know—they aren't anything fancy."

"Humph." Having stirred the slurry into the stew and edged the pot to the cooler side of the stove to finish, he found the silverware drawer and set the table, all with a casual efficiency.

From his spot on the chair, Bingley regarded all this domesticity with his usual air of disdain.

Then, to her horror, Badger picked up Mrs. Mercer's book. "*An Improved and Forthright Life for the Modern Woman*." He shook his head. "Don't see why anyone would want a modern life, let alone a forthright one."

She wiped the flour off her hands but stopped short of the snatching the book away, for something else surged through her.

"Why would you, Mr. Densmore? As a man, you have everything you want." There. She'd said it. As straightforwardly as Madeline might.

"And you don't?" he asked. "Women these days have the vote. At least here in Wyoming."

"Yes, here, but not for the greater elections, the ones that matter most in shaping our great country's future."

He leaned back and studied her. "Miss Minch, I never took you for a suffragette."

She'd never thought of herself as one either, but suddenly here she was, hands fisted to her hips. "Why not?"

"Because clearly I was a fool." He smiled, and when he did, his entire face lit up, his blue eyes merry and his lips wide and charming. Suddenly she wondered what he would look like without that great raggedy beard, or perhaps with his hair trimmed up nicely.

"So tell me," he asked, settling into the chair beside Bingley's as she gathered the shaggy biscuit dough into a pile of layers on the counter, "however do you plan on finding a forthright life here in Bethlehem?"

"WHATEVER ARE YOU DOING?"

Savannah wished she hadn't jumped at this interruption, but she had. Nearly out of her chair. Gathering her wits about her, she looked up at Inola. "Reading."

Inola gave a rueful snort. "You?"

"I read." Savannah shook out the magazine and turned her attention back to the page before her.

From the doorway, there was another snort. "*Modern Priscilla*? Since when did you start reading fashion magazines?"

"I read fashion magazines."

Inola snorted. "Not since *Godey's,* and I don't want to count the years since you pored over those pages."

"Please don't." Savannah never liked to think about the endless time that had passed since they'd come here, but it had become more obvious this afternoon as she'd looked, really looked, at the dresses everyone else wore to the Athenian Society. How had she not noticed how out of fashion she and Inola had become? They looked like relics beside the other ladies.

And it wasn't just their old dresses that set them apart.

As every year passed, it became more and more evident that she and Inola had not aged all that much, stuck as they were in Shandy's devilish trap. Not that anyone would point out such a thing, at least not in polite company.

You change by growing, Mrs. Clarke, he'd told her once when she'd complained about his timeless prison.

Change, indeed. No wonder Shandy had put that ridiculous wish in her path to nudge her along.

If there was one thing Savannah abhorred, it was being managed.

Still, she hadn't minded listening to the cheery—albeit punch-soaked—conversations that fluttered about the room like canaries set free. They chattered on about shirtwaists, pin tucks, and even something called a "motoring coat." Not that anyone in Bethlehem needed one, since there wasn't a single motoring car in town, but the very idea seemed to transfix the younger matrons.

"Just in case," Mrs. Hatchett told her audience sagely, relating a debate she'd recently had with Althea over tweed or worsted for such a costume.

The older set went on about getting the puffs just right in one's hair and the right face creams to keep one's youthful glow. It was as if Savannah had suddenly awakened after a long, dreamless sleep and found herself left far behind.

And that, she supposed, she liked least of all.

Inola shifted. "So what has you suddenly reading fashion magazines?" She cocked her head to one side. "Mrs. George L. thinks you are helping Myrtle as a way to spark Mr. King's—"

"Inola!" Savannah felt her cheeks warm at the very suggestion. "When did you start listening to that woman?"

"Well, she was rather a fount of information today." Inola smiled, her eyes twinkling.

"Only because you got her tipsy," Savannah pointed out.

"I did, didn't I?" Inola hardly sounded penitent. "I also got six months' worth of columns answered. Now I'll have plenty of time to finish the last three installments of that serial."

Which was the real benefit of the day, for Savannah knew serials were lucrative, as long as . . . "Has Mr. Wakefield promised to pay?"

Inola grimaced. "Not until publication." There was a rather lengthy pause before she added, "Of the last installment."

Savannah sat up. "That could take—"

"Months."

"More like years," she scolded. So much for her promise to pay their mercantile account by Christmas. "You can't keep agreeing to these egregious terms. The man is taking advantage of your talents. Why, you should—"

"Do what? Go to New York and march into his office? I wouldn't make it past the front door."

Now it was Savannah's turn to look away. Her eyes lit on the empty cordial bottle on the drainboard. "However did you end up in that mare's nest?"

"What was I to do?" Inola sighed. "You weren't here, and then Mrs. George L. went bullying her way up the stairs to visit your 'writing sanctum.'"

"My what?"

"You heard me," Inola said, shaking her head. "She was halfway up before I waggled a fistful of letters at her and pleaded for her help with your more pressing problems, considering how taken up you are with Mrs. Bergstrom's plight."

"Oh, Inola, that was just devious." But it still didn't explain the other thing. "Whatever induced you to stir up a bowl of Grandma Audie's Christmas punch?"

"I had to find some way to keep her from continuing her speculations about you sparking after Mr. King." Inola cocked a brow as if asking the same question.

Are you?

Savannah closed her eyes and groaned. *Of all the . . .* "You're listening to the same foolish woman who thinks public libraries lead to licentious behavior."

"That still doesn't answer why you're helping Myrtle King. Don't even try denying it."

"I helped the girl with a cake. That is hardly a cause for speculation or matchmaking."

"And this sudden interest in fashion?"

Oh, bother Inola. She could give Mrs. George L. a run for her money in the Pestering and Prying Department. "I'll have you know I'm reading a perfectly good article on mending, and I just finished an excellent one on crocheting filet lace."

"That's it. I'm taking you to see Dr. Groves tomorrow."

Savannah snapped the magazine shut—more out of a desire for Inola not to see the article she was actually reading, "Reworking Old Silks for Modern Fashions." "I have no need for a doctor. I'm in perfect health."

"Perfect health!" Inola swept the magazine right off her lap and shook it in front of her. "This says otherwise." Then she opened the magazine and thumbed directly to the spot where she'd been reading.

So she had seen it. Oh, drat.

"Reworking Old Silks—" Inola began. She stopped there and threw a wary glance over the top of the magazine. "What are you considering?"

"You know as well as I, we haven't the money for new dresses."

"True enough," Inola muttered. Then she paused and looked up. "Why do you need a new dress?" That suspicious edge returned. "Is that why you're suddenly helping Myrtle? Because you think marrying Mr. King will solve all our difficulties?"

The empty bank account. Nearly all their jewelry gone. She hadn't even worked up the nerve to tell Inola about Mr. King's warning. He wouldn't be so polite come Christmas, when he discovered they hadn't as much as a spare penny to their name and wouldn't for months.

"Is that why you've been coming up with any excuse to go to the mercantile of late?"

"We were out of tea," Savannah pointed out, even as she realized she was being boxed into a corner.

"Tea you conveniently left at the Bergstrom's."

Savannah got to her feet. "Stop this. Right now. I have no interest in Mr. King. None. Any further speculation is ridiculous and beneath you. I would never drag a respectable man like Mr. King into my past."

For there it was. The truth.

"Your past? Oh, Vanna, that was so long ago," Inola began quietly. "'Sides, it's not like anyone has ever come nosing about."

Savannah was shaking her head. This discussion was one they hadn't had in some time, but it never failed to bring with it the same spinning abyss. The sense that the world could twist precariously on its edge, dumping them into a dark chasm.

"This place isn't like others. We're safe here," Inola said. Promised, really.

"I know," Savannah agreed, finally finding some air. She took a hasty, greedy breath. "But that doesn't mean we should go out and invite trouble."

Inola shrugged. "I suppose not." After another silence, a sly smile pierced the grim air still stuck between them. "So if you aren't out sparking with Mr. King, then why this sudden interest in a new dress? Or Myrtle King for that matter."

Oh, dear, this was slinking far too close to the truth for comfort. "No reason."

"Vanna."

"Yes, well, it clearly bears repeating that we cannot afford to buy new dresses." Savannah tried to sound as nonchalant as possible. "Especially while I have several perfectly good old dresses upstairs."

That slim thread was enough for Inola. "Your green dress? You're thinking of cutting into that? We had to drag that all the way from Mississippi because you couldn't leave it behind. Now, suddenly, you want to take a pair of scissors to it?" She set the magazine aside and put her hand to Savannah's brow. "You aren't fevered, but still . . ."

"I'm perfectly well. Besides, we haven't the money to pay that quack."

"I suppose that is a problem," Inola shot back, hands on her hips. "Just promise me you aren't taking any of those snake-oil powders that woman was going on about. She's likely poisoned you."

Savannah shook her head. "Of course I'm not. I declare, Mr. Conan Doyle has addled your wits. Clearly, you're staying up too late reading *Sherlock Holmes*."

"Well, I think—" Inola's interjection was stoppered by a solid knock on the front door. She looked over at Savannah. "Were you expecting someone?"

Savannah eyed the door. "Perhaps it's Billy Poole, come for the library." The knocking resumed. "Might want to grab whatever books you want before I let him in."

Inola caught up several and tucked them aside. "Insistent, whoever they are."

Savannah nodded in agreement and went to the door. She cracked it open and then opened it wider, for she couldn't quite believe her eyes.

Certainly her first instinct was to slam the door shut. Then throw the bolt.

"Oh, you are home," Miss Drake said, edging her way inside without so much as an invitation. "I'm so sorry to intrude—"

"Then why are you?" Savannah asked.

"I just need a moment of your time." She leaned around Savannah and looked directly at Inola. "Hello, there. I'm Madeline Drake, the new owner of the Star Bright. You are Inola, are you not?"

"Yes," she replied.

"You see, Mr. Quinby thought you might be interested in some employment. I've come to ask if you would like to work for me. You see, I need a cook."

The words sank in.

Savannah straightened, indignation pushing her spine upward. "Are you mad?" A better question would be, was Mr. Quinby? How dare he send this immoral creature to their doorstep. "You need to leave," she said, holding open the door.

The apparently unflappable Miss Drake ignored her, her steady gaze set on Inola. "Mr. Quinby thought you might be interested in the work."

Savannah, arms folded, stepped into her line of sight. "Was he sober?"

But before Miss Drake could answer, Inola shocked her. "How much are you willing to pay for this cook?"

Savannah's mouth dropped open, and that was before the woman named her wage, which left them both flabbergasted.

"If it isn't enough, we could negotiate," Miss Drake hastened to add. "You see, I must have someone to cook, and I don't have a lot of time—"

"Inola is not interested. Now, if you please." Savannah tipped her head toward the darkness outside.

Miss Drake looked from Inola to Savannah and then back to Inola. "Mr. Quinby was quite specific. He said you were the best cook in town, and—"

"He was mistaken," Savannah said firmly.

"Well, I apologize for intruding," the young woman said, with one more glance toward Inola.

Once she'd closed the door firmly behind the woman, Savannah turned to Inola. "Can you believe the nerve?"

"Hers or yours?" Inola pursed her lips. "How could you?" Then she turned on one heel, changed her mind, and turned back. "Were we not just discussing the fact that we are almost destitute? Vanna, we haven't enough money to get us through this month. Even with what those women helped me with, you know Mr. Wakefield will hem and haw for months before he pays me. And now, when the chance to stave off starvation lands on our doorstep, you toss the very angel of opportunity out into the cold."

"Opportunity? Ruination more like it."

Inola rolled her eyes toward the ceiling. "You can put as much veneer and lace on our lives as you want, but you and I both know who we are."

"And who are we?"

Then Inola said it. The words that hadn't been said since that horrible night. "We are the daughters of whores and a pair of murderers, and no amount of genteel manners will remove those sins."

A brittle, cold silence stretched between them.

"So that means you should risk everything and go work for that woman?" Savannah finally managed.

Hands on her hips, Inola held her ground. "I wasn't talking about me. I already have a job."

"Then whyever were you humoring her?"

"Because you *can* cook. And we need the money." With that, she went upstairs, leaving Savannah's world tilted anew.

CHAPTER 24

Tuesday, December 10

*N*inny stood on the front steps of Mrs. Jonas's house and wished herself anywhere but here. But it was Tuesday and time for the weekly Ladies Aid Meeting.

She glanced over her shoulder at the high mountains surrounding Bethlehem and envied Badger's freedom. *However do you plan on finding a forthright life here in Bethlehem?* he'd asked.

She let out a puff of breath. She didn't know, and there was hardly time to figure it all out what with Mrs. Smith hurrying up the path behind her.

Beryl heaved a breathless sigh. "Dear me, I'm terribly late—but I see you are as well, Miss Minch. Shall we can go in together and say we just lost track of time?"

Why not? It was only a tiny white lie.

Then on a wisp of wind came a whisper of words, as honest as they were cold.

A forthright life . . . Tell them the truth.

Ninny's heart hammered away at the very idea. A forthright life.

They went inside without knocking and found the tallboy in the hallway crowded with coats and scarves.

"I might just leave my coat on, and you'll want to keep those mittens handy," Mrs. Smith whispered, adding a conspiratorial wink. "Mrs. Jonas's parlor is always colder than an outhouse in February. Why that woman doesn't put more coal in her stove, I don't know."

Ninny glanced down at her hands and realized that in her distracted state, she'd put on her old red mittens, the ones her mother had knit.

They were hardly becoming, patched and old as they were, but the cheery color lent some of its vibrancy to her growing resolve.

She'd almost laid bare her soul the previous night. Confessed everything to Badger. But the words had stuck in her throat. For telling the truth meant losing everything she'd found of late.

Friends. Admiration. Purpose.

Which, she reminded herself, was all built atop a colossal lie.

To achieve a forthright life, one needed an honest foundation. But, oh, the price.

Beryl had already hurried in—so much for the solidarity of being late together—but Ninny soon saw, or rather heard, why the woman wanted to distance herself.

As Ninny came to the parlor's wide double doors, Mrs. Jonas's voice rose above the hum of chatter. "It is unbecoming," she was saying. While she hadn't Mrs. George L.'s domineering tones, Drucilla Jonas did have a way about her. "For a woman of her age to blatantly vie for the attentions of men . . . well, it is unbecoming."

"Very unbecoming," Mrs. Hoback parroted, nodding her emphasis at the younger ladies in the room as if to remind them to *get married now*.

"If I might—" Beryl Smith began.

"I hardly think Parathinia Minch is capable of being so deliberate," said Mrs. Bohlen.

One might have mistaken the woman's statement as a defense of the postmistress, but only someone who didn't know Mrs. Bohlen.

What the mayor's wife really meant was that Miss Minch wasn't capable of wiles.

"Not deliberate, Mrs. Bohlen? I disagree. I disagree most heartily." Mrs. George L. glared at her audience as if expecting someone to disagree with her. With their quiet acquiescence, she continued, unabashed. "She's determined to turn this entire town upside down."

"If I might interject—" said Beryl, but once again, they ignored her.

"None of this calamitous business would be happening if it had been done properly to begin with," Mrs. George L. added with a grand sigh. Heads nodded in agreement. "It seems Parathinia cannot be counted upon."

"Except to bake biscuits," Theodosia Winsley pointed out. "She does bake the most excellent biscuits."

Her sister nodded in agreement. "Cakes as well."

All eyes turned toward Odella, but only for as long as it took Mrs. George L. to prise back the conversation. "The point is, she's mired the entire town with her unfathomable dithering."

Ninny wondered if this was what it was like to be a floor lamp. Unnecessary until needed. Yet, like the flicker of light that came when the cord was tugged, a spark of rebellion flared inside her, finding ignition in her own growing awakening.

How do you find a forthright life?

She was about to clear her throat to announce her arrival, if only to not be seen as an eavesdropper—which she was—but Mrs. Jonas jumped in, ruffling her lacy sleeves like a hen in a dust pile. "I declare that wreath on the door of the post office is a sign of moral decay," she warned. "I suspected something was afoot when I saw Badger carrying such an extravagant arrangement of greens down the street yesterday, and now it is hanging there on the post office. For. *All*. To. See."

Ninny's cheeks burned. The woman made it sound like her petticoats were flying from the flagpole. Then again, who was to blame for all this? That wreath wouldn't be there if she hadn't lied.

"It gets worse," Mrs. Jonas rushed to continue. "I was in Mr.

King's store yesterday afternoon, and there was that coy Goldie King wheedling poor Mr. Thayer to buy a ham so as to keep up with his 'competition.'" She paused, lips pursed. "A ham. I don't need to say who it was being addressed to for delivery."

"Yes, but—" Beryl began again, glancing over at Ninny.

Mrs. George L. wasn't about to be taken off the topic. "Oh, this will make a fine story for Cora's next edition, and once again our 'quaint' country ways will be lampooned in every East Coast paper." Her first glance went toward poor Agatha Stafford, Cora's mother, whom Mrs. George L. held responsible for every perceived slight chronicled in Bethlehem's only paper.

"How hard is it to make a choice?" Mrs. Jonas pointed out.

"Not very, when the proper choice is so obvious," said Mrs. George L.

This was met with nods from around the room.

If only they knew that there had been no proper choice that night. She'd panicked and done her best. She'd lied to save them all.

"Look how this debacle turned the bazaar into a disaster," Mrs. George L. bemoaned.

"Actually," began Mrs. Garland, the society's treasurer, report in hand, "this year's bazaar was our best year ever. Mrs. Norwood cannot boast of such a success. Why, Miss Minch's cake alone sent our balance into—"

A scathing glare ended her report. Everyone in the room knew that Josephine Lovell's cake was supposed to be the one to raise the balance sheet to such a noteworthy level.

Mrs. George L. fell back on her usual refrain. "I blame Cora for all this. She's using Parathinia's weak character and failings to her own benefit."

That was too much for Agatha Stafford. "Now see here, Mrs. Lovell—" But she was immediately drowned out.

"Not to mention seeing Mr. King profit from selling needless hams," Mrs. Jonas interjected, with yet another indignant ruffle of lace.

"That seems a great number of hams for just one woman to eat," Miss Theodosia pointed out.

"Ladies!" Beryl Smith exclaimed, catching them all and then nodding her head toward the lone figure in the doorway.

With all their gazes fixed on her, Ninny turned on one heel and fled. It was time for forthright life.

For all of them.

❄

"FOR A WOMAN of her age to blatantly vie for the attentions of men . . . Well, it is unbecoming." Mrs. George L.'s announcement rang through the room, leaving Savannah to put her hand to her forehead.

Would this never end?

Savannah had come to the Ladies Aid meeting to give her report and make a hasty exit.

As it was, she'd tossed and turned all night, with Inola's sharp, pointed words prodding her.

You can cook.

Yes, but not for *that* woman. What would people think, especially now that Inola had all but crowned her as Mrs. Livingston in the eyes of Bethlehem's respectable society?

She had to carry this mantle, if only to keep Inola's secret safe. To keep them both safe. For if Mr. Wakefield or anyone at his magazine found out Mrs. Viola Kinney Livingston wasn't *as pictured*, then she and Inola would have nothing to live on.

As the discussion continued, she took a deep breath and let her gaze flit out the window. Down the hill, she could see the steam rising from Mr. Wu's laundry.

A new dress for the Christmas ball.

For a fanciful moment she considered how she might persuade the laundryman to allow her to measure that horrid dress. An impossible notion if ever there was one.

"I blame Cora for all this. She's using Parathinia's weak character and failings to her own benefit."

Savannah glanced up and restrained herself from nodding her head along with this mean bunch of hens. Pecking at poor Miss Minch.

She hadn't heard this much disagreeable tattling since she and Inola had first arrived at Larkhall, their father's plantation in Mississippi, after their mothers had died. There had been a cackling chorus of speculation as to why Captain Vance had suddenly come home from New Orleans with a "ward" and a mulatto child after the sudden and tragic loss of his wife and children to fever.

She glanced at the clock on the mantel, but certainly that time couldn't be correct. Only ten past the hour? She pressed her hand to her forehead as her headache got worse by the moment.

Suddenly a dull silence filled the room, and Savannah looked up to see why.

Here was Miss Minch, silhouetted in the doorway, a furious blush on her cheeks. Clearly, she'd heard a good portion of their chin-wagging.

With a fair modicum of dignity, Miss Minch turned and left, the thud of the front door leaving the room in silence. While the others searched for the right words—really, were there any?—Savannah's gaze fell upon a single red mitten lying in the hallway, lost in the postmistress's haste to leave.

Like a beacon, it shone with opportunity.

"Dear me, Miss Minch dropped her mitten," Savannah said, latching onto it as a route of escape. She forced herself to rise slowly, with all the ladylike dignity her mother had drilled into her. "Allow me. I fear this situation will require some delicacy."

There. Let them all think on that a bit.

She smiled pleasantly at her hostess. "Thank you, Mrs. Jonas, for your hospitality." *What there was of it.*

She carefully unfolded the sheet of paper she'd brought with her and handed it over to Mrs. Bohlen. "Here is my report and recommendations for the booths next year."

Again, she smiled and wove her way through the crowded parlor, even as her heart thudded wildly.

A new dress for the Christmas ball. You can cook.

The two disparate threads wound together.

"Mrs. Clarke, it is hardly necessary—" Mrs. George L. began. It wasn't a suggestion but a none too subtle order.

"Oh, but it is, Mrs. Lovell." Savannah caught up the lost mitten and then swept an imperious glance around the room, in hopes of reminding them all that they were supposed to be a Ladies Aid Society.

Emphasis on *ladies*.

When she got to the hall, her calm, measured facade fled, and a sense of urgency propelled her out the door and down the steps. Miss Minch was already well ahead of her.

Oh, good heavens, this was going to be very undignified.

"Miss Minch!" she called after her. "Please wait!"

The postmistress had always reminded Savannah of a sparrow: slight, fragile, timid in manners and always flitting about, barely alighting for fear someone might notice her.

But the woman who turned around was no timorous wren. Where Savannah expected to see tears and flaming cheeks, she found herself facing a sort of Valkyrie.

Parathinia Minch planted her boots firmly in the snow. "What?" she demanded. Her hat sat askew, and a few tendrils of dull brown hair poked free from their confines.

During the war, Savannah had faced down some of the most heinous men God had ever created—on both sides. Foul-mouthed, despicably intentioned, with hate enthroned in their very marrow, all of it disguised behind the sheen of uniforms and righteous honor. But this woman of fury was a creature who set even her steel-boned corset to quaking.

"What?" Miss Minch repeated, hands fisting to her hips. "Did I miss something else that you thought I ought to hear?"

"No, it isn't like that," Savannah stammered, taking a step back.

"It isn't?" The woman's lips set in a hard line.

"I only came to say—"

"What?"

Savannah held up the mitten. "That you dropped this when you left."

Miss Minch blinked and then looked down at her bare hand. "Oh, my, I hadn't noticed." Like a pastry being pricked, the air in her wheezed out. "Thank you," she said, wilting quietly back into her sparrow's feathers. She didn't look up as she eased her hand into the errant mitten.

"I hardly thought that you'd want to return," Savannah offered quietly, glancing away, for she sensed Miss Minch needed a moment to compose herself.

"I would have had to," she confessed, resignation in her words. "You see, this pair belonged to my mother."

Savannah nodded in understanding, then tried offering a bit of consolation. "You mustn't take any of that personally."

Miss Minch's gaze flew up, feathers ruffling anew. "Mustn't I?"

There was so much raw honesty in her words that Savannah stumbled a bit as she sought to find the right words. "Yes, well, I suppose it was a bit much."

"*That* is putting it mildly."

Savannah shifted from one foot to the other, the snow crunching beneath her boots. "Miss Minch, may I ask you something?"

"Of course, Mrs. Clarke."

"Why don't you just make your choice and be done with it? Truly, I find it a lot of fuss over just a tree." And Savannah truly believed what she was saying, until Miss Minch slanted a glance at her.

"If only that were so," Miss Minch told her. "But it is much more. They may not realize it, but I was hoping to save them from themselves. I was foolish to try."

Even as she said the words, Savannah swore she saw a light go on in the woman. Something had changed within Miss Minch. Something so transformational that she felt a bit awestruck. A bit jealous. Was this Miss Drake's influence at work? And, if it could happen to Miss Minch, might it happen to anyone?

Still, Savannah had to test the waters. "Certainly choosing would make all these disagreeable matters so much easier."

Clear-eyed and straight as a pin, Miss Minch set Savannah on a new path with one simple statement. "No, it wouldn't. It would just leave everything the same." Then she set off once again.

The woman's words, her very conviction, sent gooseflesh rippling down Savannah's arms.

"Aren't you going back to the post office?" Savannah called after her, looking over her shoulder in that direction.

"No. I have a few words for Cora Stafford."

Much to her amazement, Savannah started after her, a sketchy sort of plan forming, rising out of the ashes of Miss Minch's startling transformation.

It would just leave everything the same.

Stale. Lost. Trapped. Savannah shuddered, never having felt her prison press into her so.

"Then we are both headed in the same direction," she told the postmistress as she caught up with her. "I have an errand at Mr. Wu's." Those words sawed at the bindings that had long twined around her chest. Her broken heart.

"I didn't think you and Inola used Mr. Wu's services," Miss Minch said, more in the way of polite conversation.

"We don't," Savannah said firmly and stopped there. Her mother had always said brevity was better than telling a lie.

They continued down the street, Miss Minch's pace slowing while Savannah's own feet plodded reluctantly along.

"Like you, Miss Minch, I am at a crossroads of sorts," she confessed as she came to a stop.

The postmistress gave her curt nod of understanding. "May I suggest something I read recently, Mrs. Clarke?"

"What is that?"

"*Exorior!*" Miss Minch said as she marched forward.

"Exorior?" Savannah asked, as she had no choice but to follow.

"Yes. It means to rise forth, to reach." Miss Minch's determined gaze fixed on the front door of the offices of the *Bethlehem Observer*.

Savannah shifted, as if her old coat had suddenly shrunk. "I don't think I'm quite ready to rise forth." Everything old and familiar inside her recoiled at the very notion. *Leave it all be.*

"Neither was I, but suddenly—" Miss Minch slanted a glance toward the mountains. At what was well and beyond this valley.

Savannah, against all her old instincts, needed to know. "Suddenly what?"

"I am. Ready to reach, that is." A fiery light blazed to life in the woman's eyes.

"Miss Minch, whatever does that mean?" After all, who would have thought a hawk could rise from a sparrow?

The woman fluttered to a stop, blinked several times, and then smiled with a startling glow of illumination. "I haven't the least notion. But I believe I'm about to find out." With that, the woman marched up the steps without hesitating.

All Savannah saw was the bright flash of a red mitten reaching forth.

THOUGH THE BELL overhead had jangled with a jarring note as Ninny entered the *Observer*'s offices, Cora Stafford remained bent over her press, examining whatever it was she was typesetting.

Ninny waited patiently for a moment, and then coughed slightly to gain her attention.

The woman glanced up, looking a bit startled. But she raised her glasses, blinked a few times until her sight readjusted, then smiled. "Miss Minch! Such a surprise. What brings you by on this lovely day?"

"I would think, as the town's newspaper editor, you would have a fair idea why I am here."

Miss Stafford's eyes widened, and immediately Ninny was flooded with regret. There was reaching, and then there was behaving, well, like Mrs. George L.

"My apologies, Cora," she rushed to amend. "I've just come from the Ladies Aid meeting, and I fear it's gotten the better of me."

Cora, having picked up a rag, wiped at the ink stains on her fingers and laughed a little. "I've always thought there should be an aid society for the women who attend those meetings. My mother comes home every week and declares she'll—" She coughed, set aside the rag, then approached the counter. "Well, I suppose you can imagine how she comes home."

"Indeed," Ninny said, sounding more like Mrs. George L. than she cared to admit.

Cora Stafford nodded. "You've come about the tree, I assume."

"You assume correctly."

"So you've made your choice." Cora glanced up from her notepad.

Ninny took a deep breath. "In a way." She took up the pencil on the counter and began to write on one of the order sheets Cora kept there for her printing customers. "This is what I want you to print," she said. "This, and only this."

Cora's eyes widened as she read Ninny's neat script. She began shaking her head before she even got to the end. "Oh, Miss Minch, I cannot." She looked up. "I cannot print this." She set down the piece of paper and slid it back toward Ninny. "I won't. I won't be responsible. Not for *that*."

Ninny pushed it back toward her. "You must. It's the truth of the matter."

"Truth or not, I won't." Cora crossed her arms over her chest and shook her head again, this time adamantly. "Please, Miss Minch, make a different choice."

Stubbornly, Ninny held her ground. It was an odd feeling, holding to one's convictions, but she'd taken this first step, and now that light held her fast. "You know I cannot."

Cora proved just as pertinacious. "Make another choice. Save us all."

Ninny leaned in. "Cora Stafford, if you can print the report from the Temperance Union every week and in the adjacent column print ads for Mr. Hoback's drugstore—where most of the men in this town buy their liquor—then you can hardly have any trepidations about printing this."

"Trepidations? That isn't even half of what I feel when I look at that." Indeed, the lady took a step back from the counter before she took another measured glance at Ninny. "No, I won't."

"Well, you have no other choice, because that," she said, stabbing the piece of paper with her finger, "is my decision."

CHAPTER 25

*S*avannah shook her head and continued down the road.

Reach. What a preposterous notion.

Yet Miss Minch's lost mitten and all her talk of *Exorior!* and leaving everything the same had somehow shifted everything. For here she was, standing inside Mr. Wu's laundry.

A new dress for the Christmas ball.

You can cook.

She had to admit to a keen disappointment in her surroundings. The plain counter, the bundles wrapped in brown paper and twine, and the blue curtain blocking any hint of the mysterious workings beyond.

On the counter sat a bell. *Reach*, it seemed to beckon.

Oh, this is madness, she told herself, about to turn back toward the door, but the next thing she knew here she was, reaching for the little bell, giving it a jangle.

Then she waited. For nothing happened.

So she rang it again.

After what seemed like an interminable wait, the curtain parted and Mr. Wu came out. He looked her up and down, and his mouth set in a hard line of disapproval. "Yes?"

Clearly he hadn't the same affable nature as Mr. King, who always made a point of welcoming his customers, so she tried to think of how she might compose this request.

Not that the man was of a mind to wait. "Well?"

"I . . . That is . . ."

"Do you have laundry?"

"No, but I need—" She struggled to come up with the right words.

"No laundry?" he pressed.

She shook her head.

He frowned at her. "No baths for ladies."

"Sir, I do not need a bath!" Savannah sputtered. "What I need is—"

He made a disgruntled snort and jerked his thumb toward the ceiling. "Quinby is on the second floor. Use the stairs outside." Turning, he retreated behind the curtain.

"Well, of all the . . ." She picked up her skirts and headed around the counter and through the blue curtain.

The room beyond was a circus of laundry drying on lines that crisscrossed overhead. Steam rose from large tubs. It took a moment for her to get her bearings, but she finally found Mr. Wu already seated at a table. Two of his workers sat on either side of him, but it was the fourth at the table who stopped Savannah in her tracks.

Miss Drake. The woman turned around and quirked a brow, though her expression remained coolly nondescript.

Savannah focused on the proprietor. "I have a favor to ask of you, sir," she repeated, folding her hands in front of her.

"No." He didn't look up.

"It will only take a moment." She did her level best not to look at Miss Drake, and in her attempt, her gaze fell instead on a dress hanging on one of the lines.

Myrtle's dress. Right there in front of her. Even as she took a step toward it, Mr. Wu had already made up his mind. "No."

"You haven't even heard me out."

"No favors."

This wasn't how Savannah had envisioned this happening. Not like this, in front of Mr. Wu's entire staff. In front of *her*, smiling down at the domino-like tiles on the table as if she couldn't be enjoying the moment more.

Dratted woman.

But there was no time for that, so Savannah turned her full attention to the laundryman. "I need to borrow something," she told him and as his mouth set into a firm line, she rushed to add, "but only for a few minutes."

"No."

Dear heavens, the man was impossible. "But you don't even know—"

"I don't need to know. No borrowing." He waved his hand at her, clearly indicating he'd heard enough.

Her help came from the unlikeliest of places.

"I still need a cook," Miss Drake announced.

Savannah's feet froze in place. Of all the impudent . . . "We have already settled that matter, Miss Drake."

"Maybe not." She grinned and turned. "Wu, the lady needs a favor."

He shook his head furiously. "No favors."

"You're about to lose."

At this, the laundryman made a loud snort.

Miss Drake didn't even blink. "If that's your opinion, then let's raise the stakes. If I win, you grant Mrs. . . . ."

"Clarke," Savannah provided. "Mrs. Clarke."

"Yes, of course. If I win, you grant Mrs. Clarke this favor of hers."

"I don't even know what her favor is," Mr. Wu complained, his brow furrowed as he studied the board in front of him, clearly not seeing what Miss Drake thought was so obvious. "Why should I do that?"

"Because then I won't tell Mrs. Wu how much you lost Saturday night."

Mrs. Wu? This was news to Savannah. She'd no idea the laundryman had a wife.

Nor did Miss Drake's threat have any affect. He shrugged. "She already knows."

"You're bluffing," Miss Drake replied, sitting back and crossing her arms over her chest. "What we have here is a mutual quandary. I need a cook. Mrs. Clarke needs a favor. While, you, you wily bastard, need to make sure your wife doesn't know how much you really lose at mahjong . . . *and* poker."

"This is outrageous," Savannah declared.

"Yes. Outrageous," Mr. Wu agreed, wagging his finger at his opponent.

Now it was Miss Drake's turn to shrug.

Savannah tried to regain some control over this brewing tangle. "Miss Drake, I would remind you that the matter of Inola cooking for you has been settled, and that isn't about to change."

The young woman didn't bother to look up. "Not even if I can convince Mr. Wu to grant you this suspicious—albeit highly important—favor?"

Savannah pressed her lips together. Of all the audacity. "It is hardly suspicious. It is just a . . . private matter."

Mr. Wu, and his workers, swiveled their gazes toward her. *A private matter?*

The heat of the room got the better of her. At least so she told herself to explain why she was suddenly so flushed. Perhaps leaving everything the same might be the better part of valor.

"Yes. Well, I see we have reached an impasse," Savannah managed, smoothing her hands over the front of her skirt. None of this was going the way she'd imagined. "Thank you for your time, Mr. Wu." She merely glanced at Miss Drake before she marched through the blue curtain and out of the shop as quickly as she could.

Once she got to the street, the chill of winter stole her breath. But it was a welcome theft. She drew the icy wind in deep, hoping it would chase away the humiliation of finding herself nearly indebted to that woman.

"How dare she!" she muttered as she turned toward town.

"How dare who?"

Savannah looked around only to find Shandy standing not far behind her.

"Who has left you, Mrs. Clarke, so . . . spitting mad, as you Southerners say?" He grinned slyly.

Tipping up her nose, she shook her head just slightly. "I would never say such a vulgar thing."

"No, I don't suppose you would." Much to her annoyance, Shandy fell in step beside her. "But if you don't mind me saying, you look all horns and rattles today."

"I look nothing of the sort." Still, she couldn't help herself. She touched her hat, if only to make sure it was properly set.

"Still, I have to ask myself, whyever is Miz Clarke coming out of Mr. Wu's laundry in such a state?"

Savannah came to a halt, digging her boot heels into the snow. "Mr. Shandy, is there a point to this interrogation?"

The man smiled at her. "No interrogation, just curiosity."

Oh, how the man liked to show up when he was least wanted. Nor would she be rid of him until he got his answer . . . or worse, made his point.

So she chose her words carefully. "If you must know, I went to ask a favor of Mr. Wu." She hoped that might be the end of it.

Of course it wasn't.

"A favor?" he posed as he hurried to catch up, his boots barely crunching in the snow while her footsteps sounded like the march of an entire battalion. "What sort of favor might you ask of Mr. Wu?"

A *none-of-your-business sort of a favor* was what she wanted to say, but that would only confirm his colloquial assessment of her being all "horns and rattles" today.

How this man loved to stir the pot. And stir he did.

"I'm rather surprised by you, Mrs. Clarke."

Shandy was at his wheedling best, but Savannah refused to rise to his bait.

"I've always thought of you as more of a whalebone-and-canvas sort," he prodded. "Which is why I chose you for this task."

He'd chosen her? "I haven't the least notion—"

He waved at her words. "Mrs. Clarke, let's be honest with each other."

"Whatever for?" she shot back. "You seem to already know all my secrets." She crossed her arms over her chest to hold close whatever dignity and privacy she still retained. This was exactly what happened when one strayed off the well-worn path.

"From what I can tell, you've taken it upon yourself to help Myrtle King." He paused and waited.

She held her silence tight, yet her chin notched up the barest hitch.

He continued blithely on. "Whatever your reason, I think this a most noble endeavor. And right now is no time to give up."

Give up? A pleading memory mixed with the persistent wind.

Please, Inola, just let me die.

Giving up, staying put. That was easy. Comfortable. It kept everything the same.

Savannah blinked away the snowflakes that had fallen on her lashes and obscured her vision, leaving her back where all this had begun. At the side of a river, with her hands covered in blood.

"I declare," she sputtered, gathering her horns and rattles. "I hardly—" Yet when she spun around, he was gone.

Of course he was. Shandy never stayed in one place long enough to reap what he'd sown. He was like a goose—landing where he was least wanted, making a mess of his surroundings, and then taking to wing.

And now Shandy's accusation had found a tidy roost in the idea Inola had laid the night before.

You can cook.

More whalebone-and-canvas.

A dress for the Christmas ball.

Savannah blinked. She'd remained mired all these years, letting that very whalebone and canvas wrap her up so tight she couldn't breathe, all the while telling herself it was necessary to shield her from the buffeting of an ill-cast wind.

Yet now she saw all too well how that very same buttress could raise one up. Propel one forward.

Like Miss Minch marching with purpose up the steps of the *Observer's* office.

If a sparrow could unfurl and fly like a hawk, then couldn't whalebone and canvas do the same?

Savannah Clarke decided to find out.

✳

SAVANNAH SAILED BACK into the laundry, ignored the bell on the counter, and went straight through the curtain.

Miss Drake looked up, grinned, and then launched into a lengthy lecture—scolding Mr. Wu roundly, and much to Savannah's shock, in his own tongue.

She gawked. "You speak his language!"

"Unfortunately," Mr. Wu complained, before the pair of them began another furious exchange.

Finally he sat back and crossed his arms over his chest. "No." The word came out in an emphatic puff.

Miss Drake blew out a breath as well and turned to Savannah. "He won't agree to any deal until you tell him what this favor of yours is."

She and Mr. Wu waited for her to enlighten them, and when she didn't, they went back to their game as if Savannah had never interrupted them.

After a few more tiles passed back and forth, Miss Drake glanced over her shoulder. "I'm about to win."

Mr. Wu made a remark to the man to his left. The three men at the table laughed, but Miss Drake just glanced at the ceiling as if searching for patience.

"I am," she told them before glancing at Savannah. "You'd best ask for your favor. Now or never." Her hands hovered over the tiles in front of her.

Across the way, Myrtle's dress wavered on the line, like canvas caught in a gentle breeze.

Whalebone and canvas, it whispered.

Savannah took a deep breath. "I need to borrow a dress that was brought in for washing." When this got no response, she pointed to Myrtle's mustard horror on the line. "That one."

Mr. Wu's eyes narrowed. "Why?" Clearly he shared her assessment of the dress.

"Yes, why?" Miss Drake repeated, her arms now crossed over her chest.

"I need to measure it."

Mr. Wu shrugged. "It is an ugly dress." This he said more to Miss Drake.

"Exactly," Savannah agreed. Taking another breath, she finally said aloud what she'd been avoiding since that slip of paper had blossomed open in her hand. "I wish to make the owner a new one. For Christmas. For the Christmas ball, actually." Then she got to the truth of the matter. "So she needn't wear such an ugly one."

There it was. Once uttered, the words took on a sort of magical air. It wasn't the sort of feeling that left one giddy or light, but the weight of the wish that had dogged her since that night rather fell from her shoulders.

However, the disreputable pair before her didn't share the same sense. They just sat there, staring at her, as if she'd confessed to some nefarious crime.

Oh, good heavens, why didn't they understand? In her frustration —with this wish she'd never asked for, with the women in Mrs. Jonas's parlor, with her years enduring everything at Larkhall—an unlikely confession spilled out. "Please Mr. Wu, I would like to help Myrtle King."

"King?" Miss Drake said—not to Savannah but Mr. Wu. "As in King's Mercantile?"

Mr. Wu gave a curt nod. "Yes. Myrtle. The smart one. I like her. Too bad she's not a son." The other men nodded in agreement.

Mr. Wu looked Savannah up and down with eyes that had seen every cut of clothing, and she knew that what he saw—her old-fashioned widow's weeds—did not impress him. "What sort of dress?"

"A pretty one," Savannah assured him. "I have the silk, and a pattern—a very fashionable one—from a magazine. She'll be radiant."

"So you want to be her Christmas fairy godmother?" Miss Drake studied her as well, as if she too was seeing her in a new light. A grin turned her lips. "I still need a cook. But only until Christmas."

This again? "Inola is not available—"

"Then no deal." Miss Drake's fingers toyed with her last tile, and

Savannah's path, that bit of light she'd only just discovered, began to dim.

"Then I will." The words came out of her with such force that both Miss Drake and Mr. Wu looked up, not sure that they'd heard her correctly. So she repeated her offer. "I will cook for you if Mr. Wu allows me to measure Myrtle's dress."

All of them turned and gaped at her.

"Can you cook?" Miss Drake sounded as suspicious and practical as her friend.

Savannah nodded. It was the one thing in her life she knew with certainty. Yes, she could cook.

"Let her measure the dress, Wu," Miss Drake told him, as if that settled the matter.

"No," he said, settling deeper into his seat. "No dress."

Miss Drake leaned forward. "Why not? You just said you like this Myrtle. Why wouldn't you want to help her?"

"I have a business. A reputation. I can't let strange people come in and mangle clothes. Private things."

"Isn't that the entire purpose of a laundry?" Miss Drake countered. "To have strangers mangle about with your private things?"

Mr. Wu's lips pursed together. "What if people found out?"

"No one need know, sir," Savannah rushed to assure him. "I, for one, would never tell." She'd never been more honest in her life.

"Give her the dress, Wu," Miss Drake said, having laid down her tile. From the groans about the table, it appeared she'd won, and with that, she began gathering up the coins piled in the middle. "Do a good deed. Or I'll go have tea with Mrs. Wu and explain to her as to the amount of time you spend gambling rather than doing laundry. I might forget myself and even mention something about a shed that was burned down."

He wagged his finger at her. "Madeline Drake, you are a most wicked, devious woman."

Saints preserve them all, Miss Drake laughed. "So I've been told."

❄

THE DOOR to the Star Bright opened wide, and Madeline looked up from the table where she sat. She'd been reading cocktail recipes from a book she'd found in a drawer, while Dobbs sat across from her, reluctantly practicing his handwriting.

She smiled and rose to her feet. "Mr. Quinby, this is a surprise." Having won at mahjong, she'd cajoled Wu into providing Mrs. Clarke with the dress. And she'd gained a cook in the bargain.

"A happy one, I am modest enough to say. As promised, a lease for the premises." He shook a folded sheet of paper. "The owner is delighted for you to proceed with your plans."

"That is good news." Madeline hadn't been willing to trust Shandy's assurances that she could just move in and take over, so she'd hired Quinby to make sure she wasn't being led on a fool's errand. Now, with Mrs. Clarke's help and the lease in hand, nearly everything was falling into place.

The lawyer closed the door behind him. "As for the other matter, I have a few items to finish and we should be able to proceed." He ambled to the table and paused before one of the chairs. Madeline retook her seat, and once she was settled, he sat down. "Whatever are we doing here?" he asked, looking at the sheets of paper littering the table.

"Handwriting," Dobbs complained. "Please tell her I know how to write."

Madeline wasn't about to let him muster anyone to his side, so she cut off any unwitting assistance. "You do know how, but handwriting is only useful if it is legible."

Erasmus Quinby chuckled. "I fear, my boy, she has you on that point." Then he wagged his chin at the book in front of her. "Is that *MacEvoy's Guide to Barkeeping?*"

She turned it over to look at the cover. "Why, yes, it is."

Quinby nodded approvingly. "MacEvoy is an eloquent fellow with a knack for concocting interesting libations, but sadly he hasn't the right receipt for a Brandy Crusta."

"I don't think I've gotten to that one yet."

"Page 163."

Dutifully, Madeline opened the book and read the ingredients aloud. "Lemon peel, sugar, Orchard Syrup, Boker's Bitters, lemon juice, Martell brandy." She glanced up. "Seems about right."

His hand waved a dismissal. "Never. The secret to a perfect Brandy Crusta is the addition of two dashes of maraschino. Just two."

She looked over the recipe. "Maraschino? Are you certain?"

Quinby sat back. "If you would be so kind as to mix both variations, I shall prove my point."

Now she understood. Wiley codger. She'd been maneuvered into mixing him not one free drink but two.

So she went over to the bar and began gathering what she needed. "What is the verdict, sir? On our matter of import."

"It appears you have shamed me at my own game and possess a rather advanced knowledge of Wyoming law." He paused, as if awaiting an accounting.

She could hardly explain that Nate had done an entire episode on sending a family of African American children to school. Looking back, it was almost as if he'd given her a primer on what to do for Dobbs.

And given she probably wouldn't have survived these last two weeks without Dobb's help, this was the least she owed him. But more than that, she'd grown fond of the cheery little fellow. She'd never been one for children, not even as a child, her world revolving around adults—directors, agents, tutors, her mother, and, of course, Gigi. Even on *Casey Jones*, she'd been separated from the other kids for the single reason that she was the star.

That is, until Nate had cracked that wall. Become her friend. He'd taught her how to tease and laugh and gossip and be, just goofy. And she loved him for bringing those joys of childhood into her cloistered life. He'd opened her eyes to a larger world, and if she could do that now for Dobbs, she was 'paying it forward' as Nate liked to say.

Since she had rather tacitly ignored Erasmus's question, he continued. "You are indeed correct as to the matter you asked me to investigate."

"You mean I can go to school?" Dobbs brightened, handwriting now forgotten.

Mr. Quinby nodded. "I apologize for not seeing to this matter earlier, Dobbs. The entire town owes you an apology." He pulled a folded sheet from a pocket inside his jacket and smoothed it open on the table. "May I?" He nodded at the pen and ink in front of the boy.

Dobbs happily offered up the hated pair.

Settling into his role as learned legal advisor, Quinby took on a more formal air. "All I need is your legal name, Dobbs, and this letter to the school board will be complete."

Dobbs' brow furrowed. "My what?"

"Your legal name." When, that didn't elicit a response, Quinby expounded. "The name your mother gave you when you were born."

Madeline paused, curious to hear Dobbs' answer and a bit ashamed that she hadn't asked before. Nate would have. Then again, he'd have puzzled out the kid's history, found him a good home, and started a college fund.

But that was Nate.

Meanwhile, Dobbs had hunkered down, shoulders scrunched together, curling inward as if warding off this intrusion.

"There is nothing to be afraid of, my boy," Quinby told him, glancing toward Madeline.

"It's just a name," Madeline told him, giving both drinks one last gentle stir as MacEvoy recommended. Quinby nodded with approval.

"But it's *my* name." His arms crossed over his chest in a tight hug.

Madeline tried a different tack as she picked up the concoctions and came around the bar. "My mother gave me the worst middle name ever." She cringed even as she admitted as much. "I promise you, your name can't be any worse. I'll tell you mine if you tell me yours."

That proved enough of a lure to loosen his reluctance.

Dobbs heaved a sigh and then said his name, softly and cautiously, trying it out after a long period of neglect. "Nathaniel March Hayes."

As his name slipped free, so did the drinks in Madeline's hands, punctuating Dobbs' answer with a shattering of glass against the floor.

She looked up from the mess at her feet. "Nate?"

❄

LATE THAT NIGHT, Madeline sat beside the stove, cradling a cup of hot spiced rum, while Dobbs slept on the sofa beneath a pile of blankets, his breathing soft and even.

No, not Dobbs. *Nate*. Her Nate. How the hell could that be?

After he'd said his name, Madeline had tried to argue herself out of the possibility. It couldn't be.

Yet there had been so many parts of Nate's life that had always been in the shadows. Like his birth parents. He'd never sought them out. He never even said their names. He didn't even have a birth certificate until Child Services had gone to court and had one issued for him.

But he'd always been forthcoming about two things. His birthday —December 18—and his name.

Nathaniel March Hayes.

She glanced over at the slight figure curled up on the sofa. How had she not recognized him? He was only a few years younger than when she'd first met him. But then again, those years had pushed him well into puberty, making him long-limbed and nearly a foot taller.

He'd played the cheeky, confident kid who sat in the back row of the classroom on the set of *Casey Jones*. He wasn't even supposed to have a speaking role, until one day another actor forgot his lines and Nate had piped up with a quip ten times funnier than the one written in the script. By the second season, Nate had been moved from the back row to the seat next to Madeline. He became a popular regular and Madeline's best friend in real life.

"Nate," she whispered into the dark. She looked around at the Star Bright and saw so many of her questions answered, while just as many new ones rose from every corner.

How had he gotten *here*? More importantly, how had he ended up in Los Angeles, a little more than a century in the future? How was this all connected?

"By you, of course," Shandy said as he stepped from the shadows of the back room. "You're the river."

"A river of misery and booze," she told him. She nodded at him to join her at the table, even as she went to the bar and mixed another hot spiced rum. He'd never asked for a drink before, but he seemed worn around the edges.

A feeling she knew all too well.

As she set down the mug in front of him and settled back into her chair, her gaze drifted toward Nate. "He goes home, doesn't he?"

Shandy furrowed his brow. "He can."

Madeline leaned forward, lowering her voice. "He must go back home. He does so much with his life. He's helped so many people."

He saved me. More than once, clearly.

At that startling realization, she glanced up at Shandy to find him watching her.

"So I have to stay and fix things," she said, more to herself. Oh, but that seemed impossible. "Shandy, I'll just make a mess of everything. I'm not known for making good choices. Look what happened when I urged poor Ninny to bake that cake."

"Maddie, the holidays were made for mistakes," he said, looking down at his drink. "So much rushing about, so many choices. But honestly, I brought you here for just that reason. You've pulled more loose threads than I could have hoped."

"I didn't mean to," she told him.

He laughed. "Oh, I think you did. And you'll pull a lot more if I'm not mistaken."

CHAPTER 26

Wednesday, December 11

*Y*ou're the river.

Madeline shook her head. The more Shandy had explained it the previous night, the more she'd realized there wasn't enough liquor in the bar to wrap her mind around this chicken-and-egg time tangle of his. It was all eddies and bends in time.

Speaking of time . . .

"Dobbs, we need to get going," she announced.

"I don't know about this." He regarded the lunch pail sitting atop the bar with a hefty measure of skepticism.

"Butterflies?" she asked.

He nodded. "What if they won't let me in?"

There was something to the slump of his shoulders, the resignation behind his words, that straightened Madeline's resolve. "They have to," she told him. "It's the law."

"Law is one thing. Doing is another." He didn't need to sound so certain.

Well, she had her own bit of certainty. As Gigi always said, a woman's best asset was a good lawyer.

Madeline didn't know if Erasmus Quinby met Gigi's exacting standards (fifty percent shark and fifty percent unethical ass) but she was about to find out. She closed the door and turned down the road.

Dobbs trudged behind her.

This time as she walked the streets of Bethlehem, she understood why the town had felt so familiar. Nate had recreated his childhood home when he'd written his series.

There were differences, but she supposed those were a matter of perspective, like when you returned to a beloved spot from childhood and found it smaller than you remembered.

She glanced around and shook her head at the wonder of it.

As it was, she and Dobbs reached the tidy little schoolhouse at the top of the hill all too quickly, having joined a stream of children all trickling along in the same direction.

Was this, Madeline wondered, where his love of learning had begun?

Dobbs came to a sudden halt. "I don't know . . ."

She knelt down and looked him in the eye. "I thought this was what you were saving for."

"I'm having second thoughts," he confessed, casting wary glances as the kids passed them, whispering amongst themselves.

"A friend of mine back home always says, 'Education is an opportunity.'"

Dobbs' brow scrunched up. "My mother used to say that."

So that was where Nate had gotten the phrase he repeated at every charity event. Madeline had thought it was just a good slogan to open wallets.

But that connection to his long-lost mother swept away her own trepidations.

"My friend struggled with school as well," she told him, "but he would tell anyone who would listen that it is a place where curiosity finds an open forum for exploration." She chucked her chin toward the steep steps. "That is the way to the world beyond."

"Are you certain?" he asked, for on those very steps a line of high-school-age kids silently eyed them. Boys on one side, girls on the other.

"What are you doing, Dobbs?" one of the boys asked, pushing off from the railing and coming to stand in front of them.

Dobbs, to his credit, stood his ground and shrugged.

"My dad won't like this, you know," another said. "You aren't allowed."

"You ignore them, Dobbs," a solitary figure off to one side called out.

Madeline knew she'd seen the girl in overalls before, but she couldn't quite place her. Yet here she came, swaggering her way to the forefront, and though she spoke to Dobbs, her gaze remained fixed on the largest boy blocking their path. "They're just worried you're smarter than they are. Which you are."

"You shut your mouth, *Francine* King," the kid shot back.

King. That was it.

"Gonna make me, Robbie?" Francine's hands fisted at her sides. Obviously she hadn't inherited her father's jovial manners. All elbows and knees, this one. "The last time you tried, you didn't fare so well."

For a moment, Madeline considered interjecting herself into the argument—after all, she was the only adult around. But then she saw what Francine was doing.

The girl had diverted all the attention away from Dobbs. The crowd of teenagers filed down the steps toward her, leaving Madeline and Dobbs a clear path into the school. As they made for the door, Francine winked at them and then continued to goad Robbie.

Inside the long entryway that ran the width of the school, Dobbs edged closer to her. "They don't want me. Maybe I should wait until I have enough saved for the school in Cheyenne."

"Ignore them." She nodded toward the hooks and shelf on the wall, where he could hang his coat and set aside his lunch. "You have every right to an education here. Don't let that Neanderthal or anyone else tell you differently."

Slowly and resentfully, he shrugged off his coat. "What's a Neanderthal?"

Madeline grinned at him. "Ask the teacher."

They came around the corner, and the large airy room held thirty or more desks. At the front there was a long desk, and behind that a large chalkboard, where a slight woman stood on her tiptoes, writing out lessons.

At the sound of their footsteps, she said, "I don't care how cold it is outside. I haven't rung the bell yet."

When she turned around, Madeline blinked in recognition. This was the woman Wick had been dancing with at the Ladies Aid bazaar. While she'd been a smiling, beguiling creature in Wick's arms, this woman was all business in a white pintucked shirtwaist and a plain black skirt, her hair combed into an enviable Gibson.

How the hell did these women get their hair up like that without an online tutorial? Madeline did her best not to reach up and pick at the stray strands she was certain were already falling loose.

"Yes?" Her question held all the affection of a bee sting.

Dobbs took a wary step back.

Madeline smiled warmly in return. "I've come to enroll Dobbs in school. It seems he's been overlooked."

The teacher's gaze flicked from Madeline to Dobbs and back again. "I hardly think so." She started to turn back to the blackboard.

Apparently, a different lesson was in order. "Well, if that was the case, I wouldn't be here to enroll him."

The teacher turned and stared.

One thing that all Madeline's years in Hollywood had taught her was how not to blink. She knew how to hold someone's gaze steady and hard, until they were the first to relent, to speak.

It didn't take long for the teacher to break. "Now is not convenient. Lessons begin in a few minutes."

Madeline stood her ground. "Excellent." She turned to Dobbs. "I told you we'd be on time."

Nostrils flaring, the teacher set down her piece of chalk. After a pause, she reached for the cloth hanging from a hook beside the board. "I'm sorry, I don't believe we've been introduced, Miss . . . ?"

As if she didn't know who Madeline was. The whole damn town did. But that was fine. Madeline could play along with this little farce. "Miss Drake."

"Yes, well, *Miss Drake*, apparently you don't know that this school term is nearly over. Perhaps Dobbs can start fresh in January when the new term begins."

Madeline knew this dodge only too well. "Why wait?" She smiled innocently. "He's so behind as it is, and you could use the next few weeks to help him prepare for the next term. I'll be more than happy to see he studies over the holidays, if you would be so kind as to provide some guidance."

The teacher shook her head. "He can hardly start without the right —" She'd been about to say "supplies," but at this point Dobbs held up the required items, the ones he'd been saving for and squirreling away.

"Dobbs, can you please go stand in the front hall? I would like to speak to your teacher privately."

"Yes, ma'am," Dobbs said, bobbing his head and turning to leave, though not before he cast another *I-told-you-so* look at Madeline.

Oh, he hadn't seen anything yet.

Madeline waited until he disappeared around the corner. "Yes, Miss, um . . ." she began. "I'm sorry, you neglected to introduce yourself." Two could play this game.

"I am Miss Barrett," the teacher said through gritted teeth, her gaze fixed on the empty doorway through which Dobbs had fled. As if she wished Madeline out the same way.

"Is there a problem?" Madeline asked, using the tone she reserved for the rare occasions when she was left waiting for a table.

The teacher drew in another breath through her nostrils. "Miss Drake, you being new here and all, well, you might not understand how things are done. As it is—"

"I'm not as new as you think." Madeline cut her off, done with pleasantries. "I know you're walking a line here—between what is right and what the school board demands. You see, I've done my homework. But what is lost in all this is a child who has a right to an education. Possibly more than a few—I believe there are some Japanese miners whose children are not being served." She paused and looked the younger woman in the eye. "You're a teacher with a legal and moral obligation to provide that education, are you not?"

The nostrils flared again, and Madeline knew she'd struck a nerve. Good. Let the woman squirm.

And wiggle she did. "It is a difficult situation—"

"What about it is difficult, Miss Barrett? This is a school. You are a teacher." Madeline looked her up and down, leaving the young woman mottled with anger when she added, "Or so I was led to believe."

"Of course I am."

The words came out like nails. Good. Now it was time to use a hammer.

Yet Miss Barrett wasn't done. "It was the board's decision that since there aren't enough . . ." She'd lowered her voice as she spoke.

Madeline leaned forward as if she hadn't the least idea what the problem might be. "Not enough . . . ?"

"Colored children," the teacher finally said. There was that purse of the lips again. "There are not enough colored children in the town for a school of their own, so there isn't anything that can be done. Wyoming law is very clear on the matter. So . . ." Her voice trailed off, and she did her best to look apologetic as she nodded toward the door.

Not that Madeline was going anywhere.

"Dear me," she said, putting a perfect note of sincerity to her words. "You see, I asked the very same question of Mr. Quinby, who agreed with my understanding of Wyoming law and wrote it out for you in terms that anyone should be able to comprehend." She drew the letter out of her purse and held it out. "Just so there is no misunderstanding."

Miss Barrett stared down at the paper as if she wasn't sure what to make of it. Madeline shook it a little, and still the teacher refused to take it.

"Do you need me to read it to you?" Madeline asked.

At this, Miss Barrett snatched the letter and snapped it open. She scanned the lines, her brow furrowing deeper and deeper. When she got to the end of the page, her lips thinned.

From the doorway, one of the older boys poked his head in. "Miss? Do you want me to ring the bell?"

"Not now, Robbie," the teacher snapped, her hand fluttering at him.

The boy fled back the way he'd come, most likely to give a report to his curious compatriots outside.

"Is there anything you don't understand?" Madeline asked. "I'd be more than happy to explain it to you."

"No. That won't be necessary," she replied, her gaze flitting toward the sunny windows that opened to a view of the town, as if weighing her choices.

Madeline made it for her. "Dobbs," she called out. "Come on back in. Miss Barrett just found you a desk."

Miss Barrett's brown eyes narrowed to a pair of dark slits. She spoke in a hard, sharp whisper that could have cut ice. "The school board will have a say in this."

"I'm sure they will. But the law is the law, Miss Barrett. As Mr. Quinby outlines in his letter, the school board has been derelict in its duty. Dobbs is entitled to an education, and all the parties involved"— Madeline swept a glance over the young woman to show that she included Miss Barrett in this estimation—"have failed to provide him one."

When the teacher began to stammer again, Madeline hammered her final point home. "I'd rather not ask the sheriff to intervene, don't you agree?" With that, she turned and surveyed the rows. "Which desk is to be his?"

SAVANNAH KNOCKED ON THE BERGSTROMS' door and waited. Then she knocked again.

She'd come a little early in hopes of finding some time to sew— well away from Inola's curious gaze.

Inside she could hear the plaintive cries of the baby but nothing else. A wariness spread through her. That fool man hadn't gone and left his family all alone again, had he?

Then she knocked again, and after some time—at about the point when Savannah was going to come in whether she was welcome or not, the door creaked opened, and Berta peered up at her, her mouth set in a wary frown.

"Hello," Savannah said, taken aback at this chary greeting.

Berta opened the door a bit more. "Did you remember the cookies?"

"I did."

The door opened further, and Savannah entered, but before she could exclaim at the sights before her, Mr. Bergstrom shouldered open the back door, bucket in hand. He glanced up and blinked.

"Mrs. Clarke, again you are heaven sent." He set the bucket on the counter near the sink and then wiped his hands on a towel. "The baby needs feeding. I'm afraid it was a rough night."

A rough night? That was an understatement. The small cabin looked as if it had rolled down the side of the mountain, tumbling the contents in every direction. Clothes sat piled on and beside the chair. The laundry line strung over the stove held a plethora of clothes and rags pinned together so closely they'd never dry.

Berta had settled on the bench beside Margit, who sat with her thumb stuffed in her mouth. She looked like a cat in a dog kennel. Clara was curled up in the rocking chair, staring warily at her.

"They're hungry," Mr. Bergstrom told her. "But at least the cow is still doing her part. Fresh milk and hopefully some butter from it." He sighed. "Livia had to go to school today—more tests she couldn't miss. She wants to be a teacher, you know."

"No, I didn't," she replied, still fixed on the first part of his report. The children needed feeding?

That wasn't even the half of what needed doing.

"Pelle just brought word that Mr. Tagg has some extra work at the mill, and since I can't get back to the camp right now . . ."

She'd been too busy taking an inventory of all the tasks that needed to be done to notice him tossing on his coat and gathering up his things—hat and gloves, a wide gray scarf—as he talked. Now here he was walking out the door.

He glanced at the disarray. "If you don't mind," he said, nodding toward the shambles that was his house.

Don't mind? She looked at the chaos and saw a week's worth of labors. The laundry alone would keep a person going for days.

"Livia will be home right after school," he added, as if that made all the difference.

"And Mrs. Bergstrom?" Savannah prompted, having set down her basket.

His brow furrowed—in what, an apology?—before he hurried out the door. "If only she'd . . ." He crushed his hat in his hand and shook his head before he left.

"Men!" she said to the closed door.

But before she could expound on that oath, there was a tug at her sleeve. Wide blue eyes surrounded by a halo of tousled blonde curls gazed up at her. Berta, of course. She had smudges on her cheeks and a nose that needed to be wiped and washed.

Savannah sighed. "Yes?"

"Will you make breakfast?"

"I suppose I must."

The child sighed, deep and with the air of an eighty-year-old. "That's good. Momma can't ."

"So it seems," Savannah said, looking around. There was nothing to do but do. She retrieved an apron from the laundry line and looked down at her newfound shadow. Clearly, Berta was not leaving her side. "You can help. So can your sisters."

Margit hurried over, eyes alight. Clara stayed put, blanket wound around her like a shield.

"Let's see what we can do about getting everyone fed, especially the baby," she told them as she walked over to the cradle.

There was an aggrieved sniff from the twins.

"You have a problem with that?" Savannah asked them.

"We don't like him much," Berta said with some authority.

"Why is that?" Savannah asked.

"He made Momma sick." This came from the usually quiet Margit.

"He didn't do that on purpose, child," Savannah told her, reaching down to straighten the blanket and realizing immediately that feeding wasn't the only thing the baby needed. No wonder Mr. Bergstrom had hightailed it out of the house. "You must never forget that babies are the most precious of gifts."

Berta didn't look convinced. "Someone should tell Momma that."

"I suspect she knows. She's just a little lost right now." Savannah gathered up the little fellow. So very fragile, she thought, as she brushed her fingers over his downy head. "Does he have a name yet?"

"Nope."

No name. Oh, that wouldn't do.

"He's not much," Berta commented. "Suppose that's why he probably won't live."

The breath rushed out of Savannah. Not live? She looked down at the baby and then at his sister. How could a child so young say such a cavalier thing? "Then let's see that he does."

Berta stared up at her. "Can you?"

"I don't know, but I can try." Savannah looked around, only to find what she needed in Margit's outstretched hand. The rags for changing his diaper. What the child lacked in words, she made up for in usefulness.

With that task finished, Savannah cradled the tiny mite, now bundled in a blanket, to her shoulder, carrying him toward the closed door. She found her way blocked by Berta and Margit.

"Come now," Savannah said as the stubborn little mites remained planted in front of the door. "I only want to help her. Help them both."

"We're not supposed to bother Momma," Berta told her.

"You aren't," she told the little girl. "But that rule does not apply to me." Then she sidestepped them and opened the door.

It took a moment for Savannah's eyes to adjust to the shadowed room. But since she'd been in there the other night, she went directly toward the bed, immediately wishing she hadn't. Ragged hair stuck out from the side of Mrs. Bergstrom's head, and her grief-stricken eyes, the same shade of gray-blue as the twins' eyes, held only a faint strand of light.

Savannah regarded her with no small amount of horror. "Come now . . . I can't have this . . . alone in the dark . . . it doesn't help." She settled the baby in his crib, and then returned, hoisting Mrs. Bergstrom into a sitting position. This close, she realized how much the woman needed a bath.

Wasn't anyone seeing to her?

Yes. You are. That bit of conscience whispered out of nowhere, a voice, Savannah was shocked to say, not unlike Mrs. George L.'s.

Clearly, she was not doing a very good job if she was imagining Mrs. George L. in the room. Then again, it was something of a miracle that this poor woman had not ended up with childbed fever.

She reached under the bed and pulled out the chamber pot. Turning her back while the woman relieved herself, Savannah continued her cajoling chatter. "There now. Let's move you into the chair by the stove. There's a nice bit of sunshine this morning." She wrapped a shawl around the woman's rail-thin shoulders and guided her out into the larger room.

"Momma," Berta whispered, a bit of wary awe in her voice.

Margit only stared, eyes wide, thumb jammed into her mouth, while Clara cleared out of her mother's chair, dragging her blanket after her.

Mrs. Bergstrom paid them no notice, not even when Berta brought over the washcloth and Savannah slowly began to clean her face and hands. Once she was done, she stepped back and nodded with approval. "There now. You're ready for little Thomas."

At this, the woman glanced up.

So there was still a spark inside her.

Savannah notched up her chin. "Yes, Thomas. If you won't name him, I will." She turned to the cradle and carefully brought the infant over to his mother. Mrs. Bergstrom looked away, that bit of light draining from her eyes.

"You have to feed him. You must," Savannah insisted, pressing the child to her and wrapping the woman's arms around him. Gently, she settled the baby with his face inside the opening of his mother's nightdress.

Little Thomas snuffled around, the smell of milk having aroused his instincts. So he had a spark as well.

At this, she smiled, until the baby began to cry.

"He knows what to do, you just have to help him," she quietly offered.

Mrs. Bergstrom sighed and then shifted, raising her breast to her child, letting him latch on.

Closing her eyes, Savannah said a hasty prayer for this small victory. "Thank you," she told the woman. "Now I'll see to the young 'uns." She glanced over at the small shadow beside her. "Come along, Berta."

Berta stood transfixed at the sight of her mother nursing, as if she too were starved, agony and hunger and pain in her eyes.

Mrs. Bergstrom wasn't the only one aching in this house.

"Berta," Savannah said, nudging the child.

"Yes, ma'am."

When they got to the sink, Berta glanced over her shoulder. "She doesn't look good."

"I suppose not," Savannah said as she pumped the water.

"She smells." Berta's little button nose wrinkled.

"Then we'll see that she gets a bath today."

Out of nowhere, Margit said, "And wash her hair?"

Savannah looked over at her and nodded. "A good bath always make me feel better." The little girl smiled in happy agreement.

Berta returned with a cake of soap. "Will she be better then?"

Oh, such a question.

Savannah could only answer honestly. "Most likely not. This is going to take some time, I fear." She glanced at Mrs. Bergstrom. The woman's attention was fixed on some unseen, faraway spot only she could see, and Savannah wondered if she'd ever get better.

But in the meantime, she took stock of what needed to be done and then went to the cupboards and found an odd mix of provisions. Flour. A few onions. Potatoes.

And the bucket of milk.

Flapjacks for the children—that ought to brighten their spirits. Then a decent supper of potato soup and perhaps some Parker House rolls. She took another look around the room and shuddered. Such disorder ran against her nature. Still, order was merely a matter of completing one task after another, so while the potatoes boiled and the cream separated, she'd start cleaning.

Glancing at her basket, her heart twanged a bit. There would be no sewing today, but it was still two weeks until Christmas.

With so much to be done.

CHAPTER 27

$\mathcal{N}$inny set down her cup of tea and looked down the hall toward the post office. Today was the day. With it being exactly two weeks before Christmas, this was the day that the ladies of Bethlehem awaited with trepidation and dread.

As Theodosia had so indelicately said the day before, one never knew if an invitation was a blessing or a curse.

Ninny took another look at the clock. Five to nine. Well, there was nothing to be done but get on with it, so she rinsed her cup in the sink and made her way down the hall to open the door.

Even as she got there, she could see the matron's outline on the porch. Already waiting.

So it was going to be *that* sort of year. Well, there was nothing to be done but get on with it.

Ninny hurried to open the door. Mrs. George L. held no compunctions about penning a complaint to the Postmaster General in Washington, D.C. as to the sorry state of postal matters in Bethlehem.

She'd written three such missives in the last year alone.

The woman stood waiting, watch in hand. "Ah, Miss Minch. Right on time." She almost sounded disappointed. "I do hope you have enough stamps on hand, as I have so much to mail between my

Christmas tidings and *other* things." She smiled as if her arrival on this particular day was all a mystery, then took a moment to give the wreath beside the door a disapproving sniff before she sailed toward the counter, all business. "I see you have recovered from yesterday. Excellent."

She offered this bit as if Ninny were getting over some trifling cold or a minor headache.

Ninny did her best to smile back, that is until Mrs. George L. looked up and said, "You spoke to Cora yesterday."

Not much happened in Bethlehem that Mrs. George L. didn't know, but clearly she hadn't learned everything. So Ninny waited her out.

The woman's lips pursed impatiently. "Well, I suppose I will have to bide my time with everyone else . . ." Her brows notched up as if to remind Ninny that she was not everyone else, nor did she expect to wait.

But Ninny was in no mood to enlighten her. Everyone, and she meant *everyone*, would learn the truth tomorrow when Cora published the weekly edition.

It was only fair.

With no answer forthcoming, Mrs. George L. got back to the business at hand. "Now let me see what I have here." She slowly and pointedly sorted the Christmas tidings in her hands. Postcards for those acquaintances she deigned worthy of acknowledgment but who, in her estimation, merited only a penny stamp. Next came those lofty notables worth the full expense of first-class postage, who received a card.

Once those were divided and stacked with military precision on the counter, Mrs. George L. reached inside her handbag and slowly drew out a collection of snowy-white envelopes.

The birthday invitations, crisp and neatly penned.

Laid gently on the counter beside the other two piles, Mrs. George L. looked up apologetically, as if she were holding up a vast line of customers. "It is all such a handful, and as you know, I insist on seeing to my most important matters personally." She made it sound as if she had an entire staff of servants at her beck and call, and not just poor beleaguered Annie Bell Gray at her disposal. She cocked her head and examined the piles one last time before she announced, "That's all of it."

As Ninny reached for the postcards, the door swung open, sending the bell overhead jangling like a clap of thunder.

"Columbia! Oh, dear Columbia!" Mrs. Jonas wheezed out, clutching her middle with one hand and reaching out with the other to find something or someone to support her. "I have been all over town looking for you."

Mrs. George L. eyed the outstretched hand and offered no support nor made any attempt to conceal her displeasure at this interruption. Notably, she kept her hand atop her mail and did her utmost to look unconcerned. "Heavens, Drucilla, whatever is the matter?"

"I fear *that woman*—"

Ninny hardly need a crystal ball to know exactly who "that woman" might be. Only one person could inspire such venom.

Madeline.

Nor was Mrs. George L. in need of a soothsayer. "Whatever has she done *now*?"

"Miss Barrett sent Pinky home with the most shocking news." She stole another glance at Ninny as if weighing the loyalty of her audience. When next she spoke, she lowered her voice as if to exclude Ninny. But this was Mrs. Jonas, and she could hardly speak without half the town hearing her. "A school board meeting must be convened immediately."

"A school board meeting?" Mrs. George L.'s brows knit together. "Whatever for?"

"That woman has enrolled Dobbs in school."

Mrs. George L. blinked, as if trying to decipher a telegram where all the words had been scrambled. But as the meaning finally registered, her spine straightened.

Perfectly penned invitations and Christmas tidings alike were whisked into her purse with all the care of a broom sweeping up smashed crockery from the pantry floor.

"We shall see about that," she announced, and marched out the door.

✻

As Mr. Bergstrom had promised, Livia arrived promptly at five after three. Coat flapping, tam askew, her long blonde braid loose, Livia came to a tumbling stop two steps into the house.

Savannah put a finger to her lips. Thomas, having been fretful most of the day, had finally fallen asleep in her arms. She might have put him in his cradle and sewed, but the poor mite had only settled once she'd wrapped him tight and held him close, rocking slowly and quietly. Berta and Margit sat at her feet, playing with a pair of dolls. Clara was napping.

She needn't have warned the girl to be quiet, for all Livia could do was gape at the nearly arranged cabin. The pot of soup on the stove. The wood box filled and the table set for supper.

"Livia!" Berta sprung up and barreled toward her sister, wrapping herself tight against the older girl's skirt. She looked up, smiling. "Livia, I helped. I learned to make butter."

"Me too," Margit added.

Berta continued quickly, unwilling to be outdone by Margit's accomplishment. "I helped give Thomas a bath and Momma one as well. We even combed her hair. She's sleeping."

"Thomas?" Livia asked, looking from her sister to Savannah.

She rose with the newly christened Thomas and set him softly into his cradle. Thankfully, he slept on. "The baby needed a name. Your mother can change it when she recovers."

Livia's eyes welled up. "Oh, Mrs. Clarke!" For a moment Savannah had the worrisome notion that the girl was going to hug her. Instead, she turned slowly, her gaze stopping on the closed bedroom door. "I know Momma would be so thankful—embarrassed, really— if she were herself."

"We all need help from time to time." Savannah brushed her hands over her skirt and changed the subject, for it was too uncomfortably close to home. "There is supper in the pot. And rolls ready for baking. Just brush them with a bit of milk and put them in the oven when it's hot."

"Rolls?" Having discarded her gloves and tam, Livia hurried over to the sideboard still wearing her coat, and peeked beneath the dishcloth to admire the pan of rolls rising beneath. "Oh, they're lovely."

"I helped," Berta advised her, chucking up her chin.

"So you've mentioned," Livia told her, giving her braid a gentle tug.

"Now that things are in hand, I'll be on my way," Savannah said, gathering up her basket.

"Mrs. Clarke . . . I hate to ask, but—" Livia's voice trembled.

Savannah took a step back—*now what?*—only to find her hesitation was enough for Livia to rush forward, her words tumbling out like a snowstorm. "You see, Friday is St. Lucia Day." She paused there.

"St. Lucia? I'm afraid I don't—"

"Oh, it's the very best," Berta assured her.

Margit nodded solemnly in agreement.

Before Berta could continue, Livia explained, "In Sweden, it's a very special day. Momma loves it." She stole a furtive glance at the door. "At least she does most years. I just hoped this year, well maybe, if it were done right, it might . . ." A welling of hope pushed tears to her eyes.

Get her out of bed. Put a spark of light in her sad, blue eyes.

Dashing at her cheeks, Livia continued, "On St. Lucia Day, the eldest daughter—"

"Which is Livia," Berta interjected, having held her tongue for as long as possible. "She wears a crown of candles, and there are cakes with raisins and sugar," she said, reverence in every word.

Savannah smiled at the little girl. "My, my, that sounds perfectly lovely."

"They aren't cakes," Livia corrected. "But buns. Special ones. You see, I'm responsible for making the *lussekatter*." Seeing Savannah's confusion, she added, "St. Lucia buns."

Savannah blinked. Did none of the girls in this town know how to bake?

Livia took a deep breath. "Usually Mama helps me."

"Always," Berta corrected with a solemn nod, as if she'd been witness to this tradition for decades.

"Always," Margit echoed.

Savannah's insides twisted. She glanced up to find Livia dashing at the fat tears glistening in her eyes. Oh, heavens, not this.

"I want it all to be perfect, just as if Mama was, you know, herself. I'm not the best baker. Not as bad as Myrtle," Livia rushed at to add. "It's just that I want it all to be perfect."

"My dear, I don't even know how to make these—"

"St. Lucia buns." Livia hurried to the cupboard and retrieved a small brown book. "Mormor gave this to my mother when she and Papa left Sweden. It has all the ingredients and the directions." She thumbed through it quickly, then held it open for Savannah to see.

Sure enough, just like her own cookbooks, there was a recipe, and in the margins a delicate web of handwritten notes clarifying what the author had left out. Those bits of experience that made a recipe one's own.

Here was another moment of affinity that Savannah shared with this woman. Like the sewing basket with its neatly wound and organized threads, Mrs. Bergstrom cooked with deliberate care and left her alterations and observations so others could rise from her experience.

Looking at the recipe, she realized there was one very significant problem. "Is that Swedish?"

Livia glanced down at the recipe. "Oh, dear, yes, it is. Sorry, I forgot. But I can write it out for you." Settling the book on the table, she went to her school bag and retrieved a scrap of paper and a worn pencil. Quickly she began to translate the words.

"You read and write Swedish?"

"Yes. Mama taught me in case . . ." She lowered her voice and leaned closer so Berta might not hear. "In case something happened to her. So there would be someone to write Mormor."

That was the second time Livia has used that word. "Mormor?"

"Grandmother," Livia translated.

So there it was. Mrs. Bergstrom, desperate to preserve that filament of connection, so frail and taut at this distance, had anchored it in place by teaching her daughter to read and write in her native tongue.

For when those ties broke, there was no way to cast them back across such a distance and know that there would be someone on the other side to take hold.

As Savannah knew all too well.

No, without that link of language, the thread would unravel, leaving both sides adrift.

For one brief moment, she was back in Mémé's kitchen, with all the rich spices and the heat. Oh, how the heat and steam had wrapped around her. Back then, she hadn't an inkling of just how cold the world could be.

She glanced up, and to her amazement, Livia had finished writing out the receipt and now held it out to her.

"Livia, I . . ." Yet some curious, incautious part of her had to glance down at this unknown treasure.

Flour. Sugar. Milk. Saffron.

"Saffron?" she said aloud.

"Oh, I almost forgot." Livia went back to the cupboard and sorted through the small collection of spice tins and envelopes. "Oh, no. We haven't any."

"Is it essential?" Savannah asked, for the rest of the recipe looked like any other for a sweet bun.

"Yes." Big, dewy tears threatened to spill again. "And so very dear."

Berta looked from her sister over to Savannah. Faith shone in her wide expression that yes, Mrs. Clarke would help them. Of course she would.

Savannah shook her head. "I know we don't have any."

Berta continue to gaze up to her, Margit at her side, hugging her doll, Alma, close. Even Clara had joined her sisters, taking Livia's hand.

"Well, I can check with Mr. King tomorrow." The words came out of her before she could stop them. "To see if he has any in stock."

Livia brightened but only a little. "I don't know if we can afford—"

The baby began to fuss, and Livia gathered him up, cooing into his ear, smoothing his brow. The girl had enough responsibilities. If this St. Lucia Day was something that might brighten Mrs. Bergstrom's beleaguered heart, then perhaps . . .

"It isn't that much saffron," Savannah began. "Mr. King might understand." She hurried to get her coat and hat, wondering where that bit of specious trumpery had come from. "As for those rolls there, don't forget: a fast oven and only about fifteen minutes, or they'll burn."

Berta stepped forward with her own display of aplomb. "I'll show her how."

CHAPTER 28

he knock at the door yarded Ninny's attention away from her stitches, and she dropped the one she'd been knitting. "Poppycock," she muttered as she peered down at her work to find the lost stitch. Even before she could lift it back up onto the needle, there was another knock at the door, followed by a despairing request.

"Ninny? It's me. Madeline. I've really stirred the hornet's nest this time."

That's an understatement if ever there was one. Ninny set down her knitting and caught up the lantern. As she opened the door, the shaft of light landed on a snow-crusted, woebegone figure retreating through a path of broken snow. "Goodness, what are you doing out?"

"I need some advice," Madeline said, head down, hands stuffed into the pockets of the sheriff's old sweater. "May I come in?"

"Of course." She smiled and opened the door wider. "I suppose you've had a day as well."

Madeline climbed back up the steps, and was about to come inside, but she paused, turning to knock the snow from her boots and shake out her skirt.

"So you heard?" she asked as she came inside.

"That you sent Dobbs to school? Oh, I heard," Ninny replied, reaching around her to close the door.

"It was mostly his doing. He's been saving for some time to go to some school in Cheyenne. I just sort of intervened."

"You did more than that," Ninny said, her words coming out all wrong.

"He's entitled to an education," Madeline shot back.

Ninny rushed to correct herself. "I couldn't agree more." Even as she'd heard Mrs. Jonas's news, she'd said a silent prayer of gratitude to Madeline for doing what she'd long thought ought to be done.

What are you doing? Reverend Belding's exhortation from Sunday's sermon rang anew.

Clearly, not enough.

"Ninny, why hasn't anyone spoken up for him before now?" Madeline's earnest question might have been taken as an accusation, for certainly her own silence—and that of everyone else—had been as bad as the school board's blatant disregard of Dobbs' right to an education.

"I'm ashamed to admit it, but no one looked into it more closely." Again she cursed her own timidity. "The school board ruled on the matter, and that was the end of it."

Madeline rubbed her mittens together and shivered yet again. "Well, it's done now. The school board convened at Mr. Thayer's office—for none of them trusted Mr. Quinby's opinion—but Mr. Thayer checked his copy of the statutes and agreed that Dobbs had every right. Then Mrs. George L. swore this wouldn't be the end of it." She shook off the sheriff's sweater and hung it on the hook by the hallway. "So I may have won the battle—"

"But she'll see to it you don't get your liquor license," Ninny provided. Hadn't she heard as much over the counter this afternoon?

"Erasmus warned me I'd end up in hot water," Madeline said with a shrug.

As she turned to come further into the kitchen, she stilled, staring down the long hallway, decorated as it was with parcels stacked in precarious towers against both walls, filling the entire length. She looked back at Ninny. "Wow!"

"Christmas," Ninny said, unable to keep a note of frustration out of her voice.

Madeline remained fixed at the hallway door. "Where does all this come from?"

"The catalogues, mostly. Montgomery Ward, Sears and Roebuck. Some from New York City." Ninny sighed. "By the last few days before Christmas they'll be all the way up to the ceiling, what with all the last-minute express orders from husbands who forgot to get something for their wives."

"Men don't change, do they?" Madeline said with a laugh.

"I suppose not, because it's always this way." Ninny shook her head. "Want to know something funny? I was nearly ten before I realized that Christmas decorating didn't mean stacks and stacks of parcels for other people."

Madeline laughed and rubbed her hands together again.

"Heavens, come stand by the stove and get warm, while I get us some cake." Ninny tucked a few pieces of wood into the firebox before shooing Madeline closer to the warmth. "And some tea," she added, as she set to work filling the kettle.

"Like I said," Madeline began, "I need some advice, but I think I also needed to just come over here. Your kitchen is . . ." She looked around as if struggling to come up with the right words.

Ninny glanced almost apologetically at the faded wallpaper and the open shelves. Hardly the sort of kitchen one saw in the magazines.

"It is the coziest spot I've ever been. Best of all, it always smells like heaven." Madeline grinned toward the drainboard where, atop Ninny's favorite Haviland plate, sat the coffee cake she'd baked earlier.

"Thank you." Ninny didn't know what else to say to such adoration. "Well, since you are here, you'd best settle in and help me eat this."

"What is it?" Madeline asked, inhaling with an expression of pure joy on her face.

"Just a simple coffee cake I like to make this time of year. It's nothing much."

"Nothing much. You say that, but it smells exactly like Christmas should," she said with an infectious enthusiasm.

"It does, doesn't it?" Ninny admitted, savoring the air of nutmeg and cinnamon filling the kitchen. "The truth is, I make it every year about this time, and it is far more than one person should eat."

Madeline's eyes half closed as she inhaled. "Well I'm glad I can offer some assistance in eating a slice . . . or two."

"That's very generous of you." Ninny laughed. "But I must say, it does a soul good to have someone to share it with, especially after the day I had."

"What happened?" Madeline had moved to the table, reaching out to touch the ball of gray wool waiting to be knitted up.

"Actually, it's more about what didn't happen," Ninny remarked, as she measured tea into the pot.

"How's that?"

"Mrs. George L."

"So she arrived with her birthday invitations?"

"In a sense," Ninny told her. "She came, but then Mrs. Jonas arrived with her news—"

"About Dobbs going to school?"

Ninny nodded. "That was the end of the invitations. She swept them off the counter and left." She sighed. "I've had an entire day of turning away party hopefuls. One woman broke into tears when I told her that I had no idea when Mrs. George L. would return. It's bad enough I have to do this one day a year."

"Now I see the real reason for this annual cake," Madeline offered.

"Goodness, I never thought of it that way," Ninny admitted. "But I do make it on this day." She laughed a bit, as did Madeline as she went about gathering the cups and saucers, moving through her kitchen like it was second nature.

Ninny paused in surprise. When had this companionable friendship happened? Something so rare, blossoming in the dead of winter.

Madeline had set out the cups and was looking again at Ninny's knitting. "May I?" she asked, carefully tapping the end of the needle with all the stitches.

Ninny nodded and tried her best not to feel all tangled up about someone else inspecting her handwork. Especially these very new stitches. Oh, they looked orderly on the needles, but every time she worked them, she found herself in knots.

Madeline turned the needles this way and that, her fingers trailing almost reverently over the rows of ribbing. "Your stitches are beautiful. So neat and tidy. I always end up ripping more rows than I knit, but I suppose it is just the act of making one stitch after another that is so soothing."

Ninny didn't know what to say. Somehow Madeline had put into words that quiet joy.

"What are you making?"

Ninny glanced up from pouring the tea, and once again her cheeks warmed. Dear heavens, there was nothing to be embarrassed about. "Mittens," she said, quickly turning her attention back to the tray.

Madeline set down the needles. "You must despise me for setting the entire town on fire." Again, there was that expectation that everything wrong was her fault. How was it that this confident young woman always thought she must shoulder the blame?

"Despise you?" Ninny laughed as she brought the tray to the table. "I don't make tea or put out cake for people I despise. I can't believe I'm saying this, but the look on Columbia's face when she heard the news was worth the price." She settled the tray and cake on the table, and once everything was arranged to her liking—all the silverware orderly and the plates divided—she sat down across from Madeline. "It is a rare sight to see Mrs. George L. Lovell at a loss for words. I commend you. You managed to skirt, flank, and outwit her in one move."

"It wasn't my intention."

Having passed a slice of cake to Madeline, Ninny cut a piece for herself. "If anything, it will make tomorrow's Temperance Union meeting interesting."

"You might have some good news for them," Madeline told her, taking a bite of cake. "Oh, my!"

Ninny smiled before taking a bite and sighing at the warmth of the cinnamon and nutmeg. It was good, but the real treat was having someone else enjoy it just as much. It was rather like watching Badger eating the stew the other night. It was one thing to love your own cooking, quite another to watch someone else take such great pleasure in it.

Madeline took another bite and closed her eyes as she devoured it. "Oh, Ninny, this is heaven."

Ninny tried to avoid blushing again by returning to the previous subject. "You were saying you have good news? For the Temperance Union?"

Madeline's gaze rolled upward. "All their fears of a reopened saloon may be for nothing. You see, I need a liquor license to open." When Ninny didn't say anything, she continued, "From Wick."

The sheriff had to approve the license? Ninny's eyes widened as the realization sank in. "Oh, dear."

"Yes, exactly." Madeline's fork paused over the half-eaten slice of cake. "I've been avoiding the whole license thing, and now, considering what happened Saturday, I have little hope he'll grant my request."

"Sheriff Fischer has always struck me as a fair man," Ninny offered diplomatically.

"I'm certain he's getting an earful from that schoolteacher of his." Madeline pursed her lips together.

"His schoolteacher?" After all, the town only had one teacher. "You don't mean Miss Barrett?"

"Yes, that one. What he sees in her . . ." Madeline's nose wrinkled.

Ninny put her fork down. "I'm not certain I understand." Madeline Drake had a way of turning a phrase that often left her feeling a bit behind.

"The sheriff. And Miss Barrett. I'm sure he's getting an earful from her right this very minute." Madeline waggled her brows, then took another bite of cake.

Suddenly the light dawned. "Miss Barrett and the sheriff?" She coughed a bit. "Oh, he's too smart for that."

Madeline's gaze narrowed. "But at the dance I saw . . . and then I heard—"

Ninny stopped her right there. "Oh, don't think there haven't been all kinds of plans to match those two—and how Miss Barrett loves the help. But the sheriff has been outwitting the matchmakers in this town for years."

"Years? He can't be that old," Madeline remarked before taking another bite of cake.

"He's been here for some time, now that I think about it."

Madeline's expression turned quizzical. "You mean he's not from here?"

"No. Shandy brought him. Like he did you." As he had Ninny and her father. And nearly everyone else. She refilled her teacup and Madeline's as well.

Madeline stirred a sugar lump into her tea and added a dash of cream. "From where?"

"I don't rightly know. " Ninny added a small lump of sugar to her tea as well, stirring it in slowly. Then the spoon paused. "No, that isn't quite true. He's spoken in passing of somewhere in Montana. Around Helena, I think. But I don't know many details. Doesn't really matter, as he's found his place here."

"Unlike me," Madeline remarked under her breath.

Ninny smiled. "Well, you are a different sort now, aren't you? Everything will settle where it is supposed to . . . eventually."

Madeline had taken the last bite of her cake and was even now looking with longing at the old white plate where the rest of it sat.

"Do you want another piece?" Ninny asked.

Madeline grinned. "I shouldn't, but that cake is pure temptation." She inhaled deeply, fork in hand. "My grandmother always said that the way to a man's heart was through his stomach, and Ninny, I think you could rule the world with this coffee cake."

A man's stomach.

Ninny sat up. "That's it," she said, as she added seconds to Madeline's plate.

"What's it?" Madeline managed, her mouth once again full of cake.

"Cake," Ninny began. "No, pie." She got up, fixing her gaze on her cupboards, calculating what she had on hand. She was almost certain she had everything they'd need. "Yes, yes. A pie. I know just the one."

Madeline set down her fork. "Ninny, whatever are you going on about? I don't think I have room for all this cake and pie."

"Not for us. You are going to bake a pie for the sheriff."

"Me?" Madeline shook her head, then forked another bite of cake. "There are two problems with that idea. The first being I don't cook, and, secondly, wouldn't that be construed as bribery?"

"I assure you, it is only bribery if it is a bad pie. And with me right here, that will be impossible. Besides, if you bake the right pie, the evidence will quite handily disappear, with no one the wiser."

Madeline laughed. "Ninny Minch, you put Mr. Quinby to shame."

Instead of being alarmed by the comparison, Ninny laughed.

Having finished her second piece of cake, Madeline got up and began clearing the plates to the sink. "Do you think there is a way to open a saloon so everyone doesn't hate you?"

"They don't hate you," Ninny replied, pumping the water so Madeline could wash her hands, then washing her own as the last bit of water rushed out.

"They certainly don't like me," Madeline said.

No, they don't. But Ninny wasn't going to tell her that. Instead, she took a different path. "They just need to get to know you. Besides, I'm currently the most ill-favored person in this town. Don't think of stealing my notoriety."

Madeline laughed, then shook her head. "You know, giving aid to the enemy isn't going to help your reputation."

Ninny reached out and put her hand on Madeline's forearm. "Enemy? Hardly."

Madeline squeezed Ninny's hand, her eyes alight with gratitude. For *her*.

Ninny felt that river swell around her, raising her up, carrying her forward. Madeline turned away and, if Ninny didn't know better, dashed at something in her eyes.

"That means a whole lot," Madeline began. "I haven't had that many friends in my life. You know, people I can count on."

"Neither have I," Ninny confessed.

Madeline grinned, because she understood. "I would hate to think that I'm not going to get my license, especially after I went to so much trouble to find a cook."

This was news Ninny hadn't heard. "A cook?" She moved over to the counter and reached for her mixing bowl. "Who?"

"Mrs. Clarke."

Ninny was certain she hadn't heard her correctly. Her brows knit together as she looked over at her. "You mean Inola."

"No, I mean Mrs. Clarke," Madeline said matter-of-factly.

The postmistress carefully set down the mixing bowl. After all, it was her favorite one. "Mrs. Clarke is going to cook for you?" She said it slowly because she was certain Madeline had it wrong.

Madeline had picked up the teacup Ninny liked to use for measuring. "Yes. I did her a favor, and now she's helping me."

"Well, I'll be." Ninny could barely get the words out. Then she shook off her disbelief and nodded toward the flour tin. "Two and a half teacups, if you please."

"Don't tell me she can't cook," Madeline groaned, even as she carefully measured out the flour. "She said she could, so I didn't question it. Should I have?"

"I have no idea." Ninny slid the salt cellar over. "Half a spoonful, then two of sugar." After Madeline had added those to the flour, she continued, "I was always under the assumption that Inola did all the cooking." She handed her a fork and made a stirring motion, then turned to the icebox to get the butter and lard.

She wasn't going to scrimp on this pie. A lard *and* butter crust for the sheriff.

"Oh, Ninny, I wasn't supposed to tell anyone. So please don't—"

"Believe me, I won't tell," Ninny assured her. She scooped out enough lard and pinched it into pieces, tossing them into the flour mixture.

"You didn't measure that," Madeline noted.

"It's enough," Ninny told her.

"So what do I do?" Madeline asked, looking down at the mixing bowl.

"Work it in with your fingers," Ninny told her, rubbing her fingertips together to show her how. She cut off a hunk of butter and began to roll it out on the counter, shaping it into a serviceable circle. "Even if I were so inclined—which I am not—I don't think anyone would believe me." She shook her head. Good heavens, whatever had come over Mrs. Clarke? She'd always struck Ninny as rather, well, square-toed. "Then again, I hardly believe it. You might as well have said she was tending the bar."

Madeline laughed as if she too couldn't see the staid widow with a whiskey bottle in hand. "No, that's my job."

For a moment, Ninny stopped rustling about in her shelves of canning jars. "Mixing drinks? Can you?"

Her awe and disbelief made Madeline smile. "Yes. I'll have you know I can mix a mean whiskey sour. At least Mr. Quinby says so."

"Indeed." Ninny reached for the quart jar of pie plant she'd put up early last summer. "I hope you don't mind me being a bit of a busybody."

"Not in the least," Madeline told her as she diligently worked the lard into the flour. "Busy away."

"I must warn you that Mr. Quinby is not the most . . ." Her mouth set in a line as she fished for the words.

"Reliable? Trustworthy? Forthright?" Madeline offered.

Ninny sighed with relief. "So you know?"

Madeline studied her work. "Believe me, he isn't the first shady lawyer I've encountered."

"So you've run a saloon before?"

Madeline chewed at her lower lip. "Not a real saloon. I played a saloon owner."

"Played?" Ninny opened the canning jar, and immediately the tart air of pie plant rose up. Madeline leaned over and inhaled, her eyes widening.

"Rhubarb?" she asked. "He likes rhubarb?"

"My mother always called it pie plant," Ninny replied. "I have a nice start out back. Comes in every spring. And it just happens to be the sheriff's favorite pie. I heard him say so at the Fourth of July picnic. I'd brought one, and he ate three pieces. When Mr. Thayer teased him about how much he was eating, the sheriff said his mother would make it for him every June for his birthday and it had been too long since he'd had one." After a few moments basking in the remembered warmth of that faraway summer day, she turned her attention back to the discussion at hand. "Still, I'm not sure that playing a saloon owner and being one are quite the same things."

"I do know quite a bit about saloons," Madeline assured her. "I did all kinds of research so I would be believable behind the bar."

Ninny couldn't help but show her concern. "My dear, fictional saloons—like the ones in dime novels or, dare I say it, on the stage— and real saloons are two very different creatures. I fear you might find it a bit rough." Though she suspected that actresses were well versed in some of the less genteel aspects of the greater world. She went to the pump again and filled the teacup with water.

"Men are men," Madeline was saying. "They like to have a drink, eat, and complain a bit. It can't be that hard. You'll have to come over and see for yourself."

Ninny nearly spilled the whole teacup into the mixing bowl. "Me? Oh, heavens no!" There was rebellion and there was ruin. "Ladies don't go in saloons." Carefully she drizzled a bit of water into the bowl and brought it together into a passable dough.

"They do where I come from," Madeline stated firmly.

"I never," Ninny managed, lightly dusting flour over the counter and dumping the dough atop it. She rolled it out in a quick, efficient circle, and then looked up to find Madeline gaping at her.

"You do that like a pro," Madeline said.

Not being too certain what a "pro" was, Ninny took it as a compliment. "Now here is my trick to make the crust extra special." She carefully took up the flattened circle of butter, laid it atop the crust, and folded the whole thing together.

"Like puff pastry."

Ninny glanced over. "Why, yes."

Madeline smiled. "My friend Nate loves watching Paul and Mary bake. So I guess I've picked up a thing or two over the years."

"Nate?"

"He directed the show I was in."

"But he wasn't . . ." Ninny hadn't any idea how to describe such things.

Madeline saved her from venturing down that path as she barked a laugh and shook her head. "Nate? No, never. We're friends. The best of friends. I'd do anything for him." Again, that wistful note returned.

"You miss him."

"I do. He must be worried sick over me." Madeline looked toward the window.

"Why don't you send him a postcard?" Ninny suggested. "Let him know you're safe and sound. That ought to ease his mind."

"I don't see how it will get to him," Madeline told her.

"Nonsense. As a duly sworn official of the United States Postal Office, I swear upon my honor it will find him." She folded the crust one more time then finished rolling it out. "While the pie bakes, you can write him a postcard."

Madeline seemed unconvinced, but Ninny hardly wanted to return to any conversation about ladies in saloons. "Do you like acting?" she asked as she fished out a pie tin.

"Yes. I rather love it." Madeline's expression softened. "I was in *Romeo and Juliet* two summers ago in New York."

Ninny sighed. "Oh, my favorite!" Shyly she glanced over at the other woman, seeing her anew. "O comfortable friar, where is my lord?"

Madeline's eyes widened, and she continued the stanza. "I do remember well where I should be, and there I am. Where is my Romeo?"

Here Ninny had thought Madeline wasn't much more than a fallen woman, brought to Bethlehem to find her redemption. A lost soul upon whom Shandy had taken pity.

But as Madeline said those fabled lines, her entire face changed, and her body shifted from her usual confident stance to that of an adolescent Juliet, so soon to be lost.

Ninny stepped back, her mouth opening. "Oh, how transforming!"

"Thank you," Madeline said with a small curtsy and blush.

"It is a horrible shame Shandy didn't bring you here earlier," Ninny declared.

"Earlier?"

"Yes! The Bethlehem Opera Society could use some professional help. As chance would have it, they are actually doing *Romeo and Juliet* this year for the gala." Ninny smiled. She lay the crust in the pan. "Miss Hatchett—rather, she's Mrs. Vaughn now—is playing Juliet. Oh, she's young and pretty, but her acting is, well . . . Let's just say it isn't all that. It would be ever so nice to see the play done right and proper."

"When is this supper?"

"The twenty-third. It's a busy few days, what with the Opera Society gala, then the Christmas pageant on Christmas Eve, and then the ball on the twenty-fifth. Not to mention the spelling bee the Friday before."

"Is it always like this? With all the socials and bazaars and such?"

She paused. "This time of year finds most everyone in town, so it makes the gatherings easier. Besides, it's the holidays." Ninny shrugged, for she'd never really thought about it much.

"By spring," she continued, "the men all go out into the hills, prospecting or working in the mines, while most of the others return to their ranches. So the dances and socials aren't as easy to organize."

She emptied the jar of pie plant into the pie tin, sprinkled two large spoonfuls of flour over it, and then poured in a generous teacup of sugar. She remembered her last pie being a bit on the tart side, so she wanted to make sure the sheriff smiled when he took that first bite.

"Now the trick to this pie," Ninny advised, "is making a pretty lattice on the top, so when it cooks it doesn't boil all over." She cut the crust into strips and twisted them as she put them on top. "I like to do it this way so everyone knows I baked it."

Then she brushed it with a bit of milk and tucked it into the oven. As she closed the door, she felt, instead of the usual sense of accomplishment that went with baking, an unexpected grief that this jolly evening would soon end.

Madeline had already filled the dishpan with hot water, and was starting to wash the dishes, when Ninny remembered her promise. She bustled down the hall and returned a few minutes later. "I have this postcard left over from last year. You can use it to write to your friend. It's always nice to remember those we care about with a cheery note this time of year."

At the time, Ninny had thought it too pretty not to buy, though it was a rather foolish purchase since she had no one to send cards to. But she'd liked the sentiment across the top, "*Be Merry & Bright*," along with the two cherubs decorating a fat and jolly Christmas tree with candles and strings of popcorn, while on a table behind them sat a pretty cake.

Now she understood why she'd bought it and saved it. The holidays weren't about gifts and cards and express packages.

They were about spending time with dear friends. Like tonight.

For the first time in her life, she truly understood what those words meant.

Be merry and bright.

"YOU'RE SURE the pie will be okay tomorrow?" Madeline asked, as Ninny led her down the dark hallway to the front of the post office.

"Of course. It's got to cool."

It had come out of the oven about an hour earlier, and the warmth spilled through her mittens as she carefully carried it. "I just want to make certain—"

"He'll love it," Ninny assured her.

"I hope so. I can't open without his signature on a saloon license."

"He'll sign," Ninny promised. She let Madeline out the front door of the post office so she'd have a more direct route back to the Star Bright.

Madeline turned to thank her again and found herself facing the wreath hanging beside the door jamb. "These wreaths of Badger's are beautiful, aren't they? It is from Badger, isn't it?"

"Yes. I just wish he hadn't given—"

"He gave it to you?" Madeline's eyes sparkled. "As in a bribe?"

"It is no such thing," Ninny told her tartly.

Madeline grinned. "Of course it isn't."

Ninny groaned. "I should have taken it down before anyone saw it."

"Yet you didn't," Madeline said, more in a soft hush. "You aren't the first woman to be swayed by something lovely."

Ninny glanced over at it. "It is lovely, isn't it?"

"I think this is his way of saying he's sorry. About the fight and all."

Ninny huffed. "A nicely worded note would have sufficed."

"It wouldn't be as festive."

"It would be far less public."

"But not as pretty."

"Do you want to borrow the lamp?" Ninny asked.

"No, I have the stars," Madeline told her, striding into the night in all confidence. But her confidence faded a few minutes later, after she'd crossed town and found herself in front of the two-story clapboard building across from the saloon.

There was a light on in the office and one upstairs.

So the sheriff was home and the place was open for business, and here she stood, pie in hand. Her hesitation wasn't out of fear or regret —qualities she'd never really possessed—but because the door was cracked open and voices—strident, angry ones—slipped through the opening like the warning buzz of bees.

Make that hornets.

Murder hornets.

Of all the things she should have done—turn and leave, or at the very least close her ears to this private, albeit loud, discussion— Madeline chose to move closer, right up the steps, and quietly push the door open until she found herself inside.

A solid pair of jail cells sat empty with their doors wide open. From the back room came Mrs. George L.'s strident tones, arguing forcefully to have Madeline locked away for the near future.

As the woman continued her belligerent tirade, with echoes of agreement from her unseen cohorts, the ugly words plucked at the warmth and friendship Madeline had found in Ninny's kitchen.

"She is a foul creature, determined to spoil our beloved town."

"Evil woman."

"This is the work of—"

It was rather like watching a late-night host read online comments to his audience for laughs.

"Oh gracious heavens," Madeline found herself muttering, borrowing one of Ninny's homey idioms. It was a far sight better than the one she'd usually use.

"That woman is an abomination to the godly morals of this community," Mrs. George L. intoned. "You cannot, you will not, sign a license to reopen that devil's den across the street."

Madeline looked down at the pie in her hands. It seemed it had been a wasted effort. Still, she set it down on the table by the stove and backed her way toward the door. It was, after all, the sheriff's favorite, and he'd saved her from freezing to death, and kept her fed those first hard days.

So she took one last look at Ninny's beautiful pie and closed the door. As she picked her way empty-handed through the muddy, snowy street, she rubbed her mittens together.

Leave it all behind, Maddie. Leave it all behind you.

She wondered if Shandy, when he'd offered that advice, had been referring to all those hateful online comments stacking up like bricks on her soul. Those terrible years after *Casey Jones*, years when the fans and press had been relentless as she'd made a string of flops and was no longer the pubescent child they wanted.

They only wanted the girl they remembered, the one full of sparkly charm and laughs, who wore cute outfits and sang them a sugar-coated pop song at the end of every episode.

Then Nate had come along with his wild idea for a series, *The Star Bright*, and so she'd stepped once again onto the small screen, this time as Calliope Corfield, all brass and tart. She'd been overjoyed to send the saccharine Casey Jones into the background as fans old and new embraced this new persona.

Madeline sighed. It had stopped snowing, and the hush invited her to look up. Not at the multitude of stars overhead, but at the very specific ones in front of her. The Star Bright. Her saloon. Inside, a lantern burned bright, and she could see Erasmus inside, helping Dobbs with his homework.

Now she knew why Nate had written the show, cast her as Calliope, and given her so much research and so many storylines. He'd prepared her for the greatest role of her life.

"Oh, Nate," she whispered. "Thank you."

Because for all those years, he'd been handing her more than the role of a lifetime.

He'd been giving her a map home.

AFTER DOBBS HAD FALLEN asleep on the sofa—he still refused to use the bedroom she'd cleaned up for him upstairs—Madeline settled down in front of the piano and quietly picked out a few notes. It had been a long time since she'd played, not since her days as Casey. She'd gone to great lengths to insist that her *Star Bright* contract include a clause that she never had to play or sing on the show.

But here in the lamplight, as she listened to the sad notes of the wind, something had prodded her to play. For her and her alone. Softly and quietly, she began to sing the gentle notes of "Silent Night."

She felt rather than heard the door open. A bit of wind whispering past her, but she didn't stop playing until she got to the end.

"You have a pretty voice," Wick said, having settled onto one of the barstools.

"Thank you." Her hands stilled atop the piano keys. "It needs tuning."

"I thought you sounded just fine," he teased.

Even Madeline had to smile at that.

Then he drew a deep breath. "Thank you for the pie."

"How did you know?"

"I'm the sheriff," he told her. "That, and you weren't as quiet as you thought you were."

She nodded. "Miss Minch helped."

"I thought as much. That's how I knew it was going to be edible."

She tucked her nose in the air. "You're really horrible."

"I've tried your coffee."

"How did you know Ninny helped me?" She plunked a few keys, trying to find the right notes, a song whispering to her that she couldn't quite remember.

"The crust," he told her. "She always does that fancy little twist. That, and she's the only one around these parts who has a pie plant that grows well enough to put some up."

"Ah. Next time I'll make sure we do something more mysterious. Like pecan or pumpkin."

He smiled, then straightened up as if remembering himself. "You know Mrs. Lovell came to see me."

"Really? That wasn't Santa Claus coming by for a test run?"

"I'm sorry for that. No one should have to listen to her caterwauling."

Madeline pressed her lips together to keep from smiling. "Really? Caterwauling?"

"How would you have described it? No, don't tell me—I'm certain I don't want to hear."

"Probably not."

He pushed off the stool and crossed the room. He settled a chair beside the piano before he sat down and looked over at her.

"You certain you want to open up this place?"

"Yeah, I am." She looked down at her hands and then back up at him.

"I won't cotton any trouble."

"Cotton?" She laughed a bit, but he did not.

"I'm very serious about this," he told her. "You have a way of tossing kerosene on the fire."

She shrugged.

"Any hint of trouble, and I'll pull your liquor license and toss you in jail."

She crossed her heart with her hand. "I promise." Then she had to ask. "Why are you doing this? Letting me open up."

Wick shuffled his feet a bit. He tipped his head toward Dobbs, still sound asleep on the sofa. "I couldn't let your kindness go unnoticed."

"Honestly, the kindness was all his. I wouldn't be here without him."

"I don't doubt that," he agreed. Then he turned serious again. "Don't make me regret this."

"I'll try." She knew better than to promise. Trouble had a way of finding her. "Anyway, you'd only be able to keep me locked up until Christmas."

"Why is that?

"Because Shandy promised me he'd take me back then." Madeline paused as a whisper of suspicion curled down her spine. "He can take me back, can't he?"

Wick raked a hand through his hair. "I think so. It's just that no one has ever wanted to go."

"Why didn't you?"

"Nothing to go back to."

"Really? You seem like a family man to me."

He barked a laugh. "Hardly." He looked at her, and she saw a flicker of grief there. He blinked it away just as quickly, but, oh, that honest moment wrenched her. "No, it wasn't that. I just didn't belong there anymore."

Madeline remembered something Ninny had said. "How long have you been here, Wick?" While most everyone else seemed to belong to this time, he didn't. There was this sense that Wick Fischer was just a step out of sync with the other citizens of Bethlehem.

"I don't rightly know. It's been a while, I imagine." He scratched his head and shrugged. "A few years. Time runs a bit funny around here."

"So I've noticed."

They sat there in the silence, and Madeline suddenly felt the need to fill the space between them. So she pushed the cover off the keys again, and started to play "Away in a Manger."

Gigi's favorite. When she got to the second verse, she glanced over at the sheriff. He looked only a few years older than her, but he wasn't really her age, if that made any sense. There was a timelessness to the man that put him at odds with the world she knew.

Which rather begged a question.

What world had Wick known?

She finished the song, letting the last notes settle into the silence, and asked him slowly, directly, "What year did you come here, Wick?"

He shuffled and glanced away, as if searching for something he couldn't quite put his finger on. A needle in the haystack. "Like I said, a few years ago. Just after the war ended."

A raft of bitter cold ran through her, like Dobbs had left the door open. Like time itself shifted. Even Dog sensed it, moving restlessly on his rug by the stove.

"What war?" The question came out in a quiet rush.

"What war?" He laughed. "How old do you think I am?"

"I thought you were like me. You came from . . ." She stopped. A chill descended, as time circled around the room, swirled overhead. Like a warning.

"1945," he supplied. "I came here Thanksgiving, 1945."

"1945," she echoed, clutching at the edge of the piano bench to steady herself.

Wick Fischer had come here at the end of World War II.

CHAPTER 29

Thursday, December 12

The notion that a beloved family tradition might rouse Mrs. Bergstrom from her plight had raised Savannah's hopes. According to Livia, there would be no *lussekatter* without saffron, so first thing in the morning, while Inola was typing away, Savannah made her way to the mercantile in hopes that Mr. King was in a generous mood.

Much to her chagrin, the store was busy—it always was this time of year, but today it was particularly so, with a good number of young ladies purchasing necessities for the box supper Saturday night.

The ribbon counter was doing a land office business as girls chose their favorite color to ensure their beaus would know which box was theirs. A beleaguered Myrtle stood at the helm taking their orders.

"I said the apricot one," the girl told her as the middle King daughter climbed down from the ladder for the third time. "That is champagne."

"I doubt Martin Daggett can tell the difference," Myrtle replied.

"He can barely tell you apart from Pinky Jonas," Francine added in passing.

The girl was neither amused nor willing to concede. "Apricot," she repeated, pointing at a roll on the top shelf.

Myrtle sighed and went back up the ladder. Then Savannah saw the entirety of her ensemble. A striped skirt and a checked blouse.

At least it was mostly masked by her shop apron. Oh, heavens, something had to be done. Her fingers slid into the pocket of her skirt, where she kept that restive slip of paper—having resigned herself that it was no use trying to get rid of it.

A new dress for the Christmas ball.

Yes, yes, Savannah silently promised. All she needed was time to sew.

The customer ahead of her began gathering his purchases, and Savannah saw her opportunity. "Mr. King, if I may—a moment of your time?"

"Why, Mrs. Clarke, this isn't your usual day to shop. Did you send your order in early?" He turned and looked at the stack of orders on the counter behind him.

Savannah took a breath. She was about to launch into the speech she'd planned—charity, kindness, and a bit of holiday spirit—but behind her, the bell over the door jangled with a loud clamor, and the room stilled as all eyes turned in that direction.

Miss Drake sauntered in as if she hadn't the least notion that everyone was watching her, while the knot of girls at the dry goods counter bent to whisper together as she passed.

Why wouldn't they? She was a sight. Dungarees, a man's knit cap pulled down over her head, and pigtail braids stuck out on either side. She'd knotted a bright red kerchief around her neck and walked down the aisle with a purposeful stride.

As she approached the counter, Savannah stepped out of her way, experiencing a moment of panic that Miss Drake would turn and acknowledge her. But that wasn't so. She tugged off her mittens and was all business. "Hello, Mr. King. Is my order ready?"

His easy smile tightened. "Frankie is just finishing it up. I'll get back to you when I'm done with Mrs. Clarke."

"Oh, I'm sorry!" She glanced over at Savannah, and for a second it seemed she was going to say something.

Not here. Not in front of everyone. That would never do.

Yet there was only slight quirk of her lips before she took a step back and stood silent as she waited her turn.

"Mrs. Clarke?" Mr. King said, his jovial demeanor somewhat flattened.

Savannah took a steadying breath, trying to pull together her carefully crafted speech. Nor did it help that everyone in the store was now watching.

"As you might know, Mr. King, I've been helping Mrs. Bergstrom."

"It is mighty kind of you, Mrs. Clarke. I know she's been doing rather poorly—the little mite as well."

She took another furtive glance around. A number of the real busybodies had edged closer. "Yes, well, she could use some extra cheer. I won't bore you with the details, but I have need of something that I think will help her immensely, it being nearly Christmas and all."

That was the moment Savannah knew she'd lost him. His congenial and kind expression turned to that of a businessman.

"As I understand it, it is a Swedish tradition to bake something called *lussekatter* for the thirteenth of December—tomorrow," she said, edging a smile to her lips, as much as she resented having to do as much. "Miss Bergstrom has asked me to help her bake them—but neither the Bergstroms nor I have the saffron the recipe calls for."

"Of course. Saffron. For the St. Lucia buns." He turned toward the drawer behind him and went through the small collection of papers folded around smaller amounts of spices. "It pays to know one's customers. Old Mrs. Larsen used to make them as well. I order it in every winter just for them. With her gone, I have extra."

"Bless her soul," Savannah hurried to say. "As it is, I only need a scant bit."

Mr. King quickly measured out the tiny red strands on the small scale. As he poured them into an envelope, he looked up and said, "That will be a dollar, Mrs. Clarke."

"A dollar?" she gasped.

"That is the same reaction Mrs. Bergstrom has most years, but she saves her pennies for it. Her 'Christmas pennies,' she calls them."

Then he looked at her expectantly, as if she had squirreled away those same pennies.

When Livia had said the saffron was dear, Savannah hadn't thought it *that* expensive. Heavens. Gold, frankincense, and myrrh would be a bargain in comparison. "I suppose you'll have to put it on my account."

Mr. King, to his credit, tried to be prudent about the situation. "I'm afraid I won't be able to—"

"It's for the Bergstroms," she hurried to remind him. "Those pennies you spoke of have gone to the midwife."

"I hope you understand, Mrs. Clarke, accounts need to be settled by the end of the year. I cannot in good conscience add to yours or theirs." He glanced over her shoulder at the crowded store. "Is there anything else I can do for you?"

Savannah didn't dare look left or right. It was all so humiliating. More so with Miss Drake right there at her elbow, pretending not to listen. "No, that was all I needed. I thank you for your time, Mr. King."

She turned and hurried out the door, and was no more than a block up the street when she looked up to find Mrs. Jonas bearing down on her.

"Yoo-hoo, Mrs. Clarke! How fortunate it is that I've run into you," the woman said, linking her arm into Savannah's.

"Yes, most fortunate," she replied, hoping the note of sarcasm was not too apparent.

Mrs. Jonas launched right in. "Here I had thought to corner you at the Temperance Union meeting today, but now is just as well."

Savannah didn't bother pointing out she wasn't a member, because that would only add to the conversation.

"I just wanted to ask you—"

"Mrs. Clarke! Mrs. Clarke!" someone called out behind them.

Both of them turned to find none other than Miss Drake hurrying toward them, large box in hand. "I am so glad I caught up with you."

"Whatever do you want?" Mrs. Jonas said, pulling her skirt back and eyeing the girl's ensemble with nothing less than revulsion.

The young woman returned the scrutiny, then dismissed Mrs. Jonas in a blink of an eye.

Savannah wished she could do the same so easily.

Instead, she spared a smile for Savannah, shifted the box onto her hip, and dug through the contents. "You forgot your purchase at the counter. I promised Mr. King I would catch up with you. Here it is." She drew out a small envelope.

The saffron.

"It must be something most wonderful if it requires saffron."

Savannah stood transfixed. "I never . . . that is . . ."

But it was Mrs. Jonas who snatched it away, all the while eyeing the box Miss Drake held. "Whatever is all that?"

None of your business, Savannah thought, but the young woman smiled brightly. "Oh, this? Just some of the groceries I need in order to open."

Mrs. Jonas blinked. "Open?" Like the word had some other meaning she couldn't quite translate.

"Yes," she replied, shifting the box again. "Got my license from the sheriff last night, and so I open tomorrow. We're going to serve food as well."

This, Savannah realized, was directed at her. So her duties were about to begin.

As would her wages. She looked down at the saffron and had to imagine it was an advance of sorts.

"License?" Mrs. Jonas stammered.

"Uh-huh," Miss Drake told her. "So if you'll excuse me," she said, continuing up the steps toward the door, "I've things to get ready. Drop by tomorrow if you like. The ladies' lounge will be in the back. I don't have it quite how I want it, but it will still be open for business. Tell your friends."

"A ladies' lounge?" Mrs. Jonas looked as if each word she tried came dipped in vinegar.

Miss Drake winked at her, all honey and sweetness. "Well, of course! Why should the men have all the fun?" She stepped up to the door, head held high, and continued inside, whistling a cheery carol.

Whatever Mrs. Jonas had meant to ask Savannah was now forgotten. "Someone must tell Mrs. George L!" Just before she went off in a fluff of feathers, Savannah retrieved the envelope of saffron from her plump fingers, letting out a breath as the woman hurried down the street.

Inside the saloon, Miss Drake had switched on the lights, illuminating the stained glass over the elaborately carved backbar—a bright burst of color to catch the eye.

But what Savannah really saw was her own reflection in the large mirror behind the taps. Hers and Miss Drake's, oddly juxtaposed, as if they were standing shoulder to shoulder.

A middle-aged woman clutching an envelope. A young woman whistling as she unpacked her groceries without a care in the world.

Savannah focused on her own reflection. This was not a woman who helped, no more inclined to charity than Mrs. Jonas was to restraint.

Her gaze flitted back to Miss Drake, the one person no one expected kindness from—for certainly she hadn't been shown any.

She tried to tell herself that this young woman's actions were less about altruism and more about cementing their agreement. Certainly this creature wasn't capable of doing a good turn simply because it was the right thing to do. Or was she?

She blinked hoping the reflection might shift, yet there she was, glaring back at the woman she'd become, the sort who stared out the window on a Thanksgiving morning and wished for a blizzard that would spoil everyone's hopes and wishes.

Unwilling to look any deeper, she let the sparkle of lights blur the reflection staring back at her and when she focused again, something had changed.

Her reflection and Miss Drake had blended together, and Savannah saw an altogether different picture, one that shone with the faintest of lights, a whisper of promises.

Promises of what, she knew not, but it was enough to entice her to do the last thing she'd ever thought possible.

She opened the door.

❄

"MISS DRAKE?"

The young woman stood up from behind the counter. "Madeline. My name is Madeline."

Savannah drew a line on such familiarities but continued anyway. "Why did you do this?" She held up the envelope of saffron.

Miss Drake looked up from her box of groceries. "I believe the words you are looking are 'thank you,' to which I would reply, 'you're welcome.'" She went back to her sorting.

Savannah didn't know what rankled her more—that the woman was right, or that she had the nerve to be so . . . well, direct. "If you think this makes me beholden to you beyond our original agreement—"

The younger woman glanced up again. "Beholden?" She said the word like she was trying it out. "Where the hell did Shandy find you?"

Now that rankled. "It's none of your concern."

Miss Drake sauntered down the long side of the bar. Behind her, the reflections in the long mirror flickered. "Struck a nerve, did I?"

Savannah held up the envelope again. "Why did you do this?"

"Honestly?"

Savannah nodded, short and sharp.

Miss Drake shrugged. "I didn't do it for you."

Savannah didn't know if she was relieved or piqued.

"I did it for *her*."

"Her?"

"Mrs. Bergstrom. Isn't she the one who just had the baby? She's having some problems—"

"Yes." Savannah tucked the saffron into her purse.

All the while, Miss Drake had been busy, pulling out two glasses from behind the bar, followed by a bottle. Pulling the cork with her teeth, she poured herself a shot of the amber liquid. Then she held the bottle over the second glass. "Can I interest you?"

"Not in the least." Savannah meant every word. Whiskey. How she loathed the stuff.

"Suit yourself." Miss Drake shrugged, putting the bottle on the counter and settling herself atop one of the stools with a measure of experience. She took an appreciative sip of the liquor and then glanced up. "It's bad, isn't it? This Mrs. Bergstrom and her baby, that is."

"Yes." Savannah glanced at her. "How did you know?"

"Dobbs. He's a little magpie. Gathers up all the bits around town, and then he has to share them. Makes him feel a part of something. Both of us, I suppose."

A rather painful silence drew between them, Miss Drake drinking her whiskey and Savannah standing adrift. Whatever was she doing here?

"Will she be okay?" the younger woman asked, surprising her.

The answers Savannah considered all sounded trite, in light of this girl's honest question. So she gave an honest answer. "I don't know."

"Then I hope the saffron helps."

That rather panged at Savannah's armor, so she got straight to the business at hand. "Miss Drake, do you still want a cook?"

"Yes, definitely. No one should have to eat my cooking."

"Well, I pledged my word to lend you my assistance, and so I shall."

Her brows furrowed. "Pledged your—"

"My word. I gave you my word, Miss Drake, and I am not one to shirk my obligations. However, I will not work for a drunk."

Miss Drake looked back at the glass on the bar and then right at her, as if weighing her choices. She nodded and put the cork back in the bottle.

"That's better," Savannah told her. "I have a reputation to maintain." This was becoming far too real. "I must impress upon you, Miss Drake, my desire for discretion regarding our . . . arrangement."

"Yes, I can imagine how you working for me might be misconstrued." The cheeky girl had the nerve to grin as if she was enjoying all this.

Savannah ignored the remark and turned to leave, but then she remembered her manners. "And, Miss Drake?"

"Yes, Mrs. Clarke?"

"Thank you for the saffron."

"DID YOU FORGET SOMETHING, MISS MINCH?" Miss Odella asked.

Ninny's eyes fluttered open to find the Winsley sisters staring at her as if they'd found another of their "scientific" discoveries.

How long had she been standing here in front of the Lovell residence, staring at the imposing door before her? Long enough. She knew what awaited her inside. It was Thursday. The new edition of the *Observer* was most likely all over town by now, so finally everyone knew the truth.

"I do so hate it when I forget something," Theodosia offered in consolation, absently pushing up her spectacles and taking another sweeping inspection of Ninny. Satisfied that all was well, she tucked her hand into the crook of Ninny's elbow and led the way into the Lovell residence.

"I wondered if you were coming in," Annie Bell Gray scolded, her lips taut and cheeks flushed from the exacting rigors of her duties. Late guests were the bane of Annie's existence. "I've still got to get them ka-naps"—Annie never said *canapés*—"on the trays and tea to set, and herself is in a rare mood." Shooing them toward the parlor, she shuffled back to the kitchen.

So the new edition of the *Observer* had arrived at the Lovell residence. Ninny braced herself.

The parlor brimmed over with what seemed like every member of the Temperance Union save the three of them. But an unnerving quiet filled the parlor, as if every single of one of them sat poised and waiting.

"Ah, so now we can begin," Mrs. George L. announced, and she nodded toward the only three empty seats available.

With no other choice, they wove their way through the

membership until Theodosia came to an abrupt halt in front of the low sofa table. There was a single item atop it.

This week's issue of the *Observer*.

Theodosia paused and tipped her glasses as if she wasn't sure she'd read the headline correctly. "Oh, my, that's unfortunate," she said, then glanced over her shoulder at Ninny.

No wonder.

Christmas Imperiled stared up at her. Ninny's mouth fell open.

The next column showed dueling etchings of Badger and Mr. Thayer, as if they were facing off, all heralded by another stinging headline that left Ninny imperiled.

However Can She Choose? The Battle for Bethlehem Continues.

Ninny forgot to breathe. Cora! How could she?

One glance up at the thunderous expression clouding Mrs. George L.'s features said that Cora's lump of coal had found the perfect stocking.

Worse yet, every East Coast paper, and every press from Helena to Houston, would be reprinting this tale. Then it would get reprinted and reprinted again, all the way up to Christmas. Why, the *Bethlehem Observer* would be known in every newsstand and living room.

With no other choice, Ninny settled in—if one could call it that when one was perched on needles and pins.

Mrs. George L. cleared her throat. "Yes, well, now that we are all here"—there was another pause and glance in Ninny's direction—"I had hoped that Reverend Belding would be able to attend this afternoon so we could start with a proper prayer, considering the moral imperative of the work we do. However, he was called away for something more pressing." Her tone suggested that she couldn't fathom anything more important than the work about to commence.

Mrs. Jonas looked ready to offer her own petition, but Mrs. George L. had anticipated such a likelihood and launched right in. "I fear that, despite our best efforts, we have been thwarted in our endeavors to stop that dreadful saloon from reopening."

There was a proper moment of silence, and then outrage swelled through the room like a sudden spring thaw.

"No, Mrs. George L., no!"

"How can this be?"

"We are all damned by this failure." This from Mrs. Hoback, with her usual dramatic flair.

Everyone in the room did their best to ignore that Mrs. Hoback's husband was also the town's largest purveyor of liquor. Just as they were all too well mannered to remind the woman that the fur draped over her shoulders had most likely been bought and paid for with said revenues.

"Well, this couldn't be worse," Mrs. Bohlen offered.

In that, she gave Mrs. George L. her opening. "Ladies, I haven't even gotten to the most grievous part of this news." She sat up straight, hawkish eyes bright. She had everyone's attention now. "The most heart-wrenching part? We have been betrayed by one of our own."

"You don't mean Sheriff Fischer?" Mrs. Cochrane said. "Certainly he holds some responsibility."

"The sheriff has some measure of accountability," Mrs. George L. conceded, "but I fear like all other men, Sheriff Fischer is guided more so by his stomach. Or rather his love of rhubarb pie."

Rhubarb pie.

Ninny glanced up and wished she hadn't, for here were Mrs. George L., Mrs. Jonas, and Mrs. Bohlen—the three members of the Morals committee—glaring at her.

Ninny tried to open her mouth to speak, but it had dried up like a gully in August.

How had they found out?

The answer was forthcoming. "You see, while we called upon the sheriff last night, in one last desperate effort to appeal to his decency and to the moral well-being of our entire community, it turns out there were others who did not agree with our doctrinal dictum."

Ninny tried to keep her eyes fixed on her lap. Yet for some reason her gaze rose toward the table where that dreadful headline sat atop the mast of the newspaper like a warning. *Christmas Imperiled.*

It wouldn't be if Cora had just done her job and printed what Ninny had written.

The rebellious thought startled her. Whyever was she cowering when she'd done her best to set this all to rights. And yet . . .

"Miss Minch, how could you?" Mrs. Jonas blurted out, spoiling Mrs. George L.'s grandest moment to date.

After a quick scathing glance at her de facto major-domo, the Temperance Union president wrestled the spear back into her sharp command. "It matters not how, the *why* of it is what I cannot fathom." With that, she drew out her handkerchief and dabbed it at the dry corners of her eyes as if Miss Minch had been her greatest friend, her confidante, and was now her greatest disappointment.

Everyone in the room turned toward Ninny. Shock. Dismay. She spied a flicker or two of sympathy, but not for long.

Mrs. George L. opened her mouth to rally her troops but was stopped short by none other than Theodosia. "I say, Madam President," she piped up, adjusting her spectacles and straightening with an air of concern. "How can you be so certain it was Miss Minch?"

Odella covered her face with her hands and muffled a groan.

Mrs. George L., as it turned out, was all too happy to add her evidence. "A rhubarb pie, Miss Theodosia. Rhubarb. One with a twisted lattice crust."

"Freshly baked," Mrs. Jonas added. "Sitting there on the table by the jail cell, as brazen as the sun." The woman tipped up her nose, setting her feathered hat aflutter.

"Miss Minch, is this true? Did you help that woman?" Mrs. Hoback asked.

"Yes. I did." Her confident words took most of the room aback.

"But a rhubarb pie," Theodosia said, shaking her head as if she just couldn't quite add that up. "It was pie plant, you say?" she asked the committee. When Mrs. George L. nodded her assent, Miss Winsley turned to Ninny. "Perhaps in the future an apple pie might be a more sensible choice. I fear rhubarb always hints of bribery."

"In the future?!" Mrs. George L. sputtered. "There will be no more pies. And especially no more Miss Minch. Not in our esteemed union. Not with such unconscionable sympathies."

This was met with stunned silence. Not a feather rustled.

Nor was the matron done. "I will be writing the national organization this very afternoon to demand that you, Parathinia Minch, be stricken from the rolls." Her angry gaze swept the room. "As well as anyone else who exhibits such vulgar predilections."

While most of the members looked down at the floor, out the window, or at the doorway where Annie stood open-mouthed—for she'd just arrived to ask if it was time for the tea—Beryl Smith, the Temperance Union secretary, rose to her feet, pulling everyone's attention to her tall, slim figure.

After she carefully brushed her slender hands across the front of her skirt, she cleared her throat. "Madam President, as the secretary of this esteemed union, I would be derelict in my duties if I didn't point out that, according to the rules of our charter, any revocation of membership must done by a roll-call vote, and then only by the assent of a majority of our membership."

Beryl was a regular stickler for rules and order. If she said it must be, then it must.

Nor did her interruption upend the president's agenda. Rather Columbia seemed delighted by the prospect. "Then, Mrs. Smith, please proceed, so there can be no arguments that any of us failed to act in a proper fashion."

"Then I will call each member to stand and—" Beryl started to say.

Ninny bolted to her feet.

"You needn't bother, Mrs. Smith," she told the secretary politely, glad that her voice wasn't quaking like her insides. "You can record that I quit of my own volition." Then she swept a glance around the room. "I will save all of you the humiliation of being asked to vote."

Now if only she could walk to the door without making a misstep.

She needn't have worried. She wasn't going alone.

Just as Ninny took her first step, Odella stood up. "If Miss Minch must leave, then so must we."

"We?" For all her orderly and precise questions to the president, now it was Theodosia's turn to appear scandalized. She tugged at her sister's sleeve to sit down. Immediately.

But Odella was not to be swayed. "If Miss Minch must leave for the crime of baking a pie—"

"A rhubarb pie," Theodosia pointed out, as if the issue needed to be clarified.

"A rhubarb pie," Odella conceded, "then we cannot, in good conscience, stay either."

"Oh, no, sister, you mustn't," Theodosia whispered, her gaze flitting toward the dining room across the hall. "Cannot it wait until after the tea?"

"I will not live a lie any longer, Dosia, and neither shall you," Odella told her gently. Then she turned to the room. "We keep a bottle of elderberry wine in our sideboard."

Oh, that set the Temperance Union back in their seats.

"Purely for medicinal purposes," Theodosia was quick to add. Yet now that the cat was out of the bag, or rather the wine out of the sideboard, there was no reason to remain sitting, so she shambled her way to her feet to take her place beside her sister.

"Come, Theodosia," Odella said. "Miss Minch, if you will." She nodded toward the door.

The three of them took their leave as gracefully as they could, only to find Annie already waiting with their coats in the foyer.

"You could have at least waited until after the tea to unburden yourself, sister," Theodosia whispered as she donned her coat. She cast another long, lingering look toward the dining room. "There is a nicely iced chocolate cake sitting on the table. Chocolate, sister."

CHAPTER 30

*N*inny marched ahead of the Winsley sisters, determination firing her steps.

"Miss Minch," Odella called out as she scurried along behind her. "Where are you going?"

"To see Cora Stafford." Ninny paused and let them catch up. "I have a few choice words for her."

Theodosia's brows rose a bit, even as she caught hold of Odella's sleeve. "We'd best leave Miss Minch to resolve this on her own, sister."

Odella looked ready to protest, but one glance at Ninny and she nodded in agreement. But before she turned away, she added, "You won't mention the wine to Cora, will you? There is no telling what she'll print these days."

"Have no fear. I have more than enough to say to her on my own account," she told them, and then turned down Main Street toward the *Observer's* office.

Before she even got to the door, Ninny heard shouting inside.

She stepped over Wellington and walked in to find his owner loudly voicing his own consternation. "Dammit, woman," Badger was yelling, "I will not be part of your tomfoolery! You take me out of that bloody paper and retrieve all those issues."

Ninny was taken aback by his tenor, but not Cora. She faced him down with cool resolve. "Why is that, Mr. Densmore?"

Ninny would have backed out, but she had a stake in his anger as well.

"That is none of your concern," he told her.

Cora glanced over his shoulder directly at Ninny. So much for arriving quietly or exiting quickly. "Why not take it up with my source?" She nodded for him to look. "Miss Minch, what do you have to say?"

"I have a few words of my own," she managed, wrenching her gaze away from Badger and his murderous expression.

"Seems you've said enough," he replied, before turning back to Cora. "Now leave me out of all this nonsense." Gathering himself up like a great bear, he made for the door, though he paused as he passed Ninny. "Quite a mare's nest you've managed, miss."

"But I—" Ninny began. He was already gone, the door banging on its hinges. So she turned back to the real target of her ire. "Oh, Cora, why? Why would you do this to me?" Ninny tipped her head toward the door as it stopped rattling. "I've been drummed out of the Temperance Union. And now Mr. Densmore thinks I'm . . ." She struggled for an explanation that didn't start with "a bloody liar."

"Oh, he'll come around. As for those teetotalers, I've done you a favor." Cora smiled a bit. "Never saw why you belonged to that gaggle of hypocrites anyway."

Ninny was in no mood to be cajoled. She straightened and got to the point. "I belong because I . . . Because I . . ." She pulled at her mittens and tried to summon up her reason.

"Believe in the cause?" Cora snorted. "You belong—or rather belonged—because it was expected of you." She blew out another breath. "Too much time in our lives is wasted doing what is expected."

"Whyever didn't you print what I wrote down?"

"I'm not going to divide this town." She drew a deep breath. "Parathinia, don't you see? If I'd printed the words you wrote—"

"The truth," Ninny corrected.

"If I had printed the truth, all the ugly fault lines that divide our country, that have divided men and women since time immemorial, would have ruptured the social fabric that holds this small community together."

Ninny opened her mouth to protest, but Cora kept going. "Hear me out. What you did on Thanksgiving was the best decision ever, mind you at a great personal cost and sacrifice. God willing, maybe in a hundred years or so, our beloved *e pluribus unum* will be a true nation of one heart instead of a nation in which we are divided as Catholics and Protestants on opposite sides of town, by whether one works with their hands or a pen, or uses only the language their mother spoke, or dare I say it, the color of their skin. One day, I pray we might look upon each other as brothers and sisters with one goal of common good and harmony—which, Miss Minch, is exactly what you aimed for Thanksgiving night, of all nights. If I had printed what you wrote, this town would fracture in half."

There was some truth what she was saying, but still Ninny's hand wavered over the stack of papers. "But instead you printed this falderal and left me in the suds."

The infuriating woman laughed. "Falderal, indeed!" She held up this week's edition, looking far too proud of herself. "This is the most entertaining and interesting thing that has happened to this town since Mrs. Mott's unfortunate event."

"I don't want to be interesting, or entertainment."

Or be compared to Mrs. Mott. Bless her poor departed soul.

Ninny plucked the paper out of Cora's hand and set it back down on the counter. Then as an afterthought, flipped the pages over so Mr. Thayer and Mr. Densmore weren't staring up at her so accusingly.

Cora shrugged and rustled behind the counter until she retrieved her notebook and a pencil stub. "What can you tell me about this ham Mr. Thayer has reportedly ordered from Mr. King?"

Ninny took a step back. "A ham? I don't know anything about a ham." Not that Cora stopped taking notes. "Don't write that down. That isn't news."

"I think it's my job to determine what is news."

"If you need news, then print what I told you before."

Cora looked her directly in the eyes. "When you make *your* choice—" She let that last word hang there for another moment. "Then I'll print it."

SAVANNAH CAME DOWNSTAIRS after putting away some laundry to find Inola still home. "Don't you have choir practice?" she asked, glancing at the clock.

"Tomorrow night." Inola stepped away from the table to reveal a large box. "What is all this? Dobbs just dropped it off. More of Mr. King's largesse?"

"Don't even suggest such a thing," Savannah shot back, looking down at the large roll of bologna. Good heavens, she was going to have to speak to Miss Drake. Along with the four loaves of rye bread from Larsen's bakery that had arrived earlier, they had enough to make sandwiches for the entire town.

She looked up at Inola. "I decided to take Miss Drake's offer of employment."

Inola stilled and then sank into a chair. "You what?"

"You heard me. I took the job. We need the money and, as you said, I can cook." There, it was done.

But it wasn't.

"Just like that, you decided to take the job? What aren't you telling me?"

Savannah was saved, in a sense, when there was another knock, this time at the front door.

"Oh, I can't wait to see who this is," Inola muttered as she followed Savannah to the door.

"I came a little early," Livia said, even as the door opened. "I hope you don't mind."

"Not at all." Inola edged past Savannah and welcomed the girl in. "What have we here?"

Livia held out two small sacks. "Sugar and flour. For the *lussekatter*."

"Luse-a-what?" Inola asked, as Savannah hurried the girl to the kitchen.

"I'm helping Miss Bergstrom make a special sort of bun for their celebration tomorrow." Savannah tried to make it sound like she did this all time.

Inola tipped her head. *If you think I am not going to ask . . .* "A celebration?"

"St. Lucia Day," Livia provided. "Didn't Mrs. Clarke tell you about it?"

Inola crossed her arms over her chest. "Surprisingly, she didn't."

"It must have slipped my mind," Savannah said. She turned to Livia. "You set that flour and sugar aside, child. I read over the recipe and have everything at the ready."

"Oh, you shouldn't have, Mrs. Clarke," Livia began. "You've been too kind to us."

"Hasn't she?" Inola agreed as she settled into the chair, taking a front row seat.

Savannah shot a warning glance in her direction. "Didn't you say you wanted to finish that book you were reading?"

"Finished it this afternoon," Inola replied, looking pleased. "Now what is this St. Lucia Day all about?" With an attentive audience, Livia explained the tradition—without Berta's embellishments—and Inola perked up. "Wouldn't that make the perfect article for *The Ladies Weekly* next December, Mrs. Clarke?"

"Why, yes, I suppose so," Savannah agreed, playing along.

"In the magazine?" Livia's eyes widened. "Really?"

"Indeed. I have learned to trust Inola's instincts on these matters," Savannah told her, even as Inola fetched a sheet of paper and a pencil.

She settled back down at the table. "Do you mind if I take notes about all this?"

Livia shook her head. "Not at all. Oh, mother will be so surprised."

"Then let's make sure everything is perfect," Savannah told her.

The girl explained how her mother steeped the saffron in warmed milk, and so Savannah began the process while the Livia measured out the rest of the ingredients. It was clear she knew her way around a kitchen, so why had she asked for help?

Meanwhile, Inola peppered the girl with questions about St. Lucia Day, taking copious notes. Livia didn't seem to find it odd. In fact, she retrieved another recipe from her pocket, shyly wondering if it could be included in their baking—if it wouldn't be too much bother.

To Savannah's delight, this recipe, for something Livia called *pepparkakor*, looked to be a crisp sort of ginger cookie, the sort she loved with a cup of tea. She quickly gathered the ingredients, unearthing a long-unused cookie cutter in the shape of the star.

The three of them baked a veritable Milky Way of ginger stars.

Enough, Savannah imagined, even for Berta.

In the middle of all this, Inola had gotten out her Brownie camera and taken pictures, showing Livia how to take them as well.

"I've always wanted to try taking a picture," she confessed, sounding as hungry as the twins were for cookies.

"Then please take some tomorrow," Inola said, offering her the camera. "Wouldn't that be a good idea for the article?" She nudged Savannah.

"Indeed. Pictures would make the article so much more satisfying for the readers."

"Oh, I couldn't," Livia said, staring down at the camera.

"I think you know what you're doing," Inola encouraged. "Give it a try."

Livia glowed as she turned the camera this way and that, discovering a new world. "Aren't these something? With just a click, they create a memory that will last forever."

"Everything fades with time, child," Inola told her.

Fades with time.

Savannah wondered if that was what had happened to the pair of them here—fading while the rest of the world sped along.

She changed the subject. "How did your test go today?"

Livia set down the camera and sighed. "I managed to pass."

That didn't sound very encouraging. "But you want to be a teacher, isn't that right?"

"Oh, that's a fine choice," Inola agreed quickly, having put the kettle on for tea.

"For someone else," Livia told her.

Savannah shared a glance with Inola. "But your father said—"

The girl heaved a sigh. "That is what Mama and Papa want me to do, but I don't want to be a teacher. I've had enough of little children and runny noses." She stole a glance at Savannah, as if she held all the answers.

Ah, now it was coming through. She didn't need help baking. She needed a sympathetic ear. And because she thought she was standing before Mrs. Livingston. Which she was, in a manner of speaking.

"But now Mama is so . . ."

"Lost," Savannah provided.

Livia shook her head, so adamantly Savannah was taken aback. More so when she spoke. "If only it were that, Mrs. Clarke. If she were merely lost, then we could find her. But I don't think she wants to come home. Ever again."

There it was. What Savannah had been ignoring all these days. What she hadn't been telling Inola.

Livia continued in a rush. "I've seen her like this before. After the twins it was bad, but nothing like this." Tears welled up in her eyes.

"It seems bad now, but I'm certain—" Savannah began.

"You can't be certain," Livia shot back, past the point of reaching for even a silver of hope. "No one can. Have you ever seen anyone this bad before?"

Savannah looked up. She saw not her kitchen, not the dark night beyond, but a faraway river that had pulled the life from her heart.

That question stopped Inola in the middle of the kitchen, the steaming kettle in her hands. "Yes, we have."

Livia glanced up from swiping at the tears on her cheeks.

"Did she find her way home? Did she recover?"

Savannah couldn't breathe. Couldn't say the words. Didn't think she could manage to force the lie past her lips.

"How? How did she come back?" the poor, desperate girl begged.

"With patience and love, child," Inola said, rescuing Savannah from having to lie. "Isn't that always the way?"

Livia hiccupped and sniffed back any more tears. Savannah slid her handkerchief over and went to the stove to retrieve the last tray of cookies.

Inola followed. "Vanna," she whispered.

"Not now," Savannah shot back, under her breath. As she put the cookies on the rack to cool, she turned to Livia. "You have had a long day. I'll bring these over early tomorrow morning. Then we'll see those rolls baked properly so everything is in order before your parents wake up."

Livia nodded and gathered her things. "Thank you so much, Mrs. Clarke." She turned. "And you, Inola."

"You are most welcome, child." Inola handed her the Brownie. "Don't forget this."

Livia stammered more thanks and left.

Savannah closed the door and took a deep breath as if she had just avoided a runaway train—that is until she turned to find Inola in the middle of the hall, arms crossed over her chest.

"Oh, Vanna, what have you gotten yourself into? Tell me this isn't going to be Sybilla all over again, is it?"

CHAPTER 31

Friday, December 13
St. Lucia Day

"*D*o you think they are done?" Livia asked quietly, as she and Savannah leaned over the pan she'd just pulled from the oven.

Savannah tapped one with the tip of her finger, and the hollow thud told her all she needed. "Perfectly."

"I couldn't have done it without you," Livia whispered, taking a furtive glance at her parent's door, clearly worried that such a sentiment was disloyal to her mother.

"You don't give yourself enough credit," Savannah told her. "Now let's put the tray near the window so you can get a good picture."

Livia smiled and retrieved Inola's Brownie. "Will my pictures truly be in a magazine?"

"That is the hope," she replied. "Of course, you will be credited."

Livia shook her head. "You did all the work."

Savannah demurred. "You gave Inola and me a lovely gift last night, sharing your family tradition, and you are the one taking the pictures. Of course you deserve the credit."

A slight figure slid between the two of them. "Are they done?" Berta whispered.

"What are you doing up?" Livia asked, trying to look imperious. But it was impossible with Berta, who stood there all sleep-tousled, a spark of hope in her eyes.

She still believed in the magic of Christmas. Thought that anything was possible.

"I couldn't wait," Berta told her sister. "I want to help."

"Go get the other plate," Livia offered, well used to tasking the little ones.

Berta scurried off and returned with the plate. "Can I help you put on your crown?"

"Yes. But, even better," Livia said, "you can help me with this." She pulled a tin out of the cupboard and tipped it so that Berta could see inside. She opened it slowly, and the scent of ginger and cloves and cinnamon filled the air.

"Pepparkakor," Berta reverently whispered, standing on her tiptoes.

"Can you put them on the plate while I arrange the *lussekatter* on another?"

"If I break one, can I eat it?"

"Only if you want to lose your wish," her sister reminded her.

Thus chastened, Berta carefully and slowly placed the cookies on the plate.

"A wish?" Savannah whispered over the little girl's head.

Livia nodded. "You place the cookie in your palm and tap it. If it breaks into three pieces, your wish will come true."

"It is a season of wishes," Berta reminded her solemnly.

Once, Savannah would have told the child that wishes were for the foolish. But when she looked into those starry blue eyes, something inside her flickered with a word she couldn't name. A wish of her own.

"I think she will be pleased," Livia said, her gaze traveling to the closed door. Margit and Clara, hand in hand, had quietly come to stand beside her. Even Peter, the eldest, had climbed down from the loft and joined his siblings.

Livia took off her apron. Beneath, she was wearing a plain white dress with a red sash. Berta hurried over to the window and gathered up the crown twined with evergreen sprigs and candles.

"I want to light them, Pelle," Berta declared, reaching for the box of matches.

"No, little sötnos," Peter told her. "That's my job. Your job is to wake Papa and have him bring Mama and Thomas out."

Peter, who until now Savannah had thought of as a bit of braggart, lit the candles with stately care. As the circle of illumination from each candle grew, sending dancing slivers of light all around the young girl, Savannah fell awestruck at the transformation.

So much so that she nearly forgot to capture this moment. She carefully framed the shot as Inola had instructed, and held her breath in the hope that the film might encapsulate even a wisp of the wondrous scene before her.

Peter lighting the last candle. The twins gazing up in rapt awe at their older sister. The Bergstrom children, bound together by light and tradition.

In a click of the shutter, her work was done. They had an image to hold this memory safe. Until it, too, began to fade.

Savannah didn't want to think of what was lost when memories faded and the past drifted out of reach.

She slid her coat on, determined to slip away.

Livia looked up from straightening her crown. "Please, Mrs. Clarke, stay. You've done so much."

"I don't know—"

But then the door to bedroom opened, and Mr. Bergstrom came out, guiding his wife with one hand and holding baby Thomas in the other.

Despite Livia and Berta's assurances that she should stay, Savannah backed toward the door, the scene so intimate it felt a sacrilege to intrude.

Berta broke away and caught hold of her hand, drawing her closer and anchoring her with them. "Isn't Livia beautiful?"

"Very much so," Savannah agreed.

Mr. Bergstrom settled his wife into the rocking chair and then carefully placed the bundled baby in her arms, while her gaze remained fixed on the crown of lights atop Livia's head.

Then Mrs. Bergstrom smiled ever so slightly, returned to them, and Savannah's hopes found a slender thread to weave upon.

They all began to sing a song in Swedish, soft and beautiful. The words and tune rose around them like the light from the candles, illuminating each of them. Most amazing of all, here was Mrs. Bergstrom, her lips moving over the words, and while no sound came forth that Savannah could discern, candlelight and family curled protectively around her.

Savannah held her breath. Might this be, as Livia had hoped, the nudge that would lift her mother's spirit from those unfathomable depths and settle her back into her rightful place?

As Mrs. Bergstrom's lips began to turn into a real smile, Thomas stirred and began to fret. The noise turned into a weak squall, a stark reminder that his place, his weave in the fabric of this family, was as frayed as his mother's.

Mrs. Bergstrom looked away, to that faraway place only she should see, the darkness finding its toehold yet again. Absently, she rose from her chair, handed the baby to Peter as if she were passing along a bit of folded laundry, and walked quietly back into the sanctuary of her bedroom, closing the door behind her.

Just as quietly, Livia took off her crown and, one by one, blew out the candles.

NINNY WANTED nothing more than to board up the post office and hide from the entire town. For if they hadn't heard of the dressing-down she'd received at the Temperance Union meeting, they'd most definitely read this week's issue of the *Observer*. Yet there was nothing to be done but tie on her apron and sort the sack of mail that had come in on the morning freight wagon.

Besides, she had only herself to blame for all this mess.

Postal and otherwise.

Dragging the heavy canvas bag around the corner, she opened it up and sighed. There was a good hour or more of sorting here and—she glanced at the door—there would be a steady stream of customers and the curious today.

After all, Mrs. George L. had yet to mail her birthday party invitations, and, being such a stickler for social rules, she would have to mail them today.

With a shrug and a sigh, Ninny dug into the sack and began to sort. The letters and postcards moved through her fingers quickly, finding their respective mail slots with an economy that came from years of practice.

Daggett.

Hoback.

Groves.

Densmore.

Already? She'd known who the letter was for even before she looked at it. Her fingers running over the crisp, thick envelope that had traveled so far.

The Honorable Sterling McCandish Densmore.

So Badger's annual letter had arrived. The one and only solicitation he received from the outside world.

Even that no-account Denny Herlan had a daughter who wrote to him faithfully every month. But not Badger. No one wrote him, save the sender of this one mysterious letter.

It was notable because it was unlike anything else that arrived in the Bethlehem post office in so many ways, starting with the precisely typed return address.

CAMPBELL, McKAY & FREY, SOLICITORS
LINCOLN'S INN
LONDON

Atop this thick envelope sat a multitude of stamps and postmarks that lent an air of gravitas to the missive. Yet each year, Badger gruffly picked it up and stuffed it in his pocket like a scrap of paper one might use to light a stubborn stove.

"Miss Minch!"

Ninny spun around. She hadn't heard the door open or the bell ring. There, standing at the counter, was Mrs. W. H. Vaughn, done up as if she had a number of very important social engagements to attend besides checking in to see if she'd gotten her hoped-for invitation.

"Good morning, Althea," Ninny said, tucking Badger's letter into the general delivery slot, reserved for the people who got little to no mail. "I'm sorry, I didn't hear you come in."

"Apparently not," she replied, her nose in the air. The former Miss Althea Hatchett had gone to the university in Laramie and come back to Bethlehem quite taken with herself and her degree. She used every opportunity to remind anyone listening that she had been a member of not only the Dramatic Society but also the Mandolin Club. "Is there anything for us? Mr. Vaughn is expecting a particularly important letter."

More so his wife, Ninny thought none too charitably, but she managed to paste a smile on her face. Mrs. Vaughn was only the first in a parade of hopefuls who would be dropping by today. "Sorry, there isn't anything new since you checked yesterday afternoon, but I've just begun sorting the stage mail."

The door opened in a hurry, the bell jangling wildly.

"Miss Minch! Miss Minch!" Miss Odella called as she bustled inside. "Has she been—" Her chatter ceased the moment she spied Althea at the counter. "Miss Hatchett," she managed in greeting, her brow crinkling.

"Mrs. Vaughn," Althea corrected with a sniff.

"Oh, yes, so it is," Odella replied, even as she pressed past the younger woman and made her way to the front of the counter. "The mail, Miss Minch?"

Ninny shook her head slightly. "Not yet, I'm afraid."

Odella sighed. "Sister warned me that my travails this early would be for naught and that my time would be better spent cataloging. Though I so hate returning with no success, for she'll quite crow about it the rest of the day." She glanced over at the Althea. "I see others share my opinion."

Althea bristled. "I hardly know what you mean, Miss Winsley."

"Of course you don't, dear," Odella replied, pushing up her spectacles and giving Mrs. Vaughn another glance. "Then again, you haven't been invited before, have you?"

The color drained from Althea's face. There had been a long-simmering air of discord between the pair. When Althea had left for the university, Odella and Theodosia had been her most adamant supporters, for they had thought she was pursuing the sciences. As it turned out, her degree was in domestic science and hardly provided the sort of learned discourse upon the subjects—natural and ancient—so dear to the sisters.

Althea was saved from making an unfortunate response by the arrival of Mrs. George L. herself. Mrs. Vaughn and Odella immediately melted out of the way so the woman of the hour could swan unobstructed to the front of the line.

"While I have been most grievously delayed in posting these invitations," Mrs. George L. announced to no one in particular, "it has been a fortunate blessing in that I've been able to make amendments to my previous intentions." She handed over the stack to Ninny. Taking a glance over her shoulder, she asked, "Miss Winsley, where is Theodosia this morning?"

"I daresay she wouldn't come out today, it being, well, today," Odella replied, doing her best to unobtrusively rise up on her tiptoes to see the directions written upon the invitations as Ninny stamped them one by one.

"Whatever is the matter with today?" Mrs. George L. asked.

Odella cringed. "It is Friday the thirteenth, and sister is convinced that the day is ill-favored."

A cruel flicker of delight lit Mrs. George L. expression. "Well, the day is young."

Odella paled to the same grayish white of her gloves.

With Miss Winsley put in her place, Mrs. George L. turned to Ninny. "As you can see, Miss Minch, a ladies' entrance is required for this institution. Any sort of riff-raffish man could come in right now, and we would be obliged to mingle in his company. If such a convenience is good enough for Denver, I do not understand why it cannot be contrived here."

"A ladies' entrance?" Odella inadvisably asked. She looked around the narrow space, clearly calculating the impracticality as well as the impossibility of such a demand.

Mrs. George L. ignored her. "Will *all* of these be posted today, Miss Minch?"

As if all her mail wasn't completed in a timely fashion every day of the year. Now it was Ninny's turn to bristle. "Yes, after the stage mail has been sorted," she replied, stacking up the invitations and adding them to the pile of letters that had come in overnight through the slot in the door.

"After?" Mrs. George L. huffed. "This will be going into my letter to the Postmaster General." She turned crisply and marched out the door. Then she paused. "Mrs. Vaughn, were you leaving? I have much to discuss with you about the Opera Society." She held open the door and waited.

The young matron had no choice but to oblige. "I would be delighted. It seems I have unexpected time on my hands, since Miss Minch hasn't completed the sorting as yet." She underlined this with a sniff of dismay.

"That is the sorry state of things around here," Mrs. George L. remarked. "But I do recommend returning later, as I think you will find what you were hoping for. Do have a care on the steps, they haven't been swept yet. We cannot have the shining star of our recital coming to any harm."

"Your concern is most touching, Mrs. Lovell," Mrs. Vaughn said, smiling in triumph at Odella before making an exit that would have made her Dramatic Society proud.

As the door closed, Odella turned nervously to Ninny.

Ninny pressed her lips into a tight line, not sure what to do.

For as she stamped the letters, she'd also been seating the guests around the table, and recognized immediately that Mrs. George L.'s birthday party had been reordered into an unholy reckoning.

Starting with the Winsley sisters. Ninny slid the two invitations across the counter.

Odella gasped. "No, Miss Minch. It cannot be!" Her gloved hands trembled as she gathered them up, her eyes dewy with tears. "I fear sister had the right of things. This day is misaligned."

No, Ninny thought, that day would be next Wednesday.

INOLA LOOKED up from her desk. "How did it go?"

Savannah shook, but not from the cold. She stripped off her mittens and tossed them down on the chair. Her hat followed with a plop.

"That well?" Inola muttered as she straightened the pages of notes in front of her.

"I thought . . . well, I—" *Wished.* How foolish had she let herself become.

Inola leaned back in her chair, a study in patience.

Savannah's chin wavered. "You should have seen their faces, Nola. So full of hope and joy, and then . . . and then she . . . she . . ." Her eyes filled, and she swiped at the tears threatening to spill.

Tears. What was she coming to?

"Let me guess," Inola began as she rose from her chair. "She closed the door?"

Savannah sucked in a breath, trying to curl around the maelstrom inside her to keep it from roaring free. "How did you know?"

Inola arched her brow.

"Yes, I should have realized." The tears welled up again, threatening to overflow their banks.

Then Inola was there, enclosing her into her arms, holding her close. Letting her cry.

"Well, I hardly expected a miracle." A wish that the past could be erased.

"I know, honey. I know."

But she had. She'd let Livia's hopes fill her own desires.

Savannah stepped back and struggled to regain her equilibrium.

"But it's Christmas, Nola. Well, nearly Christmas. And she has all those children. Such lovely young 'uns, and I fear she'll . . ."

"Do what Sybilla did?" Inola said the words they'd both been avoiding. For a lot longer than just the past few minutes.

Savannah nodded. "You saw her the other night. She's not getting better. I don't know what to do."

"I don't think anyone does," Inola told her. "It is a journey only she can take. Just as Sybilla chose hers."

"No," Savannah told her. "I won't let it happen again."

"It wasn't your fault the first time. Sybilla was never the strongest creature, and that awful mother of hers—"

"You say that, but—" Whatever she wanted to say was lost in a babel of accusations and recriminations, ones she couldn't blot out. It was a reckoning she'd avoided for too long.

How could you have left her alone?

I was only gone for a moment . . .

The empty bed. The cradle still rocking.

The silence that stretched through the house.

Through the window, a figure at the river's edge.

The blur of trying to get to her. Down the stairs. Out the door. The wide, endless expanse of the lawn.

By the time she'd gotten there, there was only an empty spot beside the spring-swollen river. The thick, dark water had claimed its spoils.

Dropping to her knees, Savannah sobbed. She was ever so far from that voracious river, yet she was drowning in it.

Inola knelt before her, encircled her with her warm arms, and held her fast. "Just cry. Just cry, Vanna. Let go."

The tempest tore at her, but Inola kept her moored, and Savannah did something she hadn't done before.

She let the currents carry the past away.

AFTER SUCH A LONG day in the post office, Ninny hardly wanted to go to the mercantile.

Land sakes, Beryl Smith had broken into such a spate of tears over her empty mail slot that Ninny thought she'd need to fetch smelling salts. But it was Friday, and she always picked up her regular order Friday afternoon.

"Miss Minch, good to see you," Mr. King said as she came into the crowded store. "I was just about to send Frankie over with your order and a special delivery." He leaned in and lowered his voice. "So today was the day, eh? The guest list is the talk of the town. Though not all the guests have been tallied." He grinned at her as if she might enlighten him.

After a hopeful pause, he gave up and nodded to Frankie to get the order. The girl, who sat atop a barrel, pushed off it, landing square on both feet, and hurried to the back room.

"Perhaps the special delivery that arrived for you today will brighten your spirits," he offered.

"Special delivery?" Ninny didn't know if she needed any more surprises, especially with Josephine Lovell and Pinky Jonas choosing ribbons at the opposite counter.

"Myrtle King," the Lovell daughter complained, looking down at the roll of ribbon in Myrtle's hand, "that is Turkey red. My mother would never approve of such a shade. I want Christmas green. The green I always get."

Myrtle huffed and set the roll of ribbon aside before scrambling up the ladder once more in search of "Christmas green."

"I predict that ham sandwiches will be awfully popular at the box supper tomorrow night," Mr. King was saying to her as he took money from another customer.

"Ham?" Ninny had quite forgotten that the box supper was tomorrow night. Thank heavens the evening was managed by Mrs. Norwood and the Catholic Women's Auxiliary.

Just then, Frankie returned with her box of groceries, and Mr. King reached in and brought out a large bundle, unwrapping the brown paper to reveal a lovely ham. "Now please don't tell Mr. Friedrich," he advised as he wrapped it back up. "He gets quite put out when people from these parts order up fancy Christmas hams from Cheyenne."

"But I didn't . . ." Ninny shook her head. Then she remembered that nonsense Mrs. Jonas had been spouting the other day and realized she shouldn't have dismissed it out of hand.

Not when Goldie leaned on the counter with her elbows and grinned. "It's from an admirer."

"An admirer?" Josephine parroted as she spun around. The girl had her mother's sharp ears and instincts. "Have you acquired more of them, Miss Minch, or is this one of the usual ones?"

Pinky Jonas snickered.

Myrtle climbed down the ladder, roll of ribbon in hand. "This is the only green we have left."

"That is apple green," Josephine sniffed. "I said Christmas green."

Goldie went to her sister's side and chimed in happily. "If you wanted the green you usually get, you should have come by earlier in the week. Clemmie Bohlen bought the last of what we had yesterday."

"You sold it to her?" Josephine turned to Pinky, and the pair shared a venomous look that didn't bode well for poor Clemmie. "Goldie King, you know that is *my* color."

Goldie hardly appeared the penitent. "First come, first served," she said, nodding to the sign that hung on the wall above the register.

That hardly suited Josephine. "How dare she? Clemmie knows I always have green. Everyone knows that."

"Which makes it easy to avoid bidding on your box," Francine remarked as she joined her siblings.

After glancing around to see if anybody had heard the spiteful remark, Josephine's sharp gaze found another target. "Miss Minch, have you come to get a length of ribbon for your box?" She and Pinky snickered. "Certainly now that you have suitors, it would be a shame not to make the most of this rare opportunity. The Women's Auxiliary will undoubtably raise enough money to buy two fire engines from your box alone."

Frankie snorted. "Thank goodness for that." She pushed back from the counter and crossed her arms over her chest. "Because everyone here knows your box won't raise enough money for a bucket of water."

Josephine's lips puckered into an outraged moue.

Pushing away from the counter, Frankie winked at Miss Minch. "Anything else you need?"

"Some extra tea, if you will, Francine." She was nearly out, what with all the company she'd had of late.

"*Francine*," Josephine mocked, while Pinky tittered like a goat. "Come along, Pinky. I suppose Miss Minch wants the color of her ribbon to be a mystery."

Her sniping tone dug into Ninny and frayed at her last nerve, especially because it had burrowed into Frankie as well. Before she could stop herself, she piped up in a voice that carried, "Myrtle, don't put away that roll of ribbon."

Everyone stopped and turned.

Myrtle did her best to act as if this was nothing special. "Which one, Miss Minch?"

"The red," she told her, not even bothering to spare a glance at the door where Josephine and Pinky were certainly gaping like a pair of trouts. "Turkey red."

MADELINE DISCOVERED QUICKLY that while the women of Bethlehem had a multitude of objections to the reopening of the Star Bright, the men held no such qualms.

The saloon was filled with both the curious and those outright content to have their sanctuary back open. They claimed their favorite stool or table and, with little fanfare, ordered up a shot of whiskey or a beer.

Or both, in some cases.

In the back corner sat the more esteemed citizenry of Winslow Jonas, Doc Groves, and no less than the town's mayor, Roswell Bohlen. They'd chosen their spot well, for it was out of eyeshot of the front windows.

Those whose wives didn't belong to the Temperance Union— Gabe Lundy, Dodge Tallack, and a few of the miners—filled the front tables.

About ten o'clock, Shandy ambled in. So the old coot had decided to show up. She poured him a drink and slid it down the bar, all the while chatting with Denny Herlan, for he'd been the first through the door and now sat ensconced in his seat.

"Arthur," Shandy said in greeting to the man on his left.

"Shandy," the fellow replied, reaching for his glass and taking a long swallow of beer.

"Surprised to see you here," Shandy remarked as he tried his drink.

"You wouldn't be if you'd been at my house earlier."

"How's that? Is something wrong with Beryl?"

"Everything is wrong, according to her. She didn't get one of them fancy invitations. Ten years in a row she's been invited to that luncheon, and now . . ." He shook his head as if it was all beyond his ken.

That confession brought ashore a raft of comments and grievances.

"Arthur, tell her she can have Althea's invitation," one of the fellows at the front table called out. "If I have to listen to 'I need a new dress' for the next week—"

"Oh, just wait," Mr. Higgins advised from across the table. "It isn't just a new dress. She'll be adding shoes and a hat to that list before Sunday is out." After a rare moment of masculine introspection, he sagely added, "I think Coralie is less upset about the slight than she is about not having an excuse to buy some lace or other doodad." He tapped his glass, and Madeline carried over a pitcher to refill his beer.

Shandy turned on his barstool. "Did you get an invite, Maddie?"

She laughed as she filled glasses all around the table and collected the coins. "No, my dance card remains wide open for next Wednesday."

"Then who did get invited?" Denny asked. "'Cause I sure as heck didn't."

As laughter and a few hoots filled the room, Madeline returned to the bar and pulled out a slate that she'd thought to use to advertise the food. "Let's see what we can figure," she said as she picked up a piece of chalk and began to write. When she was finished, she held it up for all to see. There was a column of numbers, one through twelve, down the side. "Who got an invitation?"

Just then, the door opened and Erasmus came in. Madeline had been wondering where the old chiseler had taken himself off to.

"Invitations to what?" Erasmus asked, as he claimed an empty spot at Mr. Thayer's table. Thayer didn't look all that happy to have his legal opponent—in nearly everything—seated across from him.

"Miss Drake was not invited to Mrs. George L.'s luncheon," Thayer supplied.

Erasmus snorted. "Maddie, I am aghast that you've been slighted. Parched, one might add."

The disreputable old coot. She grinned back at him and started to mix his drink. "I wouldn't want to take an invitation from someone who would truly appreciate the honor."

"Take Althea's, please," Mr. Vaughn grumbled. "When I left, she was going on with some fiddle-faddle about a gift. What do you give the richest woman in town?"

"A one-way train ticket to Denver?" Madeline offered as she finished stirring the Manhattan. Her suggestion had the entire room hooting with glee.

"So who is going?" Madeline asked.

The names came fast and furious.

Mrs. Jonas.

Mrs. Bohlen.

Mrs. Vaughn . . . with Althea's husband bemoaning the expenditure one more time.

"What is this?" Mr. King asked, having just arrived. He looked over the list with a keen eye. "Let me guess, the birthday luncheon."

A round of applause followed.

"I may be able to help, because I know for a fact that the Winsley sisters were invited." He paused while Madeline added their names. "As well as Mrs. Belding."

"Lucky old gal," Mr. Smith remarked. "She's deaf as a post and won't have to listen to the speeches."

Madeline added three more names. "Dobbs says Mrs. Hoback is going, as well as Cora Stafford."

"Cora Stafford?" Mr. Higgins shook his head. "No, that can't right."

Madeline shrugged. "According to Dobbs, she got an invitation. He fetches her mail every day."

"She'll be pleased as punch to have a front row seat when all hell breaks loose." One of the fellows laughed and nudged the man beside him. "Hey, Brisbin, your wife expectin'?"

The man turned a bit red in the face but laughed. "With our sixth. Not that she's invited." He grinned. "Ever again."

There was another round of laughter.

"What? You don't want to pay for another new carpet at the Lovell place?" Shandy asked.

"Didn't pay for the last one," he told them, tipping his glass in salute. Everyone roared in laughter in return.

"Ah, it is a joy and a delight to have this place opened again," Erasmus declared, raising his glass to the scandalously carved figurehead over the bar. "To Poppy!"

"To Poppy," the crowd cheered back.

That was when the door opened, and George L. Lovell walked in, to the dumbfounded amazement of most everyone. The room fell silent immediately, with one and all quickly burying their noses in their drinks or returning to their card games and conversations.

Denny caught Madeline's eye and tipped his head toward the blackboard, which she quickly tucked out of sight.

Mr. Lovell, for his part, hung his coat on the rack and his hat on the hook above, and entered like a king. Every man he passed nodded a respectful "Mr. Lovell" or "sir."

He paused at the back table, then slowly turned to Madeline. "A Tom Collins."

She got out a large bar glass and the gin bottle.

"Old Tom, if you have it," he specified.

"Of course." She turned the bottle toward him.

He nodded appreciatively and sat down with his cronies, and the room returned to its previous level of disorderly fraternity.

"I got a fine word or two for him," Mr. Smith muttered before he gulped down his drink.

Madeline reached across the bar and grabbed hold of the man's sleeve. "No trouble. I got rules, mister."

"I got something to say to him," he told her. "His wife is a—"

"A regular battleaxe," Madeline supplied. "You aren't the only man in here with a miserable wife back home. That there list proves it. But I didn't go to all this trouble"—she waved her hand around the room—"to have Mrs. Lovell win and see me get shut down." She let go of him and he straightened up, shaking out his sleeve. "Now help me out so I can continue to be a thorn in her side."

For a moment she thought she might have gone too far, but he turned, slapped Shandy on the back, and walked out.

Madeline shook her head. *Men.*

As Mr. Smith exited, a rough-looking pair entered, and suddenly Ninny's warning rang anew in her head. *A real bar and a fictional one* . . . That warning took on new meaning when one of them nudged the other as he spotted her. The two men shared a word or two that left them both laughing in a way that was both unsettling and sadly familiar.

Her hand slid under the bar, where she had a brand-new Honus Wagner bat tucked away.

As they passed the table where Thayer and Quinby sat, one of them nodded at Erasmus.

"Stay out of jail, Jenson," Erasmus advised him. "I'll charge you double if you cause trouble for Miss Drake."

"I'd like to trouble her," his friend said, jabbing an elbow into his companion's ribs.

Madeline curled her fingers around the solid maple.

Thayer glanced up and looked about to say something, but Jensen beat him to it. "Hey, ain't you the fella trying to catch that old postmistress?"

Thayer ignored him.

"Hams won't do the trick," he told the lawyer. "Not with an old girl like that."

From the corner, Badger, who had been keeping to himself near the stove with Wellington and Dog at his feet, rose in one smooth movement. Dog got up as well and moved to Madeline's side, letting out a low growl.

"You know what spinsters like," the fellow continued.

"I'd be very careful with what you say next, young man," Badger warned him as he crossed the room.

"What are you going to do about it, you crazy old fool? As desperate as she might be, she ain't idiot enough to let a lunatic like you up her skirt."

There was a suck of air in the room, a universal acknowledgment as to this deep insult as well as an understanding of what needed to be done. The saloon's occupants all seemed to melt toward the walls, drinks safely in hand.

All except the arrogant lummox who had tossed those heinous words and his pea-brained companion who chortled in agreement.

Madeline had the bat up and ready, anger flaming hot and white inside her, but she was nowhere near as fast as Badger.

His fist slammed into the man's face, sending him toppling to the floor in a heap.

Thayer took out the other one before he even saw it coming.

SOME HOURS LATER, Madeline set a glass of whiskey atop the arm of the piano and took a seat on the bench, her back to the room. She stared at the keys but was too tired to even pluck out a few notes. Instead, she reached for her glass.

The front door opened, but she didn't look. No need when her guest gave himself away.

"This should be locked," Wick complained. "Didn't tonight teach you anything?"

"I've had enough lessons tonight."

"Not as easy as it looks, is it?" he asked as he looked around the room, shadowed though it was.

She knew what he was seeing. The broom against the bar. The tray filled with empty glasses. The bin filled with broken glass.

"Came over here to gloat?"

"No, I came over here for some peace and quiet. I got two cells filled with angry citizens."

You're welcome probably wasn't the response he was looking for, so Madeline held her tongue.

"But I see you've got your hands full as well."

At least the tables were all righted. But they needed scrubbing, as did . . . well, everything. Her beautiful saloon, a tumbled wreck of masculine posturing.

All in her first night open.

To her chagrin, there was no set crew to put it all to rights. This was her mess to clean up.

"I can stick it out for the next ten days."

"Can you?" His shoulders tightened. "Make sure you lock your doors from now on. I'll keep those two overnight, but they are a pair of troublemakers."

"You didn't lock up Thayer or Badger, did you?"

"Of course I did."

"They didn't do anything other than—" She stopped there, afraid she might inadvertently add to their list of troubles.

"Other than . . . ?"

"Never mind. Do you want a drink?"

"Didn't I shut you down for the night?"

"You told me not to sell any more liquor," she told him as she went to the bar and found a clean glass. "I'm offering."

"You've been spending way too much time with Erasmus. You're starting to sound like him."

She grinned, poured a measure, and carried it over to Wick. She also brought the bottle and topped off her own drink. "You should let Thayer and Badger go."

"No, I shouldn't. I can't have it be seen that fighting will be tolerated. It might save you some damage in the days to come."

She nodded. "Sorry about the trouble." She sat down on the bench again.

"Are you?"

"How can you even ask?" Madeline settled the glass on the edge of the bench beside her. "I don't even want to think about how embarrassed Ninny is going to be when she hears."

"Ninny?"

"Miss Minch."

"Ah," Wick murmured. He slid a chair toward the piano and straddled the seat, his arms resting on the back. "Ninny, is it? So you've made a friend. I wondered how you got Miss Minch to bake you a pie."

"I baked that pie," she told him.

He snorted. "She helped. A lot."

"She might have," Madeline conceded, and then they both laughed. But it wasn't long before Wick was back to business.

"Those two are going back to the mining camp tomorrow," he told her. "I'll let Mr. Norwood know what they said. He'll have them working double shifts for a good long time." He smiled a little at her. "Miss Minch won't hear."

"You have a higher opinion of the wagging tongues in this town than I do. She'll know the moment she opens the post office. And it's all my fault, and she's about the only friend I have here."

An admission that was both a balm and an open wound.

"Your only one?" Wick sat back. "You've got Dobbs. And, for some reason I can't fathom, Mrs. Clarke is cooking for you." He held up his hand to fend off the required protest. "Don't even try to deny it. She's cooking for you. Not to mention Thayer and Badger are over in their cell right now, claiming you were innocent of any incitement. I won't even tell you what Erasmus, that old devil, threatened on your behalf." He shook his head. "Miss Drake, you have your fair share of defenders around here. Friends, even."

"I don't see why or how," she murmured into her glass.

Wick snorted. "Don't you?" He glanced at her, and an odd light shone in his eyes. Then he looked away and took a sip from his glass. "Where did you get this whiskey? This isn't Hoback's usual."

"Found a bottle of it upstairs. Not bad, eh?" She saluted him and swallowed the rest of it.

Wick glanced over his shoulder toward the stairs. "What is up there?"

Now it was Madeline's turn to sit back. "You asking to go upstairs, Sheriff?" Those words slipped out with practiced ease. As Calliope, she'd said that line more times than she could count, but in this shadowed room, she wasn't playing a role, and it held more power than she'd ever realized. Especially when it wasn't Wick who was ensnared by the offer, but her.

He finished his drink, his gaze never leaving hers. Blue eyes steady as the sky. He put down his glass, and for a moment she thought he was going to take her up on her flippant offer. She wasn't sure if she should be horrified or grateful.

Instead, he rose to his feet and retrieved his hat.

"Good night, ma'am."

Ma'am. That rather pinched in all the wrong places.

He opened the door and turned to her. "Lock up after I leave."

She suspected he wasn't talking about just the doors.

CHAPTER 32

Saturday, December 14

*B*y the time Madeline finished getting the Star Bright ready for the Saturday evening crowd, it was nearly time for her to reopen and the post office to close.

Convenient, or just the unwitting timing of procrastination? Well, there was only one thing to be done, she realized as she hung up her apron. She hurried over to see how much Ninny had heard.

Too much, Madeline learned as she entered the post office.

"I'm glad to see you all in one piece," Ninny said, scarcely glancing up from a stack of letters and cards in front of her. Methodically, the postmark stamp went *thunk* from the ink pad to the stamp on the letter. The poor stamp bore all the markings of her deliberate air of indignation.

So, yes, she'd heard.

"Why wouldn't I be?" Madeline replied as she closed the door, trying to sound nonchalant.

"I understand there was a bit of ruckus last night." *Thunk.*

"Just a misunderstanding." Madeline shrugged.

"Hmmm." *Thunk.*

Madeline rather pitied the poor stamps.

Not that Ninny intended to prolong the agony. "What started that fight last night?" *Thunk.*

As good as Madeline was at acting, she couldn't help but cringe. "What fight?"

"Madeline." Ninny came around the counter, holding a large mailbag by the strings, and faced her. "I want to hear it from you. Why did Mr. Thayer and Mr. Densmore end up in jail again?"

"They weren't fighting each other."

Ninny took a step back. "No?"

"No." At least Madeline could say that much honestly.

The postmistress dug in. "If they weren't fighting each other, then who was fighting?"

"Just some miners who said—" Madeline snapped her mouth shut. She'd been lulled into revealing too much. Not even the best of late-night hosts had ever rattled her this badly.

"Said what?"

"You know, stupid things men say." Madeline tried to sound off-handed. "They were just popping off."

"'Popping off'?"

"Speaking out of turn." Madeline pivoted. "So are you going to the box supper tonight?"

"Don't even try to change the subject," Ninny told her. "I know very well that the sheriff wouldn't have filled up his jail merely because a couple of miners spoke out of turn."

Madeline chewed at her lip. Now she was in a corner.

Ninny, with her fists tucked atop her hips, knew it as well.

"How I heard it was that Mr. Thayer and Badger took exception to something that was said about me, and then a brawl ensued." Ninny paused by the door. "Is that about right?"

"Ninny—"

"Madeline! I will not be cozened or coddled. Tell me."

Not knowing what else to do, Madeline repeated the ugly words. There was no point in making less of them than they were, for she had the sense that lying to a friend in that moment would be a more grievous crime.

Almost immediately she regretted her honesty. Her friend, this kind, gentle soul who had shown her nothing but generosity and compassion, began to cry.

Then everything turned upside down, but not in the way Madeline could have ever supposed.

"You could have been hurt," Ninny managed to blurt out between sobs. "I could have lost you."

Her? Ninny was worried over *her*?

"You didn't lose me," Madeline said quietly, gently. But her words fell like snow on a warm day, melting before they were heard.

Ninny struggled to compose herself, insisting all the more, "Hurt, I say. And it's all my fault."

Her fault? "I hardly see how—"

Thunk. The mailbag hit the floor like a giant exclamation point. "Yes! My fault. I'd never be able to forgive myself if you were hurt because of my mistake." The sobbing took on a hysterical note, great wrenching sobs and tears that flowed as if they'd been stoppered for decades.

"Ninny, I don't see how you can keep insisting that any of this is your fault," Madeline told her. "You weren't even there."

"No, it is all my fault. All this mess—the drawing, the cake dance, and now this. It is my fault because I lied. I lied about everything."

"What do you mean?" Madeline blinked. Clearly they were no longer talking about the same things. "About what?"

"The names. The drawing," she said. "I didn't draw Mr. Thayer's name, nor Badger's. I stood up in front of the entire town and lied."

"Oh, my."

Since neither of them had said it, they both turned to find Mrs. Clarke standing in the open doorway. They had no idea how long she'd been there, but clearly long enough to have heard the entirety of Ninny's confession.

※

"I FEAR I must unburden myself now," Miss Minch was saying as she opened the door to her house and started down a long hallway.

"Miss Minch, I can leave if you prefer," Savannah said. Confessions smacked of a familiarity that she wasn't comfortable with. Not in the least.

Besides, she'd had her own unburdening the day before, and everything was still too raw. For as much as her tears had washed many of her agonies loose, one didn't walk away from years of grief that easily.

"No, no," Miss Minch said, stopping. "I must explain, or you'll think the worst of me."

It was hardly good manners to confess that, for her part, she rarely gave the postmistress a second thought.

"Please," the woman continued.

Then, of all things, Miss Drake gave her a slight nudge and a glance that said two things quite clearly. *Please. Indulge her.*

"Well . . . " There was another glance from Miss Drake. This time it was hardly subtle. "Yes. Of course."

Miss Minch hurried on, muttering something about the kettle.

Perfect. Now there would be tea involved. This was becoming more complicated with every step.

She glanced back toward the post office. She'd merely come to see if Mr. Wakefield had finally sent the check he'd promised.

"Mind your step," Miss Drake advised as they wound past a myriad of packages stacked up on both sides of the hall.

"Are all of these for Christmas?" she couldn't help asking.

"Apparently so," Miss Drake told her, weaving the route with practiced ease.

"My goodness." Savannah drew her skirt close. She had to admit she'd never indulged in even a bit of curiosity as to how Miss Minch lived, but here was a glimpse into a life surrounded by so many pieces of other people's lives. So many entanglements, so many secrets. Her thoughts flitted back to the previous morning, when that bit of Christmas sparkle had brightened the Bergstroms' house—and then just as quickly flitted up the chimney. Now whatever was she about to witness?

Yet as she stepped into the small, intimate kitchen—an embroidered dishcloth hanging on the rack, a wide counter and a fine stove—she approved of the room immediately. Best of all, there was an airy window over the sink that let one daydream as they went about the mundane work of washing up the dishes.

Yes, she liked this tidy, cozy room.

Especially when she spied the table in the corner, topped with a bit of knitting, a book, and a small vase with a sprig of holly tucked inside.

Nothing alarming here. Why, Miss Minch's kitchen was as welcoming as a dear friend.

Miss Drake, for her part, had already settled down at the small table near the door, having displaced a large ginger cat that fled up a set of stairs on the opposite side of the room, vehemently meowing his displeasure.

Having ventured into the very depths of Miss Minch's quiet, ordinary domestic life, it was nigh on impossible to believe that this woman had done anything that required a confession.

Miss Minch hastily stacked up things to one side of the counter. "Madeline, do you mind filling the kettle?"

"Not at all," Miss Drake told her, catching it up off the stove and going over to the sink.

It shocked Savannah to see such easy familiarity between this odd pair. However was it that in such a short time, the two had forged a friendship?

Exorior!—the word Miss Minch had used the other day—came bubbling up as if to say, *See what can happen when you reach?*

Madeline had paused in front of an assortment of things on the counter. "What is all this, Ninny?"

"Foolishness," the woman replied, tucking it all aside and putting her back to it. She busily put a tray together while Miss Drake got down the cups and saucers.

Once they were all settled at the table, the teapot steeping before them, Miss Drake got straight to the point. Of course she did. "So what do you mean, you lied? About what?"

Ninny looked up from checking the tea. "The Christmas tree drawing. All of it. I lied."

"You didn't draw two names?" Savannah asked. Dear heavens, she was as bad as Miss Drake. Then, to save herself, she added, "Inola was quite firm on that point."

"Oh, I drew two names," Miss Minch said. She took a deep breath. "Just not the ones I announced to everyone."

A moment of silence passed, and Savannah glanced over at Miss Drake. Prodded, really.

"Why?" Miss Drake asked.

"Because it would have been—" Miss Minch pressed her lips tightly together.

"What names, Miss Minch?" Savannah's quiet question startled all of them, including herself. "What names did you draw?"

Miss Minch went over to the cupboard and pulled out a spice tin marked *Thyme*. She brought it over to the table and shook out two slips of paper.

Savannah, having had her own run-in with errant slips of paper, was reluctant to pick them up. Miss Drake had no such compunctions and gathered them up, reading aloud the first one.

"Mrs. George L." She blinked and looked at Miss Minch. "Not Badger?"

Miss Minch shook her head.

Then Miss Drake opened the other slip. "Mrs. Neville Norwood." She looked at it again, brow furrowed. "Who's that?"

Savannah's mouth fell open. "No! What are the chances?"

"I know," Miss Minch agreed. "Oh, the odds are incalculable. Mrs. George L. and Mrs. Norwood."

"Dear heavens." Setting down her cup of tea, Savannah took a deep breath. "Dearest heavens above."

Miss Drake looked from one to the other. "I don't understand. I mean, I get it about Mrs. George L." She pulled a face to emphasize just how much she got it. "But who is this Mrs. Neville Norwood?"

"You've done a noble deed," Savannah told Miss Minch. "You all but saved Christmas, I estimate. And the town itself."

"I don't feel all that noble now. It's all gone awry. So terribly awry."

"It does seem to have run into a bit of trouble," Savannah agreed.

"Who is Mrs. Norwood?" Miss Drake repeated.

"Her husband owns the mine," Miss Minch supplied in a hasty aside.

Savannah nodded. "Among other things." Goodness, what an upheaval Miss Minch had averted. "Mrs. Norwood and Mrs. George L. have a rather infamous rivalry."

Miss Minch got to the point. "I fear each feels she is the first lady of Bethlehem."

Savannah snorted. That was putting it mildly.

Miss Drake's brow furrowed. "Rivalry? How so?"

"How not?" Miss Minch huffed. "When Mrs. George L. founded the Temperance Union, Mrs. Norwood founded a chapter of the Suffrage Society."

"I can't imagine Mrs. George L. approves," Madeline noted.

"Precisely," Savannah agreed. "But it doesn't stop there."

"While Mrs. George L. has charge of the Ladies Aid Society—"

"Mrs. Norwood steers the Catholic Women's Auxiliary."

"Mrs. George L., the Athenian Society."

"Mrs. Norwood, the Library Guild." Miss Minch paused to amend that. "The Public Library Guild."

"Oh my, yes," Savannah agreed.

"I take it Mrs. George L. doesn't approve of public libraries," said Miss Drake.

Miss Minch shook her head. "Declares them dens of sin and promiscuity."

"We are talking about libraries, right?" Miss Drake asked. "Books, shelves, card catalogue?"

"Is there any other?"

"I don't know," she said. "I thought it must be a euphemism for something else. I mean, what sort of person disparages a public library? Or considers them dens of promiscuity?"

"Mrs. George L." Savannah and Miss Minch said together.

Miss Drake shook her head. "I'd hate to hear what she says about the Star Bright."

Savannah busily picked up another lump of sugar and stirred it into her tea, while Miss Minch reached for her knitting.

Savannah looked up from her tea. "Miss Minch, you haven't told anyone else, have you?"

Miss Minch drew a deep breath. "Cora Stafford."

"You told Cora?" she blurted out.

Miss Minch held up her hands. "Not that it mattered. She refused to print any of it. She said that she couldn't, especially if we held any hope of living with a 'mutual goal of common good and harmony' or some such thing."

Savannah let out a breath. "Oh, thank heavens. For once she's to be praised for showing some restraint and good sense."

Miss Minch's lips trembled, and her eyes began to well up.

"Oh, come now, Ninny, don't cry." Miss Drake took hold of her friend's hand and gave it a squeeze. "Whatever it is, we can help you out of it. Can't we, Mrs. Clarke?"

With the two of them looking across the table at her, there was nothing she could do but nod in agreement. "Yes, of course."

In for a penny, in for a pound, as her father used to say.

"But what am I to do about Mr. Thayer and Mr. Densmore?"

That stopped Savannah. "Mr. Densmore?"

"Badger," Miss Drake supplied.

Miss Minch sank into her chair and folded into a defeated slump. "I can't continue to beggar those two under false pretenses."

"Seems to me men have been doing that to women since the beginning of time," Miss Drake remarked.

Savannah found herself nodding in agreement.

"I'm using them in a most shabby fashion," Miss Minch bemoaned.

"That's up to interpretation." Miss Drake's gaze strayed over toward the kitchen counter. "Ninny, I know I asked before, but what is all that?"

Savannah looked as well and saw the telltale evidence. The box.

The ribbon. The jar of bread-and-butter pickles. "Oh, Miss Minch, you can't be thinking of . . ."

Miss Minch cringed. "It was purely a moment of weakness. I regretted it immediately. Why, I even considered—"

"Considered what?" Miss Drake interjected, looking from Savannah to Ninny and back to Savannah.

"Those are the makings of a box supper," she told her.

Again, the younger woman looked from one to the other. "A box supper?" Her brow crinkled again. "That isn't anything like that cake dance, is it?

"In manner of speaking."

Miss Drake groaned. "What is it with you people that your only entertainment involves women lining up like beauty contestants and auctioning themselves off?"

"Don't be vulgar. It's not the lady but the box that is being auctioned off," Savannah informed her. Yet even as she said the words she had the sense of being hoisted with her own petard.

One Miss Drake held fast. "There's a difference?"

Savannah struggled to explain how it wasn't anything like that. Yet how could she, when that was exactly what it was?

"It was a weak moment," Miss Minch said. "I was at King's yesterday and Josephine Lovell—"

Miss Drake's teacup halted in midair. "Josephine again?"

Miss Minch nodded.

The cup rattled back onto its saucer. "What did she say this time?"

The postmistress recounted the story, and Savannah mused that the King sisters had encouraged this madness. "And all of a sudden I found myself buying a ridiculous length of that turkey-red ribbon."

They all looked over at the innocent length of silk curled up like a sleeping cat.

Miss Drake's expression changed. In fact, her entire demeanor took on a calculated air. "Will Josephine be at this supper dance?"

"Box supper," Savannah corrected.

"Yeah, that thing," Miss Drake agreed, wagging her finger at Savannah while her attention remained fixed on the postmistress.

"Of course," Miss Minch told her.

Miss Drake sat back and grinned. "Oh, you have to go. You must."

"What?" Miss Minch looked up at Savannah for help.

"No, she shouldn't," she replied, shaking her head.

"Of course she should," Miss Drake argued, her grin turning devilish. "When her box brings in more money than that horrible Josephine's—"

"Madeline!"

"Miss Drake!" Savannah inhaled deeply. "A lady doesn't go to a box supper to win."

Again, Miss Drake looked at her as if she should know better.

"It is all for charity," Miss Minch rushed to explain. "The Catholic Women's Auxiliary hopes to raise enough to make a good contribution to the fire engine fund."

"So if this box supper is all for charity, then how can it be wrong to want to bring in a lot of money?" Miss Drake asked.

Again, neither woman had an answer. Savannah was afraid to say anything lest she give this impossible woman more ammunition.

Not that she needed any help, for Miss Drake continued, grinning like a cat in the cream. "My money's on Badger."

"Madeline Drake!" Miss Minch sputtered, blushing furiously.

"Well, it is," the younger woman said without the least bit of repentance. "Mr. Thayer is all well and good, but there is a mystery to Badger."

Savannah blew out a breath. "Of all the—"

"What?" Miss Drake continued unabashedly. "He's got the most beautiful blue eyes, and that Scottish accent of his could melt my . . ." She paused as if considering her words for once. "Well, it melts. You can't tell me that neither of you hasn't wondered—more than once— what he would look like all cleaned up." She looked from one to the other. "Don't even try to deny it."

"A time or two," Savannah conceded without thinking. Then, to her amazement, she laughed, more at her own confession than anything else, and Miss Drake and Miss Minch began to laugh as well.

As the delight that had wrapped them together faded, Savannah didn't know what to do: catch hold of these tenuous threads, this odd connection that seemed to be weaving between the three of them, or dash for the door.

A moment or two more and she'd be on a first-name basis with the pair of them.

With that rebellious thought, she rose abruptly. "I must be going."

Miss Minch jerked up out of her seat. "If you must." Then her eyes widened. "Oh, I nearly forgot. You came for your mail."

"Dear me, so I did."

"As it happens, you do have . . ." She paused and drew a breath. "Let me get that for you." Miss Minch hurried down the crowded hall.

Taking advantage of a moment of privacy, she leaned over toward Miss Drake. "Dobbs came by and got the soup for tonight. Make sure it stays at a simmer." She folded her hands in her lap, having almost regretted saying that much. What if Miss Minch heard?

Madeline laughed. "What's a simmer? Oh, never mind. I'll ask Ninny."

Ninny? Against her better judgement, Savannah sat back down. "Whyever do you call her that?"

"Who?"

"Miss Minch. You keep calling her Ninny."

"Because that's what her friends call her."

Miss Minch had friends? Savannah shifted in her seat. Truly, it was rather unbelievable. But as she glanced around the table at the half-drunk cups of tea and a cookie plate that now boasted only crumbs, an odd bit of envy prodded her to ask, "She's your friend?"

"Absolutely."

"Hmm." Here Savannah had thought there couldn't be anything that surprised her about Miss Minch. Yet, if they were friends, perhaps Miss Minch would listen to this ruinous young woman. "As her friend, you should be cautioning her not to pursue some reckless course."

Miss Drake's brow furrowed.

"Consider where she will be in this community after you leave if she is made friendless by all this."

Miss Drake dropped a lump of sugar into her tea and began to stir.

Savannah pressed her point. "Don't you understand how precarious life is for a single woman?"

The woman stopped stirring but didn't look up. The spoon stood stock still while the milky tea swirled slowly. "I know."

Pain and grief shouldered those two words and silently bound Savannah and Miss Drake into an unholy sisterhood.

Not that Savannah would admit to it. Not now. Not ever.

Thankfully, Miss Minch returned with two pieces of mail, breaking up their grim reverie. One was a familiar enough envelope— perhaps that weasel Wakefield had finally sent the money he owed Inola—and, to her surprise, an envelope that looked far too pristine to have journeyed from New York.

Miss Minch put them both down in front of her.

"Oh, my!" Miss Drake exclaimed, her teacup rattling in its saucer. "You've got a golden ticket."

"Madeline Drake!" Miss Minch sank into her seat. "That is a confidential postal matter."

"We are not in the post office," Madeline teased. "We're in your kitchen."

Savannah had been so relieved to see Mr. Wakefield's correspondence she hadn't paid much heed to the other envelope, a crisp white square that seemed out of place.

"Now there's only one left to discover," Miss Drake said to herself.

"How do you know that?" Miss Minch asked, both shock and surprise in her question.

"We're keeping a tally at the Star Bright," she explained without the least bit of shame.

"Tally of what?" Savannah asked without thinking, lulled again into their affable banter, as teasing and warm as Miss Drake's manners and Miss Minch's pot of tea.

Miss Drake leaned over and tapped the envelope with her finger. "A tally of who's been invited to Mrs. George L.'s birthday party. You, Mrs. Clarke, appear to be lucky number eleven."

❅

I LIED.

Savannah wondered at Miss Minch's words as she knocked on the Bergstroms' door that evening, a canteen of soup in one hand and her workbasket in the other.

Miss Minch wasn't the only one with an honesty conundrum. For here she was, apparently offering Mr. Bergstrom and the older pair the chance to go to the box supper and dance while she charitably stayed with Mrs. Bergstrom and the younger fry.

She would have considered herself a very martyr of charity if it weren't for the pieces of silk in the bottom of her workbasket that needed basting.

Basting that needed to be done well out of Inola's sharp-eyed view.

Mr. Bergstrom grinned as he opened the door. "Mrs. Clarke! As ever, a godsend."

"How is Mrs. Bergstrom today?" Savannah asked, stepping in the house. Once again, the room was clouded in shadows, and the door to the bedroom was closed. She set down her workbasket and handed the canteen of soup to Livia, who set it on the table.

"She's been . . ." Mr. Bergstrom began, but he trailed off as he shuffled his feet and glanced away.

"She hasn't been out of bed all day," Livia provided as she shrugged on her coat. Tugging on her hat, she offered a sort of mumbled apology. "I tried. We all did."

As Mr. Bergstrom, Livia, and Peter all clustered at the door, looking more than happy to flee, Margit, Clara, and Berta came forward.

"We want to go. It's not fair," Berta complained.

"This is not a dance for children." Livia leaned over and kissed the top of her sister's head. "You get to go to the spelling bee and the school pageant."

"And candy?" Berta asked, rocking on the heels of her stocking-clad feet.

"Candy?" Clara echoed.

Livia nodded. "Yes, there will be candy at the school pageant."

"Still, I'm a very good dancer," Berta reminded her, as if hoping that was enough to get her included in tonight's festivities.

Savannah caught hold of Berta's hand. "You get to stay with me. I brought soup and—"

"Cookies?" Margit asked.

"I might have," Savannah told her, trying not to smile. "Come now, let them go. We'll have our supper, and I have a very important task for the two of you after we've washed the dishes."

Neither child looked very impressed with such an agenda, but Margit went to get the bowls while Berta collected the spoons.

As the door closed, Savannah looked around, her eyes having adjusted to the shadows. At least the house wasn't in a complete mishmash. When she lit the lamp on the table and the one on the kitchen counter, a cozy glow enveloped the room, the shadows now consigned to the corners.

"That's better," she said under her breath, and set the soup to warming. Once she had the trio settled over steaming bowls, she turned to the quiet cradle. Baby Thomas lay within, curled up, pale and thin. "This will not do," she muttered, looking over at the closed door.

Girding herself, she opened the door. And once again, the close smell nearly overwhelmed her. Oh, heavens. No wonder the rest of the family had hurried out so fast.

She lit the lamp by the bed and began getting out clean things, not bothering to ask for permission.

When she returned with a wash bowl, she set everything down on the dresser. "You can help me, or I'll do it despite you. That baby needs to be fed, and you need to be upright and clean to do it."

While she wasn't certain how much English Mrs. Bergstrom spoke, her tone must have translated, for the woman rolled over and eyed her through narrowed slits.

Then slowly she sat up.

The children were finishing off the last spoonfuls of their supper when Savannah led their mother from the bedroom.

Mrs. Bergstrom had submitted to being washed and having her hair brushed and braided.

"Here's a warm spot by the stove," Savannah said, as she settled her in the rocking chair even as the baby began to stir. The fragile sound nearly broke Savannah's heart anew.

So she gave Thomas the attention he needed, gently cleaning him, finding a new nappy, and then bundling him tightly before handing him back to his mother.

Although she'd anticipated another stonewall, this time Mrs. Bergstrom—though she didn't look at either her baby or Savannah—took the infant and settled him in to nurse.

"Well, that's an improvement," Savannah told her, unable to stop the sharp words.

Mrs. Bergstrom glared up at her. Savannah skittered back, vanquished by a revenant from her past.

There now, Sybilla. Please, for the baby.

Go away. Let me die.

Savannah tried to breathe as the shadows pushed against the confines of the lamplight and that familiar need to bolt whispered in her ear. Yet in that moment, soft and gentle like a fair mouse, Margit caught Savannah's hand, her gaze fixed on her mother as if she wasn't certain who she was seeing. "Mama?"

"Your mother is tired, angel." Savannah did her best to still her racing heart. "That's all."

Berta came to stand beside her sister. The little girl shook like a tiny aspen in winter, empty of color and naught but trembling limbs. Savannah didn't know which was more heartbreaking, the sister who longed to crawl into her mother's arms or the one shaking with something akin to fury.

"I put our dishes in the sink." Berta slanted a glance at Margit to indicate her lack of participation.

"Cookies?" Clara reminded.

"Let's get some soup for your mother and then finish the dishes. After that, I have a task for you three." They went about their domestic chores, the girls rewarded for their hard work with a large cookie each. Savannah had kept an eye on Mrs. Bergstrom, who had finished feeding Thomas and now held him at her shoulder, gently rocking, her eyes closed.

Savannah settled into the chair beside her, opening up her workbasket and bringing out three small balls of yarn. She handed one to each of the girls. "These balls were wound in the wrong direction," she told them solemnly.

"Is that bad? Margit asked, looking sideways at the offering she held.

"It isn't good," Savannah informed them.

"Who wound them?" Berta could put Mr. Quinby to shame with her direct questioning.

"That matters not," she told her. "All that matters is that I need you to make them right again." She paused a moment and looked at the trio as if measuring their ability for such an important task.

Berta straightened, and Margit and Clara followed suit.

"This is a job that cannot be rushed, or it will need to be done over."

Berta's brow wrinkled as she looked down at the yarn and nodded as if it all made perfect sense.

After a quick demonstration on how to wind a ball of yarn, the children quietly set to work, slowly and carefully winding the wool. Inola's mother had used this trick more than once to keep Savannah and Inola busy in the quiet lull of the afternoons before the customers began to arrive.

Satisfied they were fully occupied, Savannah took out her sewing. Out of the corner of her eye, she caught Mrs. Bergstrom looking over at her, and for a second she thought she saw the woman's lips twitch.

Savannah smiled back before gathering up the silk that needed to be basted and reaching for her basting threads.

Savannah paused and sorted through the basket again. Wherever were her basting threads? She'd put them in, of that she was certain, but they were nowhere to be found.

"Bother," she muttered.

She looked up and found Mrs. Bergstrom reaching over to touch the silk. "Beautiful."

"Isn't it?" Savannah replied quietly. She hardly wanted to move lest she startle the woman back into her dark silence. At her feet, the girls stilled, the yarn in their hands held in place.

"For you?" Mrs. Bergstrom asked, once again in a soft, wistful voice.

She shook her head. "No. A gift."

The woman nodded.

Savannah sorted through her basket one more time and sighed. She held up the pieces of dress to add context to her words. "I forgot my basting thread."

Mrs. Bergstrom leaned over and reached into her own long-neglected basket of mending and sewing. She pulled out a spool— much like the one Savannah had—rewound with old threads. "Yes?" she asked, holding it out.

"Thank you," Savannah told her, taking it gratefully.

She looked down at the colorful spool—faded blues from old chambray shirts, white from sheets and petticoats, all picked loose to be given a second life. "During the war, I reused some thread so many times it up and deserted me."

Those threads had told their own story. The soft pink thread from the dress Sybilla wore all those long months after Lucius left. The thick linen thread leftover from sewing shrouds.

What had happened to that spool? she wondered, wound as it was with the very fibers of her life. Her past.

Yet instead of mourning its loss, she realized something. There would always be more threads waiting for her. Just like the spool she held now.

Berta looked up from her winding. "What is a war?"

"A terrible thing, child," Savannah told her. "I hope you never see one in your lifetime."

Clara began to yawn, and Savannah realized it was time to put them all to bed. Nor did they argue, settling their tangles of yarn back into the basket and getting on their nightclothes.

She tucked them into bed and settled the quilts around them.

Margit went right to sleep, her thumb tucked in her mouth and her doll, Alma—more rag than dolly—firmly held in the crook of her elbow.

When Savannah returned to the chair, she found Mrs. Bergstrom had quietly settled the baby back in his cradle. But instead of silently seeking her refuge in her bedroom, she'd sat back down in the rocking chair to eat the soup.

Savannah smiled at her, threaded her needle, and began to sew long, even stitches to hold the pieces together.

Some people skipped this step, preferring to pin the fabrics together, but she'd found with silk that basting first kept the final seams even.

The simple, steady stitching lulled her, her thoughts picking and pulling at Berta's question like a loose thread. *What is war?*

She could have told the child the truth. War is death in a thousand different ways. To the boys and men on the battlefields. To the wives and sisters and mothers and children they leave behind.

Not the sort of death that is an ending, but a death that stubbornly holds any hope of light at bay. A death that ekes upon one, clinging to the soles of boots that are more hole than leather, to the hem of a tattered skirt, reaching for one's very soul.

It is an evil of hunger and want, capable of erasing all that has come before.

In this quiet, sleepy room, Savannah's memories stirred and demanded telling, so as not to be forgotten. No. She suspected they were clamoring to be set free.

Or to be lost, like a tangle of old threads.

"When I was young," she began, pulling the needle through the layers, "I did not live in my father's house. Rather, Inola and I lived with our mothers in New Orleans, in a house of . . ."

Well, some parts of the story didn't need telling.

So she sallied past that part. "My father, Captain Vance, had his own family—his real family, as I would be reminded so often. But they perished—his wife and all his children—in a terrible hurricane that ravaged and wiped away an entire island. That same hurricane brought disease to town, and our mothers perished." She glanced down and got her bearings, begin to sew again. "In his grief, and because Inola and I were his only living relations, he brought us to his plantation outside of Vicksburg. It was called Larkhall."

As she told her story, it felt as if the room stilled, the world outside paused, and the clock stopped ticking.

"Not long after, he remarried a woman who had a daughter, Sybilla. Since she was not all that much younger than us, it seemed a good fit. A family was restored, and Papa found peace again. It was all well and good, though Inola's place in the house was always fraught with tension, the new Mrs. Vance not being as understanding as one might hope. Then, as the drumbeats of discontent grew louder between the North and South, Papa took Inola to a college in Ohio— against Mother Vance's vehement objections. But Inola longed for education, and it was illegal for her to get schooling in Mississippi, never mind that she'd sat through the lessons being given to me and Sybilla over the years. Papa, being Scottish on his mother's side, believed education was a self-evident truth for everyone and anyone who wanted it."

She reached for the teapot and filled her cup, then filled one for Mrs. Bergstrom. After adding a teaspoon of sugar, she continued.

"I should have gone with Inola, left Mississippi, but I refused for all the wrong reasons. You see, I'd fallen in love. At least I thought it was love."

Taking a sip of the tea, she settled the cup back onto the saucer and went back to her seams.

"A neighbor, Lucius Maddox, began paying calls that summer. His family was wealthy, and their land ran alongside ours. A match with me would give the Maddoxes riverfront access and fertile fields. All I saw was a handsome man with charming manners."

Savannah drew a deep breath. She hardly wanted to continue, for it was like wading into the darkest parts of the river where one can't see the bottom.

"The trip north had been arduous for Papa, and he became sickly. I think it was his heart. You see, he had loved Inola's mother more than any other woman in his life, and leaving their child so far away had broken what was left of his spirit. Then war was declared."

She glanced over at the children to make sure they were asleep. Restive, she rose to check on Thomas, and found him thankfully asleep in the warm comfort of his crib. So she settled back down in her chair.

Picking up her needle, she looked for where she'd left off. "War is a terrible thing," she said softly, not wanting the words to touch the sleeping children. "I see no point to it, though for some reason men go rushing into the fire, their heads stuffed with a vainglorious notion of victory." She huffed. "I wish they had the foresight to see how it always ends. Lines of men, broken and haunted, having discovered that the promise was bound in greed and lies."

"But here I am, getting ahead of myself." She looked down at the pieces in her hands and realized she'd gone astray and would need to pick back her work.

"The Maddoxes were a most influential family, and Mother Vance had raised herself up when she'd married Papa. What she wanted was for Sybilla to rise as well, and me marrying Lucius went against that plan. Then Papa died, and his will left everything—much to my surprise—to Sybilla. Oh, I was to be cared for until such time as I married, but the land and the house went to Sybilla. I didn't blame her—she was a sweet child who knew nothing but to patter along in the wake of her mother's ambitions." Her needle wavered. "Though more the fool me, for I was still of the opinion that Lucius would marry me. Especially by then."

Taking a deep breath, she rethreaded her needle and started anew. If only the seams in life could be redone so easily.

"To my horror, Lucius eloped with Sybilla, with her mother's blessing. And before he left to join the regulars, he saw to it she was carrying his child. Then again, so was I."

Thomas began to fuss. Savannah waited a few moments, watching to see if this would stir his mother, but when she continued to sit as still as the sphinx, she rose and went to the crib herself. Discovering the source of his woes, she changed his nappy and brought him over to his mother. "I think he's still hungry."

Mrs. Bergstrom nodded and reached for the baby, settling him in close. The baby snuffled a bit beneath her robe, latched hold, and suckled happily.

Savannah sighed with relief. At least one of them was improving.

If only Sybilla could have.

Savannah settled back into the chair but didn't pick up her work, or her story, letting the memories ebb and flow around her.

Lucius and Sybilla.

The green grass of the Larkhall running down to the river.

The chatter of a tow-haired child as he followed her through her day.

She didn't realize it, but her eyes drifted shut, the weight of the last few days enveloping her. Somewhere in the distance, she heard a baby crying. A woman keening.

Leave me be, Nola. Let me die.

Not yet. We still got plenty of living to do.

She woke with a start and bolted to her feet as the door creaked open. A winter chill worried its way in, carrying away the thick, smothering hold of memories.

A shadow crossed the threshold and, for a moment, the past returned.

Lucius. She sucked in a deep breath.

"Mrs. Clarke?" The man stayed where he was. "Mrs. Clarke, it's me."

"Mr. Bergstrom," she said, the name anchoring her in this time, in this place. She looked around, taking a quick inventory. Thomas asleep in his cradle. The girls curled up in their bed. Her sewing neatly folded and stacked atop her basket. The spool of thread atop had unwound like so many memories. "Oh, my. I fear I fell asleep."

He looked toward the empty chair across from her, as did Savannah.

Empty? She got to the feet. "Oh, no! She was here—"

Mr. Bergstrom's face went from concerned to stricken as he rushed to the bedroom. Savannah followed, filled with the same sense of panic, but there Mrs. Bergstrom lay, on the far side of the bed beneath a faded and patched quilt.

Both of them heaved a sigh and backed out of the room. When the door clicked shut, Mr. Bergstrom tugged off his hat and ran a hand through his hair. "I came home. I was worried. Suddenly felt as if—" His gaze flicked to the door.

"Something might be wrong?" Savannah quietly offered.

He nodded and slumped. The man looked as lost as his wife.

She rushed to reassure him. To remind him of all he had. "I got her to bathe and eat. And she fed the baby."

He was still shaking his head, tears in his eyes, as if she were mistaken. "I had this horrible feeling. I thought I was coming home to find—"

Savannah turned away and began gather up her things, if only to give the man some privacy. Yet here were all the pieces of silk, neatly basted, ready for proper seams. How was this? She'd barely begun. Then she glanced at the empty chair, and the snips of threads on the table beside it. "No, Mr. Bergstrom. I think she's turned a corner."

Definitely a corner turned, for when she went to tuck the dress pieces back in her basket, there was another surprise.

The balls of yarn, perfectly wound, the wool plied back into order by someone who had taken this path before.

CHAPTER 33

*M*adeline looked up from wiping the bar as the door opened. "What the devil are you doing here?"

"Looking for something to drink," Thayer told her as he settled in at one end of the bar. At the other sat one of the saloon's few customers, Badger, who'd ambled in a half an hour earlier and sat moodily nursing a beer.

"Didn't a night in jail rather convince you of the evils of such a habit?" she teased, even as she poured Thayer a whiskey.

The man shot her a warning glance, so Madeline retreated into the kitchen and returned with two bowls of soup and plates with sandwiches, setting one down in front of each of them. "On the house," she told them. "You did me a real favor last night."

Thayer spoke up first. "Then do us a favor, will you?"

"What is that?" she asked. If she thought they'd appreciate her gesture, she'd thought wrong.

"Stay away from Miss Minch."

Badger nodded in agreement.

"Stay away from Ninny?" The words tumbled out, sounding almost childlike. "I think that is up to Miss Minch," she told them, and went to refill a beer.

As she left, she heard Badger's rough voice asking a question down the bar. "Didn't expect to see you here. How was your supper?"

"I was about to ask you the same thing," Thayer replied.

Madeline looked over her shoulder. The two fools sat there glaring at each other, hunched over their drinks. She set the pitcher down on the table and left it, returning to the bar. "You mean to tell me neither of you went to that box supper thing?" Her hands fisted on her hips. "After I went to a lot of trouble to get Ninny all fixed up? Not to mention put together a box." Now it was her turn to glare.

For after Mrs. Clarke had left, Madeline had followed the exact opposite of her advice and cajoled Ninny into going to the box supper. By the time Madeline had left, the shy postmistress practically glowed with her hair all done up like one of the younger set.

"Don't you think you've interfered enough?" Thayer shot back.

"I haven't even begun," she warned them. "Look at the pair of you. Sitting here like a couple of adolescent chumps. She's over there, probably sitting by herself, humiliated. While the two of you are to blame."

"Us?" Badger protested. He looked to be about to say a lot more when the door opened and Erasmus wandered in.

"Close the damn door, Quinby," Mr. Thayer growled out.

"Lovely to see you as well," Erasmus replied as he ambled over and settled in the exact middle of the bar. He looked from one occupant to the other. "Well, that answers two out of three of my questions." He set his hat on the hook. "Maddie, my love, something to warm my soul."

"You sure you have one?" she asked, which elicited a snort from Badger. Filling a tall glass with ice, she reached for the whiskey and then the vermouth.

Erasmus slapped his hands down on the bar, hard, and then looked from his right to his left to make certain he had their attention. "Why aren't the two of you over yonder? Ira just struck up his fiddle."

"Don't even try," Madeline told him, giving his drink a final gentle stir before she strained it and slid the dry Manhattan across the bar. Wiping her hands on her apron, she tipped her head toward Badger, but her ire spilled onto both him and Thayer. "Shame on the pair of you. I would have thought by now one of you would have gotten up to make sure that Mrs. George L. hasn't roasted poor Ninny alive."

Taking an appreciative sip of his drink, Erasmus sat back and smiled. "That is where you would be wrong, Miss Drake."

"How so?" she asked as she put away the bottles.

Erasmus took a long drink and savored both the concoction and his moment in the spotlight. "I mean that Miss Minch never showed up."

Madeline stopped wiping the bar and stared at him. "Never?" A shiver crawled down her back.

Had she pressed the shy woman too far? She was about to rip off her apron and set off for the post office but realized she couldn't leave the bar unattended. She was pretty certain Wick would consider that a dereliction of duty. Nor could she leave Erasmus in charge.

Which would most definitely be a dereliction of duty.

"That is what I said." He finished off his drink and set the empty glass down in front of her. "Just a dash more of bitters this time. And no, Miss Minch has not shown her face at the box supper. I for one might have been enticed to bid if it weren't for my own marital vows."

"You're married?" Madeline looked up from chipping ice from the block.

"To my profession, my dear girl. To the law."

"And probably half a dozen once-wealthy widows between San Francisco and New York," Thayer remarked, to which Badger guffawed in agreement.

"I take offense to such a suggestion—" Erasmus began, pushing his empty glass toward Madeline. "I never venture east of St. Louis."

No one bothered to ask why.

But Madeline had other concerns. She looked from one end of the bar to the other. "Well?"

"Well what?" Badger finally replied, tipping his head and eyeing her. It was like being stared down by a bear.

Not that his grizzly mien intimidated her any more than Thayer's broody, aristocratic air did. "Which one of you idiots is going to see if she's okay?"

They both settled deeper into their barstools as if suddenly planted there.

"Shall we draw lots?" Erasmus suggested with a chuckle, though he was universally ignored.

"If one of you doesn't go, then I will, and when I do, I'll throw all three of you out into the snow for good," Madeline told them, collecting the bowls of soup and setting them down for Dog and Wellington, who happily lapped up the remains. She stared defiantly at both of them. When they still didn't move, she caught up the plates of sandwiches, though Erasmus managed to snag half of a bologna sandwich before Madeline could pull it out of reach.

The wily man grinned as he began to eat.

Mr. Thayer threw back the rest of his whiskey and pushed off his barstool first. "I only came in for a drink. I have a few legal matters to catch up on as it is."

"Such as how not to lose?" Erasmus asked, all innocently.

Badger chuckled, but Thayer ignored them both. "I shall check in on Miss Minch on my way home." Taking down his coat and hat, he left.

As the door closed, Badger got up. He whistled softly, one short note, and Wellington looked up from the bowl he was continuing to clean. With one last swipe of his tongue, he ambled over to his owner's side. "I'll go see if she's at the supper."

"She's not there," Erasmus repeated.

"Like I'd trust your befuddled word on it."

"Hardly befuddled," Erasmus told him. "Why, it's merely eight o'clock. I'm rarely befuddled before nine."

Badger huffed a sigh as he pulled on his coat.

"Old Widow Daggett's box is still in the bidding," Erasmus offered, happily eating his purloined sandwich. "She makes a fine diced egg salad, or so I hear."

"Listen here, you damned pettifogger—" Badger began.

Erasmus waved aside the threatening words as if he were batting at a fly. "I prefer shyster."

"You would," Badger remarked.

"You'll see that she's okay?" Madeline asked him as he turned to leave.

The craggy lines on Badger's face deepened. "Don't trust me, do you?"

"It's not that," Madeline told him. "I'm more disappointed."

He cocked his head to get a good look at her. "How's that?"

"I'd have bet this saloon you'd be the first off that barstool, but I see I was wrong. Very wrong."

A flicker of something crossed his craggy face, and then Badger left without another word, Wellington at his heels.

THE KNOCK on the door brought Ninny's head up. She'd been so lost in her knitting she'd nearly forgotten the muddle and mess that lay outside her four walls. Knitting had a way of soothing all the wrinkles in her life.

Dropping her handiwork into her workbasket, she got up and smoothed her apron over her skirt. Her regular old black wool skirt. As another knock came, Ninny hurried to the door.

"Madeline, I hope you aren't disappointed, but I changed my mind," she said as she opened the door. "I just couldn't—" That's where her words stopped.

For it wasn't Madeline on her back porch, but Mr. Thayer. Hat in hand. Snow on his shoulders.

"Oh, dear. Come in before you freeze," she told him, even as she nudged her knitting basket under the table with her foot.

"I apologize for barging in," he began, shuffling his feet a bit. "I am here at Miss Drake's behest."

Ninny didn't know quite how to take that, but that didn't mean good manners weren't in order. She closed the door and nodded toward the stove.

Since she hadn't said anything, he rambled on as he held out his hands. "She was under the impression . . . That is, she thought . . .

well, she grew concerned . . ." He glanced around and then looked down at the floor.

"Mr. Thayer, you are a man of words—at least I've always had that impression. Can you please use some? In complete sentences, if you don't mind."

He paused and looked at her, his gaze sweeping over her as if seeing her anew. Then he grinned. "I like what you've done to your hair."

Ninny's hand went to the grand pompadour that Madeline had managed to wrangle. After she'd changed her mind about going to the box supper—after all, what had she been thinking?—she hadn't had the heart to take it down and put it back in its usual knot.

In the face of this rare, if not completely foreign, compliment, words rather escaped her.

Her hand went unconsciously up to the precariously pinned strands. "I . . . That is Madeline . . . I mean, Miss Drake . . ."

Oh, heavens, however was she supposed to explain this vanity?

Mr. Thayer laughed. "She is quite in everyone's business of late, isn't she?"

Ninny huffed out a breath. "Indeed, she is, Mr. Thayer." Then they both laughed. "But I don't mind."

He looked her over again. "No. Neither do I. And I would like it if you called me Archie."

"I couldn't," Ninny demurred.

He glanced up at her hair again. "I think you can."

"Then please, call me Ninny."

He tipped his head. "I would be honored, Ninny." As he straightened, his feet paced a bit but he hardly seemed to move— something he must have perfected standing before a jury. "You know, I think this is the first time I've ever been in your kitchen."

"It isn't much," Ninny said

"It reminds me of home," he told her.

"Boston? Truly?"

"Oh, no, not my parents' house, but the kitchen at my grandparents' home on Nantucket. I think I mentioned it before. I spent my summers there as a child. It's the sort of place you never wanted to leave." He inhaled slowly. "Exactly like this. All spices and freshly ground coffee."

Ninny didn't know what to say, and apparently neither did the usually loquacious Mr. Thayer.

After another uncomfortable moment or two, he took a deep breath. "I'm usually not so sentimental."

"Would you like a cup of coffee?"

"Why, yes. I think I would."

She took another glance at him—gracious heavens, how hard had Badger hit him last week, when that eye of his was still rimmed with a yellowing bruise?—then held out her hand for his hat and coat, which she hung on the hook. With a nod toward the empty chair opposite hers, she made herself busy.

It was far easier than talking.

Ninny filled the pot with water and then ground the coffee. Settling it on the back of the stove, she turned and came to a halt. There, in front of her, sat the box, tied up with its bright red ribbon and conjuring all the unwanted reminders of why Mr. Thayer had found her here, sitting alone in her kitchen. She glanced back to find him looking at it as well.

"Is it too late to bid?" There was a tip to his grin that wasn't usually there.

"Yes—I mean no," she told him. "I mean, of course you needn't bid."

"You never know, someone else may outbid me." He looked over at Mr. Bingley curled into a yellow loaf atop his cushion. "Good sir, are you considering bidding?" He cocked his head to listen, then looked back over at Ninny. "No, I do believe he is of a mind to pass this time."

"Oh, do stop." She shook her head and pressed her lips together to keep from laughing. Straightening, she glanced from her imperious cat to the equally imperious man and confessed, "If you must know, Mr. Bingley's credit is most unreliable."

"Some would say the same of me," Mr. Thayer remarked.

She blinked and looked at him. "I wouldn't."

The weight of her words pulled at her, and she looked around for something to anchor her. To her surprise, her gaze fell on the lone box on the counter.

The one she'd so carefully packed before she'd allowed all her old fears to convince her she was being foolish. She'd abandoned it there on the counter, unwilling to even unpack it, because eating it alone had seemed even worse. But now she wasn't alone, was she?

Suddenly propelled by a rush of *Exorior*, she got down two plates, grabbed up the box, and carried them all over to the table. Silverware followed, and mugs for coffee. After another glance at Mr. Thayer, she brought over the creamer and the sugar. He seemed the sort of man who would like his coffee strong and sweet.

With everything in its proper place, she took her seat, carefully untied the ribbon—no need to ruin a good piece of silk—and unpacked the contents onto the plates. The sandwiches wrapped in paper, the small jar of . . .

"Pickles!" He rather inhaled the word.

"Bread-and-butter."

The man sighed. "My favorite. The competition has no idea what they are about to miss." Gathering up his sandwich, he peeked inside the thick slices of bread. "Ham? What an incredible happenstance. My favorite."

Ninny had the decency to blush.

He laughed and took a bite. After a few moments of enthusiastic chewing, he sighed. "Oh, Ben King did not lie. This ham from Cheyenne is incredible. Worth every penny."

"Pennies you shouldn't have spent," Ninny chided him.

"I disagree. Turned out to be a smart investment," he said, wagging the sandwich as if that alone proved the point. He took another bite and then reached for the jar of pickles.

After he fished out two of them and added them to his plate, where the other half of his sandwich waited, he went back to the box. He looked inside, inhaled, and then gazed back up at her. "What are those?"

She laughed a little at the wonder in his voice. "Jam puffs."

"Raspberry?" Again, that note of hope.

She nodded.

That was enough for him. He reached for one and popped it in his mouth before she could protest.

"Mr. Thayer, those are for dessert!"

"My box, I can eat it in any order I choose. Also, I thought we'd agreed you'd call me Archie," he reminded her, brazenly stealing another puff out of the box and popping it in his mouth.

Oh, of all the cheek!

He tipped the box toward her. "You had best get one before I eat them all."

"No, you go ahead," she told him, taking on a martyred air.

Mr. Thayer held one out to her. "Come, now. No need to be the epitome of good hospitality and kindness, for I insist."

Now it was her turn to laugh. "It isn't necessary." She nodded toward the cupboard. "I have an entire plate of them hidden away."

Now it was his turn to laugh, a deep rich sound that she sensed surprised even him. For as quickly as he laughed, he stopped and settled back into his seat in a cloud of silence.

"Is something wrong?" she asked, having taken up one of the quarters of sandwich. She'd always liked a sandwich cut like a butterfly.

"Not at all. It's just been a long time since I ate supper with anyone. Or laughed like that."

"Don't you eat over at the hotel?" she asked, ignoring the other part. She hadn't laughed much before Madeline had come to town.

"I do, but I have a table to myself. It isn't like this." He smiled at her, and they went back to eating in companionable silence, for she hardly knew what to say.

But, being a lawyer, Mr. Thayer went on to add, "I have to say this isn't my typical Saturday night fare. Far too festive."

"Festive, indeed!" she shot back. "I'm not sure what would be regarded as 'festive' these days. I haven't had much company over for dinner since my father died." She glanced away. "We'd play backgammon on Saturday nights," she added for no particular reason.

"Backgammon? I haven't played in years. My sister and I would play for hours." His face lit up. "You still have your board?"

Ninny had already gotten to her feet and was beginning to clear the table. "I do."

At that he grinned and got up, taking the plates from her. "I'll clear the table if you'll go get it. If you are of a mind to play?"

She paused. "I warn you, I don't like to lose."

He began picking up the rest of the table. "Neither do I."

With that, Ninny retrieved the board from its long hibernation in the parlor sideboard while Mr. Thayer cleared the table. When she returned, she found the plate of jam puffs had been liberated from the cupboard and now sat beside the coffee pot on the table.

Archie glanced up at her. "I would hate for them to go bad."

"Incorrigible," she said as she sat down, taking one and popping it in her mouth.

"You have mistaken me for my colleague, Mr. Quinby."

"No, I definitely have not." She looked over the pieces already set up on the board. How many years had it been since she'd played? She couldn't really recall. She handed him a die and rolled her own, as he did his. He won the start.

"How is it you and your sister spent your evenings playing backgammon? In Boston of all places." Ninny paused and then considered what she'd asked. "If I'm not speaking out of turn."

"I don't think you could."

He rolled and made his first move, boldly forging out across the board. "My parents were always out. Later when my Saturdays were filled with the socials and balls and the clubs—everything that was expected of me as a Thayer—I often missed those quiet evenings. Mostly, I missed my sister."

"Expectations. How they bind us to a life that is not our own," Ninny said, rolling the dice and taking her own turn.

"They do indeed," he offered as he gauged the board and then rolled the dice. A pair of ones. He pressed forward, exposing more pieces. "If we let them."

She had certainly let others make her choices. About her entire life. After her father had died, it had never occurred to her that there was anything else for her other than running the post office.

She rolled the dice. "What became of your sister?" she asked as she counted out her turn, knocking one of his pieces to the bar.

Then she realized how quiet he'd become. Dear heavens, what had she just asked?

"She died. Of a fever. Just after I went to study law." He rolled again and brought a checker back into the game, this time laying it atop another to protect them both.

"I'm so sorry," she told him. To have someone so dear and to lose them . . . Ninny pushed the plate of jam puffs closer. He took two.

She knew she was straying into uneasy territory, but with the door cracked, she couldn't help but widen the gap, a whisper of *Exorior!* prodding her. "I hardly think you would have wanted to leave. Boston, that is."

This time his eyes held nothing of their earlier humor, only a stark sheen. "Things changed. As they do." He rolled again and this time, he had few choices, or none that helped him, and his brow furrowed in frustration.

"Excuse my impertinence," she told him. "Will you tell me about her?"

"My sister—"

Ninny shook her head. "No, Archie, not her. You know very well who I mean. Please, tell me about your wife."

CHAPTER 34

Sunday, December 15
The third Sunday of Advent

Ninny glanced at the clock for the hundredth time. Five minutes to noon.

Behind her, the empty mail slots were evidence enough that all her usual Sunday customers had come and gone. It had been an exceptionally busy morning, leaving her no time to reflect on her conversation the previous night with Mr. Thayer. Nor had the man attended church. Not that he went every week, rather he attended just enough to maintain a proper mien in good society.

She hoped he wasn't embarrassed at having unburdened himself by answering her forward question.

A wife. A betrayal. A child. All left behind. The story was rather too familiar.

One more glance at the clock. Four minutes to noon. Behind her, all that was left was one mail slot nearly filled with a stack of letters. They were quickly penned replies to the invitations received, the lines inside most likely cribbed from *Hill's Business & Social Forms*:

My dear Mrs. Lovell,

I shall be charmed to join your birthday luncheon on Wednesday, the 18th of December. It is most kind of you to include me.

Yours most sincerely . . .

"Charmed" was not the word Ninny would use, but there they sat. Eight prompt and perfectly polite replies.

Though the recipient had yet to arrive and claim them.

Now normally, Ninny wouldn't expect Mrs. George L. to come to the post office on a Sunday, especially given Columbia's frequent comments on the sacrilege of conducting business on the Sabbath. Never mind that Sunday hours gave those who came to town only for church services an opportunity to claim their mail.

So hopefully she wouldn't make an appearance, given that there were only eight envelopes in the Lovell slot. She'd expect eleven. A complete compliment of guests. Not three holdouts.

Ninny knew exactly who would bear the brunt of her indignation at this social affront.

So as the hand on the clock ticked another minute closer to closing, Ninny hurried around the counter, tugging at her apron as she went. Having reached the sign in the window to flip it to "closed," there was an ominous creak on the stairs out front, and the thud of a determined heel on the front porch, right before the door swung open.

"I assume you are still open, are you not, Parathinia?" Mrs. George L. asked, glancing over at the clock to confirm her question.

Two minutes to the hour.

Ninny, tangled in her apron strings, tamped down a groan. Instead, she managed a forced smile. "You've arrived just in time."

"You weren't about to close early, were you?" Mrs. George L. glanced again at the clock and sniffed as if Ninny were trying to pull a fast one on the citizens of Bethlehem.

"Hardly, when I knew you'd most likely be coming by for your mail," Ninny said, heading straight to the Lovell box. Gathering up the envelopes there, she handed them over.

Instead of taking her collection of tidings home, Mrs. George L.

stayed put, sorting them slowly, inspecting and cataloguing each one until she got to the end. She looked up, her brow furrowed. "There seems to be an error."

"How is that?" Ninny feigned a surprise she didn't feel.

She held up her mail, brows arched. "There are only eight. There should be eleven." She shook the envelopes at Ninny. "Can you explain this?"

"Explain what?"

"The others," she ground out. "There should be eleven."

"I cannot say." Ninny turned and looked at the now-empty slot. "Those are all I have received."

"Perhaps, *Parathinia*, they have been misplaced," she persisted.

Ninny ruffled. "I can assure you, *Columbia*, I have been exceedingly thorough."

"But there should be eleven. Why, everyone knows that a prompt reply to an invitation is the mark of civility and good manners." She reshuffled the envelopes in her hands, making an occasional *tsk-tsk* as she went. "Such indecision . . . Such tardiness." Then she glanced up, "Shocking. When one doesn't make up their mind with due diligence, it reflects a fault of character."

"Perhaps you will have a full accounting by tomorrow afternoon," Ninny told her, taking a pointed glance at the clock, which now only had a minute to go.

"As if I have time to shilly-shally back and forth when I have a luncheon to plan." She straightened, a formidable creature in her Sunday finery of a fox fur and a grand hat. "I cannot fathom any reason for a delay. When one receives an invitation, one responds immediately." She paused as if to allow that word to sink in.

Immediately. Not in a few days. Not next week. Immediately.

The clock on the wall made a loud clunk as the big hand met the little hand at the top of the hour.

Noon.

Even Mrs. George L. could take a hint. But she wasn't about to leave without the last word. "When indecision rules your life, it will leave you behind. Your fatal flaw, if you don't mind me saying, Parathinia Minch, is an inability to take a firm grasp of opportunity."

✳

WICK STOOD in the doorway of the saloon and looked around. He arched one brow slightly, but he said nothing.

"Welcome, Sheriff," Madeline said. "If you're coming in, mind closing the door?"

"Certainly, ma'am."

Ma'am. So they were back on those terms. *You asking to go upstairs, Sheriff?* Her and her big mouth.

"You aren't open, are you?" he asked, glancing over at the table where Erasmus and Thayer sat with Dobbs, and at Badger, who sat on one of the barstools. "I got an earful from Mrs. George L. that the saloon was open. On. A. Sunday." The last part was a rather spot-on imitation of the lady, which left Badger chuckling.

"Not at all," Erasmus informed him. "Mr. Thayer and I are helping young Dobbs with his homework, while I know not what Mr. Densmore is about. As for our lovely proprietress, she has quite refused us any sustenance, other than leftover sandwiches and soup, in compensation."

"Does that violate my license?" Madeline straightened.

"I suppose not," Wick said, hanging his hat on the hook. So he was going to stay. Great. "Not if there are any more of those sandwiches."

Madeline had planned on checking in with Ninny, but with her saloon filled up, she could hardly leave this lot unsupervised. She'd quizzed Thayer and Badger when each had shown up, and all she'd gained in return were mumbled responses about the post office being open, and she'd been seen earlier at church. But still . . . she wanted to check on her friend herself.

Now, added to this mix was Wick. "Didn't see you around last night," she said, swiping at the counter. Even as she said the words, she realized she'd been rather disappointed that he hadn't checked in on her.

He ambled in, his gaze sweeping the room. "No one was causing problems here, so I had the evening off."

"Glad I could oblige you." She had hoped to leave it at that, but one more question came nagging up. "Did you go to the supper?" She did her best not to sound *too* interested.

He nodded and made his way over to the table.

Dobbs glanced up from his homework, pencil in hand. "Who'd you eat supper with?"

The sheriff got all sheepish suddenly, his mouth working back and forth before he admitted the truth. "The Winsley sisters."

While Madeline clamped her teeth together so as not to laugh, the rest of the room stilled. In horror, it seemed, for Thayer and Badger spoke at once.

"No."

"Are you mad?"

Wick shuffled his feet a bit. "No one else was bidding, and so—"

"You thought to throw yourself on the train tracks?" Erasmus shook his head. "There is kindness, and then there is being foolhardy. Maddie, my love, a plate for this poor devil, if you will."

She nodded and went to the kitchen, returning with a plate of sandwiches and a bowl of soup. As she set them down on the table, she asked, "Whatever is wrong with Theodosia and Odella? They seem quite harmless. And you ate more than one of Miss Theodosia's ginger cookies—which, by the way, were for me."

"Cookies, yes, but anything else—" Thayer shuddered. Every man in the saloon, including Dobbs, nodded their head in solidarity.

Badger was more direct. "Sheriff, you might want to go by Doc's and see if he has a good purgative."

Erasmus barked a laugh, but then turned more reflective. "It is a loathsome shame what this town has come to of late," he announced. "One cake dance gone awry, and every spinster and widow in town is dusting off her dance card. A man can't go anywhere now without being the subject of speculation."

Now Thayer laughed. "I assure you, Quinby, no one is speculating about you."

Erasmus bristled with indignation. "I'll have you know that in my day, there was a young woman from—" He scratched at his bristling chin as he tried to remember.

"Nantucket?" Thayer offered.

Wick coughed and stopped the tale in its tracks. "So you haven't discovered who the other two guests are?" he asked, nodding at the chalkboard on the backbar.

"Nope," she said, tucking the foolish thing away.

That didn't stop the jovial speculation from running back and forth, while Madeline continued to straighten the bar and clean the shelves.

All her life, the people surrounding her—with the exceptions of Nate and Gigi—had always wanted something from her. A piece of her fame. A percentage of her earnings. A splash in her spotlight. But nothing in her life had felt like this.

Being surrounded by friends.

How that had happened, and so quickly, she couldn't fathom. But here it was. Her gaze strayed to the calendar by the door. The fifteenth of December.

Nine days left. She glanced up and caught her own reflection in the glass—a figure she barely recognized. Not a role, not a character. Something more.

The clock on the backbar gave a shuddering *tick*. And then a few more, as if it too was reaching toward some stirring of time.

"If it isn't Miss Minch," said Erasmus, his voice rising to make his point, "then who might—"

Madeline opened her mouth to argue the matter when the back door creaked open and a figure strode in.

"Now what am I being defamed for?"

They all turned to find the lady in question standing in the back room doorway. Ninny marched into the center of the saloon, hefting a pair of snowshoes, and came to a stop between Badger and Mr. Thayer. "I thought I might find the two of you here," she said, in a tone that suggested the location didn't play in their favor. "But it was my presumption that saloons aren't open on Sundays. Is that not true?" This she addressed to Wick.

"It is not open," he told her.

"Unfortunately, we are not imbibing, madam," Erasmus added. "Simply helping Dobbs with his studies and having some leftover sandwiches."

For whatever reason, Ninny drew in a sharp breath and stole a surreptitious glance at Mr. Thayer, before she seemed to recover. She held out the snowshoes. "This needs to stop." Looking from Mr. Thayer to Badger and back again, she asked, "Which of you did this?"

"Is there something wrong with them?" Wick asked with an innocent air.

Madeline thought him either really brave or entirely foolhardy, for Ninny looked like she might wallop him with them.

"Since you asked, yes." She turned them this way and that. "Someone took them off my shed, and then went to the trouble of restringing and varnishing them."

Wick whistled. "That doesn't sound like a crime, Miss Minch."

"I know it isn't a crime," she shot back. "But the two of you must cease this nonsense."

Her words found no purchase. Thayer whistled. "Damn you, Densmore. That is some fine work."

"You know, Badger, I've got an old pair that could use some sprucing up," Erasmus offered.

"Sod off," Badger shot back, then he looked up at Ninny. "Do you like them?"

She blushed and stammered a bit. "Well, yes. I've always loved this pair. But I haven't been snowshoeing in ages." An uncomfortable silence filled the room, as everyone else looked anywhere in the room that wasn't occupied by the two of them.

All except Mr. Thayer. "Looks like you've left me no choice but to step up to the plate, Densmore."

"No one is doing any more stepping," Ninny told him, wagging a finger at them both. "I will not stand for it. As a matter of fact, I have something to say about the entire proceedings."

"MISS DRAKE, I WAS WONDERING IF—"

Savannah stumbled to a halt as the room before her came into focus.

Instead of just Miss Drake and Dobbs, there was a regular party happening. On a Sunday, no less.

So much for finding a place where she could sew in private. The saloon had been her last resort.

But now it seemed a good part of the town was gaping back her as she tried to think of a good explanation for her sudden appearance in the town's saloon. Her mouth opened, but it wasn't so much the number but the mix of people that left her speechless. Badger, that disreputable Mr. Quinby, the sheriff, Mr. Thayer. And Miss Minch, holding, for whatever reason, a pair of snowshoes.

Yet as much as they all cut their own separate paths, this motley collection of souls belonged here.

Just as she did, she realized. And that rather staggered her.

She closed her mouth, still scrambling for an explanation. Then her gaze fell once more upon the postmistress, and suddenly she had her excuse.

"Ah, Miss Minch. I thought I saw you coming in here," she lied. She pulled out the RSVP she'd penned earlier and the two pennies she'd tucked in for postage. "I know this is highly irregular, and I do apologize for not being more prompt in my arrival to the post office during your regular Sunday hours, but if you don't mind . . ." She set the envelope down on the table.

Mr. Quinby leaned over and snorted loudly. "Well, I'll be." He nodded toward the envelope. "Mrs. George L. Lovell. That's another one, I'd bet my entire practice on it."

Savannah bristled. "Mr. Quinby, I daresay your entire legal practice wouldn't buy a round of sarsaparilla at the drugstore, so it is a wager hardly worth considering."

Her reply left Badger and Mr. Thayer chortling.

Mr. Quinby straightened his jacket. "Mrs. Clarke, I've always suspected you would make a formidable opponent in the courtroom, and now I see I am correct."

She sniffed. "It doesn't appear to be a very taxing profession if it leaves one time to loaf about a saloon most days."

Badger looked over. "She's got you and Thayer pegged to a T.

But, more to the point, I think we've got number eleven covered now."

All eyes turned toward her, and Savannah had a horrible feeling that her hasty entry had just landed her in the soup.

Dobbs voiced the question everyone wanted to ask. "Are you going to that birthday luncheon, Mrs. Clarke?"

Savannah pressed her lips together and then stunned them all. "Yes. I must."

"Why wouldn't you go?" Dobbs asked, twisting around in his seat. "I bet there'll be ice cream."

"Most likely," Savannah told him. "But ice cream is not always an inducement."

"Would be for me," he muttered, turning back to his homework.

"When is your birthday, Dobbs?" Miss Minch asked.

Dobbs and Miss Drake answered as one. "December eighteenth."

"Hey, how'd you know?" Dobbs asked her.

"Lucky guess," she offered.

"If I was having a party, I'd have ice cream," he declared. More like suggested.

"So you shall," Miss Drake told him. "Because on Wednesday I'm closing the Star Bright, and we are having the grandest birthday party this town has ever seen."

"Closing?" Mr. Quinby protested.

"For Dobbs' birthday party," Miss Drake told him firmly.

"Really?" Dobbs grinned.

Savannah caught herself warming at his starry-eyed delight.

"Truly," Miss Drake told him.

"And a cake?"

"Wouldn't be a birthday without one," she promised. "We'll invite everyone."

Dobbs' tutor had a different question. "Will the bar be—"

"Erasmus." The sheriff's warning tone stopped the man.

"Just asking for the concerned citizens of our good town," he said, tapping on the pages in front of Dobbs to remind him what he needed to finish.

"Yes, well, I've completed my business and must be going."

Savannah turned to leave and found Miss Drake studying her. Seeing right through her.

"You are most welcome to stay." She nodded toward the chair next to the stove. "If you would like."

An invitation to belong, as if she were part of this unspoken alliance.

She shook her head. "No, I have matters to attend to at home." With that, she hurried out the way she'd come, lest that thread had a chance to wind around her, to anchor her amongst this strange collection of souls.

For there was the rub. She could stay. Gather friends, acquaintances. But once they learned the truth, the why of her existence here in Bethlehem, they'd cast her aside soon enough.

Friendship came with confidences, and truth, and inadvertent confessions. So the best course of action, she'd decided long ago, was to keep her distance so no one would discover what she'd done.

As she hurtled out the door, she nearly ran headlong into someone else.

Shandy.

Of course.

"What are you scurrying away from, Mrs. Clarke? he asked, reaching out to steady her. "Place catch fire?" He nodded at the saloon.

"Hardly, on both counts," she told him, straightening and stepping around him.

To her chagrin, he followed.

"Did you know? That spot, where the saloon sits, is where this town began."

"No, I did not," Savannah told him, done with his nonsensical meanderings.

"Most think it's the mine," he continued, "but it was the Star Bright. It wasn't much more than a tent and Poppy, all determined to start over. And boy, did she." He smiled at the false-fronted building. "A fine spot to start over, don't you think? For a new beginning?"

"I'm hardly one of your lost souls, Mr. Shandy." She went to move around him, but he just managed to fall in step with her.

"Aren't you? I consider you one of my greatest challenges."

"You are most mistaken."

"Mistakes are not the last word in a life," he observed as he strode along beside her.

It was like being followed by a stray mutt. One with fleas.

She edged away from him, but he tracked her course and stayed right in step, even as she quickened her pace.

"Mistakes only count when you look at how one moves forward from them," he continued.

"I apparently cannot move fast enough."

He laughed. "You should have taken up Maddie's invitation and stayed."

She came to a stop. How did he know?

She sighed. He always knew. Why, after all this time, was she surprised?

He stopped a few steps later and looked back, examining her much as Miss Drake had, as if looking for something lost.

Before he could find it, she told him directly, "I haven't time for more obligations."

"An obligation? Is that how you look at a gathering of folks on a Sunday afternoon?" He shook his head. "Is it an obligation or an opportunity?

Now it was her turn to scoff. "I'll not play your games, sir." She shook the snow and ice off the hem of her skirt. "Good day."

"You know what the real mistake in life is, Mrs. Clarke?" he called after her.

Against her better judgment, Savannah turned.

"Not recognizing the friends we have standing right in front of us."

CHAPTER 35

Tuesday, December 17

$\mathcal{M}$adeline hurried up the steps to Ninny's back door with a large box in hand.

"Goodness, did you empty the mercantile?" Ninny asked as she opened the door.

"I got everything you said we'd need," Madeline told her, coming in and opening up the bundle on the table. On Sunday, Ninny had offered to help her bake Dobbs' birthday cake. "The eggs and sugar," she said as she handed them over to Ninny. "Chocolate."

"He'll be over the moon," Ninny said, but suspected it was Madeline who would be floating on air.

"I've invited the usual suspects, as well as the Kings and Savannah and Inola."

"Savannah?" Ninny asked.

"Rather a prickly sort, but once you get to know her, she's interesting."

"Are you referring to Mrs. Clarke?"

"Yes." Madeline paused, hands on her hips. "Why is everyone so surprised about her?"

A heavy knock at the door startled them both. "My heavens," Ninny exclaimed as a second set of staccato raps set the rafters to rattling.

"Get out the vanilla while I see to this," she said to Madeline, nodding toward the upper cupboard. As Madeline began searching for the vanilla, Ninny opened the door.

Without any greeting or invitation, a gust of wind brought in a bundled crone of a woman. Her hands were encased in patched mittens, and she thumped her cane on the floor as if testing for soft spots in the hardwood. "I went to the front door and found you closed," she croaked out as she unwound a long (and also patched) scarf. "What sort of tomfoolery is this?"

"You know as well as everyone else I'm closed on Tuesday afternoons," Ninny told her.

"Closed? Closed, you say?" the woman all but shouted. "Not to me, Parathinia Minch. I've known you since you were knee-high, and you can't naysay me. Now I need my mail, so go fetch it. That highfalutin daughter-in-law of mine wants me to write her a note to say I'll be at her party. Bah! As if I'd turn down an opportunity to see her hoity-toity luncheon turn into yet another disaster. Still, Georgie wants me to play nice, so I'm here to get my invitation." All through this speech, she'd been unwinding her great scarf, a rainbow of patches, and she croaked a laugh as she finally got the last of it, revealing snow-white hair and bright pink cheeks.

She glanced around the kitchen and her narrowed gaze lit on Madeline. "Land sakes, who the hell are you?" She stepped closer. "I suppose you're that hussy who has my daughter-in-law in a state. The one Quinby came to see me about. Nice to meet you. Now pour me a glass of that, and then you can tell me what the devil you're doing *here*."

Pour me a glass . . . To Ninny's horror, there was Madeline with a bottle that was definitely not the vanilla.

McKinnon's Fine Whiskey.

"Girl, are you hard of hearing?" the old gal complained. She drew in a deep breath through her nose and looked as if she wanted to spit. When no suitable receptacle presented itself, she gargled the . . . well, contents back down and then prodded at Madeline with her cane. "I said, pour me a glass. Get a tall one for Ninny there. She looks like she's been caught outside in her bloomers."

Madeline's gaze flew to Ninny because she wasn't quite sure what to do.

Ninny heaved a sigh. "Madeline, may I present, Mrs. George J. Lovell."

MADELINE LIKED HER IMMEDIATELY.

Until the old crow whacked her in the shinbone. "Drinks, gel. You'll never keep my saloon afloat if you can't pour a drink with some speed. Men don't like to be kept waiting. If you know what I mean." She paused and eyed her. "I think you do." She turned to Ninny, "What are you gaping at? My mail, if you please. The sooner I get it, the less drunk I'll be when I leave."

Ninny immediately turned tail and hurried down the hall to get the woman's mail.

Madeline returned to the table with three glasses. Tall ones. Mrs. Lovell had already pulled the cork and was taking a sample. It was hard to tell how old she was. There was a hazy cast to her faded blue eyes, but she was spry of movement and clearly quick of wit. Madeline doubted she missed a thing. Age spots dotted the backs of her curled hands, and her wrinkled face was framed by a braid pinned in a crown around her head.

"I like her," she was saying, wagging her chin toward the hall. "Wish my son hadn't jilted her for that pretentious social climber he married."

Madeline choked. "What?"

Mrs. George J. barked a laugh. "Oh, yes. Ninny and my son were quite the item. Then something happened, and next thing I know he's off to Denver and bringing home that show pony. Joke's on him. Turns out she's more of a draft horse."

Now it was Madeline's turn to laugh. She held up the bottle for Mrs. George J.'s inspection then filled all three glasses.

Ninny was definitely going to need a drink.

The woman's nose wrinkled. "McKinnon's. Go easy if you haven't had it before. Bites on the way down and won't do you any favors in the morning."

Madeline raised her glass. "To being forewarned."

"To hell in a handbasket," Mrs. George J. returned. Their glasses clinked, and they both drank.

"Oh, dear," Ninny exclaimed, having returned with two pieces of mail. "Here you are, Mrs. Lovell."

"You know better than to call me that," the woman told her. "My name is Poppy. No fancy manners for me." She tipped her glass to Madeline. "Goes for you as well."

"Poppy it is," she agreed.

Madeline had never known Ninny to be anything other than exceedingly polite to all she met, but here she was giving Poppy side-eye nudges toward the door.

Not that Poppy noticed. "No wonder they threw you out of the Temperance Union, Ninny-girl."

Ninny went to gather up the bottle, but Poppy was faster and caught hold of it in a vise-like grip.

"That's an old bottle of Father's."

Poppy had no boundaries. "How long has it been since Machias blew his brains out?"

Madeline choked in shock and then turned toward Ninny, who'd gone as white as her tea towels.

"Twenty-two years ago," Ninny said in a cold, strangled voice.

"So unless you put him back together, I doubt this was his," the old woman replied with a huff, holding the bottle, her finger tapping at the lower part of the label. *Bottled 1902.* "Oh, drink up, child. Good riddance to that pack of mangy crows."

"A murder of crows," Madeline corrected, swirling the amber liquid in her glass.

"Huh?" Poppy said, looking up from the label.

"It's properly a murder of crows, not a pack."

"You'd best realize that I've never been proper a day in my life," Poppy replied.

"Then we are going to get along famously," Madeline told her.

Ninny set her glass down and folded her arms over her chest. "I have hopes of finding my way back into the Temperance Union." She pursed her lips. "With some time."

"You would," Poppy said, shaking her head as if she had higher hopes for Ninny. Then she turned back to Madeline. "So how do you like my saloon?"

"I had no idea it was yours."

"Well, it was, until Shandy came around a couple of months ago and asked to borrow it." She laughed. "Can't refuse that man anything, try as I might. He's a regular devil, he is."

"Devil?" Madeline shook her head. "He makes himself sound like he's some sort of angel doing everyone a favor."

Poppy snorted. "He would. I'll never admit it to him, but the best thing he ever did was bring me here. Oh, don't get me wrong, I cursed him roundly for years, but then in time, I saw that he'd given me the chance I needed. I've lived a far better life because of him. Harder, but better."

For a moment, there was a spark of something in her faded blue eyes that must have carried her through some very challenging times.

But living in the past wasn't Poppy's style. "How is the Star Bright?"

"Odd as it sounds, it feels like home," Madeline admitted. Probably because her insides were beginning to warm with whiskey.

Poppy nodded in approval. "Funny how that happens, eh? Did you find my gold?"

"Under the counter, behind the star."

"Well, I'll be dammed," Poppy said. "Shandy show you that?"

"Nope." Madeline took a slow drink, dragged the moment out. "Found it on my own."

"Gonna tell me how?"

"Nope. You wouldn't believe me anyway."

"You'd be surprised what I'm willing to believe after all this time here."

"I've spent a good portion of it," Madeline confessed. "Didn't know it was yours."

"You're welcome to it. It's nice seeing the place lit up again. Besides, the fool men in this town will fill that drawer back up in no time, given how hell-bent the women are to close you down." At this, she shot a scathing glance at Ninny. "Still want to be a member of that hypocritical lot?"

They both turned and caught Ninny taking a tentative drink from her glass. "Yes, well, I have my own dilemmas."

"That tree nonsense?" Poppy made a bark of a laugh. "Best thing that ever happened to this town."

Ninny shook her head and set down her glass. "Not that problem. Another one." She pursed her lips and worried her hands together.

"Well, spit it out," Poppy told her.

Ninny sighed. Madeline suspected no one stood up to Poppy for long.

"You see, you aren't the only one who hasn't answered your daughter-in-law's invitation," Ninny admitted. With that, she opened her knitting bag and pulled out a white envelope.

"Ninny!" Madeline gaped at her. "You never said a word!"

Poppy wagged a finger at the postmistress. "Look at you, Ninny Minch. I've always said you were a dark horse. My hat is off to you."

"I've been remiss in not making up my mind. I should have sent a reply forthwith."

"Bah! Columbia's never had anyone refuse her. She knows you'll be at her party. Just wants to see everyone dance through hoops to get there." She nudged the bottle back toward Ninny.

"I can hardly arrive tomorrow smelling of spirits. Why, I'd be a scandal," Ninny pointed out.

"Who says you aren't already?" Poppy shot back. "And good company it is." She tipped her glass at Madeline, and then that rheumy gaze pierced the veil, seeing far more than just what was in front of her. "You aren't from this . . ." She paused, searching for the right words. "These parts."

But Madeline had the eerie sense that the woman had meant something else. *You aren't from this time . . .*

Poppy looked down at the contents of her glass as if she could see the portents swirling in the whiskey. "We all get our start somewhere, don't we? And eventually we all find ourselves here. By the grace of chance or that son of a bitch Shandy."

CHAPTER 36

Savannah was about to serve supper when there was a hurried pounding on the back door. Even before she got there, Dobbs rushed in with a geyser of words.

"Mrs. Clarke, there's trouble. I didn't know who else to get."

"Dobbs, slow down. What's happened?"

Inola came around the corner of the dining room with silverware in hand. "What's this?"

"Miss Drake's in trouble," Dobbs said. Then he lowered his voice for Savannah's hearing only. "And Miss Minch."

"Then you'd best go get the sheriff," Inola told him, having come to stand beside Savannah.

"No!" Dobbs and Savannah said at once. Savannah hurried to the hooks at the back door and began to put her coat on. Both of them? What could have happened that had Dobbs looking like his world was falling down?

Inola rushed over and caught her by the arm. "Vanna, whatever are you doing?"

She nodded toward Dobbs, who was going out the door. "I've got to go help him." Then she corrected herself. "Them. I've got to help them."

"You've got to help them?" Inola repeated each word slowly. "You don't even know them."

Shandy's words rang anew, carrying with them the truth from which she had fled. *Not recognizing the friends we already have.*

"But I do know them." Savannah plopped her hat on. "So I must go."

"You never help. Now, suddenly, you are rushing about town like Clara Barton. What has happened to you?"

Savannah almost laughed because she barely believed it herself. For the first time in years, decades really, she was doing what she should have been doing all this time. "First you badger at me for not participating, and now for helping."

Inola crossed her arms and took a deep breath, ready to argue the point, but instead she went in a different direction. "You haven't been right since Thanksgiving. Sneaking off. Crying until you can't breathe. Explain what is going on. Right now. Do you hear me?"

"Mrs. Clarke?" Dobbs practically begged from the bottom of the steps outside.

"Yes, Dobbs, I'll be right there." She tugged on her mittens and caught up the lantern. "I'll explain everything when I get back. Don't wait supper for me."

"I won't," was all Inola said. She whirled around, her skirts making a thick *whoosh*, and stomped back into the dining room to finish setting the table. Clearly for one.

Savannah sighed, for her reckoning was fast approaching.

"Mrs. Clarke!" came the plaintive cry. That alone hurried her steps, and she followed Dobbs toward the cottonwood grove.

When they got to the main street, instead of turning left, the boy went right.

"Dobbs, I thought you said Madeline was in trouble." Savannah nodded toward the saloon.

Dobbs shook his head and pointed down the road toward the post office. "Her and Miss Minch. And someone else."

Savannah was still looking at the saloon, all lit up and full of customers. "Who's running the Star Bright?"

"Mr. Quinby," Dobbs told her. "When Miss Drake didn't show up, he insisted I open the door and let him conduct business. Said he had a proprietary investment in the establishment."

"Did he now?" Savannah said, her breath coming out in a steamy huff.

"What does that mean?" Dobbs asked.

"That he's a rapscallion thief."

"Thought so." Dobbs frowned over his shoulder at the saloon. "That's why I went to find Miss Drake. After that, I came for you."

"What's happened?"

Dobbs' pace quickened. "They're all drunk."

"Drunk?" Savannah shot a side glance at Dobbs. "Surely not Miss Minch."

He nodded, his eyes wide.

Oh, gracious heavens. This was worse than Savannah thought. Miss Drake wasn't a surprise, but Miss Minch?

It's always the quiet ones, Mémé used to say. Then it occurred to her that there was one more in this party of debauchery. "You said there is someone else with them."

Dobbs stumbled a bit. "It's *her*." He stopped and turned around. "Mrs. George."

Now Savannah stopped. "Dobbs, are you playing a prank on me?"

"No, ma'am."

"So why are you telling me that Mrs. George L. is drunk?"

"No, not her. *Mrs. George*." He tugged his coat close and shuddered. "The old one."

Savannah looked up at the post office. "Oh, Lord have mercy." She slanted a glance at Dobbs. "How did *she* end up with *them*?"

"I don't know," he said. "But it ain't good."

"No, I suppose it wouldn't be."

Dobbs led her along a deep path in the snow that circled around back. She followed, holding the lamp high. Even before they got to the door, she could hear singing. Or rather some sort of lewd caterwauling.

"Let's get it on . . ."

She marched up the back steps and straight into the kitchen. What had been a cozy, homey spot just a few days ago was now a regular sirens' den.

The line of empty bottles on the counter said much, but here was Miss Minch waltzing and swaying in the middle of the room with her cat in her arms. The poor thing peered over her shoulder, wearing a disgruntled moue, like a boy pressed to dance with his wallflower cousin.

Meanwhile, Mrs. George and Madeline moved in a circle around the postmistress in a frenzy of waggling hips and hands fluttering overhead.

"Let's get it on," Madeline wailed in a deep husky voice, bottle held high.

"Let's get it on," Mrs. George echoed, before she took a swig of her own libation.

"What the devil?" Savannah exclaimed, and they all came to a stumbling halt.

"Told ya," Dobbs said, looking around her.

Savannah whirled around. "Go get the sheriff."

Dobbs shook his head. "He'll take away the saloon if he catches her like this."

"No, he won't. I'll see to that," she promised, though she had no idea how she was going to keep such a bargain. "Believe me, we'll need his help." She nodded toward the door. "Go quick, and don't tell anyone else."

He nodded and left.

Savannah turned around, hands on her hips, and took that stance that Mémé had used when things got out of hand. "Ladies. Enough!"

Mrs. George, empty bottle in hand, wagged it at Savannah. "I've only just started."

That elicited drunken giggles from Miss Minch.

From Miss Minch.

Savannah groaned and looked over at Madeline. Hands in the air, hips swaying in slow circles, eyes closed and a sly smile on her lips, she was still going, like some sideshow hoochie coochie girl looking for extra tips. Or work after the show.

Savannah shook her head. Oh, she had questions, but for another time. Right now she had to shut down this illicit party before . . . word got out.

"Where did all this liquor come from?" This she posed to Madeline, for it looked like she'd emptied the Star Bright shelves.

But it was Miss Minch who came staggering forward. "That's all mine." She paused, considered that statement, and then corrected it. "At least it was."

That brought a round of laughter.

Mrs. George was no fool, even drunk. "Did that boy bring more whiskey? I told him to get the good stuff from Mr. Hoback and charge it to my Georgie." She finished off the bottle she held and then shook her head. "For we've gone and drunk the post office dry."

This elicited howls of laughter from the threesome.

Savannah took the bottle and added it to the collection on the drainboard. Vermouth. Whiskey. Rum. Brandy. Oh, dear heavens. She was surprised they were still standing, more or less.

Miss Minch toddled forward. "I am gloriously drunk, Mrs. Clarke." She wavered in place, her gaze unfocused, her lashes batting back and forth.

"Yes, you are, dear." Savannah divested her of her cat and let the creature go. He stalked up the stairs, tail high, showing not the least hint of appreciation for his rescue.

"Sour old lemon," Mrs. George called her before she turned to Madeline. "Told you. Dobbs will fetch the men of this town any bottle they want, but when a lady needs a little bit of ease, something to help her forget, he goes and fetches one of them." She chucked her chin toward Savannah.

"We should have tipped him more," Miss Minch offered, more astutely than her state of inebriation might have indicated, then went back to her tuneless waltzing, completely unfazed by the abdication of her partner.

"He'll be a fine man one day," Madeline announced. "Famous, even. Known all over the world."

"Go on with you," Mrs. George said, waving her hands.

"He will. It's his birthday tomorrow. Going to have a party. At the Star Bright."

"Why wasn't I invited?" Mrs. George complained. "I have to go to that wretched luncheon of Columbia's. Might as well have something to look forward to."

"Then you should come," Madeline offered, before she went back to her one-woman show, sliding about the room and singing something about kissing a girl.

The door opened, and here was Dobbs back again, and a few seconds later the doorway filled with the tall, steady figure of the sheriff. He gaped at the scene before him. Clearly, even for the sheriff, this wasn't an ordinary call.

Savannah sagged in relief. "Oh, thank heavens. I wasn't too sure what to do."

"Neither am I," he confessed.

"Told you," Mrs. George complained, shaking a finger at Dobbs. "No liquor, just the law."

"He'll be a fine man," Madeline repeated, taking the old woman's hand and swirling her in a circle. "He wrote me an instruction book for here."

"Could have used that a time or two when I first got here," Mrs. George said with a throaty laugh. "But things improved immensely when this one showed up." She sauntered over to the sheriff and winked at him.

"We're going to need help," Mr. Fischer said quietly to Savannah, even as he kept his eyes on Mrs. George, who was checking the empty bottles on the table in search of one last drop.

Savannah grimaced. "The fewer people who know—"

"Trust me, this isn't my first party with Poppy." He leaned over and whispered to Dobbs, who groaned but then took off yet again. "Can you make some coffee, Mrs. Clarke?"

"If you think that will help."

"It isn't for them, it's for us. This is going to take some time."

A half an hour later, there was a knock on the door. Savannah answered and found both Mr. Thayer and Badger outside.

"Has something happened to Miss Minch?" Badger asked, shouldering his way in. Within two steps, he came to a dead stop.

Mr. Thayer followed, and the two of them turned and looked at the sheriff and then Savannah.

"What is going on here?" Badger demanded.

"I think the answer is rather obvious," the sheriff told them, tipping his coffee mug at the line of empty bottles on the drainboard.

Badger's head swiveled back toward Madeline. "You did this," he barked out, wagging his finger at her. "I told you not to let Miss Minch come to harm."

"Mr. Densmore, the liquor was all mine," Miss Minch scolded him.

"And a fine sampling it was," Mrs. George added.

There was another unholy chorus of laughter from the pot-valiant trio. Then Miss Minch caught hold of Badger's hand and put it on her hip, and then caught his other and began waltzing with him. "You make a much better partner than Mr. Bingley. He's abandoned me yet again." She leaned in. "Cats and men are never reliable."

Poor Badger gaped over the lady's head at the sheriff, in a silent plea not all that dissimilar to the one Mr. Bingley had made earlier.

"Let's sort out the blame later," the sheriff said. "We need to get every one of them home and into bed without raising any sort of hue and cry."

"Sheriff?" Badger's voice trembled a bit, for here was Miss Minch passed out in his arms, her head lolling on his shoulder. "What do I do?"

"Take her upstairs. Can you manage?"

"She's a wee mite of thing. I can manage." He hoisted her into his arms.

Miss Minch blinked a few times and then smiled at him. "Mr. Bingley would never offer such a kindness."

"I'll help," Savannah assured the poor, befuddled man and led the way up the stairs.

"Are you going to give me the same service, Sheriff?" Mrs. George asked in a throaty purr, curling up to him and batting her eyes.

Savannah pressed her lips together to keep from laughing and continued up the stairs.

"Oh, Poppy," he replied, as he disengaged himself from her grasp. "We've done this dance before."

"And we'll do it again," she promised.

Badger stopped at the head of the stairs and turned to look at Savannah. "Where to?"

Savannah shrugged. "I don't know." She eased past him in the narrow space and looked around. Three doors. The first one she opened had a wide bed and a bureau. For a moment she thought she'd gotten lucky, but a faint scent of bay rum and cigars lingered in the room, so she closed the door. "Not this one." Her second try found a small, narrow bedroom under the eaves, and an air of lavender led her in. She fumbled for the light switch and pressed the button.

The solitary lightbulb hanging in the middle of the room revealed a narrow bed, an old bureau, and a rocking chair. Faded lilacs sprayed across the curling wallpaper. It was a sad, cold room that left Savannah bereft with a sort of loneliness she hadn't realized could exist. As much as she thought herself quite alone in the world, Miss Minch's life was a veritable desert of solitude.

If Badger noticed, he didn't say anything. He just gently lay the woman down and then rolled her on her side. After he surveyed the scene, he pulled the chamber pot from under the bed, set it close, and took off her shoes. Finally, he unfolded the blanket at the foot of the bed and gently settled it over her.

Miss Minch snored lightly and never moved, so the two of them quietly left her to whatever the morning would bring.

Meanwhile, downstairs, a kerfuffle was brewing.

"I'm not going home," Poppy complained. Threatened, more like.

"I'll put you both in jail," the sheriff argued back.

Madeline snorted. "Is that supposed to scare me? It wouldn't be the first time."

"I like her, don't you, Sheriff?" Poppy cackled, wagging her finger at Madeline.

"She's a regular pip," he ground out.

"You'll miss me when I'm gone," Madeline warned him.

"I'll have a lot less to do," he shot back.

"One more song, Maddie," Poppy declared, winding her hand into the curve of the sheriff's arm. "For the road."

"For the road," Madeline repeated, taking the sheriff's other arm.

"*Let's get it on,*" Poppy howled.

"*Let's get it on,*" Madeline purred right back.

"I'll clean up here and then lock up," Badger told them. The sheriff nodded, and Savannah caught up her lamp.

They started down the main street, the pair singing at the top of their lungs. Curtains drew back, spilling light into the street and allowing a raft of unforgiving witnesses watch their parade.

"Might want to turn that down," he advised Savannah. "Less to see then. Less to gossip about."

"Oh, I suppose so," she said, dampening the light.

When they came to the saloon, Erasmus came out, along with Denny. Thayer guided Madeline up the steps. "We'll see to her, Sheriff." They steered her into the saloon, even as she blew kisses over her shoulder at Poppy.

"See that she comes to no harm," the sheriff warned them.

"My best-paying client?" Erasmus huffed. "I will guard her with my life, you can count on that."

"Do you think you should trust him?" Savannah whispered.

"With Miss Drake?" he began. "She's not just his best-paying client. I'd guess she's his only paying client."

Savannah clucked her tongue and looked back at the saloon.

"Don't worry," the sheriff told her. "I have every intention of coming back and making sure she's safe and sound."

At this, Savannah nodded.

As they turned onto Prospect Avenue, the sheriff's boots dragged. "Mrs. George L. is going to have my badge," he muttered as they trudged along. "Or worse."

"If I were a few years younger, I'd have your badge," Poppy teased him. "And a whole lot more."

"Mrs. George!" Savannah scolded.

"Oh, don't you go all high and mighty, *Mrs. Clarke.*" Mrs. George stumbled to a stop, and there was a stillness to her, a soberness that had Savannah rubbing at the gooseflesh rising beneath her sleeves.

"You can cast your fancy Southern airs all you want, gel. But I've had my eye on you since the day you arrived, and of late, something's changed. It's more than just Maddie. *You've* started to move. No longer stuck in the past. And about damn time. You want to know what will happen next?"

The cold night air rushed into Savannah's lungs.

Mrs. George finished with eerie, prescient words. "You'll be just like me."

Like her? Savannah shook off whatever witchery had overcome her. "I doubt that."

Poppy Lovell winked at her and grinned. "What? Don't you want to be free? Living your authentic life, as they liked to say back where I came from? Trust me, no one cares who you were or what you did. It's what you make of your time here that counts. The past—it's just a prison."

Savannah hadn't the time to consider what that meant, because they'd arrived in front of the Lovell house and Poppy was the last to notice. But when she did, she balked.

"Well, shit. I forgot to say goodbye to my hostess. I'd best go back." She turned to flee, but the sheriff had her in hand quickly.

"You can thank her tomorrow," he told her.

"True enough. I'll see her at Columbia's damned lunch."

Savannah tipped her head, for certainly she hadn't heard her correctly. "What do you mean, Mrs. George?"

"Ninny. She's number twelve. Coming to the luncheon, but I wish she wouldn't. Columbia's got something up her sleeve for tomorrow. I know it."

"But Miss Minch never mentioned . . ." Savannah began. "No, you must be mistaken."

"About Columbia?" Poppy barked a laugh. "I doubt it. I knew what she was the minute Georgie got off the train with her on his arm. Hasn't changed an iota since." She looked up at the grand house and shuddered. "I ain't going in there." She backed up, her feet pedaling, but she didn't get far.

Wick caught her by the elbow. "Yes, you are. Eventually every chicken has to come home to roost."

"Not when they know they are about to be fricasseed," Poppy muttered.

The Lovells must have been looking for their errant octogenarian, for here was the front door flinging open. "Mother! There you are! We've been worried sick as to—" Mr. Lovell stopped at the top of the wide steps, gaping down at the odd collection in his front yard.

"Like I'd get lost in this town," Poppy grumbled. She shook off the sheriff's hold on her elbow and took a step forward, but her evening caught up with her. She pitched forward and would have landed headfirst in a snowbank were it not for Wick's quick movement. He righted her and held her fast, ignoring the slew of profanity and threats bubbling up.

Mr. Lovell blanched. "Oh, good Lord, how drunk is she?"

"Drunk enough," Wick replied, hanging onto the scrappy handful.

"Where did she get the liquor?" Mrs. George L. had joined her husband on the porch and surveyed the scene before her with a curl to her lip.

Savannah was about to lie, to say anything but the truth, when the sheriff spoke up before she could manage a decent fiction.

"The post office."

"The post office?" The Lovells echoed with an air of disbelief even as Savannah blanched.

Mr. Lovell's brow furrowed. "You mean she had it mailed—"

Poppy grinned. "First-class whiskey it was. Better than that second-class piss you call bourbon."

Mrs. George L. tacitly ignored her mother-in-law, turning her attention to the sheriff. "Are you telling me she got . . ." Words failed as she tried to finish the sentence in the most dignified manner possible.

Poppy did it for her. "Loaded? Half-shot? Cock-eyed?" She shook herself free once again. "For God's sake, Columbia, just say it. Stop mincing about with pretensions you haven't a right to."

Mrs. George L. set her jaw and turned to the only person who hadn't spoken. "Mrs. Clarke, I demand an accounting!"

Savannah cringed. "Dobbs came and asked for my help, and when I realized the situation, I sought the sheriff's assistance."

There. The truth, without all the recriminations. She hoped that would be enough.

Hardly. Mrs. George L. was a stickler for details. "And the liquor?"

"Ninny," Poppy declared. "She's the dearest girl, that one."

Mrs. George L. gaped. "Ninny? You mean Miss Minch?"

"Is there another?" Poppy jabbed the sheriff in the ribs with her elbow and laughed.

Mrs. George L. turned to Savannah. "Is this true?"

Savannah nodded, and hated herself for having to be the one to deliver Miss Minch to the judge, jury, and hangman.

Mr. Lovell shook his head. "That can't be right." He looked over at the sheriff. "Truly? Miss Minch?"

Wick shrugged.

"Well, I'll be damned," Mr. Lovell muttered.

"Good stuff," Poppy told him. "None of that horrid currant wine or watered sherry you keep in the back of the sideboard, Columbia."

Mrs. George L. opened her mouth to protest such a scenario, but here was Poppy ready to air all their sins. "Oh, don't you get all high and mighty, Columbia Wright. So what if I like to get jiggered from time to time? Makes no matter to you."

"Mother Lovell, we have a standing in this community—"

Poppy wagged her finger. "Don't you 'mother' me. Your standing comes from that bank. A bank I financed with a saloon. Gambling, liquor and ill-gotten gold bought you this fine house and your beloved standing, and don't you ever forget it."

A strained, stunned silence followed, and Poppy took advantage of it to gain her freedom again. She stalked through the snow toward the back of the house.

Mr. Lovell hurried down the steps. "Mother, where are you going? Your room is upstairs."

Poppy huffed a laugh. "And my house is behind this gingerbread monstrosity. I'll be spending the night there." She continued to stomp off, her son following in her wake.

"Need anything?" the sheriff asked him.

Mr. Lovell paused. "I'll see to her. Thank you, Sheriff." Then, as an afterthought, he nodded to Savannah. "Ma'am." He followed his mother around back. "I had Junior light the stove just in case . . ."

The pair disappeared into the darkness, leaving Mrs. George L. on the porch, towering over them like a veritable gargoyle. Her bellicose gaze landed on the sheriff. "Parathinia, you say?"

"Yes, ma'am."

"*Harrumph!*" With that, she stalked into the house and closed the door. Firmly.

Savannah spun around. "Whyever did you do that?"

"Do what?"

"Cast Miss Minch into the fire?"

He crossed his arms over his chest. "What am I supposed to do? Lie?"

Savannah blinked. "Yes!" Dear heavens, how hard could it be to figure that out? She hefted the lantern and stalked down the road.

The sheriff followed.

She glanced over at him as he caught up with her. "Now I will have to fix all this."

"Fix this? We just did," he said, as if delivering Poppy home was the end of it. "Besides, none of this is your fault."

His confidence that the entire debacle was a *fait accompli*, as Inola liked to say, left Savannah shaking with rage.

She came to a stop, the light from the lantern encircling them and floating across the snow in waves. "If there is any fault to be had, it is yours."

His eyes widened. "Mine? I didn't pour a bottle of whiskey into Poppy Lovell." No, but he'd done more damage than that, as evidenced by his next statement. "This will all blow over in the morning. It always does."

"It certainly will not," Savannah shot back, leaving him gaping in bewilderment. Men! She wheeled sharply onto the path through the aspens and left him gaping after her.

Come morning, there was only one thing to be done. Thwart the slaughter that was certain to be held over Mrs. George L.'s luncheon table.

❄

SAVANNAH BARELY GOT through her door before she found herself wrapped in a fierce hug.

"You've come home," Inola said in a thick voice.

Shaking herself free, Savannah straightened. "Where else would I go?"

Inola wasn't done. She took her by the shoulders and gave her a good shake. Like Mémé would have. "I was so worried. You scared me half to death!"

Savannah took a step back. "Whatever are you going on about? I just went over to help Miss Minch. You knew that."

Inola moved into the kitchen, giving her room to take off her coat, her hat. "I don't know you anymore," she was saying, as she went to put the kettle on. "Sneaking around town, crying in great jags. You even cut up your dress!"

"How did you know?"

Inola had the decency to blush. "Vanna, what has happened? You know I couldn't go on without you."

"Nor I you, sister," she told her.

"Then are we sisters again?" Inola asked.

"Always."

"Sisters don't keep secrets."

"No, they shouldn't." Savannah nodded in agreement, as she rinsed the teapot and got down the tea tin. "Why don't you sit down."

"You *are* dying! I knew it!" Inola sought out her chair.

"You've been writing that tragic serial again, haven't you?" Savannah laughed.

"I hardly think . . ." Her jaw worked back and forth.

"I'm not dying." Savannah stilled for a moment. "In fact, quite the opposite."

Setting the teapot down on the table, she took the chair opposite Inola. Her dearest friend. Her sister.

She retrieved the wishes from of her pocket and slid them onto the table. Then she told Inola everything. As she should have from the start.

❄

WHEN SHE FINISHED HER CONFESSION, Inola burst into tears. Savannah reached across the table and caught her hand. "Please—no more tears."

"I thought you were trying to make amends. I thought you were trying to make some peace with this world before you . . ." Inola said the words quietly, as if afraid that lending them voice might give them life. "I didn't think you were coming home tonight."

"I thought we'd settled that. Where else would I go?"

"I thought you had done what Sybilla did."

The depth of those words sank into Savannah. *What Sybilla did.*

"I feared I'd have to spend tomorrow walking the river's edge to find you."

"I could never do that."

Not now. She was no longer stuck in that dark place. She'd been nudged out of her prison by a slip of paper and the myriad consequences it had wrought.

"But what about this one?" Inola asked, turning over the other wish, the one Savannah hadn't dared unfold. "I don't think I've ever seen this language before."

Savannah leaned over to look at it, trying to recall where she'd seen such lettering. But she couldn't place it. Well, one thing at a time, she supposed. "When I picked those up that night, Nola, everything changed."

"I'll say everything changed," she agreed, "if it got you cooking for that woman."

"Madeline," she corrected.

Inola sat back, her mouth open. "You like her!"

"I do," she admitted, surprising herself. "She's quite the going concern. She's been here no more than three weeks, and already she's found her place, built a family around herself. Miss Minch. The sheriff. She's been good by Dobbs. And Mr. Quinby, Mr. Thayer, and Badger aren't in the saloon because it's open. I think they genuinely like her. Just like that."

"So you envy her." Inola smiled, her eyes crinkling at the corners.

Savannah hadn't quite thought of it that way. "I suppose I do."

"But she can't cook," Inola pointed out.

"Oh, no, she can't," Savannah agreed with a chuckle. "She didn't even know what a simmer was."

They both laughed over that.

"No wonder she's paying you too much," Inola pointed out.

Here was another thing Savannah had left out. "Sadly, it won't last for long." She took a breath. "Miss Drake is leaving at Christmas. She's not staying here—she's returning home. I didn't think such a thing was possible."

Now it was Inola's turn to confess. "It is."

Those two little words. Savannah could hardly believe it. "What?"

"It's possible."

"Inola, what are you saying?"

"Shandy offered us . . . Well, he offered me the choice for both of us—since you were so lost at the time—to stay or go. I didn't see how we could go back, so I told him we wanted to stay. I'm sorry. I should have told you ages ago, but I didn't see how it would help." She glanced up. "Did I do the right thing?"

All this time she'd thought herself trapped. In an identity that wasn't her own. In a life she'd crafted to hide her past.

Inola had crafted that life too, it seemed. Crafted a world to protect them both.

"Yes. Of course you did the right thing," Savannah assured her, before she glanced out the window, into the darkness, toward the line of aspens. She couldn't see them, but they were there, as they'd always been, solitary and yet standing shoulder to shoulder, branches reaching toward each other, waiting for the summer breezes and the spring leaves to renew their familial whisperings back and forth.

"Poppy Lovell said the most interesting thing tonight."

Inola barked a laugh. "Poppy Lovell says a lot of things. Especially when she's three sheets to the wind."

"Truly, she is quite adept at prying open locked doors. She said no one cares about one's past. Not here. Those things, those secrets, anchor you to a world that no longer exists. Once you let go of all that, you're not bound by it. You're . . ." She searched for the word.

"Free," Inola offered.

"Yes, that's it. Free." Savannah looked down at the trace of leaves in the bottom of her cup. There had been a woman in New Orleans who claimed to tell the future by looking at their arrangement. Savannah always thought it odd that the future could be found in the dredges of a teacup.

The future, she realized, was found by looking up. "Do you think she's right?"

Inola smiled at her. "I think you've already figured that out."

"Not everything," Savannah said, reaching over and taking Inola's hands in hers. "I must apologize to you. Not just for the last few weeks. I never intended to worry you."

"I know . . . Well, I know that now," Inola said, giving her fingers a squeeze.

"I've taken so much from you. You could have made a life out in the world. You are Mrs. Viola Kinney Livingston, and the world should know that. I can't wear your mantle anymore. It is properly yours."

Inola began to shake her head. "You and I both know the world is not ready for a Viola who looks like me. I don't know if it ever will be." Savannah was about to say something, but Inola stopped her. "To my way of thinking, we are both Viola. We come up with the recipes and the advice. I am lucky enough to get to write the words—which, by the way, is what I always wanted to do."

"You don't just write. You breathe life onto your pages." Savanah shook her head. "No, you are Viola. All I've done is swan about like I'm too important for all of them. I've been horrible."

Inola glanced away. Notably, she didn't argue the matter. She only asked the most pertinent question. "What do you propose to do now?"

"To begin with, I need to figure out a way to save Miss Minch."

Inola snorted. "You've got a tall order there. Mrs. George L. isn't the most forgiving of souls."

"I don't think she knows what the word means."

Inola looked up and grinned. "I would have liked to see Miss Minch all tipsy."

Savannah grimaced. "She was dancing with her cat."

"No!" Inola couldn't help herself, she laughed. They both did. But they quickly sobered to the fact that tomorrow's luncheon was going to be a different sort of hangover, a reckoning of biblical proportions.

Inola let out a long, deep breath. "Are you certain there's no way to hush this up?"

"No. Half the town witnessed Poppy's promenade down Main Street."

"Why on earth did the sheriff bring her home that way?" Inola stopped herself there. "Never mind. Men!"

Savannah nodded. But they had a more difficult problem to solve. "You know Cora will mention this episode in the *Observer*."

"Of course she will. She can't help herself." Inola cringed, most likely remembering the brief but telling reference Cora published the last time Poppy went on a bender. *The disagreeable disturbance Tuesday night involved a noted citizen of our township . . .*

Mrs. George L. didn't venture out of her house for nearly a month after. But this time, she could hardly hide. Not with tomorrow being, well, tomorrow.

"You should have seen Mrs. George L." Savannah shook her head. "Up on her porch, all fire and brimstone. I can well imagine what she'll do to poor Miss Minch tomorrow." The *thud* of the Lovells' front door had sounded like the lid of a coffin being slammed shut. "She'll carve her up and serve her as the second course."

"I wish you were going," Inola said. "Too bad you weren't invited."

Savannah flinched. "I was invited." She retrieved her sewing basket and took out the invitation. "Rather, Viola was invited."

She held it up so Inola could see the ingratiating lines.

It would be my deepest honor to have our dear Viola at my humble celebration . . .

"Did you send your acceptance?" Then Inola drew a deep breath. "Of course you did."

"What else could I do? She'll make my life—our lives—

miserable for the rest of the year if I don't go. We are in such a precarious situation as it is."

Inola scoffed. "Too bad we can't send her to New York City to give Mr. Wakefield a chewing. He'd never be late with a check again."

Savannah sat up. *Mr. Wakefield.*

"Why didn't we think of that before?" She got to her feet, recalling the list on the blackboard at the saloon. The guests for the luncheon. "Cora Stafford is going to be at the luncheon."

Inola's gaze narrowed. "If only to ensure the entire ordeal is properly reported."

Properly reported. Mr. Wakefield.

Inola got to her feet. "Are you thinking what I'm thinking?"

"I don't know, but I've got a notion to do something completely mad." Savannah stilled.

Now Inola grinned. Like she used to when they were kids and stole sweets from her grandmother's kitchen. "Like save the day?"

"Do we dare?"

"Unless you have Mr. Wells' time machine stashed away, I don't see how we can do it any other way." Now Inola paced.

"Consider that guest list," Savannah said, running through the names. "Miss Minch. The Winsley sisters. Cora Stafford."

"She's plotting a regular slaughter," Inola said with a shiver. "But what if we were to give her exactly what she really wants? In the flesh."

"Miss Minch's head on a plate?"

"No." Inola slid back into her chair. "We'll give her Mrs. Livingston. The *real* Mrs. Viola Kinney Livingston."

Savannah's mouth opened then closed before she finally managed the words. "Do you know what you're saying?"

"I'm saying we should do everything we can to save four kind women from being publicly humiliated. Or worse, in Miss Minch's case—she could lose her position. Her livelihood."

"But what you're suggesting could ruin Viola's very existence. *Our* very livelihood. All you've worked for."

Inola smiled. "Not if we do it right."

CHAPTER 37

Wednesday, December 18

*N*inny awoke the next morning and immediately wished she hadn't. Her hand went to her brow as if trying to tamp down the pain thudding beneath.

Whatever was the matter with her?

A bit of sunshine peered through the curtains, splitting the room in half and sending her ducking back beneath the covers. She closed her eyes and tried to make sense of all this.

Heavens, she couldn't remember how she'd gotten to bed. Madeline had come over, and then . . . things got terribly muddled.

She tentatively opened her eyes and pulled back the covers, sucking in a deep breath. Her clothes. She'd gone to bed in her clothes.

As she sat up, the bed springs groaned even as the room spun around her. Ninny added her own whinge, for here was a slate of memories dancing and swirling in the rising river of her upended senses.

Madeline had come over. That much she was certain of . . .

Tentatively she put her feet down on the rug. The floor seemed to be the only solid certitude of her life at this moment.

Madeline had come to get help making Dobbs a cake. Yes. That was it. Then . . .

Poppy. She'd come to get her mail. And then . . .

No. Ninny bolted upright and then immediately sat back down on the bed, certain she was about to throw up more than just an unbalanced merry-go-round of memories.

Papa's whiskey. The brandy. Oh, not the currant wine!

Ninny groaned, slowly getting to her feet. She blanched and looked again toward the window. The sun was well above the mountain, which meant . . .

It was nearly eight. Or, worse, well past.

She needed to get dressed. Get downstairs. Get the post office open before someone noticed.

Before she lost her nerve.

Well, she didn't need to get dressed, she realized.

She looked around for her shoes and found them sitting on the chair in the corner—a place she would never have put them. Someone must have helped her. But who?

A problem for another time, she decided.

Giving her hair a quick fix, she set out warily down the stairs, teetering like a newborn calf, concentrating on what she needed to do.

Get the mail bag in. Hope it was a slow day. Wednesdays usually were.

Wednesday.

She caught hold of the railing. Wednesday the eighteenth. Mrs. George L.'s birthday party.

Ninny—though she was loath to admit it—had turned to flee back up into her bedroom, when her nose caught a distinct sharp odor. *Coffee.*

Coffee?

Cautiously she continued past the landing. Below, at the bottom of the steps, sat the mail bag. Might Madeline have returned?

But it wasn't Madeline she discovered in her kitchen as she reached the final step. It was the last person she expected.

Well, maybe not the last.

"Good morning to you, Miss Minch. How are you faring this fine day?" Badger asked. He sat at the table, a mug of coffee in hand and, most startling of all, Mr. Bingley curled up in his lap. "I'd get up, but this fool cat of yours is quite content."

A woebegone Wellington took up most of the space in front of the stove. She stepped around him and poured herself a cup of coffee, adding an extra bit of cream. She looked out the window and tried to breathe. There was a man in her kitchen. At this hour!

If what she vaguely remembered from last night wasn't enough, his presence in her house at this hour would certainly ruin her.

"I know what you're thinking," he said, as she made her shaky way to the table.

"I doubt you do," she said tartly. "Tell me you haven't been here all night."

"Of course I have. Where was I supposed to go? I couldn't leave you alone in that condition."

A memory of dancing with Mr. Bingley waltzed through her thoughts, and when she closed her eyes, Mr. Bingley became Mr. Densmore.

Oh, dear heavens. *That* condition.

"I must apologize," she rushed to say. "I don't know what—"

He blew out a breath. "Just stop right there. So you tied one on. We all do that from time to time."

"I assure you, I do not." She had no idea where to look, so she stared at the swirling bit of cream in her coffee.

"Last night rather begs to differ."

The whirl of cream began to make her head spin, and she thought she might be sick. "Oh, heavens, what have I done? How will I ever face today?"

"Open the post office, hold your head up, and be done with it," he suggested.

"That isn't all I face today," she replied, reaching for her knitting bag and pulling out the invitation. She tentatively pushed it across the table.

"What's that?" he asked, eyeing the card.

"You know exactly what that is."

His eyes widened. "I hardly think you're going now."

"Of course I'm going." She got to her feet and glanced at the clock. "I have no choice."

A growing list of things ran through her head. Get the mail sorted. Open the post office. Sacrifice herself, come eleven o'clock, at the Lovell altar.

"You know what she'll do to you," Badger was saying. As if he needed to. "Especially now, what with Poppy and all. She can't be happy."

"Yes, Poppy complicates matters, but that is what she does best. My real problem is that I haven't decided on a gift yet."

Badger huffed. "You're expected to bring that harridan a gift?"

"A speech as well," Ninny told him, finding a modicum of amusement in his dismay.

He crossed his arms over his chest. "I wouldn't go."

"You weren't invited." Ninny tapped a finger to her lips and considered what she had in her pantry. Currant jam? No, Mrs. Clarke would be bringing her prized gooseberry most likely. Perhaps a pot of rhubarb compote?

No, definitely not rhubarb.

But as it turned out, Badger gave her the most inadvertent solution to her problem. "I wouldn't give that woman the time of day. Why, I wouldn't give her that old tin of thyme."

Ninny gaped at the spice tin sitting on the counter. Oh, heavens, if he only knew what was inside it. Why, consider if Mrs. George L. knew the contents of that tin.

If she knew . . . That was it.

Ninny reached over and picked it up. "Mr. Densmore, you are brilliant. That is exactly what I intend to give her. A bit of thyme."

❄

SAVANNAH TURNED to find Inola a few steps behind her. "Are you certain about this? Most likely she'll shut the door in our faces."

"No, she won't. We've worked this all out," Inola said.

"This is Mrs. George L. we've 'worked out.' We might as well take up juggling dynamite," Savannah pointed out.

Inola glanced behind them. "Not with a witness." Down the road came Cora Stafford, hurrying along toward them, right on time. Or rather five minutes late, as she usually was. The perfect unwitting key to this entire scheme. "Besides, it would be bad form to turn away an invited guest. Or so Mrs. Livingston always says."

Inola had even tucked the invitation into her purse in case there was any question as to their hostess's intent. Mrs. Viola Kinney Livingston, in the flesh.

"When one of these crows goes squawking the truth all over, then what will we do?" Savannah pointed out yet again. "Can you imagine Mrs. Jonas holding her tongue with such a secret? She'll nigh on burst before the cake is cut. Mrs. Livingston will never sell another story."

"It isn't like we haven't changed our names before and survived," Inola reminded her. "As for Mrs. Jonas and the rest of the ladies, we are about to give them a boon." Inola tucked her hand into the curve of Savannah's arm and tugged her along toward the fine house at the end of the road.

Savannah smiled at her. "A boon indeed. Now they can claim an acquaintance with a celebrated writer."

Inola tipped up her chin. "Oh, I'm celebrated, am I now?"

"You are about to be," Savannah told her. "Though I will point out—"

"Again."

"—that we are wagering everything that these women will keep our secret."

Inola took a deep breath. "They will. Every single one of them will have a share in Mrs. Livingston's future success. Recall how they all wanted to lend their advice at the Athenian Club?"

"Yes. But—"

"Once they've given their advice, they will be waiting with bated breath to see if Mrs. Livingston uses their suggestions in her column.

They will buy and clip that article and share it with everyone they know. 'I helped her with this bit,' they'll say. 'She's a particular friend of mine.' If they spill the secret, there goes Mrs. Livingston, and with her, their chance at seeing their ideas, their advice, in the *Ladies' Home Monthly*." Inola preened a bit. "There's a very Holmesian logic to it all."

"Let's not get ahead of ourselves," Savannah said. "We haven't even got through the front door." She plucked at her gloves.

"That's why we have Cora," Inola reminded her. She slowed her pace a bit to give the newswoman the opportunity to catch up to them. "She is going to eat this up."

Savannah remained skeptical. "Think of the notoriety she'll gain by printing Mrs. Livingston's true identity across the front page of the *Observer*. Mark my words, she'll publish a special edition. Probably two."

"Not when she gets"—Inola waved her hands like a magician— "'An Exclusive Interview with Mrs. Viola Kinney Livingston, Celebrated Authoress.'" She grinned a little. "How nice of me to write her headline for her. And best of all, when Mr. Wakefield reads her article and discovers the suggestion that I'm taking my columns elsewhere—"

"He'll pay up." Savannah grinned.

It was a masterful plan, yet there were so many *ifs*.

"Though we mustn't forget we're asking for trouble, Vanna. Some people are not going to like this." She looked again at the Lovell residence. "And most of them are inside that house."

Savannah agreed. "But I'm tired of living a lie, aren't you?"

"I suppose I am." Inola drew a deep breath.

"Then let's put the record to rights. Let's take Poppy Lovell's advice and live our authentic lives." Savannah shook her head. "There's something I never thought I'd say."

When they got to the wide steps up to the door, they both stopped. Savannah gave Inola a sweeping glance. "You're pretty as a picture today. Though your hat is crooked."

Inola's hand shot up to fix it, and Savannah grinned at her. "You always fall for that."

Then Inola smiled. "You haven't pulled that one in a long time."

"I haven't felt like myself in a long time." Savannah looked her up and down yet again and smiled. "You have your speech ready?"

"Certainly you were teasing about the speech," Inola said as they began their ascent to the front door. "Watch out, Vanna. There is a bit of ice there."

Savannah stepped around the slippery bit. "No, I was serious. You'll have to give a speech. Miss Minch said as much."

"Miss Minch must have been teasing," Inola insisted. Though very quickly they both realized the sheer unlikelihood of such a thing. As the notion sunk in, she added, "No wonder you've managed to avoid this affair all these years."

Savannah nodded and then remembered something else. "You have the gift?"

Inola held up the jar of gooseberry jelly, the recipe for which was one of Mrs. Livingston's most famous contributions to *The Ladies' Home Monthly*. It was featured every summer as the one thing every homemaker should put up.

"'This delicate and elegant jelly will make the perfect gift come the holiday season,'" Savannah said, quoting the description that usually appeared before recipe. The door loomed before them.

"Do be quiet," Inola told her as she straightened. "I know what I wrote."

"Tell them you put a bit of nutmeg in yours. That it is your special secret," Savannah advised.

"Nutmeg," Inola repeated.

"And don't stare at the elks in the parlor," Savannah advised, "or you'll be regaled with the story of how she shot them on her honeymoon."

"Now you are joking," Inola scolded.

"If only." Savannah tipped her head and looked behind them. "Cora is at the gate, so go ahead and knock."

"Oh, Lord, what was I thinking?" Inola muttered as she knocked and the door swung open.

Annie might have been done up in a frilly apron and a starched cap, but she was still Annie. She gaped at the pair of them and then, after taking stock of the situation, just as promptly shut the door.

"That went well," Inola declared. But Savannah opened the door and marched inside, bold as brass. The hall tree looked quite festive, like a Christmas tree decorated with bright-colored scarves and coats.

At the end of the hall, Annie stood conferring with Mrs. George L. and nodding toward the door. "Told you, missus, it were both of them."

"So I see, Annie," Mrs. George L. said. "Please go arrange the canapés. I don't want them just tossed onto the platter."

Annie snorted her opinion at the need for such an instruction but shuffled toward the kitchen nonetheless, shooting glances over her shoulder every few steps, determined to get her share of this how-do-you-do.

"Ah, Mrs. Clarke. I was beginning to think you might be having one of your headaches, but I see . . ." She faltered to a stop and then, in an afterthought, pulled the door of parlor partially closed, if only to shield her guests inside from whatever *this* was.

"Inola," she said, her features curling into a question mark. Her gaze returned to Savannah as if to say, *I don't understand.*

Oh, you will, Savannah thought. She glanced behind her, and here came Cora Stafford through the front door, as dependable as her blazing headlines.

Savannah began her carefully scribed speech, courtesy of Inola. "My dear Mrs. Lovell, the happiest of returns upon the occasion of your birthday. It is with immense pleasure that I present to you the guest of honor you so kindly requested." She stepped aside slightly so Inola had the spotlight, as it were, and paused to give Cora just enough time to hang up her coat and turn toward them. "May I present the honored and celebrated writer Mrs. Viola Kinney Livingston."

At this, both ladies stilled. And, though Mrs. George L. had thought to keep this from her guests, there was an abrupt halt to the chatter within the parlor.

Cora Stafford didn't stay still for long. Even as she digested this revelation, her hand went to her skirt pocket for her pencil and notebook.

Meanwhile, Mrs. Lovell's gaze darted from Savannah to Inola to Cora and then back to Savannah. This time she did get the words out. "I don't understand."

Cora clearly did, for she was already scribbling notes, her pencil scratching as fast as she could.

Savannah did her best to appear puzzled, then drew the crisp white invitation from her purse. "Oh, but you must. Your note was quite clear." She cleared her throat and spoke up. "It would be my deepest honor to have our dear Viola at my humble celebration." She looked up and smiled. "So it is my sincerest pleasure to bring her to you, Mrs. Lovell. Mrs. Livingston, in the flesh."

Cora wedged herself into the conversation. "Are you telling me— that is—that Inola is—" She didn't wait for an answer, instead began scribbling madly in her notepad, as if afraid to miss a single detail.

"Mrs. Viola Kinney Livingston. Yes, that's correct. Inola has labored under the veil of anonymity for far too long, don't you agree?" Savannah looked to Mrs. George L. and smiled. "Given that you always say, 'Credit is due where the work is done,' I thought you would appreciate having her at your celebration."

Mrs. George L.'s lips moved but no words came out, even as the occupants of the parlor began to stir. At the door, Mrs. Jonas peered out, then turned to pass along the news to the others.

Savannah took advantage of the moment. She turned to Cora. "You've asked any number of times for an exclusive interview with Mrs. Livingston, and I believe Inola would be more than happy to provide you any answers you might need for a most thorough and exclusive article."

"It would be my pleasure," Inola agreed.

Cora began to smile, as if awakening to find this party had been planned for her and her alone. "Oh, my. Oh, my heavens." She flipped to a new page.

"Think of it, Mrs. Lovell," Savannah said, turning back to their hostess. "Such an interview would be reprinted from coast to coast, all beginning with the most edifying line, *Mrs. Livingston was delightfully entertained in the gracious home of Mrs. George L. Lovell.* Oh, look at me, writing your first line for you, Miss Stafford. I do hope you don't mind."

"Mind? No, not at all," Cora said, her eyes alight. She saw the line for what it was—a hook and a lure. "It is exactly how I would phrase it. I imagine the Chicago papers will rush to reprint such an article—at the very top of the social page."

"The social page?" The words came out of Mrs. George L. in a reverent hush. "The Chicago social page?"

"Pages, I'd imagine," Cora said. "Not just Chicago's. New York. Boston, even. Why I'd guess every paper from coast to coast, given how popular Mrs. Viola Kinney Livingston is with her readers." Cora's gaze was still half-fixed on Inola, as if she feared she'd vanish at any moment. But, wrenching her attention back to her hostess, she did the work they'd counted on her doing. "Why, every matron in fine society will be left to wonder how it is that Mrs. George L. Lovell of Bethlehem, Wyoming, managed such an esteemed guest. Such a social coup."

"Fine society . . ." Mrs. George L. stammered as she recovered her wits. The transformation was something to watch as the lady went from disbelief to radiant welcome. "My dear Inola! You are most welcome to my humble yet, dare I say, gracious home. Why, I've always suspected there was more to you than met the eye, considering what an amiable and perceptive lady that you are."

Savannah found herself elbowed aside and forgotten as Cora Stafford hurried behind her hostess, muttering, "I'll have to work all night to make sure this is on the front page."

NINNY WOULDN'T HAVE BELIEVED it if she hadn't seen it for herself: Inola seated on Mrs. George L.'s sofa, confessing to being Mrs. Viola Kinney Livingston.

Ninny had long suspected as much, but that secret like so many other secrets that passed through the Bethlehem post office, remained tightly held.

Yet here was the entire dispatch of Inola's life, laid out for all to see. No envelopes. No twine tightly wrapped around the contents.

"Are you saying your father was white?" Mrs. Hoback asked, sounding incredulous that such a thing could happen.

"Yes, ma'am," Inola told her.

"Are you certain?" she pressed.

"Decidedly certain. His name was Captain Thomas Vance."

"Vance?" Miss Theodosia repeated, her words like a thunderbolt into the silence that had followed. "Why, isn't that Mrs. Clarke's maiden name? I do believe she once mentioned her father's name was Vance. Isn't that right, sister?" She glanced over at Odella and then back at Inola. "Goodness, you could be related!"

Odella closed her eyes and looked to be praying.

"We are sisters, Miss Theodosia. Half-sisters."

Miss Theodosia blinked a few times. "Oh, my. Rather like dear Odella and I. Though not the half part." She smiled—brightened, really—and reached over and squeezed Inola's hand. "It is lovely having a sister for a companion, is it not?"

"It is, Miss Theodosia," Inola agreed. "A most precious gift. There is always another set of hands to pick up and row when one tires. Don't you find that so?"

Theodosia nodded and wiped at her eyes. "Exactly."

Mrs. George L. looked to be about to say something, but Cora beat her to the punch. "You said you went to college?" Her pencil hovered at the ready above her notepad.

Inola sat primly on the edge of the sofa, her hands folded in her lap. "I did. At my father's insistence. He took me himself to be enrolled at Oberlin College in Ohio just before the war broke out."

"Ah. To escape slavery," Mrs. Bohlen offered.

"That wasn't the case, ma'am," Inola replied. "I was never a slave. Nor was my mother. She was a free woman, a Creole. She made her own life and wished the same for me. As did my father."

"Did Mrs. Clarke go to this college as well?" Mrs. Hoback asked.

"No, ma'am, she did not. She remained in Mississippi."

"All alone, during the war?" Mrs. Jonas shook her head. "How terrible for her."

"She had an awful time of it, though she was not alone. She lived with our stepmother and her daughter, Sybilla." Inola glanced away. "I had only two letters from her during that time."

"However did you manage that?" Ninny asked, for her father had often talked about the difficulties of postal service between the warring states. All mail between the North and the South had been banned, with the exception of a few exchanges, those occurring only under a flag of truce.

"We used our father's agent in London to relay our correspondence. One of mine made it to her, and two of hers made it to me. The last one came just after the war ended."

As Cora scratched away, Mrs. Jonas spoke up again. "Whatever did you study at this college?" She glanced around as if she couldn't quite believe any of it. Clearly there were others who shared her skepticism.

"Oberlin offered a ladies' literary course, which I completed," Inola told her. "After that, I obtained my teaching certificate."

"Truly? A teacher?" Mrs. Bohlen sat up. "I didn't know such a thing was possible."

"Oh, it is, Mrs. Bohlen," Mrs. Vaughn noted, from her seat next to Mrs. George L. "Why, there was a colored girl studying at the university in Laramie while I was there. Carrie was her name. Surprisingly talented at the piano."

"Why is that surprising, Mrs. Vaughn?" Inola asked.

Cora's lips twitched toward a smile.

Mrs. Vaughn blinked, her mouth opened, and the words seemed to fail her. Then she composed herself and added, "I recently heard she's going to go to Howard University in Washington, D.C. I do wish her well."

Mrs. Jonas rushed back in. "Mr. King says Goldie is just mad to go to college. Constantly badgering him to let her enroll." She huffed a sigh. "Girls and education. It seems to me a colossal waste of time and money. I am ever so thankful that my dear Pinky has no head for knowledge."

A few shared glances suggested Pinky wasn't the only one in the Jonas household with that particular endowment.

"I disagree, Mrs. Jonas, most emphatically." All eyes turned in amazement, for old Mrs. Belding, the reverend's wife, rarely made a peep. She cleared her throat and straightened in her chair like a veritable Athena. "I, for one, went to college, and am thankful for my education."

When no one seemed to know what to make of this, Inola spoke up. "Where did you go, Mrs. Belding?"

"Elmira College in New York." The old woman brightened, clearly proud of her alma mater. "Oh, such times. Such glorious times."

Inola smiled back, and the two of them shared a shiny moment of collegiate sisterhood.

"Yes, but however do you use your education, Mrs. Belding?" Mrs. Jonas asked with a small sniff.

"Mr. Belding always asks me to review his Sunday sermon as he writes it, and he often includes my suggestions."

"Your suggestions?" Mrs. Jonas choked out. She turned her goggling eyes toward their hostess as if to say, *Did you hear this? A woman . . . giving theological counsel?*

"Why wouldn't I have suggestions?" Mrs. Belding told them, stirring out of her usual cocoon, her words like the beating of new wings. "I studied the testaments—in Greek, I'll have you know—*and* took an entire semester on Butler's *Analogy Of Religion, Natural And Revealed.* Faith and religion are not solely the domain of men. When we allow men to dictate our choices, we are doomed to servitude."

"Why, Mrs. Belding, you rather sound like a suffragette," Cora remarked, flipping the page of her notebook.

Mrs. Belding's usually rheumy eyes cleared, and shone bright and defiant. "Why shouldn't all women be allowed to vote and express their ordained rights—"

Mrs. George L. bounded to her feet. "I do believe Annie has our luncheon ready."

"But the speeches," Mrs. Jonas protested. "I have mine all prepared." There were some nods in agreement. There was a strict order to this luncheon. The gathering in parlor, the speeches, the luncheon . . .

"Not now, Drucilla." Mrs. George L.'s brittle smile silenced any further rebellion. Her birthday luncheon was teetering toward anarchy, with all this talk of votes and rights, and she'd salvage it however she must, even if that meant deviating from her carefully scripted agenda. "Ladies, shall we?" She led the way and did not look back.

"Oh, this is only going to get better," Poppy whispered to Ninny as they trailed the others into the dining room.

"You have no idea," Ninny replied, the little box of thyme rattling about in her handbag.

CHAPTER 38

*U*pon entering the dining room, Ninny found there was a bit of a scramble with the place cards as Mrs. George L. made some hasty changes to her previous designs.

"I am surprised to see you," Poppy whispered to her.

"No more than I," Ninny admitted as they hung back and allowed their hostess to shuffle her guests.

"What made you change your mind?" Poppy persisted.

"A friend."

"I doubt it was only your friend who convinced you," Poppy said, as they made their way around the table. "You have more backbone than you give yourself credit for, Ninny-girl." As they settled into their seats, Cora, now seated beside Inola, began another round of questions.

Poppy leaned over and whispered, "We both owe Mrs. Clarke and Inola a huge debt of gratitude. Their decision to make this confession here and now has completely derailed whatever mischief Columbia had cooked up."

"Indeed," Ninny agreed. The moment she'd collected Columbia's neatly addressed invitations at the post office, she'd known she would be walking into a reckoning—and grieved inwardly for Cora Stafford as well as Odella and Theodosia. Not that the sisters would realize what Inola and Mrs. Clarke had done, but it was nice to know they would be spared whatever humiliation or set-down Mrs. George L. had hoped to serve between the courses of scalloped cheese and lobster salad.

Yet, whyever had Mrs. Clarke, and Inola especially, taken it upon themselves to wade into this fray?

"How did you start writing for *The Ladies' Home Monthly*?" Cora was asking.

"It was Mrs. Clarke's suggestion. We'd read a column they'd published about the proper way to clean one's house. The magazine had suggested doing it all in one day, and Savannah and I both knew the only way to clean thoroughly is to divide the chores equally across the week."

"So very true," Mrs. Bohlen agreed. "Otherwise one is subject to the worst sort exhaustion."

Inola nodded. "Mrs. Clarke said someone ought to write to the magazine and correct them. So I did."

"Oh, bravo, Inola," Mrs. Belding declared.

"Yes, well, the next month there was an article on the most efficient way to cream butter and sugar, which I wrote in to correct as well. Then Mr. Wakefield, the editor-in-chief, replied and asked if I would be interested in writing a regular column, since my advice had a tone of experience." She looked down at her plate. "The rest just followed. The columns, the stories, the opinion pieces."

"And the recipes?" Mrs. Bohlen asked. "As if there is anyone who doesn't know Mrs. Livingston's gooseberry jelly is perfectly divine."

There were nods all around the table.

"The recipes all come from Mrs. Clarke. She's the cook," Inola told them, reaching under the chair for the bag she'd brought, and revealing the small jar of jelly inside. "But I will tell you all Mrs. Clarke's secret. When she makes this jelly for us, she adds a scratch or two of nutmeg."

"Nutmeg!" was the collective gasp. All eyes fixed on the bright jelly before them as if they'd been let into the very sanctum.

Inola held the jar out toward the head of the table. "For you, Mrs.

Lovell, with Mrs. Clarke's compliments on the occasion of your birthday."

"Oh, my," Mrs. George L. managed as the jar was passed down the table and found its place of honor in front of her plate.

Even Ninny was surprised. Nutmeg. Well, why hadn't she thought of that?

"But that isn't all," Inola was saying. "I have my own gift for you." With that, she passed a folded piece of paper over to their hostess.

Mrs. George L. opened and read the words within. Her sharp expression softened as she continued, until finally her mouth opened. "Oh . . . my. Why, I never!" The usually verbose woman stammered, suddenly at a loss.

"Whatever is it?" Mrs. Jonas asked impatiently.

Mrs. George L. cleared her throat. "I do believe this is Mrs. Livingston's next column."

Inola nodded. "It is, to be precise, my June column for *The Elegant Home*."

This brought out a raft of murmurs. *The Elegant Home!*

"Why, I had no idea you meant to use my advice."

"No, you didn't," Inola agreed. "But I believe credit is due where it is given."

Mrs. George L. drew a deep shaky breath and held it up. "May I?"

Inola bowed her head a bit. "I would be honored."

"Do listen," Mrs. George L. began, as giddy as a schoolgirl. "'It is the rule and guiding principal of my dear esteemed friend and celebrated hostess, Mrs. George L. Lovell, that a gathering should never be so crowded that one's guests are elbow to elbow. Keeping an airy, graceful space should be considered when numbering one's guests.'" The woman's eyes misted. "This will be published in *The Elegant Home?*"

"It will indeed. As will the advice of Mrs. Bohlen and Mrs. Jonas," she added, smiling at both the ladies, who responded with open mouths and no words as the implication and honor sank in. "I receive so many letters seeking advice about children and husbands, and it would be ever so helpful if I could, from time to time, rely upon you fine ladies to assist me—with all due credit, of course."

Annie came in with a tray of something, but Mrs. George L. waved her away with a quickly whispered, "Not now."

"All of us?" Miss Odella asked.

"Of course," Inola told her.

The sisters clasped hands and beamed.

"But what of Mrs. Viola Kinney Livingston?" Mrs. Hoback asked. "Whatever became of her?"

Inola smiled politely. "There never was a Mrs. Livingston. Mr. Wakefield suggested the name. Apparently most of the writers at the magazine use a nom de plume."

"Oh, a *nom de plume*," Miss Theodosia repeated. "That sounds ever so sophisticated."

"But the photograph. That isn't you," Mrs. Vaughn added, as if it needed pointing out.

"No, it isn't. Mr. Wakefield also provided a photograph."

"Then he knows." This sharp indictment came from Mrs. Jonas.

"Knows what?" Inola asked.

"Well, that you . . . aren't a . . . That you aren't a . . . Viola," she finally finished.

"If you mean that I am a Negro, no, he does not," Inola said. There it was, the truth teetering on razor-thin line.

Ninny's breath caught as she saw with sharp clarity the great personal risk Inola and Savannah were taking in divulging all this.

One word, and Mrs. Livingston would be consigned to the dustbin. Their self-sufficiency swept away.

It was a fate every woman at this table knew could come to her doorstep. One accident, a year or two of lost crops, a husband with a penchant for poker, and all that they had and held dear could be lost. Forever.

How often had Ninny worried that one too many nattering letters from Mrs. George L. could prod the Postmaster General to take action, and then where would she be?

The silence stretched taut as, one by one, all eyes turned toward the head of the table.

"Nor will he," Mrs. George L. announced, rapping her fan against the table. "Ever." The authority in her voice brought everyone to attention. This was their social commander, and she was issuing an order. She sat up straight. "Inola, there would never be a moment's consideration of unveiling your nom de plume. Would there?" Her hawk's gaze swept the room, resting a moment longer on Mrs. Jonas, but every head nodded.

All except Cora's. "But what about my interview? My exclusive interview?" She held up her notepad. "What will I print?"

"Miss Stafford," Inola interjected before Mrs. George L. could react, "I have a perfect solution for that." She drew a small packet of papers from her purse. "This ought to do the trick. It is a thorough interview with Mrs. Livingston, detailing her harrowing and brave life, and it mentions every lady at the table, especially her dearest friend, Mrs. George L. Lovell, as well as the intrepid journalist who managed to track her down for an exclusive interview. It's a fine story, if I do say so myself. You're welcome to print it, free of charge. I suspect such a convenience will give you the time you need to make tomorrow's edition."

Cora eyed the pages like one might eye a sleeping snake.

"Oh, do read it aloud, Inola," Mrs. Jonas begged. "We would all love to hear Mrs. Livingston's story." As if they hadn't already.

"Oh, yes, it will be most diverting," Mrs. Bohlen added, reaching for the pages. "I do want to know if my new hat is mentioned." After a pause, she added, "Cora, I will need extra copies to send to my cousin in St. Louis."

Cora leaned over and snatched up the pages. "You can all read every word in tomorrow's edition."

"Do promise to print extra copies for all of us. I shall want to send clippings to all my friends from college, and I shall need one as well for my scrapbook," Mrs. Vaughn said. There was resounding chorus of requests for extra copies, giving Cora all the push she needed to accept Inola's proffered pages.

Poppy leaned over to Ninny. "That is how a coup is managed."

"A what?"

"A coup d'état," she said. "My hat is off to Inola and Mrs. Clarke. They have routed my daughter-in-law and left her hog-tied."

"Now it is my turn to overturn the cart," Ninny told her, reaching into her pocket and drawing out the small spice tin. She cleared her throat and spoke up. "I know it is rather out of turn for this gathering, but I also have a gift for our hostess, and this moment seems most opportune." She handed the tin down the table, and it passed from guest to guest, each more puzzled than the last as they handed it along.

"Whatever is this?" Mrs. George L. asked as she looked down at the small box.

"Thyme?" Mrs. Vaughn suggested, with a bemused light in her eyes. "Wouldn't we all love more time?" A few others laughed lightly at her play on words.

Ninny just smiled back, and then nodded at Mrs. George L. "Please open it."

Mrs. George L. did so, but once she looked inside, her brow immediately furrowed. "Parathinia, whatever is this?"

"I would think it is obvious."

"Should it be?" She turned the tin over and shook out the slips into her hand. Then her gaze narrowed as she saw the names on them, and the realization hit her.

Mrs. Vaughn leaned over. "Oh, my. Are those what I think they are?"

She reached for them, but Mrs. George L. tucked them quickly back in the tin. Out of sight.

Mrs. Vaughn turned to Ninny. "Whatever do you mean by such a gift, Miss Minch?"

But Ninny didn't have to answer.

"I believe Miss Minch means for Columbia to choose for her," Poppy said. "Well, who is it going to be?"

Again, everyone turned to their hostess, awaiting her pronouncement, but Mrs. George L.'s gaze remained fixed on Ninny, who held her head high. That was her gift to Mrs. George L. To allow her to feel the consequences of such a choice. To bear the real burdens of Bethlehem. To hold their secrets inside you and never let them out.

The lady pursed her lips with concentration. "Who else has seen these, Parathinia?"

"Would it matter?" Cora Stafford asked, flipping open her notebook to a blank page and smiling.

Mrs. George L. turned her hard-edged stare from Ninny to Cora, most likely remembering that while Ninny had visited Cora, nothing had come of that meeting. Nothing had been printed.

At least not yet.

Nor was it past her notice that Cora was not the only one entertaining Ninny's confidences of late. Her mother-in-law would have no compunction against sharing the volatile and inflammatory contents held inside the little tin of thyme.

"Who are you going to pick?" Mrs. Jonas asked. "Oh, how foolish of me. The choice is so very obvious." She settled in her seat like a hen on the nest, as well pleased with the decision as if she'd been tasked with making it herself.

"An obvious choice? I suppose many would see it that way," Mrs. George L. began, more to herself than her guests, staring down at the tin. "But I can hardly be held accountable for every decision that needs to be made in this town." Then, as if remembering herself, she added in a more conciliatory tone, "Besides, Parathinia, I trust your judgment in this matter."

"If you are certain?" Ninny left the question hanging in the air.

Mrs. George L. looked down at the tin and then slanted a quick glance at Cora. "Yes. Decidedly so. I will concur with whatever choice you make." She passed the tin back down the table and didn't take it out of her sights until Ninny had it safely tucked back inside her handbag.

The other guests looked around with a shared sense of puzzlement. What had just happened? Cora set her pencil down beside her plate and sought solace with a large gulp of tea.

"Well, I'll be," Poppy muttered. "You did what I never thought possible."

"What is that?" Ninny asked, finally daring to draw a breath.

"You humbled her at her own game."

For now.

❄

No disaster had fallen as Mrs. George L.'s birthday celebration came to its inevitable conclusion. Ninny was only too happy to see the birthday celebrant rise from her chair to signal that it was time for one and all to depart.

Badger's inadvertent suggestion—that, and the revelation that Inola was Mrs. Viola Kinney Livingston—had worked. There hadn't been any public flogging for Ninny's involvement in Poppy's, shall one say, intemperate display.

Not that Ninny thought for a moment that all was forgiven and forgotten, for she knew Mrs. George L.'s forgiveness was always temporary at best, and an infraction—even the slightest indiscretion—would certainly never be forgotten.

As the ladies filed into the hall where Annie handed out coats and accoutrements, Althea Vaughn took her place front and center.

"Just how do you propose to play Juliet, Mrs. Vaughn?" Theodosia was asking, as Ninny caught up her coat from a nearby chair and hurried past the gathered knot of women.

Odella spoke right up. "With an overarching air of tragedy, perhaps?"

Ninny thought she sounded rather hopeful. Then again, Odella was known to love a good three-hanky cry.

"Tragedy? No, no, sister. Juliet should be done with an air of exuberance and the passionate heart that is so evident in Mr. Shakespeare's prose," Theodosia countered.

Ninny went out the door and was about to hasten off, but she paused as she looked down at the stairs. They had been icy coming up, and they had only gotten worse. She shook her head. And to think how many times she'd had to hear Mrs. George L. complain about the post office entry.

Behind her, Althea continued to hold court. "Oh, never," she told Theodosia, allowing Odella a moment to bask in her superiority. "Passion has no place on the stage." She paused, if only to ensure she had an audience. "In my humble opinion, it too easily becomes altogether unbecoming."

"Bravo, my dear," Mrs. George L. declared. "Understated and demure have always been my guiding principles."

Poppy snorted and bullied her way down the steps to come to Ninny's side. "Understated and demure. What a load of twaddle. Juliet is one hot mess of a teenager."

Meanwhile, Althea had taken her hat from Annie and settled it just so before parading out onto the porch. The gaggle of guests followed.

"What do they say in the theater, sister?" Theodosia asked in an aside.

Odella's brow furrowed. "I haven't the least notion."

Ninny looked over at the pair and smiled. "Break a leg, I believe, is customary."

Althea moved to the edge of the porch. "I shall portray dear Juliet with the same grace and poise that my dramatic teacher would often call out for others to emulate."

To demonstrate her upcoming crowning glory, she raised one hand in the air, her angular nose tipped upward, and took a mincing step down.

"Oh, Mrs. Vaughn, have a care—" Ninny began.

Giving Ninny scant regard, the young woman flounced as she went. The moment her boot hit the step, it slipped right out from beneath her and sent her tumbling, her skirt flipping up to reveal long, stocking-clad legs. The tableau finished with a horrible thud and crack, and the lady ended her one-woman show in a heap on the walkway, her leg bent in the most unnatural position.

A stunned silence followed, until Mrs. Vaughn began shrieking like an unhinged Lady Macbeth or a dying Desdemona.

"I don't think anyone wants to emulate that," Cora noted, before she got out her notepad and began to scribble furiously.

"I say pride goeth before the fall," Badger declared. "It was not your fault, Miss Minch." He adjusted the pool stick in Dobbs' hands and stepped back so the boy could take his shot.

All around the Star Bright, a number of Dobbs' birthday guests nodded in agreement. As it was, Madeline was pleased to see the saloon nicely filled with a mix of young and old guests, the King sisters having brought along a number of their friends.

And it wasn't just that youthful circle, but a wide collection of the town's residents, all of whom came to thank Dobbs for all he did—the errands, his kindness, the chores, his cheery news. A few bringing gifts, others plates of food to add to the celebration.

"We couldn't do without his help," Miss Theodosia had said when she'd arrived with a large plate of molasses cookies.

"Not my fault? But I uttered those fateful words," Ninny said. "Break a leg. What was I thinking?"

"You were there, Miss Inola," said Mr. Thayer. "What is your opinion?"

"Oh, that gel wasn't listening to anything other than her own conceit. Miss Minch tried to warn her about the step."

"It was not a matter of how, but when," Erasmus noted. "Disaster never fails to show up for that woman's birthday celebration."

The balls on the pool table clinked and clattered together, and one dropped with a thud in the corner pocket.

"There you go, my boy." Badger winked. "You'll be hustling strangers in no time."

"Don't encourage him," Madeline told him, knowing only too well that Nate would do just that to make ends meet after he aged out of the foster care system.

"Who likes cake?" Savannah asked, carrying a large candle-topped cake she'd hastily baked at Madeline's request.

As all eyes turned toward her, the door to the saloon unexpectedly opened, and in marched—even more surprisingly—Mrs. George L., bringing with her a cold wind.

The candles wavered and seemed to shudder at this late arrival.

"Celebrating, I see," she announced, stopping in the middle of the room. "What does this signify? The ruination of my birthday celebration? My family's reputation in tatters? Or could it be that you are rejoicing over poor Mrs. Vaughn's grievous injury and the doom of the Opera Society gala?" She looked around. "No takers? Then allow me."

She turned toward Madeline. "You may have Shandy's favor for now—for reasons that are unfathomable to the good citizens of this once respectable town—but mark my words—your residence in this business will not last. Not as long as my husband holds the lease on this property."

Madeline snorted. "If your husband actually held the lease to this property, I would have been evicted weeks ago. She threw a glance over at Erasmus. "I have a lease, do I not?"

"Indeed you do. At my insistence. Signed by Mrs. George Lovell." He cleared his throat. "The original one."

"Which would be me," Poppy said from her spot at bar.

Mrs. George L. gaped. "Mother Lovell! What are you doing here?"

Poppy grinned at her daughter-in-law. "I was invited. You can't, I note, say the same."

Mrs. George L. Lovell straightened and swung her sights toward a new target, marking Savannah and Inola for her next tirade.

"Don't think I don't know what you did today. While I am grateful for the distraction it provided, I cannot overlook the deception that preceded such a necessity. Mrs. Viola Kinney Livingston, indeed!"

Savannah and Inola shared a look. "I don't believe we made our decision with your difficulties in mind," Savannah replied. "Rather, we chose to help someone who has always shown herself to be indispensable to the citizens of Bethlehem, and who we assumed— rightly so—would be persecuted for a slight and momentary indiscretion."

Ninny's arms rippled with gooseflesh. Momentary indiscretion? Her smile wobbled and she bit her lip. She only wished she could remember her indiscretion.

Badger, the irrepressible rascal, grinned at her. Apparently he did.

Before she could warm to that notion, here came Mrs. George L., having spied fresh hunting grounds. "I have not forgotten your part in all this, Parathinia Minch."

"I wouldn't expect that you would, Columbia," she said, surprised at her own fortitude.

"You deliberately distracted poor Mrs. Vaughn and thus . . ."

"Now, wait just a minute," Ninny replied sharply, surprising everyone.

Not that Mrs. George L. was of a mind to listen. "As it is, with our leading lady indisposed, the hope of raising the needed funds for a fire engine are now dashed. And the fault is all yours, Parathinia."

"I'd say she's gone and done us a service," Erasmus remarked. "Althea sings off-key and prances about like a lame peacock, if you ask me."

"No one did," Mrs. George L. snapped back.

Though he did his best to look contrite, his gaze twinkled as he turned back to his glass of punch, for he knew his words had hit the mark.

Ninny was still trying her best to reply when Mrs. George L. arrived at the true reason for her errand.

"Parathinia, I shall be writing the Postmaster General about your moral qualifications to handle our precious mail—given the questionable company you have chosen to keep of late." Her gaze flitted toward Badger.

The company you have chosen.

The names. The names she'd picked and the names she'd made up. That was the true reason Columbia was here.

Ninny swallowed, for she'd been ready for an onslaught over Poppy and Madeline, but oh, my, she hadn't thought the rest of this out when she'd given the slips to Columbia for her birthday.

The real slips. Now that Mrs. George L. knew . . .

Mr. Thayer slid off his barstool. "Are you done, madam?"

The matron's brows lifted in a stormy arc. "I believe I have said my piece."

Badger straightened and set down his pool cue. "Then go." He pointed toward the door.

Mrs. George L. knew how to make an entrance, but she also knew how to take her leave with grace and timing. She wasn't about to be bullied out of any situation. Even one of her own making. Taking her time, she tugged at her gloves and then shook out her coat, leaving a circle of snow on the floor. Before she turned and left, she tipped her gaze toward Ninny one last time. "Oh, one more thing, Parathinia."

Ninny braced herself.

"I understand why you did what you did, but does everyone else involved know of their part in your mischief?" Her question was the very swirl of poison in a cup, and with that lingering in the air, the woman departed.

"Good riddance," Erasmus muttered before the door shut with a definitive thump.

The room shivered in the ensuing silence.

Poppy came to stand by her side and whispered, so no one else could hear, "Mark my words, she'll use those slips against you the first opportunity she finds."

Wick cleared his throat and nodded his head toward the piano. "Come now, Miss Drake, show them all how it's done. How about a song?"

From behind the bar, Madeline shook her head. "I think everyone would rather a slice of cake."

"You sing?" Inola asked. "That might be just the thing right now."

Savannah set the cake on a table. "It would definitely clear the air."

Madeline demurred and then nodded. "I suppose. And as it is, I know the perfect song."

"Oh, indeed yes," Ninny added. "Dear Dobbs, how is it we didn't know this was your birthday?"

"No one asked," Dobbs told her in his matter-of-fact way.

"We should have," Badger told him, giving his head a tousle.

"Miss Drake?" Wick waved the way across the bar.

Madeline wiped her hands and sat down at the piano. She patted the bench beside her so Dobbs could join her. "I need all of you to sing along."

Her fingers went to the keys and, with a grand flourish, she began to play, *For He's a Jolly Good Fellow.*

Everyone quickly gathered around the now grinning Dobbs, and in just a few notes, blew the ill will from the room, Mrs. George L. and her threats all but forgotten.

Well, mostly forgotten. Ninny glanced at the calendar by the door. Six days to Christmas. Six days to find her way out of this mire.

CHAPTER 39

Thursday, December 19

*N*inny had tossed most of the night, Poppy's warning ringing in her ears. Unable to sleep, she stole out of bed in the wee hours and stood by the window. A panorama of stars clung to the edges of darkness as they always did, sparkling a surety down on the sleeping occupants beneath them, offering her a lesson she'd never considered.

The stars shone without any concerns for tomorrow—for they knew with certainty that the next day, and the next night, and the ones to follow would be waiting for them. They sparkled with a smug confidence that never disappointed those willing to look up.

To reach.

In that moment, Ninny understood what Mrs. Mercer had meant with her rallying cry. Oh, yes, *Exorior!*

She, Parathinia Minch, would set things to right.

As she went down the stairs, she felt as if she were speeding along in a motoring car—she never had, but she could imagine it was much the same heady feeling. She'd have to ask Madeline if she had ridden in one. She most likely had.

She opened the post office door and to her surprise—truly, she was going to have to stop being surprised when she opened her door these days—there were her old snowshoes.

Rather her new ones. Dear heavens, she'd quite forgotten them over at the saloon the other night. Yet they'd found their way home, along with a note:

Sunday?

She glanced at the mountains rising behind Bethlehem. She'd mentioned to Badger how she envied his treks through the quiet of the hills and how she'd loved going for rambles in the snow as a girl.

Now he'd asked her to join him. She ran her fingers over the smooth wood and imagined tramping through the hush of the trees, that stillness of snow blanketing the world, wrapping it up and promising rest until the busy days of spring.

But thoughts of such a tranquil ramble brought a hitch. With the specter of Mrs. George L. hanging over her head, she needed to come clean to Badger and Mr. Thayer as soon as possible.

Mrs. George L. could have revealed the truth the night before but had chosen not to—most likely, as Poppy had warned, so she could foul the waters when it best suited her.

Once, that very thought would have held her in its thrall for months.

No longer.

Ninny straightened, ready to strike her own course from here on out.

THE FIRST THING Ninny came face to face with in Mrs. George L.'s parlor was that wretchedly miserable elk. The one on the right—the poor haunted creature that seemed to be warning the entire room what was in store for them.

The author of its untimely demise looked up from her desk, scissors in hand and a stack of newspapers beside her. "Miss Minch, I have no time today. So much correspondence to look after. Perhaps you saw the *Observer* today?"

Truly, Cora had outdone herself. Competing headlines—*A Gala in Peril* and *Famous Authoress Graces Local Birthday Celebration*—positioned Mrs. George L. front and center in the issue, alongside the exclusive interview with Mrs. Viola Kinney Livingston. Given the stack of newspapers beside her, clearly Mrs. George L. had bought out every last copy.

So much for her constant threats of canceling her subscription.

"If you've come to apologize, please be done with it and then see yourself out."

Before, Ninny might have done just as the woman directed, mumbled out a string of dull words and left. But no more.

"I see no need to apologize. I've done nothing wrong."

Mrs. George L. set down her scissors and turned to fully face her. "Tell that to Mr. Thayer and Badger."

Her heart twisted out of habit. She might have crumbled if it hadn't been for the gift of certitude the stars had given her.

They'd pointed the way. Badger and Thayer were not her immediate problem. But like the stars, an answer would rise soon enough, and she'd deal with that disaster then.

So, before Mrs. George L. could lecture or bluster or explode, Ninny continued with a serenity she didn't know she even possessed. "I have come with a solution to the problem of which you spoke last night."

"Which one?" came the icy reply.

"Mrs. Vaughn's unfortunate *accident*." She placed the emphasis where it belonged, all but daring the woman to contradict her. Ninny took a cue from her nemesis and tugged at her mittens for a moment as if she was already bored with the subject but was here out of duty nonetheless. She looked up and found a flushed Mrs. George L., vexed by her own tactics. "I have another person in mind for Juliet. A choice that will fill the Opera House with guests."

Mrs. George L. laughed. A cruel, barking yap. "Who, you?"

"Certainly not. That's a foolish notion, especially when we have a trained actress, who is also a singer, in our midst."

"I think I would know of such a person—"

Ninny got straight to the point. "Miss Drake." Madeline might have made a mess of things when she'd first arrived, but she needn't be perpetually flogged for her mistakes. "She would fill the role admirably. If you apologize to her."

The woman's mouth fell open. Whether it was at the suggestion that such a creature be featured at the Opera Society gala, or at the notion that she was due an apology, or both, Ninny didn't know.

Or care. She didn't care what Columbia Lovell thought of her. Not anymore.

Now she knew why, when she'd looked down at those two names in her hand—Mrs. George L. Lovell in her bold penmanship, and Mrs. Neville Norwood in a delicate, neat script—why she hadn't panicked, but made the necessary decision in that moment born out of a strength and foresight that she hadn't realized she possessed.

But now she saw it. How it had always been there. For that multitude of stars had also reminded her that she was surrounded. By friends. People who had proven they would give up anything for her. Madeline. Badger and Mr. Thayer. Savannah and Inola.

Meanwhile, Mrs. George L. wiped at her eyes as she finished laughing. "Have you been tippling again, Parathinia?"

Ninny ignored the dart. "Miss Drake is a professional actress—she's been on the New York stage. And she can sing."

"Are you certain what sort of stage she was performing upon?" Mrs. George L. asked. "Whatever does she sing? Ribald songs for the unwashed?"

"She can sing anything you set before her."

Mrs. George L., scissors back in hand, picked up another paper. "I will not entertain—"

Ninny cut her off. "Yes, you will, Columbia." Because this wasn't about her or Mrs. George L. It was about Bethlehem and what they all needed, which was a proper fire engine.

Mrs. George L. stilled. "How dare you—"

"Oh, she dares," came another voice. Poppy stood in the doorway, dressed to go out. How long she'd been there, Ninny didn't know, but clearly long enough. "I've heard that gel sing. She's got pipes."

But Mrs. George L. wasn't in the mood to be consoling. "Your hearing might have been impaired at the time."

"She can sing," Ninny repeated. "Far better than Althea, for all her Dramatic Society credentials. Better yet, Miss Drake's presence will ensure the funds are raised for the new fire engine."

Poppy nodded in agreement, coming to stand at Ninny's side, another unlikely but most welcome friend.

Mrs. George L. folded her hands in her lap. "Have either of you considered that not a single decent woman in this town will attend such a spectacle?"

Poppy, bless her heart, had a ready answer. "But every man will."

Mrs. George L. ignored her and turned to Ninny, brow raised. "I've already made the decision that the dinner will need to be canceled. There is no question of if going on without Mrs. Vaughn."

Ninny nodded, but not in defeat. "Then I will ask Miss Drake to sponsor an event to raise money for the fire engine. When she does— and secures the funds—the dedication plaque on the engine will credit her, reminding everyone who wanted all of us safe in our beds."

Poppy's gaze swiveled toward Ninny as if she hadn't expected the postmistress to counter so perfectly.

For one triumphant moment, Mrs. George L. and the elk shared the same look of shock and dismay as karma found its bullseye.

MADELINE FINISHED STRAIGHTENING the chairs and turned toward the stove where Mrs. Clarke sat sewing. "That is going to be a pretty dress."

The usually prickly woman blushed. "I think it is better than the original."

"The original?"

She sighed. "I couldn't afford new silk, so I cut apart an old gown and remade it into this." She shook it out and held it up.

"That's remade?" Madeline sucked in a deep breath, drawn to the chartreuse color. She didn't dare touch it, but, oh, it was so pretty. "That's amazing. Why, the color is perfect for you."

Mrs. Clarke shook her head. "It isn't for me. Though I wish it was —then I could get the hem right. I'm too tall." She paused for a moment and eyed Madeline. "As are you."

"Is that the one for Myrtle?" Madeline asked. For a moment she thought she'd gone too far with the normally terse woman, but something had changed with Mrs. Clarke since the other night. Her corset of restraint had loosened, the strings broken free of their previous knots.

She didn't look up, her hands returning to stitching. "Yes, it is."

"Thank goodness," Madeline told her. "I've seen how that girl dresses, and it's a crime. Stripes and plaid. Some days she blinds me when I go in the store." Studying the dress again, she noticed something else. "What are you going to do for the buttons?"

Mrs. Clarke shrugged. "I don't know. Cut them off one of my dresses, I suppose."

Madeline was already shaking her head. "No need." With that, she dashed upstairs and returned in a thrice with the button jar that sat on her dresser. "There are some really pretty ones in here." She turned the jar this way and that, showing off the bits of brass and enamel, tin and wood, mother-of-pearl, and even some paste gems that sparkled like diamonds.

Without any further fanfare, she spilled the buttons out onto a table. In no time, she had a handful of delicate little buttons, encircled by tiny gems that winked in the light.

"I couldn't," Mrs. Clarke told her.

"Of course you can," Madeline said, holding them out. "They work, don't they?" She set them against the silk to prove her point.

Yet another piece of Mrs. Clarke's armor fell away. "Thank you, Madeline. They are exactly what I need."

"They are, aren't they?" Madeline agreed, more pleased than she cared to admit. "What's left to do?"

Mrs. Clarke, having tucked the buttons away in her basket, glanced over it with a critical eye. "Just the finishing touches. Though I do wish I could try it on Myrtle to make sure I have the waist and the hem length correct."

Madeline nodded, having done more than her fair share of fittings. She looked again at the gown and then over her shoulder toward the mercantile, as if measuring it up against the girl. "You know, you could try it on Ninny. She and Myrtle are about the same size."

She thought she might have finally overstepped, for the woman frowned slightly, but then just as quickly she smiled, a radiant dawning. "What an excellent idea. I wonder if Miss Minch would be so indulgent."

"She's a romantic at heart," Madeline confided. "She'll be pleased to be included. I'll ask her later." She glanced over at the clock. "Is that the time? I've got to get ready for the lunch crew."

Mrs. Clarke nodded and carefully put away the dress. "I should check on the soup," she was saying, when all of a sudden the door opened, and in swept Mrs. George L. Lovell.

Even more surprising, Ninny and Poppy followed in her wake.

"Mrs. Clarke," Mrs. Lovell began, slanting a mere glance at Madeline before launching in. "You continue to surprise me." She was not a woman to waste an opportunity. "How fares poor Mrs. Bergstrom? I hate the very thought of her being neglected."

Mrs. Clarke sallied right back. "I checked in on her this very morning."

Mrs. George L. sniffed. "At least you haven't forsworn all your obligations."

"As it is, she is much improved." Mrs. Clarke tugged on her gloves. "I actually interrupted her morning chores, and she appeared quite energetic." Her brow arched elegantly, as if questioning the very need for this interview.

"Indeed," Mrs. George L. mused. "Energetic, you say?" She pursed as she chewed on this bit of information. "I wonder if we shouldn't consult Grace. I don't recall Mrs. Bergstrom ever recovering so quickly."

Madeline thought she might have discerned a note of concern in the woman's words, but certainly Savannah wasn't giving the suggestion any consideration, for she turned to Madeline. "Send Dobbs around when he's done with school to fetch the sandwiches. Don't let that soup get above a simmer." Then she left through the kitchen.

"Sandwiches?" the matron sputtered. She turned her ire to Madeline. "So that's where you're getting them. Here I suspected Elias Turner."

"No, he refused me. On the grounds that you wouldn't approve."

Mrs. George L. huffed a bit, watching the doorway through which Mrs. Clarke had fled. "I don't know how you've persuaded poor Mrs. Clarke to your side, but she was a perfectly respectable woman before you arrived."

Madeline picked up a rag and moved behind the wide cherrywood bar. "Why are you here?"

"To prove a point, though very much against my will," Mrs. George L. complained.

"That's not why I'm here," Poppy declared, shouldering her way past her daughter-in-law and making a beeline for the bar. She hopped up on the stool like a twenty-something and grinned. "How's your Cosmo?"

"My . . . wha-a-t?" Madeline stammered. Certainly she hadn't heard that correctly.

"Haven't had one in an age and, oh, how I've missed them." Poppy leaned across the bar and jerked her thumb over her shoulder. "I suppose herself would disapprove."

"Herself would decidedly object," Mrs. George L. told her, in a voice frosty enough to chill an entire tray of Cosmos.

"Now is not the time," Ninny told them, finally speaking up.

"*Et tu*, Miss Minch?" Poppy winked at Madeline. "Another day, eh?" She turned in her seat and barked a laugh, for here was Mrs. George L., standing stiff as a board, her gaze fixed on the cherubic form over the bar.

"Ah, me in my younger days. I was a real looker back then," Poppy told her. "A fellow from Italy passed through and offered to carve that for the bar. He usually worked on ships, but no matter. I think he just wanted to spend a month looking at my tits. Not that I can blame him. They were spectacular, weren't they?"

No one in the room could help themselves. They had to give the siren overhead another once-over. Mrs. George L. broke first, blinking and wrenching her gaze away before hastily getting to business, though her cheeks appeared to glow with a rare blush. "Shall we finish this nonsense?"

Madeline opened her mouth to make a quip, but with one look at Ninny's pleading expression, she chose a more innocuous route. "To what do I owe this honor?"

Mrs. George L. cleared her throat. "I've been advised that you sing."

"I've been known to," Madeline replied nonchalantly, wiping at the bar. After a few swipes, she looked up. "What of it?"

A steely silence followed, both women staring at the other.

"Madeline," Ninny said, coming around the bar, "I recommended you for the part of Juliet. In the Opera Society gala."

"I sort of figured that out," Madeline told her, her gaze never moving from Mrs. George L.'s. The woman was good. She hadn't moved a muscle. Hadn't blinked. She reminded Madeline of her first agent, a battleaxe of a crone who had decades earlier represented Gigi with a singular, ruthless zeal that had made grown-ass men cry.

Mrs. George L. added, "The gala is for the town. You would be the lead."

There. That was her offer. Help the town. Be the lead. It wasn't a boon she was offering, but a plea. And Madeline could see clearly it had cost the overbearing matron every ounce of pride she possessed.

"Come on now, sing," Poppy said, waving her hand at the piano. "I'd like see how one eats crow when it is well served."

"Poppy, I don't know . . ." Madeline was enjoying this triumph as much as Poppy clearly was, but her old resentment at being prodded into that old role raised her hackles.

"This is all ridiculous," Mrs. George L. announced, and began backpedaling toward the door. "I shall not waste my time." She glanced over her shoulder at the rest of her party in an unspoken command to follow.

Poppy wasn't moving. Not now that she was happily ensconced on a barstool, gazing up at the figurehead with a fond light in her eyes.

But it was Ninny who surprised them all. "I doubt Mrs. Norwood would find this a waste of time." Ninny's words, her *threat*, stopped the old girl in her tracks. Then the once-shy postmistress honed her thrust. "Mrs. Norwood never allows pride to go before the welfare of Bethlehem."

While Mrs. George L. sputtered in indignant rage, Ninny turned to Madeline. "Please." She tipped her head toward the piano.

A few weeks before, Madeline would have laughed at such a request. Trying out for a community charity play.

The lead, a wry voice amended.

Even now, as she walked over to the piano, she didn't know whether to laugh or to snidely explain that this was all entirely beneath her.

Her. Madeline Drake.

Yet Ninny's faith smoothed that sense of indignity roiling around inside her. The gala was for a new, much-needed fire engine. And, not for the first time, she wondered what would have happened if that fire in the shed had spread. To some other part of town, say, to Ninny's house.

So she went to the piano and settled down on the bench, her hands coming to rest lightly atop the keys. As they brushed over the smooth ivory, she realized that for Ninny, this wasn't about fame, regard, status, or any of the things Madeline usually fought and clawed for.

For Ninny, this was about this odd town. Her town.

Madeline thumbed through the music sheets in front of her and found just the right song. So she began to play, and the words moved up from inside her, and she sang.

O little town of Bethlehem, how still we see thee lie . . .

This wasn't just Ninny's community. It was hers.

At least in this moment. In this bend of the river. The words rose up, carrying off those last bits of resistance, those clinging threads that had held her in the endless churn of a solitary channel. They sent her into an entirely new runnel, a stream that ran swiftly toward a grander tributary.

Above thy deep and dreamless sleep, the silent stars go by . . .

This was what Shandy . . . what Wick . . . what Nate, in his own way, had tried to tell her.

The choices one made in the moments—those awkward, rare, but oh-so-important moments—steered our lives. Tiny decisions sent the course of that brook down ever-changing paths.

Life was never the smooth stillness of a quiet pond. It was a discordant river running hither and fro in the flux of daily choices.

As Madeline got to the second verse, she forgot her audience, the weight of indignities, everything, and gave in to the singular pleasure of singing.

Over the years, she'd sensed this path of transcendence, of being filled with genuine joy, but she'd never felt that unseen scale tipping toward her, rewarding her for nothing more than being herself.

For the first time, that long-sought-after balance poured forth into her heart.

She finished with a little flourish of notes and closed her eyes, even as Ninny and Poppy clapped enthusiastically. She turned on the bench, and there was Mrs. George L., standing in the middle of the Star Bright, wide-eyed with genuine surprise.

The woman who carried her pride and arrogance like the fox mantle draped around her shoulders had let her prejudice and preconceptions be washed away.

"My dear," she enthused. "Your voice . . . Why, it's lovely."

Madeline nodded, though she could hardly take credit for it. Gigi's dogged determination had brought her here.

If you are going to do this, she'd say, *you'll do it right and not embarrass the Drake legacy.*

Madeline understood that now better than she had as a nine-year-old being dragged to singing lessons.

"I am all astounded and humbled." Mrs. George L. turned to Ninny. "Parathinia, you have done us all a great service."

It was as close to an apology, Madeline suspected, as one would ever get from the woman. But more rewarding was the look of triumph in Ninny's tear-filled eyes as her steady faith in Madeline found its reward.

While Mrs. George L. aired her effervescent praise and plans, Ninny stood steadfast behind her, wiping at her eyes, once again overshadowed.

But this time, Madeline saw her. Knew what she'd done. This was a testament to Ninny's remarkable skill to connect others. And not just as the town's postmistress. She had an instinct to knit people together, to share the load, to ease the burden.

Then, for some reason, Madeline's gaze traveled to the empty chair by the stove. The one where Mrs. Clarke liked to sew, just on the edge of the crowd. Away from the currents.

As Mrs. George L. waxed on about her role and responsibilities as Juliet—for to her way of thinking, Madeline had already said yes— she couldn't help but wonder what would nudge the widow out of the last tangles to which she was so tightly bound.

CHAPTER 40

Friday, December 20

*N*ot long after Ninny opened the post office Friday morning, Madeline arrived, a letter in hand.

"I spotted this partly tucked under the doormat." She handed the letter across the counter.

"How many times do I have to tell people not to—" Ninny turned the letter over to discover the culprit. "Oh, my."

Miss Parathinia Minch
Bethlehem, Wyoming

"Thought you might find that interesting." Madeline grinned. "Whose handwriting is that?"

"Mr. Densmore's," she replied, setting it into the pile that needed to be sorted and canceled.

"Aren't you going to open it?" Madeline's eyes sparked with curiosity.

"Not before it is posted." She continued sorting the mail that had come in from the mailbag.

"Oh, come on!" Madeline complained, reaching for the letter, but Ninny was faster. "Don't you want to know what it says?"

"I imagine it says exactly what this one does." She reached under the counter and pulled out the correspondence she'd found earlier atop the mailbag. Her distraction upon finding Mr. Thayer's missive explained how she'd missed Badger's letter in the first place.

"How do you know? Neither of them are opened," Madeline pointed out.

"I can't open them until I postmark them," Ninny told her, clinging to postal regulations and her own dread of what the contents might hold.

"Oh, good heavens," Madeline muttered, reaching across the counter and snatching up the postmark stamp and the letters.

Even as Ninny yelped in protest, Madeline postmarked both letters and handed them back. "There. No more excuses."

"Madeline Drake! You are not authorized to—"

"I swear, Ninny, if you don't open those letters, I will." Her hand began to snake out, but Ninny was forewarned and stepped out of reach.

"Just open them," Madeline urged.

With no more excuses—and her suspicion that Madeline wouldn't leave until the contents were discovered—Ninny opened the one from Mr. Thayer.

She read the lines, and with each word her brow furrowed deeper. "This is terrible news."

Madeline lowered her voice. "Did he find out?"

"Worse," Ninny declared, glancing up from the scrawling handwriting. "He's invited me to be his guest at the Opera Society gala."

Madeline's brow furrowed, but for different reasons. "How is that bad news?"

"Because I have every suspicion that Mr. Densmore's letter bears the same request."

"And that is bad because . . . ?"

"I don't know which letter came first. However can I choose? And, even if I wanted to go, I have nothing to wear to a gala." Even as she said the words, she knew how ridiculous they sounded, because that was exactly her problem. Not choosing.

Madeline leaned against the counter. "Go with both of them."

Ninny stuffed the letters in her apron pocket. "This is no time for jests. As I said, I have nothing to wear."

Madeline pushed back, arms folded over her chest. "Who says I'm joking? Besides, you can wear one of my dresses."

Ninny stepped back. "Now you are joking!"

"Sure would set tongues wagging."

"I would prefer a little less wagging." She shook her head and got back to sorting the incoming mail. "I can't accept either. Not in good conscience, not after what I've done."

Madeline sighed. "Not this again. If that is what is holding you up, then tell them! That would certainly sort things out."

All her resolve from the other day, well, it had run right into her very real fears as to what the truth would unleash.

"You know they'll find out eventually."

"Not necessarily," she hedged.

This time, Madeline groaned. "Ninny, a secret is only a secret when one person knows it."

"Yes, well—"

"No 'well.' How many people now know what you did?"

Her lips pursed. "You. Mrs. Clarke. Most likely Inola." She hedged, hoping that was enough. But Madeline was too sharp by half.

"And Cora over at the newspaper," she added.

Ninny closed her eyes. "Yes, and Cora."

"And that doesn't concern you? That she'll print the entire story when she runs out of everything else?"

Yes, Ninny could well imagine that Cora, despite her claims of some lofty, higher goal, would finally succumb to the inevitable headline of *The Truth Behind Christmas!!*

She looked down and realized she'd mixed the mercantile's mail with the drugstore's. Heavens.

Then Ninny admitted the rest. "Mrs. George L."

Madeline coughed. "No! Oh, Ninny, no!" She shuddered. "That tears it. You have to tell them the truth. You know darn well that woman will wreak havoc the first chance she gets."

"Hardly. Not when she's included you in the gala." Ninny glanced at the clock. "Well, look at the time. When is rehearsal today?"

"Don't you dare try to change the subject, Ninny Minch. I see right through you."

"I prefer to think Mrs. George L. has seen the error of her ways."

"Do you now? You really think she's changed? Really?"

Well, when she put it that way. "No. Probably not."

Madeline nodded. "So you have your answer. You need to tell them. Sooner rather than later. Tonight. You can come by the saloon —" She held up her hand to stave off the protest rising on Ninny's lips. "Come into the kitchen. No one will see you."

"I can't tonight."

"Whyever not?"

"I'm busy."

"Busy? You?"

"You needn't sound so incredulous. I judge the spelling bee every year. Which happens to be tonight."

"The spelling bee? How convenient."

"I always judge," she told her. "I hold the all-time record for most wins."

"Ninny, you must clear the air. Face this head-on. I could have avoided a lot of problems in my life if I had been upfront and honest. Would you also like me to spell it? H-O-N—"

"I know how to spell *honest*. Now don't you have a rehearsal to attend?" She turned her back and returned to sorting the mail into the proper slots.

"You can't put this off much longer." The bell jangled like a warning as she left.

Of course she couldn't put it off, but however could she let go of this life she'd discovered?

And who could blame her for wanting just a few more golden memories?

LATER THAT AFTERNOON, Madeline hurried into the Star Bright, flush and happy from the gala rehearsal—no matter that she and Mrs. George L. had clashed at every turn. She'd nearly forgotten how much she loved being on stage. She glanced around. All the tables were in place, and everything was ready for a busy Friday night.

Dobbs sat in the corner with Wick, working on his homework. Their heads were bent together.

The sight of them stopped her, like *déjà vu*. A homey warmth surrounded her as she looked again. Dobbs chewing at the end of his pencil, Wick's brow furrowed with concentration. A big book open in front of them.

The entire tableau tugged at her. *Remember this?* It seemed to say. *Remember how much this means?* But the memory wasn't hers—or was it?

She shook her head and hurried to the kitchen. To her surprise, Mrs. Clarke was still at the stove, giving the soup, or whatever she'd made today, a stir.

"Keep this at a simmer," the woman cautioned yet again as she wiped her hands on her apron. "At the very least, give it a good stir now and then."

Madeline walked over and inhaled. Potatoes and onions and cream. "Oh, what is this?"

"Just potato soup."

Madeline loved how the women of this town always described their food as "just." "Just" a stew. "Just" a bit of pot roast. Now it was "just" potato soup. By Madeline's scale, "just" always smelled like heaven.

But she knew better than to correct Mrs. Clarke. She turned prickly when it came to praise.

"How is Mrs. Bergstrom?" she asked instead.

"Much improved."

"So the soups and breads must be helping?"

Mrs. Clarke flinched a little. Madeline had guessed correctly. Her cook was skimming from the Star Bright offerings to feed the Bergstroms. Not that Madeline minded.

"I thought she was in a bad way," she began. "Isn't she improving a little too fast?" She hated to sound like Mrs. George L., but she'd been a bit surprised by this turn of events, given what little she knew about postpartum depression. Not for the first time, she missed having her phone handy to give her quick answers.

Mrs. Clarke straightened with that impenetrable pride. It was like bricks being tossed in the air and landing perfectly to form a high wall. "That would be a problem?"

Madeline knew one certainty about walls—they could always be breached. "I heard about her standing in front of the house, incoherent and wearing only her nightgown."

"How did you—"

"Dobbs."

The wall notched higher as Mrs. Clarke turned her back, removed her apron, and hung it on the hook. "Well, that was a few weeks ago, and in the meantime, she seems to have found her footing."

"If you say so," Madeline remarked, stacking her coat and hat on a chair and reaching for her own apron that hung nearby. Mrs. Clarke pursed her lips as she glanced at the untidy bundle of clothes.

Clearly she adhered to the same standard as Gigi. "A place for everything, everything in its place." It wasn't until Madeline had gotten older that she'd discovered Ben Franklin had said it first.

"Until tomorrow," Mrs. Clarke said, all crisp words and a dismissive tip of her head.

Perhaps Ninny would know what to do. Madeline made a note to ask her tomorrow, as Mrs. Clarke's heels clicked out the door.

At the bar, Erasmus had already claimed a seat.

"I'm not open yet."

"I'm not just anyone," the lawyer told her. "My lips, two blushing pilgrims, ready stand, to smooth that rough touch with a tender kiss."

Madeline laughed, but was hardly caught flat-footed. "Good

pilgrim, you do wrong your hand too much, which mannerly devotion shows in this."

"You've learned your lines quickly." Erasmus smiled and tapped the bar with a finger.

Madeline grinned back and began to mix him his Manhattan. "As luck would have it, I did that very same play not too long ago."

"Mrs. George L. must be in the pink."

"Sadly so," Madeline supplied as she wiped at the bar and then strolled around the room, checking the tables again and adjusting some of the chairs. "She's already planning next year." She shook her head.

"What's wrong with that?" Erasmus asked.

Madeline stopped. "I won't be here. I'm leaving."

"Leave?" Dobbs twisted around in his seat. "Why would you want to leave? I thought you liked it here. This is . . . home."

Madeline found herself pinned as all eyes turned on her. "I'm only here until Christmas. You all know that. Besides, you'll come back with me," she told Dobbs.

He shook his head. "No, I won't. My place is here."

This was the last thing she expected of him. Of course he would be coming back. He had to.

"This is home," he insisted. She recognized that tone. Nobody could be more stubborn than Nate when he set his heels.

How she longed to tell him what his future held. *Oh, Dobbs, you are going to find a family who adores you. A life where you will flourish and grow.*

Those happy images flitted through her, but she also recalled all the times Nate had taken off to explore Wyoming. Hiking the hills, always searching for lost townships, ghost towns. Scouring the archives at the college in Laramie, all in the name of "research" for the show.

She had thought at the time that he was merely being a perfectionist, but now she saw his obsession with Wyoming's history as something different.

He'd been trying to find his way home. Here. Right now.

When he couldn't find it, he'd recreated what he'd lost by writing and producing the show. The home she'd taken from him when she'd somehow drawn him through time into the future.

Madeline's throat dammed up, the arguments tangled like flood debris under a bridge.

"You okay there?" Wick asked. His quiet question seemed to cut through the room.

"Yeah. Just fine," she said, borrowing the word from Mrs. Clarke. *Just fine.* But if Nate didn't go back with her, would he still be there when she returned?

Wick nudged Dobbs. "Best you get ready for your big night."

Dobbs nodded and headed toward the back room.

"Big night?" Madeline asked.

"Spelling bee," Wick supplied.

Madeline did a double take toward the back room. "He didn't tell me."

"Didn't want you to feel bad because you can't be there," Erasmus said.

Erasmus knew as well? "He just started school . . . Is that wise?"

"He wants to try," Wick told her, "so you'll be proud of him."

"He doesn't need to spell to do that," she huffed, taking another glance at the door. Did she dare?

Even as she looked toward Erasmus, the wily lawyer was shaking his head. "I cannot help you with the bar tonight."

"How did you—"

He tapped his skull. "I know. But I have to be there as well. I'm one of the judges."

"You?"

"Words are my stage," Erasmus told her, with a great flourish.

"Whole town will be there," Wick added. "No one misses it."

"Really?" She couldn't quite fathom that a spelling bee was the social event of the season, but here it was.

Erasmus nodded and then finished off his drink. "Only one round tonight. Can't show up podgy. I'd lose my place at the judge's table." He pushed off his barstool and gathered up his hat. "As always, a pleasure to drop by, madam."

Madeline rapped the bar with her knuckle. "The real pleasure would be you paying for a drink."

"Did I forget?" he asked, then patted his pockets, coming up empty-handed. Yet again. "I do believe you'll have to put it on my tab."

"Your tab is growing longer than my patience will extend."

"Patience is a priceless commodity. You should thank me."

LIVE AN AUTHENTIC LIFE.

Poppy's words had haunted Savannah all week. She was doing that, wasn't she? She'd helped Miss Minch. She was no longer hampered by accolades that were not hers to claim. Why, she'd even joined in at Dobbs' birthday party.

Heavens, that statement alone was more than she'd thought possible a few weeks earlier. Her, at a party. With friends. In a saloon.

Yet as she walked down to the house by the river, she wondered why her steps still dogged her, dragged at her.

The dress was nearly done and would be in time for Christmas. She'd succeeded at everything.

Or had she?

Livia opened the door before she got there, then hurried down the path past her, Clara in her arms. "Mrs. Clarke, you are too kind to help us. I've got to get to the Opera House and get my name on the list for the bee."

"Good luck," she offered as she went into the house. There she found the girls, along with Mr. Bergstrom and Peter, all scrubbed and shrugging their way into coats. Mrs. Bergstrom sat in her chair, rocking, with Thomas in her arms.

For a moment she thought perhaps she wasn't needed. Everything looked well in hand.

"We are going to the spelling bee, even though there won't be a dance," Berta told her.

"Stop complaining, little *sötnos*," Peter told her, tweaking her braid before he caught hold of her hand. "You get to walk with me."

Margit already held his other hand. He led the beaming twins out the door.

Mr. Bergstrom nodded for Savannah to follow him, and for a second she thought she was being dismissed.

Not at all.

"I know she looks well," he said quietly, "but I'm worried."

"Then let me help with that," Savannah told him. "I will be here, tonight, tomorrow, for as long as you need me." The man looked ready to choke up and cry. That would never do. "Now off with you, or you won't find a seat."

He nodded and hurried after his family, leaving Savannah all alone in the dark, save for the shaft of light coming from the half-open door.

When she went back inside, Mrs. Bergstrom was laying the baby back down in his cradle. She expected the woman to turn and flee to the sanctity of her bedroom, but she surprised her by settling back down in her chair and reaching for her knitting: a nearly finished sock in a thick wool. She glanced up at Savannah and nodded toward the empty chair beside her.

Well, this was an improvement.

Still, there was an air to the room that left her feeling undone, unfinished. Like the dress in her basket. The sock on the needles. Savannah never liked leaving anything incomplete. Dirty dishes in the sink. A story half told.

She wasn't quite sure it was the right time. She wasn't sure she was ready. She'd come this far, but there was still a wide, swift river to cross.

She sat and unfolded the dress, looking it over for the hundredth time. Tonight, she'd finish whipstitching the buttonholes. Truly, the buttons Madeline had given her were perfect, but she needed something else, something . . .

Beside her, Mrs. Bergstrom murmured a few soft words, then dug into her sewing basket. She pulled out a card of white bobbin lace in an elaborate partridge-eye pattern, picked from something old and once treasured, and wrapped with care so it could reused. She held it out against the silk.

The white of the lace, the chartreuse silk, the pink hue of the buttons twined together. Borrowed thread. Bits and pieces gathered into a new whole. Like spring blossoming in a barren land.

Yet how could she take such an exquisite treasure?

Mrs. Bergstrom must have seen Savannah's hesitation. "*Ja*," she insisted, with a determined shake of her head.

Savannah stared down at the lace with a growing sense of understanding. "It came from before."

"*Ja*. Before." She set the lace on the end table between them and pushed it toward Savannah. "Before."

She knew what that meant, and the name came out of her in a whisper. "Shandy."

"*Ja*, Shandy." This time, Mrs. Bergstrom looked away.

So he had brought them as well. To her shame, she'd never really paid any attention to Shandy's flock of lost souls. She never wanted to know what sins, what tragedies, had brought them to this place. Just as she liked to keep her own buried away.

Taking up her needle, Savannah continued her sewing, picking up where she'd left off—with the dress and her story.

"I said the other day that war changes men, but for women it is a misery and an endless fear that leaves every day cursed in shadows." She glanced over at her companion, but Mrs. Bergstrom continued to knit as if Savannah hadn't said a word. So she waded further in. "But life continues in its endless turns, no matter the vagaries of men. Or because of them. I am not ashamed of what I did. I loved him. Lucius made promises I was willing to believe. Some months later, I gave birth to a fine, healthy son, and not long after, Sybilla bore a wee child too early. Sybilla despaired into silence. I tried my best to help her, but there was my son, healthy and the very image of his father—and her son, barely alive."

Savannah finished one buttonhole and tied the thread into a knot. "Then, one day, Sybilla—poor, sweet Sybilla—found the wherewithal to get up and go for a walk. Unfortunately, she walked into the river and let the deep waters swallow her into their cold grasp." Savannah paused, saying the same prayer she always did when she thought of that nightmarish afternoon.

Forgive her, Lord. She knew not what she was doing.

"Not long after—though I tried my best—her baby slipped away as well."

Something stirred beside her, and she looked up to find Mrs. Bergstrom not so much watching her but, by the tip of her head, listening, as if the tone of the words conveyed Savannah's deep loss.

"I'd like to say that after we mourned, Mrs. Vance and I pulled together, for by this time, the slaves had left—not that I blamed them. I'd always abhorred slavery, and when the last of them ran off, I silently wished them well. But Mother Vance would not be consoled. It wasn't the loss of her daughter that left her bereft, but rather that the land we lived on now belonged to Lucius Maddox. It had become his property the day he married Sybilla. If there was no way to connect ourselves—well, herself—to him, he could cast us out the moment he returned. So that wretched woman wrote to him that his wife had died giving birth to his son. *My child.*"

Another lie. Another knot. Her entire life a series of tangles and deceptions.

Rethreading her needle, she started on the next buttonhole. "You would have thought that by this time, I would have known better. But I lived a lie greater than the promise of conquest and victory. I thought that I could turn her desperation to my advantage, that Lucius would return and marry me—the woman he truly loved. Oh, how I was wrong."

Her needle snagged on the silk, and Savannah paused to survey for any damage. Satisfied it was just a tiny rive the button would conceal, she went on.

"So I become Aunty Vanna, and I raised my son for a man who never wrote. Never sent word. We survived the arrival of Union troops as they took Vicksburg. They raided the countryside, taking what they wanted and leaving hunger and fevers behind. Just as the war ended, a terrible sickness swept through, first taking Mother Vance and then, to my unending horror, my dearest boy." She glanced away and swiped at her eyes, now moist and filling quickly. "I buried them both with my own hands. There was no one else. Then I crawled into my bed and begged the Lord to take me."

The baby snuffled again, and Mrs. Bergstrom's brow furrowed.

"Into my despair, Inola returned. How she managed it, I don't know, but she did, bringing the light back into my life. She bullied me back onto my feet, and we made our plans to leave. There was nothing left for us there, and she wanted to return to Ohio. She'd made a life there and wanted me to join her. Yet before we finished packing, Lucius found his way to our doorstep. Or, rather, his."

Savannah closed her eyes as she went on. "He was not the man I thought him to be. He probably never was.

"Filled with pride and greed, he'd marched off to war. In defeat, he returned a scavenger, picking angrily over the scraps that remained of his previous self-divined glory, plaguing his ills on everyone within his reach like the worst sort of pestilence.

"And straight to Larkhall he'd come. Demanding his rights. Drinking for hours, blaming everyone for his losses. He accused me of all kinds of crimes. Letting Sybilla die. Killing his child—that one near did me in. My own darling Thomas."

At this, Mrs. Bergstrom glanced up. "Thomas?"

"Yes, Thomas." Savannah glanced over at the cradle. They both did.

She shivered for a moment, as if someone had tread upon that faraway grave.

The rest of her story came out in a haunted rush. "I won't go into what Lucius did that night. I think every woman knows what a man in that state of mind is capable of meting out. If she doesn't, she finds out quickly. But when he turned his anger on Inola, threatened her with what he'd savaged upon me, swore she'd never see the light of day again, something inside me snapped. I'd lost so much, and I wasn't about to let him take away my last bit of family. He turned his back to me and went toward the cellar where he'd locked her away earlier. I grabbed up the clock from the mantel and hit him as hard as I could. I had listened to that clock tick away as he'd done his worst to me, and I never wanted to hear that sound again."

Silence filled the small house, much as it had the night Savannah had felled Lucius. No more of his ugly insults, his ranting. No more endless ticking of the clock. Just stillness and silence.

"I got Inola out of the cellar, and we knew when the Maddox family—what was left of them—discovered what had happened, both of us would hang. So in the dark of that night, we consigned him to the same waters that had taken Sybilla. Let him sink and drift away with the currents. By that time I was near mad with the entirety of it. I was halfway into that unholy river myself, as Inola pleaded from the banks for me to stay with her, when . . ." She glanced away, toward the shadows in the corners.

"Shandy," Mrs. Bergstrom finished. "*Ja?*"

"He caught hold of my hand and stopped me from taking that last step into the depths. Instead, he pulled me into an entirely different sort of flux. And here I've been, all these years."

She finished the buttonhole and clipped the last thread.

TRUE TO ERASMUS and Wick's prediction, the entire town seemed to be at the spelling bee. Though, regular as clockwork, Denny came in at eight, claimed his barstool, and ordered a bourbon.

"Why aren't you over at the spelling bee?" Madeline asked him, as she pulled the bottle from the shelf.

"I was, but then they started using made-up words, and I wasn't going to stick around and listen to nonsense," he complained.

She slid the drink across the bar. "Made-up words?"

"I mean whoever heard of the word"—he paused to take an appreciative drink of his bourbon—"obstreperous?"

A derisive snort came from the corner, where her only other customer, Badger, sat by the stove, Wellington curled up on one side of his boots and Dog on the other. He'd come in earlier for soup and a sandwich.

"Is that even a word?" Madeline asked, glancing over toward him.

"I'm rather surprised you two don't know it," Badger said, getting up and shaking on his coat, "considering it means noisy and difficult to control."

Madeline grinned, but Denny took exception to the description.

"Says you," he shot back, settling in with his bourbon and a sour expression.

Not long after Badger left, Denny followed, leaving Madeline all alone.

She cleaned up what little needed to be done and eventually drifted to the piano. She plunked out the Christmas carols she knew by heart, but without a chorus of drunken folks around her to sing, it wasn't as much fun.

She was about to slam the lid down over the keys when the door opened and Wick came sauntering in. Her heart lightened, until she realized he'd come back without Dobbs.

"Forget someone?" she asked, spinning around on the bench, arms crossed over her chest.

"I came to tell you about that," Wick began, "so you didn't worry."

She got to her feet. "I'm worried now. Where is Dobbs?"

"He's going to sleep over at the hotel so he can help Mr. Turner first thing in the morning. There's a lot of people who came into town for the spelling bee and are staying the night."

Madeline's jaw worked back and forth as she hunted for the words that expressed the tossing storm inside her. "He didn't need to do that."

"He's a bit out of sorts," Wick shot back.

Clearly Dobbs wasn't the only one.

Madeline rounded the bar and got out two glasses. She chucked her chin toward the table closest to him as she caught up the bourbon bottle. "Tell me about this spelling bee."

He snorted. "Is that what you want to talk about?"

She shook her head. "Hardly, but it seemed a good opening." She settled into a chair, and Wick took the one opposite her. She poured for the both of them, pushed his glass across the table, then corked the bottle. Settling back with her glass in hand, she got to the point. The one that had really been bothering her all night. "How is it Dobbs ended up here?"

Wick shifted and looked away. He took a quick drink.

"I need to know," she persisted. Because one thing was certain. This was all tied to Nate, or rather Dobbs. And what held him here.

Wick took another sip and set down his glass. "He arrived before me. From what I know, he's been here some time."

Shaking her head, Madeline tried to make sense of any of it. "How could that be? He's all of nine."

"Time is funny here," Wick said, giving the bourbon in his glass a churn so it whirled and curled around itself. "Some people seem to move with it. Others seem to be stuck."

In time. Out of time. Wasn't that how Shandy had explained it? She ticked through the various people she knew. Savannah had mentioned the war the other day, and Madeline had gotten the sense that she wasn't talking about World War II, or even the Great War. Then there was Poppy and her talk of drinking Cosmos.

The entire town was one big Twilight Zone. Yet they all held something in common: they'd been brought here.

"But Dobbs. Why is *he* here?" She straightened. "If you won't tell me, I'll ask Shandy."

Wick's gaze snapped up. "Don't."

Madeline sat back, stunned by his sharp tone.

Wick glanced away and took a deep breath. "Don't ask Shandy. He was the one who found him. Got him here. After—"

The silence of the night pressed in again. The shadows edged closer. Still, she had to ask. Had to take that step. "After what?"

He reached for the bottle and topped off both their glasses. "His parents were murdered."

"Murdered? Why?"

"Why is anyone murdered? Greed. Hate. Revenge. None of it matters once the crime is done."

"It matters to me." That gaping hole in Nate's life had been spun by whatever had happened to his parents. To him.

It was Wick's turn to shake his head. "It isn't a fit subject."

"I have to know."

He set down his glass so that it rattled atop the table. "You really want to know?"

"Yes."

"His parents were good people, teachers from what I understand, moving to an all-black township near the Nebraska border. On their way, a group of locals found them. They weren't happy about this new town and the people headed there."

"And?"

"Madeline." Not Miss Drake, but Madeline. He leaned on his elbows and rested his forehead on his palms as he stared at his glass.

"I need to know."

"Shandy blames himself. He got there too late. He found Dobbs standing beneath his father. He'd been hung. Kid was covered in so much blood, Shandy thought for sure he must have been cut up as well."

"They cut up his father?"

"Yeah. Before they hung him." So much for sparing the details.

Madeline tried to fathom such violence. Such hate. "Who would do such a thing?"

Wick just looked at her. "Who do you think?" He shook his head. "My grandfather was a sheriff, and he always said, 'You judge a man by how he does a day's work, not by the color of his skin.' My father held the same opinion when he became sheriff. Never tolerated people or his deputies taking matters into their own hands. 'They got no right to do that,' he'd say. But not everyone thinks that way."

"His mother?" A quiet question with the weight of a millstone.

"She was nearby. Left in a ditch."

Madeline didn't press. She didn't need to. Whatever horrors they'd visited on Dobbs' father meant they hadn't any compunction, any humanity, about what came next.

Wick raked a hand through his hair. "So Shandy brought Dobbs here. Over the years, different folks have tried to help. Poppy looked after him for a long time, then he just sort of made do. As if he tries on one place like a winter coat, and then the next year it doesn't fit, so he moves on, as if he's waiting for—"

"A home," Madeline supplied. "He only ever wanted a home." She glanced away as her eyes began to well up. *Oh, dammit Nate, why didn't you tell me?*

Wick slid his hand across the table. He'd managed to fish a

handkerchief out of his pocket. Ever the boy scout, of course he had a clean one at the ready.

As she wiped at her eyes and tried to tell herself it would all come to rights, he asked, "Why are you so set on taking him back and uprooting him? He's safe here."

"He can get a real education where I'm from. From teachers who are willing to teach him instead of being forced to."

"I doubt Shandy will allow that."

"Screw Shandy," she told him. "He shouldn't have been late. Besides, what if I told you that where I come from, Dobbs is a grown man? He's creative and successful, and has the power to take on whatever he wants to do."

He looked at her sideways. "Dobbs?"

"Yes."

"I'd say the world has changed a whole lot. 'Specially if he's safe from the sort of people who took his folks."

Madeline opened her mouth but realized she couldn't give Wick that kind of assurance. Because those very things—ignorance, hate, racism—they hadn't gone away. Nate wasn't any safer at home than he was here.

"What you should know is that I've never seen the kid so content, so happy, since you got here." Wick shifted in his seat. "He made a good showing at the spelling bee. He has a way with words. Surprised everyone."

You have no idea, Madeline wanted to say.

"So did your girlfriend take all the credit?" The catty question slipped out before Madeline could stop herself.

Not that Wick seemed to mind. Rather he laughed. "If you mean Miss Barrett, I can assure you she's not my type."

This pleased Madeline more than she cared to admit. She leaned back in her chair. "What is your type, Sheriff?"

"I'm starting to figure that out."

CHAPTER 41

Sunday, December 22
The fourth Sunday of Advent

*B*uried as she'd been in mail and parcels for the past two days, and weathering the constant interruptions of customers sending off their final Christmas tidings, Ninny had nearly forgotten Badger's invitation to go snowshoeing. But when she got up Sunday morning and spied the fresh layer of snow and the sun brightening the tops of the mountains, a longing awakened inside her.

To hear the crunch beneath her snowshoes. To wander amongst the trees, their boughs low and laden as if dipped in thick frosting.

Trees.

She grimaced and hurried to get ready for church. She hadn't forgotten *that* dilemma, since half the customers who'd come into the post office of late had posited their worry as to the perilous state of the upcoming holiday parties.

How could any of the celebrations be held without a Christmas tree?

As if Christmas would be canceled all because the hall didn't have a tree adorned with the children's paper chains and the odd bits that had been collected over the years.

Ninny considered it a personal victory that she'd managed not to tartly remind Mrs. Jonas that Christmas had been around long before their little town grew into existence and that it had fared quite well without their contribution to the festivities.

Downstairs, she found Mr. Bingley sitting by his small chipped dish, as confident in his expectation of breakfast as Ninny was that the next few days would roll by, one after another, until suddenly it was Christmas.

Christmas. She shook her head and poured a bit of cream into his dish.

"What do I know of Christmas?" she asked him.

Mr. Bingley had no reply. After all, in all his years under her roof, the holiday had never been celebrated, except to provide him a plethora of packages to explore and climb.

She filled the kettle, set it on the stove, and got the fire going. By rote, she put together her breakfast. The same one she had every morning. A bit of toast, apple preserves, and a cup of tea.

It was no different than the sameness of every December.

Until this year. Ninny stopped, plate in hand, and stared at the table.

For there lay the pair of mittens she'd sat up late into the night to finish. Every row knit with anticipation and joy. She'd hurried last night to get them done, and for a moment she admired her handiwork. The gray wool, sturdy and thick, would keep the wearer's hands toasty even on the most bitter of days. She smiled shyly and wondered how he would like them.

Suddenly, in that quiet moment of joy, she understood why the rest of the world chased that deep-seated hope, that spark of something unseen that she'd carefully knit into each stitch.

Love was what made a present a gift.

Ninny teetered between what this realization meant and what lay ahead. Maybe that was the reason she hadn't wanted to make up her mind—so she could find her way to this very spot of joy and hope, trepidation and exuberance.

Never mind that she was living in a lie, or that the truth would only see her banished back to the unseen margins. Wasn't it better to find this spark, to marvel at its tiny, transformative light, than to have lived alone in darkness for the rest of her days?

Yet, having wrapped herself in its warmth, however would she go back to her old life?

On the porch, her snowshoes waited for the promised ramble. If she told Badger the truth, he'd turn his back on her and there would be no joyful tramp through the woods. Just a solitary afternoon spent sorting Christmas packages meant for others.

She set her plate down beside the mittens.

"I'll tell them," she promised Mr. Bingley, who took his seat across from her. He cast a skeptical glance. "I will," she insisted. "Just not yet."

THEY WERE LEAVING MASS, and Savannah was woolgathering over the finishing details for Myrtle's dress, when Inola nudged her.

"Here comes Mrs. Always-and-Never," she said under her breath.

Sure enough, Mrs. George L. bore down on them like a runaway coal car. "Dear Mrs. Clarke—and my favorite authoress! Oh, Inola, you will not believe the week I'm having."

"Certainly I could not," Inola replied, taking a tentative step back from this new and unnerving attention.

"We have no tree," the matron declared. "No tree. Well, we might as well cancel Christmas."

A child passing by looked up in horror and then burst into tears.

Mrs. George L. shooed the youngster along with a dismissive wave of her hand. "Dear heavens, look at me. I'm in such a state, I've made the Catholics cry."

"You'll find we are made of sterner stuff," Inola advised.

"I certainly hope so, for we have dark days ahead. Dark days, indeed."

"At Christmas?" Savannah asked, looking around at the happy knots of people socializing despite the frigid temperatures.

"As I said, there will be no Christmas if this matter isn't decided. So I've come to ask you to speak to her, Mrs. Clarke. Posthaste."

"Her?" Savannah played the innocent, while Inola pressed her lips together to keep from laughing.

"Miss Minch, of course," Mrs. George sputtered. "It hasn't escaped my notice that you and she have developed an acquaintance of late, and I would consider it a special favor if you would impress upon her the importance of a decision."

"She appears to be in a bit of quandary, I will give you that," Inola noted, glancing over to where the lady in question was being boxed in by her two suitors.

"She is in the thrall of that shiftless pair," Mrs. George L. declared.

"I thought you rather preferred Mr. Thayer," Savannah remarked.

"I would take a blind, three-legged hog at this point, if he were capable of sniffing out a Christmas tree."

"Miss Minch will not fail the good citizens of this town," Inola assured her.

Savannah nodded in agreement. "I'm certain she'll make her choice soon. If anyone understands prompt attention to detail, it is Miss Minch."

"I would have agreed with you before, but now . . ." Mrs. George L. glanced over at the trio in question and shook her head. "In my day, I was known to entertain a bevy of suitors—at an age when such things were expected—but I was also mindful of my reputation and my duty. Heaven help us, I don't think it needs pointing out that Parathinia is well past her first bloom, and she is making a spectacle of herself."

"Since Inola and I have never been inundated with suitors, wouldn't you be more qualified to address this issue with her?" Savannah asked, trying to add a gravitas to her words that her quaking insides contradicted.

"Miss Minch and I have never developed those bonds of

friendship that would lend to such a conversation," Mrs. George L. confided, glancing down at her gloves.

"I don't see how that can be," Savannah replied, biting at her lip as if working out the conundrum of it all. "Miss Minch is one of the most affable women in this town. I find I have only myself to blame for not availing myself of her company sooner."

Mrs. George L. blinked a few times, as if trying to see how this information applied to her, while Inola had the decency to cough into her mitten and look away.

"Yes, well, it is most important that you impress upon her the importance of this matter. The gala is tomorrow night, and the tree needs to be up in time or the spirit of the season will be lost."

"I suspect no one will be looking at a tree tomorrow night," Savannah offered.

"Heavens, don't I know it! Why, the Opera Society is in open rebellion over Miss Drake's inclusion," Mrs. George L. admitted. "If they would only open their eyes and see what a blithe spirit that dear girl carries."

Inola shot a glance at Savannah. *Wasn't she the very one just the other day who said—*

"It's all been made into a scandal by people who have no understanding of the arts," Mrs. George L. continued, with a most put-upon puff of breath.

"Is that all, Mrs. Lovell?" Savannah would quickly regret the question. "I have so much to see to this morning, it being nearly Christmas and all."

"Nearly Christmas? Haven't you heard a word I've said? Christmas is likely to be canceled."

"How has it become so dire?" Inola asked. "I heard Miss Barrett just yesterday tell Mrs. Garland that the children's pageant was well in order."

"Yes, yes, for once," Mrs. George L. conceded with a lofty wave of her hand. "But there will be no candy afterward. Mrs. Pelham is still ill. The children will make such a fine showing, and with none of Ellen's mints as a reward after."

"Those mints are a reward?" Savannah asked without thinking, and then she grimaced. Whatever had come over her that she could no longer govern her tongue? Then again, she'd always thought those ghastly candies were more a lump of coal than a favor.

"Be that as it may," Mrs. George L. said, choosing to ignore Savannah's comment, "who takes sick at Christmastime when there is so much to be done? I declare I've never heard of such a careless disregard for duty."

"I'm certain Mrs. Pelham didn't take ill on purpose," Inola soothed.

"That doesn't solve the problem." Mrs. George L. drew a deep breath and sighed. "There is no candy for the children, and for some of them, that is their only Christmas present."

For once, Savannah saw beyond the woman's bluster and high-handed ways. In this moment, she saw not the grand hat and expensive fox muff, but a little girl with an empty stocking.

"We'll make the candy," Savannah announced.

Mrs. George L. blinked. "You will?"

"We will?" Inola echoed.

She nodded. "But we won't make mints."

"But you must. Those are traditional," Mrs. George L. began.

"Not where we come from," Savannah told her. "Those children are getting pralines. And fudge."

"Mrs. Clarke! When I suggested Dr. Timonius Stevens's powders, I never imagined they would work such a miracle. Why, you and Inola will save the day. Thank you." She hurried off, dabbing at her eyes.

"Was she truly crying?" Inola remarked.

"I do believe she was," Savannah said, not a bit bowled over to witness what could be described only as, well, a miracle.

"You aren't taking those powders, are you?" Inola asked.

"Heavens, no," Savannah said with a shudder. Then she glanced up at the clear blue sky overhead. "Forget the pralines and fudge. Do you think we could manage some divinity?"

Inola looked up as well. "I do, if this dry weather holds. But we would be remiss if we didn't make fudge." Her eyes lit as if she could already smell the chocolate. Nor had her confection-loving heart finished overflowing. "What about some taffy? When was the last time we made taffy?"

The Kings happened to be walking by at that moment, and Goldie came to an abrupt halt. "Are you going to make taffy?"

"Yes," Savannah told her. "Mrs. Lovell has asked us to make candy for the children's pageant."

"Then you'll want to do it tomorrow night. Won't that be fun? Of course you'll need help," the girl declared as she turned to her sister. "Myrtle, there's to be a taffy pull."

Myrtle's entire face brightened.

"Oh, you needn't—" Savannah began, but it was too late. Goldie had gotten the bit between her teeth and hitched her sisters to the plan.

"I can help," Francine offered.

"No," both sisters declared.

"We had to cut it out of your hair the last time you helped," Goldie reminded her. "You looked a horror for six months after."

Francine folded her arms over her narrow chest. "I was seven."

"This isn't a party," Savannah tried to explain, "but a serious endeavor."

"More hands lighten the load," Goldie informed her, as if that decided the matter. To prove the point, she rose up on her tiptoes and called to another girl. "Hazel, there's to be a taffy pull tomorrow night at Mrs. Clarke's. Wanna help?"

Hazel lit up much as Myrtle had. "Hattie and I will be there. Are the boys invited?"

"I was getting to that," Goldie said, throwing a blinding smile at Mrs. Clarke. "Boys do make the evening so much more fun."

Behind her, Inola began to chuckle.

Then the shameless girl was off, gathering more comrades for her madcap plans. Her departure left an opening for her father to step forth.

"Mrs. Clarke, if you don't want them all over your house, I'd suggest putting a stop to this now," he suggested.

Yet there was Goldie, already explaining her grand plans to a group of boys, her hands fluttering about, her animated features bright with excitement.

Dear heavens, when was Savannah going to learn to govern her tongue? Still, she smiled at Mr. King. "Inola and I welcome the help, but I daresay I have no idea how I'll fit them all in the house."

"Goldie will find a way," he said with a chuckle.

"I HAVEN'T DONE this in a long time," Ninny told Badger as he finished fitting her boots to her snowshoes.

"From the state of those snowshoes, I assumed as much." He looked up, blue eyes alight with a devilish twinkle, and winked, which only made her insides flutter the more. "But you're ready for a ramble now."

She shivered a bit at the suggestion, and then shook off such nonsense by stamping her feet, testing how the snowshoes held. They fit perfectly, and she grinned in delight. "I suppose I am. It's such a perfect day." The sun stood bright and high in the deep blue sky. "Now where do you propose we go?"

"Up," he said, getting to his feet. In no time, he'd put on his snowshoes, and he led the way. Or rather, Wellington led the way, loping through the snow like a giant puppy.

Ninny followed in their tracks and realized immediately this was a familiar path for the pair who tramped easily through the progressively deeper snow, up into the thick stands of pine, where their breath came out in puffs of clouds.

With each step, Ninny let the whispers at church, and the pointed remarks made across the post office counter, all fall beneath her feet.

On this side of the valley, the old trees hadn't been cut away for railroad ties, or houses, or timber sets for the copper mine. As they drew higher, Ninny heard the noisy rush of a creek. Gauging where they stood, she imagined it was the one that ambled through town and emptied into the river near the Bergstroms'. While it made a more civilized gurgle down below, up here the water rushed and tumbled headlong down the hillside.

Not much further on, as they left the thicket of trees, the roar of the creek dulled to a distant whisper, and Badger stepped aside. Almost immediately Ninny saw why he'd led her to this place, and she stilled in wonder.

There, in the middle of what was probably a small green meadow in the soft summer months, grew a singular tree. As perfect a Christmas tree as could be imagined. Straight and true, the branches reached outward and upward as if welcoming the world around it.

Such a beauty would have been a sight with just the sparkle of snow on its boughs, but someone had added a long garland of shiny tin stars, as well as strings of popcorn and bright cranberries. Finishing the holiday adornments were a dozen or more candles in those pretty tin holders Mr. King carried at the mercantile.

"Oh, my." The words, so full of her heart, came out in a breath, warming and clinging to the crisp air around them. She glanced over at Badger. Had he done this?

Of course he had.

He shrugged and kicked at the snow a bit. "I take that to mean you like it."

She reached over and laid her hand on the crook of his arm. A steadier, more solid place she'd never imagined. "I've never seen anything prettier."

He tipped his head and studied his own handiwork. "I gotta admit it is a fine sight prettier than that tree Mrs. Baumgarten chose."

"That wasn't a tree. It was a broom handle with tinsel," Ninny corrected.

They both laughed, and Ninny drew back her hand, regretting the loss of his steady presence immediately. Then again, it wouldn't do to get too used to such an intimacy. She began to put more distance between them, circling the tree and admiring Badger's festive attempts.

Then a horrible thought struck her, and she rounded the tree to face him. "You don't mean to cut this down, do you? You can't!" She glanced at the tree, and this entire beautiful place. "Please tell me you'll leave it be."

Let this always be here.

Badger chuckled. "Want to keep it all to yourself, do you, Miss Minch?"

She notched her chin up even as her cheeks flamed a bit. "I do. I can't imagine it being hacked down and dragged into town. It will never look lovelier than it does in this moment."

"Yes, lovely is the right word," he said, looking at her and not the tree. "But I disagree on one point. It will look quite fetching Christmas Eve, when I light all those candles."

The thought of being up here in the hills on that dark solemn night, with only the light from the heavens and the sparkle of candles against the deep evergreen, sent a shiver through her. "That sounds perfect."

"Nearly perfect," he told her. Then he began to cut a new path. After a few steps, he turned and said, "Never fear. I have no intention of cutting this tree down. Ever."

"That's good news, but what if someone else finds it and decides to make off with it?" The tin stars winked in the sunshine, and Ninny was loath to leave just in case someone happened upon this sacred little spot.

"Then they'll have me to answer to," he told her, nodding beyond the tree to where a jumble of a cabin sat tucked between the trees.

Ninny squinted into the sunshine and wondered how she hadn't noticed it before.

The cabin, once probably a one-room homestead, boasted a hodgepodge of additions poking out of the original structure. More amazing was that atop this jumble sat a second story.

Ninny might have called it ramshackle at first glance. But as she stepped closer, spellbound, it was clear from the painted casements around the windows, the snug fit of the logs, and the heavy door in front that it had been built with care and even a bit of whimsy, for the door was painted bright blue and decorated with a wreath. Of course. A narrow covered porch ran across the front, and two chairs sat under the eaves, waiting for warmer days.

Wellington had already laid down in front of the door, watching the pair of them. Badger made his way as well.

"So this is where you live," she said, planted in his wake.

He stopped and looked back at her. "Thought I lived in a cave, did you?"

Her cheeks warmed. "Not in the least. But it isn't quite what I expected."

"What did you expect, Miss Minch?"

"I didn't expect a turret," she said, nodding up toward the second story. "Can you see the town from there?"

"I can," he said, glancing up at it as well.

"Truly?"

"See for yourself." He strode up to the porch and sat down to take off his snowshoes.

Go up there? Into the far reaches of his house? Follow a man she barely knew into . . . Ninny paused. His house. Where he lived and ate and slept. The color returned to her cheeks, for if it was her house, she'd sleep up in that tower. Did he?

Goodness, she was becoming as bold as Madeline.

Yet as that frisson of worry urged her to hie her way back to Bethlehem with all due haste, her gaze fell on the single tree standing in the grove.

It will look quite fetching Christmas Eve when I light all those candles.

Ninny took a deep breath as she looked anew at the string of tin stars, the garlands of white and red. This wasn't the first time he'd decorated that tree or adorned its boughs with fat white candles. He did this every year. All by himself. All for himself. All alone.

This solitary man—without kith and kin to surround him, to sing carols before the flickering candles—knew the meaning of Christmas, something she'd never understood until this morning.

Until now.

She, who faithfully went to church every Sunday. Who had stamped and carried and handed over hundreds upon hundreds of Christmas greetings. She'd passed that joy from one person to the next and never held any of it for herself.

So, ignoring her usual fears, she let that new spirit fill her heart.

She glanced back at Badger. He'd hung up his snowshoes on a hook by the door. She wasn't surprised to find an empty hook waiting for another pair.

He smiled to her. "Come on in. You'll find I make a passable cup of tea."

CHAPTER 42

Monday, December 23

*M*adeline opened the door to the laundry as an explosive howl rang out from the back room, followed by a loud argument. In English and Cantonese.

"Are you trying to cook me, you bastard? You'll boil off my skin with that water." There was only one person with that Scottish burr.

Badger.

The response, in Cantonese, came back just as hotly. *Someone should have a decade ago.*

Madeline covered her mouth to keep from laughing. Not that Mr. Wu was wrong.

"I'm not taking off my long johns," Badger continued. "Not with all them standing round gaping. Send 'em away or I'll toss 'em into the river."

Madeline couldn't help herself. She chuckled, rounding the counter and not even hesitating to part the curtain into the familiar room. Laundry hung from every available line, turning the space into a maze of petticoats, sheets, and pants waving over the steaming tubs. From the look of things, the entire town had dropped off their dirty clothes in anticipation of the coming holidays.

Including Badger. "Get them out!" he roared.

She looked under the flapping sheets and spied a scramble of feet and the back door swinging open and shut. So Badger's threats had worked. Perhaps Mr. Wu's staff understood English a far sight better than they let on. Then again, a raging, bear-sized Scot was probably enough to send any sane person hurrying away, no matter the language.

Still, she'd be more careful with her words the next time she played mahjong with them.

Next time.

She shook her head and corrected herself. *If* she ever played mahjong with them again. There wasn't much time left. She glanced over at the table where the tiles usually sat, but even they'd been packed up given the tremendous amount of work at hand.

"What's that?" Badger roared. "Say it again so I can understand it, or I'll knock the words out of you."

Wu's response was, in Madeline's estimation, unprintable.

She wasn't even sure it had a translation, but she could offer a version that wouldn't see the man tossed into the river. She wove her way through the laundry and came around to find Badger standing in his long johns beside one of the bigger laundry tubs. A newly pressed suit hung to the right. "He says there is no point in wasting his hot water if you don't take off everything and get clean down to your skin."

Wu crossed his arms over his chest and snorted.

"Blast it all to hell, woman! What are you doing in here?" Badger plucked a sheet from the line and wrapped it around himself like a maiden aunt caught in her altogether.

"Merry Christmas, Badger," she said, grinning with all the cheek she could muster. "Decking the halls, are we?"

The man glared and pointed a finger toward the door. "I'll deck your halls if you don't leave immediately."

Madeline laughed, rocking on her heels. "You'll have to drop that sheet to do it. Besides, I'm with Wu. You aren't going to improve the situation by bathing in your long johns. Peel them off and get clean. Everywhere."

The man's nostrils flared, and for a moment, Madeline wondered if she was about to find herself dunked in the river. Then he turned his back, muttering to himself. "Entire town is conspiring against me. First Silvio refused me service until I had a bath, and now he"—a long finger pointed at Mr. Wu—"thinks he has the right to tell me how to wash myself."

Madeline pointed at the tub. "I'll tell you how to bathe. Strip. Get in there. Use a copious amount of soap." She laughed more. "Do you want me to spell *copious* for you?"

"Demmit woman, get out of here!"

She grinned. "Shall I stop by the barbershop and tell Silvio you'll be by in, say, an hour?"

"I don't think I need an hour to get clean."

She nodded. "You're right. I'll tell him two."

Madeline was still laughing over his profane retort well into the middle of the street. Yet there she paused. Whatever had gotten into Badger to prompt such a momentous change?

Not what, but who.

Madeline muttered a curse. If he meant to show up at the gala clean and shaven, in a new pressed suit, then . . .

She whirled toward the post office, but changed her mind mid-step and turned in a very different direction.

Badger wasn't the only one who needed their halls decked.

"I CAME AS SOON as I could close the post office," Ninny began, as Madeline opened the door at Mrs. Clarke's house. "Dobbs said there was an emergency." He had been vague about the problem, just telling her that she was needed immediately. Yet here stood Madeline, fit as a fiddle, Mrs. Clarke beside her, grinning like a cat in the cream, and no sign of any emergency.

"What's all this?"

Madeline slanted a glance at Mrs. Clarke. The older woman stepped aside to reveal a dress hanging on the wall behind her. Not just any dress—a pale green silk overdress set off by an ivory underskirt. A sparkle of buttons ran down the front, and an intricate filet lace ran around the hem. Why, it was like something out of a magazine.

"I still don't understand," Ninny insisted, pulling her gaze away from the dress and back to Madeline.

"You can't go to the gala in your old Sunday dress," Madeline told her, shooing her into the parlor, taking her coat and hat, and depositing them unceremoniously on the sofa.

"No, definitely not," Mrs. Clarke agreed, casting a stray glance at Ninny's accoutrements, which should have been hanging on the hall coat tree and not cast adrift on the furniture.

"But I haven't anything else . . ." Ninny began, her gaze straying to the dress. It was like something out of a fairy tale.

"You do now," Madeline told her, nodding at the dress. "We are determined that you outshine every lady there tonight."

"Oh, I couldn't," Ninny protested, looking from one to the other.

"Miss Minch, you must," Mrs. Clarke told her. "It is my dearest wish for you to accept this dress."

INOLA PRIDED herself on knowing everyone in Bethlehem, but here was someone she'd never met coming down their front steps, looking like one of those come-hither Gibson girls. Her hair sat piled perfectly atop her head, with a few quaint curls winding around her ears.

"Inola. Lovely evening, isn't it?" the woman said in greeting, before she continued down the path.

"Miss Minch?" Inola turned just in time to see a flash of chartreuse silk poking out from beneath the postmistress's stylish navy wool coat. At the hem was the lace Mrs. Bergstrom had given Savannah for Myrtle's dress.

More shocking was the two women standing in the doorway,

looking as cozy as a pair of robins in a nest as they watched their fledgling take wing.

Savannah and Miss Drake.

Then Miss Drake gave Savannah a hug as if she were her dearest companion. "Thank you so much, Mrs. Clarke."

"How many times do I have to ask?" she told her. "Please call me Savannah."

"Savanah, then," Miss Drake agreed, and she hurried down the steps to catch up with Miss Minch.

Inola stopped, unsure if this was even her house. "Vanna?"

"Yes?"

"Whatever did you do?" She took another look back into the gloaming and watched as the pair were swallowed up in the deepening night. "Why is Miss Minch wearing Myrtle's dress?"

"Because I think she needs it more than Myrtle does."

Inola dug for her handkerchief even as she tried to put it all together. Oh, it was an answer to her prayers. Like seeing a miracle.

But Savannah misunderstood. "Don't cry. Myrtle is young, and we'll help her in other ways. Won't we?"

"Oh, bother the tears. I couldn't be prouder of you. Of course we'll help that child," Inola told her in a rush as she hurried up the stairs and pulled her dearest sister into a hug. For once, Savannah didn't shake free. It was Inola who pulled back first and held her at arm's length. "I just can't believe you gave that dress to Miss Minch after . . . well, everything."

Savannah shrugged. "I see now that dress was never for Myrtle."

Inola glanced down the road again. "No, I suppose it wasn't." She smiled after the woman. "She looks pretty as a picture."

"She does, doesn't she?"

"But why? And what is Miss Drake's part in all this?"

"She came just after you left, full of plans to help get Miss Minch gussied up for the gala. When she described what Badger was doing—"

"Badger?"

"He invited Miss Minch and apparently spent the day bathing, shaving, and getting a haircut."

"Badger?"

"The same. And that's not all. Mr. Thayer invited her as well. And she's accepted them both."

Inola collapsed more than sat on sofa. She shook her head. "Our Miss Minch?"

"Dear little wren that she is, she's found her wings."

"So you decided to gild them."

"I did." Savannah glanced around the room, which was now a clutter of hairbrushes and clips and pins and ornaments that had been tried and dismissed until the perfect combination had been found. "I realized all of it—taking apart my old gown, the thread, the lace, the buttons, all given out of kindness—had provided me a new life, stitched together by a collection of friends I never imagined. All because I picked up a wish and came to believe."

Inola began to cry anew, for if anyone's wish had come true, it was hers.

Savannah settled on the sofa next to her and picked up her hand. "Merry Christmas, Nola."

"Merry Christmas, Vanna."

Savannah gave her a short curt nod, then got to her feet, smoothed her hands over her apron, and took a quick survey of the cluttered room. "Now, do put away those tears. We have a taffy pull to host and the opportunity for some very necessary matchmaking."

MADELINE'S HANDS curled around her stomach as a veritable parade of butterflies danced a rowdy version of the two-step in her stomach. She wasn't usually prone to jitters, but tonight proved to be the exception.

"Whatever is the matter?"

Madeline twisted around and forced a smile—not that it was really that hard. For here was Ninny looking quite the picture.

With even this friendly bit of scrutiny, Ninny patted at her hair and smoothed her skirts.

"A case of nerves," Madeline said, turning back to the small oval mirror.

"You done this before," Ninny pointed out, as Madeline dabbed on more lip rouge.

"Yes. More times than I can count," she admitted. *Casey Jones* had been filmed before a live audience, so she'd learned very early to be the consummate professional. Still . . . She spun around and caught hold of Ninny's hands. "What if I go out there and fail? What if I'm a horrible flop? I could never forgive myself if I ruined everything."

"I hardly see how it matters," Ninny said in that pragmatic way of hers. "You won't be here much longer, so it isn't as if you'll have to live down the shame."

Madeline shook her head, for she'd missed the point. "I don't care about me. It's you I am doing this for. You recommended me. You put your faith in me." She let go of Ninny and wiped at the tears threatening to ruin her makeup.

"Oh, go on," Ninny said, as she rummaged through her handbag and quickly produced a hanky. "Madeline Drake, you are an odd key, I'll grant you that. But you are my friend now, whether you like it or not. You've opened my eyes beyond my small word, beyond my post office."

"You dear—" Madeline took the hanky and dabbed again at the tears toppling down her cheeks.

"No, please let me finish." Ninny took a deep breath, as if delivering a speech she'd put much thought into. "I thought myself quite worldly because the world passed through my fingers—but in truth, it was just passing me by. You helped me see that."

"I hardly—"

"Your arrival," Ninny insisted, pushing back into the conversation where once she would have let her words be trampled, "was the spark that illuminated everything I needed to do. Everything I needed to risk. So I thank you."

Madeline shook her head at all this, for Ninny's confession had only kindled her own apprehensions. "I can't bear the idea of you being left responsible if I go out there and bomb."

Ninny wiped at a few tears as well. "Then might I suggest you do me one last favor?"

"Anything," Madeline told her with all her heart.

Ninny grinned. "Don't 'bomb.'"

They both laughed, and then Ninny hurried out.

Don't bomb.

Madeline chuckled a little as she turned back to the mirror. It was like having Gigi in the dressing room with her again.

A Drake does not suffer nerves.

A Drake performs because this is what we do.

Madeline sucked in a deep breath. *What we do.*

There it was. The Drake dictum.

She'd lived under that edict her entire life, as she was photographed and dissected in the tabloids, picked apart on social media, graded and examined and haphazardly plotted, like a bad script.

Now Madeline saw how she'd been caught in that turnstile, much as Ninny had been caught in hers—ceaselessly spun round and round by expectations that had nothing to do with her own desires. She'd let others row her boat—Dahlia at first, then a series of agents and producers. Even Gigi.

It was only in the safe harbor of Bethlehem that she'd found the wherewithal to pick up the oars and set her own course.

She quaked when she thought back to those first few days—okay, weeks—when she'd been the very worst of Madeline Drake. Dear, sweet Ninny had seen beyond all that. As had Dobbs, and Shandy, and even Wick. She could even count Savannah among their number now.

Slowly, through some miracle, she'd found a place where she could be herself. Madeline, without all the Drake baggage. Yet she couldn't deny that her past, her name, and all those years had been a training ground for this very moment.

She wouldn't fail Ninny and her unceasing faith, because she was a Drake.

There wasn't a chance in hell she was going to bomb tonight.

After all, she was making history as the very first Drake to hit the boards.

That idea rather pleased her.

When she glanced back up at the mirror, there was Mrs. George L.'s reflection peering back, brows furrowed. Having discovered that she had Madeline's full attention, she launched in.

"My dear, are you certain you have all the songs memorized?"

"Yes, Mrs. Lovell," Madeline tipped her head to make sure her elaborate hairdo wouldn't topple over mid-song, and to search for whatever imperfection had Mrs. George L. so transfixed.

"You're certain where you should be and when?" the woman pressed.

"My marks? Yes. I hit every single one this morning at rehearsal." She straightened and shook her head. Not a hair came loose. She'd have to thank Savannah later.

"But in that second song, I was uncertain if—"

The *thump* of a cane brought the woman's fault-finding to a halt.

"Leave her be, Columbia." Poppy thumped her cane again and shooed her daughter-in-law aside to make space. "The gel knows more about this than any of us."

Not one to relinquish easily, Mrs. George L. bullied on. "Now, Mother Lovell—"

"Don't 'Mother Lovell' me," Poppy shot back like a cannon. "I only came back here to wish Maddie luck." She winked into the mirror. "Knock 'em dead, kid. I know you got the pipes and the talent." She smiled and, after an uncharacteristic moment of silence, looked as if she were about to dash a tear away. She huffed instead. "Can't dally. There's a handsome stranger out there, and I have high hopes that he wants the empty seat beside mine, though I suspect he has other quarry."

That single word, *stranger* caught her daughter-in-law's attention, and bless Poppy's heart for diverting her.

"Stranger? I don't see how that can be. Why, I reviewed the guest list this very morning and—"

"I believe he was buying his tickets from Mrs. Baumgarten as I came in."

Even as Mrs. George L. turned to leave, Ninny returned, her cheeks a rosy pink. "Madeline, you'll never believe—"

Mrs. George L. reacted by rote. "Miss Minch! What are you doing here? If you think your unorthodox friendship with Miss Drake allows you the liberty to come uninvited . . ." Then her complaint rather faltered to a halt, for in front of her was hardly the mousy postmistress she was used to bludgeoning with her opinions and orders. "Parathinia, whatever have you done to yourself?"

No one missed the note of envy.

"Doesn't she look lovely?" Madeline pointed out more than asked. "Savannah was right—that dress sets off your coloring perfectly, Ninny. You'll shame the stars tonight."

Ninny appeared flustered for a moment, then gathered her wits and got back to the matter at hand. "Did you know?"

"Ah, so he's arrived. I am dying of curiosity," Madeline admitted.

Mrs. George L. struggled to take command of the situation, but had a hard time pulling her gaze away from Ninny's transformation. When all else failed, she reverted to habit. "Miss Minch, this event is for ticketed guests only. I don't recall you on the guest list."

"Miss Minch was invited," Madeline provided. "Twice."

"Twice?" Mrs. George L. shook her head. "Why that's—" She was most likely about to say "impossible," but as she glanced yet again at Ninny's transformation, she couldn't get the word out.

"So they both asked you. Ha! Well done," Poppy interjected, giving Ninny a nudge with her elbow.

Mrs. George L. cleared her throat. "At least you finally had the good sense to say yes to Mr. Thayer. The tree he chose is perfect."

"Tree?" Ninny said, shaking her head. "I haven't made a choice on that."

"But you must have," Mrs. George L. insisted. "When I arrived this morning, there was a perfectly lovely tree in the stand. I couldn't have picked a finer one."

"But I never—" Ninny continued.

Poppy barked a laugh. "Best Christmas season ever, with all these mysteries and shenanigans. But I must know which one of those two rogues you said yes to. You wouldn't be here if you hadn't made that bargain."

"Both," Ninny told her.

"Both?!" Mrs. George L. sputtered.

"In my day, 'both' would have been a slow night," Poppy quipped, with a loud cackle and spark in her eyes. "All this talk has me in mind to find out who that handsome fellow is and just where his boundaries lie."

"That's no stranger," Madeline told Poppy. "Rather an old friend. Surprised you didn't recognize him." She went back to applying one last layer of lip color.

Poppy glanced over her shoulder toward the hall. "I've never seen that man before."

Madeline turned in the chair, resting her hand on the top rail. "Want to bet on it?"

CHAPTER 43

*N*inny should have been delighted that the Opera Society gala turned out to be a smashing success. Madeline wowed her skeptical audience, bringing even the most strident objectors to tears with her final song.

But in the same breath, the metaphorical spotlight had spent most of the night shining not on the stage but on Ninny and her supper companions. The entire room whispered and speculated as to the postmistress's dramatic transformation, not to mention Badger's startling changes.

He'd shaved off his great beard, revealing a strong jaw and a deep cleft in his chin. With his hair cut and brushed back—showing a bit of gray at his temples—he was causing hearts to flutter, especially in a dark suit that looked like it had come from the very best sort of tailor, along with new boots, and a smart hat. Being a gentleman, the Honorable Sterling Densmore took no notice of the stir, sitting next to Miss Minch with elegant ease.

Adding to all this was the scandalous inclusion at the table of Mr. Thayer—also done up to the nines—seated at Ninny's other elbow.

The situation was not missed by Mrs. George L., who had the

horrible misfortune of hearing the arrangement off-handedly referred to as a "threesome" by none other than her gleeful mother-in-law.

Now here she was, prowling the room, greeting the guests at each and every table.

Ninny shifted miserably in her seat, for it was only a matter of time before the lady reached them and exacted her revenge.

"Miss Minch, that is a look," Mr. Thayer remarked, as he finished up his supper.

"Whatever do you mean?" Ninny smiled, doing her best not to look in *that* direction.

"You appeared lost in a rather dark deliberation." He turned his head and followed her previous line of sight. Mrs. George L. was only two tables away now, smiling and chatting amiably with the Garlands. "Ah. I see. That woman is—"

"The chairwoman of this event and just doing her job," Ninny told him primly as she rearranged her silverware and then changed her mind and settled it all on her plate.

Badger cast a glance in that direction and growled. "She ought to take her seat and leave folks be so they don't end up with indigestion."

Now it was their turn as Mrs. George L. crossed the last divide.

"It's my habit to see that everyone has had a perfectly delightful evening." She paused and waited for an enthusiastic round of compliments—as was her due—but when none were forthcoming, she tried again. "Well, then, how was your supper?"

The other guests at the table gave their nervous compliments.

"Excellent."

"Lovely."

"You've quite outdone yourself, Mrs. Lovell."

This fatuous comment allowed the woman to preen. "Oh, I'm hardly alone for such kind laudation, for in this sphere there are many hands to carry the load." She then turned to Ninny and awaited her tribute. When her new nemesis remained quiet, she took another path. "I worried that my unorthodox choice of Miss Drake would have lent a less charitable spirit, but as always, the citizens of our beloved

Bethlehem have turned out in force to support our dear Opera Society with their generosity."

Another round of careful compliments rose from the other guests at the table, but not to the level that Mrs. George L. usually enjoyed, and her brow furrowed. "So, Parathinia, you've had quite the triumph tonight." Her gaze darted from Mr. Thayer to Badger and back to Ninny.

"As have you, Columbia," she replied. "This dinner is a credit to your determination and planning."

Badger began to cough, something Ninny remedied by kicking him under the table. His brows arched, but he managed to hide a grin behind his napkin.

Mrs. George L. paid him scant regard. "One would think, however, the only thing anyone wants to discuss is your remarkable arrangement here."

"Arrangement?" Badger began with a sort of growl.

Ninny slanted a glance at him. That bluster would only egg her on.

"Yes. Why, your three names are on every pair of lips."

"I hardly see why," Mr. Thayer said. "After all, I didn't get my hair done."

Mrs. George L. gave him a sweeping glance that suggested she'd carried the wrong measure of him all these years and her new estimation was not to his credit.

"But this." She finished with a wave of her hands over the three of them.

"Whatever is wrong with 'this'?" Badger asked.

A wiser woman would have discerned the tone in his voice and trod lightly. Mrs. George L. knew no such caution. "I so dislike an empty chair in a table arrangement. I have very strict rules about these things when I entertain in my home."

"Whatever is the problem with an empty chair?" Mr. Thayer asked.

"An empty seat in the house means that somewhere"—her hand fluttered absently toward the door—"a truly generous pair were left out."

"Fortune favors the bold," Badger provided.

"So I've heard," she murmured, her eyes narrowing. "How fortuitous—or rather ironic—to hear you, of all people, say that, Mr. Densmore."

Mr. Thayer settled back in his seat, arms crossed over his chest. "Mrs. Lovell, it is actually rather fortunate you are here. We were just about to tell Miss Minch our plans."

"Plans?" Ninny said, startled out of her silence.

"Mr. Thayer and I are forming a partnership."

The matron's brow furrowed. "A what?"

"A law firm."

"Densmore and Thayer," Badger supplied.

"Thayer and Densmore," Mr. Thayer corrected.

Badger's jaw worked back and forth. "We are still working out the particulars."

"A law firm? How can that be?" Mrs. George L. asked. "To do that, you would have to be a lawyer." This she said with a pointed glance at Badger.

"Which I am," Badger told her. "I studied the law at the University of Edinburgh."

The woman goggled.

"It's not Harvard," Mr. Thayer commented.

"It's better," Badger shot right back. "It'll make the firm actually respectable."

"You still have to be admitted to the bar," Thayer reminded him.

"I don't think your district judge will find my acumen lacking," he replied.

Thayer laughed, glancing up over his shoulder at Mrs. George L. "You're the first to hear the news, madam," he told her, eyes sparking. "Now we don't have to pay for an advertisement in the *Observer*."

There was a guffaw from across the table by Mr. Wallace, whom the rest of the occupants tacitly ignored—though, from the way he winced, Ninny guessed he'd received a good kick from Mrs. Wallace.

Badger sat back in his seat. "As it is, we have Miss Minch to thank."

"And Miss Drake," Mr. Thayer added.

"A wee bit," Badger conceded.

"Yes, yes," Mrs. George L. began, again with the fluttering wave of her hand. "You have much for which to thank Miss Minch, I imagine."

"Well, she did bring us together," Mr. Thayer said.

That was all the entry Mrs. George L. needed. "Has she shared with you the particulars of this fortuitous union?"

"Columbia!" Ninny sank in her seat. She could almost feel herself crawling back to the post office in disgrace.

Now Mrs. George L. was smiling. "Credit is due, Parathinia."

"Hardly credit. More a matter of chance," Badger supplied.

"Chance, was it?" Mrs. George L. smiled like she had yet another elk in her sights. "More like chicanery."

"Columbia, please. Not now," Ninny pleaded.

"Oh, I think now is the perfect time," the matron replied. She tipped her head and swept a glance from one man to the other. "Did you know, Mr. Thayer, Mr. Densmore, that on Thanksgiving, when Miss Minch pulled out that pair of slips, your names were not on them?"

Ninny got up to flee, but Badger caught her hand, his grip warm and sure. His steady presence lent her the strength to hold fast.

And she would, but she wasn't so sure that he would continue to keep her moored in place once he knew the truth.

Worse, the entire room had stilled, having sensed that something of import was happening at their table.

Ninny closed her eyes, for there was nothing left to do but drown.

Mrs. George L. raised her voice. "Indeed, she did not pull out your names. Rather, she made it all up. This entire business, this ridiculous competition, was her concoction."

The packed room fell into a deathly silence as everyone waited for Ninny to speak. To deny this outrage.

As it turned out, she didn't have to.

"Of course I knew," Badger said. His voice carried through the room.

"And I as well," Thayer echoed, leaning back in his chair, crossing his arms over his chest as if bored with the entire proceeding.

"You knew?" Ninny and Mrs. George L. blurted out, at the same time. It was hard to tell who was more shocked.

"How could I not know?" Badger glanced at Mr. Thayer. "You?"

"Immediately," he replied. "Most likely for the same reason."

"How is that possible?" Mrs. George L. asked, when Ninny couldn't find the words.

"It is possible," Badger told them, "when you consider that neither of us entered our names in the drawing to begin with."

"WALKER! Travis! You are just in time, and exactly who we need," Goldie King said as she opened the door to the Stafford brothers. "Wilda and Fanny are over there, and they need partners. Do be the pair of pips I know you to be and help them, won't you?" In a blink, she had gathered their coats and herded the handsome brothers into the dining room.

"I don't see how she does it," Inola said to Savannah as she stirred up another pot of taffy on the stove.

"Who does what?" Savannah asked as she carefully put a few drops of vanilla in the cooling slab of taffy and then nodded at Francine King and Rosemary Tuttle to continue pulling.

Inola tipped her head toward Goldie, who now held court in the hallway. "However has she managed to fit another soul in this house? I swear we'll find them in the morning, tucked in the rafters."

"Stuck to the rafters is more like it," Savannah noted. "There won't be a square inch of this house that isn't sticky."

But even that wasn't the case. Goldie had come by earlier, taken a measure of the house, and returned not long after with a small parade of friends and all the necessary accoutrements: sheets to cover the furniture and floors, extra chairs, and a few additional pots and pans, along with a large sack of sugar, a jug of syrup, and several bottles of flavorings. Savannah had ordered the ingredients when she'd gone into the mercantile first thing to pay their bill in full, courtesy of her wages from Madeline.

As each guest arrived, Goldie assigned them work—pulling

candy, cutting the pieces, or wrapping—until the entire house hummed along like an elaborate candy factory.

But that wasn't all Goldie had done. Her true talent lay in pairing partners for the taffy pull and making sure every girl was matched with her sweetheart, or perhaps the boy she fancied. After all, her mercantile eye was well used to matching customers to goods— whether they needed them or not. Now, couples took up spots in the dining room and even, to Savannah's horror, the parlor.

In between, Goldie quizzed Inola about going to college, conferred with Savannah about how she'd done Miss Minch's hair, and kept up half a dozen conversations with her collection of friends.

Indeed, their house had never seen such a jolly assembly or shaken with so much laughter.

What a change from only a few weeks before, when she'd sat in this very house, alone in the dark, miserly telling herself that her bitter existence was a far cry better than celebrating with her neighbors.

Now every ring of laughter and the high-spirited conversations made her heart swell with delight and hope.

"However did this happen?" she wondered aloud.

Inola heard her. "You offered to help."

"I was steamrolled into helping," she corrected.

Looking her up and down, Inola grinned. "You look like you've recovered."

"Good as new," Savannah told her.

"Better," Inola told her firmly.

Savannah turned again to the door as Goldie hustled another pair of helpers inside and quickly sorted them out. "She does have a way about her. I think she's granted more wishes tonight than Shandy has in his entire career."

"She isn't the only one with a knack," Inola remarked, slanting a glance at the small table in the corner where Myrtle and Jacob Kearns sat, pulling a long rope of taffy and smiling at each other.

That had been Savannah's doing, for she'd kept a keen eye out for the lad, and when he'd come in, she extracted him from Goldie's clutches and brought him to the kitchen to help Myrtle.

Savannah crossed her arms over her chest. "That did work out, didn't it?" she said quietly.

The pair sat with their heads together, whispering something that had Myrtle blushing. For it seemed, all the girl needed was just a bit of help.

"So you don't regret giving that dress to Miss Minch?" Inola said quietly.

"Not at all," Savannah confessed. "Perhaps I'll get to make her wedding dress." Besides, all it had taken to make Myrtle's wish come true was nothing more than a gentle push. More so, she'd wager, that at the moment, neither of these two cared a whit about fashion.

Her work in this matter now done, Savannah turned to eye the pot on the stove.

Inola tipped her head. "Are you supervising me?"

Savannah crossed her arms over her chest. "I might be."

"I think I know how to boil up of a pot of taffy."

"Then you'd best stop and let it get to work," Savannah advised. "That sugar doesn't need any more stirring."

Inola snorted, but after a glance, put the spoon on the rest and grinned. "This is the last batch," she announced.

All the young people groaned and protested.

Savannah came to stand beside Inola. "Look at all the candy you've turned out," she told them. Your work will save Christmas for all the little ones. You've done a great service."

Their faces beamed back at her.

"To Mrs. Clarke and Inola," Myrtle declared, getting to her feet. "For welcoming all of us to their home and being such bricks in all this."

A cheer rose, and Savannah's eyes welled up. Happily, here was Inola at her side, pressing a handkerchief into her hand. "Welcome to Bethlehem, Vanna."

"You knew?!" Ninny had held her temper until they were well away from the rest of the dispersing guests. "You knew and said nothing?"

"I might remind you, Miss Minch, that you were the one who tied this knot," Badger pointed out, walking alongside her.

Mr. Thayer, on her other side, glanced at him and shook his head. *Novice.*

Meanwhile, Ninny did her best to compose herself, and failed. "I . . . I . . ."

"Yes, you," Badger pressed. He reached up and fumbled with his tie and collar, but eventually gave up as it wouldn't loosen.

Ninny considered offering to help, but then again, she thought he deserved to choke a bit.

"Since my esteemed colleague brought it up," Mr. Thayer began in his smoothest tones, "why did you do it?"

"Yes, indeed. A man has a right to know why he was dragged into a holiday pantomime." Badger returned to grappling with his collar.

Oh, heavens. The moment she'd been dreading. "If you must know—"

"Yes, I must," Badger insisted.

"I did pull two names out by accident. I assure you that much was not a lie. But once I saw the names there, I knew immediately I couldn't read them aloud."

"And adding our names to the fray made it better?" Mr. Thayer was starting to sound as skeptical as Badger.

She took a deep breath. "Please forgive me, but I'm not very good at conjuring lies."

The pair shared a glance and then began to laugh. Loudly.

"We would respectfully disagree," Mr. Thayer told her. "You fooled everyone but us."

"I was starting to believe it myself," Badger teased. Then he chucked his chin in a prodding motion. "So, who *did* you pull out of that fool jar?"

"If anyone deserves the truth, it's us," Mr. Thayer added.

Ninny took another breath. "Mrs. Neville Norwood."

"Whatever could be wrong with her?" Mr. Thayer hurried to say.

"Not a bad egg, that one," Badger agreed. "That is, when she and that old—" Right there he stopped and blinked. "No."

"Yes," Ninny agreed.

Thayer looked from one to the other, shifting his feet in the snow. "Yes what?"

Badger huffed in exasperation, for he could see the answer clearly. "She went and pulled Mrs. Norwood *and* Mrs. Lovell."

Thayer gaped for a moment and then he remembered himself. "Good thing Mrs. Lovell doesn't know."

Ninny turned and trekked toward the post office. "She knows."

The pair hurried after her.

"How?" Badger asked as he caught up.

"I told her."

Thayer shook his head as if he hadn't heard her correctly. "Miss Minch, you are either the bravest woman I've ever met or you're determined to meet an early end."

Badger nodded. "How is it your head isn't mounted on her parlor wall by now?"

"Because Mrs. Norwood doesn't know."

That bit of logic took both men aback.

Oh, dear how did one explain this? "You see, Mrs. George L. won't kick up a fuss because Mrs. Norwood doesn't know. If they both knew, then Mrs. George L. would feel obliged to rally the troops to her cause, while the rest of the ladies would decamp to Mrs. Norwood's side, dividing the town. It is such a tenuous situation between the two already, but oh, this would have ruined everything."

Neither man disagreed, for Bethlehem's female denizens operated in ways far beyond their ken.

"Which one of you brought in the tree?" Ninny asked. The question had puzzled her all night.

Thayer straightened, his chest puffing out a bit. "I did. Well, I hired the Stafford boys to cut it and bring it into town last night."

Badger drew himself up to his full height. "Oh, you did, did you?"

Thayer shrugged off the posturing. "Well, of course she was going to ask me. It's the sensible choice."

Snort.

Thayer came to a stop. The post office was just in sight. "After all, it seems to me that she's chosen you for a far worthier task, my good man."

With that, he bowed over Ninny's hand, placing an indecently long kiss atop her fingers. "Thank you for a most memorable evening, dear Ninny," he murmured. When he rose, he winked at Badger and left them both gaping after him.

CHAPTER 44

Tuesday, December 24
Christmas Eve

The school's Christmas Eve pageant was winding down to its usual conclusion. Exuberant children, full of candy, were excitedly showing off the present they had received. Savannah thought the Christmas Committee had outdone itself with donations from the community businesses. They'd seen to it that every child had something that had appeared on the wish lists they'd written for Miss Barrett just after Thanksgiving.

How this town loved their wishes, she mused, as the warmth of the evening surrounded her. How had she not seen it before?

Even Mrs. George L. brimmed with congenial spirits. "Mrs. Clarke! Inola!" Her voice rang with a relief and joy that made it seem as if she hadn't seen them in an age. "Why, the children couldn't be more pleased with their candy horns! Such pretty things!" she exclaimed, showing hers off as if she were suddenly eight again.

"Taffy, fudge, and—oh, what are these called?" She plucked a sugary piece for them to see.

"Pralines," Savannah supplied.

"Ah, yes!" she enthused. "So very decadent and delicious." With that, she popped it in her mouth, her face alight.

"Mrs. Lovell, those are for the children," Savannah teased.

"Someone had to sample one or two to ensure they were suitable for the young." Her gaze was already wandering toward her next victims.

"Are they?" Inola asked, prodding her attention back toward them.

The woman blinked. "Are they what?"

"Suitable."

Mrs. Lovell dimpled. Actually dimpled and blushed. "Yes. Very much so. I insist both of you make an abundant supply for next year's Ladies Aid bazaar. That alone will double our candy sales."

"We shall look forward to helping," Savannah told her. Normally such a request would have startled her into a panic. But last night had changed so much.

The night before, after everything had been cleaned up and the young people sent on their way home, she and Inola had dug out their grandmother's recipe book and waded through her sketchy notes to make up a large batch of pralines, laughing and reminiscing like they hadn't in ages.

In that halo of caramel and toasted pecans, Savannah had found herself transported home. Not in the sad, old way, but with a light of remembrance that gave her hope.

A lamp pointing the way toward how things could be.

Should be.

"Oh, and Miss Inola—" Mrs. George L. began.

Inola's brows perked and she glanced at Savannah as if to say, *Did you hear that?* Miss *Inola.*

While Inola basked, Savannah smiled inwardly. She knew what *that* tone meant.

With her next breath, Mrs. George continued true to form. "Now that we've discovered your secret, don't think you are going to be out of the fray. A writer and a college graduate. You are quite the feather in my cap. So it is no surprise that I've secured you a spot in the Athenian Society. How could we not put your erudite views and experiences to good use?"

The woman paused, always starting with the cake. With her next breath, she would lather on the icing as if it were too glorious to behold.

And so she did, as if bursting to tell Inola the news. "I would like you to take over the selection of our new books and magazines."

So there it was. Membership *and* the highest honor. Now it was Inola's turn to blink and gape, while Mrs. Lovell beamed. "I told Mrs. Jonas you'd be speechless."

"Mrs. Lovell, that is such a kind offer," Inola replied, "but I fear I must decline."

Mrs. Lovell's fingers crinkled the paper candy horn, pinching it a bit too tightly. "Decline?" she managed. "You must have misunderstood me. We want you as a full member in the Athenian Society."

Savannah rushed in to help. "I'm afraid Inola must refuse. Her time is in such demand."

This had the lady ruffling like a wet hen. "I hardly see how the Athenian Society wouldn't be a priority."

"It would be, Mrs. Lovell," Inola told her, "but yesterday afternoon, Mrs. Norwood called upon us to ask me to join the Library Guild. She feels I would be an enormous aid to the committee." When Mrs. Lovell had no reply, Inola continued. "She has every intention of securing a Carnegie grant for a library here in Bethlehem. A library of our very own. Can you imagine anything more wonderful?"

"A *public* library?" Mrs. George L. shuddered a little. "Here?"

"And the entire town will have you to thank, Mrs. Lovell," Savannah offered innocently. Well, not all that innocently.

"Me?" The woman drew back.

"But of course," Inola told her, winding her arm into the crook of Mrs. Lovell's and drawing her along. "If you hadn't invited me— well, Mrs. Livingston—to your birthday party, Mrs. Norwood would never have discovered my identity."

"That was supposed to be a secret," Mrs. George L. complained.

"Is there such a thing in a small town?" Savannah asked, flanking Mrs. George L. on the other side.

"I suppose not," she agreed.

"Which is exactly why Mrs. Norwood hastened to ask me," Inola told her. "She believes that the signature of Mrs. Viola Kinney Livingston on the request for funding will take our application directly to Mr. Carnegie's attention."

Mrs. George L. shook her head. "But a public library—"

"Is the greatest investment a community can make in its future success," Inola assured her. "Every child should have access to books so they can start their lives with a love of reading and a curiosity for lifelong education. Why, it is the duty of our generation to usher them into a changing world of motoring cars and aeroplanes and who knows what else. A library will ensure their success. Don't you agree?"

As the children swirled around them, boisterous and happy, a very democratic obligation found its way into Mrs. George L.'s heart. "I suppose so," she admitted. Even if it did sound more like, *As if I have a choice.*

"Excellent," Inola told her, uncoiling her arm and stepping aside. "I told Mrs. Norwood you would be delighted to host the first fundraiser." Before the woman could refuse, Inola continued, "Let me tell you what I have in mind . . ."

Savannah smiled at the unlikely pair. "A very merry Christmas to you, Mrs. Lovell," she whispered after them.

Moving smoothly into the crowd, Savannah was still smiling when she nearly collided with Shandy. "Ah, just the man I hoped to see."

"Mrs. Clarke, you surprise me," he said, tipping his candy horn toward her.

She smiled again and took a piece of taffy.

He did the same and then tucked the horn into his pocket. "You wanted to see me?" he asked as he unwrapped the bit of candy. "I usually have the impression you are endeavoring to avoid me."

"Not today, Shandy," she told him. "We have a few things to discuss."

He nodded for her to continue as he chewed.

"I fear I am going to disappoint your efforts in prodding me to make Christmas wishes come true."

Shandy's brow furrowed, and he murmured something, but his teeth were well caught by the thick taffy.

Savannah took advantage of the opportunity. "The dress you arranged for me to make for Myrtle King found another home."

"A dress?" he asked, having unstuck his jaw. "I never—"

"Oh, don't try to deny it, sir." She dug into her skirt pocket and drew out the worn slip of paper. "This one here. A wish for a new dress for the Christmas ball. While I did make the dress, I was convinced it should go to someone else. So I'm afraid that Myrtle—"

"Myrtle King?"

"Yes. As I was saying—"

Shandy shook his head. "Mrs. Clarke, Myrtle King makes that wish every Christmas." He scratched his chin. "If I intended anything, it was for you to help Mrs. Bergstrom."

"No, Mrs. George L. asked me to help Mrs. Bergstrom," Savannah corrected.

But Shandy got that stubborn look of his. "That meddling woman wasn't the first to ask you for assistance."

Suddenly, that warning note that had whispered in her ear on Thanksgiving night sounded again. Like an owl hooting a lonely cry, heavy with trepidation.

Savannah dug frantically into her pocket again until her fingers closed upon the other folded bit of paper, the one she had studiously ignored. "You mean this?"

She hastened to open it, but the handwriting was illegible.

"Of course." His gaze scanned the words and he shook his head. "Those words just cut through, don't they? That's exactly why I wanted you, of all people, to—"

"You can read that?" Savannah looked again, and now she saw the similarity to the writing in Mrs. Bergstrom's recipe book. *Of course.* "That's written in Swedish."

"Swedish?" He looked again. "Well, I'll be. It is. Still, chills the heart, those words."

Those words.

She didn't even ask him to translate. Her gaze flew from table to table. Finally she spotted Livia and pushed past Shandy to reach her. "Where is your mother?"

Livia shook her head. "She's not here."

A chill raced down Savannah's spine. All the way down to her boots. "Where is she?"

"She stayed home. She was tired. She did too much today and—"

"Alone?" Savannah asked. "Tell me she's not alone."

"No. The baby is with her."

Savannah staggered back a step. "No."

Mr. Bergstrom rose from his table and came over, saying something to Livia.

The girl turned and replied in English. "She's worried about Mama."

He shook his head. "She's merely tired. Why, she cleaned the house for Christmas, and got all the laundry done. She even started the supper for tomorrow. All in preparation for—" He paused, his eyes widening as if that owl's wary cry now sent a raft of trepidation through him.

Savannah held out the slip. "What does this say?"

Mr. Bergstrom took the little piece of paper in his big maw of a hand, and his entire face fell, as if he'd just been plunged through a sheet of ice into an abyss he couldn't escape.

"No," he managed, even as he went bolting for the door.

"What does it say?" Savannah repeated as she turned to Livia.

The girl stared at the slip, unbelieving at first before recognition set in. Finally, she read it aloud.

"Let me die this time."

MADELINE STILLED as she looked across the crowded room. Savannah's cry sent a ribbon of panic through her. "Something is wrong," she said, even as she began a quick visual search for Dobbs. Relief flooded her when she spotted him at a table playing checkers with Mr. Thayer. Changing direction, she hurried toward her friend, who knelt on the floor, keening.

"Mrs. Cla—" she began, and then dropped down beside her, laying her hand on the woman's forearm. "Savannah, what is it? What's wrong?" When she got no response, she went all in, taking her in her arms and holding her close. "There now, we'll fix this."

Once she found out what "this" was.

Ninny had followed on her heels and knelt down as well. "Oh, heavens, how can I help?"

"This," Savannah said, as she thrust out a slip of paper with a trembling hand.

Madeline took it, then shook her head. "What does it say?"

"It's terrible. And now I fear the worst. It's all my fault."

Ninny glanced at the paper. "That's Mrs. Bergstrom's writing."

Madeline did a double take. "How could you know that?"

"I know everyone's handwriting. From their mail," Ninny reminded her.

"Yes, but what does it say?" Madeline pressed, for now Savannah was trembling from head to toe. With no response, she and Ninny got her to her feet and steered her toward the table where Dobbs and Thayer were sitting.

"I don't know," Ninny told her apologetically. "I only know addresses."

Mr. Thayer took one look at them and offered his chair. "What is it?"

"Something has Mrs. Clarke in a state," Ninny supplied as they got the distraught lady seated. "It has to do with Mrs. Bergstrom, we think."

Savannah caught hold of Madeline's hand. "It is just like before. Worse, I imagine." Her gaze remained fixed on the door. And when it finally opened, there stood Mr. Bergstrom, holding the frame, his face mottled with tears. Savannah began to cry out again, then tucked her fist into her mouth like a stopper.

Madeline looked down at the slip. The lettering was so shaky and fragile, and this time she shivered with disquiet. Those words held no glad tidings.

"She's missing," Mr. Bergstrom sobbed out. "The babe as well."

"No," Savannah blurted out. "No."

Madeline glanced at the gaping door, the darkness beyond, and shivered. What if it had swallowed up that poor woman? A uneasy slate of memories flooded her. The swirl of flakes in front of the windshield, tantalizing yet blinding. The shadows that lurked at the edges of the lamplight. The train whistle, so lonely, luring her into the night. She gave herself a shake.

Inola pushed through the curious knot of people and knelt at Savannah's side. "Vanna, what is it?"

"It's the same as before."

Madeline quaked. *The same as before.* With those words, the mystery of Mrs. Clarke fell into place. She didn't need the particulars. "We won't let that happen. *We won't,*" she told her, looking for Wick. She glanced around the room, pulling on every thread she'd gathered over the past few weeks. "Dobbs, get all the older boys. We need to organize quickly. Ninny, get Badger. He'll be a big help."

"What can I do?" Mr. Thayer asked, his gaze fixed on Mrs. Clarke's woeful expression as she got to her unsteady feet.

"Tell everyone to collect every lantern they can find." Madeline looked again toward the door, toward the night. Lanterns to banish the shadows, she reasoned. Yet it was the sparkling strings of lights overhead that gave her strength.

This is your path, they seemed to whisper. *Yours, Madeline Drake.*

Her fear and panic on the train that lonely afternoon she'd tried to run, the anger that had sent her into that snowy night in Jackson, her fury at finding herself trapped here—it all melted away.

She needed to stay calm for Savannah's sake. She needed help.

"Wick," she whispered, raising up on her toes and searching the room. He'd help her.

She wrapped her arms around her friend one more time, whispering fiercely. "Take courage. We'll find her in time. We will. It's Christmas Eve, after all. A night of miracles."

"A Christmas Eve spent finding a mother and babe," Badger said, shaking his head.

"It would be ironic if it weren't so frightening," Ninny said, hugging her coat around her, trying to fend off the voices from the past that threatened to undo her. Oh, heavens, they just had to find the poor woman before it was too late.

Please, Machias, let me in. I'm so very sorry.

Helplessness crawled out of Ninny's very soul, which had heard those words and been powerless to help—to defy her father and let her mother back into the warm house.

And yet she'd opened the door to Madeline, and now to this man beside her.

"What is it?" Badger asked, tipping his head and studying her.

As much as she didn't want him—or anyone—to see inside her distress, she knew eventually she could tell him. And just that knowledge, that this man was a safe harbor, was enough to ease her panic. "Not now," she told him, and to her surprise and relief, he nodded in understanding and willing acceptance.

Madeline's quick instructions had managed to gather a search party in no time. Now they all stood in front of the Opera House while Wick got them organized.

"What are we waiting for?" Mr. Thayer asked as he came up beside Ninny. "I won't have them lost."

"Aye," Badger added.

"I want everyone to fan out," Wick explained to the assembled party. "Be mindful of the tracks in the snow. Since it's been coming down all evening, this new layer has erased most of our incoming prints, and might reveal where Mrs. Bergstrom has gone. "Please don't go running about. I know we want to hurry up and find her—"

"Damn straight," Denny called out from the back.

"Yes," Wick agreed, "but if we make a mess now, we may lose our chance of finding her. We'll move slowly, in a big circle. Those behind can fill in when the gaps between people get too wide. Look for a single track of fresh prints."

"Stay with me," Badger told Ninny in an aside. "I won't be losing you in all this."

"I have no intention of going anywhere else," she told him. The words were a pledge of sorts, to which he nodded in agreement.

Madeline came hurrying up. "Do you mind if I join you? I feel lost all over again."

"You?" Ninny said, surprised. Her friend always appeared so self-reliant.

"Always, Ninny," Madeline confessed. "Less so, I think, since I came here. I found all of you."

"Oh, go on with you," Ninny told her, letting the warmth of those words chase at her own chills. But there was something else that Madeline could do better than anyone else. "Can you see to Mrs. Clarke? I think she trusts you." She tipped her head in that direction. "She's in a terrible way, and I can't find Inola."

"Inola's gone to the Bergstrom house to get it ready for when we return," Mr. Thayer told them.

So Madeline made her way to Savannah, who was as pale as the moon and pacing back and forth in agitation. It was a wonder she could still stand. "Come now, we can't have any of this," she told the woman, curling a hand around her elbow.

"I left her alone. I told myself she was improved. I should have known better."

Madeline squeezed her arm. "It wasn't your burden to carry. Not alone. We all should have been helping."

Ninny came up on Savannah's other side and steadied her as she began to sob anew. "We're helping now, and we will find her. Don't fret."

From across the street, Wick called out for them to begin, and the entire community fanned out, their feet crunching into the soft stillness of the night. No one spoke. A grim determination bound them all in a single purpose.

As the circle widened and they reached the outskirts of the town, Dobbs, who had been trailing behind Badger, stopped and tipped his head as he studied the hillside that rose up before the dark mountains beyond. "I saw a light." He pointed into the darkness. "There's a light up there."

"Don't be daft," one of the Stafford boys said. "There ain't nuthin' up there."

Badger shared a glance with Ninny. He had the same thought, she realized. "Where, Dobbs? Where did you see it?"

He pointed. "There!" Then he shook his head. "It was just a flicker, and now it's . . . No! There it is again."

"I see it," Savannah said, shedding her anguish like an old coat in the spring. "A light where there shouldn't be one."

Ninny blinked into the darkness, then turned to Badger. "You lit the candles, didn't you?"

"I did, but I don't see how they could have lasted this long." He looked again, and then his eyes widened.

This time when Ninny peered into the night, she spied the faint flicker as well.

"If we can see it, Mrs. Bergstrom might have as well." She looked up to find Badger holding his lamp close to the ground.

"Aye, I think she did." He grinned and held the lamp higher so she could see what he'd discovered: a single track of prints leading up the mountainside.

WITH BADGER TAKING the lead and a grim-faced Mr. Bergstrom now at his side, Savannah grasped at that flicker of hope, even though it seemed as far away as the stars. But there it was, twinkling again, and she took another step closer in expectation.

"What if it isn't her?" Mr. Bergstrom shook his head.

"Who else would it be?" Badger asked. "No one ever comes this way but me. Not this time of year."

Already, word was spreading, and a good number of searchers followed in their wake, a string of lights stretched out behind them, bright with that very same sense of hope.

The further they climbed, the more convinced Savannah became that this was naught but a fool's errand. Then they broke through the trees, the mysterious twinkle now revealed.

A lone tree, alight with candles, stood in the middle of a clearing. Sparkling across the boughs, a garland of tin stars caught those bits of light and reflected them well beyond the reach of those solitary wicks.

Savannah's breath caught in her throat. She was looking at the very lesson she'd learned over the past season. The night Madeline arrived, she had changed her focus, let her see her own light and how it could be strung together with others to reflect well beyond her reach.

In front of the tree stood a solitary figure looking up at the candles in starry awe, and in her arms, a bundle. Mrs. Bergstrom and Thomas. Safe and unharmed.

Savannah sobbed at the sight of them.

Mrs. Bergstrom turned, her blank expression barely registering their arrival. Her husband choked out an indecipherable word and then rushed over to her, gathering her into his arms.

As overcome as she was, Savannah didn't hesitate to shrug off her coat and come to her side. "My dear, there you are. I fear you forgot a coat," she offered gently. She tucked the dark wool around the woman then gently prised Thomas from her arms. The baby cooed back, snuggling closer.

"I must get her home," Mr. Bergstrom said, sweeping his wife into his great meaty arms as if she were a feather.

"I'm right behind you," Savannah told him. Before she even took a step, Mr. King put his coat over her shoulders, sheltering her and the baby.

"You've a kind heart, Mrs. Clarke," he told her. "It would be a shame to see it freeze over."

She nuzzled her nose into Thomas's downy head. "If I possessed a kindly heart, I would have had the sense to be there with her tonight, and none of this would have happened."

"Well, as I always say, there is time enough tomorrow to fix those mistakes and forge ahead." He stole a peek at the baby and smiled. "He seems a right fine lad."

"He is. He will be," she promised. To herself. To Thomas. To Mrs. Bergstrom.

Savannah stole a glance over her shoulder and found the rest of the searchers circling the miraculous tree in wonder, and someone—Badger, she guessed, by the rich tone of his voice—began to sing.

"O, little town of Bethlehem . . ."

MADELINE FOLDED the last note and tucked it into its envelope, then wrote the name on the front and added it to the stack of letters she'd written. With one last look around the empty Star Bright, she took a deep breath. It seemed everything was ready. All the chairs lined up, all the tables wiped, and the stained glass sparkling. She wanted the place tidied up before . . .

Well, before she left.

After they'd found Mrs. Bergstrom, the entire town had paused and sung an array of carols around Badger's Christmas tree. She'd added her voice to the grand chorus, and never in her life had she felt so close to something. To everything. She and Wick and Dobbs had trooped back here to the Star Bright, and she'd made hot cocoa for the three of them.

But as they finished their mugs, Wick had glanced at the clock and reminded Dobbs that they would need to get to midnight Mass.

"It will be Christmas soon," Dobbs had reminded her, and then he'd rushed forward and hugged her—long and hard, as if he didn't want to let her go. "I'll save you a seat in case you change your mind."

She'd glanced over his head at Wick, that infuriating stoic look on his face. He knew what midnight would bring. She let go of Dobbs and held out her hand to him.

"Take care of him," she'd whispered as Wick shook her hand quickly and then let go. "Take care of both of them," she added, with a glance toward Dog.

He'd nodded, a tight jerk of his head, and then turned and left. As the door closed behind him and Dobbs, something shuttered inside her.

Now, as the minutes ticked closer, she tried to smile. "Somehow I managed it," she announced.

"Yes, you did."

She whirled around, and there was Shandy near the back-room door.

"I always forget to lock that one, don't I?"

Shandy shrugged. Perhaps, as she'd suspected all along, locks weren't a real impediment to the man.

"You missed all the excitement," she told him, hanging up the rag on the hook under the bar.

He settled onto a barstool and said nothing.

"You ordering?"

"You still serving?"

"I suppose I am," she replied. She took a glass out of the icebox, filled it with beer, and settled it on the bar in front of him.

"How did you know?"

"It's my job."

"I thought your job was being an actor. Or a producer. Being someone."

Madeline straightened. "I am someone. I am the owner and proprietress of this establishment. At least until midnight."

"Owner?"

She opened the cash register and pulled out the piece of paper the bank had sent over earlier. She laid it down in front of him and tapped the signature lines. "Poppy signed it over to me."

He squinted at the writing and leaned closer. "Well, I'll be jiggered. How did you manage that?"

"I won it. Poppy and I made a little wager, and she lost."

"I'd wager George Lovell didn't like that."

"That is a bet you would win. He bellowed something about being swindled. But a bet is a bet, Poppy reminded him." Madeline carefully folded up the title and tucked it back into its hiding spot in the register.

"What do you plan on doing with that? You can't have it both ways, Madeline."

She knew what he meant. Both lives. "Are you here to take me back?"

"It's Christmas, isn't it?"

"Nearly." She took another glance at the clock. Suddenly the currents she'd found herself tossed into seemed so very narrow, running swift and silently in one direction. *Home.*

But where was that?

"I've made friends here," she said, more to herself. Who was going to take care of Dobbs? She had hoped tonight to ask Ninny or Mrs. Clarke to take him in, but in all the hullabaloo, she'd never had the chance. The notes she'd written would have to do. "Shandy, how does Dobbs end up in my time?"

He had been about to drink, but paused. "That's not my story to tell . . . yet," he muttered under his breath.

"What will happen to Ninny? Do she and Badger marry? What about Savannah? Does she find some measure of happiness? Then there's—" Madeline's string of questions ended abruptly as a heart-wrenching realization struck her.

She'd never know.

"There's who?" Shandy nudged.

Madeline took a deep breath. "Wick." Then she rushed to explain. To both of them, she supposed. "He doesn't judge me. Well, he judges me—don't mistake the matter—but he also sees who I am. Who I could be. And when I'm about to make a big mistake, he lets me. Then he comes back with a broom and dustpan and helps me clean up all the broken parts."

"Sounds about right," Shandy said, sitting back a bit and watching her.

"If I left . . . I'd never see him again, would I?"

Shandy shook his head. "Can't say that you would."

"Nor Ninny or Savannah?"

He sighed and shook his head again.

"I don't know what to do." Her gaze rose toward the clock, and the ticking hand was like the roar of an ever-growing flood. "If I go back . . ."

"You go back for good."

Something nudged her hand and she looked down to find Dog standing there, staring up at her with those trusting brown eyes. *Oh, what will happen to you, my friend?*

"If I were to stay—I'm not, mind you, but if I were—"

"Then you'd be here for good."

Dog's tail thumped against the wooden floor, adding his vote. *Stay.*

"And I have to decide now?"

"Now or never."

In the deep silence of the night, the church bells began to toll for midnight Mass, where Dobbs sat with an empty seat saved just for her.

"I'm ready," she whispered as tears began to fall down her cheeks.

CHAPTER 45

Wednesday, December 25
Christmas Day

"I'm sorry, but this seat is taken," Dobbs told the man who went to take the place beside him.

Wick leaned over. "You can't keep holding that spot. She might not come."

Dobbs face set in deep furrows. "I just know she will."

"I'm not so sure."

The bell overhead continued to toll the midnight hour, the solemn tintinnabulation bringing the parishioners to their feet. For in the deep tones, there was a joyous echo that announced the arrival of Christmas. It rang over and over until it reached twelve, and then a stillness, a waiting, filled the church.

"Excuse me. Is this seat taken?"

Dobbs and Wick turned together as Madeline slid into the empty spot. Dobbs shot a triumphant glance at Wick. *Told you.*

Up front, Miss Barrett had begun the entrance hymn, and down the nave came the altar boys and Father O'Brien, in a celebration both old and familiar.

The words, the music, and the perfume of incense wrapped around her, filling her heart, welcoming her home, enfolding her in this time and place. She reached over and took Dobbs' hand.

"Honestly, I thought you might not come," he whispered.

"I wasn't sure myself," she confessed. "But I'm here now."

"Shh," Wick added, nodding toward the front.

After a second, one more came into their row. Dog.

"You brought Dog?" Dobbs said in delight, hugging his canine friend.

"He led me here," Madeline told him, but she was looking at Wick. "Oh, and he has a name now."

"Really? What is it?" Dobbs asked.

"Scout," she told them. "Because I realized he always knew what was ahead. I just had to trust and follow."

Wick leaned over and twined his sturdy, warm fingers around hers. "Merry Christmas, Miss Drake. And welcome home."

Madeline blushed, probably for the first time in her life. "Thank you, Sheriff Fischer. Merry Christmas to you."

And for once, she didn't let go.

SAVANNAH KNOCKED ON THE BERGSTROMS' door just after supper. There was a scramble of feet from within, and of course Berta managed to get there first, swinging the door open wide and tumbling out into Savannah's skirts.

"Mrs. Clarke, you're here!" She took Savannah's hand and drew her inside. "Margit's doll got a new dress for Christmas." She paused for a moment and threw a glance at her family. "Livia got a Brownie camera—and no one knows who it is from! If you didn't know already, my birthday—and Margit's," she added as an afterthought, "is in two weeks. So there is still hope for the blue mittens I wished for. If only I was going to dance tonight. Pelle and Livia get to go."

Savannah laughed at the little schemer, hinting and complaining at the same time. Berta would be a going concern when she got older.

Not that anyone was listening to Berta's wheedling. Peter and Livia were too busy gathering up their coats, while Mr. Bergstrom stood nearby, his loving gaze set on Thomas in his arms. Margit hung back, assessing everything in her silent way, but after a moment, a slight smile lifted her serious expression, and she came over and took Savannah's other hand.

"Have you had a nice Christmas, child?" Savannah asked her.

Margit smiled shyly and held out her doll so Savannah could see Alma's new dress. Clearly, she had no complaints about her Christmas gift.

Mrs. Bergstrom sat in the rocking chair, staring into space, lost again in her own darkness.

Settling Thomas in the crib, Mr. Bergstrom came over and said quietly, "She hasn't said a thing all day. Truly, you don't mind?"

The two older Bergstroms stilled at their father's question. If he stayed behind, they would have to as well.

Savannah smiled. "I can't think of any place I would rather be. After such a busy few days, a quiet evening will be a gift of sorts. For all of us."

The three of them got their coats and hats settled, and Mr. Bergstrom went to his wife and placed a kiss on her forehead, murmuring a few words for only her ears.

They all went to leave, but Livia paused at the doorway. Seeing her hesitancy, Savannah took hold of the door and ushered her out. "Enjoy yourself. Dance all night if you can."

"But Mama—"

"Isn't going anywhere. Not with me here." Savannah nodded for her to hurry after the others. "You are only young for a short time. Enjoy yourself, Livia."

When she closed the door, she sighed. "Oh, now this is perfect," she announced. "I thought they would never leave."

Berta and Margit shared a glance and trailed after her as she set to work, first washing the supper dishes and showing the girls how to help dry them. Clara sat before the rocking chair, her head resting against her mother's legs.

Finally, Savannah settled the teakettle on the stove and hummed a Christmas song as she put together a tea tray.

"Do we get to have tea?" Berta asked, eying the pot.

"No," she told her. Then she leaned down. "You three get cocoa and cookies. Do you want to help?"

They all nodded and grinned.

Very quickly, they had everyone sorted, the girls with their mugs of cocoa and a plate of cookies between them, Savannah in the chair beside Mrs. Bergstrom. She didn't say a word as she set a cup of tea and a plate of cookies beside the woman.

As the air of cinnamon and nutmeg and cloves rose in the air, Mrs. Bergstrom slowly turned.

Savannah didn't have to wait long for the woman to spy what was on the plate.

"Pepparkakor," she said, staring down at the cookies with awe. Like Margit over Alma's new dress.

"I was told they are your favorite. Merry Christmas, Mrs. Bergstrom."

"*Tack så mycket*," she replied.

To Savannah's surprise, it was Margit who turned and translated. "She says 'thank you.'"

"How do I say 'you're welcome'?" Savannah asked.

Berta rushed to help. "*Igen fara.*"

Savannah repeated the words and the girls giggled at her, as did Mrs. Bergstrom. Soon, all four of them were laughing, and she couldn't think of anything she wanted for Christmas more than to hear such a merry sound.

This night was a beginning, she realized. As it should be.

SHANDY JOINED Mrs. George L. at the side of the dance floor. "Is that Miss Drake I see dancing?"

"Yes, with Sheriff Fischer," the woman said, with a note of pride.

"Look at how that dear girl has transformed. All under my careful direction."

"Yours, Columbia?"

She ignored his implication. After all, tonight was her triumph. "I have had a very successful Christmas season, if I do say so myself."

"You have and you can," Shandy conceded, not that she didn't see the smirk in his smile. "Where is Mrs. Clarke?"

"Seeing after Mrs. Bergstrom, according to Inola."

"On Christmas? I daresay that's a surprise."

"I am modest enough to admit that I can take full credit for her transformation," Mrs. George L. confided.

"You, Mrs. Lovell?"

She sniffed. Shandy needn't sound so incredulous. He wasn't the only one in Bethlehem who could enact miracles. "Indeed. Not three weeks ago—or was it four?—I advised Mrs. Clarke to take Dr. Timonius Stevens's Miracle Powders." She smiled. "I daresay I should direct a testimonial to Dr. Stevens, for our dear Mrs. Clarke has blossomed."

"Indeed."

"Not to mention how I helped Miss Minch rise above herself." She nodded toward Ninny and Badger, who were dancing. "I do think we might have a wedding in the new year." She paused as she watched the happy couple, and then got straight to business. "And then all too soon it will be Thanksgiving again, and this time a new minister is needed, sir. A Presbyterian one."

"Mrs. Lovell, you know I don't have any say in all this."

Her hand fluttered in dismissal. "I only ask that *when* you bring the new minister, you don't deposit him in the saloon. Can we not find a more dignified setting into which you introduce our miraculous arrivals?"

He considered her complaint and came up with a suggestion of his own. "Perhaps the stable?"

ACKNOWLEDGMENTS

The idea for this story blossomed out of a bad day on a family vacation in 2010. Long story short, there was about 237 miles of crying from the backseat and no way to console our unhappy youngster. But as we drove from Cody, WY to Gillette, WY amidst an unending cacophony of sobs and "go home now" hiccups, I gazed out the window and began daydreaming—having run out of every maternal trick I possessed. Passing through Ten Sleep, a story kernel began to sparkle, and by Gillette I was off to the nearest Barnes & Noble for research books and a new journal.

With that, my *O Little Town of Bethlehem* journey began. Since that fateful day, I think I've poked around nearly every corner and county in Wyoming, digging through libraries—large and small, through museums and towns, both ghost and real, to breathe life into my fictional Bethlehem.

As an unapologetic museum and library junkie with insatiable curiosity, this wasn't such a hard task. One might suggest that this nosiness was kindled by my grandfather, who for a time, oversaw a state museum and let us kids run around the back, opening all the collection drawers. Yes, even as I write that I can see modern museum staff cringing in horror, but it was the 60s, and Grandpa was a bit of a rebel. As an adult writer who has researched history now for nearly 30 years, (and done so without an indulgent grandparent) I have learned that if I ask nicely, I can often find my way into those same back rooms, into old Masonic Temples, and into the locked cabinets of libraries.

This is where I found the history of Wyoming that I wanted to encapsulate into my writing and I owe a debt of gratitude to the guardians of these archives and collections, these wonderful old buildings, for allowing that part of me that still wants to open drawers to do just that.

So in that vein, bowers of love to the patient volunteer docents I peppered with questions and who willingly shared their love and pride of their corner of the world, and equal amounts of appreciation to those history guardians I emailed with questions when travel wasn't possible.

And again, my apologies to the police in one small Wyoming town, who mistook my interest in the architecture of their bank. Note to others: never forget your business cards.

But research gaffs aside, I want to first and foremost, thank the Grand Encampment Museum in Encampment, Wyoming for being my home base for researching and developing my dear town of Bethlehem, as well as the characters you've come to know—and I hope, love. This delightful museum with its array of historical buildings and amazing library and photo collection, allowed me to walk through time and see everyday life at the turn of the 20th century with all its eccentricities.

Believe me, writers adore eccentricities.

And thank you to Christy Gobbersmith, who helped me navigate my early research in Encampment and around the state.

Beyond Encampment, the state of Wyoming is filled with not just breath-taking scenery, but a string of wonderful local museums that happily share their history and are, through diligent and careful cultivation, repositories for artifacts, items, and vivid personal histories that reveal the past in ways stories can only hope to share. Among these, I would like to especially thank the Little Snake River Museum in Savery, the Sweetwater County Historical Museum in Green River, the Hotsprings County Museum & Cultural Center in Thermopolis, the Buffalo Bill Center of the West in Cody, the Uinta County Museum and Chinese Joss House Museum in Evanston, and South Pass City—definitely, South Pass City.

And in the category of research homes, I owe a deep debt to the American Heritage Center at the University of Wyoming in Laramie. I spent countless hours there combing through archival collections that filled my creativity and story dreams. Thank you for sharing your archives and library, as well as your endless patience with my countless requests.

And speaking of libraries, get ready for the love.

My undying gratitude to the generations of librarians, who, through the decades collected so many valuable and extensive personal histories of Wyoming, including the Cheyenne branch of the Laramie County Library, where the kind librarian led me to the Wyoming Room. An entire room. Be still my heart. Also, thank you for opening that cabinet, even when it took you an hour to find the keys. Believe me, it was well worth it.

And in the category of wonderful rooms filled with Wyoming history, include in that list the collection at the Buffalo branch of the Johnson County Libraries. Also helpful were the librarians at the Cody branch of the Park County Library system and The Wyoming State Library in Cheyenne—their online Wyoming Newspaper Project is an invaluable resource and a hoot to read just for the local 1907 gossip.

Oh, and I nearly forget. My thanks to the hot springs in Thermopolis, as well as the ones in Saratoga. They had nothing to do with research, but this author does love a good hot soak under the stars.

I was also lucky enough to visit the National Postal Museum Library, a part of the extensive Smithsonian library system in Washington, D.C. The gracious librarian there was invaluable in helping me find first-hand accounts from postmistresses across the American West. These brave, unflappable women brought connection and community to often hard to reach corners beyond the Mississippi. They are unsung heroines, as are the librarians who have saved their stories.

And last but never least, my heartfelt and deep love for my home libraries—The King County Library System and the Seattle Public Libraries—their wonderful inter-library loan librarians tracked down my countless requests for obscure books as well as keeping their shelves stocked with nearly everything an author who loves to dig deep into history might need to know.

Finally, a book is never written without a lot of support. First, to my husband, Terry, who held down the fort when I took off to do research for weeks at a time or bury myself in my office trying to get this book finished. His unwavering support of "I have this wild idea," and then giving me the freedom to pursue my story dreams is the real reason why this book is here.

To my amazing writing group, Eileen Cook, Kathy Chung, Crystal Hunt, Liza Palmer, Nephele Tempest, Susanna Kearsley, and Mary Robinette Kowal. We are a wildly different collection of souls, and I am so glad we found each other. Your support kept me tapping along when I wanted to give up.

To those who helped put the finished book in order: Anne Ricci, an early reader and later proofreader extraordinaire; my editor, Shannon McKeldron; my copy editor, Amanda Bidnall; and Crystal Hunt, who coached me through indie publishing, and helped me pull this all together and get this book out the door—she is singularly brilliant.

And I cannot forget all of you.

Every bit of my heart goes to you, my faithful readers, who emailed and nudged and urged me to get this book done. Your faith and love of my stories gives me the courage to keep writing every day. Thank you.

ABOUT THE AUTHOR

Born and raised in the Pacific Northwest, Elizabeth Boyle loves to garden as long as it isn't too hot out. She won't swim in water if she can't see the bottom. And her sons will tell you not to poke the bear or let her loose in a yarn shop.

When not being sassy and quirky and passionate about her friends and family, Elizabeth is the *New York Times* and *USA Today* bestselling and award-winning author of 28 novels and novellas. Her stories have captivated the world and been translated into dozens of languages.

For news and random oddities, sign up for her newsletter on her website at ElizabethBoyle.com, or connect with her online. Or, all of the above.

If you loved *O Little Town of Bethlehem* please consider adding a review to your favorite site or telling all your friends. Books are meant to be shared.

facebook.com/AuthorElizabethBoyle

instagram.com/elizboyle

bookbub.com/authors/ElizabethBoyle

threads.net/@threads.net@elizboyle

9 781733 676540